THE MAMMOTH BOOK OF EROTICA

The Mammoth Book of

EROTICA

NEW EDITION

Edited by
Maxim Jakubowski

RUNNING PRESS
PHILADELPHIA · LONDON

Collection and introduction © 1994, 2000 by Maxim Jakubowski
First published in the United States in 2000
by Carroll & Graf Publishers
This edition published in 2007 by Running Press Book Publishers
All rights reserved under the Pan-American and International
Copyright Conventions
Printed and bound in the EU

9 8 7 6 5 4 3
Digit on the right indicates the number of this printing

Library of Congress Cataloging-in-Publication Data is available on file

ISBN 978-0-7867-0787-4

Running Press Book Publishers
2300 Chestnut Street
Philadelphia, PA 19103-4371

Visit us on the web!
www.runningpress.com

CONTENTS

ACKNOWLEDGEMENTS

"A" by Alice Joanou, © 1992 by Alice Joanou. First appeared in TOURNIQUET. Reproduced by permission of the author.

THE ISLE OF THE DEAD by Thomas S. Roche, © 2000 by Thomas S. Roche.

PURE PORN by Dion Farquhar, © 1992 by Dion Farquhar. First appeared in FICTION INTERNATIONAL. Reproduced by permission of the author.

AT ONCE by Robert Silverberg, © 1992 by Agberg Ltd. First appeared in PENTHOUSE LETTERS. Reproduced by permission of the author.

A LONG LETTER FROM F. by Leonard Cohen, © 1967 by Leonard Cohen. Excerpted from BEAUTIFUL LOSERS. Reproduced by permission of Black Spring Press Ltd/Stranger Music Inc.

DEATH AND SEDUCTION by Catherine Sellars, © 1992 by Catherine Sellars. First appeared in THE JOURNAL OF EROTICA.

TENDER FRUIT by Vicki Hendricks, © 2000 by Vicki Hendricks.

THE AUCTION IN THE MARKET-PLACE, BEAUTY ON THE BLOCK, THE PLACE OF PUBLIC PUNISHMENT and SOLDIERS' NIGHT AT THE INN by Anne Rice, © 1984 by A.N. Roquelaure. Excerpted from BEAUTY'S PUNISHMENT. Reproduced by permission of Little, Brown, UK and Dutton Signet, a division of Penguin Books USA Inc.

OOH BABY, YOU TURN ME ON by Stewart Home, © 2000 by Stewart Home.

THE K.C. SUITE by Maxim Jakubowski, © 1990 & 1994 by Maxim Jakubowski. RITE OF SEDUCTION first appeared in a different form in NEW CRIMES 2. Reproduced by permission of the author.

HOLLOW HILLS by Michael Hemmingson, © 2000 by Michael Hemmingson.

A CARCASS OF DREAMS by Marco Vassi, © 1975 by Marco Vassi. Excerpted from METASEX, MIRTH AND MADNESS. Reproduced by permission of the author's agent, Serafina Clarke.

NEEDLESS TO SAY by Lisa Palac, © 1992 by Lisa Palac. First appeared as STOP N' SCHTUP in SCREW. Reproduced by permission of Black Ice Books.

BETWEEN SIGNS by Cris Mazza, © 1993 by Cris Mazza. First appeared in FABRIC OF DESIRE. Reproduced by permission of the author.

EVIL COMPANIONS by Michael Perkins, © 1968 by Michael Perkins. Excerpted from EVIL COMPANIONS. Reproduced by permission of the author.

THE GIRL IN BOOTH NINE by Adam-Troy Castro © 1994. First appeared in LOST IN BOOTH NINE from Silver Salamander Press, 1994. Reproduced by permission of the author.

THE SAFETY OF UNKNOWN CITIES by Lucy Taylor © 1994. First appeared in UNNATURAL ACTS AND OTHER STORIES from Richard Kasak Books, 1994. Reproduced by permission of Richard Kasak Books.

LESSONS IN SUBMISSION by Mark Pritchard, © 2000 by Mark Pritchard.

VIOLENT SILENCE by Paul Mayersberg, © 1991 by Paul Mayersberg. Excerpted from VIOLENT SILENCE. Reproduced by permission of the author.

THE PARIS CRAFTSMAN by Lucienne Zager, © 1993 by Lucienne Zager. First appeared in THE JOURNAL OF EROTICA. Reproduced by permission of the author's agent, The Akehurst Gallery.

FRAME GRABBER by Denise Danks, © 1992 by Denise Danks. Excerpted from FRAME GRABBER. Reproduced by permission of the author's agent, Scott-Ferris Associates.

MARRIED LOVE by David Guy, © 1991 by David Guy. Excerpted from THE AUTOBIOGRAPHY OF MY BODY. Reproduced by permission of the author's agent, the Virginia Barber Literary Agency Inc.

EQUINOX by Samuel R. Delany, © 1973 by Samuel R. Delany. Excerpted from THE TIDES OF LUST. Reproduced by permission of Rhinoceros Books.

THE BUTCHER by Alina Reyes, translated by David Watson. © 1989 by Alina Reyes. Excerpted from THE BUTCHER. Reproduced by permission of Reed Book Services.

CHAPTERS IN A PAST LIFE, © 1993 by Marilyn Jaye-Lewis, © 2000 by Marilyn Jaye-Lewis.

BAUBO'S KISS by Lucy Taylor © 1994. First appeared in UNNATURAL ACTS AND OTHER STORIES from Richard Kasak Books, 1994. Reproduced by permission of Richard Kasak Books.

DESIRE BEGINS by Kathy Acker, © 1974 by Kathy Acker. Excerpted from I DREAMT I WAS A NYMPHOMANIAC IMAGINING. Reproduced by permission of the author.

INTRODUCTION

Back in 1993, I gingerly proposed to Robinson Publishing that they add a volume of erotic stories to their successful Mammoth series. For some time, I had been coming across a plethora of fascinating writings about sex and sexual matters both in the UK and America, and felt I was not the only potential reader with an interest in exploring the subject further from a literary angle. After some hesitation, we soon came to an agreement and the first *Mammoth Book of Erotica* appeared in 1994.

As we now embark on a new millennium, I look back with astonishment at the success of the project. The book's printings go well into two figures, it has been a bestseller both in England and America, and with book club audiences, and has spawned a further four volumes, which I greatly enjoyed compiling: *The Mammoth Book of International Erotica*, proving that sensual pleasures are not just the privilege of English-speaking sensualists; *The Mammoth Book of New Erotica*, which for the first time mainly consisted of specially written new stories; *The Mammoth Book of Historical Erotica*, demonstrating that our forefathers also had the knack for pleasure; and, finally, *The Mammoth Book of Short Erotic Novels*, confirming the oft-mentioned fact that size does count.

And still they all keep on selling. There is not only a thirst within the reading public for literate erotic stories, but in the years that I have been somewhat active in the field (also personally giving birth to several erotic novels of my own) the growth of quality erotica has grown in leaps and bounds, and a whole new generation of absolutely wonderful new writers of erotica have made their debuts (many of them in the Mammoth series).

This revised edition of the initial volume in the series is of course a celebration and features six brand new stories which were specially commissioned from authors who were not around when the book was originally compiled. They all sit comfortably with some of the earlier classic tales we featured.

London-based Stewart Home is well known for his provocative fiction and the recently notorious novel *Cunt*, which many printers refused to print. Vicki Hendricks is a Miami academic and crime writer whose first two novels *Miami Purity* and *Iguana Love* are delightfully lurid and unputdownable. Michael Hemmingson and Thomas Roche have become regulars in the series and are two of the best young California practitioners in the art of erotic writing. Marilyn Jaye-Lewis is an ex-New York singer whose first book *Neptune and Surf* has made an immediate impact on the field and is a great hope for the future, as she is completing her first novel right now. Mark Pritchard is another California talent whose first collection, *Too Beautiful*, has just appeared and offers rare examples of exciting erotica over the gender lines.

Erotic writing at its best is not pornography. Yes, there is sex, tons of it, but it's also about people, flesh and blood, with feelings, imagination and a radiant sense of discovery of the joys the flesh can bring. Since I embarked on the adventure in 1993, I've had the opportunity to meet many of the writers it's been my privilege to publish in this series – in London, Paris, New York, New Orleans, San Francisco and further afield. They are all quite normal, delightful people, who have an invaluable talent for choosing the right words, the perfect description to seize the unseizable. I have lived in their minds, felt their deep-seated obsessions, absorbed their words, experienced their sensuality, known them better than if I had even had sex with them. It's been quite a trip.

I hope you enjoy this new swim in the seas of erotica as much as I've enjoyed floating there for the past seven years.

Maxim Jakubowski

"A"

Alice Joanou

THE WAY WE fucked each other had the precision and focus of cruelty.

His face, my breasts, our lips and skin grating together – all the bleeding, all the noise, all the decorations, all the esoteric and aesthetic niceties of seduction became inconsequential when we were making love. Finally, it was the act, the pure act of wrong that we were executing that allowed everything else to exist. As our bodies matrixed into the transgression, our pleasure was informed. The flavor of sex was made better by the adultery.

Our nearly sublime moment was reached when anything was possible, when finally any false morality had dissolved, when reason and compassion and pity were nothing more than weak excuses to keep him from my bed.

Last night I dreamt we were in his house again, her inert body there beside us on the kitchen floor. She looked prone and vulnerable in my dream, exactly the same way she had really been all those years ago. I dreamed that I was fucking her husband, rounding my back over him, bringing my hips to his with a deliberate languor. I was forcing him to keep an almost cautious rhythm, drawing his pleasure up into my own body with excruciating exactness. It was a dissection of pleasure, fucking him that way. It was clinical, and I liked the detached, powerful

feeling overwhelming my sensibilities. I was thinking how they
were both really helpless to me at this moment, and I knew it was
a moment that would pass so I thought to draw it out, to measure
each breath. I remember wishing that her eyes were open, and
more clearly I recall scrutinizing her drunken, slack face as I
pulled my body taut over him, my breasts lifted into the air, my
belly flat as I reached behind my ass to hold his balls. I turned my
attention to my own body and remember feeling pleased at how
powerful it looked at that moment, how strong and able. I felt
victorious and this urged my pleasure to a mysterious, darker part
of my psyche. I can still almost feel the motion of going down
slowly over him, using the hard, round tendons on his shoulders
to brace myself, pulling up again and again and then falling all
over his cock like an unpredictable tide. I was hoping that she
would wake up, thinking our crime really wouldn't be complete
unless she knew about it. If she had, by chance, woken, she would
have known the worst of the transgression by watching the way
his body was betraying him, by the way his body was betraying
her, she would've known she was being robbed by the way he was
lifting his body, the way his neck pulled tight and his face
torsioned into an erotic grimace straining to meet me with every
contraction, every pull, and every bend of my sex. She would
have known that night that I possessed him in a far deeper way
than she had ever conceived of desiring.

In real time, in the past, she lay on the floor next to us,
victimized, dead to passion, dead to our world. That last night
I took her husband and baptized him when he came between my
legs. Our lovemaking that night was an event that shaped many
others, an historical act of fucking, and I could feel this. I could
feel the power of the temporal, the celestial, the demonic culminating inside the mysterious wet flesh of my body. I could feel his
cock leaving definite impressions on the softer part of my internal
flesh, and I knew that my sex, my hands, and my lips were
marking his body, his life. There are infinitesimal tattoos on the
inside of my cunt from him.

When I think of him I often think of tattoos, a criminal's mark,
a street stigmatic's sign that he is other. When we fucked that last
night, we left little red A's all over each other's bodies, red A's
that never come off, never really wash away. Certainly, he has
faded in my mind. She has nearly disappeared and I may not even

recognize her. Her face, her personality was never important to me. But though the red A's have faded, they exist, just as the three of us continue to exist.

"Nobody is going to die from this," I told him, when the guilt started to panic him.

There are times now that I find her trying to infiltrate my dreams, as if she has tried to make me feel shame or regret when I am vulnerable, sleeping. Of course, I only took pleasure in remembering the guiltless grace of my transgressions, the perfection of fucking her husband. I refuse any offer of redemption, any false promises of salvation if I admit an even more false sense of guilt. When I wake after these dreams, I think mostly of the electricity that ignited my body when I was taking him. I was so powerful, so omnipotent that I let him believe that it was he who was taking me. It was never that way.

The dreams and memories are never sentimental, but they lack the beauty of the actual event. There was a purity to our crime. There was a clarity that infidelity sometimes affords liars. We were liars, and, being supplicant to all the lies we were constructing, we became intoxicated with the complexity, drunk with the shame and fun of being bad.

When we were making love, there was a bald, rude nakedness that only fed our need to consume the moment, a raw excess of light, a heat, a sun emanating from the reflection of sweat on our arms, on our foreheads. As our breasts were bruising the soft surface, sparks of glaring diamondic light rained down on us.

One night soon after he had tasted me, after he had poured his diabolic, toxic truths into my mouth, into my ears, into my sex, one night after I had held his head between my legs, making him drink more than he should have, he was drunk from my juice.

"You're crazy drunk from the juice in my pussy," I said to him.

He was drunk with criminal passions, intoxicated with champagne. He was absolutely smashed with the idea of leaving a life he hated, a life that oppressed him. He was drunk with the possibility of freeing himself, as if the key were located somewhere inside my body. His hands pried into me, searching for an escape, but my body did not relent.

"I don't have the key," I said, "but you can look."

Desperately he looked into my organs. He peered into my eyes, my breasts, looking for a way out.

"Show me where you live. Show me your wife. I want to see this horrible life you are so ready to destroy. Show me the whole fucking picture." I thought he would deny me the pleasure, but he thought it was a swell idea. My body pulsed with excited meanness. We were going to invade his sanctum, his home, his wife. This, I suppose I was thinking at the time, would validate all our sweating, all our grunting, all our criminally great fucking.

"You're in me deeper than I thought. You've fallen all the way inside," I said, raising my eyebrows.

Early on in our game, his wife had tried, in a rare display of strength, to frighten me away. Sadly, the weapons she used had no effect on me. I didn't give a fuck about compassion, or morality, or what she called "the sanctity of marriage."

"There's no going back now," I said without any expression on my face, while I stroked his hair. I was holding his head on my breast.

"He's my husband!" she screamed at me over the phone one night. I could tell she thought her words were going to change the fact that he was putting his cock deeper and deeper into my life every day.

With every push, the mutability of her world was more remote. She didn't realize that we could hardly hear her voice over the rain of sweat pelting the sheets of my bed, couldn't hear her over the orgasms that were washing the wooden floor of my house.

His body was like morphine, and he had become this particular addict's attraction. The way we came together, the way that gravity hurled our bodies at one another, seemed predetermined.

Without hesitation, I took what I wanted.

Her attempt to wrest his attention, to turn his gaze away from the maze of my flesh was weak-hearted, while the purposefulness, the single-minded focus with which I straddled and attacked his body with the lips of my mouth, the teeth of my sex, the way I held his shoulders between my fingertips, the way I wanted him had a honed quality to it. I felt expert when I was fucking him, I knew the pleasure of a murderer's discipline when we made love. And some portion of my psyche knew that the existence of his wife allowed for the intensity of our pleasure. He denied this. He wanted to attach the desire, the dizzying draw of one another's body, to love.

"Don't be silly, darling. You don't love me. You're just going through a mid-life crisis," I said to him.

He protested louder. He protested too much.

But I knew that the orgasms, the wild flowering orgasms that shattered windows and tore holes in the walls, in my lungs, in my heart, were hinged on his wife's existence.

His wife flinched and backed pathetically away like a wounded animal, trying to hide her face from the bestial truth of his desire for me, his unnatural attraction to my pussy. When she recognized the lunacy of his desire, she threw herself upon him, begging him in clumsy girlish pleas to stay. He instinctively moved toward me when she showed her weakness, as though the power of my sex could shield and preserve the perfection of our affair from the disease of their mutual weakness.

Our transcendent moment was reached when anything was possible, when finally any false morality had dissolved, when reason and compassion and pity were nothing more than weak excuses to keep him from my bed.

One night we agreed to go see her to declare our victory. He really believed our passion was going to conquer the banality of his middle-class life. He was electric with the knowledge of our fucking and how it had sealed his fate. He was ready.

"I'm ready," he announced.

"You're drunk," I replied.

He had the look of a polite man, a little sorry as he declared he was ready to commit metaphorical suicide. We went there to gloat, to glow all over her loss. To punish her, for she had committed the sin of banality.

When we walked into his house, I shuddered at the sharp edges of his reality. There were so many little objects around the house, millions of papers, books, flowers, photos, millions of little anchors and weights. There was plenty in the rooms of this house to keep him from jumping off. I thought perhaps the terrible weight of a lifetime of knic-nacks would keep him from any really great passion. His world, his home, was so material it was a glaring opposite to our world: a bed, flesh, fingernails, and hair. Our reality was housed in the juices our bodies provided. My pussy was home to him now.

"You really don't need much more," I assured him.

When we walked through the front door, I realized he was not strong enough to crawl out from underneath all this earthy, comfortable excess. No matter how warm and inviting my sex was. His existence was informed by the furniture, the paintings on the wall. I was offering him only my body, my breath. For the time being.

I felt the walls move in close around me. I felt the oppression of all his nice things, the tyranny of objects. The life in this house smelled like slow death. A life without tangible passion. I could see his weakness in every beautiful object that decorated his home. It was as though the more frantic his attempt to regain some sense of being, the more things he collected, and the more he vanished. Until he found me. My legs were open, my mouth dirty, my hunger for wrong so great that I simply wanted to eat up his life and spit it out.

"A prelude to much greater wrongs," I said, seducing him.

"She knows we're coming. I warned her. I told her."

"Bastard," I said, and squeezed his hand, encouragingly.

He whispered as we moved slowly through the treacherous labyrinth, as though, if he raised his voice, he would wake the objects in this house. At last we found his wife, lying on the kitchen floor, wearing what appeared to be a wedding dress.

I put my hand to my mouth when I started to laugh. This tableau, it seemed, was his wife's last little burst of energy in this hysteric drama. Her desperation had a kind of suburban sentimentality to it that I could appreciate. I kept laughing even as I felt a rare desire bloom, unusual in its strength and form. It grew up from the bottom of my abdomen and motivated my body to act. I desired him more greatly than before. It was a feeling of such great ambition that my laughter grew more full bodied and loud. I wanted to wake up all the lovely objects in his house. Especially his wife. Then my laughter became explosive, because, for a perfect and prolonged moment, I thought she was dead.

He turned to meet the sound that came out of me, and on his face was a horrified, maybe even a disgusted, expression I had never seen before. But I didn't stop laughing.

"We killed her," he whispered in shock.

"Don't be so hopeful, she's not dead. She's drunk." I gestured to the wine bottles on the floor next to her body. "But what about that dress?" I started to laugh again.

I was wiping my eyes. I felt nothing more than a need, a hunger to satisfy my desire in his house.

When I reached toward him, he flinched. His gesture was microscopic, but it was visible.

He moved away from me. He went to her and knelt next to her as she lay there, her mouth open, the dated wedding dress wrinkling up around her waist.

I could see that he was humiliated by the sordid B-movie quality his passionless life had taken, and I was glad he was ashamed since I knew now that he was never going to leave her, or this house, or all the things in it. He looked at me quizzically, almost accusingly, as though he were still wishing that all the answers in the world, all the meaning of the universe lay some-where deep within my pussy. I could tell by the expression on his face that he was crushed that I was not going to be his kinky Pandora, the one who would unlock his oppressed body.

He sat bent over her, unmoving, and I watched his power wane. Every moment in this house, his heart was shrinking back to its normal middle size, a heart that had grown huge with the lust of a criminal act.

"You only pity her," I said, accusing him. I lit a cigarette. I could tell that he wanted to tell me not to smoke in the house, but of course he didn't humiliate himself further.

As I studied him bent over his silly, suburban Ophelia, I realized that my hunger for him would last only as long as this great, absurd moment. Breathing in the importance of my disappointment, the greatness of my aching, I took this last moment. I seized it. I wished then that the brilliance of our lovemaking could have extended beyond my mattress. I was vaguely insulted. I was relieved and I was angry. I wanted to see to it that the memory of our lovemaking would outlast any true recollection of the body. I wanted to make certain that this night would become a seething, palpable memory throughout his life. I wanted him to always be uncertain that he did the right thing by staying with his wife. Even though I knew that he did precisely what he was meant to do. The certainty of this knowledge urged me forward in this drama.

"Fuck me," I said, walking toward him.

"What?" he said, shocked, not moving from his wife's side. She was as drunk as a bum on the Bowery.

"Fuck me right now. In front of her. Fuck me," I whispered, smiling a little, feeling the potency of our tragedy. I didn't want him to see it in my face, so I unbuttoned the front of my shirt.

I was looking at her wedding dress bunched up around her waist. I focused on a little wine stain that marred the bodice.

Suddenly I felt the kind of control one knows only in rare moments, usually moments of deathly terror or rage. My fingers were moving with a poetic precision, pulling my clothes away from my body. He turned to face me and, in doing so, his own weakness. The accusation was in my body, in my hand reaching to pull his clothes away from his body. My offer of taking him, my promise of fucking him back to life was unbearable, his inability to accept the invitation an admittance of defeat. He had lost his faith.

The strength of his face was fading quickly, the edges of his character falling away. I reached out and put the palms of my hands on his chin, wanting to hold him together, feeling that he might literally fall apart, or perhaps that I might tear him apart. His personality, like hers, was becoming small, a boat on the ocean, expertly swallowed by the sharp edge of the horizon.

His wife's inert body on the kitchen floor was fast becoming the apogee of my attention, the stained and wrinkled dress the clichéd symbol of our wrong. He desperately tried to move me away from her, to lead me out of the kitchen.

"No. I want to have it here. Now." I suppose the sound of my voice told him that being near her body was exciting me.

I was standing closer to him now, naked as he was kneeling nearer to her.

"I feel like I should genuflect," he gasped, looking wildly into my nudity.

"Yes. You really should," I said, pulling his head toward my pussy.

He put his tongue inside me, and with growing force let his body involve itself once again in our crime. While he kissed me, I wrapped his hair around the tips of my fingers, watching his wife lying there near us. I was ready to come almost instantly, so pulled away from him, teasing him with the warm sex smell emanating from my hair, the odor of promise coming from between my legs. There was a force issuing from every orifice of my body, a destructive, erotic force coming out of my hands and eyes. My nudity shamed him because it was fearless, even though it was clear that this fuck was the big crash and burn.

"Shame on you," I said quietly. It was the only rebuke I could conceive of for his inability to take what life offered.

A few seconds passed. I wondered if he were considering the price of his infidelity, tallying the months, the years of penance he was going to have to pay his wife for exposing the ugly truth that their marriage was a bore and a failure. She would say he was a liar, but his crime was not a lie. His transgression was the truth. He had acted on real impulses and, like every good puritan, he knew he would have to pay. As I stood there, he knelt in front of me, his face resting on my belly, and I imagined that he was trying to count the purgatorial nights he would have to sleep beside her. I was hoping with a vengeance that he would come to understand the tangible pangs of regret.

Suddenly it was as though a physical roar emitted from his hands, from his eyes, from the entire expanse of his skin and he yanked my body to him hard. He pulled me apart and down on him. In a fleeting moment of courage, he relented to my minor perversity. We fell to the floor, next to his wife, and, as our bodies clashed and sparked, we rolled and tumbled against her inert body. The backs of my thighs brushed her arms, and I could feel the slick, cool satin of her white dress on the warm flesh of my ass. I pushed my body against her dead dress. I was in union with both of them now.

For a last time, his body was an accomplice to my body.

I wanted to fall on her, smell her hair. I wanted to moan and cry into her skin, leaving the sound of my pleasure on her forever.

I bit him on the neck. I held him still with my teeth as I sucked the bite hard, forcing him to focus on the pain of his actions. I had never known such power between my legs, made stranger because I knew it was not an organic lust that has time to grow and flower. It would certainly destruct at the moment following climax, and I felt driven to that finality. Before I abandoned him, I was going to capture his orgasm and keep it in my mouth forever.

I tore at his body, pulled him into me. His wife still lay motionless, her dress rustling with the breath tearing from my lips. As our bodies fused, our encounter seemed more and more anonymous, as though our terrestrial bodies were vanishing, erased with every caress, the flesh pared away, at each inhalation a soldering cell shaved away, making the reality of the other impossible and we were nothing more than genital and breath. I watched to see where we met. With almost clinical detachment I saw his cock disappear into the invisible folds of of my body. I watched his personality, his fear, his life, disappear into the folds of my own life. I was swallowing his history for a moment so he could enjoy me once more.

He opened his eyes and looked at me very hard, fucking me slowly but more forcefully with every thrust. He was digging into me as though seeking reassurance that with every graceful push of his hips, with every perfected contraction of his ass, of the arch and bend of his lovely belly, that he was pleasantly careening, falling recklessly toward momentary nothingness. Every time his body demanded that mine meet his, I complied and mirrored the demand. We were accomplices. I felt every indelible mark my mouth, my teeth, my vagina made on his body. I was fascinated with the translucent, vulnerable flesh of our genitals, the clear white of our pelvises, the delicate skin like two razors coming together. Our bodies were slicing. He was making a deep, close-eyed call into my neck, a sound far beyond the capacity of his temporal body, leaving rosy echoes on my skin.

I was coaxing him, holding him together with my thighs. I could feel my body filling more and more with him, with his smell, his sounds, his sex. I continued to watch his wife, still unconscious. In a sudden impulse, I reached over and touched her.

This was a new sensation of transgression. I touched her skin, her cheek. I put my hand in her hair. He opened his eyes and saw that I was touching her, tracing her lips with the tip of my finger.

"Don't do that . . .," he said helplessly, knowing that I would do what I pleased, to him and his wife tonight.

I dragged my finger down her chin and over the soft, sexy grotto of her neck. She didn't respond at all. I was excited, filled with limitless possibilities.

I was still holding him inside me, feeling the pulse of him drive toward a conclusion. I rolled over so that he could take me from behind, so that I could concentrate on both husband and wife. He was mortified as I let my breasts touch her dress, covering the stain on her bodice.

"Fuck me. He's fucking me," I whispered into to his wife's face.

I was close enough to smell her boozy breath. Her face was quite pretty. He pulled at me, trying to draw my body away from hers. I don't know whom he was trying to protect at that moment, but I don't imagine it was me. I fell forward and put my lips over her mouth. I kissed her slowly, letting my tongue sip her lips, feeling the creases of her soft, dead mouth, feeling the impressions of her husband's cock. He was gasping, but I could hardly hear it, my head muffled and drowning in her hair. I couldn't take my mouth from hers, so great was the pleasure. The sensuality of her warm, unresponsive tongue was radical in sensation and sensibility. He was holding my flesh hard, reaching for my breasts, and I could feel his warm breath in my hair. I took her hand and brought it to my nipple, a grotesque elocution of desire. I imagined she was dead. The more fiercely he fucked me, the more he pushed the air out of my lips and into hers. He was fucking me into his wife. He had one hand on my clit, my clit that had turned into a big, red ruby between his fingers. His other hand had secreted itself under the white lace of her dress. He pushed away the fabric and took her nipple between his fingers, caressing it, mirroring the way he was touching me. I was swelling with a great scream.

By equal increments we moved closer and closer to finishing the deal. I tore my mouth from hers before I was going to come, not wanting to give her that. I pulled his hand from her breast and guided it to my hips. In one last effort, he pulled me into him, and I pushed against her breasts, using her, bracing myself against her for our orgasm.

I took him, I sucked him through her mouth, and when I ate his breath it was regenerated back out of my mouth in a terrible victorious yell. It was a scream that should have awakened her, but it didn't.

I remember that her dress smelled like mothballs.

THE ISLE OF THE DEAD

Thomas S. Roche

THIS IS NOT a true story: What I'm about to tell you concerns a goth high priestess named Lucrezia Borgia. Of course she's not *the* Lucrezia Borgia – well, not unless you believe in reincarnation. Even then it seems unlikely. This particular Lucrezia Borgia is one hot goth bitch with a foot-long schlong, who sings a real nice dirge and fakes one hell of an orgasm on stage. She's got kind of a weird thing going with death, but don't worry, she's not a necrophile or anything. Just a little unusual. Oh yeah, and speaking of death, rumour has it she blew Keith Richards once, but that must've been years ago.

L.B. and the Deathtones, live at the Orphanage: Lucrezia, my reflection. Six foot five, if she's an inch. Hovering above the audience, moaning out her best Linda Blair impression, dancing with the currents of sandalwood-scented mist from the smoke machines. Cleavage deep and white with silver ankh delicately swaying from one breast to the other. Tight black rubber dress, laced up the front, strapped down in back. Tight across the crotch, not quite showing what everyone wants to see. So short that you'd almost think you could get a glimpse of her cock if she had one, which is what keeps everyone wondering. Fishnets at half-mast, mid-thigh, sans garters. High-heeled deathrock boots. Lucrezia is a Thing of Satan, and damn is she proud of it. Heaven help the poor fucker who calls her a chanteuse. The Deathtones, generally speaking, do their lead singer justice. Lizzie Borden: five foot two, stretch jeans, lace bra delicately cupping little tits, stainless steel rings forming a gauntlet around her face. Gibson SG with a *Slow Death* bumper sticker across the front. No visible tattoos or genitals – rumour has it she's post-op, the old-fashioned way. Mata Hari: Birth female? Who knows? Who cares? Gorgeous like no one else in the band, traditional gothgirl–wraithboy accoutrement: thick red lipstick, whiteface, black bob. Steinberger bass turned up to maximum distortion, eliciting a rumble not unlike that of an earthquake. Sleazy Johnson: only guy in the Deathtones, which would really fuck things up if he wasn't an FTM. That gets you a lot of mileage, even in San fucking Frisco. Tight black jeans with the outline of a thick cock visible, white T-shirt, non-Euclidean geometry tattooed cruelly up and down both arms – don't look too close! Flattop gelled flawlessly, wrap-around Lou Reed-style shades, jetblack hormone-induced Satan-goat framing an evil seductive smile that, had it been present at Gethsemane, might have made things go a bit differently. Slamming the drums like he's really pissed off at them, but doesn't see the need to work up a sweat.

It is still Walpurgisnacht, and has been since at least 1982. Maybe longer.

Pressed hard up against the stage, eyes wide as she looks up at Lucrezia, Alice's blackberry lips form an "o" of desperation and amazement. The seethe of the crowd fills her with need for Lucrezia, all the longing of the children of the night and the drinkers of blood focused through her. She is a lens projecting their need into the singer. Alice's black-rimmed eyes weep tears of ecstasy as Lucrezia moans and wails and whispers her seductive prayers to dark gods and goddesses. Alice: white-skinned goth girl, black-haired wraith, earringed wunderkind of black-lace mourning. She's wearing a black lace wedding dress, not quite a full train, but enough to get Lucrezia's attention. Alice sings along inside her head, knowing all the words by heart but afraid to hum or whisper them for fear of upsetting the magical sound of Lucrezia's voice which touches her like the heartbreaking loss of an ancient love. Alice crosses herself as the band launches into another song. It's Alice's all-time favorite Deathtones song: *Isle of the Dead*.

Alice considers, deliciously, all the stories she has heard about

Lucrezia. Drag Queen. Pre-op transsexual. Post-op transsexual. Or the most delectable rumour of all. Alice has run the scene a thousand times in her mind, ever since she heard it whispered to her in the bathroom the last time the Deathtones were in town. The rumour: Lucrezia is the lone graduate of a highly secret experimental programme, one financed by the government of Switzerland (whose current president is a MTF transsexual) in the most complicated variety of organ transplantation, known as Living Tissue Splice. The technique is called Genetically Operative Doctoring on the street, and it remains, probably, an unrealized wet dream of science. Alice heard the same rumours about that Fuck person, who used to hang around here. Alice has never found out first-hand whether GOD exists. It seems unlikely. But Alice can believe the stories when it comes to Lucrezia. It's a chilling thought. Multiple genital capacity. It's enough to soak the wedding dress with nuptial fervour.

Alice feels her knees go weak as Lucrezia blows her a kiss – a sad, mournful kiss. "In pace requiescat," murmurs Lucrezia, looking directly at Alice. Alice's eyes go wide, the "O" of her blackberry lips widening as she is struck with terror and erotic excitement.

Alice can't be sure when she mentally reconstructs the incident later, but she is virtually certain that she had an orgasm at that moment – how else to explain the throbbing ecstasy which suddenly explodes through her young body like the fireball of a kerosene-soaked funeral pyre? Alice lets out a faint moan, unable to control herself, the vision of Lucrezia filling her eyes. The heat rushes through her. Alice faints and dissolves into the crowd.

Heaven/Hell/Purgatory: Alice slowly awakes, aware of a sensuous warmth surrounding her body. She is in flickering candlelight. A gentle, warm wind seems to pass over her face. The scents of sandalwood and roses, musk and jasmine, all mix in a seductive caress. Alice feels drained, exhausted. Her eyes gradually adjust to the dim light and she sees that she is on a canopied bed, with white lace curtains pulled closed around her. The faint glimmer of candles is all that lights the room. Thorned red roses are scattered about Alice's head on the silken pillows. From somewhere, soft music plays. Alice recognizes it instantly: Rachmaninov's "Isle of the Dead". Music for the afterlife. Alice breathes warm sandalwood, not caring if she is alive or dead.

She remembers the kiss, blown to her by the apparition on the stage. It couldn't have been real, Alice tells herself. Lucrezia is the deathgoddess of deathwave – she would never take notice of a humble little wraithgirl like me.

Then Alice recalls the orgasm, unsure whether it was real or hallucinated. Regardless, her thighs still tremble with the intensity and her body seems wrapped in its sensuous afterglow.

Perhaps Lucrezia did blow Alice a kiss, and orgasms granted by Lucrezia are the sweet kiss of death.

Alice wonders, for a long, gentle time, whether she might be in heaven or in hell. She imagines heaven, with its naked angels feeding her lotus petals and pouring nectar for her, and soothing her with harp and cello music. She considers hell, with its leather-and-spike dominatrixes snapping bullwhips and suspending her from dungeon walls by thick chains and manacles, tormenting and perverting her malleable flesh.

Either one would be OK, she supposes . . .

Alice's eyes flutter as she looks around at the white lace curtains blowing in the warm wind, and at the candlelight scattering through the lace. Heaven or hell. Could be either.

So Alice lies still and devours the sensations.

She becomes aware of a presence on the other side of the white lace curtain. A dark presence, enveloping, dangerous. Unable to lift herself onto her elbows, Alice whispers a gentle query: "Who's there?"

There is no answer. But Alice sees the form dancing a slow dance to Rachmaninov. Alice speaks again. "Who is it?"

The dark form stands there for some time, outlined in candlelight, shrouded by white lace, as Alice comes to recognize it.

"I am become Shiva, the destroyer of worlds."

"How can it be?" whispers Alice, unmoving.

Slowly, Lucrezia draws the white lace curtain and stands before Alice.

"You have come to me from beyond the grave," whispers Lucrezia, her words as seductive to Alice as those in any of her songs. "You have come to me from the sweet arms of Death. You have tasted the ice-cold tongue of Persephone and returned to bring me pomegranate seeds. I was afraid you had gone there forever. . . ."

"I fainted," whispers Alice as Lucrezia crawls onto the bed and closes the white lace behind her. "Your kiss . . . you blew me a kiss from the stage."

"And you thought it was a kiss from the Angel of Death," says Lucrezia. "You imagined that she had placed her lips against yours and sucked the very life out of you – and so you died."

"I passed out," murmurs Alice, as she feels Lucrezia settling down upon her. "I . . . I climaxed. The heat . . . I passed out."

Lucrezia shakes her head, her beautiful face and lush, thick lips inches from Alice's. "You tasted my tongue, without tasting it. You went to your grave, but only for a moment. Was it sweet, Death's embrace?"

Alice sighs. Why argue? Alice settles into the softness of the bed as she feels Lucrezia's lips touching her throat. "It was sweet," whispers Alice. "Sweet death . . ."

Lucrezia begins to kiss Alice's throat, nibbling gently between words. "The taste of Death was like absinthe upon your lips. Her embrace was like that of a lover. She wrapped you in ecstasy . . . and brought you here to me . . ."

"How did I get here?" whispers Alice, suddenly afraid.

Lucrezia senses her terror. "Shhhhhh – don't worry. I had my boygirls bring you back here, where my physician Dr Faustus ensured that you would return from the land of the dead. Bringing your knowledge for all of us . . . what did you see there, my sweet Alice?"

"I do remember seeing heaven," says Alice, vaguely confused. "And hell . . ."

"Ah, hell is the more delicious of the two," said Lucrezia as she crawled on top of Alice. Alice did not wonder how Lucrezia had known her name – it seemed only right that she should know everything. "Hell . . . to atone for your sins, for all eternity, to suffer immeasurably, knowing there is no release – I look forward to it so . . ." Lucrezia considers the problem, absently, as she sets to work on the soft triangle of flesh just under Alice's jaw. "Then again, Heaven would be acceptable, as well . . . or Purgatory . . ."

Alice moans faintly as she feels Lucrezia's tongue trailing down her throat. Lucrezia pauses before the swell of Alice's bosom in the black lace wedding dress. In fact, Dr Faustus has checked the girl's identification to make sure she is of age. "Alice," whispered Lucrezia. "Such a pretty name." But it occurred to her that the girl might have a fake ID. Was it possible? No, Lucrezia decides. Not with retina scans.

"Oh, Lucrezia . . ." it is all Alice can manage to choke out as Lucrezia unlaces the front of the wedding dress. Alice's mind slips into a trance of unbelieving ecstasy – she cannot be sprawled in bed with Lucrezia Borgia, about to find out all her secrets – such bliss is denied mortal wraithgirls . . .

Lucrezia's mouth descends on Alice's nipple. Alice feels a surge go through her body. Moaning softly, she settles into the rapture, suckling Lucrezia gently. "Drink of me," whispers Alice. "Drink all of me . . ."

Lucrezia's hands work their way underneath Alice's wedding dress. Alice gasps as Lucrezia touches her between the parted thighs.

"Is it true?" moans Alice softly, ecstasy flowing through her.

Lucrezia kisses Alice, nibbling her lower lip.

"Is it true?" says Alice, more mischievously this time, her lips curving in a smile. "Tell me if it's true." She nibbles at Lucrezia's fingertips. "What they say about you?"

Lucrezia lifts herself onto her knees, most of her six-and-a-half feet towering over Alice. She laughs cruelly. "That I am become Shiva, the destroyer of worlds?"

Alice catches her breath. "Um, no, not that. I mean . . . the Swiss thing."

Lucrezia laughs. She snuggles down against Alice, spreading her legs. "You tell me, my sweet. Death is yours to embrace."

Holding her breath, Alice slides her hand up Lucrezia's thigh. Lucrezia opens the black silk robe. Lucrezia holds Alice's eyes in hers, willing the girl to discover with her hands, not her eyes, so that she will believe. Alice's frail hand closes around the thick shaft of the multi-veined cock, feeling its hardness and its smooth, throbbing power. She moans faintly. Slowly, working her way down the shaft, Alice discovers the truth. Lucrezia's scrotum is a smooth-shaved sac enclosing her hard nuts. Behind that, Alice feels the slick wetness, the hard clit, the full lips and tight hole of a flawless, fully operational, anatomically correct vat-grown vagina. Her mind races, unable to believe. Alice's eyes roll back as she shudders in climax and loses consciousness again.

"Lovely Death," weeps Lucrezia. "Her kiss hath come for you

again, my delectable Alice. I can only pray her lips, once again, were sweet . . ."

Shiva, the Destroyer of Worlds: Alice relinquishes the embrace of death to find herself quite as effectively embraced by Lucrezia. Lucrezia has removed Alice's wedding dress – figuring the wedding was already over. Now, Alice finds herself overwhelmed by sensation as Lucrezia whispers her prayers between Alice's parted thighs. Alice, spread wide, squirms underneath the weight of the goddess. She feels Lucrezia's fingers working their rhythmic wonders, sending surges of power through her body.

"You have returned," whispers Lucrezia. "My prayers have been answered."

"Oh, Lucrezia," moans Alice. "Death's embrace was so much sweeter this time . . ."

"You're beginning to learn, my delicious . . ."

And Lucrezia's mouth descends once again upon Alice. Naked against the silk of the bed, Alice gives herself over to ecstasy. She feels Lucrezia repositioning herself, reaching out to the nightstand, rolling an unlubricated condom over the thick shaft of her cock. Then Lucrezia settles down atop Alice as Alice greedily swallows. Lucrezia comes to rest with her body against Alice's, the tip of her tongue just reaching Alice's clit. Grasping the smaller woman's thighs, Lucrezia rolls her over so they can more effectively trade favours. Lucrezia's tongue buries itself in Alice as Alice descends upon cock and cunt with equal vigour, trading off and finding technology to be equal to nature.

When Alice cries out, Lucrezia rolls her over onto her belly. Lucrezia settles upon Alice's body with newfound fervour, entering her from behind. Alice does not faint this time, but she most certainly sees Heaven and Hell both, simultaneously. It is then that Lucrezia climaxes, cock and cunt spasming simultaneously.

Curling up, embraced by Lucrezia's strong arms, feeling the reality of the death-goddess androgyne against her, Alice finally allows herself to hum, softly, the lyrics to one of Lucrezia's songs. *Isle of the Dead*.

Isle of the Dead: As far as Lucrezia's fascination with Alice's narcolepsy, if that's what it is, I can't vouch for its erotic value or safety. I'm not yet sure if Lucrezia brings Alice along with the

Deathtones on their Australian tour, maybe keeping her in a coffin between shows. On the other hand, maybe Alice replaces the flute-player who fled to Sweden a couple of months back. Or perhaps Alice, having visited the Isle of the Dead, becomes bartender at the Orphanage. It's also possible that Mata Hari goes mad with jealousy, since she and Lucrezia used to fuck, and takes a cleaver to the poor girl. That last one seems unlikely, unless you believe in reincarnation. Even then, it doesn't seem possible. It doesn't really matter much, does it? Alice got a good fuck, and tasted the kiss of the angel of death, and probably got her picture in *Propaganda* to boot, maybe even *Blue Blood*. Shit, that's a good enough reason for anyone to return from the Isle of the Dead. It'd bring me back, and I don't even own a wedding dress.

PURE PORN

Dion Farquhar

. . . [the uncanny as it is depicted in literature] is a much more fertile province than the uncanny in real life, for it contains the whole of the latter and something more besides, something that cannot be found in real life.

–Freud

ON THE EL from the airport, they sat next to each other in a molded plastic seat designed to boundary two strangers via a slightly raised bump that travelled down the middle. Which they could feel as they sat very close to each other, bodies pressed left to right, leaning slightly against each other's side. He reached up and across her chest, grazing the front of her leather jacket with a prickly wool sleeve to grasp the raw silk scarf that lay around her neck. He slowly pulled on it until her face was very close to his, never breaking the gaze. She inadvertently fanned her fingers out to touch the side of his body as he pulled her toward him, feeling his chest through layers of wool and cotton as they sat on the rattling train, thighs warm and pressed against each other. They could only get together every other week, living as they did in different cities during the school term. But they were relatively mobile and able to arrange four- and five-day weekends.

They walked together, hip to hip, through the courtyard right up to the stairway of his building, where they separated to walk up the two squeaky flights to his apartment. She watched him walk ahead of her. In the apartment, she dropped her brown suede backpack into a Breuer chair by the door. They watched each other unzip and take off their jackets, flinging them onto the backs of chairs. Holding the gaze. Unwavering control. Unsure about what they were doing. In part. Playing with tropes. Mutual recognition. He lifted her bag from the floor to place it on a chair, saying, "You travel light. It's good." Then he walked away into the kitchen to pour them each an ice-cold seltzer. Coming back with two glasses, he handed one to her and then raised his glass in a gesture of acknowledgement. Which she responded to by leaning toward him, kissing his neck with a sweep of tongue and lips cooled by the liquid.

He walked slowly toward her. His hand reached over to her shoulder, gently pulling her body into contact with his. Her arms met his, embracing him back, pulling him toward her, feeling him along the length of their bodies. Noting her soft breasts against his hard chest, pubic bone to hardening cock, the firmness of their touching thighs. They began to kiss, slowly and gently at first. With a sweep of his tongue, he took her entire mouth in his, then resting his tongue at the entrance of her open mouth, poised, moving it only when he felt her tongue envelop his. Then, opening his mouth to contain hers, he sucked her in and released her, over and over, resting his lips against hers, for a moment resisting her tongue meeting his, then pushing against her with closed lips, now seeking out and trying to suck her tongue into his mouth.

They loved to kiss, she thought, running her tongue along his cheek all the way down to his chin. She licked the tiny ridge under his lower lip, feeling the pull of the rough texture of his nascent beard offer resistance. If she stayed more than a moment kissing or licking a cheek, or lip, or eyelid, he couldn't bear it. His tongue would then seek out her mouth, moving over her lips from side to side, savoring their moist pliancy. Their tongues darted around each other, slowing down and speeding up, drawing back, then hurrying on for more. He would moan and move to nibble her ear, to take the bird from her earlobe with his lips. In the same way he would kiss and lick her belly down to the top of her underpants, sometimes grasping the elastic band in his mouth and pulling them off with his mouth.

Their bodies pressed into one another, seeking out the radiant center of their genitals. They move against each other. She cannot stop herself from moaning slightly. Suddenly he grasped her, hands squeezing her shoulders, and pushed her away. "Not so fast," he says, reaching for her scarf. Which he placed over her eyes, winding it around her head and tying a knot with an emphatic tug "Now, you will feel it more," he said, sucking and biting her lips before opening his mouth to kiss her deep and long and hard.

Then he stopped. Grasping her hand firmly by the wrist, he pulled her to walk with him, and led her around the apartment until she could feel her legs touch the side of the bed. He pushed her slightly so that she sat down, one hand caressing a breast with increasing firmness as he leaned into her until they were lying along side of, then under, and on top of each other for long intervals. Until one of them would indicate a desire to vary position. Slipping his hand underneath her blouse, he brushed her erect nipple with the side of his hand, running his fingers around the aureole. Then he pulled her shirt over her head, and nuzzled his head between her breasts, pillowing into her with a sweep of his head, then rising to take as much of a breast into his mouth as he could. He nibbled and sucked her breasts until she moaned, feeling some direct connection to her clitoris that pulsed in rhythm to the firm pressure of his tongue.

When he stopped, she would seek his mouth strongly, falling into him and opening herself to his eager lips. Their bodies pressed up hard against each other, moving their hips in sync with each other. She sighed to feel his hard cock through their clothes, delighted but almost alarmed by its hardness, her wetness, the power of their desire for each other. "Enough of this," she said suddenly, pulling the scarf-blindfold off her head and holding it as she looked at him, reaching over to stroke the outline of his erect cock through his jeans.

"Now, I will tie you up," she said to his moan, pushing against her hand. "Stand up," she said, grasping his belt and pulling him toward her. "Take your clothes off," she said, rubbing him through the thick jeans material. As he pulled off a cotton sweater and unbuttoned a flannel shirt, she unbuckled his belt and unzipped his fly. Then his hand met hers, cupping it and pressing it against him through his clothes for a moment before finally shedding his jeans. She sat down on the bed, savoring the sight of his body, naked now except for his shorts. She looked at his erection, tight up against the white cotton material, seeing a few drops of preejaculate, a circle of wet against the shorts. Lifting them over his cock in order to pull them off, she smiled, noticing a drop quivering on its glistening tip. Following her gaze, he smiled and said, "I'm very wet." Touching him lightly and smiling broadly, she said, "So I see." He moved closer to her, bringing his head close to hers. "Kiss me," he said, before wrapping her mouth in his.

Tying two long silk scarves together, she wrapped one scarf around his right wrist, running it like a chain under the mattress until it met his other wrist from the opposite side. Next, she attended to his legs, knotting old silk ties together to secure his feet. She made one loop gently but firmly around an ankle, proceeding under the mattress to the other. This way each wrist and ankle were held as widely spread as seemed comfortable. She looked at his legs spread far apart but held tightly in position, centering his outstretched body on his pelvis. She had tied him spreadeagle to the bed. She wanted to see him struggle, beg her to release him, entreat her to fuck him, to never let him loose.

He had watched her as she tied him up, a slight sweat bathing his forehead. "Kiss me," he said, "please." She watched him thrust his pelvis up as much as the bonds limiting his motion allowed, craning his neck up towards her. Coming over to the bed, she lay down next to him and began to kiss him, caressing his cock with her hand, as she rubbed herself against his leg, feeling her slippery wetness as she slid her hardening clitoris back and forth against the bone of his knee, noting that he moved slightly to meet her motion. "You're very hard," he said, with a deep sigh, head thrown back, as she moved to kiss him deeply in reply.

"What would you like to do?" she paused to ask, raising an eyebrow as she looked at him. She inclined her body towards his from her position stretched out next to him, resting her head on her hand, supported by an elbow. She had one leg slung over the "X" his body made on the middle of the double bed. Her knee slowly rubbed his penis lightly back and forth. With her free hand, she grazed his chest, stroking and pinching a nipple until it grew hard, bending over him to tongue it and suck it until he groaned. "So, are you going to tell me what you want to do?" she asked, moving her knee away from his hard penis and resting it on a thigh. "Well . . ." he said, casting a glance over his immobilized torso, the erection quivering slightly, delight and embarrassment mixing in his look.

She began to kiss him again, taking his lower lip between hers and sucking hard on it, then running her tongue over it from side to side, moving to his upper lip until his tongue came to meet hers. She opened her mouth to take him inside her, gulping him down with tiny sucking motions, their tongues finding each other and twisting around and around until one of them would alter the motion.

She moved over to lie on top of him, holding herself up with her arms so that their bodies were touching only at the groin. He thrust his hips up, pushing his cock hard up against her belly, and she leaned into him, savoring his hardness. "Fuck me," he said, "please. I can't stand it any more." "We'll see what you can stand," she said, moving herself over him so that his penis slid effortlessly against her totally slippery wet vulva, rippling against her hard clit with each stroke. "Oh. Fuck me," he moaned, straining to push his cock against her as far as his bonds would allow. "Take me inside you," he said, looking hard at her. "Stop torturing me."

"Not so fast," she said, as she rolled off of him and lay next to him. She reached for the seltzer bottle on the night table and filled her glass again, greedily sipping it because she was parched. "Do you want some," she offered. He nodded, so she refilled a glass and held it to his lips until he had drunk his fill. Then she slowly began to kiss his face, making her way down from his lips to his ears, then biting and sucking his neck until she rested at a nipple. "Oh, I love it when you do that," he said of her hardening a nipple with her tongue. She loved the absurdity of mouths on breasts.

Moving herself slowly over him, she changed directions on the bed to suck his toes, tickle and rub his feet, making her way to the center of his body, to nibble the inside of his thighs, alternately licking, sucking, kissing, and biting him there with her mouth while her hand kneaded and softly caressed his other thigh and leg.

Taking his balls into her mouth made her dizzy with his smell, anchored by their rougher texture. He moaned continuously now, moving his hips and straining against the scarves that spread him open, setting a rhythm to her sucking and biting, which had not yet reached his penis. "Oh, God. Suck me. I can't stand it. Not another minute." She nipped at the many tiny folds of skin around its base, then licked him from base to tip, first hard, then softly, alternating the top and then the underside of her tongue, back and forth. He lifted his pelvis to meet her mouth, emitting cries and tossing his head from side to side. His body shuddered in waves of desire.

She ran her tongue around and around the top of his penis, taking his head between her lips and making shallow thrusting motions with her mouth and tongue. With one hand, she grasped his penis, encircling it and taking special care to press hard against the ridged area just below its lip that connected the sides. She sucked him, especially forcefully down the backside of its shaft, which he had told her was particularly sensitive. With each thrust she would rest her half-closed mouth firmly around the lip of its head and pressing her lips against him for intervals that she varied, until his groans urged her on. "Oh, more. More, more," he said. Then she swept her tongue around the head of his penis, sucking him deeply into her mouth and moving her tongue over its length, while her hand ringed him at the same time, attentive to his most sensitive spot.

Sliding her hands under his ass on one of his lifting motions, she grasped his cheeks, rubbing and working them along with the motion of her mouth on his cock. "Put your fingers inside me," he moaned, "fuck me." In answer, she moved her fingers back and forth along the crack of his ass until she felt the tiny wrinkled opening, warm and moist, throb against her gently circling finger. Pausing to lubricate her fingers thoroughly with the bottle of almond massage oil they kept on the night table, her hand followed the line from the base of his balls right up to the crack of his ass.

He opened to meet her like a flower, and she eased her middle finger into him, hearing him cry out in pleasure, feeling his sphincter tighten around her finger, release, then tighten again. She worked it to his rhythms, never going further until invited, but stopping only when her finger could easily enter him no further. She moved her finger inside him, slowly back and forth, pressing up against the front of his rectum, allowing his thrusting to work her hand, setting the pace. "Now try two fingers," he said in between gasps. All the while her mouth and other hand never left his cock, moving over him, in rhythm to her fingers fucking him easily as he pressed his ass against her fingers with each inward motion, allowing her more deeply inside him.

They fucked each other like this for a long delicious while. She had no idea. Her awareness contracted almost completely to the sensate liquid cosmos of her mouth and fingers and the sounds of their pleasure. Her world the feel and heat of him between her lips, reaching deep into her throat, the rhythm of his cock back and forth at the same time her fingers slid deeply in and out of his ass, feeling his thrusts meet her fingers. Then, his cock reached all the way down into the curve of her throat at the same time his ass took her fingers all the way in. His body pushed against her hard, stilling into a strong thrusted orgasm that she felt go on for what seemed to be minutes. Her mouth registered the spurts of semen, warm and briny like seawater, flowing into her mouth in several short spasms at the same time she felt his anus contract in little pulses of ringing afterpleasure. After a moment, she swallowed the ejaculate, and slowly leaned over him to kiss him. "Taste," she said.

"Oh, God. Oh, God," he spat out, rolling his head from side to side, still breathing in gasps, "it's too much." "Untie me, so I can torture you." She kissed him on the lips. "Twist my arm," she said, fiddling with the silk knots around his wrist.

They took a break to pee, wash a little, and refill seltzers. "We forgot to smoke," he said, returning to the bedroom with a joint and an ashtray. "And here's an extra bathrobe in case you get chilled," he said, draping a terry robe over her shoulders, and pausing to kiss her neck. "It's a smooth strong green," he said, sitting down next to her and lighting the joint, taking a long, slow puff. He held it out to her. "Hmm," she said, reaching for the joint, "smells great." "What shall we do now?" he said, looking playfully at her. "That depends on what you want to know," she said, as she coughed, laughing and exhaling a mouthful of smoke. Leaning back into a cluster of pillows, she passed the joint back to him. "I can't smoke too much. I want to do some work later," she said. "Good, I have tons to do myself. You can have the computer if you want. I have stuff to read." "Great. And let's get some takeout, then we'll work."

"Thai, all right?" "Fine." He put the joint out, moved the ashtray, and began to kiss her until they were rolling around again on the bed. It was so easy when they weren't cripples or psychos, she thought, her arms around him, tongues intertwined, completely happy being with him.

Never predictable, he chose to replicate for her the spreadeagle position from which he had recently been released. "It had a lot going for it," he thought, as he looked at her body extended in a classic "X". He loved the way she looked tied up – helpless and completely open to him, her hipbones prominent and breasts flatter and rounder because of her raised and out-stretched arms, her pubic hair wet with surplus secretions. Maybe they liked the trust and the hypothetical risk. Though they had each never felt safer.

After he had tied her up in the same spreadeagle position, he sat up next to her, leaning down to kiss her, tonguing her deeply. Pulling away slightly, he bent over her and kissed her belly, continuing down to her pubic triangle. Moving his hand over her body to cup her vulva, he rocked her with his hand. "Let's see how turned on you are," he said, feeling her wetness even on the longer pubic hair that he grasped and pulled at, twirling a small clump around his fingers, absorbing its wetness.

Then he skilfully parted her inner lips with two fingers, sliding his middle finger far inside her, feeling her wetness and the ever-changing texture of her vagina. "Oh," he said, "very nice," working a second finger into her and moving in and out with harder and faster thrusts until she moaned and strained against the scarves, meeting his hand. Suddenly, he took his fingers out of her and began to work the area just a tiny bit above her clitoris with gentle firm rhythmic caresses that made her scream in pleasure. Moving down to cover its length and circle the small knob of hard flesh, he moved his middle finger higher up to grasp its hood. Then he opened her inner lips with a separating sweep of his second and fourth fingers, holding them apart as he slid his middle finger firmly over her clit, a gesture he knew she loved because she would always moan more. He worked his middle finger rhythmically back and forth over her clit, rubbing it ever so slightly harder in time to her increasing pelvic movement against his hand. With his other hand, he thrust two, then three, fingers all the way up inside her, faster and faster until her body tensed into immobility, lifting her into a high-pitched moan of an orgasm that rippled through her, rising and falling for a long time.

He immediately arranged himself on top of her in order to enter her while her orgasm went on in wave after wave, which his fucking now skimmed and rode, taking his cues from her thrusting. After slowing to meet her subsiding motion, instead of stopping altogether, he slowly began to increase the rhythm knowing that she could often be brought back into another pitch of pleasure following immediately upon a first. She opened further to this quick thrust fucking, raising her hips to meet his cock, burning with such exquisite feeling she felt almost faint. "Oh, God. Oh, God," she moaned, "it's so good."

He leaned over her, kissing and biting her breasts, sucking hard on one and then another as he thrust high into her, or licking her neck as he withdrew to the entrance of her vagina, then plunging all the way into her until she screamed with pleasure, rocking with him, tightening her vaginal muscles to grip him when he was deepest inside her, making him gasp, squeeze his eyes shut, and whisper, "Oh, God. It's so good."

He stopped for a moment to bend over and untie her legs so she would move more. They both reached for pillows to slide under her hips, and she lifted her legs high, wrapping them tightly around his neck, and guiding him back into her. Each thrust pleasured her differently. After a while, she lost the ability to know which one of them initiated a stroke or set of strokes. She couldn't feel their borders. Who was who. What was what. Sometimes it felt as if they moved in and out of each other fast, fast, fast, with strokes that were close together. Other times their fucking was long and slow, it reaching so deeply into her that she would cry out. Sometimes there was anger in the force of their fucking, and they fucked as much from need as from desire, hate as much as love. She never knew in advance of their bodies joining who or what would move the other or how. Loving invention.

They fucked for a long time until he pulled out of her in order to move to her mouth. "I love being inside all of you," he said as he straddled her, bringing his cock very near her mouth. Opening to him with a sucking kiss, she could taste the mixture of their secretions, licking and moving her mouth over him, taking him all the way into her, then pulling back on him. Just as she was falling into a smooth rhythm of taking him in and wrapping her mouth around him as he rocked back on each thrust, he pulled out of her mouth, saying, "It's getting very sensitive."

He began to kiss her mouth, running his hands over her entire body, pausing to slide his fingers over her vulva, again seeking her inner labia and finally, as she moaned more and more, her clitoris. He opened her slowly, separating the inner lips carefully with his fingers, and pulling the hood firmly back until her clit lay completely exposed to his tongue. He knelt over her, his erect cock resting against her belly, and began to lick her there with wide gulps, wrapping his mouth around her. Her entire body shuddered with pleasure. Then he held her lips apart with the fingers of one hand as he slowly worked the tip of his tongue back and forth over the length of her clit, returning to the spot just above its most sensitive area for a more intense tonguing.

With each motion, she moved to meet his tongue and lips, breathing herself into his mouth, and pushing her pelvis against him when she wanted him to suck her harder and stronger, and moving ever so slightly up or down in the bed to guide his tongue. His other hand reached into her, thrusting hard and slipping partly out of her, then thrusting into her again with gathering force while his tongue worked her clit steadily. He sensed her lifting herself up to him and pressed his tongue harder onto her, moving back and forth faster until her moaning looped itself into an orgasmic cry that seemed to go on for minutes. Her arms strained hard against the scarves that held her taut, his tongue blanketing her vulva hard and safe, and his fingers pressing up hard against her as far into her as he could go, evoking strong sensation inside her as well.

Again, he entered her, though this time their pleasure was even more strong, pushing himself all the way into her, thrusting up, over and over, coming partly out only to come hard back into her, sighing and moaning more with each motion. She could feel his sweat mix with hers as he nuzzled his face against her neck. They smelled of sex. Yum. When he finally came, crying out, she felt, not orgasm, but a series of tiny but pleasurable ripples in her vagina reverberating from the cessation of motion, that she could intensify by contracting her muscles against his ejaculating penis.

Their weekend continued much in the same vein, their being talking sex, *pace* Foucault.

TWO AT ONCE

Robert Silverberg

"YOU NEVER HAVE?" Louise asked. "Not ever?"

This was in the glorious seventies, when everyone was doing everything to everyone, in every imaginable combination. I was young, healthy, prosperous and single. And we were in Los Angeles, city of year-round summer and infinite possibility.

"Not even once," I said. "Things just haven't clicked the right way, I guess."

"Well," Louise said, "let me think about this."

What we were discussing – over Belgian waffles and mimosas at a favorite breakfast place of mine on the Sunset Strip – was my primo fantasy, the one sexual act – well, not the only one, but the only one that really interested me – that I had never managed to experience: making love to two women at the same time. Fucking one, amiably caressing the other, then switching, then maybe resting for a little while and watching as they amused each other, and then starting the whole cycle again, Ms. A. followed by Ms. B – the good old sandwich game, me as the filling, double your pleasure, double your fun.

Louise sipped her mimosa and thought about it. Her brow furrowed; her wheels were turning.

"Janet?" she said. "No. No, that won't work. Martine? Probably not. Kate?" She shook her head. Then: "Dana, maybe?"

It was maddening. Delicious possibilities flickered one by one in her eyes, rose briefly to the level of a bright gleam, and died away with a shake of her head just as each of the girls she named started to assume a thrilling reality in my mind. I had no more idea who Janet was, or Kate or Martine, than you do. They were only names to me; but for the single dazzling instant that they dangled in the air between us as potential members of our trio they were glorious names already turning into delectable flesh, and in the hyperactive arena of my imagination I could see myself rolling around in bed with lovely Louise and lissome Janet (blonde, leggy, slim-hipped) or luscious Louise and languid Martine (dark ringlets, heavy swaying breasts) or lascivious Louise and lubricious Kate (bright sparkling eyes, tiny tattoo on left buttock). But as fast as the tantalizing visions arose, Louise dismissed them. Janet had moved to San Francisco, she remembered now; Martine was in a relationship; Kate's motorcycle had gone into a ditch in Topanga Canyon the week before. Bim, bam, boom: all three vanished from my life just like that and I had never even known them.

"Dana, though," she said. Louise's eyes brightened again and this time they stayed that way. "Yes. Yes. Very probably a yes. Let me see what I can do about Dana, all right?"

"Dana's a female?" I asked uneasily.

Louise giggled. "For Christ's sake, Charlie, what do you think?"

"I knew a Dana in college once. A man."

"You said two women, didn't you? Come on, then." She tossed me a mischievous look. "Unless it's the other kind of threesome you were thinking of."

"Not exactly, Louise."

"I wouldn't mind that, you know."

"I bet you wouldn't. But I would."

"Well, then. All right." She winked. "I'll see what I can manage."

A hot little quiver of anticipation ran through me. Louise would manage something: I was sure of it. This was the giddy seventies, after all, when the whole planet was in heat. We were in Los Angeles, global capital of carefree copulation. And Louise, slim, agile, raven-haired, uninhibited Louise, was very resourceful indeed. She made her living setting up window displays for the innumerable little women's clothing boutiques that had

sprouted up all over Venice and Santa Monica and West Hollywood, and she knew hundreds of women models, fitters, de-
signers and boutique owners, nearly all of whom were young,
attractive and single.

"Finish your mimosa," Louise said. "Let's go to the beach."

Louise did her window work between three in the afternoon
and half past eight at night. Plenty of time for play, before or
after.

"Isn't it too cool today?" I asked.

"The radio says it'll be seventy-five degrees by ten o'clock."

January 13th. Seventy-five degrees. I love L.A. in the winter.
We went to the beach: the old nude beach at Topanga, the one
they closed down around 1980 when the people in the expensive
beach houses began to get tired of the show. The water was a little
chilly, so all we did was run ankle-deep into the surf and quickly
out again, but the beach itself was fine. We basked and chatted
and built a sand castle – more of a bungalow, really – and around
noon we got dressed and drove down to Louise's place in Venice
to shower away the sand. Of course we took the shower together
and one thing led to another, and between that and lunch Louise
was a little late getting to work. Nobody would mind.

We were such good friends, Louise and I. We had known each
other for three years and at least once a week, usually on a
Tuesday or Wednesday morning, we had breakfast together
and went to the beach. Then we went to her place and balled.
We liked each other's company. Neither of us expected anything
more than that from the other: company. She was twenty-eight; I
was a couple of years older. Good friends, yes. I had met her at a
bookshop on Melrose and we had liked each other right away and
there we were. We didn't give a thought about getting married,
either to each other or anyone else. What a nice decade that was!
The stock market went to hell, the government was a mess,
inflation was fifteen per cent, sometimes you had to wait on line
for an hour and a half to buy gas. But for Louise and me and a lot
of others like us it was the time of our lives. Yes. The time of our
lives. Everybody young, everybody single, and we were going to
stay that way forever.

Two days later she called me and asked, "Are you free Saturday night?"

"I could be." We rarely saw each other on weekends. "Why?"

"I talked to Dana."

"Oh," I said. "Well, then!"

"Will you spring for dinner for three at Le Provence?"

"I could do that, yes." Le Provence was a small and very authentic French restaurant in Westwood that we liked. Dinner for three would run me close to forty bucks in the quaint money of the era, a nice bottle of wine included. But I could afford it. I was writing continuity for Saturday morning TV then – Captain Goofus and His Space Brigade. Don't laugh. Captain Goofus kept me solvent for four seasons and some residuals, and I miss him very much. "Tell me about Dana," I said.

"New York girl. Been here about a year. Medium tall, brown hair, glasses, nice figure, very bright. Smokes. You mind that?"

"I can survive. Stacked?"

"Not especially. But she's built okay."

"How do you know her?"

"She's a customer at Pleasure Dome on Santa Monica. Came into the store one night in November while I was setting up the Christmas window. We've had lunch a few times."

"You sure she'll go for this, Louise?"

"Le Provence, Saturday night, half past seven, okay?"

My first blind date in years. Well, all right. Louise vouched for her. The two of them were already there, sitting at a table in the back, when I showed up at the restaurant. In half a minute I knew that things were going to work out. Dana was around twenty-five, slender, pleasant-looking if unspectacular, with big horn-rimmed glasses and quick, penetrating eyes. Her whole vibe was New York: alert, intelligent, fearless. Ready to throw herself joyously into our brave new California world of healthy, anything-goes erotic fun. I didn't sense any tremendous pheromonal output coming from her that related specifically to *me*, no instantaneous blast of lust, just a generalized willingness to go along with the project. But that was okay. We had only just met, after all. Expecting a woman to fall down instantly at my feet foaming with desire has never been any prerequisite of mine: simple willingness is quite sufficient for me.

My ever-active mind began to spin with fantasies. I saw myself sprawled out on the big water bed with Louise to my left and Dana to my right, all of us naked, both of them pressing close against me, squirming and wriggling. I imagined the sleek texture

along the inside of Dana's thighs and the feel of her cool firm
breasts against my hands while the rest of me was busy with
Louise. And then slipping free of Louise and turning to Dana,
gliding into her up to the hilt while Louise hovered above us
both, grazing my back with the tips of her breasts –

Back in the real world Dana and I started to make polite first-
date chitchat, with Louise sitting there beaming like a match-
maker whose clients are going in the right direction.

"So, Louise tells me you write for television?"

"Saturday morning cartoons. Captain Goofus and His Space
Brigade."

"Far out! You must make a mint."

"Half a mint, actually. It's not bad. And you?"

"A word processor," she said.

"A what?"

"Typist, sort of. Except I use a kind of computer, you know?
In a law office in Beverly Hills?"

I didn't know. Computers were something very new then.

"Must be movie lawyers," I said. "They're the only ones who
can afford a gadget like that."

She named the firm. Entertainment law, all right. But actually
Dana wanted to write screenplays; the word-processing thing was
just a way station en route to success. I smiled. This city has
always been full of ambitious would-be screenwriters, two-thirds
of them from New York. I expected her to pull a script out of her
purse any minute. But Dana wasn't that tacky. The conversation
bubbled on, and somewhere along the way we ordered, and I felt
so up about the whole thing that I selected a nine-dollar bottle of
Bordeaux. Nine dollars was a lot for a bottle of wine in those days.

We'd be done with dinner by nine, I figured, and it was a five-
minute drive over to my apartment on Barrington just above
Wilshire, and figure half an hour for some drinks, brandy or
sherry or whatever, and a little music and soft lights and a couple
of joints – this was the seventies, remember – and the clothes
would begin to come off, and then the migration to the water bed.

Two women at once, at last! My dream fulfilled!

But then a waitress we hadn't noticed up till then brought the
wine to the table and things started to go strange.

She was standing next to me, going through her elaborate
bottle-opening rigmarole, cutting the red seal and inserting the

corkscrew and all, paying all the attention to me because obviously I was the one who would be picking up the bill, when suddenly she happened to glance toward Dana and I heard her gasp.

"Oh, my *God*! Dana! What are *you* doing in LA?"

Dana hadn't looked at the waitress at all. But now she did and I saw a flush of amazement come over her face.

"Judy?"

They were both babbling at once. Imagine! Coincidence! Terrific to see you again! Old friends from New York days, I gathered. (High-school chums? Pals in Greenwich Village?) Lost touch, hadn't seen each other in years. Judy, an aspiring actress, just passing time as a waitress. Sure. Been here five years; still hoping. Must get together some time. Maybe tonight after work? Apartment on Ohio between Westwood and Federal, practically around the corner from here. Listen, see you in a little while – can't stay and gab. Is the wine okay, sir? Glad to hear it. My God, Dana Greene, imagine that!

Judy poured us our wine and moved along.

Dana couldn't get over it. Imagine – Judy Glass, waiting tables right in the restaurant where we were eating!

My guess was right on both counts: they had gone to high school together in the Bronx, hung out together in the Village afterward. Really close friends: wonderful to rediscover her. Three sips of wine and Dana jumped up and went across the room to talk to her newfound old pal some more. I didn't like that: diversion of interest. Broke the rhythm of mutual seduction. Little did I know. I saw them giggling and whispering and nodding. About what? I would have been amazed. You too. The chitchat went on and on. Old Pierre, the boss, scowled: get on with your work, Mademoiselle. Judy went in back. Dana returned to the table. Said something to Louise that I couldn't hear. Louise grinned. The two of them got up, excused themselves, went toward the bathroom together. Judy was still back there somewhere too. What the hell was brewing? Gone a long time. Louise returned; Dana didn't. I gave her a quizzical look.

Louise said, looking mischievous, "How would you feel if Judy comes home with us tonight, Charlie?"

That startled me. "Instead of Dana?"

"Also."

"Three women?" I was utterly floored. "Jesus Christ."

"Think you can handle it?"

"I could try," I said, still stunned. "God Almighty! *Three!*"

"Dana thought it might be fun. A really Los Angeles thing to do. She can be very impulsive that way."

It took a couple more bathroom conferences for them to work everything out. Somehow they thought it was crass to discuss the logistics in front of me. But finally it was all set up. The restaurant would close around eleven; it would take a little time for the employees to cash out, but Judy could be at my place by half past. A late evening, but worth it, all things considered.

The rest of dinner was an anticlimax. We talked about the weather, the food, the wine, Dana's screenwriting ambitions. But we all had our minds on what was coming up later. Now and then Judy, busy at other tables, shot a glance at me. Second thoughts? I wondered. Or just sizing me up? I shot a few glances at her. I felt dizzy, dazzled, astounded. Would I be equal to the task? A foursome instead of a threesome? A one-man orgy? Sure. God help me, I had to be equal to it. Or else.

We dragged the meal out till half past nine. I drove to my place, Dana and Louise following in Louise's car. Upstairs. Soft music, low lights. Drinks. Kept clothes on while waiting for Judy. Not polite to jump the first two ladies before number three shows up.

Long wait. Eleven-thirty. Quarter to. Judy getting cold feet? Midnight. Doorbell.

Judy. "I thought we'd never finish up tonight! Hey, what a cool place you have, Charlie!"

"Would you like a drink? A joint?"

"Sure. Sure."

We were all a little nervous. The big moment approaching and nobody quite certain how to start it off.

Things simply started themselves off: a sudden exchange of glances, grins, nods, and into the bedroom we went and the clothes dropped away. And then we were one naked heap on top of the water bed.

So it began, this extraordinary event. The wildest fantasy you could imagine? Sure. But I'm here to tell you that it's possible to get too much of a good thing. Go ahead, laugh.

They certainly were gorgeous. Louise trim and athletic and darkly tanned, Dana pale beneath her clothing and breastier than she seemed when dressed, Judy plump-rumped, red-haired, freckled down to her belly. We were all pretty stoned and piled on each other like demented teenagers. I got my right hand onto one of Judy's soft, jiggling breasts and my left onto one of Dana's firmer ones and put my tongue into Louise's mouth, and somebody's hand passed between my thighs, and I brought my knee up between somebody else's thighs so she could rub back and forth on it, and then abruptly I was fucking Louise – start with the familiar one, work into it slowly – while trying to find Dana and Judy with my fingers or toes or anything else I didn't happen to be using on Louise.

The perfect deal, you say? Well, maybe. But also a little confusing and distracting. There were all sorts of things to think about. For example I didn't want to get so carried away with Louise that I'd have nothing left for the other two. Luckily Louise always came easily and quickly, so I was able to bring her to her pleasure without expending a lot of my own energy, and I turned to find one of the others.

But they were busy with each other. Licking and grappling, slurping away merrily. I realized now that they had been better chums back in the old New York days than they had mentioned. It was a turn-on to watch them, sure, but finally I had to slide myself between them to remind them I was here. I peeled them apart and Dana came into my arms and I went into Dana. She was heated up and ready, wild, even, and as her hips began a frantic triple-time pumping I had to catch her and slow her down or she would finish me off in six seconds flat. A little humiliating, really, having to ease her back like that. But for me the first come is always by far the best, and I didn't want this once-in-a-lifetime event to be over so fast. So that was something else distracting to think about. I clung to Dana for as much of the ride as I could take, but finally I had to pull out and finish her by hand, while sliding over into Judy. Louise was moving around in the background somewhere. She was one more thing to worry about, really, because I didn't want to ignore anyone even for a minute, and there wasn't enough of me to go around. I shouldn't have worried all that much. Louise could take care of herself, I knew, and would, and did. But I am a conscientious sort of guy in these matters.

I know, I make it sound like it was a lot of work, and there you are sitting there telling me that you'd have been happy to have taken my place if I found it all that much of a bother. Well, let me tell you, I know there are a lot worse things to complain about than finding yourself in bed with too many women at once. But it *was* a lot of work. Really. A stunt like that has problems as well as rewards. Still and all, I have to admit it wasn't such a terrible ordeal. Just a little complicated.

I was in the rhythm of it now – you know how it is, when you get past that first fear of coming too soon, and feel like an iron man who can go on forever? – and I swung around from Judy to Louise again, and back to Dana, and on to Judy. While I was with Louise, Dana and Judy seemed very capable of keeping each other occupied. While I was with either of the other two, Louise improvised with one or another or all three of us at once. It went on and on. I was swimming in a sea of pussy. Wherever I moved there was a breast in my hand and one in my mouth and somebody's thighs wrapped around my middle. Our bodies were shiny with sweat; we were laughing, gasping, dizzy with the craziness of it.

Then I knew I would drop dead if it went on one more minute, and I reached for Louise and entered her and began to move in the special rhythm that brings on my orgasm. She knew at once what I was doing: she slipped into a reciprocating rhythm and whispered little encouraging things into my ear and I cut loose with the most gigantic come I am ever going to have.

And rolled off the bed, chuckling to myself, and lay on the floor in a stupor for I don't know how long while sounds of ecstasy came from the bed above me. Somewhere in the night I found enough strength to get back into the fray for another round or two. But by three in the morning we had all had enough, and then some. I opened the bedroom windows to let the place air out, and one by one we showered and the girls dressed, and we went into the living room, weary and dazed and a little sheepish, all of us stunned by everything that had passed between us this weird night. Dana and Judy left first. Louise lingered for one last joint.

"Well?" she said. "Satisfied now?"

"Am I ever," I said.

What I didn't tell her then, but will confess to you now, is that I wasn't. Not really. Three at once is a remarkable thing. Extraordinary. Unbelievable, almost. But not really satisfying, in terms of my original fantasy. It was too hectic, too mechanical, more work than play. Or so it seems to me, looking back on it now.

Is that hard to believe? Maybe I'm being too picky, I guess. Some guys are never satisfied with anything.

But really: all I wanted was *two*. Not three. Just two. Fucking one, caressing another – switching – switching back – calmly, attentively, sharing my bed with two lovely women, concentrating on them both, fully, without any extraneous distractions. Not an endurance contest or a circus event but a divine adventure in sensuality.

Well, it was never to be, for me. We set it up and then by accident a third woman got involved and I could never set it up again the right way. Louise met a real-estate tycoon a few weeks later and moved to Phoenix. I phoned Dana but she told me she was going back to New York. Le Provence closed and I don't know where Judy went. And the seventies ended and life got a lot more sedate for most of us, especially where stuff like threesomes were concerned. So I still haven't ever been to bed with two women at once, though I once did it with three. Ironic, I guess.

Two at once – I still fantasize about it.

I guess it's not ever going to come to pass. But I live in hope.

A LONG LETTER FROM F.

Leonard Cohen

MY DEAR FRIEND,

Five years with the length of five years. I do not know exactly where this letter finds you. I suppose you have thought often of me. You were always my favorite male orphan. Oh, much more than that, much more, but I do not choose, for this last *written* communication, to expend myself in easy affection.

If my lawyers have performed according to my instructions, you are now in possession of my worldly estate, my soap collection, my factory, my Masonic aprons, my treehouse. I imagine you have already appropriated my style. I wonder where my style has led you. As I stand on this last springy diving board I wonder where my style has led me.

I am writing this last letter in the Occupational Therapy Room. I have let women lead me anywhere, and I am not sorry. Convents, kitchens, perfumed telephone booths, poetry courses – I followed women anywhere. I followed women into Parliament because I know how they love power. I followed women into the beds of men so that I could learn what they found there. The air is streaked with the smoke of their perfume. The world is clawed with their amorous laughter. I followed women into the world, because I loved the world. Breasts, buttocks, everywhere I followed the soft balloons. When women hissed at me from brothel windows, when they softly hissed at me over the shoulders of their dancing husbands, I followed them and I sank down with them, and sometimes when I listened to their hissing I knew it was nothing but the sound of the withering and collapse of their soft balloons.

This is the sound, this hissing, which hovers over every woman. There is one exception. I knew one woman who surrounded herself with a very different noise, maybe it was music, maybe it was silence. I am speaking, of course, about our Edith. It is five years now that I have been buried. Surely you know by now that Edith could not belong to you alone.

I followed the young nurses to Occupational Therapy. They have covered the soft balloons with starched linen, a pleasant tantalizing cover which my old lust breaks as easily as an eggshell. I have followed their dusty white legs.

Men also give off a sound. Do you know what our sound is, dear frayed friend? It is the sound you hear in male sea shells. Guess what it is. I will give you three guesses. You must fill in the lines. The nurses like to see me use my ruler.

1.—

2.—

3.—

The nurses like to lean over my shoulder and watch me use my red plastic ruler. They hiss through my hair and their hisses have the aroma of alcohol and sandalwood, and their starched clothes crackle like the white tissue paper and artificial straw which creamy chocolate Easter eggs come in.

Oh, I am happy today. I know that these pages will be filled with happiness. Surely you did not think that I would leave you with a melancholy gift.

Well, what are your answers? Isn't it remarkable that I have extended your training over this wide gulf?

It is the very opposite of a hiss, the sound men make. It is Shhh, the sound made around the index finger raised to the lips. Shhh, and the roofs are raised against the storm. Shhh, the forests are cleared so the wind will not rattle the trees. Shhh, the hydrogen rockets go off to silence, dissent and variety. It is not an unpleasant noise. It is indeed a perky tune, like the bubbles above a clam. Shhh, will everybody listen, please. Will the animals stop howling, please. Will the belly stop rumbling, please. Will Time call off its ultrasonic dogs, please.

It is the sound my ball pen makes on the hospital paper as I run it down the edge of the red ruler. Shhh, it says to the billion unlines of whiteness. Shhh, it whispers to the white chaos, lie down in dormitory rows. Shhh, it implores the dancing molecules, I love dances but I do not love foreign dances, I love dances that have rules, my rules.

Did you fill in the lines, old friend? Are you sitting in a restaurant or a monastery as I lie underground? Did you fill in the lines? You didn't have to, you know. Did I trick you again?

Now what about this silence we are so desperate to clear in the wilderness? Have we labored, plowed, muzzled, fenced so that we might hear a Voice? Fat chance. The Voice comes out of the whirlwind, and long ago we hushed the whirlwind. I wish that you would remember that the Voice comes out of the whirlwind. Some men, some of the time, have remembered. Was I one?

I will tell you why we nailed up the cork. I am a born teacher and it is not my nature to keep things to myself. Surely five years have tortured and tickled you into that understanding. I always intended to tell you everything, the complete gift. How is your constipation, darling?

I imagine they are about twenty-four years old, these soft balloons that are floating beside me this very second, these Easter candies swaddled in official laundry. Twenty-four years of journey, almost a quarter of a century, but still youth for breasts. They have come a long way to graze shyly at my shoulder as I gaily wield my ruler to serve someone's definition of sanity. They are still young, they are barely young, but they hiss fiercely, and they dispense a heady perfume of alcohol and sandalwood. Her face gives nothing away, it is a scrubbed nurse's face, family lines mercifully washed away, a face prepared to be a screen for our blue home movies as we sink in disease. A compassionate sphinx's face to drip our riddles on, and, like paws buried in the sand, her round breasts claw and scratch against the uniform. Familiar? Yes, it is a face such as Edith often wore, our perfect nurse.

– Those are very nice lines you've drawn.

– I'm quite fond of them.

Hiss, hiss, run for your lives, the bombs are dying.

– Would you like some colored pencils?

– As long as they don't marry our erasers.

Wit, invention, shhh, shhh, now do you see why we've sound-

proofed the forest, carved benches round the wild arena? To hear
the hissing, to hear wrinkles squeezing out the bounce, to attend
the death of our worlds. Memorize this and forget it. It deserves a
circuit, but a very tiny circuit, in the brain. I might as well tell you
that I exempt myself, as of now, from all these categories.

Play with me, old friend.

Take my spirit hand. You have been dipped in the air of our
planet, you have been baptized with fire, shit, history, love, and
loss. Memorize this. It explains the Golden Rule.

See me at this moment of my curious little history, nurse
leaning over my work, my prick rotten and black, you saw my
worldly prick decayed, but now see my visionary prick, cover
your head and see my visionary prick which I do not own and
never owned, which owned me, which was me, which bore me as
a broom bears a witch, bore me from world to world, from sky to
sky. Forget this.

Like many teachers, a lot of the stuff I gave away was simply a
burden I couldn't carry any longer. I feel my store of garbage
giving out. Soon I'll have nothing left to leave around but stories.
Maybe I'll attain the plane of spreading gossip, and thus finish
my prayers to the world.

Edith was a promoter of sex orgies and a purveyor of narcotics.
Once she had lice. Twice she had crabs. I've written crabs very
small because there is a time and a place for everything, and a
young nurse is standing close behind me wondering whether she
is being drawn by my power or her charity. I appear to be
engrossed in my therapeutic exercises, she in the duties of super-
vision, but shhh, hiss, the noise of steam spreads through O.T., it
mixes with the sunlight, it bestows a rainbow halo on each bowed
head of sufferer, doctor, nurse, volunteer. You ought to look up
this nurse sometime. She will be twenty-nine when my lawyers
locate you and complete my material bequest.

Down some green corridor, in a large closet among pails,
squeegees, antiseptic mops, Mary Voolnd from Nova Scotia will
peel down her dusty white stockings and present an old man with
the freedom of her knees, and we will leave nothing behind us but
our false ears with which to pick up the steps of the approaching
orderly.

Steam coming off the planet, clouds of fleecy steam as boy and
girl populations clash in religious riots, hot and whistling like a

graveyard sodomist our little planet embraces its fragile yo-yo destiny, tuned in the secular mind like a dying engine. But some do not hear it this way, some flying successful moon-shot eyes do not see it this way. They do not hear the individual noises shhh, hiss, they hear the sound of the sounds together, they behold the interstices flashing up and down the cone of the flowering whirl-wind.

Do I listen to the Rolling Stones? Ceaselessly.

Am I hurt enough?

The old hat evades me. I don't know if I can wait. The river that I'll walk beside – I seem to miss it by a coin toss every year. Did I have to buy that factory? Was I obliged to run for Parliament? Was Edith such a good lay? My café table, my small room, my drugged true friends from whom I don't expect too much – I seem to abandon them almost by mistake, for promises, phone calls casually made. The old hat, the rosy ugly old face that won't waste time in mirrors, the uncombed face that will laugh amazed at the manifold traffic. Where is my old hat? I tell myself I can wait. I argue that my path was correct. Is it only the argument that is incorrect? Is it Pride that tempts me with intimations of a new style? Is it Cowardice that keeps me from an old ordeal? I tell myself: wait. I listen to the rain, to the scientific noises of the hospital. I get happy because of many small things. I go to sleep with the earplug of the transistor stuck in. Even my Parliamentary disgrace begins to evade me. My name appears more and more frequently among the nationalist heroes. Even my hospitalization has been described as an English trick to muzzle me. I fear I will lead a government yet, rotten prick and all. I lead men too easily: my fatal facility.

My dear friend, go beyond my style.

Something in your eyes, old lover, described me as the man I wanted to be. Only you and Edith extended that generosity to me, perhaps only you. Your baffled cries as I tormented you, you were the good animal I wanted to be, or failing that, the good animal I wanted to exist. It was I who feared the rational mind, therefore I tried to make you a little mad. I was desperate to learn from your bewilderment. You were the wall which I, batlike, bounced my screams off of, so I might have direction in this long nocturnal flight.

I cannot stop teaching. Have I taught you anything?

I must smell better with this confession, because Mary Voolnd has just awarded me a distinct signal of cooperation.

– Would you like to touch my cunt with one of your old hands?

– Which hand are you thinking of?

– Would you like to depress a nipple with a forefinger and make it disappear?

– And make it reappear too?

– If it reappears I will hate you forever. I will inscribe you in the Book of Fumblers.

—

– That's better.

—

– I'm dripping.

Do you see how I cannot stop teaching? All my arabesques are for publication. Can you imagine how I envied you, whose suffering was so traditional?

From time to time, I will confess, I hated you. The teacher of composition is not always gratified to listen to the Valedictorian Address delivered in his own style, especially if he has never been Valedictorian himself. Times I felt depleted: you with all that torment, me with nothing but a System.

When I worked among the Jews (you own the factory), regularly I saw a curious expression of pain cross the boss's Levantine face. This I observed as he ushered out a filthy coreligionist, bearded, shifty, and smelling of low Romanian cuisine, who visited the factory every second month begging on behalf of an obscure Yiddish physical-therapy university. Our boss always gave the creature a few groschen and hurried him through the shipping exit with awkward haste, as if his presence there might start something far worse than a strike. I was always kinder to the boss on those days, for he was strangely vulnerable and comfortless. We walked slowly between the great rolls of cashmere and Harris tweed and I let him have his way with me. (He, for one, did not resent my new muscles, achieved through Dynamic Tension. Why did you drive me away?)

– What is my factory today? A pile of rags and labels, a distraction, an insult to my spirit.

– A tomb of your ambition, sir?

– That's right, boy.

– Dust in the mouth, cinders in the eye, sir?

– I don't want that bum in here again, do you hear me? One of these days they're going to walk out of here with him. And I'll be at the head of the line. That poor wretch is happier than the whole caboodle.

But, of course, he never turned the loathsome beggar away, and suffered for it, regular as menstruation pain, which is how the female regrets life beyond the pale of lunar jurisdiction.

You plagued me like the moon. I knew you were bound by old laws of suffering and obscurity. I am fearful of the cripple's wisdom. A pair of crutches, a grotesque limp can ruin a stroll which I begin in a new suit, clean-shaven, whistling. I envied you the certainty that you would amount to nothing. I coveted the magic of torn clothes. I was jealous of the terrors I constructed for you but could not tremble before myself. I was never drunk enough, never poor enough, never rich enough. All this hurts, perhaps it hurts enough. It makes me want to cry out for comfort. It makes me stretch my hands out horizontally. Yes, I long to be President of the new Republic. I love to hear the armed teen-agers chant my name outside the hospital gates. Long live the Revolution! Let me be President for my last thirty days.

Where are you walking tonight, dear friend? Did you give up meat? Are you disarmed and empty, an instrument of Grace? Can you stop talking? Has loneliness led you into ecstasy?

There was a deep charity in your suck. I hated it, I abused it. But I dare to hope that you embody the best of my longings. I dare to hope that you will produce the pearl and justify these poor secreted irritations.

This letter is written in the old language, and it has caused me no little discomfort to recall the obsolete usages. I've had to stretch my mind back into areas bordered with barbed wire, from which I spent a life-time removing myself. However, I do not regret the effort.

Our love will never die, that I can promise you, I, who launch this letter like a kite among the winds of your desire. We were born together, and in our kisses we confessed our longing to be born again. We lay in each other's arms, each of us the other's teacher. We sought the peculiar tone of each peculiar night. We tried to clear away the static, suffering under the hint that the static was part of the tone. I was your adventure and you were my adventure. I was your journey and you were my journey, and

Edith was our holy star. This letter rises out of our love like the sparks between dueling swords, like the shower of needles from flapping cymbals, like the bright seeds of sweat sliding through the center of our tight embrace, like the white feathers hung in the air by razored bushido cocks, like the shriek between two approaching puddles of mercury, like the atmosphere of secrets which twin children exude. I was your mystery and you were my mystery, and we rejoiced to learn that mystery was our home. Our love cannot die. Out of history I come to tell you this. Like two mammoths, tusk-locked in earnest sport at the edge of the advancing age of ice, we preserve each other. Our queer love keeps the lines of our manhood hard and clean, so that we bring nobody but our own self to our separate marriage beds, and our women finally know us.

Mary Voolnd has finally admitted my left hand into the creases of her uniform. She watched me compose the above paragraph, so I let it run on rather extravagantly. Women love excess in a man because it separates him from his fellows and makes him lonely. All that women know of the male world has been revealed to them by lonely, excessive refugees from it. Raging fairies they cannot resist because of their highly specialized intelligence.

– Keep writing, she hisses.

Mary has turned her back to me. The balloons are shrieking like whistles signaling the end of every labor. Mary pretends to inspect a large rug some patient wove, thus shielding our precious play. Slow as a snail I push my hand, palm down, up the tight rough stocking on the back of her thigh. The linen of her skirt is crisp and cool against my knuckles and nails, the stockinged thigh is warm, curved, a little damp like a loaf of fresh white bread.

– Higher, she hisses.

I am in no hurry. Old friend, I am in no hurry. I feel I shall be doing this throughout eternity. Her buttocks contract impatiently, like two boxing gloves touching before the match. My hand pauses to ride the quiver on the thigh.

– Hurry, she hisses.

Yes, I can tell by the tension in the stocking that I am approaching the peninsula which is hitched to the garter device. I will travel the whole peninsula, hot skin on either side, then I will leap off the nipple-shaped garter device. The threads of the stocking tighten. I bunch my fingers together so as not to make premature contact. Mary is jiggling, endangering the journey. My forefinger scouts out the garter device. It is warm. The little metal loop, the rubber button – warm right through.

– Please, please, she hisses.

Like angels on the head of a pin, my fingers dance on the rubber button. Which way shall I leap? Toward the outside thigh, hard, warm as the shell of a beached tropical turtle? Or toward the swampy mess in the middle? Or fasten like a bat on the huge soft over-hanging boulder of her right buttock? It is very humid up her white starched skirt. It is like one of those airplane hangars wherein clouds form and it actually rains indoors. Mary is bouncing her bum like a piggy bank which is withholding a gold coin. The inundations are about to begin. I choose the middle.

– Yesssss.

Delicious soup stews my hand. Viscous geysers shower my wrist. Magnetic rain tests my Bulova. She jiggles for position, then drops over my fist like a gorilla net. I had been snaking through her wet hair, compressing it between my fingers like cotton candy. Now I am surrounded by artesian exuberance, nipply frills, numberless bulby brains, pumping constellations of mucous hearts. Moist Morse messages move up my arm, master my intellectual head, more, more, message dormant portions of dark brain, elect happy new kings for the exhausted pretenders of the mind. I am a seal inventing undulations in a vast electric aquacade, I am wires of tungsten burning in the seas of bulb, I am creature of Mary cave, I am froth of Mary wave, bums of nurse Mary applaud greedily as she maneuvers to plow her asshole on the edge of my arm bone, rose of rectum sliding up and down like the dream of banister fiend.

– Slish slosh slish slosh.

Are we not happy? Loud as we are, no one hears us, but this is a tiny miracle in the midst of all this bounty, so are the rainbow crowns hovering over every skull but tiny miracles. Mary looks at me over her shoulder, greeting me with rolled-up eyes white as eggshells, and an open goldfish mouth amazed smile. In the gold sunshine of OT everyone believes he is a stinking genius, offering baskets, ceramic ashtrays, thong-sewn wallets on the radiant altars of their perfect health.

*   *   *

Old friend, you may kneel as you read this, for now I come to the sweet burden of my argument. I did not know what I had to tell you, but now I know. I did not know what I wanted to proclaim, but now I am sure. All my speeches were preface to this, all my exercises but a clearing of my throat. I confess I tortured you but only to draw your attention to this. I confess I betrayed you but only to tap your shoulder. In our kisses and sucks, this, ancient darling, I meant to whisper.

God is alive. Magic is afoot. God is alive. Magic is afoot. God is afoot. Magic is alive. Alive is afoot. Magic never died. God never sickened. Many poor men lied. Many sick men lied. Magic never weakened. Magic never hid. Magic always ruled. God is afoot. God never died. God was ruler though his funeral lengthened. Though his mourners thickened Magic never fled. Though his shrouds were hoisted the naked God did live. Though his words were twisted the naked Magic thrived. Though his death was published round and round the world the heart did not believe. Many hurt men wondered. Many struck men bled. Magic never faltered. Magic always led. Many stones were rolled but God would not lie down. Many wild men lied. Many fat men listened. Though they offered stones Magic still was fed. Though they locked their coffers God was always served. Magic is afoot. God rules. Alive is afoot. Alive is in command. Many weak men hungered. Many strong men thrived. Though they boasted solitude God was at their side. Nor the dreamer in his cell, nor the captain on the hill. Magic is alive. Though his death was pardoned round and round the world the heart would not believe. Though laws were carved in marble they could not shelter men. Though altars built in parliaments they could not order men. Police arrested Magic and Magic went with them for Magic loves the hungry. But Magic would not tarry. It moves from arm to arm. It would not stay with them. Magic is afoot. It cannot come to harm. It rests in an empty palm. It spawns in an empty mind. But Magic is no instrument. Magic is the end. Many men drove Magic but Magic stayed behind. Many strong men lied. They only passed through Magic and out the other side. Many weak men lied. They came to God in secret and though they left him nourished they would not tell who healed. Though mountains danced before them they said that God was dead. Though his shrouds were hoisted the naked God did live. This I

mean to whisper to my mind. This I mean to laugh with in my
mind. This I mean my mind to serve till service is but Magic
moving through the world, and mind itself is Magic coursing
through the flesh, and flesh itself is Magic dancing on a clock, and
time itself the Magic Length of God.

Old friend, aren't you happy? You and Edith alone know how
long I've waited for this instruction.

– Damn you, Mary Voolnd spits at me.

– What?

– Your hand's gone limp. Grab!

How many times must I be slain, old friend? I do not understand the mystery, after all. I am an old man with one hand on a
letter and one hand up a juicy cunt, and I understand nothing. If
my instruction were gospel, would it wither up my hand? Certainly not. It doesn't figure. I'm picking lies out of the air.
They're aiming lies at me. The truth should make me strong.
I pray you, dear friend, interpret me, go beyond me. I know now
that I am a hopeless case. Go forth, teach the world what I meant
to be.

– Grab.

Mary wiggles and the hand comes to life, like those ancestral
sea ferns which turned animal. Now the soft elbows of her cunt
are nudging me somewhere. Now her asshole is rubbing the ridge
of my arm, not like rosy banister reverie as before, but like an
eraser removing dream evidence, and now, alas, the secular
message appears.

– Grab, please, please. They'll start to notice at any second.

That is true. The air in O.T. is restless, no longer golden
sunshine, merely sunny and warm. Yes, I've let the magic die.
The doctors remember that they are at work and refuse to yawn.
A fat little lady issues a duchess command, poor thing. A teen-
ager weeps because he has wet himself again. A former school
principal farts hysterically, threatening us all with no gym. Lord
of Life, is my pain sufficient?

– Hurry.

Mary bears down. My fingers brush something. It is not part of
Mary. It is foreign matter.

– Grab it. Pull it out. It's from our friends.

– Soon.

Dear Friend,

It comes back to me.

I sent you the wrong box of fireworks. I did not include the Pimple Cure in my famous soap and cosmetic collection. I cured Edith's acne with it, you know. But of course you do not know, because you have no reason to believe that Edith's complexion was ever anything but lovable to kiss and touch. When I found her her complexion was not lovable to kiss and touch, nor even to look at. She was in an ugly mess. In another part of this long letter I will tell you how we, Edith and I, constructed the lovely wife whom you discovered performing extraordinary manicures in the barber shop of the Mount Royal Hotel. Begin to prepare yourself.

The soap collection, though it includes transparent bars, ghosts of pine, lemon and sandalwood, Willy jelly, is useless without the Pimple Cure. All you will achieve is scrubbed, fragrant pimples. Perhaps that is enough for you – a demoralizing speculation.

You always resisted me. I had a body waiting for you, but you turned it down. I had a vision of you with 19-inch arms, but you walked away. I saw you with massive lower pecs and horseshoe triceps, with bulk and definition simultaneously. In certain intimate embraces I saw exactly how low your buttocks should descend. In no case, when you were squatting in front of me, should your buttocks have been lowered so far down that they sat on your heels, for once this occurs the thigh muscles are no longer engaged *but the buttocks muscles are*, ergo your rocky cheeks, a very selfish development that gave me no happiness and is a factor in your bowel predicament. I saw you oiled and shining, a classic midsection of washboard abdominals fluted with razor-edged obliques and serratus. I had a way to cut up the serratus. I had access to a Professional Greek Chair. I had the straps and stirrups to blitz your knob into a veritable sledgehammer, mouthful for a pelican. I had a Sphincter Kit that worked off the tap like washing machines and bosom aggrandizers. Had you a notion of my Yoga? Call it ruin, or call it creation, have you a notion of my work on Edith? Are you aware of the Ganges you insulted with a million mean portages?

Perhaps it is my own fault. I withheld certain vital items, an apparatus here, a fact there – but only because (yes, this is closer to truth) I dreamed you would be greater than me. I saw a king without dominion. I saw a gun bleeding. I saw the prince of Paradise Forgotten. I saw a pimpled movie star. I saw a racing hearse. I saw the New Jew. I saw popular lame storm troopers. I wanted you to bring pain to heaven. I saw fire curing headaches. I saw the triumph of election over discipline. I wanted your confusion to be a butterfly net for magic. I saw ecstasy without fun and vice versa. I saw all things change their nature by mere intensification of their properties. I wanted to discredit training for the sake of purer prayer. I held things back from you because I wished you greater than my Systems conceived. I saw wounds pulling oars without becoming muscles.

Who is the New Jew?

The New Jew loses his mind gracefully. He applies finance to abstraction resulting in successful messianic politics, colorful showers of meteorites and other symbolic weather. He has induced amnesia by a repetitious study of history, his very forgetfulness caressed by facts which he accepts with visible enthusiasm. He changes for a thousand years the value of stigma, causing men of all nations to pursue it as superior sexual talisman. The New Jew is the founder of Magic Canada, Magic French Québec, and Magic America. He demonstrates that yearning brings surprises. He uses regret as a bulwark of originality. He confuses nostalgic theories of Negro supremacy which were tending to the monolithic. He confirms tradition through amnesia, tempting the whole world with rebirth. He dissolves history and ritual by accepting unconditionally the complete heritage. He travels without passport because powers consider him harmless. His penetration into jails enforces his supranationality, and flatters his legalistic disposition. Sometimes he is Jewish but always he is American, and now and then, Québecois.

These were my dreams for you and me, vieux copain – New Jews, the two of us, queer, militant, invisible, part of a possible new tribe bound by gossip and rumors of divine evidence.

I sent you the wrong box of fireworks, and this was not entirely by mistake. You got the Rich Brothers' All-American Assortment, which claims to be the largest selection offered at the price, over 550 pieces. Let us be charitable and say that I didn't know exactly how long the ordeal should last. I could have sent you the Famous Banner Fireworks Display, same price as the other, with over a *thousand* pieces of noise and beauty. I denied you the rocking Electric Cannon Salutes, the good old-fashioned Cherry Bombs, the Silver Rain Torch, the 16-report Battle in Clouds, the suicidal Jap Pop-Bottle Night Rockets. Let charity record that I did this out of charity. The explosions might have drawn malicious attention. But how can I justify withholding the Big Colorful Family Lawn Display, a special package made up for those tuned to a minimum of noise? Musical Vesuvius Flitter Fountains I hid from you, Comet Star Shells, Flower Pots with Handles, Large Floral Shells, Triangle Spinning Wheels, Patriotic Colored Fire Flag. Stretch your heart, darling. Let charity argue that I spared you a domestic extravagance.

I am going to set you straight on everything: Edith, me, you, Tekakwitha, the A————s, the firecrackers.

I didn't want you to burn yourself to suicide. On the other hand, I didn't want the exodus to be too easy. This last from professional teacher's pride, and also a subtle envy which I have previously exposed.

What is more sinister is the possibility that I may have contrived to immunize you against the ravages of ecstasy by regular inoculations of homeopathic doses of it. A diet of paradox fattens the ironist not the psalmist.

Perhaps I should have gone all the way and sent you the submachine guns which the firecrackers concealed in my brilliant smuggling operation. I suffer from the Virgo disease: nothing I did was pure enough. I was never sure whether I wanted disciples or partisans. I was never sure whether I wanted Parliament or a hermitage.

I will confess that I never saw the Québec Revolution clearly, even at the time of my parliamentary disgrace. I simply refused to support the War, not because I was French, or a pacifist (which of course I'm not), but because I was tired. I knew what they were doing to the Gypsies, I had a whiff of Zyklon B, but I was very, very tired. Do you remember the world at that time? A huge jukebox played a sleepy tune. The tune was a couple of thousand years old and we danced to it with our eyes closed. The tune was called History and we loved it, Nazis, Jews, everybody. We loved it because we made it up, because, like Thucydides, we knew that whatever happened to us was the most important thing that ever happened in the world. History made us feel good so we played it over and over, deep into the night. We smiled as our uncles went to bed, and we were glad to get rid of them, because they didn't know how to do the H. in spite of all their boasts and old newspaper clippings. Good night, old frauds. Someone worked the rheostat and we squeezed the body in our arms, we inhaled the perfumed hair, we bumped into each other's genitals. History was our song, History chose us to make History. We gave ourselves to it, caressed by events.

In perfect drowsy battalions we moved through the moonlight. Its will be done. In perfect sleep we took the soap and waited for the showers.

Never mind, never mind. I've gone too deep into the old language. It may trap me there.

I was tired. I was sick of the inevitable. I tried to slip out of History. Never mind, never mind. Just say I was tired. I said no.

– Leave Parliament this instant!

– Frogs!

– They can't be trusted!

– Vote him dead!

I ran off with heavy heart. I loved the red chairs of Parliament. I cherished the fucks under the monument. I had cream in National Library. Too impure for empty future, I wept old jackpots.

Now my fat confession. I loved the magic of guns. I sneaked them in under the skin of firecrackers. My old monkey made me do it. I planted guns in Québec for I was hung between free and coward. Guns suck magic. I buried guns for future History. If History rule let me be Mr. History. The guns are green. The flowers poke. I let History back because I was lonely. Do not follow. Go beyond my style. I am nothing but a rotten hero.

Among the bars in my soap collection. Never mind.

Later.

Among the bars in my soap collection. I paid big cash for it. Argentine vacation hotel week-end shack-up with Edith. Never mind that. I paid equivalent U.S. $635. Waiter giving me the eye for days. He not cute little recent immigrant. Former Lord of few miserable European acres. Transaction beside swimming pool. I wanted it. I wanted it. My lust for secular gray magic. Human soap. A full bar, minus the wear of one bath in which I plunged myself, for better or for worse.

Mary, Mary, where are you, my little Abishag?

My dear friend, take my spirit hand.

I am going to show you everything *happening*. That is as far as I can take you. I cannot bring you into the middle of action. My hope is that I have prepared *you* for this pilgrimage. I didn't suspect the pettiness of my dream. I believed that I had conceived the vastest dream of my generation: I wanted to be a magician. That was my idea of glory. Here is a plea based on my whole experience: do not be a magician, be magic.

That weekend when I arranged for you to work in the Archives, Edith and I flew down to Argentine for a little sun and experiments. Edith was having trouble with her body: it kept changing sizes, she even feared that it might be dying.

We took a large air-conditioned room overlooking the sea, double-locking the door as soon as the porter had left with his hand full of tip.

Edith spread a large rubber sheet over the double bed, carefully moving from corner to corner to smooth it out. I loved to watch her bend over. Her buttocks were my masterpiece. Call her nipples an eccentric extravagance, but the bum was perfect. It's true that from year to year it required electronic massage and applications of hormone mold, but the conception was perfect.

Edith took off her clothes and lay down on the rubber sheet. I stood over her. Her eyes blazed.

– I hate you, F. I hate you for what you've done to me and my husband. I was a fool to get mixed up with you. I wish he'd known me before you.

– Hush, Edith. We don't want to go over all that again. You wanted to be beautiful.

– I can't remember anything now. I'm all confused. Perhaps I was beautiful before.

– Perhaps, I echoed in a voice as sad as hers.

Edith shifted her brown hips to make herself comfortable, and a shaft of sunlight infiltrated her pubic hair, giving it a rust-coloured tint. Yes, that was beauty beyond my craft.

> Sun on Her Cunt
> Wispy Rusty Hair
> Her Tunnels Sunk in Animal
> Her Kneecaps Round and Bare

I knelt beside the bed and lay one of my thin ears on the little sunlit orchard, listening to the tiny swamp machinery.

– You've meddled, F. You've gone against God.

– Hush, my little chicken. There is some cruelty even I cannot bear.

– You should have left me like you found me. I'm no good to anyone now.

– I could suck you forever, Edith.

She made the shaved hairs on the back of my neck tingle with the grazing of her lovely brown fingers.

– Sometimes I feel sorry for you, F. You might have been a great man.

– Stop talking, I bubbled.

– Stand up, F. Get your mouth off me. I'm pretending that you are someone else.

– Who?

– The waiter.

– Which one? I demanded.

– With the mustache and the raincoat.

– I thought so, I thought so.

– You noticed him, too, didn't you, F.?

– Yes.

I stood up too suddenly. Dizziness twirled my brain like a dial and formerly happy chewed food in my stomach turned into vomit. I hated my life, I hated my meddling, I hated my ambition. For a second I wanted to be an ordinary bloke cloistered in a tropical hotel room with an Indian orphan.

> Take from me my Camera
> Take from me my Glass
> The Sun the Wet Forever
> Let the Doctors Pass

– Don't cry, F. You knew it had to happen. You wanted me to go all the way. Now I'm no good to anyone and I'll try anything.

I stumbled to the window but it was hermetically sealed. The ocean was deep green. The beach was polka-dotted with beach umbrellas. How I longed for my old teacher, Charles Axis. I strained my eyes for an immaculate white bathing suit, unshadowed by topography of genitalia.

– Oh, come here, F. I can't stand watching a man vomit and
cry.

She cradled my head between her bare breasts, stuffing a
nipple into each ear.

– There now.

– Thankyou, thankyou, thankyou, thankyou.

– Listen, F. Listen the way you wanted us all to listen.

– I'm listening, Edith.

> Let me let me follow
> Down the Sticky Caves
> Where embryonic Cities
> Form Scum upon the Waves

– You're not listening, F.

– I'm trying.

– I feel sorry for you, F.

– Help me, Edith.

– Then get back to work. That's the only thing that can help
you. Try to finish the work you began on all of us.

She was right. I was the Moses of our little exodus. I would
never cross. My mountain might be very high but it rises from the
desert. Let it suffice me.

I recovered my professional attitude. Her lower perfume was
still in my nostrils but that was my business. I surveyed the nude
girl from my Pisgah. Her soft lips smiled.

– That's better, F. Your tongue was nice but you do better as a
doctor.

– All right, Edith. What seems to be the trouble now?

– I can't make myself come any more.

– Of course you can't. If we're going to perfect the pan-
orgasmic body, extend the erogenous zone over the whole fleshy
envelope, popularize the Telephone Dance, then we've got to
begin by diminishing the tyranny of the nipples, lips, clitoris, and
asshole.

– You're going against God, F. You say dirty words.

– I'll take my chances.

– I feel so lost since I can't make myself come any more. I'm not
ready for the other stuff yet. It makes me too lonely. I feel
blurred. Sometimes I forget where my cunt is.

—You make me weary, Edith. To think I've pinned all my hopes on you and your wretched husband.

—Give it back to me, F.

—All right, Edith. It's a very simple matter. We do it with books. I thought this might happen, so I brought the appropriate ones along. I also have in this trunk a number of artificial phalli (used by women), Vaginal Vibrators, the Rin-No-Tam and God-emiche or Dildo.

—Now you're talking.

—Just lie back and listen. Sink into the rubber sheet. Spread your legs and let the air-conditioning do its filthy work.

—O.K., shoot.

I cleared my famous throat. I chose a swollen book, frankly written, which describes various Auto-Erotic practices as indulged in by humans and animals, flowers, children and adults, and women of all ages and cultures. The areas covered included: Why Wives Masturbate, What We Can Learn From the Anteater, Unsatisfied Women, Abnormalities and Eroticism, Techniques of Masturbation, Latitude of Females, Genital Shaving, Clitoral Discovery, Club Masturbation, Female Metal, Nine Rubber, Frame Caress, Urethral Masturbation, Individual Experiments, Masturbation in and of Children, Thigh-Friction Technique, Mammary Stimulation, Auto-Eroticism in Windows.

—Don't stop, F. I feel it coming back.

Her lovely brown fingers inched down her silky rounded belly. I continued reading in my slow, tantalizing, weather-reporting tones. I read to my deep-breathing protégée of the unusual sex practices, when Sex Becomes "Different". An "Unusual" sex practice is one where there is some greater pleasure than orgasm through intercourse. Most of these bizarre practices involve a measure of mutilation, shock, voyeurism, pain, or torture. The sex habits of the average person are relatively free of such sadistic or masochistic traits. NEVERTHELESS, the reader will be shocked to see how abnormal are the tastes of the so-called normal person. CASE HISTORIES and intensive field work. Filled with chapters detailing ALL ASPECTS of the sex act. SAMPLE HEADINGS: Rubbing, Seeing, Silk Rings, Satyr-iasis, Bestiality in Others. The average reader will be surprised to learn how "Unusual" practices are passed along by seemingly innocent, normal sex partners.

– It's so good, F. It's been so long.

Now it was late afternoon. The sky had darkened somewhat. Edith was touching herself everywhere, smelling herself shamelessly. I could hardly keep still myself. The texts had got to me. Goose pimples rose on her young form. I stared dumbly at Original drawings: male and female organs, both external and internal, drawings indicating correct and incorrect methods of penetration. Wives will benefit from seeing how the penis is received.

– Please, F. Don't leave me like this.

My throat was burning with the hunger of it. Love fondled. Edith writhed under her squeezes. She flipped over on her stomach, wielding her small beautiful fists in anal stimulation. I threw myself into a Handbook of Semi-Impotence. There were important pieces woven into the theme: how to enlarge the erect penis, penis darkness, use of lubricants, satisfaction during menstruation, abusing the menopause, a wife's manual assistance in overcoming semi-impotence.

– Don't touch me, F. I'll die.

I blurted out a piece on Fellatio and Cunnilingus Between Brother and Sister, and others. My hands were almost out of control. I stumbled through a new concept for an exciting sex life. I didn't miss the section on longevity. Thrilling culminations possible for all. Lesbians by the hundreds interviewed and bluntly questioned. Some tortured for coy answers. Speak up, you cheap dyke. An outstanding work showing the sex offender at work. Chemicals to get hair off palms. Not models! Actual Photos of Male and Female Sex Organs and Excrement. Explored Kissing. The pages flew. Edith mumbling bad words through froth. Her fingers were bright and glistening, her tongue bruised from the taste of her waters. I spoke the books in everyday terms, the most sensitivity, cause of erection, Husband-Above 1–17, Wife-Above 18–29, Seated 30–34, On-The-Side 35–38, Standing & Kneeling Positions 39–53, Miscellaneous Squats 54–109, Coital Movement In All Directions, both for Husband and Wife.

– Edith! I cried. Let me have Foreplay.

– Never.

I sped through a glossary of Sexual Terms. In 1852, Richard Burton (d. aet. 69) submitted calmly to circumcision at the age of 31. "Milkers." Detailed Library of Consummated Incest. Ten

Steps on Miscegenation. Techniques of Notorious Photographers. The Evidence of Extreme Acts. Sadism, Mutilation, Cannibalism, Cannibalism of Oralists, How To Match Disproportionate Organs. See the vivid birth of the new American woman. I shouted the recorded facts. She will not be denied the pleasures of sex. CASE HISTORIES show the changing trends. Filled with accounts of college girls eager to be propositioned. Women no longer inhibited by oral intimacy. Men masturbated to death. Cannibalism during Foreplay. Skull Coition. Secrets of "Timing" the Climax. Foreskin, Pro, Con, and Indifferent. The Intimate Kiss. What are the benefits of sexual experimentation? Own and other's sexual make-up. Sin has to be taught. Kissing Negroes on their Mouths. Thigh Documents. Styles of Manual Pressure in Voluntary Indulgence. Death Rides a Camel. I gave her everything. My voice cried the Latex. I hid no laces, nor a pair of exciting open-front pants, nor soft elasticized bra instead of sagging, heavy wide bust, therefore youthful separation. O'er Edith's separate nipples I blabbed the full record, Santa Pants, Fire Alarm Snow, Glamor Tip, plain wrapper Thick Bust Jelly, washable leather Kinsey Doll, Smegma Discipline, the LITTLE SQUIRT ash-tray, "SEND ME ANOTHER Rupture-Easer so I will have one to change off with. It is enabling me to work top speed at my press machine 8 hrs a day," this I threw in for sadness, for melancholy soft flat groin pad which might lurk in Edith's memory swamp as soiled lever, as stretched switch to bumpy apotheosis wet rocket come out of the fine print slum where the only trumpet solo is grandfather's stringy cough and underwear money problems.

Edith was wiggling her saliva-covered kneecaps, bouncing on the rivulets of lubrication. Her thighs were aglow with froth, and her pale anus was excavated by cruel false fingernails. She screamed for deliverance, the flight her imagination commanded denied by a half-enlightened cunt.

– Do something, F. I beg you. But don't touch me.
– Edith, darling! What have I done to you?
– Stand back, F!
– What can I do?
– Try.
– Torture story?
– Anything, F. Hurry.

– The Jews?

– No. Too foreign.

– 1649? Brébeuf and Lalemant?

– Anything.

So I began to recite my schoolboy lesson of how the Iroquois killed the Jesuits Brébeuf and Lalemant, whose scorched and mangled relics were discovered the morning of the twentieth by a member of the Society and seven armed Frenchmen. "Ils y trouuerent vn spectacle d'horreur. . . ."

On the afternoon of the sixteenth the Iroquois had bound Brébeuf to a stake. They commenced to scorch him from head to foot.

– Everlasting flames for those who persecute the worshipers of God, Brébeuf threatened them in the tone of a master.

As the priest spoke the Indians cut away his lower lip and forced a red-hot iron down his throat. He made no sign or sound of discomfort.

Then they led out Lalemant. Around his naked body they had fastened strips of bark, smeared with pitch. When Lalemant saw his Superior, the bleeding unnatural aperture exposing his teeth, the handle of the heated implement still protruding from the seared and ruined mouth, he cried out in the words of St. Paul:

– We are made a spectacle to the world, to angels, and to men.

Lalemant flung himself at Brébeuf's feet. The Iroquois took him, bound him to a stake, and ignited the vegetation in which he was trussed. He screamed for heaven's help, but he was not to die so quickly.

They brought a collar made of hatchets heated redhot and conferred it on Brébeuf. He did not flinch.

An ex-convert, who had backslid, now shouldered forward and demanded that hot water be poured on their heads, since the missionaries had poured so much cold water on them. A kettle was slung, water boiled, and then poured slowly on the heads of the captive priests.

– We baptize you, they laughed, that you may be happy in heaven. You told us that the more one suffers on earth, the happier he is in heaven.

Brébeuf stood like a rock. After a number of revolting tortures they scalped him. He was still alive when they laid open his breast. A crowd came forward to drink the blood of so courageous an enemy and to devour his heart. His death astonished his murderers. His ordeal lasted four hours.

Lalemant, physically weak from childhood, was taken back to the house. There he was tortured all night, until, sometime after dawn, one Indian wearied of the extended entertainment and administered a fatal blow with his hatchet. There was no part of his body which was not burned, "even to his eyes, in the sockets of which these wretches had placed live coals." His ordeal lasted seventeen hours.

– How do you feel, Edith?

There was no need for me to ask. My recitals had served only to bring her closer to a summit she could not achieve. She moaned in terrible hunger, her gooseflesh shining in supplication that she might be freed from the unbearable coils of secular pleasure, and soar into that blind realm, so like sleep, so like death, that journey of pleasure beyond pleasure, where each man travels as an orphan toward an atomic ancestry, more anonymous, more nourishing than the arms of blood or foster family.

I knew she would never make it.

– F., get me out of this, she moaned pitifully.

I plugged in the Danish Vibrator. A degrading spectacle followed. As soon as those delicious electric oscillations occupied my hand like an army of trained seaweed, weaving, swathing, caressing – I was reluctant to surrender the instrument to Edith. Somehow, in the midst of her juicy ordeal, she noticed me trying to slip the Perfected Suction Bracers down into the shadows of my underwear.

She lifted herself out of her pools and lunged at me.

– Give me that. You rat!

Bearlike (some ancestral memory?) she swung at me. I had not had the opportunity to fasten the Improved Wonder Straps, and the Vibrator flew out of my embrace. Thus the bear, with a swipe of his clawed paw, scoops the fish from the bosom of the stream. Crablike, the D.V. scuttled across the polished floor, humming like an overturned locomotive.

– You're selfish, F., Edith snarled.

– That's the observation of a liar and an ingrate, I said as gently as possible.

– Get out of my way.

– I love you, I said as I inched my way toward the D.V. I love

you, Edith. My methods may have been wrong, but I never
stopped loving you. Was it selfish of me to try to end your pain,
yours and his (you, dear old comrade)? I saw pain everywhere. I
could not bear to look into your eyes, so maggoty were they with
pain and desire. I could not bear to kiss either of you, for each of
your embraces disclosed a hopeless, mordant plea. In your
laughter, though it were for money or for sunsets, I heard your
throats ripped with greed. In the midst of the high jump, I saw
the body wither. Between the spurts of come, you launched your
tidings of regret. Thousands built, thousands lay squashed beneath tubes of highway. You were not happy to brush your teeth.
I gave you breasts with nipples: could you nourish anyone? I gave
you prick with separate memory: could you train a race? I took
you to a complete movie of the Second World War: did you feel
any lighter when we walked out? No, you threw yourselves upon
the thorns of research. I sucked you, and you howled to dispense
me something more than poison. With every handshake you wept
for a lost garden. You found a cutting edge for every object. I
couldn't stand the racket of your pain. You were smeared with
blood and tortured scabs. You needed bandages – there was no
time to boil the germs out of them – I grabbed what was at hand.
Caution was a luxury. There was no time for me to examine my
motives. Self-purification would have been an alibi. Beholding
such a spectacle of misery, I was free to try anything. I can't
answer for my own erection.

I have no explanation for my own vile ambitions. Confronted
with your pus, I could not stop to examine my direction, whether
or not I was aimed at a star. As I limped down the street every
window broadcast a command: Change! Purify! Experiment!
Cauterize! Reverse! Burn! Preserve! Teach! Believe me, Edith,
I had to act, and act fast. That was my nature. Call me Dr
Frankenstein with a deadline. I seemed to wake up in the middle
of a car accident, limbs strewn everywhere, detached voices
screaming for comfort, severed fingers pointing homeward, all
the debris withering like sliced cheese out of Cellophane – and all
I had in the wrecked world was a needle and thread, so I got down
on my knees, I pulled pieces out of the mess and I started to stitch
them together. I had an idea of what a man should look like, but it
kept changing. I couldn't devote a lifetime to discovering the
ideal physique. All I heard was pain, all I saw was mutilation. My

needle going so madly, sometimes I found I'd run the thread right through my own flesh and I was joined to one of my own grotesque creations – I'd rip us apart – and then I heard my own voice howling with the others, and I knew that I was also truly part of the disaster. But I also realized that I was not the only one on my knees sewing frantically. There were others like me, making the same monstrous mistakes, driven by the same impure urgency, stitching themselves into the ruined heap, painfully extracting themselves –

– F., you're weeping.

– Forgive me.

– Stop blubbering. See, you've lost your hard-on.

– It's all breaking down now. My discipline is collapsing. Have you any idea how much discipline I had to use in training the two of you?

We both leaped for the Vibrator at the same instant. Her fluids made her slippery. For a second in our struggle I wished we were making love, for all her nozzles were stiff and fragrant. I grabbed her around the waist, before I knew it her bum popped out of my bear hug like a wet watermelon seed, her thighs went by like a missed train, and there I was with empty lubricated arms, nose squashed against the expensive mahogany floor.

Old friend, are you still with me? Do not despair. I promised you that this would end in ecstasy. Yes, your wife was naked during this story. Somewhere in the dark room, draped over the back of a chair like a huge exhausted butterfly, her Gal panties, stiffened by the slightest masonry of sweat, dreamed of ragged fingernails, and I dreamed with them – large, fluttering, descending dreams crisscrossed with vertical scratches. For me it was the end of Action. I would keep on trying, but I knew I had failed the both of you, and that both of you had failed me. I had one trick left, but it was a dangerous one, and I'd never used it. Events, as I will show, would force me into it, and it would end with Edith's suicide, my hospitalization, your cruel ordeal in the treehouse. How many times did I warn you that you would be whipped by loneliness?

So I lay there in Argentine. The Danish Vibrator hummed like a whittler as it rose and fell over Edith's young contours. It was cold and black in the room. Occasionally one of her glistening kneecaps would catch a glint of moonlight as she jerked her box up and down in desperate supplication. She had stopped moaning; I assumed she had approached the area of intense breathless silence which the orgasm loves to flood with ventriloquist gasps and cosmic puppet plots.

– Thank God, she whispered at last.

– I'm glad you could come, Edith. I'm very happy for you.

– Thank God it's off me. I had to blow it. It made me do oral intimacy.

– Wha –?

Before I could question her further it was upon my buttocks, its idiot hum revved up to a psychotic whine. The detachable crotch piece inserted itself between my hairy thighs, ingeniously providing soft support for my frightened testicles. I had heard of these things happening before, and I knew it would leave me bitter and full of self-loathing. Like a cyanide egg dropped into the gas chamber the D.V. released a glob of Formula Cream at the top of the muscular cleavage I had labored so hard to define. As my body heat melted it to the trickle which would grease its shameful entry, several comfortable Latex cups assumed exciting holds here and there. The elastic Developer seemed to have a life of its own, and the Fortune Straps spread everything apart, and I felt the air-conditioning coolly evaporating sweat and cream *from tiny surfaces I hardly knew existed*. I was ready to lie there for ten days. I was not even surprised. I knew it would be insatiable but I was ready to submit. I heard Edith faintly calling to me just as the Foam Pad rose the full length. After that I heard nothing. It was like a thousand Sex Philosophers working over me with perfect cooperation. I may have screamed at the first thrust of the White Club, but the Formula Cream kept coming, and I think a cup was converted to handle excreta. It hummed in my ears like alabaster lips.

I don't know how long it swarmed among my private pieces. Edith made it to a light switch. She couldn't bear to look at me.

– Are you happy, F.?

I did not answer.

– Should I do something, F.?

Perhaps the D.V. answered with a sated whir. It pulled in the American Laces fast as an Italian eater, the suck went out of the cups, my scrotum dropped unceremoniously, and the machine slipped off my quivering body meat. I think I was happy. . . .

– Should I pull out the plug, F.?

– Do what you want, Edith. I'm washed up.

Edith yanked at the electric cord. The D.V. shuddered, fell silent, and stopped. Edith sighed with relief, but too soon. The D.V. began to produce a shattering sonic whistle.

– Does it have batteries?

– No, Edith. It doesn't have batteries.

She covered her breasts with crossed arms.

– You mean –?

– Yes. It's learned to feed itself.

Edith backed into a corner as the Danish Vibrator advanced toward her. She stooped queerly, as if she were trying to hide her cunt behind her thighs. I could not stir from the puddle of jelly in which I had been buggered by countless improvements. It made its way across the hotel room in a leisurely fashion, straps and cups flowing behind it, like a Hawaiian skirt made of grass and brassières.

It had learned to feed itself.

(O Father, Nameless and Free of Description, lead me from the Desert of the Possible. Too long I have dealt with Events. Too long I labored to become an Angel. I chased Miracles with a bag of Power to salt their wild Tails. I tried to dominate Insanity so I could steal its Information. I tried to program the Computers with Insanity. I tried to create Grace to prove that Grace existed. Do not punish Charles Axis. We could not see the Evidence so we stretched our Memories. Dear Father, accept this confession: we did not train ourselves to Receive because we believed there wasn't Anything to Receive and we could not endure with this Belief.)

– Help, help me, F.

But I was fastened to the floor with a tingling nail, the head of which was my anus.

It took its time getting to her. Edith, meanwhile, her back squeezed into the right angle, had sunk to a defenseless sitting position, her lovely legs spread apart. Numbed by horror and the prospect of disgusting thrills, she was ready to submit. I have stared at many orifices, but never have I seen one wear such an expression. The soft hairs were thrown back from the dripping lips like a Louis Quatorze sunburst. The layers of lip spread and gathered like someone playing with a lens opening. The Danish

Vibrator mounted her slowly, and soon the child (Edith was twenty) was doing things with her mouth and fingers that no one, believe me, old friend, no one has ever done to you. Perhaps this was what you wanted from her. But you did not know how to encourage her, and this was not your fault. No one could. That is why I tried to lead the fuck away from mutual dialing.

The whole assault lasted maybe twenty-five minutes. Before the tenth minute passed she was begging the thing to perform in her armpits, specifying which nipple was hungriest, twisting her torso to offer it hidden pink terrain – until the Danish Vibrator began to command. Then Edith, quite happily, became nothing but a buffet of juice, flesh, excrement, muscle to serve its appetite.

Of course, the implications of her pleasure are enormous.

The Danish Vibrator slipped off her face, uncovering a bruised soft smile.

– Stay, she whispered.

It climbed onto the window sill, purring deeply, revved up to a sharp moan, and launched itself through the glass, which broke and fell over its exit like a fancy stage curtain.

– Make it stay.

– It's gone.

We dragged our strange bodies to the window. The perfumed sticky tropical night wafted into the room as we leaned out to watch the Danish Vibrator move down the marble stories of the hotel. When it reached the ground it crossed the parking lot and soon achieved the beach.

– Oh, God, F., it was beautiful. Feel this.

– I know, Edith. Feel this.

A curious drama began to unfold beneath us on the deserted moonlit sand. As the D.V. made slowly toward the waves breaking in dark flowers on the bright shore, a figure emerged from a grove of ghostly palms. It was a man wearing an immaculate white bathing suit. I do not know whether he was running to intercept the Danish Vibrator with the intention of violently disabling it, or merely wished to observe at closer range its curiously graceful progress toward the Atlantic.

How soft the night seemed, like the last verse of a lullaby. With one hand on his hip and the other scratching his head, the tiny figure beneath us watched, as did we, the descent of the apparatus into the huge rolling sea, which closed over its luminous cups like the end of a civilization.

–Will it come back, F.? To us?

–It doesn't matter. It's in the world.

We stood close to each other in the window, two figures on a rung of a high marble ladder built into the vast cloudless night, leaning on nothing.

A small breeze detached a wisp of her hair and I felt its tiny fall across my cheek.

–I love you, Edith.

–I love you, F.

–And I love your husband.

–So do I.

–Nothing is as I planned it, but now I know what will happen.

–So do I, F.

–Oh, Edith, something is beginning in my heart, a whisper of rare love, but I will never be able to fulfil it. It is my prayer that your husband will.

–He will, F.

–But he will do it alone. He can only do it alone.

–I know, she said. We must not be with him.

A great sadness overtook us as we looked out over the miles of sea, an egoless sadness that we did not own or claim. Here and there the restless water kept an image of the shattered moon. We said good-by to you, old lover. We did not know when or how the parting would be completed, but it began that moment.

There was a professional knock on the blond door.

–It must be him, I said.

–Should we put our clothes on?

–Why bother.

We did not even have to open the door. The waiter had a passkey. He was wearing the old raincoat and mustache, but underneath he was perfectly nude. We turned toward him.

–Do you like Argentine? I asked for the sake of civil conversation.

–I miss the newsreels, he said.

–And the parades? I offered.

–And the parades. But I can get everything else here. Ah!

He noticed our reddened organs and began to fondle them with great interest.

– Wonderful! Wonderful! I see you have been well prepared.

What followed was old hat. I have no intention of adding to any pain which might be remaindered to you, by a minute description of the excesses we performed with him. Lest you should worry for us, let me say that we had, indeed, been well prepared, and we hardly cared to resist his sordid exciting commands, even when he made us kiss the whip.

– I have a treat for you, he said at last.

– He has a treat for us, Edith.

– Shoot, she replied wearily.

From the pocket of his overcoat he withdrew a bar of soap.

– Three in a tub, he said merrily in his heavy accent.

So we splashed around with him. He lathered us from head to foot, proclaiming all the while the special qualities of the soap, which, as you must now understand, was derived from melted human flesh.

That bar is now in your hands. We were baptized by it, your wife and I. I wonder what you will do with it.

You see, I have shown you *how it happens*, from style to style, from kiss to kiss.

There is more, there is the history of Catherine Tekakwitha – you shall have all of it.

Wearily we dried each other with the opulent towels of the hotel. The waiter was very careful with our parts.

– I had millions of these at my disposal, he said without a trace of nostalgia.

He slipped into his raincoat and spent some time before the full-length mirror playing with his mustache and slanting his hair across his forehead in just the way he liked.

– And don't forget to inform the *Police Gazette*. We'll bargain over the soap later.

– Wait!

As he opened the door to go, Edith threw her arms about his neck, pulled him to the dry bed, and cradled his famous head against her breasts.

– What did you do that for? I demanded of her after the waiter had made his stiff exit, and nothing remained of him but the vague stink of his sulphurous flatulence.

– For a second I thought he was an A –.

– Oh, Edith!

I sank to my knees before your wife and I laid my mouth on her toes. The room was a mess, the floor spotted with pools of fluid and suds, but she rose from it all like a lovely statue with epaulets and nipple tips of moonlight.

–Oh, Edith! It doesn't matter what I've done to you, the tits, the cunt, the hydraulic buttock failures, all my Pygmalion tampering, it means nothing, I know now. Acne and all, you were out of my reach, you were beyond my gadgetry. Who are you?

– Ισις ἐγῶ εἰμί πάντα γεγονός καί ὄν καί ἐσόμενον καί τό ἐμόν πέπλον οὐδείς τῶν θνητῶν ἀπεκάλυψεν!

–You're not joking? Then I'm only fit to suck your toes.
–Wiggle.

DEATH & SEDUCTION

Catherine Sellars

GABRIEL'S BODY CUTS through the heat curtain dividing street from arcade. For a moment external and internal are indistinguishable, until all the sounds and scents of the exterior are sucked back into their rightful place.

The drone and chime of conversation and cutlery fill the dome above her, recalling memories of tastes and sensations that become more exquisite with each recollection. Gabriel's eyes become adjusted to the warm light and focus on the faces of shoppers, rendered beautiful by the carefully created glow. They stroll in calm contentment, with expression of reverence and awe, complimenting and admiring, more like an audience at a great exhibition than consumers in a mall.

Through the delicately wrought iron and engraved glass, Gabriel spies her victim. She eyes her prey, wets her lips and crosses the expanse of jewelled mosaic like a society courtesan making a path through a crowded ballroom to her potential Prince.

The prey, a young man with a touch too much red in his cheeks and his locks too brassy to be those of a classic beauty, is comely enough nevertheless. Track-suited and chain-smoking, he slouches against the wooden-fronted candle shop, a squat shape with a halo of flickering flames. He has as little sense of style as he has of his impending doom.

Gabriel uses her clipboard like an antique fan. The delicate movements of a courtly ritual long dead tug unconsciously at the cultural memory of the youth, for he smiles and bows his head on cue, saying all the right things at all the right moments. Each flutter and tilt of the clipboard beckon him closer to his destruction.

A little polite conversation gives way to a few simple questions concerning his habits as a consumer. Gabriel once again employs her clipboard as a fan, but this time in its more conventional fashion, for she grows warm with anticipation of coming pleasure. The format of the questionnaire you see, and her promises of a reward at its completion are cunningly designed to appeal to all the vices in man, playing on the human frailties of laziness, greed and lust with expert skill, and coaxing white lies from his lips in defence of his frail ego.

Flattered into a sense of stupid pride at his ability to recognize brands of toothpaste by their logo, his good taste in cars and the amount of alcohol-free lager he might consume in a month, the young man's defences begin to crumble. Vanity parades his vices in an unwitting confession of guilt.

Then comes the invitation, and a promise that he might discover something to his advantage or receive his reward should he follow her. Greed and lust chain him to her, and Gabriel triumphantly trots her mortal specimen out of the centre, through the crowds of consumers and into the night.

The city's floodlights glow into life at the perfect moment to illuminate the lowering heavens and turn the sudden squall into a crystal light show, immediately the dull pavement becomes a dark mirror to the cityscape. At this impressive piece of celestial stage management, Gabriel picks up the skirts of her coat, deeply inhales the ozone-charged air and flies along the sparkling streets homeward to the Merchant City, her captive in morbid pursuit. The setting is ideal and the atmosphere inspiring, but totally lost on the unsuspecting victim, whose whole being is now focused on the body of his seducer. Nights like this give meaning to her existence, for on a night like this her true genius can reveal itself and her powers of creative destruction flourish.

Entering the hallway of her home, Gabriel sways free of her sable coat. The shock of metal heels on marble is muffled by the shuffle of his rubber-soled Reeboks as the sounds merge high up above the picture rail. A long bronze lady on an onyx plinth obligingly raises a globe of light to the crazed and ancient mirror, her back arched in an ecstasy of lunar worship. Gabriel's sepia-toned reflection, a Theda Bara in this amber glow, gazes out at the breathless youth on the doormat. As the last sounds of their entrance die away, the muted sounds of a tragic melody filter from the room ahead, Gershwin or Porter, Puccini or Rachmaninov – an irresistible and passionate keening.

Gabriel glides down the long corridor past fatal beauties with sailors entwined in their hair and disarmed knights at their feet: mermaids and sirens and *belles dames sans merci*. The wan faces of their victims, tragic and lovely, gaze down from the captivity of their picture frames at the unsuspecting youth. Blind with lust and ignorant in his certainty, he takes no heed of their silent warning. Water nymphs lure Hylas to his airless end, while Morgan le Fay eternally bewitches, but they perform their terrible function unrecognized. The young man does not even glance at them.

GABRIEL, COATLESS, is dressed to kill. Her body is a metronome that swings hypnotically before him to the throb of the melancholy music, accompanied by the murmur of velvet on silk as her skirts sigh against her stockings. Gabriel leads the man along the endless corridor of panels and paintings, exhaling myrrh and spices and charging the air with rich scents and ozone. She leaves a trail of musk that the man must follow. At last they reach the door at the corridor's end. Gabriel glides a hand over her waist and hips and waves the prey into her room. She strolls in behind him, eager to embark on her fatal labours.

The light in the room is cool silver and blue. The stormy night, viewed in panorama through the room's enormous windows, is huge and indigo. Despite the casements flung wide, the air is heavy with the scent of three great lilies.

Gabriel takes a liquor glass, silver vines entwining its stem, and pours a slick of noxious liquid into it. It shines with emerald light. The stupid youth takes the glass without a question, bewitched by the ruby, amethyst and jet that are her lips, eyes and hair. As he sips the poison and inhales its fumes, he does not notice its bitter taste, for his senses are dazzled into dullness. Gabriel looks on in satisfaction and drapes herself in ecstasy over the vast blue velvet sofa.

The youth falls helpless into her arms and she absorbs all the life from him, drinking in his strength and watching all that disgusted her seep slowly away. At last he is no longer an uncouth sinner. He has become her object. An object with more potential than she ever imagined on first setting eyes on his rough, un-refined form. He will make a most beautiful corpse, and his death will be magnificent.

SHE CARRIES the senseless young man into a high-ceilinged bathroom of dolphins and sea nymphs and, despite his weight, glides effortlesly over the floor. She undresses him slowly and carefully, and places his limp, damp clothes in the fire of the fire of the polished copper boiler. They hiss disagreement before bursting into flames. Gabriel then takes a gleaming silver blade from the bathroom cabinet, a bottle of peroxide, some scissors, scented oils, a razor, soap and a shaving brush, and lines them up on the shelf beside the great cast-iron bath. While she runs the water she cuts the young man's hair into a tousled cap of curls. She then undresses and steps into the steaming, scented water with her victim in her arms.

Gabriel washes away all traces of his mortal life – the stale stench of cheap deodorant and sweat, and the rancid smell of smoke in his hair. Unable to move or speak, only the look of terror in the dying man's eyes show that he has any awareness of his situation. Gabriel runs her hands over the hard muscle and taut sinews, stroking and massaging his malleable form, then shaves his entire body. She applies the peroxide to his brassy locks and, while she waits for it to take effect, she glides the silver blade across each wrist and lies back to watch her terrible bath turn red with the blood of her victim. The life pours out of him and she captures a little of it in a small glass vial. He labours to breathe his last, succumbing to the poison and the loss of blood. Gabriel feels an involuntary spasm in the walls of her stomach as he releases his final sigh. She rinses the chemicals from his now silver hair, and after wrapping his body in great warm towels she moisturizes the smooth, white skin.

Gabriel dresses the beautiful corpse in a pure silk shirt, voluptuous in the generosity of its cut, and a pair of high-waisted trousers of the finest fabric. She applies kohl to his lids, mascara to his lashes and a wine-coloured stain to his lips. She carries her beautiful work out of her room, along the endless corridor and out into the city. In her pocket is the vial of blood and beneath her coat are white narcissus and orchids. She passes unhindered through the sleeping city and enters its cultivated parkland. The storm is over, the night is still, crisp and clear. A huge pewter moon illumines a dark sapphire sky and lights the way to the final resting place.

GABRIEL LAYS HIM gently in the frozen fountain at the centre of the botanical gardens. In a pose of carefully engineered disarray, his head rests casually on one arm, the limbs draped over the marble, everything arranged to the greatest aesthetic effect. Only one task remains. She plunges the gorgeous blade into the heart of the dead man, between the folds of his shirt. She arranges the narcissus and orchids about his body, placing one in his dangling fingers and others around his shining hair and at his feet.

She drips a little of the contents of the vial around the bloodless wound in his chest, perfectly choreographing the trickle of blood so that it curves delicately over the line of his pectorals. She places a single drop at the corner of his burgundy lips and delicately strokes a wisp of platinum hair from his heavy blue lids. She lingers a moment to gaze at her work, gleaming white against the moonlight, the perfect man reclining on a crystal throne, shimmering with purity, untainted by life, released from bestiality for a brief moment, before the sun rises, melts the fountain and sets the machinery of decay into motion.

Gabriel records the scene in her memory and disappears back into the city.

TENDER FRUIT

Vicki Hendricks

SHE WAS MAKING a long, loud crunch, every bite she took of the apple. The motion was painfully slow. Her teeth pierced the slick skin and buried themselves in the firm grainy flesh until they struck against the core. Ronny heard the snap as she freed the bite. Then she chewed, and chewed. Her mouth was open. A piece of white pulp dropped from one corner.

He would bet he'd pumped her ten times for every bite, and another ten for the chewing and swallowing. She was sitting back on her heels rocking a little atop him, her weight pressing him down into the mattress. She was looking out the window at the Marlboro ad.

The evening wasn't going like he'd planned. From the time he saw her pull the apple out of her large gold bag and shine it against her pubic hair, he had an inkling that he wasn't in control of the situation. Ronny glanced at the other bed. Dan's whore wasn't eating an apple. Dan's whore wasn't looking out the window. They'd both paid the same. Ronny knew he was going to hear the incident repeated later, always.

He stopped thinking about it and let his mind move down to the spot where their bodies were mashed together. Round peg in the square hole. He felt the warmth gathering. It spread over his thighs and stomach, and a shudder took hold. A sound pushed up from deep inside him. "Umph." He checked to see if Dan was watching, but all Ronny could see was the outline of muscular thighs and ass pumping strong over the girl on all fours.

Ronny's girl dropped her apple core onto his abdomen. It rolled to his sunken navel. "Time to git goin," she said. She lifted her solid chunk of a leg across his body, stepping down to the floor. He remembered how pretty she'd looked when he spotted her standing in the moving shadows of the palm on U.S. 1 in Fort Lauderdale. Her long carroty hair, the color his mother's had been, was looped around her left hand to keep it from blowing. Her right hand moved a cigarette away from her lips like Bette Davis.

She stooped, found her panties in the dim light from the window, and stepped into them, dimpled buttocks grazing his shoulder. Sometimes in the movies a whore fell in love with her customer. She would see beyond the silly imperfections that put other women off, to the caring human being underneath. He guessed it wasn't going to work for him this time.

He picked up the apple core and nibbled idly as he looked over at the other bed. Dan's muscular form moved in push-ups against his girl, and she kept the rhythm. His hips hit hers with a sweaty smacking sound. She sucked in breath and let it out in a hoarse growl.

The next morning at work, Ronny stood in the filtered sun under the mango tree and flicked some sawdust from his moustache, thinking about the night before. He wanted to forget it. He wanted a change in his life, a steady girl, somebody to do regular things, like read the comics to him and tell him fondly when his zipper was down or he had a splatter of spaghetti sauce on his chin. He was always being teased, as if he was the only one who ever did something silly. He heard Dan's voice coming from the branches above him.

"Hey, Buddy, if you don't have any plans, you could come along on the boat Sunday." Dan paused to tighten the blade on the chainsaw. "Tina's sister just moved down. You could be her date."

"Sure. I'll go. Sure, man. I always like to go on the boat." He decided he was going to play it cool, but already he could feel the excitement building for meeting the new woman.

The chainsaw started up and Dan dropped a heavy limb. It came crashing through the lower branches and landed at Ronny's feet. It sounded like sea spray. He pictured a tan, wet body. Two small branches dropped to his left, and a log clipped his right shoulder on its way to the ground. The whine stopped. "Think you can handle it?"

"Sure," he said and brushed dirt from his shoulder. He wasn't certain whether Dan meant the big branch or the date. "No problem." He grabbed an end and began dragging the limb toward the chipper. "What's she look like?" he yelled up. The saw started again and he could hear its scream as it nipped off more branches, and the rustle, like spray, as they fell through the live canopy and hit the ground.

He made five more trips to the tree and back to the chipper, but the saw never stopped its scream long enough for him to get in a word. He decided it didn't matter. He was standing near the trunk looking up at the V-shaped crotch where Dan was ready to make the next cut to sear off a log the size of a man's thigh. He saw him jerk his head to the side to get a clear view below.

"Christsakes, man, I told you not to stand under the tree when I'm dropping branches," he yelled. "Quit dreamin' – you're going to get your fucking head knocked off."

"Sorry, thought you were finished. I was wondering, how old is –?"

Dan was jerking at the cord to start the saw again and Ronny quickly moved out to the perimeter of the tree. A branch ricocheted and landed behind him. What difference did it make? He'd go anyway.

He chipped the thin branches while Dan stacked the log. He flinched every time he fed a slender branch into the hungry machine. It sucked in the stems and slivered them with the ease of chopping ripe bananas. He feared the power that could suck him in just as smoothly, the searing pain on his tender limbs. He stared fascinated into the chute trying to see the cutting edge as it came around, but it was a whirling blur.

"Here, catch," Dan yelled and flung a mango at him. It was part of Ronny's job to pick up all the smashed fruit. He stuck out his left hand to grab it, but missed. It hit his belt buckle and bounced off, rolling a few feet until it rested against a root. He bent and picked it up. Still good. Just one small bite gone – probably a squirrel or a rat got at it. He unclipped the Swiss Army Knife from his belt loop and peeled away the tough green skin. He opened his jaws wide and cut his teeth into the orange flesh. The sweet piney juice ran down his chin and onto the neck of his tee-shirt. He thought of a girl's sweet lips.

They finished the job before lunch, and would have been done sooner, if Ronny hadn't laid the keys in to grass and caused a twenty-minute search.

On Saturday he went to Sears to get a new pair of bathing trunks. He wanted a loose, comfortable pair, something dark so the tar wouldn't show when he went to the beach, but the clerk suggested a bright green "lycra sling". It was cut low and would fit snug to his body. "You're lean," the salesman told him. "You can wear something stylish." Gangling was the word his mother had always used to describe him. He guessed it was about the same thing. He fingered the slinky fabric. Thirty dollars was a lot, but this was for a special day.

When Tina introduced them at the dock, he saw right away why Crystal had come to Florida to stay with her sister. She had an inch of stitches beneath her blackened left eye and a bruise on her cheek the color and size of an immature eggplant, light purple fading to green around the edges.

"Her old man gave her a couple of hard shots when she left," Dan told him as they took turns stepping over the rail, down into the white glare of the twenty-foot open fisherman. "He drinks, hits her."

"The son-of-a-bitch won't beat on me again," she said. She pointed her finger down at Ronny to make the point before she stepped next to him. He felt a warmth toward her, wanted to hold her. The two of them could face the world together.

He looked at the other side of her face. She was a pretty girl, short, dark like Tina, nice skin, a Sophia Loren type. Probably around his age too, twenty-eight to thirty. He looked down – big tits. I've got a chance with a nice girl, he thought.

The ocean was flat and they headed out a few miles to the weed line to fish. The women sunbathed. Ronny and Dan got a few bites, but no keepers. They smoked a couple joints, worked through a case of beer. Ronny couldn't think of much to say to Crystal, but she smiled and nodded when he asked her if she needed a beer or passed her a joint. She gave him the second half of her crab salad sandwich.

After lunch Ronny put the used napkins and empty wrappings

into a trash bag. Dan stood watching him. "I knew there was something funny, but I just couldn't figure it out," Dan said. He laughed. "What's wrong with this picture?"

Tina and Crystal stared at Ronny. He stared down at himself. He couldn't see anything humorous. There was no zipper, just a little bagginess in front. "I know I'm lean," he said and laughed, "but it's in style."

"I see it. I see it," Tina yelled. "He's got his trunks on backwards." She and Dan began to laugh like idiots.

"I wondered why there was so much extra fabric," Crystal said. She sipped from her can and giggled. Suddenly a spray of beer exploded from her mouth and she doubled down to the deck snorting and choking. Ronny stepped up and leaped over the side. He swam around behind the boat. As he held onto the small wooden dive platform and pulled out his legs to switch the suit, he wondered what were the chances of a barracuda nipping off his dick. It could only happen to me, he thought. He watched the tender flesh waving weightless below the surface until he pulled up the trunks.

After several hours, Dan suggested that they stop at a bar along the water to have a few drinks and get something for dinner on the way in. Tina agreed.

"Yes, let's go somewhere dark and cool," said Crystal. "I've had enough sun."

"Me too," Ronny said. He pulled out the front of his trunks and saw the clean pink line against the white stomach skin, like an Easter egg half-dipped in rose tint.

The girls walked on ahead. Dan put down the bumpers and tied the lines. He and Ronny pulled on tee-shirts and walked into The Sand Bar. The place was dim with smudgy porthole windows and dark paneling. The cold, dry air brought up gooseflesh on Ronny's stinging arms as he headed toward the back end of the bar, but he spotted Crystal with an empty stool next to her, and he felt great.

He sat down on the padded plastic stool facing the mirror. He could see the reflection of his thin face framed by bottles of bourbon and gin that sparkled in the scant light, and for a second, he felt he was in a movie. Crystal sat down to his left, and put her cool fingers on his sunburnt thigh. She was drunk and high, but even so, he couldn't believe it. Dan and Tina were sitting a few stools away since the bar was crowded. He wished Dan could see Crystal's hand.

"Did you get any sunburn?" he asked her. He used the question as an excuse to brush her thigh like butterfly wings with his fingertips. A few pubic hairs had strayed from the crotch of her suit.

"I don't think so," she said, "but that sure felt good." She leaned over and kissed him on the side of his neck. He jerked, but recovered immediately and leaned over to kiss her on the cheek. She started walking the fingers of her left hand from his knee toward his thigh. The goosebumps were really standing up. He leaned forward, enjoying the sensation, his arms crossed on the edge of the bar. Suddenly he felt a jolt run through his frame. She was headed for his dick in front of twenty people at nearby tables.

"Stand up closer to the bar," Crystal said. "I'm going to make you feel real good." She stuck her index and middle fingers under the edge of the green slinky fabric at his groin. He jumped up and mashed his gut into the bar top.

"I don't think you should do this," he said, standing, looking around, trying to appear casual. "Somebody will see." Dan and Tina were absorbed in conversation down the bar.

"Just keep quiet," she said. "Stand close. Most men like when I do it."

By this time she had her thumb and index finger curled around his penis outside his trunks, working up and down. He liked it all right, not only because it felt so good, but because it was her idea. He started to relax his posture.

"You're huge," she said. He could see her elbow moving up and down under the smooth wood overhang of the bar. He was frightened that someone would see, but he couldn't make himself stop her. He watched his face in the mirror – no one would notice a little shallow breathing. His eyes widened and his jaw dropped.

"I'm coming, I'm coming," he whispered. She stopped moving her hand and held still with her tits mashed hard into his side. He tried to keep his face calm in the mirror. He saw his lips open slightly and the corner of his mouth pull downward.

"Jesus," she said.

"Umph." He came and came, all over inside the bright green lycra.

"Shit. You're just a big kid. I swear." She looked between his legs at the suit. "Jesus. You weren't supposed to come. We were just playing."

"I didn't know."

Crystal looked away and lit up a cigarette. Ronny tugged down the T-shirt to cover the dark splotch and walked to the men's room. He heard laughter behind him.

When Dan said it was time to go, Crystal walked out in front of Ronny while he tugged down on his T-shirt trying to cover the dark splotch on the front of his suit. He heard some laughter behind him.

"I'm sorry I embarrassed you," he said when they got back to the parking lot by the dock. "I shouldn't have –"

She shrugged. "Forget it."

"I mean I really –"

"Shut up about it."

He decided not to try for a kiss. "Can I call you sometime?"

"Yeah. I guess." She turned and got into the truck beside Tina. Ronny's face spread out in a big grin.

"I don't think my sister wants to talk to you," Tina said, when he called up the next night. "She's going back with her husband. He drove all the way down to see her."

"Dan didn't mention it at work," Ronny said.

"He just got here an hour ago."

He hung his head forward and expelled some air that made his lips puff out. "Well, you tell her to give me a call if she changes her mind," he said.

"I sure will, Ron. I'm sorry you two didn't hit it off."

He lay on his stomach on the linoleum in front of the TV. A nature show came on, an underwater habitat. He'd seen it a million times. A pitiful hermit crab was nibbling at a fish head left by a barracuda who'd sliced it off below the gills and swam away to digest the prime parts. The announcer was talking about the cruel competitive world under the sea. The passive and gentle creatures didn't have a chance at live prey. They had to feed on the leftovers that drifted their way.

He lunged to his feet from the floor and nearly fell back down. He had to do something. He steadied himself against the wall. He had to find himself a woman.

★   ★   ★

Dan passed his fries down to Ronny at lunch the next day. "Eat, eat." It was a sort of joke between them, how Ronny could never get filled up.

"No, thanks," he said. "I still have some of my own." He was thinking of his plan.

He began to relax in the dark coolness of the tavern and he leaned on his forearms on the smooth lacquered bar. "How do you put an ad in the *Herald*?" he asked, lapping his bottom lip over the fringe of his moustache to suck off the beads of ketchup. He knew Dan used ads for his tree service.

"You call 'em up and send a check. Why? You trying to sell something?"

"No, I've got some kittens. A mother left babies under my trailer." He didn't worry about the lie. Dan would never ask to see them.

"Just drop 'em at the Humane Society. They'll take care of it."

"No, I want to give them a chance at a home first."

"I think it's useless, but you gotta do what'ya gotta do," said Dan. Dan got him the number from the truck. Ronny went right back into the men's room to call. He told the woman he wanted to put an ad in the "Person-to-Person" section of the Sunday magazine.

"I can't take it over the phone. Too many mistakes. Write it out and send it with your check," she told him. "If you get it in the mail tomorrow, it'll be in the paper on Sunday. Be sure to print."

That evening he studied the personal ads from the last Sunday. Shit. He hadn't even thought about what to say. His spelling was terrible, and so was his handwriting. What could he tell about himself? What did he seek?

"Marlboro man seeks female for . . ." He looked around the room. His eyes stopped on a pillow he'd thrown on the couch. ". . . comfortable . . . relationship." He looked at his swim trunks hanging on the doorknob. I am a tall, lean, stylish, employed gentleman, age 29, interested in water sports." No, no watersports this time. He ran the nail of his middle finger between his two front teeth. He tasted ketchup from lunch. ". . . dining." It sounded good. He tried to print clearly.

He needed a few more words to fill out his minimum and get his money's worth. "Looking for another of similar tastes. Send note and photo." He wrote it out quickly. "Not bad. Not bad," he said out loud as he slipped it and the check into the prepared envelope.

The rest of the week he had trouble concentrating on dragging branches and chipping. He kept thinking of his message on its journey from post office to newspaper to a beautiful, sweet, sophisticated woman. Twice he pushed the shovel too far into the chute of the chipper and it hit the blade, causing him to jump at the loud noise and nearly drop in the shovel. Dan came running from the tree thinking he'd swan his arm off, or worse, broken something.

"You must need to get laid, buddy," Dan said on Friday. "You know, an apple a day." He chuckled.

"Yeah, fuck you, man." He didn't want to hear about it. He knocked the safety glasses off his forehead and into the chipper. They became splinters in barely a screech.

He was up at four that Sunday when the paper was delivered and ran outside in his jockey shorts to get it. He flung it to the floor and plopped down to whip through the sections, not noticing the headlines, not glancing at the comics. Finally, he found the magazine and turned to the "Person-to-Person" pages. Where was it? Where? Where?

It was there. In the middle column, toward the bottom. He read it over. ". . . comfortable relationship . . . tall, lean, employed . . . interested in dining. Looking for a mother of similar tastes."

"A mother?" he said aloud. "A mother!" They fucked it up. Jesus, what now? Why always him?

The next morning he got on the phone while Dan was in the Seven-Eleven. No time for Twinkies. He had serious business with that newspaper woman.

"I have your ad right here in my hand," she said. "It's not our fault. If that's supposed to be an n, it has too many humps, and I can see a separation between the two characters. You have a combination of script and block.

"What can I do to fix it?"

"It's too late now. You can write a new ad for next week or just wait and see what happens. You still might get a response that fills your needs."

He was amazed by the number of letters and photos he got in the first week after the ad came out. Each day after work he picked two or three envelopes from his mailbox. He'd never gotten so much mail before, and despite the mistake, he was enjoying the popularity. There were perfumed notes on expensive looking stationery and interesting close-written letters on lined school paper. The photos were fifty-cent booth shots, polaroids, even professional shots with the company name in gold imprinted on the bottom, like graduation pictures, except all of the women were way past graduation. He decided to keep the mail together so he could study the faces and compare their statements. He wrapped the packet in foil and put it in the freezer. He didn't want any of his bar buddies to see it, especially Dan, if he happened to come around. Ronny hadn't seen much of him outside of work since that Sunday on the boat. Tina was taking up more of Dan's time.

On the ninth day he only got one letter, and one more on day twelve. He set the weekend aside to choose. It wasn't difficult. Most of them were old. Old enough to be my mother, he thought, and laughed. A few were too intellectual for him, three school teachers, a nurse. Others just didn't appeal to him because of their starchy hair or heavy make-up. His mother hadn't worn any make-up and he'd never gotten used to it.

Two women were fine. Although their looks were opposite in coloring, he liked them both. And both were secretaries, probably not too smart for him or too controlling. He didn't want to be "pussy-whipped", as Dan would say. Neither seemed much older than he was. Their names were Jane and Martha.

He phoned Jane first because her letter came first, but he never could reach her, even trying at different hours of the day and night. He wondered why someone would reply to an ad and then leave town or move. It worried him, but there was still Martha. She answered on the first ring.

"Hello. Dinkelacker residence." Her voice was deep and a little husky. She sounded gruff and businesslike. Nothing wrong with that.

"This is Ronny," he said, "from the 'Personals'".

"I don't buy intimate apparel over the telephone," she said flatly.

"No, this is Ronny Magee. You sent me a letter and your picture – the ad in the Herald."

"Oh, it's you," she said. "I'm so happy you called." Her voice became as sweet as he expected it to. "When can we meet?"

The receiver pressed against his cheek as he grinned. He was sick of pot pies and doing his own laundry, and most of all he wanted a nice soft breast to cuddle up to at night. He was the only man he knew who'd never had a live-in girlfriend. Suddenly it seemed possible.

They arranged to meet at the supermarket on Singles Night. He'd gone to the event before and come home disappointed, but this time he had a date. His luck was changed. He suggested meeting in the meat department. She said she would like to cook dinner for their first night. "We can pick out a roast together," she said. They talked for three hours about their likes and dislikes, their favorite meats, vegetables, desserts. They finally settled on a beef tenderloin. Ronny wasn't sure why he picked it – he'd never had it before.

After two more hours on the phone, he knew everything important about her. She had a house and enjoyed cooking. He was ready for love.

That evening he wore a new pair of jeans and his plaid Western shirt with the mother-of-pearl snaps. He felt good, on target. He strode down the bright dairy aisle without even stopping for a sample of Colby cheese with jalapeno. He took a direct left to the meat cooler that ran across the rear of the store. From fifty feet off, Ronny recognized the solid middle-aged woman, although she was probably twenty years older than her picture. Her hair was soft and long, but had streaks of iron gray on the sides. She wore a dark skirt and a loose cotton blouse. She was looking into the meat case. He turned and walked back up the dairy aisle.

"Have a sample, Sir? It's very good."

He reached over the tray, took the cracker, and pitched it into his mouth. He paused to chew. Maybe he should go back and meet Martha Dinkelacker. He grabbed another cracker. After all, they'd planned to have a meal. He didn't want to leave her standing there picking out meat all night, and he was starved.

He stepped up and introduced himself. She looked happy to see him. She had a pretty smile, even for late forties, and nice white teeth, full lips, teasing eyes.

She had already chosen a tenderloin. Potatoes and corn on the cob were also in her basket.

"I bet you like your brownies without nuts," she said, after he'd introduced himself. "Just like my Johnny." She was comparing him to the son she'd mentioned on the phone, who was now working on an oil rig off the coast of Norway.

"Let's get it straight right off," Ronny said, "The 'mother' in the ad was a mistake. I don't need a mother at all, just a regular relationship."

"Sure, Babe. Whatever you want." She tilted her head to the side and took a long look at him. He decided he liked the gutsy sound of her voice.

They dated every night for six weeks. Martha showed him how to live. She taught him to like wine, took him to foreign films, bought him vitamins. Ronny was finally getting the things everyone else took for granted, except for sex – he was worried about that. She had removed his hands from her breasts the only time he'd dared put them there. He knew her husband had left her. Maybe sex was a problem.

He spent many evenings in her tidy home, comfortably resting his head in her lap, his long legs curled up to fit on her embroidered sofa, watching television until it was time to go home. He thought of asking Dan about it, but the chance never came up.

"You have to try these," Martha said one evening and pointed to a tray of crushed ice, covered with rows of slick gray clumps in rough irregular shells. She'd ordered the oysters especially for him from the raw bar. He'd never even looked at one up close before. He'd rather have had the little cocktail dogs in barbeque sauce, but Martha said he ought to try new things. They were sipping wine and watching *Body Heat*, sitting on the carpet next to her heavy antique coffee table. It was her favourite film.

"Now see," she said, and she squeezed a wedge of lemon over one of the slimey blobs and followed it with a dot of horseradish. She stabbed it with the tiny three pronged fork and headed it toward his mouth. "Open up, here it comes."

He opened, then closed. "I can't," he said, and closed his mouth again tightly. She stopped the motion of her arm and the oyster slipped off and plopped onto his thigh just below the edge of his shorts, as he sat cross-legged. It slipped down and caught in the gap of the leg near his crotch. It was icy.

She clicked her tongue. "Now be a good boy, Babe. Martha knows what's best for you." She bent forward and slurped between his groin and the fabric. He felt her warm tongue lap against his skin. It lapped again, again. A tingle turned to pressure that he could feel hard against the inside of his pants. "Delicious, delicious," she said as she raised up and chewed.

She bent forward again and aimed her face at the same spot. "You're a big boy." She nuzzled and licked.

"Whew," he said. "Oooh . . . Ouch." She'd bitten him in the tender skin of his inner thigh. "Ouch." She bit him again. "That hurts." She took the advantage of his mouth hanging open, grabbed an oyster with her fingers and popped it in.

"You love it," she said. She was on top of him immediately and covered his mouth with hers forcing the oyster farther back with her tongue. He swallowed. He gathered saliva and swallowed again to wash away the slimey tang. She got up and pulled him by the belt and he stumbled along dazed behind her.

She undressed him on her antique-style waterbed and pressed him down into the flowered waves. She opened her soft cotton dress and put a large dark nipple to his lips, guiding his hand down into her thick pubic hair. He noticed her muscular arms as she stroked his forehead. She bent her neck to kiss his eyes. Then she moved down and bit his neck. It didn't hurt too much.

"Stay still," she whispered, and she lowered herself onto his hard cock. She pinned his wrists above his head and pumped him hard and fast and long.

The next morning he told Dan about her.

"She's a little older," he said, "but we have all the same interests. And she cooks as well as my mother." He took a breath. "I think I'm going to ask her to marry me."

"I don't know, Buddy. Are you sure this is what you want?" Dan asked.

"I sure am happy."

"Maybe you should wait a while, live together. I've been living with Tina for six months and I still don't know if it would work for a marriage."

"I don't think so. Not with Martha. I better do it now."

The next day he asked Martha to marry him. She suggested a no frills wedding at the courthouse on the following weekend. He moved out of the trailer and into her home among the dark antiques and jangling chimes.

A few months later, Dan and Tina were over for Sunday

dinner. "I'm proud of you, man," Dan said after they had
finished eating a pile of Martha's pasta and clam sauce. He
motioned toward the kitchen where Martha and Tina were doing
dishes. "You got everything you could want – a nice house, a
good cook, a warm waterbed. Martha's a good woman. I used to
wonder what might happen to you, but you've got it made,
buddy."

"She's a little rough sometimes," he said.

Dan shrugged. "PMS."

Ronny wanted to mention a couple of slaps Martha had given
him, and the bites, but before he could say anything more, she
walked out of the kitchen drying her hands on a towel. "You boys
ready for dessert?"

"Strawberry shortcake," Ronny said to Dan, lifting his eyebrows. He licked his lips at Martha and she smiled.

He crawled into bed early that night after the huge meal. The
sun was still setting, but he couldn't keep his eyes open.
Suddenly he felt a burning crack at the back of his thighs. It
was Martha with his belt. He knew he'd done something, but he
didn't know what. She came around to the other side of the bed
and went for the insides of his thighs. He rolled onto his
stomach to protect his genitals. She didn't stop. "You're a
bad boy," she yelled.

He flung himself to the upper corner of the waterbed where she
had difficulty reaching him. "Get your ass over here." He
cringed as he looked at her. Her eyes were squinted and her hair
caught light from the sunset and glowed red in a fringe around
her face, like a crown of lightning. She threw her arms and torso
down on the bed and began to make waves, bouncing him again
and again, striking his head against the antique headboard until
his skull throbbed and his cut scalp stung.

When she stopped he shrank into a tight ball. He heard the belt
drop and Martha crawled slowly toward him on the bed. Her robe
hung open and he focused on the brown nipples, almost the size
of saucers, until he was buried in her warmth and opened his
mouth wide to take her in.

It would happen again and again and again, he knew it, the
hurricane in the waterbed – he didn't understand it, but he knew
it. Dan would say leave her. Dan would say there are plenty of
women. Ronny nuzzled and sucked harder at the soft, sweet skin

of Martha's breast, and she lowered her wet slit on his cock, huge
and sensitive with the blood of pain and passion. A thought came
to him through his clouded mind – he didn't have to tell Dan, or
anyone.

BEAUTY'S PUNISHMENT

Anne Rice

I The Auction in the Market-Place

THE CART HAD come to a stop, and Beauty could see through the tangle of white arms and tousled hair the walls of the village below, with the gates open and a motley crowd swelling out onto the green.

But slaves were being quickly unloaded from the cart, forced with the smack of the belt to crowd together on the grass. And Beauty was immediately separated from Tristan, who was pulled roughly away from her for no apparent reason other than the whim of a guard.

The leather bits were being pulled out of the mouths of the others. "Silence!" came the loud voice of the Commander. "There is no speech for slaves in the village! Any who speak shall be gagged again more cruelly than they have ever been before!"

He rode his horse round the little herd, driving it tightly together, and gave the order that the slaves' hands should be unbound and woe to any slave who removed his or her hands from the back of the neck.

"The village has no need of your impudent voices!" he went on. "You are beasts of burden now, whether that burden be labor or pleasure! And you shall keep your hands to the back of your necks or be yoked and driven before a plow through the fields!"

Beauty was trembling violently. She couldn't see Tristan as she was forced forward. All around her were long windblown tresses, bowed heads, and tears. It seemed the slaves cried more softly without their gags, struggling to keep their lips closed, and the voices of the guards were miserably sharp!

"Move! Head up straight!" came the gruff, impatient commands. Beauty felt chills rising on her arms and legs at the sound of those angry voices. Tristan was behind her somewhere, but if only he would come close.

And why had they been put out here so far from the village? And why was the cart being turned around?

Suddenly she knew. They were to be driven on foot, like a gaggle of geese to market. And almost as quickly as the thought came to her, the mounted guards swooped down on the little group and started them forward with a rain of blows.

"This is too bitter," Beauty thought. She was trembling as she started to run, the smack of the paddle as always catching her when she did not expect it and sending her flying forward over the soft, newly turned earth of the road.

"At a trot, with heads up!" the guard shouted, "and knees up as well!" And Beauty saw the horses' hooves pounding beside her, just as she'd seen them before on the Bridle Path at the castle, and felt the same wild trepidation as the paddle cracked her thighs and even her calves. Her breasts ached as she ran, and a dull warm pain coursed through her sore legs.

She couldn't see the crowd clearly, but she knew they were there, hundreds of villagers, perhaps even thousands, flooding out of the gates to meet the slaves. "And we're to be driven right through them; it's too awful," she thought, and suddenly the resolves she had made in the cart, to disobey, to rebel, left her. She was too purely afraid. And she was running as fast as she could down the road towards the village, the paddle finding her no matter how she hurried, until she realized she had pressed through the first rank of slaves and was now running with them, no one before her anymore to shield her from the sight of the enormous crowd.

Banners flew from the battlements. Arms waved and cheers rose as the slaves drew closer, and through the excitement there came the sounds of derision, and Beauty's heart thudded as she tried not to see too clearly what lay ahead, though she could not turn away.

"No protection, nowhere to hide," she thought, "and where is Tristan? Why can't I fall back into the flock?" But when she tried, the paddle smacked her soundly again, and the guard shouted to her to go forward! And blows were rained on those around her, causing the little red-haired Princess on her right to break into helpless tears. "O, what's to happen to us? Why did we disobey?!" the little Princess wailed through her sobs, but the dark-haired Prince on the other side of Beauty threw her a warning glance: "Quiet or it will be worse!"

Beauty couldn't help but think of her long march to the Prince's Kingdom, how he had led her through the villages where she had been honored and admired as his chosen slave. Nothing like that was happening now.

The crowd had broken loose and was spreading out on either side of them as they neared the gates. Beauty could see the women in their fancy white aprons and wooden shoes, and the men in their rawhide boots and leather jerkins, robust faces everywhere alight with obvious pleasure, which made Beauty gasp and drop her eyes to the path before her.

They were passing through the gates. A trumpet was being sounded. And hands reached out from everywhere to touch them, pushing them, pulling at their hair. Beauty felt fingers brush roughly across her face; her thighs were slapped. She let out a desperate scream, struggling to escape the hands that shoved her violently forward, while all around came the loud, deep, mocking laughter, shouts and exclamations, random cries.

Tears were flowing down Beauty's face and she hadn't even realized it. Her breasts throbbed with the same violent pulse she felt in her temples. Around her she saw the tall, narrow half-timbered houses of the village opening broadly to surround a huge marketplace. A high wooden platform with a gibbet upon it loomed over all. And hundreds crowded the overhanging windows and balconies, waving white handkerchiefs, cheering, while countless others choked the narrow lanes that led into the square, struggling to get close to the miserable slaves.

They were being forced into a pen behind the platform. Beauty saw a flight of rickety wooden steps leading to the boards above and a length of leather chain dangling above the distant gibbet. A man stood to one side of the gibbet with arms folded, waiting, while another sounded the trumpet again as the gates of the pen were shut. The crowd surrounded them, and there was no more than a thin strip of fencing to protect them. Hands reached for them again as they huddled together. Beauty's buttocks were pinched, her long hair lifted.

She struggled towards the center, desperately looking for Tristan. She glimpsed him only for a moment as he was pulled roughly to the bottom of the steps.

"No, I must be sold with him," she thought and pushed violently forward, but one of the guards shoved her back into the little cluster while the crowd hooted and howled and laughed.

The red-haired Princess who had cried on the road was now inconsolable, and Beauty pressed close to her, trying to comfort her as much as to hide. The Princess had lovely high breasts with very large pink nipples, and her red hair spilled down in rivulets over her tear-stained face. The crowd was cheering and shouting again now that the herald had finished. "Don't be afraid," Beauty whispered. "Remember, it will be very much like the castle finally. We will be punished, made to obey."

"No, it won't be!" the Princess whispered, trying not to move her lips visibly as she spoke. "And I thought I was such a rebel. I thought I was so stubborn."

The trumpet gave a third full-throated blast, a high echoing series of notes. And in the immediate silence that fell over the marketplace, a voice rang out:

"The Spring Auction will now commence!"

A roar rose from all around them, a near-deafening chorus, its loudness shocking Beauty so that she couldn't feel herself breathe. The sight of her own quivering breasts stunned her, and in one sweeping glance she saw hundreds of eyes passing over her, examining her, measuring her naked endowments, a hundred whispering lips and smiles.

Meantime the Princes were being tormented by the guards, their cocks lightly whipped with the leather belts, hands plumping their pendulous balls as they were made to "Come to attention!" and punished with severe cracks of the paddle to the buttocks if they did not. Tristan's back was to Beauty. She could see the hard perfect muscles of his legs and buttocks quivering as the guard teased him, stroking him roughly between the legs. She was miserably sorry now for their stolen lovemaking. If he could not come to attention, she would be to blame.

But the booming voice had sounded again:

"All those of the village know the rules of the auction. These disobedient slaves offered by our gracious Majesty for hard labor are to be sold to the highest bidder for the period of no less than three months' service as their new Lords and Masters shall see fit. Mute menials these incorrigibles are to remain, and they are to be brought to the Place of Public Punishment as often as their Masters and Mistresses will allow, there to suffer for the amusement of the crowd as much as for their own improvement."

The guard had moved away from Tristan, giving him an almost-playful blow with the paddle and smiling as he whispered something in Tristan's ear.

"You are solemnly charged to work these slaves," the voice of the herald on the platform continued, "to discipline them, to tolerate no disobedience from them, and never an impudent word. And any Master or Mistress might sell his slave within this village at any time for any sum as he should choose."

The red-haired Princess pressed her naked breasts against Beauty and Beauty leaned forward to kiss her neck. Beauty felt the tight wiry hair of the girl's pubis against her leg, its moisture and its heat. "Don't cry," she whispered.

"When we go back, I will be perfect, perfect!" the Princess confided, and broke into fresh sobs again.

"But what made you disobey?" Beauty quickly whispered in her ear.

"I don't know," the girl wailed, opening her blue eyes wide. "I wanted to see what would happen!" and she started to cry piteously again.

"Be it understood that each time you punish one of these unworthy slaves," the herald continued, "you do the bidding of her Royal Majesty. It is with her hand that you strike the blow, with her lips you scold. All slaves once a week are to be sent to the central grooming hall. Slaves are to be properly fed. Slaves are to be given time to sleep. Slaves should at all times exhibit evidence of sound whipping. Insolence or rebellion should be thoroughly put down."

The trumpet blasted again. White handkerchiefs waved, and all around hundreds upon hundreds clapped their hands. The

red-haired Princess screamed as a young man, leaning over the
fence of the pen, caught her by the thigh and pulled her towards
him.

The guard stopped him with a good-natured reprimand but
not before he had slipped his hand under the Princess's wet sex.

But Tristan was being driven up to the wooden platform. He
held his head high, hands clasped to the neck as before, his whole
attitude one of dignity despite the paddle soundly playing on his
narrow tight buttocks as he climbed the wooden steps.

For the first time Beauty saw beneath the high gibbet and its
dangling leather links a low round turntable onto which a tall
gaunt man in a bright jerkin of green velvet forced Tristan. He
kicked Tristan's legs wide apart as if the Prince could not be
addressed even with the simplest command.

"He's being handled like an animal," Beauty thought, watching.

Standing back, the tall auctioneer worked the turntable with a
foot pedal so that Tristan was turned quickly round and round.

Beauty got no more than a glimpse of his scarlet face and
golden hair, blue eyes almost closed. Sweat gleamed on his hard
chest and belly, his cock enormous and thick as the guards had
wanted it, his legs trembling slightly with the strain of being so
widely spread apart.

Desire curled inside of Beauty, and even as she pitied him, she
felt her organs swelling and pulsing again, and at the same time
the terrible fear, "I can't be made to stand up there alone before
everyone. I can't be sold off like this! I can't!"

But how many times at the castle had she said these words. A
loud burst of laughter from a nearby balcony caught her off-
guard. Everywhere there were loud conversations, arguments, as
the turntable went round again and then again, the blond curls
slipping off the nape of Tristan's neck to make him appear the
more naked and vulnerable.

"Exceptionally strong Prince," cried the auctioneer, his voice
even louder, deeper than that of the herald, cutting through the
roar of conversation, "long-limbed, yet sturdy of build. Fit for
household labor certainly, field labor most definitely, stable labor
without question."

Beauty winced.

The auctioneer had in his hand a paddle of the long narrow

flexible leather kind that is more a stiff strap almost than a paddle, and with this he slapped Tristan's cock as Tristan faced the pen of slaves again, announcing to one and all:

"Strong, attentive organ, capable of great service, great endurance," and volleys of laughter rose everywhere from the square.

The auctioneer reached out and, taking Tristan by the hair, bent him from the waist suddenly, giving the turntable another whirl while Tristan remained bent over.

"Excellent buttocks," came the deep booming voice, and then the inevitable smacks of the paddle, leaving their red blotches on Tristan's skin. "Resilient, soft!" cried the auctioneer, prodding the flesh with his fingers. Then his hand went to Tristan's face, lifting it, "and demure, quiet of temperament, eager to be obedient! And well he should be!" Another crack of the paddle and laughter all around.

"What is he thinking," Beauty thought. "I can't endure it!"

The auctioneer had caught Tristan by the head again, and Beauty saw the man lifting a black leather phallus, which hung from the belt of his green velvet jerkin by a chain. Before she even realized what he meant to do, he had thrust the leather into Tristan's anus, bringing more cheers and screams from all quarters of the marketplace, while Tristan bowed from the waist as before, his face still.

"Need I say more?" cried the auctioneer, "or shall the bids begin!"

At once they started, bids shouted from everywhere, each topped as soon as it was heard, a woman on a nearby balcony – a shopkeeper's wife, surely, in her rich velvet bodice and white linen blouse – rising to her feet to call her bid over the heads of the others.

"And they are all so very rich," Beauty thought, "the weavers and dyers and silversmiths for the Queen herself, and so any of them has the money to buy us." Even a crude-looking woman with thick red hands and a soiled apron called out her bid from the door of the butcher's shop, but she was quickly out of the game.

The little turntable went round and round slowly, the auctioneer finally coaxing the crowd as the bidding grew higher. With a slender leather-covered rod that he drew from a scabbard like a sword, he pushed the flesh of Tristan's buttocks this way and that, stroking at his anus, as Tristan stood quiet and humble, only the furious blush of his face giving his misery away.

But a voice rose suddenly from far back in the square, topping all the bids by a broad margin, and Beauty heard a murmur rush through the crowd. She stood on tiptoe trying to see what was happening. A man had stepped forward before the platform and, through the scaffolding beneath it, she could just see him. He was a white-haired man, though he was not old enough for such white hair, and it sat upon him with unusual loveliness framing a square and rather pacific face.

"So the Queen's Chronicler wants this sturdy young mount," cried the auctioneer. "Is there no one to outbid him? Do I hear more for this gorgeous prince? Come on, surely . . ."

Another bid, but at once the Chronicler topped it, his voice so soft it was a wonder Beauty heard, and this time his bid was so high that clearly he meant to shut off all opposition.

"Sold," the auctioneer cried out finally, "to Nicolas, the Queen's Chronicler and Chief Historian of the Queen's village! For the grand sum of twenty-five gold pieces."

And as Beauty watched through her tears, Tristan was roughly pulled from the platform, rushed down the stairs, and driven towards the white-haired man who stood composed with his arms folded, the dark gray of his exquisitely cut jerkin making him look the Prince himself as he silently inspected his purchase. With a snap of his fingers he ordered Tristan to precede him at a trot out of the square.

The crowd opened reluctantly to let the Prince pass, pushing at him and scolding him. But Beauty had only a glimpse of this before she realized with a scream that she was herself being dragged out of the gaggle of crying slaves towards the steps.

II Beauty on the Block

"No, it can't be happening!" she thought, and she felt her legs give out from under her as the paddle smacked her. And the tears blinded her as she was almost carried to the platform and the turntable and set down. It did not matter that she had not walked in obedience.

She was there! And before her the crowd stretched in all directions, grinning faces and waving hands, short girls and boys leaping up the better to see, and those on balconies rising to get a more careful look.

Beauty felt she would collapse, yet she was standing, and when the soft rawhide boot of the auctioneer kicked her legs apart, she struggled to keep her balance, her breasts shivering with her muffled sobs.

"Lovely little Princess!" he was calling out, the turntable whirling suddenly, so that she almost fell forward. She saw behind her hundreds and hundreds crowded back to the village gates, more balconies and windows, soldiers lounging along the battlements above. "Hair like spun gold and ripe little breasts!"

The auctioneer's arm wound round her, squeezing her bosom hard, pinching her nipples. She let out a scream behind her closed lips, yet felt the immediate surge between her legs. But if he should take her by the hair as he had done Tristan . . .

And even as she thought it, she felt herself forced to bow from the waist in the same fashion, her breasts seeming to swell with their own weight as they dangled beneath her. And the paddle found her buttocks again, to the screaming delight of the crowd. Claps, laughs, shouts, as the auctioneer lifted her face with the stiff black leather, though he kept her bent over, spinning the turntable faster. "Lovely endowments, fit surely for the finest household, who would waste this pretty morsel in the fields?"

"Sell her into the fields!" someone shouted. And there were more cheers and laughter. And when the paddle smacked her again, Beauty gave out a humiliating wail.

The auctioneer clamped his hand over her mouth and he forced her up with her chin in the air, letting her go to stand with her back arched. "I will collapse, I will faint," Beauty thought, her heart pounding in her breast, but she was standing there, enduring it, even as she felt the sudden tickle of the leather-covered rod between her pubic lips. "O, not that, he cannot . . ." she thought, but already her wet sex was swelling, hungering for the rough stroking of the rod. She squirmed away from it.

The crowd roared.

And she realized she was twisting her hips in horrid vulgar fashion to escape the sharp prodding examination.

There was more clapping and shouting as the auctioneer forced the rod deep into her hot wet pubis, calling out all the while, "Dainty, elegant little girl, fit for the finest lady's maid or gentleman's diversion!" Beauty knew her face was scarlet. Never at the castle had she known such exposure. And as her legs gave out from under her again, she felt the auctioneer's sure hand lifting her wrists above her head until she dangled above the platform, and the leather paddle slapped at her helpless calves and the soles of her feet. Without meaning to, Beauty kicked helplessly. She lost all control.

Screaming behind her clenched teeth, she struggled madly as she hung in the man's grip. A strange, desperate abandon came over her as the paddle licked at her sex, slapping it and stroking it, and the screams and roars deafened her. She did not know whether she was longing for the torment or wildly trying to shut it out.

Her own frantic breaths and sobs filled her ears, and she knew suddenly that she was giving the onlookers precisely the kind of show they adored. They were getting much more from her than they had from Tristan, and she did not know whether or not she cared. Tristan was gone. She was forsaken.

The paddle punished her, stinging her and driving her hips out in a wild arc, only to stroke her wet pubic hair again, inundating her with waves of pleasure as well as pain.

In pure defiance, she swung her body with all her force, almost pulling loose from the auctioneer, who gave a loud astonished laugh. The crowd was shrieking as he sought to steady her, his tight fingers biting into her wrists as he hoisted her higher, and out of the corner of her eye Beauty saw two crudely dressed varlets rushing towards the platform.

At once they bound her wrists to the leather chain that hung from the gibbet above her head. Now she dangled free, the auctioneer's paddle turning her with his blows as she sobbed and tried to hide her face in her upstretched arm.

"We haven't all day to amuse ourselves with the little Princess," the auctioneer cried, though the crowd urged him on with shouts of "Spank her," "Punish her."

"Calling for a firm hand and severe discipline for this lovely lady, what am I bid?" He twisted Beauty, smacking the soles of her naked feet with the paddle, pushing her head through her arms so that she could not conceal her face.

"Lovely breasts, tender arms, delectable buttocks, and a sweet little pleasure cleft fit for the gods!"

But the bids were already flying, topped so quickly he did not have to repeat them, and through her swimming eyes Beauty saw the hundreds of faces gazing up at her, the young men crowded to the very edge of the platform, a pair of young women whispering and pointing, and beyond an old woman leaning on a cane as she studied Beauty, raising a withered finger now to offer a bid.

Again the sense of abandon came over her, the defiance, and she kicked and wailed behind her closed lips, wondering that she didn't shout aloud. Was it more humiliating to admit that she could speak? Would her face have been more scarlet had she been made to demonstrate that she was a thinking, feeling creature, and not some dumb slave?

Her sobs were her only answer to herself, her legs pulled wide apart now as the bidding continued, the auctioneer spreading her buttocks with the leather rod as he had done to Tristan, stroking her anus so that she squealed and clenched her teeth, and twisted, even trying to kick him if she could.

But he was now confirming the highest bid, and then another, and trying to coax more out of the crowd until she heard him announce in that same deep voice:

"Sold to the Innkeeper, Mistress Jennifer Lockley of the Sign of the Lion, for the grand sum of twenty-seven pieces of gold, this spirited and amusing little Princess, surely to be whipped for her bread and butter as much as anything else!"

III The Place of Public Punishment

THE SUNLIGHT was too bright for a moment. But Beauty was busy folding her arms and marching, lifting her legs as high as she could, and finally the square became visible as they entered it. She saw its shifting crowds of idlers and gossips, several youths sitting on the broad stone rim of the well, horses tethered at the gates of the Inns, and then other naked slaves here and there, some on their knees, some marching as she was.

The Captain turned her with another one of those large soft spanks, squeezing her right buttock a little as he did it.

Half in a dream it seemed, Beauty found herself in a broad

street, full of shops much like the lane down which she had come, but this street was crowded and everyone was busy, purchasing, bargaining, arguing.

That terrible feeling of regularity came back to her, that all of this had happened before, or at least that it was so familiar that it might have. A naked slave on her hands and knees cleaning a shop window looked ordinary enough, and to see another with a basket strapped to his back, marching as Beauty was being marched, before a woman who drove him with a stick – yes, that too looked regular. Even the slaves, bound naked on the walls, their legs apart, their faces in half-sleep, seemed just the ordinary thing, and why shouldn't the young village men taunt them as they passed, slapping an erect cock here, pinching a poor shy nether mouth there? Yes, ordinary.

Even the awkward thrust of her breasts, her arms folded behind her to force her breasts out, all of that seemed quite sensible and a proper way to march, Beauty thought. And when she felt another warm spank she marched more briskly and tried to lift her knees more gracefully.

They were coming to the other end of the village now, the open marketplace, and all around the empty auction platform she saw hundreds milling. Delicious aromas rose from the little cook-shops, and she could even smell the wine that the young men bought by the cup at the open stands, and she saw the fabrics blowing in long streams from the fabric shop, and heaps of baskets and rope for sale, and everywhere naked slaves at a thousand tasks.

In an alleyway, a slave on his knees swept vigorously with a small broom. Two others on all fours bore baskets full of fruit on their backs as they hurried at a fast trot through a doorway. Against a wall, a slender Princess hung upside down, her pubic hair gleaming in the sun, her face red and flushed with tears, her feet neatly tethered to the wall above with wide tightly laced anklets.

But they had come into another square opening off the first, and this was a strange unpaved place where the earth was soft and freshly turned as it had been on the Bridle Path at the castle. Beauty had been allowed to stop, and the Captain stood beside her with his thumbs hooked in his belt, watching everything.

Beauty saw another high turntable, like that at the auction, and on it, a bound slave was being fiercely paddled by a man who worked the turntable round and round with a pedal as the auctioneer had done, whipping hard at the naked buttocks each time it spun to the proper position. The poor victim was a gorgeously muscled Prince, with his hands bound tight on his back and his chin mounted up on a short rough column of wood so that all could see his face as he was punished. "How can he keep his eyes open?" Beauty thought. "How can he bear to look at them?" The crowd around the platform squawked and screamed as stridently as they had done at the earlier bidding.

And when the paddler raised his leather weapon now to signal the punishment was at an end, the poor Prince, his body convulsing, his face twisted and wet, was pelted with soft bits of fruit and refuse.

Like the other square it had the atmosphere of a fair, with the same cookshops and wine vendors. From high windows hundreds watched, their arms folded on sills and balcony edges.

But the turntable paddling was not the only form of punishment. A high wooden pole stood far to the right, with many long leather ribbons streaming down from an iron ring at the top of it. At the end of each black ribbon was a slave tethered by a leather collar that forced the head high, and all marched slowly but with prancing steps in a circle around the pole, to the constant blows of four paddle-wielding attendants stationed at four points of the circle like the four points of a compass. A round track was worn in the dust from the naked feet. Some hands were bound behind the back; others were clasped there freely.

A straggle of village men and women watched the circular march, commenting here and there, and Beauty looked on in dazed silence as one of the slaves, a young Princess with large floppy brown curls, was untethered and given back to a waiting Master, who whipped at the slave's ankles with a straw broom as he drove her forward.

"There," said the Captain, and Beauty marched obediently beside him towards the high Maypole with its turning bands of leather.

"Tether her," he said to the guard, who quickly pulled Beauty over and buckled the leather collar around her neck so her chin was forced up over the edge of it.

In a blur, Beauty saw the Captain watching. Two village

women were near him and talking to him, and she saw him say something rather matter-of-factly.

The long band of leather running down from the top of the pole was heavy and carried along in a circle on the iron ring by the momentum of the others, and it almost pulled Beauty forward by the collar. She marched a little faster so that it would not, but it tugged her back, until she finally fell into the right step, and felt the first loud spanking blow from one of the four guards who rather casually waited to punish her. There were so many slaves trotting in the circle now that the guards were always swinging their bright ovals of black leather, Beauty realized, though she was blessed with a few slow seconds between blows, the dust and the sunlight stinging her eyes as she watched the tousled hair of the slave ahead of her.

"Public Punishment." She remembered the words of the auctioneer telling all Masters and Mistresses to prescribe it whenever they felt it necessary. And she knew that the Captain would never think, like her well-mannered, silver-tongued Masters and Mistresses at the castle, to give her a reason for it. But what did it matter? That he wanted her punished because he was bored or curious, that was reason enough, and each time she made the full circle she saw him clearly for a few moments, his arms at his sides, his legs firmly apart, his green eyes fixed on her. What were all the reasons but foolishness, she mused. And as she braced herself for another smart blow – losing her footing and her grace for an instant in the powdery dust as the paddle swept her hips forward – she felt an odd contentment, unlike anything she'd known at the castle.

There was no tension in her. The familiar ache in her vagina, the lust for the Captain's cock, the paddle's crack, these things were there as she marched, the leather collar bouncing cruelly against her uplifted chin, the balls of her feet smacking the packed earth, but still it was not that terrible quavering dread she had known before.

But her reverie was broken by a loud cry from the crowd near her. Over the heads of those who leered at her and the other marching slaves, she saw that the poor punished Prince was being taken down from the turntable where he had remained for so long an object of public derision. And now another slave, a Princess with yellow hair like her own, was forced into place, back arching down, buttocks high, chin mounted.

Coming round the dusty little circle again, Beauty saw that the Princess was squirming as her hands were tied behind her back, and the chin rest was being cranked up by an iron bolt so that she couldn't turn her head. Her knees were bound to the turntable and she kicked her feet furiously. The crowd was as thrilled as it had been by Beauty's display on the auction block. And it showed its pleasure with much cheering.

But Beauty's eye caught the Prince who had been taken down and she saw him rushed to a nearby pillory. There were several pillories, in fact, in a row in their own little clearing. And there the Prince was bent over from the waist, his legs as always kicked apart, his face and hands clamped in place, the board coming down with a loud splat to hold him looking forward and quite unable to hide his face, or for that matter to do anything.

The crowd closed in around the helpless figure. As Beauty came round again, groaning suddenly at an unusually hard crack of the paddle, she saw the other slaves, Princesses all, pilloried in the same way, tormented by the crowds, who felt of them, stroked them, pinched them as they chose, though one villager was giving one of the Princesses a drink of water.

The Princess had to lap it, of course, and Beauty saw the pink dart of her tongue into the shallow cup, but still it seemed a mercy.

The Princess on the turntable meantime was kicking and bouncing and giving the most marvelous show, her eyes shut, her mouth a grimace, and the crowd was chanting the number of each blow aloud in a rhythm that sounded oddly frightening.

But Beauty's time of trial at the Maypole was coming to an end. Very quickly and deftly, she was released from the collar and taken panting from the circle. Her buttocks smarted and seemed to swell as if waiting for the next spank, which never came. Her arms ached as they lay doubled behind her back, but she stood waiting.

The Captain's large hand turned her around and he seemed to tower over her, gilded with sunlight, his hair sparkling around the dark shadow of his face as he bent to kiss her. He cradled her head in his hands and drew on her lips, opening them, stabbing his tongue into her, and then letting her go.

Beauty sighed to feel his lips withdrawn, the kiss rooting deep into her loins. Her nipples rubbed against the thick lacing on his jerkin, and the cold buckle of his belt burned her. She saw his dark face crease with a slow smile and his knee pressed against her hurting sex, teasing its hunger. Her weakness seemed complete suddenly and to have nothing to do with the tremors in her legs or her exhaustion.

"March," he said. And turning her around he sent her with a soft squeeze of her sore buttock towards the far side of the square.

They drew near to the pilloried slaves, who writhed and twisted under the taunts and slaps of the idle crowd milling about them. And behind, Beauty saw closely for the first time a long row of brilliantly colored tents set back beneath a line of trees, each tent with its canopied entrance open. A young man handsomely dressed stood at each tent and though Beauty could glimpse nothing in the shadowy interiors, she heard the voices of the men one by one tempting the crowd:

"Beautiful Prince inside, Sir, only ten pence." Or "Lovely little Princess, Sir, your pleasure for fifteen pence." And more invitations like these. "Can't afford your own slave; enjoy the best for only ten pence." "Pretty Prince needing punishment, Madam. Do the Queen's bidding for fifteen pence." And Beauty realized that men and women were going and coming from the tents, one by one, and sometimes together.

"And so even the commonest of the villagers," Beauty thought, "can enjoy the same pleasure." And ahead at the end of the row of tents, she saw a whole gathering of dusty and naked slaves, their heads down, their hands tethered to the tree branch above behind a man who called out to one and all: "Hire by the hour or the day these lovelies for the lowliest service." On a trestle table at his side was an assortment of straps and paddles.

She marched on, absorbing these little spectacles almost as if the sights and the sounds were stroking her, the Captain's large firm hand now and again punishing her softly.

When at last they reached the Inn, and Beauty stood in the little bedchamber again, her legs wide, her hands behind her neck, she thought drowsily, "You are my Lord and Master."

It seemed in some other incarnation she had lived all her life in the village, had served a soldier, and the mingling of noises coming from the square outside was a comforting music.

She was the Captain's slave, yes, utterly his, to run through the public streets, to punish, to subjugate totally.

And when he tumbled her on the bed, spanked her breasts, and took her hard again, she turned her head this way and that, whispering, "Master, and then Master."

Somewhere in the back of her mind she knew it was forbidden to speak, but this seemed no more than a moan or a scream. Her mouth was open and she was sobbing as she came, her arms rising and encircling the Captain's neck. His eyes flickered, then blazed through the gloom. And there came his final thrusts, driving her over the brink into delirium.

For a long time she lay still, her head cradled in the pillow. She felt the long leather ribbon of the Maypole prodding her to trot as if she were still lost in the Place of Public Punishment.

It seemed her breasts would burst as they throbbed from the recent slaps. But she realized the Captain had taken off all his clothes and was slipping into the bed naked beside her.

His warm hand lay on her drenched sex, his fingers parting the lips ever so gently. She drew close to his naked limbs, his powerful arms and legs covered with soft curly golden down, his smooth clean chest pressed against her arm and her hip. His roughly shaven chin grazed her cheek. Then his lips kissed her.

She closed her eyes against the deepening afternoon light from the little window. The dim noises of the village, thin voices from the street, the dull bursts of laughter from the Inn below, all merged into a low hum that lulled her. The light grew bright before it began to fade. The little fire leapt on the hearth, and the Captain covered Beauty with his limbs and breathed in deep sleep against her.

IV Soldiers' Night at the Inn

FOR HOURS Beauty slept. And only vaguely was she aware of the Captain jerking the bell rope. He was up and dressed without an order to her. And when she fully opened her eyes, he stood over her in the dim light of a new hearth fire, his belt still unbuckled. In one swift movement he slipped it from around his waist and snapped it beside him. Beauty couldn't read his face. It looked hard and removed and yet there was a little smile on his lips, and her loins immediately acknowledged him. She could feel a deep stirring of passion inside, a soft discharge of fluids.

But before she could break through the languor, he had pulled her up and deposited her on the floor on her hands and knees, pressing her neck down and forcing her knees wide apart. Beauty's face flamed as the strap walloped her between the legs, stinging her bulging pubis. Again came a hard slap to the lips, and Beauty kissed the boards, wagging her buttocks up and down in submission. The licking of the strap came again, but carefully, almost caressingly punishing the protuberant lips, and Beauty, fresh tears spilling to the floor, gave an open-mouthed gasp, lifting her hips higher and higher.

The Captain stepped forward, and with his large naked hand covered Beauty's sore bottom, rotating it slowly.

Beauty's breath caught in her throat. She felt her hips lifted, swung, pushed down, and a little throbbing noise came out of her. She could still remember Prince Alexi at the castle telling her he had been made to swing his hips in this ghastly, ignominious fashion.

The Captain's fingers pressed into Beauty's flesh, squeezing her buttocks together.

"Wag those hips!" came the low command. And the hand thrust Beauty's bottom up so high that her forehead was sealed to the floor, her breasts pulsing against the boards, a throbbing groan choked out of her.

Whatever she had thought and feared so long ago at the castle didn't matter now. She churned her bottom in the air. The hand withdrew. The strap licked up at her sex, and in a violent orgy of movement she wagged and wagged her buttocks as she had been told to do.

Her body loosened, lengthened. If she had ever known any other posture but this she couldn't clearly remember it. "Lord and Master" she sighed, and the strap smacked her little mound, the leather scraping the clitoris as it thickened. Faster and faster Beauty swung her bottom in the circle, and the harder the strap licked her the more the juices in her surged, until she could not hear the sound of the strap against the slick lips, her cries coming from deep in her throat, almost unrecognizable to her.

At last the licking stopped. She saw the Captain's shoes before her and his hand pointing to a small-handled broom beside the fireplace.

"After this day," he said calmly, "I won't tell you this room is to be swept and scrubbed, the bed changed, the fire built up. You will do it every morning when you rise. And you will do it now, this evening, to learn how to do it. After that you'll be scrubbed in the Inn yard to properly serve the garrison."

At once Beauty started to work, on her knees, with swift careful movements. The Captain left the room, and within moments Prince Roger appeared with the dustpan, scrub brush, and bucket. He showed her how she must do these little tasks, how to change the linen, build up the wood on the hearth, clear away the ashes.

And he did not seem surprised that Beauty only nodded and didn't speak to him. It didn't occur to her to speak to him.

The Captain had said "every day." So he meant to keep her! She might be the property of the Sign of the Lion, but she had been chosen by its chief lodger.

She could not do her tasks well enough. She smoothed the bed, polished the table, careful to kneel at all times, and rise only when she must.

And when the door opened again, and Mistress Lockley took her by the hair and she felt the wooden paddle driving her down the steps, she was softened and carried away by thoughts of the Captain.

Within seconds, she'd been stood in the crude wooden hogshead tub. Torches flickered at the Inn door and on the side of the shed. Mistress Lockley scrubbed fast and roughly, flushing out Beauty's sore vagina with wine mixed in water. She creamed Beauty's buttocks.

Not a word was spoken as she bent Beauty this way and that, forcing her legs into a squat, lathering her pubic hair, and roughly drying her.

And all around Beauty saw other slaves being coarsely bathed, and she heard the loud bantering voices of the crude woman in the apron and two other strong-limbed village girls who went at the task, now and then stopping to smack the buttocks of this slave or that for no apparent reason. But all Beauty could think of was that she belonged to the Captain; she was to see the garrison. Surely the Captain would be there. And the volleys of shouts and laughter from the Inn tantalized her.

When Beauty was thoroughly dry, and her hair had been

brushed, Mistress Lockley put her foot on the edge of the hogshead and threw Beauty over her knee and swatted at her thighs hard with the wooden paddle several times, and then pushed Beauty down on her hands and knees as Beauty gasped for breath and sought to steady herself.

It was positively odd not to be spoken to, not even sharp impatient commands. Beauty glanced up as Mistress Lockley came around beside her, and for one instant she saw Mistress Lockley's cool smile, before the woman had the chance to remember herself. Quite suddenly Beauty's head was lifted gently by the full weight of her long hair, and Mistress Lockley's face was right above hers.

"And you were going to be my little troublemaker. I was going to cook your little buttocks so much longer than the rest for breakfast."

"Maybe you still should," Beauty whispered without intention or thought. "If that's what you like for breakfast." But she broke into violent trembling as soon as she finished. O, what had she done!

Mistress Lockley's face lit up with the most curious expression. A half-repressed laugh escaped her lips. "I'll see *you* in the morning, my dear, with all the others. When the Captain's gone, and the Inn's nice and quiet, and there's no one here but the other slaves waiting in line as well for their morning whipping. I'll teach you to open that mouth without permission." But this was said with unusual warmth, and the color was high in Mistress Lockley's cheeks. She was so very pretty. "Now trot," she said softly.

The big room of the Inn was already packed with soldiers and other drinking men.

A fire roared on the hearth, mutton turned on the spit. And upright slaves, their heads bowed, scurried on tiptoe to pour wine and ale into dozens of pewter flagons. Everywhere Beauty glanced in the crowd of dark-clad drinkers with their heavy riding boots and swords, she saw the flash of naked bottoms and gleaming pubic hair as slaves set down plates of steaming food, bent over to wipe up spills, crawled on hands and knees to mop up the floor, or scampered to retrieve a coin playfully pitched into the sawdust.

From a dim corner came the thick, resonant strumming of a

lute and the beat of a tambourine and a horn playing a slow melody. But riots of laughter drowned the sound. Broken fragments of a chorus rose in a full burst only to die away. And from everywhere came shouts for meat and drink and the call for more pretty slaves to entertain the company.

Beauty didn't know which way to look. Here a robust officer of the guard in his vest of shining mail pulled a very pink and pale-haired Princess off her feet and set her standing on the table. With her hands behind her head she quickly danced and hopped as she was told, her breasts bouncing, her face flushed, her silvery blond hair flying in long perfect corkscrew curls about her shoulders. Her eyes were bright with a mixture of fear and obvious excitement. There another delicate-limbed female slave was being thrown over a crude lap and spanked as her frantic hands went to cover her face before they were pulled aside and playfully held out before her by an amused onlooker.

Between the casks on the walls, more naked slaves stood, their legs apart, their hips thrust out, waiting to be picked, it seemed. And in a corner of the room, a beautiful Prince with full red curls to the shoulders sat with legs apart on the lap of a hulking soldier, their mouths locked in a kiss as the soldier stroked the Prince's upright organ. The red-haired Prince licked at the soldier's coarsely shaven black beard, mouthed his chin, then opened his lips to the kissing again. His eyebrows were knit with the intensity of his passion, though he sat as helplessly and still as if he had been tied there, his bottom riding up with the shift of the soldier's knee, the soldier pinching the Prince's thigh to make him jump, the Prince's left arm hanging loosely over the soldier's neck, right hand buried in the soldier's thick hair with slow, flexing fingers.

A black-haired Princess in the far corner struggled to turn round and round, her hands clasped to her ankles, her legs apart, long hair sweeping the floor as a flagon of ale was poured over her tender private parts and the soldiers bent to lap the liquid playfully from the curling hair of her pubis. Suddenly she was thrown standing on her hands, her feet hoisted high above, as a soldier filled her nether mouth with ale to overflowing.

But Mistress Lockley was pulling Beauty so that she might take a flagon of ale and a pewter plate of steaming food in her hands, and Beauty's face was turned to see the distant figure of the

Captain. He sat at a crowded table far across the room, his back to the wall, his leg outstretched on the bench before him, his eyes fixed on Beauty.

Beauty struggled fast on her knees, her torso erect, the food held high until she knelt beside him and reached over the bench to place the food on the table. Leaning on his elbow, he stroked her hair and studied her face as though they were quite alone, the men all around them laughing, talking, singing. The golden dagger gleamed in the candlelight and so did the Captain's golden hair and the bit of shaven hair on his upper lip, and his eyebrows. The uncommon gentleness of his hand, lifting Beauty's hair back over her shoulders and smoothing it, brought chills over Beauty's arms and throat; and between her legs the inescapable spasm.

She made some small undulation with her body, not truly meaning to. And at once his strong right hand clamped on her wrists and he rose from the bench lifting her off the floor and up so she dangled above him.

Caught off-guard, she blanched and then felt the blood flooding to her face, and as she was turned this way and that, she saw the soldiers turning to look at her.

"To my good soldiers, who have served the Queen well," the Captain said, and at once there was loud stomping and clapping. "Who will be the first?" the Captain demanded.

Beauty felt her pubic lips growing thickly together, a spurt of moisture squeezing through the seam, but a silent burst of terror in her soul paralyzed her. "What will happen to me?" she thought as the dark bodies closed in around her. The hulking figure of a burly man rose in front of her. Softly his thumbs sank into the tender flesh of her underarms, as, clutching her tightly, he took her away from the Captain. Her gasps died in her throat.

Other hands guided her legs around the soldier's waist. She felt her head touch the wall behind her and she tucked her hands behind her head to cradle it, all the while staring forward into the soldier's face, as his right hand shot down to open his breeches.

The smell of the stables rose from the man, the smell of ale, and the rich, delicious scent of sun-browned skin and rawhide. His black eyes quivered and closed for an instant as his cock plunged into Beauty, widening the distended lips, as Beauty's hips thudded against the wall in a frantic rhythm.

Yes. Now. Yes. The fear was dissolved in some greater unnameable emotion. The man's thumbs bit into Beauty's under-arms as the pounding went on. And all around her in the gloom she saw a score of faces looking on, the noises of the Inn rising and falling in violent splashes.

The cock discharged its hot, swimming fluid inside her and her orgasm radiated through her, blinding her, her mouth open, the cries jerked out of her. Red-faced and naked, she rode out her pleasure right in the midst of this common tavern.

She was lifted again, emptied.

And she felt herself being set down on her knees on the table. Her knees were pulled apart and her hands placed under her breasts.

As the hungry mouth sucked on her nipple, she lifted her breasts, arching her back, her eyes turned shyly away from those who surrounded her. The greedy mouth fed on her right breast now, drawing hard as the tongue stabbed at the tiny stone of the nipple.

Another mouth had taken her other breast. And as she pressed herself against the mouths that suckled her, the pleasure almost too acute, hands spread her legs wider and wider, her sex almost lowered to the table.

For one moment the fear returned, burning white-hot. Hands were all over her; her arms were being held, her hands forced behind her back. She could not free herself from the mouths drawing hard on her breasts. And her face was being tilted up, a dark shadow covering her as she was straddled. The cock pushed into her gaping mouth, her eyes staring up at the hairy belly above her. She sucked the cock with all her power, sucking as hard as the mouths at her breasts, moaning as the fear again evaporated.

Her vagina quivered, fluids coursing down her wide-spread thighs, and violent jolts of pleasure shook her. The cock in her mouth tantalized her but could not satisfy her. She drew the cock deeper and deeper till her throat contracted, the come shooting into her, the mouths pulling gently at her nipples, snapping her nipples, her nether lips closing vainly on the emptiness.

But something touched her pulsing clitoris, scraped it through the thick film of wetness. It plunged through her starved pubic lips. It was the rough, jeweled handle of the dagger again . . . surely it was . . . and it impaled her.

She came in a riot of soft muffled cries, pumping her hips up and up, all sight and sound and scent of the Inn dissolved in her frenzy. The dagger handle held her, the hilt pounding her pubis, not letting the orgasm stop, forcing cry after cry out of her.

Even as she was laid down on her back on the table, it tormented her, making her squirm and twist her hips. In a blur she saw the Captain's face above her. And she writhed like a cat as the dagger handle rocked her up and down, her hips spanking the table.

But she was not allowed to come so soon again.

She was being lifted. And she felt herself laid over a broad barrel. Her back arched over the moist wood, she could smell the ale, and her hair fell down to the floor, the Inn upside down in a riot of color before her. Another cock was going into her mouth while firm hands anchored her thighs to the curve and a cock pushed into her dripping vagina. She had no weight, no equilibrium. She could see nothing but the dark scrotum before her eyes, the unfastened cloth. Her breasts were slapped, sucked, and gathered by strong kneading fingers. Her hands groped for the buttocks of the man who filled her mouth and she clung to him, riding him. But the other cock pummeled her against the barrel, plugged her, grinding her clitoris to a different rhythm. Through all her limbs she felt the searing consummation, as if it did not rise from between her legs, her breasts teeming. All her body had become the orifice, the organ.

She was being carried into the yard, her arms around firm, powerful shoulders.

It was a young brown-haired soldier who carried her, kissing her, petting her. And they were all over the green grass, the men, laughing in the torchlight as they surrounded the slaves in the tubs, their manner easy now that the first hot passions had been satisfied.

They circled Beauty as her feet were lowered into the warm water. They knelt with the full wineskin in their hands and squirted the wine up into her, tickling her, cleansing her. They bathed her with the brush and the cloth, half playing at it, vying to fill her mouth slowly, carefully with the tart, cool wine, to kiss her.

She tried to remember this face, that laugh, the very soft skin of the one with the thickest cock, but it was hopeless.

They laid her down in the grass beneath the fig trees and she was mounted again, her young captor, the brown-haired soldier, feeding dreamily on her mouth, and then driving her in a slower, softer rhythm. She reached back and felt the cool, naked skin of his buttocks and the cloth of his breeches pulled halfway down, and touching the loosened belt, the rumpled cloth, and the half-naked backside, she clamped her vagina tight on his cock so that he gasped aloud like a slave on top of her.

It was hours later.

She sat curled in the Captain's lap, her head against his chest, her arms about his neck, half sleeping. Like a lion he stretched under her, his voice a low rumble from his broad chest, as he spoke to the man opposite. He cradled her head in his left hand, his arm feeling immense, effortlessly powerful.

Only now and then did she open her eyes on the smoky glare of the whole tavern.

Quieter, more orderly than before. The Captain talked on and on. The words "runaway Princess" came clear to her.

"Runaway Princess," Beauty thought drowsily. She couldn't worry about such things. She closed her eyes again, burrowing into the Captain, who tightened his left arm about her.

"How splendid he is," she thought. "How coarsely beautiful." She loved the deep creases of his tanned face, the luster of his eyes. An odd thought came to her. She had no more care what his conversation was about than he had care to talk to her. She smiled to herself. She was his nude and shuddering slave. And he was her coarse and bestial Captain.

But her thoughts drifted to Tristan. She had declared herself such a rebel to Tristan.

What had happened to him with Nicolas the Chronicler? How would she ever find out? Maybe Prince Roger could tell her some news. Perhaps the dense little world of the village had its secret arteries of information. She had to know if Tristan was all right. She wished she could just see him. And dreaming of Tristan, she drifted into sleep again.

OOH BABY, YOU TURN ME ON

Stewart Home

THERE WAS someone else, of that I was certain, or at least certain that something had changed in our relationship. It isn't easy to date this transformation. I'm not particularly jealous. Suspicious yes, but not possessive. I wasn't suddenly seized by the idea that horns had sprouted from my temples. The feeling that I was a cuckold grew on me, slowly, with stealth and subtlety, then all at once burst forth into conscious conviction, a conviction that shaped itself into words during the course of a fleeting glance through a window.

I could see her, or rather I could see her reflection, a shop window opposite our flat acting as a mirror. She was standing beneath our apartment, the door to our dwelling just to her right. Just to her right as I saw the scene inverted in the glass frontage of Derek's Traditional English Fish & Chips. The door actually stood to her left. She stood there, as rush hour traffic thundered along Essex Road, in her typist's uniform, like some small erect commander of a siege. Her black stiletto shoes polished and perfect. Her black stockings straight and tight and trim. Her short black skirt drawing my gaze, or rather what her short black skirt partially revealed and largely kept hidden drew my gaze. Her black jacket well tailored and set off against a white blouse, which since I knew she'd trained as an art historian brought to mind Bridget Riley. Indeed, we'd met and moved in together during our first term at university, so I'd been living with her as she pursued these studies. Over her shoulder a shiny black handbag. The black handbag, a deeper black against her black jacket, bringing to mind Rothko and Malevitch paintings. I'd never shared her enthusiasm for abstract art. She'd never shared my ardour for her work as a secretary, work that enabled me to pursue my postgraduate studies in English. Work performed on the never never, on the understanding that once I had my doctorate I'd become the breadwinner and she'd get to follow up her interest in the minimalist painter Frank Stella at an accredited academic institution. When we were in our early twenties she'd planned to take her doctorate at the Courthold, but as the years passed this scheme receded as an immediate possibility, until it had been diminished to a mere hope – a kind of alchemical transmutation but, like so many of our youthful expectations, done in reverse.

He had his back to the traffic, so that what I saw reflected of him was a pair of broad shoulders and the back of his head, which was topped by a shock of silver hair. His hair made me think of Andy Warhol. She didn't share my taste for pop art. She considered pop imagery vulgar. She sought cosmic vibrations from canvas (I refer to paintings not tents, although that said, she was fond of camping holidays in the wilds). She did not – as she put it, and she often put it in this manner to me – seek confirmation of what she already knew from art. She did not like banality and she particularly hated banality in art and to her pop art was banal. She insisted the prices paid for Warhol's output (she favoured denigrating it with the term throughput) would gradually fall until his works became worthless. According to her Warhol's success was a temporary blip, a fluke of fashion, he was no master.

I put down the eighteenth century translation I was studying – *Grobianus; or, the Compleat Booby. An Ironical Poem in Three Books. Done into English by Roger Bull, Esq.* – and pushed up the window. I'd forgotten, or at least I'd learnt to forget, why I'd chosen eighteenth century translation as my specialised area of study. It had been a foolish move, foolish at any rate in one who had aimed to complete his doctorate quickly (in say three or four years) and thus end his dependence on another, making her instead dependent on him. At that point in time, if time can be said to have a point, my studies had stretched over seven years and would stretch out for a few more with much ease and little trouble. When I'd begun these studies I'd been interested in languages. Making English translation my speciality gave me an excuse to learn other tongues. I liked using my tongue, I wanted to lick time and this was time consuming. Looking back with hindsight and coming face to face with my lack of foresight, I see my chief mistake or blunder or error or fault or whatever, as opting for the eighteenth century. The sixteenth century, even the seventeenth century, might have proved more manageable and would have certainly been less intractable. Too many translations had been published in the eighteenth century and not enough had been lost to posterity to bring the total down to reasonably orderly proportions. The British Library was filled with eighteenth century works written in various languages and translated into English (and much else besides written in both English and a great many other tongues).

All I gained for my pains as I pushed my head into the foul outside air was the sting of traffic fumes in my throat, eyes and nose. He was disappearing into the pharmacy beneath our flat and while no longer a bloodless image, all I saw of him was a pair of broad shoulders and the back of his head. She too was revealed – but revealed is too strong a term, since I'd known her intimately, indeed cohabited with her, for the best part of ten years – as palpitating flesh and blood. What I saw of her was no longer inverted, although the image reaching my retina had been reversed. She had her back to the street and was opening the door that gave access to the stairs that led up to our flat. She disappeared, or at least she disappeared from my field of vision. Our dirty brown, fume stained, flimsy front door closed behind her. A door that reminded me of Gary Hume's art. Neither she nor I liked our front door. Neither of us liked the paintings it brought to mind. Neither of us liked Essex Road. We liked Islington and would have opted for Upper Street or somewhere close to the canal if we'd been able to afford it. To return, however, to our front door (a door that she had just opened, walked through and closed), in referring to our front door I'm speaking in the plural, by which I don't just mean her and me or me and her – I'm also thinking of the couple who live in the flat above us, and not just the two adults (Brian and Brenda) but also their two small children (Scott and Harris).

Had I withdrawn my head from where I held it in that indeterminate space that was both outside our flat and above the street, I'd have heard her footsteps on the stairs as she made her way up to the first floor. The stairs creaked, or at least three of them did, the first three of the second flight. Or rather those were the only stairs that creaked on the two flights that led up to our rooms. There was another stair that creaked on a third flight that led from our modest abode to the turning for a fourth flight that provided access to the top floor flat. With my head outside the window I didn't register the protests of the three creaking stairs that undoubtedly groaned beneath her stiletto heels as she made her way up to our quarters. I know full well that those stairs creak with a predictability that is monotonous but I didn't hear their moans on this occasion. I'd often listened for the creak of those three stairs, particularly when she'd been out late without me. The groan of the stair on the third flight, the fourth creaking stair if you count from the bottom to the top of our building, I didn't care for – and I had a particularly strong dislike of being disturbed by it at night. It was a stair that went unsounded by her feet, except for those rare occasions when we made social calls on our upstairs neighbours Brian and Brenda. I didn't hear her key turn in the yale lock of the unmorticed door that when I say it was ours I mean it belonged solely to me and my wife – was solely ours, that is, in terms of use (obviously as tenants we didn't own it, possession may be nine tenths of the law but legally this door was the property of Mr Hunt, our landlord). Until my wife entered our front room I'd not been able to hear any noises coming from inside the building. The roar of traffic on Essex Road had prevented me from registering the click of her stiletto heels as she entered our flat.

I'd hoped to see his face but he'd not emerged from the pharmacy during the time it took her to get up the stairs. I had, however, seen four number 73 buses and felt thoroughly poisoned from the fumes they and a number of other diesel-driven vehicles which passed by my window had belched. I withdrew my head from the window and closed it. That is, I closed the window. Native

English speakers do not at present talk about closing their heads and besides, I try to keep my mind open. At least I consider myself to have an open mind, open – at any rate – within certain limits. My wife had thrown down her handbag and removed her jacket before entering the room. They'd be in the kitchen; she always left her jacket and handbag in the kitchen when she came in from work. She was still wearing her stilettos and the kitchen floor bore scars from the heels of these shoes, and not just this new pair which she'd only bought the previous Saturday but also the pair that she'd thrown out after purchasing this replacement footwear. My wife also had a pair of red stiletto shoes that had damaged the kitchen floor. The red stilettos lasted longer than her black stilettos since she never wore them to work, reserving them for evening wear. She also possessed a pair of white stilettos which she'd had for a very long time and wore chiefly but not exclusively when we made love, since this greatly pleased me.

"Is he married?"

"Who?"

"He."

"Who?"

"The guy you were talking to in the street."

"You ought to know as well as I do that Frank is widowed. He's been our landlord for more than two years."

"I only saw the back of his head and he looked, well he looked different."

"Make me a cup of tea."

I kissed her and she sat down. I stood for a few moments staring at the flimsy material of the short black skirt that covered the top of her legs. We'd been together for ten years and I still found her attractive. Indeed, I found her very attractive, very attractive indeed. I took in the black stockings covering her shapely legs. Shiny black stockings. As I took in the burnished black stockings I wondered what he was like. The fact that I had a rival merely added fuel to the flames of my passion. I'm not the jealous type and when we made love we often inflamed each other with intimate words. We had a number of shared and long-standing fantasies involving threesomes. We'd often had sex in public places, places where we might be seen by other people. Indeed, I knew that at least one of my wife's friends had watched us making love. It was when we were still undergraduates in Norwich, and living together in a big bedsitter room.

Katie, my wife's best friend from school, had come up from Canterbury to stay for the weekend. Katie slept on a battered imitation black leather sofa that the landlord supplied as part of the furnishings. The plastic cover was ripped and yellow foam showed through, so it was permanently covered with a white blanket. On Sunday morning, when we thought Katie was soundly asleep, we'd made love. She'd woken and watched us. My wife, at that point she was still my future wife since we didn't get married until after we'd graduated, suspected we'd woken Katie and got confirmation out of her as they walked to the train station later that day. I've always regretted that I didn't accompany them since at that point Katie didn't have a boyfriend. My future wife, my girlfriend as she was then, had snogged Katie several times when the two of them were in their mid-teens and they'd even talked about becoming girlfriends. There were no secrets between my wife and her friend, so Katie was ordered to divulge the thoughts and fantasies that had passed through her mind as she'd watched us making the beast with two backs on a feather soft double bed. As she'd watched Felicity sitting on my face with my tongue darting between Felicity's legs, Katie admitted that she'd really wanted to come over and suck what she described as my big blunt cock. Seeing how excited I became when I was told this, my wife (or future wife as she was then) encouraged Katie to indulge in fantasies about a threesome. Katie eventually agreed that we could go down to see her in Kent for a monster sex session, but the visit was cancelled when she started seeing a boy called Graham, whom she later married. At that point both of them were studying politics at the University of Kent.

I knew Felicity hadn't had a bad day at the office, she smiled – even troubling herself with the effort of making the smile appear coy – as I gazed down at her. If she'd had a bad day she would have told me I looked stupid with my mouth open, or picked up the paper, or told me to hurry up and get her some tea. Felicity had changed, or if she hadn't actually changed, then she had grown younger and changed back to her old sweet self. It wasn't that Felicity was vicious or mean but sometimes her work made her short-tempered – well it was a combination of the temporary office work that no longer seemed temporary, and the fact that she was not getting on with the real business of her life, her researches into minimal painting. It was a long time since she, a long time since we, had graduated from the University of East Anglia.

"What is it?" Felicity asked me.

"You're different."

"I'm eight, no, nine hours older than when you last saw me."

"More like nine years younger, you've changed."

"For the better?"

"For the better."

"Are you jealous?"

"You're seeing someone else, who is he?"

"I'm not interested in other men."

Then it dawned on me, or rather, what was going on half dawned on me. When I mentioned Katie's name Felicity laughed but I knew I was on the right track. She was seeing another woman. I looked at the hem of Felicity's skirt and then I looked at her face. I was trembling with emotion but the emotion was not anger. I felt happy, I felt very very happy. I put my arms around Felicity and told her everything would work out, that we would work it out, that I had worked it out. I told Felicity that this was what I'd always wanted. She was to phone her girlfriend right away, invite her over. I looked at the hem of Felicity's skirt and wanted to wrench it up but I restrained myself. What I wanted to do – and I wanted to do this far more than simply wrench up Felicity's skirt – was sit on a chair. I wanted to strip off and sit naked in a chair and watch Felicity and her girlfriend make love. I'd look at Felicity and her girlfriend, drink them in with my eyes. I'd get off on Felicity and her girlfriend getting it on. As I watched them – or so I thought or imagined – I might even touch myself. These touches would be gentle enough to qualify as caresses. Nothing so vigorous that it would bring forth pollution. I wouldn't spasm or spend what I was now determined to save, at least not until Felicity had brought her girlfriend to complete submission. Then I would get up and, and, and spurt into the other woman's face. That was what I really wanted, what I really really wanted, and to get it I had to wait. And not just wait, but wait and wait and wait.

Felicity was reluctant to make the phone call, she did not want to make that phone call, she told me to ease up, let her break it to me gently. I stopped up my ears, refused to listen, until eventually she did my bidding. She sent me out of the room, made the call, then told me her girlfriend – how I relished those words her girlfriend (or as she put it "my girlfriend") at that point in time, if time can be said to have a point. I could hardly wait but wait I must and wait I did, not just the full hour casually mentioned after she'd made the phone call but an extra fifteen minutes on top. The prospects I saw opening up before me during that wait carried my imagination off into infinite spaces. I imagined her, the girlfriend, her tight bodice cracking with vivacity, her desperation to suck my thing as I waggled it provocatively in her face. But the girlfriend, the other woman, she was, she was, she was . . . Well, she was shapely but not my type. I knew and still know many men who find her attractive but I am not one of them. I'd known Felicity's girlfriend since boyhood and she'd long been my rival for family affections. When I saw Felicity's girlfriend, when she walked through the door of the front room in which I stood expectantly awaiting her, the mask of fantasy fell away. I would not, I could not, engage in an unnatural relation with my mother's daughter, my father's pride and joy. She came into the flat and shortly afterwards she left with Felicity. She left with Felicity and a bundle of Felicity's clothes under her arm. In the interval I did not speak but you could hear the silence vibrate.

THE K.C. SUITE

Maxim Jakubowski

My original sin was to need you who could live without me . . .
I resisted as best I could, not knowing that the struggles of the
soul are intended to be lost.

Marie-Victoire Rouillier

I SING THE SACRED. I sing the bodies, I sing the sex, the union
between man and woman, the ever so shocking intimacy of bodies
moving towards each other, of copulation, of fornication, on beds
of starched linen sheets, on floors of unclean carpet squares, on
rickety sofas, in bath tubs under the drip of a leaking shower
head, in adulterous beds where the smell of deceived partners still
lingers on, in public places, in private places. I sing the fucking,
the thrusting, the sighs, the pain and the pleasure.

I sing what is no longer. I mourn what we once were and if you
say I am betraying you thus, I say you are wrong. It might be a
wake, but it is also a celebration. Of the way our naked flesh met
and connected and of a joy supreme.

This is what happened.

This is a crime story I wrote and published somewhere. At one
stage I thought it might actually become the opening chapter for a
novel I was mentally toying with, about violence and desire along

the American highways and a desperate race for love and money moving from Florida to Seattle. I read it in public at some festival. She was in the audience. As I hesitantly lingered over the particularly sexual elements, aware that my tale was so much more personal and explicit than the preceding stories by my fellow authors, my eyes suddenly connected with hers. She was sitting in a middle row. For weeks afterwards, I would wrack my brain to try and recall the actual colour of her eyes, with no success. I would find out later, of course. I was sitting with three others on a slightly elevated platform, two microphones shared between the four of us, a carafe of water and glasses, green baize covering the table on which our books were scattered. I wonder what I must have looked like to her. I was wearing a black Wranglers shirt with metallic poppers, open at the collar, and my usual black Farah trousers. That shirt still is a favourite of mine, I enjoy the way the cuffs sport three poppers instead of the traditional lone button most shirts have. I don't remember what she wore. At the end of the reading, one or two people came over with questions. I lost sight of her as the audience trouped out of the large room.

This is the story I read that day. It was raining outside, pouring down with rage. The woman in the story was a composite of so many I had known and, in fact, was even more a creature of my imagination. When I wrote the tale, I had not yet visited Miami.

Rite of Seduction

"Kill me," she had asked.

So I had.

It seemed the only thing to do. I can't pretend I was confused, I wasn't. I knew exactly what I was doing. I remember the night still: there was a full moon over Miami Beach, the ocean lapped the shore quietly and the cheap motel sported some odd Spanish name that somehow reminded me of a bad Elvis Presley song. It was fast, reasonably painless. The look in her eyes. Then she died.

She was a $100 a night starlet in a $2.5 million B-movie. I'd been hanging round the studios for a week or so. I had an assignment to cover the making of a big project financed by Spielberg's Amblin' company for one of his young hot-shot screenwriter-turned-directors. My interviews were in the can, my notepad full of okay anecdotes and I was ready for the road home and a first draft on the laptop. That evening, I'd walked into this small projection room towards the back of the studio lot. Some indie outfit was screening its dailies. The assistant director had shared reviewing chores with me on a now defunct magazine some years back, and hearing I was schmoozing around town had suggested we have a drink together for old time's sake after the screening.

It was hot and sticky in the projection room. The conditioning had a bad case of terminal cough and it smelled inside there of dry sweat, stale cigarettes and dime store perfume.

On the screen, following disjointed shots that a clever editor would later knit into the semblance of a car chase with explosions and bruised metal galore, came take after take of a nude shower scene and graphic enactment of a rape. Shot with three different cameras, one hand-held, the sequence repeated and repeated punctuated by clapperboards snapping, seen from various angles, at times literally pornographic as the camera lingered on details of the girl's body, the ambiguous smile on her lips as some Latin American-looking hood first slapped her before throwing her onto the bed, her breast tips stiffening as both naked bodies made contact, a fleeting view of her slightly open pubes as the hand-held camera moved to a better vantage position, a candid shot which would no doubt land on the proverbial cutting-room floor. It was all badly filmed, but these soundless, imperfect images had an unsettling effect on me. In the smokey darkness, I could feel the dryness in my throat and the beginning of an involuntary erection.

For the other spectators in the uncomfortable room, it was nothing new or anything wild, just a strip of unformed celluloid that would fit into a larger visual puzzle once it had been cleaned up, aseptised. Most of them would have been present at the shooting anyway and this was just a bunch of flickering second-hand thrills.

The screen went dark as the projectionist threaded some new footage into the system. A bar scene with different protagonists I'd never seen before. The knot in my throat was beginning to hurt. I just had to get out of this room, hankered for a cold drink.

"I need some fresh air," I whispered to my pal sitting in the next row. "I'll see you outside later."

As I rose from my seat, I noticed a woman in the back row of the small audience also heading for the exit.

Once in the open air, the cold was like a slap in the face following the suffocating atmosphere of the screening room. The woman who had preceded me out was standing with her back against the building's wall, a long filterless cigarette hanging from her lips.

"Do you have a light?"

It didn't take me long to recognize her. Clothing was no disguise. It was that ambiguous smile, part come-hither invitation, part crooked rictus, half small girl ingenue and half downtown hooker.

"Sorry, I don't smoke. But I badly need a drink of some sorts. There's a bar around the block, you can light up there."

She appeared so much smaller than on the screen, but this was not unfamiliar. I introduced myself. Even minor film journalists might prove useful to a career girl, she must have initially thought, and followed me across the lot.

The bar was called something like The Mark of God, or some other patently stupid or irrelevant name. It just sticks in my memory somehow. The lighting inside was gentle and soothing. I had my customary cola, no ice; she had a vodka and orange.

"Quite a sequence, hey?"

"Yeah."

"It must feel odd," I said, "to see yourself up there so big, so . . . so . . ."

"Nude, you mean, naked?"

"Yes, I suppose that's what I was trying to say," I answered.

She smiled gently. I wasn't blushing, but neither did I feel altogether comfortable. After all, I had already seen so much of her, her exposed flesh, her concealed self.

"How does it feel, to have to do a nude scene for the cameras?" I asked, slipping into journo mode, as she sipped her alcohol in the non-descript, almost empty bar.

"Well, you feel in a way violated, there are all these people around. In a way, it all becomes a bit impersonal, but you know what, it's also something of a turn-on. Gives you power over all these men. They can look but they sure can't touch."

"Really?"
"Oh yeah."

That first night, we returned to my hotel room.

As I undressed her in the full, bright light I finally witnessed the true colours of her body. Seeing her on a cinema screen being touched by another man was one thing, and was quite enough to give me a hard on, but here, smaller, open to nobody but me, she was something else. Her skin felt softer than the skin of any woman I had been with before. For all that, she was hard and firm, her breasts pointing gently upwards, stiffening as my fingers began to skim their tips, her buttocks clenched together as I lowered her onto the bed.

Inside her, it was like fire, all-consuming heat that reached so deep, so far. It wasn't like love, it was desperation and we merged like strangers, uncomprehending witnesses to the mad urges of our bodies.

On the second night we went to her room in another mediocre beach motel with would-be art nouveau trimmings and a crumbling balcony overlooking the ocean.

This time I undressed her slowly, mentally filming every square inch of her flesh for memory everlasting. The curve of her neck, the almost invisible dimple in her chin, the forgotten trace of a scar on her forehead hidden by a lock of stray hair, the mole at the top of her back, the way her pubic hair curled and curled. We never did say much. We didn't really have that much to say to each other when we were not in bed. We soon realized we were creatures of lust and little else mattered.

For I think an hour I kissed, caressed, gently bit, made studied foreplay with her until she could stand it no longer and screamed out:

"Enough, I want you inside me now," as she wrapped her hand around my cock.

Then, "It feels so big, I don't know how it's going to fit," and guided me in.

On the third day, we rented a room for the night in a better class of hotel, up north on Collins Avenue, towards the Aventura Mall. At the other end of the room, facing the bed, was a large circular mirror. She insisted I take her from behind and watched attentively in the mirror, as I laboured in her rear, thrusting for her appreciation and my own pleasure and hers, fascinated by the look on her face as sweat dripped from her forehead over our private cinema screen.

It was simple fucking, it wasn't love by any means. But I couldn't escape, all of me just wanted more. I should have returned to the magazine and the city by now, but she was here for a further week, with one final sequence, a death scene to be shot, where the script dictated she meet her fate at the hands of some sordid Mexican pimp (I did say it was a B-movie, didn't I?).

"I'm so raw."

"Me too, but it feels good."

"Look at me down there, I'm all red."

I kissed her open wound, savouring the strong taste and pungent smell of her insides.

"Your curls are too long," jokingly.

"So trim me, shave me."

I did, and later that day when I made love to her for the first time in her utterly nude incarnation, she got so wet and excited that she lost all control and peed all over the sheets.

From that moment onwards, we both knew we were going too far but there was nothing to hold us back. The moments of desire when our energy returned and we could make love again were the only thing we could look forward to.

It was summer and I suppose we weren't that young any more. You know how sometimes you're doing something you shouldn't and you just can't help it, you're just a spectator watching yourself at play and wrong. Ah, summer . . . The sun comes out at last and women, girls, now unencumbered of their thick sweaters, long skirts, dresses and their heavy coats, move like a lightweight symphony in the streets outside, the shape of their bodies so sweetly visible like never before, and you want them all.

Summer and you think: this is wonderful, this is terrible. But the fear is there lurking deep inside, telling you it's the last time something this special is going to happen to me, and I want it to last forever, even if there is pain and heartbreak at the end of the road. Live now, pay later. Seize the bloody fucking day.

Summer and she's more than a fantasy, a pornographic centerfold dream. You hold her breasts in a vice, twist her nipples counter-clockwise until you think she will complain of pain, but she smiles and says nothing. You make love in the bath, and you slide in and out of her like in an ocean. You fantasize about making love in a public place. You eat in a fancy restaurant and she is deliberately wearing no underwear, and only your eyes, silent accomplices, know.

Summer never lasts forever.

"What's the matter?"

"It hurts like hell when I go to the bathroom. We've been making love too much, my cystitis is playing up."

"I didn't know."

"Yeah, a lot of us girls suffer from it, but it's been a long time, I must say. Don't worry, I've got some pills for it. There is a side-effect, though, you know."

"What?"

"For a few days, whenever I go to the bathroom, I'll be pissing all blue . . ."

"What are you doing?"

"Just taking the belt from your pants."

Afternoon, the sun is setting outside the window, the curtain drapes fluttering in the air, somewhere in the distance, I imagined, the Cuban coast. A tropical fantasy.

She is standing by the bed, threading the belt out of his beige slacks, her lips wet, her short, brownish hair tousled the way he loves it dearly. She is wearing a black bra, cut low, upholding her long, dark nipples. Mental photographs. They've already made love once today, both sniffing a capsule of amyl nitrate, their bodies bucking like wild horses when the chemical rush reaches their brain. Afterwards, she had washed her hair, and returned to the room with a white towel wrapped around her head, otherwise nude. He had been lying on the bed, resting, daydreaming, and he had looked at her moving nonchalantly through the room, his gaze fixed on her lower stomach, the lips of her shaven sex, pink and bruised like the petals of some exotic flower.

"Come here," he had asked. "Take me in your mouth."

She now holds the belt in one hand, a red silk scarf taken from her bag in the other, picks up two stockings hanging on the door and comes towards him.

"Tie me up," she asks him.

"Really?"

"Yeah, you've never tried that before, have you?"

"Can't say I have."

"Well, there always has to be a first time. Tie me hard, tie me firm, both hands and feet."

She couldn't move and moaned under the weight of my body as I forced myself into her brusquely without foreplay. Later, she tied me down also. Then she licked every part of my body, starting from my toes, sucking on them in a way I had never experienced before, sending shivers through the whole length of me. In time, not only my cock, but my balls in her mouth.

Tomorrow, they would be shooting her final scene in the movie, where Ramon, the Mexican pimp (played by an elderly French utility actor), catches her red-handed concealing part of the take from the heist and knifes her in the stomach, leaving her to die in a pool of blood, in the back room of the cantina.

Then, she would be returning to California where her agent had managed another good-time girl small cameo in some other movie no doubt bound straight for the video shelves.

"Go to the fridge and get a cube of ice."

"What for?"

"Squeeze it inside me, I want to feel what it's like."

"There?"

"No, behind."

And later she would do it to me, too.

We were on the road to nowhere, prisoners of our senses. She returned from the studio that day, wearing a thin white cotton tee-shirt through which her sharp nipples were clearly visible.

I felt a pang of jealousy that other men might have seen her breasts thus on the drive back from the shoot.

"Well, that's it. I'm now officially out of work," she said.

"How did it go?" I asked.

"Well, he killed me cleanly. We only needed three takes."

"How does it feel to be killed?" the journalist in me asked her.

"It turned me on. I almost wet myself."

"You slut," I said, jokingly.

"Yeah, well, that's what I am," she answered, laughing. "But now, listen, I want you to do absolutely everything I tell you to. It's important, this might be our last time together and I want you to remember it forever."

"Yes, boss."

I undressed her, her body was on fire, feverish, burning with emotional incandescence, she bit my lips to the blood as I pulled her head back by her hair. I tied her up, watched her crucified body spread-eagled over the bed. I prepared to undress. My short-sleeve shirt was sticking to my torso like an unwanted skin.

"Cover my eyes," she begged, as I lowered my body over hers.

And as we made love, it was as if we were buried in a deep well of despair as we both knew all too well this must be the last time. There was nowhere else to go. Nothing more that we could do. We had tried everything, every position and most perversities and still we wanted more, but it just wasn't there. Is this all there was to love? Togetherness and future domesticity surely could not be the answer, felt rather ridiculous a concept in fact, any-thing further would only dull the immediacy, the passion, the desire, the lust.

As we came, almost together, I opened my eyes and saw a tear rolling down her cheek. "What is it?" I asked her solicitously.

"You know what it is," she answered calmly.

Yes, I knew.

It was then she asked:

"Kill me."

The sweat was drying over our bare bodies. There was a full moon over Miami Beach.

So I did.

The sound of her neck breaking was muted and gentle.

Outside, it's now raining. In the distance, I can hear the jets hovering over Coral Gables on their way to landing at the International Airport, ferrying passengers to and from South America. It's been a few days already. I'm feeling hungry. I still haven't dressed and sometimes I disgust myself as unwanted erections manifest themselves when I gaze at her dead body, laid out like a cross over the grey bedsheets. Her crooked smile is now permanently carved into her face, her pubic hairs are shyly growing back and her fixed eyes keep on watching me.

I wonder what she is thinking now.

*   *   *

Yes, that's the story that started it all.

I came across her late in the evening at the bar of the hotel where all the delegates to the festival were staying. I'd ventured into town with a bunch of other writers, in a group of twenty or so, and we had ended up in a decent curry place. I'd somehow managed to get myself squeezed in between two local nincompoop librarians, half the length of the table away from a small, flame-haired Murdoch Empire book editor I sort of fancied. Through the spicy meal, I kept on thinking of how our eyes had crossed paths at the reading. It was almost midnight when we all returned to base and the small bar was crowded. There she was, standing in distracted conversation with a couple of reviewers. I realized who she was: a junior editor for some small publishing outfit whose books you never actually saw in shops but who seemed to profitably stay in business mainly stocking library shelves with totally unpromoted novels and churning out badly designed cookery books, new age clap-trap and self-help and how to dress manuals.

She stood out like a beacon. All blonde, curly-haired, wonderfully tall five feet ten of her. I looked at her. My heart skipped a proverbial beat. I walked over.

"Hello."

"How are you."

My imagination no sooner ran out of things to say to her in this artificially social context.

"I'd like to talk about things someday," I clumsily blurted out and made my excuses, as she probably gave me a strange look while I moved away.

The next morning, the final hours of the festival, I spotted her on her own on a seat in the hotel's reception area reading a paperback crime and mystery novel by one of the previous day's main speakers. She looked up as I passed by, moving towards the bar where I had some business with an American film director. Half an hour later, I returned, she was still sitting there, a picture of vulnerable beauty, wearing a long loose black dress with small white polka dots. I moved towards her.

"Have you enjoyed the festival?" I asked her.

She looked up at me, smiled, the dress slid slightly down her left side, baring her pale left shoulder and revealing a thin black bra strap.

"How are you getting back to London? I have spare passenger space in my car if you're interested." I enquired.

"I have a lift," she replied.

Then someone called me away, and when I looked back in her direction, she was gone.

I thought of her a lot on the motorway back.

The Secrets of Her Anatomy

Dear K.C.

You were probably wondering on Sunday morning what the hell I wished to talk to you about. Sorry I left you guessing. I just didn't know what to say and how to say it, I suppose. The propriety of making a gentle pass at a beautiful woman eludes me when she has witnessed me the day before reading "dirty bits" aloud in public.

At any rate, I must confess I found you wondrously attractive and have thought about you a lot since the weekend.

I'd love to see you again, if only to talk or have a meal. Would you?

Until then I remain,

Lustfully but respectfully yours,

Maxim J.

Dear Maxim,

I somehow guessed that you were not really interested in discussing the art of crime fiction with the likes of me.

Your letter made me smile. Yes, I'd love to meet up for a drink. Give me a call.

Yours,

K.C.

Three weeks elapsed before they finally met. She had been on holiday to Ireland in the meantime. Searching for her roots, she joked over the telephone.

On that first evening, following a drink and a meal, he found out she was married while they sat in the basement of a noisy Soho pub. All the wrong tunes were blaring out from the juke-box.

"So where do we go from here?" he wondered.

But when he drove her to her train station, she gently put her hand on his while they waited in the queue to exit the Central London underground car park.

Everything was unsaid, but they could feel the mutual attraction simmering in the air like electricity. All they had done was partly exchange life stories and publishing gossip, but she said: "We must meet again."

"Yes," he concurred.

On the occasion of their second meeting a week later, they quickly agreed after the first round of drinks that all Soho pubs were much too noisy in the evening, and they must find somewhere else to talk. He suggested his office. As a director of the company, he had a set of keys and knew no one else would likely be in at that time of evening. She readily agreed.

As he switched the lights on, she said:

"Don't, it's too bright," and pulled out a metal candle holder with a large candle speared in its centre from a Habitat paper bag, which had been buried in her backpack full of manuscripts. "I thought this might come in useful."

He found a match. In the flickering of the candle, he looked in awe at her amazon figure. He'd never been with a woman this tall before, he thought. Her tousled hair was a mass of Medusa-like curls. Her eyes, he now saw, were dark brown. He moved towards her and kissed her. She responded.

The thin coat of scarlet lipstick melted under his tongue, tasting slightly sweet. She opened her mouth wider and allowed him to insert his exploratory tongue. A warm stream of air from her lungs raced inside him. She skipped a breath.

That evening, he kissed her deep and passionately, touched her knee, her thigh but no higher. She wore an open neck short sleeve white sweater and after delicately moving his roving fingers repeatedly over her face, her nose, her chin, his hand moved downwards to her soft shoulder. There was a light brown mole at the onset of her cleavage. He caressed it, and moved his hand further and cupped her small left breast. She looked deeply into his eyes, anxious, interrogating, hopeful, but kept on saying nothing. His fingers slipped behind the thin fabric of the shirt, inside her bra and kneaded her nipple, then as she still offered no resistance he delicately pulled the breast away from the flimsy texture of her black bra. Then, the other. A black beauty spot peered at him close to the aureola of the right breast. She stood there, her breasts unceremoniously, wantonly on display, as he drank in this exquisite vision of her. The colour of her nipples was a discreet pink in the overall pallor of her torso.

Later:

"I have to catch the train home," she said, her upper clothing in disarray, her cheeks flushed, some buttons of his shirt undone.

"Where did you tell him you were?"

"With one of my authors."

"Stay longer, please. I want to make love with you," he asked her in the office penumbra.

"Not today, we just haven't got the time. Next time."

"Are you sure?"

"Yes."

"I'll find it difficult to wait. Every minute until I see you again, I shall doubt you, I will fear that in the cold light of day all tonight's fumblings will appear foolhardy and wrong to you and you will change your mind."

"I won't," she replied, but once they were walking along the night road to Charing Cross station, she moved faster and faster, in her characteristic manly and slightly gawky way, and she said little, almost as if embarrassed to be with him in public, swimming through the evening crowd.

The next day, he sent a single red rose to her office, bought from a flower stall in Covent Garden.

Two days later, he received a letter telling him he had been right, and that the reality of their circumstances had appeared to her all too clearly as they had been walking towards her train. She just couldn't, she wrote. She didn't wish to hurt her husband, she just felt she could not deceive her husband, and how anyway could they conduct an affair without it becoming sordid, cheap hotel assignments, stealing time out of time, deceitful. No, she just couldn't. He felt right gutted and answered as best he could, with a long letter justifying his feelings, the state his life was in and could not help himself evoking the erotic feelings she stirred inside him, how he already dreamed of their lovemaking, the caress of flesh against flesh, how their skin touching would feel. Please, he implored, change your mind. But he didn't really think she would and after receiving no answer, all he could do was write again. The hours and the days were heavy and lasted forever those weeks. Then another letter, and another. The tone moved from loving, suggestive, explicit to angry, resigned, desperate.

She phoned.

"Your last letter made me very angry (he could not for the sake of him recall what he had said in it that he he had not written before). But I just keep on thinking of you in spite of myself. We must meet again and talk."

They settled for the bar of a big hotel.

He explained again, she nodded her understanding; he told her how he did not wish to harm anyone, that this was just between the two of them, that no one else would know, and as long as no one was hurt, why did they not accept what was happening between them and the way they felt?

Sipping her drink, she looked breathtakingly radiant. His heart was just ragged, being with her, detailing every facet of her features, the way her nose turned slightly upwards, her hair hid her ears, how the faint trace of a scar on her right cheek revealed itself in the bar's muted lighting.

She acquiesced in silence, her eyes piercing through him, her sadness touching him in parts he didn't know he had, her long dark stockinged leg like an endless object of desire parting her orange slit skirt.

He looked back at her, he hadn't asked a question.

Their eyes, soundless.

"Yes," she said, almost inaudibly, under her breath, and looked down at her lap.

"You mean?"

"Yes, I will," she firmly answered.

He was overcome with naked fear rather than joy. She was saying she would become his lover, did she? Or was he interpreting her wrong?

"But we must agree we must not ever harm others, it's very important. You said so yourself."

Immense relief coursed through him. And irrational disbelief. This can't be happening to me, surely.

"You won't change your mind again, will you," he asked her, falling into fourth gear into a pit of newly-found insecurity.

"I promise I won't," she assured him.

At last, he allowed himself to smile, to relax. The waiter brought some more peanuts and olives to their table.

"When?" he finally asked, after what he felt was a decent interval, after they had become more talkative and managed to cast the ghost of the coming affair away to laugh a bit about publishing and writers' gossip. He loved the way she tittered when he said anything a touch witty or mischievous.

"I don't know. I hadn't thought about it, really."

"I don't want the first time to be vulgar or sordid," he said. "Not at the office. I'll think of some hotel where no one knows us or is likely to recognize either of us. I'll make the arrangements."

She nodded.

It would be two weeks. In the meantime, she came once more to his office a few nights later, and she allowed him to undress her when they embraced on the uncomfortable sofa he kept for visitors. But when he wanted to pull her black knickers down over her wide, ample hips, she said "Not now, we must keep something for next time." She had arranged a day away from her company, under pretext of some imaginary contracts seminar. He agreed, and touched her sex through the dark, thin material, she felt wet and so warm.

> Cos I know that you
> With your heart beating
> And your eyes shining
> Will be thinking of me
> Lying with you on a Tuesday morning.
>
> The Pogues

They became lovers on a Tuesday morning in August, in the identikit room of a chain hotel in the metaphorical shadow of the Heathrow runways. J.G. Ballard territory almost.

He had brought along a bottle of white wine and strawberries bought earlier that morning from a small greengrocer near Hampstead Pond, before picking her up in front of the tube station. She wore dark glasses during the drive.

"You're sure you still want to go through with this?"

"Of course I do."

"I thought you might have changed your mind."

"I thought you would."

"Well, I was going to give you a few more minutes and then I was going to leave, thinking how can the bastard be late or not come?"

"I was here on time, but I was looking out for you in front of the cinema on the other side of the road. I almost missed you . . ."

He undressed her first. Item by item. Layer by layer. Her waistcoat. Her long flowing skirt of many colours. Her quaint lace-up boots. Her wedding and engagement rings. Kissed her throat, then her lips, then bit gently on her ear, nonchalantly licked her forehead and her smooth shoulders. Pressed his lips against her throat and held her tight against him. She wore a black bustier, garter belt and stockings.

"How lovely. It's been ages since I've seen stockings, old-fashioned but so nice, watching you like this is enough to turn anyone into a raving fetishist . . ."

"I thought you would like them."

After rolling the warm silk down her endless legs and briefly tickling her funny-shaped toes, he got up from where he had been kneeling, drank in her sheer splendour and pulled down her final piece of underwear.

Her pubic hair was darker than he expected, all flattened curls against the marble expanse of her lower stomach. He kissed her bush with reverence, like a priest in holy homage.

He pulled back.

She was now nude.

The look in her eyes said a million things.

"I want to know everything about you," he blurted out.

She turned round, took a few steps towards the window and closed the curtain.

"It's too bright," she said.

It was only eleven fifteen in the morning. The sun shone outside. All that could be seen from the hotel room window was a car park.

Her arse was slightly square and also heart-shaped, a tad too large, but he wanted his hands all over her pale cheeks. Venus on a Tuesday, he distractedly thought. The straps of the garter belt had left a small indent at the top of her hips, outlining the majesty of the pelvis where her dark cunt beckoned.

"Aren't you getting undressed?" she said.

He did, holding his stomach in as he pulled his trousers off. She looked him up and down.

He took her by the hand and pulled her towards the bed.

*   *   *

Later, when he would recall their first time together, the image of her body next to him with the filtered light that came through the curtains shadowing it delicately, would remind him of a postcard he had in his study of a sand dune, where a dip in the sand evoked a woman's navel and a rise the gentle slope of her small breast.

After the initial, obligatory nervousness, he surprised himself by managing erection after erection anew and making love repeatedly, entering her three times before the time came to clean up, leave the room rented for half a day and drive back to Charing Cross station for her 6.14 train.

"Oh, God," he says, entering her, feeling the ridged texture of her cunt walls against the taut skin of his cock.

"Oh, Jeeeeezus," she says, as he slides, thrusts in and out of her, realizing this is it, she has done it, she has a lover, she is an adulteress, and no longer fighting the pleasure coursing through her body.

"Oh, Christ," he moans, his body convulsing as he comes inside her, and this is the first time, I want it to last forever, for eternity, and opens his eyes and notices she had kept hers open all along, the first woman he remembers making love to who has done so. What a wonderful quirk, he thinks. It strikes him deep. It touches him intensely.

Both speechless for a long time after the initial orgasm; he finally disengaged from her, pulling his now limp and moist penis from the warmth of her vagina and kissed her lips with all the tenderness he could muster, even as he knew that neither gestures nor words could properly express the epiphany he had just experienced. The cover of the bed is rumpled, they had not even bothered pulling it down to uncover the sheets. He gets up, pours her a glass of wine. His throat is dry.

"Shall we take a bath?" she asks.

Together in the regulation-size Trust House Forte bath tub which barely contains the two of them, he sees the dark bruises on her thighs and legs.

"Oh, it's nothing, I'm always catching the corner of my desk at the office. I bruise so easily."

He soaps her, his fingers lingering more than hygiene demands in the gaping crack of her cunt, caresses her breasts with lather until they shine like wet jewels, she rubs his back, remarks on the hairy birth-mark there, he kisses her and their wet bodies entwine in the lukewarm water, he tries to manipulate himself into a position where he can enter her, but the geometry of the bath tub defeats him. He is hard. Dripping over the bathroom tiles and then the bedroom's grey carpet, they rush to the bed. Here, unbidden she opens her mouth over his prone body and takes his penis into her mouth. He closes his eyes, thinking, Christ, and this is only our first time, and feels her teeth graze against his glans. He watches her tousled hair, the million and one blonde curls bob up and down over his stomach, the regal expanse of her back and her rising anus as she sucks with loving gluttony on his cock. He extends his hand and touches her back, a finger circling the black beauty spot just below her right buttock, the soft invisible golden down in the small of her back that reminds him of sheer silk in its tactile delight. He feels a surge pass through his body and pulls her off his member, lays her out on the white sheets, spreads her legs wide, slips a wet finger into the gaping aperture of her vagina and guides his cock in to the hilt. He feels harder, thicker and longer than he has ever been. He digs in as deep as he can, scraping, thrusting, aiming at her most intimate innards, she moans, her eyes open, gazing deep into him, her hair falling back from her face, revealing her overlarge forehead, her exquisite innocence, her torn ear from a past accident with an earring that got caught somehow and was wrenched away, he pulls her legs up and places them over his shoulders, to increase the depth of his invasion, his hands move convulsively from her lips, to her shoulders, her breasts and move downwards to her arse. Impulsively, feeling the wetness in the valley separating her arse cheeks, he slips a finger into her anus. She screams with pleasure and comes instantly with a violent shuddering that courses in overdrive through her body from scalp to toes.

"Oh, Jeeeeezus, Jesus."

They managed to get together again a week later. Initially, they were only going to see a movie. Some American indie effort. Throughout the film, he kept on wanting to touch her every-where and found it difficult to concentrate on the pyrotechnic action on the screen.

"Me too," she said to him as the credits rolled.

They rushed to his office, where they quickly stripped. Again she was wearing stockings and suspenders. He wondered, was it only for him? They fell on the hard floor and embraced, his cock straining for her in physical agony, his tongue inside her mouth, coming up for air when the pressure became too much. He kissed her everywhere, between her toes where she was ticklish, he licked her breasts, her stomach, counted every mole and mark on her body, imagining he knew every square inch of her flesh so much better than her husband, he moved his tongue from cheek to cheek on her backside and slid it down the valley of her arse and into her rear hole. She shivered. Later, he slipped his finger in, and then two.

"You're so sensitive there," he remarked.

"I know, I know," she replied.

Later, in the days apart, he would dream of buggery. He knew she did.

He then moved her round onto her back and moved his mouth towards her sex.

"You can't," she said. "I have a tampon in. It's my period."

Nonetheless, he slipped a finger into her sex and felt the moistness and the unbearable heat.

"Let me pull it out," he asked her.

"Oh, you wouldn't," she said.

And he began to tug gently on the thin string that peered out shyly from the folds of her labia, below the hood of her clitoris.

"I'll do it myself," she said and stood up, all 5ft 10 of nude pallor and unforgettable flesh, and walked to the toilet in the corridor of the empty building.

When she returned, he entered her with joy. Later, when his cock slipped out of her, it was baked with blood, and when she moved over, there was a dark red stain on the brown sofa which he cleaned as best he could. To this day, there is a remote trace of it, and his heart stops every time he looks at the damn sofa, to the extent that he feels he should get rid of it as the memories assault him all too painfully.

There were many more encounters in his office over the months that followed. Often crazed coupling punctuated by doubt and guilt and snacks on the floor, sate sticks, prawns from Tesco, sushi pieces. Because both their backs ached every next day after lovemaking on the hard carpeted floor – they never did use the sofa again – he bought a thick orange blanket which they would drape over the floor, their bed of illicit sex, and later, when autumn came, he even acquired a cushion, and a quilted bed cover to keep them warm. He wondered what his secretary thought if she ever came across the blanket, cushion and cover, at the bottom of his personal filing cabinet.

And then came the fateful weekend away in Brighton, after he had begged her repeatedly for a whole day, a whole night at least together for the first time. It had been her birthday the day before. Her husband had bought her a brown leather waistcoat and taken her to *Miss Saigon* in the evening. She had found the performance dreary and, somehow, nerves about the coming weekend, impatience with him or guilt, they had begun quarrelling and he had ended up sleeping apart from her on their small apartment's sofa bed.

The hotel was on the sea front. They took a cab from the station. Their alibi was another writers' conference. In the room, as he had previously promised he would when guessing randomly at her many secret fantasies, he borrowed the lipstick from her handbag, and pressed the soft tube against her breasts and rouged the nipples a dark red, then squeezed her body tight against his own, slashes of colour blending into the hair on his chest. Then he laid her out on the bed, set our her limbs in a semblance of crucifixion, held the fleshy folds of her cunt apart and applied the lipstick to its outer lips. Then, they fucked and he told her that he loved her, and he whispered suggestively to her what they would do throughout the coming night, how he would wake her and enter her in the small hours of morning, how he would remain embedded in her warm cunt while they briefly slept. Fingers, almost his whole hand, then his tongue in her various apertures, bringing her to climax again and again in moist abandon while he waited for his cock to grow hard between the successive bouts of lovemaking. Fish and chips on the promenade for lunch. Back to the room. Sex. Ice-cream at the local Haagen-Dasz parlour. Sex. Tying her hands against the foot of the bed with the belt he thredded out of his trousers, wrapping one of her black stockings around her neck as he took her from behind. A late night meal at a noisy Mexican joint a few yards from the hotel. The room, a small isolated world away from the real world. Washing her in the bath, joining her there, listening to her pee from behind the bathroom door, furtively sniffing her knickers. Shaving in the morning, naked, with his back to her while she relaxed in the tub, it all felt so familiar, so comfortable, so natural.

He had soon realized he was hopelessly in love with her. It wasn't just the sex, he knew. He just wanted to be with her all the time, holding her in his arms, buying her things, clothes, discovering books, music and movies together and he counted the interminable hours that would elapse between their stolen evenings and their furtive lunch hours in pubs none of their acquaintances frequented. He wanted more of her, all of her, and began pressing her, which made her nervous. Her husband and her had sold their small, claustrophobic flat and had to find a new house to move into soon. Irrationally – even though he would eventually be proven right – he felt this new house would be the cause of the end of their relationship.

"Of course not," she defended herself. "We have to live somewhere, you know."

On the Sunday morning, after breakfast, she rang her husband from the hotel lobby as she had agreed to and found out, to increasing panic, through talking to his brother when she could not reach him, that he had been trying to get hold of her the previous evening and had discovered she was neither registered at the conference nor resident at the hotel where the event was taking place. He had to drive up to Oxford unexpectedly and had only wanted to warn her. She burst out in tears when she returned to the room.

He clumsily attempted to comfort her, only for her to turn viciously against him. He was blamed for breaking up her marriage and she insisted they leave for London – immediately. It turned out to be a false alarm, and she lied her way through it, blaming matters on a mix-up between the hotel and the conference organizers. She said her husband was so immersed in his own job that he never even suspected. But the rot had set in. Having almost lost her, he now knew how much she really meant to him and he became absolutely terrified of losing her for good. He could no longer envisage life without her.

In his mind's eye, he no longer wanted her to be the wave, but the sea.

Autumn deepened.

She had to go to the Frankfurt Book Fair as all dutiful

publishers do. He had a book to promote in America. From her bleak German room, she ached for him and wished he was there with her, she said. In his impersonal mid-West motel suite, he pined for her and feared she would no longer wish to see him after their return from foreign climes. She was due to move house a few days after Frankfurt.

They did meet up again a few times, and the sex was as intense as the pain they both felt about the future. Searing, savage, filthy, entering her again and feeling a desire to literally impale her, tear her apart from orifice to orifice. Shades of Bertolucci's *Last Tango*, he carried a small amount of butter in a plastic bag in his attache case, meaning to use it with her and penetrate her anally, but he never did, the tenderness of entering her normally sufficing in the gentle heat of the moment.

The fear and the uncertainty were driving him crazy. Should they part or should they stay together, where was it all leading to, did the others suspect, was the pain stronger than the joy the affair gave them? During a pub lunch break, she suggested they might stay apart for at least a month to consider their feelings and the situation. She was now thinking of him too much, she said, in the nights, at the weekends (as if he bloody well didn't suffer in the same jealous, atrocious manner, too), and her husband was wondering why she was so distant, and after all this new house meant so much to him, and the shopping at IKEA for new furniture and knick-knacks he kept dragging her to in his cheery insouciance, and it all made her feel so guilty, she explained.

If this was it, he said, give me at least one more night. He could see how torn she was, how despite all her best intentions, she couldn't bear to be the one to say it was possibly over. One night, he thought, and I will make love to her like never before and force a positive decision out of her. Not that he even believed himself. She agreed for the next day. Not tonight, her husband was doing the cooking at home and she was already late and he would be angry at yet another late night, and why was it that recently she had to work late so often, it wasn't like that before, was it?

The next day, her husband received an anonymous letter at work.

At seven o'clock, just as he was laying out the blanket on the office floor ready for her arrival, and sucking on Polo mints to freshen his breath, she rang. She was in tears, full of rage. It could only be him. What could he say? It all pointed towards him. Things in the damn letter that only he could know. He had once even joked about an envelope with her company's logo he had kept back, unused, from a note she had once given him at the pub. He wracked his brain in vain; sure, they hadn't really been taking too many precautions, hadn't always been discreet, but who? Her husband was an industrial journalist, could he have made enemies? Duplicitous friends who had pieced things together? Colleagues? Staff at his office who had assembled the clues of the puzzle together from his irrational behaviour, the stain on the sofa, the blanket, their regular telephone conversations? At any rate, she was heading home to save her marriage. She now hated him and nothing he could ever do or say would ever make her want to have any further contact with him again. He just stood there, paralysed, as she hurled abuse at him over the telephone line. He protested his innocence, too shaken to probably even sound convincing. The last time he saw her was standing at his building's door, the look in her eyes so withering, come to reclaim her letters and the two photographs she had once given him of her. He supposed they had been taken by her husband. Their memory remained etched forever in his brain. One with her hair short and uncurled, disturbed by what looked like a cold wind on the Beaubourg Plain in Paris, taken soon after her graduation from Cambridge. The other, just some months before he had met her, in the Northumberland countryside, her tousled hair almost orange, her eyes small and remote, wearing a black jacket, jeans and heavy DM shoes. A few months later, he took his courage in both hands and rang her at home on a day he knew she had taken off to catch up on manuscripts, and confronted her about this certainty she had that he was the sender of the letter. It turned out the letter was too well written and spelt difficult words correctly, as well as giving his private phone number. In her grief, this was now damning and incontrovertible evidence, it appeared. She made him swear to never write, call or try to see her again. Even threatening police action. He felt he couldn't fight. She was even now accusing him of a series of strange phone calls her husband and her had been getting for some months, conveniently forgetting they had begun long before their affair, as she had told him about them then.

For a few months, his life fell apart.

Living with pain is a boring story.

He masturbated often, thinking of her endlessly and fishing up to the surface of his troubled mind desperate images of her body, stroke up, the look in her eyes, stroke down, the maddening curls of her hair, stroke up, the colour of her lips, stroke down, the moving shades of pink in her cunt when he chewed on her and his eyes immodestly peered deep inside. It didn't help much, but he managed to come, the white glue of his seed dripping into his fist.

Why does it have to hurt me, bruise me so? he reflected as he gazed at his drawn features in the small mirror in the toilet while he cleaned the mess off his hands. After all, millions have affairs, fall in lust, spiral in love, come apart. But at the back of his mind, an insidious voice also whispered that, somehow, some also did stay together in the end.

Christmas and its desert of longing and loneliness. Then the February torment of Valentine's Day – would her husband send her a doggerel card, take her out for a meal, buy her flowers?

Came the time of writing stories again.

The Amputated Soul

–You know, I'm very angry at you.

–What have I done?

–You never even took any precautions, used a condom, asked me if I was on the pill.

–You're married, I'd somehow assumed.

–Well I wasn't.

–But your husband and you?

–We've always used condoms.

–Always?

–Yes.

–How bizarre. I know I have no right to say so, but it's a strange comment on the state of your marriage.

–Maybe. Anyway, I've gone on the pill now.

–And how have you explained such a momentous change to him?

–Well, buying the new house. It's going to be expensive, the new mortgage. He understands. Couldn't afford a kid right now. He knows I don't really want children.

– But does he?

– Yes, he does.

– I was still a virgin when I went to Cambridge. I'd misbehaved quite a bit before, but somehow I never did do it.

– And when was the first time?

– At University, at a party. This guy suggested we go together, and I decided, why not, and we just did. It was nothing special.

– And afterwards?

– I caught up for lost time. You know how it can be when you're a student, you're away from home for the first time. Don't think I was promiscuous, I wasn't really. There were only three other guys. And some of them didn't really last long. I met my husband in my second year. He was then going out with a friend of mine, and I was with another guy. But all our friends sort of said we looked good together. So it happened. There, you're only my fifth lover.

– I'm madly jealous of every man who touched you then, you know.

– I miss you awfully. So, anything interesting at the office today?

– They've finally agreed I could make an offer for that novel I was telling you about. I'm really excited. It won't be much money, but I hope the author accepts it. The book still needs some work done to it, but I think he will be willing to listen to my suggestions. He sounds a bit weird, but the novel is really good.

– I miss you. I thought about you all weekend, tried to imagine what you were cooking, when you were doing your shopping at Sainsbury. I can't seem to get you out of my mind.

– I know, I know.

– At one stage, I wanted to talk to you so bad, I even phoned.

– You didn't!

– Yes. He picked up, so I slipped on a Liverpudlian accent, and said 'Sorry, wrong number, mate'.

– That was you . . . He was fuming. He hates being called 'mate'.

– It's unfair. You always undress me first. Why can't it be the other way around?

–Sure.

. . . .

–There you are. This is me. Look at me. I'm so much older than you. I'm a bit overweight. There's more and more grey in my hair and I can never comb it properly. And this is you, standing there, so beautiful. Shit, what do you see in me?

–I like your hair. The curls on your chest, it's wonderful.

–Here, put your hand on my cock. See how you make it grow so effortlessly. Just being with you gives me a hard on. I am in awe of you, of your nudity. Yes, squeeze it more. Yes.

–I like it when you give me orders. You can be so authoritative.

–It's the old managing director in me . . .

– The other night in bed, next to him, I just kept on tossing and turning so much. I had to get up and go to the other room to read. It was an old book I'd already read; I couldn't really concentrate. Dickens or Jane Austen, I think. My body ached for you so much, even though we had only parted a few hours before. Why is it so strong? I feel I just want to be consumed by you, eaten alive.

–I feel the same. I just hate the idea that ten miles away, some nights, he might be caressing you, making love to you, it almost makes me feel sick. That he invades you where the imprint of my cock still lingers inside you.

–I just can't make love to him after the time I spend with you. I'm not that wicked. Most times, by the time I get home, he's already sleeping.

–Jesus, I don't know how you do it. You're the best lover I've ever had.

–You're not just saying that, are you, because we're together right now? It's ever so dangerous. It's the sort of thing that's likely to stay in a man's mind forever. I'm touched. Deeply.

–No, of course not. You're also my first circumcised penis.

–Really?

–And you have so much hair on your chest.

–Yes, a proper monkey, that's me.

—At the conference, you know I was sitting in the lobby on that Sunday morning hoping you would come across and see

me. It was something about you. The way you read, the way
you looked.
  – Premeditation, hey?

– He hates it when I clip my fingernails in the bath. I don't know
why, it's just so natural. Why should it bother him.
  – I agree.
  – He's so involved with his new job. He takes me for granted.
He's a few years younger than me, and some times I feel he just
sees me as a convenient substitute for his mother.
  – And the sex?
  – It's okay, I suppose. Not like in the early days of when we
were together at Cambridge. We lived together for some time
before we married. We almost didn't. We had some terrible rows.
I have such a temper. I even throw things. See, you don't really
know me.
  – I wouldn't mind you throwing things at me, if it was a
condition of living with you.
  – Oh, it was nothing hard, just an old ham and tomato sandwich.
  – Beware the mad sandwich hurler!

– We finally went to see *The Piano* yesterday night. It was good,
as you said. There was a difficult moment. He remarked on the
fact that we had never been to this particular West End cinema
before, and I stupidly blurted out that I had, forgetting briefly it
was with you. But he didn't make anything of it.
  – Yeah, London's a dangerous city. Soon, too many bars,
restaurants and places will be part of our own private geography.
We have to keep both worlds apart.

– The whites of your eyes are so . . . white when you're above me,
making love to me.
  – They're nothing special, really.
  – No, they are so white. Oh, look at the time, I have to go.
  – Do you really want to?
  – No. Some evenings, I just want to stay here in this office
forever, with the candle light flickering over us. But I can't.
  – Stay. I will become hard again and make love to you in every
conceivable pornographic position, missionary, rear, sideways,

upside down, make you scream, groan, cry. Stay a little bit longer. God, the tenderness is swelling inside of me and I feel I'm like some bomb, ticking away, that I desire and need you so.

– Why does lust make us feel that way?

– Because it was meant to be, I suppose.

– Jesus, Jesus, Jesus, I could let you do absolutely anything to me. I trust you implicitly. It's crazy.

– Would you let me put my fingers around your neck and squeeze gently until the pain comes? Would you let me distend the rim of your arsehole, making it more pliant so that I might insert myself there and fill you, mark you forever in that forbidden place? Look at my finger, you're already so wet down there. Lick it. See how I dip my finger in cunt and arse and sip your juices so naturally, so fragrant, my mistress, my lover.

– Yes, my lover.

– Come with me to New York. I want you for a whole week. I want to spend whole nights fucking you, worshipping you in strange hotel rooms. I want to wake up beside you, I want to smell your breath in the morning when you awake, I want to see your tired cheeks without make-up and the wrinkles of our lovemaking carved like a tattoo under the surface of your skin, all over your body.

– You know I can't. How would I explain it? Anyway, you know I no longer have any holidays left at the office.

– I'm sure those are not love bites. I'm always very careful.

– Let me see in the mirror. No, it's just orgasmic flush.

– It's all over your neck and the top of your chest. What's he going to say when you get home?

– Don't worry, it will fade away . . .

– I know, I know.

A LONG LETTER TO K.
(with apologies to Leonard Cohen)

I obsess over you, K. Here I am at my typewriter,
unshaven for the last four days, all grey sharp stubble,
probably more than ever looking my age, in what has

now become my room, surrounded by the paraphernalia
of my life, the piles of books, countless magazines,
record albums and CDs, the mattress against the back
wall, the reality of what is left of me after your passage
through my days. Outside the window, a thin layer of
frost whitens the green manicured surface of the lawn,
and the bare winter branches of the trees. I wonder what
you are doing right now. Whether you are wearing your
long skirt of many colours which appeared so transparent
with the sun in your back that morning I picked you up
in Camden Town, outlining the dazzling shape of your
legs, rising from small black boots all the way up to the
volcano of your crotch. What perfume you are wearing;
maybe one from the amusing assortment of small fancy
flasks I'd bought in duty-free at Kennedy. When was the
last time you even thought of me, of our so few hours
together? If you did actually get around to buying that
CD of Nanci Griffiths' or finally got a raise at your job·
for the New Year. A trade magazine revealed how much
your boss was earning; yes, you certainly deserved a
better salary, considering. I miss the sound of your
voice, the drawn out "Helloooo" when you pick up the
phone and I daily resist the temptation to dial your
number. The last time we did speak, you almost
suggested that I needed psychiatric assistance and why
did I have this compulsion to write you sordid letters? I
had no pat answer to give you. And that my lines, my
sad pleas caused you distress and could I not do the
decent thing and just fade away and let you get on with
your life? Understand me, I cannot. I have lost you, I
know, but you will not in your anger deny me the
memories, the tenderness of what we fleetingly possessed
before events and your sense of guilt and craving for
respectability bid you throw it all away, handed as you
were a perfect excuse. You see, I am not a respectable
person; I am unbearably selfish. Well, what would you
expect of a romantic pornographer, you of all women
with your cold heart of glass and your passion for
independence, secure in the knowledge of your beauty
and your damning pride. But I am a good person, I

assure you. You made me that way. Earlier today, I was
browsing through a collection of photographs with a nice
introduction by Jayne Anne Phillips, *The Last Days Of
Summer*. Full of images of naked teenagers on far
beaches, their bodies full of an expression of innocence
not lost by knowledge, luxuriating in textures of sand,
flesh, cloth, tide pools and gentle waves. So call me a
paedophile, then. I remembered how much I would
dream during our nights apart of taking you to the sea,
not just a sordid dirty weekend in Brighton, but under
some blazing tropical sun, where I would see you for the
first time in a bathing suit, your fluid limbs sprawled
akimbo in the light of the falling sun. Or even a nude
beach, where I would admire how natural you would
stand in the buff and would feel both proud at how I
was exhibiting your charms to the insidious gaze of other
men and jealous of the fact they could not be blind and
allow me the exclusivity of your voluptuous nudity.
Then I fantasized about how I wanted to adorn your
exposed flesh, setting a diamond in the jewel-case of
your navel, shaving your pubic hair away, setting clamps
of gold around your nipples and piercing your labia, to
feel the thrill of a ring dangling from the lips of your
cunt, twisting it under my tongue when I licked you,
sucked you, ate you, my cock rubbing against the metal
that would now be part of you every time I moved
within. Silk threads carefully wound around your neck,
wrists and ankles. Oh, K, I know you would have
allowed me. And all the places I wanted to take you. To
a bed and breakfast in old San Francisco at Christmas,
with antique elevators inside wrought-iron cages, to New
Orleans for New Year's Eve, to stand on the banks of
the Mississippi river nearby the Jackson brewery to
listen to the hooting funnels of the riverboats at
midnight amongst the boisterous crowd and later to
cruise, plastic glasses in hand, down Bourbon Street,
past the wonderfully shameless topless and bottomless
joints and myriad bars with overhanging balconies full of
revellers and happy drunkards. I know this lovely hotel
in the French Quarter, you see, where all the rooms are

distant from the lobby building, old slave houses set in a
circle around drooping vegetation, so private that I could
allow myself to scream your name to high heavens when
I come like a river inside you, and no one can hear the
disturbing noise of my excess. Yes. A hotel room in
Paris, on the Left Bank, on a top floor, with a vista of
wet roofs and latticed metal gratings, where the walls are
so thin you can't help listening to couples in
neighbouring rooms making love with all the sounds of
indecency. 'The Algonquin in New York, where the
rooms are small but the furniture is delicately antique
and breakfast can be taken outside in bagel places close
by, where I would introduce you to the Jewish delights
of garlic bagel with lox and cream cheese, a meal of
kings in its own right. A beach under the fierce Barbados
sun, staying in a cabin, licking away the grains of sand
that have crept up inside your sex whilst on the beach,
washing the crack of your arse clean of all impurities and
wading out, both naked, to the water at midnight and
admiring the shadow of a yellow moon illuminate your
erect wet nipples. Or oysters by Puget Sound in Seattle.
The world's best roast duck at the Water Margin in
Golders Green, in North London. The human
geography of pleasure unbound. See how I obsess. I take
the Northern Line daily to my office, a lump in my
throat when I pass Goodge Street and guess you might
be alighting there from a train going in the opposite
direction. Sometimes, I even get off at my own station
and wait on the other platform if a train has stopped
there, peering inside as it speeds away for a vision of you
and your crazy curls on the way to your own office.
When I wash in the morning, my mind wanders and
imagines what you might be wearing that day, whether
your fool of a husband made love to you the evening
before, how in darkest hell he found deep inside himself
the generosity to forgive you when he discovered the
facts of our affair. And even when I try not to think of
you, he then reminds me without fail when he appears
on my television screen standing in some factory car park
pontificating about the state of the industry on the

regional news, or crusading for victims of Stock
Exchange swindles in his cheap suit. Of course, I hate
him, I move closer to the screen when he appears to peer
at the landscape of his pimples – how the hell do they let
him appear on the box with all those blemishes, look,
there's a big red one near his eyebrow almost ready to
burst! When we were still lovers, I feared him and
noticing him for the first time during a live appearance,
I even thought him handsome in a bland sort of way. No
longer, he looks like a clumsy amateur, a few more years
and he will be hopelessly going to fat. But would I be
any better for you, I ask myself? The pain of your
absence is killing me softly, day by day, hour after lonely
hour. Do you still listen to the Grant Lee Buffalo album
I turned you onto? I've made a few other great rock
discoveries since: the Walkabouts, Counting Crows.
Somehow all these callow musicians manage to express
so many of the things I seem incapable of with only the
power of words. If only I had learned how to play an
instrument when I was younger. So what more can I
say, apart from repeating the boring litany of how I miss
you and want you still? Oh yes, I'm no saint, I fuck
other women, but I detest myself as I always feel
compelled to evoke images of you when I am with these
others, to help me stay hard inside them, to furnish me
with the rage to plough my furrow of infamy inside their
bodies. I feel sweaty, dirty in these hurried embraces and
my cock softens, so I close my eyes and think of the
lunar expanse of your great arse, the delicate lack of
opulence of your breasts, the jutting geometry of your
hip bones, the heartbreaking pallor of your body. See
how low I stoop. Forgive me. I have written you letters,
yes, letters full of hate and anger, letters that made no
sense, letters that bled and roared, but none of them
were sent and I sit here imagining stories I might write
one day. Tales of sound and fury where the red flowers
of the mountain will scream Yes to the returning sailor
home from the wars, where St Germain des Prés in Paris
after WW2 will bear witness to the lovelorn passions of a
group of expatriates Yes I might complete that novel

about passions out of erotic control against a panoramic landscape of mythical American highways and love on the run taken to its orgasmic conclusion Yes or that crazy tale of lovers who fuck themselves to death to explore what lies on the other side Yes I obsess and the ghost of you is taking over my life Yes my love. And I never saw you dance. So, night falls and a cloak of darkness surrounds me, snow is falling, Boston and New York airports are closed, and the roads out there are treacherous and deadly. I imagine myself in a car, blocked by the snowdrifts, with the temperature falling, my breath visible in the restricted space of this odd cockpit, even with gloves on my fingers are becoming numb and outside there are no lights for miles and miles. What a stupid way it would be to die like this, just because I wanted to get away from you and foolishly thought the road was the answer. So, I return to London and now my life begins again, my mind still engulfed in hopeless passion, buried in the folds of her flesh, the dark brown vulnerability of her sad, married eyes. Today is the first day of the rest of my life (or what is left of it). I wonder what bodies will come my way again, how will they compare? Will they shudder and hold their breath back as she did when I slipped a finger inside the pliable tightness of her anal aperture? I know they won't.

– Why, when you touch me, do you always seem to do all the right things?
– I don't know, I suppose it just comes naturally.

HOLLOW HILLS

Michael Hemmingson

"THIS IS THE last night of my life," Cynthia says, "I mean, this is the last night of my life as a single woman, a single girl, this is the last night of that life and tomorrow I'll begin a new life so I want to do something I've never done before – well, I guess I am: I am doing something I've never done before. I'm here, aren't I? This is something I've never done before."

We're all crammed into Ralphie's 1971 Mustang. She's in back, wedged between Ajax, Mookie, and Fortanbras. They're passing around a bottle of Jim Beam. I'm up front, shotgun to Ralphie, who's driving.

"I hardly ever drink," Cynthia goes on, "but tonight I think I'll drink."

"Drink all you want," Mookie says.

Ralphie speeds up the speed, the Mustang's engine growls.

"I want to go somewhere I've never been before," Cynthia is saying, "somewhere strange, somewhere where you shouldn't go, somewhere with pizzazz and danger." She plays with her hair, which is pulled back into a bouncy-bouncy ponytail. "You know?" she says. I turn, take a quick glance at her, up and down. She wears a long, simple skirt; blue blouse; light green unbuttoned sweater. Her gold-rimmed glasses keep falling to the end of her nose. She doesn't wear any make-up.

"How about Hollow Hills?" Ajax says. "You ever been to Hollow Hills?" he asks Cynthia.

"No," she says. She was valedictorian in high school – "Miz Goody-Two-Shoes" in the locker-room.

"Hollow Hills," Ajax says to Ralphie.

"Yeah," says Mookie.

Fortanbras nods, taking the bottle of Jim Beam from her.

Ralphie makes a turn.

I look at him.

He shrugs.

"Time to open some beer," Mookie says.

"Beer indeed," Fortanbras says.

"Shriek," Mookie says, "break out the brewskis!"

"I could go for a beer," Cynthia says.

I have the case of beer in my lap. I open it, pass beers out to all, except Ralphie. He doesn't drink and drive. I don't think I've ever seen him drink. I have a beer. I look in back. The guys seem to be squeezing Cynthia in more and more. Her glasses fall into her lap. "Oops," she says, picking them up, putting them on, drinking beer. "I'm getting buzzed," she announces.

"Only way to be," Ajax says.

"I feel good," she says.

"Only way to be," Ajax says.

There's an odd silence, the engine roars.

"Music," Cynthia says, "is there any music?"

"Thing with Ralphie," Mookie says, "is he don't like to hear tunes when he drives."

"Only the engine," Fortanbras says.

"Yeah," Ajax says.

Ralphie speeds up the speed.

"Where's these Hollow Hills?" she asks.

"We're getting there," Mookie says.

"Boy are we," Fortanbras says

"You two up there sure are quiet," Cynthia says to me and Ralphie.

"That's why they're up there," Ajax says.

"You should talk more," she says, directing this to Ralphie, "you should go blah-blah-blah."

I say, "Blah-blah-blah."

"You see?" she says. "You see how different things are when you go blah-blah-blah?"

Ralphie makes another quick turn.

"I spilled my beer," Fortanbras says.

"Here." I give him another.

I look back and see that Ajax is practically falling into Cynthia's lap. She's red in the face.

"It sure is getting cramped," she says.

"That's what happens when you try to squeeze four people into the back," Mookie says.

"Someone's touching me," she says.

"That's me," Ajax says, "I have my hand caught under your ass."

"Stop that," she says.

"Are we there yet?" Mookie says.

"Not yet," Fortanbras says.

"Shriek," Cynthia says, "can I have another beer?"

I hand her one.

"You drank that other fast," Ajax says.

"I hardly ever get drunk," she says. "If I ever drink, it's one glass of wine, one can of beer, that's it. Tonight, I want to get smashed. I want to do something I've never done before. This is my last night, the last night I have to be a single person, and I want – I keep saying the same thing over and over, don't I?"

"Hey," Mookie says, "you can blah-blah-blah all you want."

"Yeah," Ajax says, "talk."

"Your hand is under my skirt," she says.

"It can't help itself."

"You're bad," she says.

"Um-hm," Ajax says.

"Stop that," she says again.

I see Ajax getting his hand higher in there and she doesn't protest.

Ralphie makes another quick turn and the four fall into each other more and more. Cynthia's head pokes up from a mass of bodies, arms, legs. "Help," she says, "help."

"Soon we'll be there," Mookie says, "then we can all get out."

"Maybe I should have sat up front," Cynthia says.

"Where would you sit?" Ajax asks.

"I could sit in Ralphie's lap," she says.

"He's driving."

"I could sit with Shriek," she says. "On his lap."

"That would keep it in the family," Fortanbras says.

"They're not family yet," Mookie says.

"Tomorrow," Cynthia says, "hey!"

"Hey hey," Ajax says.

"Those are my panties," Cynthia says.

"Cotton," Ajax says, "I love cotton."

"I'm spilling my beer," she says.

"We all are," Mookie says.

Ralphie makes another sharp turn and the four in back make sounds like they're on a roller coaster. Wherever Cynthia is, back there, I can't see her. She's under the guys.

"Help," she says, muffled, "help."

"Oh," Fortanbras says, "everything is okay."

"Does he always drive like this?" she asks.

"Always," Ajax says.

"Get your hand out of my panties," she says, and her head emerges.

"It likes it there," Ajax says.

"My beer is all over the floor," she says.

"That's okay," Fortanbras says.

"You want another?" Mookie asks.

"Yes."

I give her one. Her arm struggles for it. Ajax's face is in her pony tail, Fortanbras' in her breasts.

"She's wet," Ajax says.

"She's hanging nip," Fortanbras says.

"Stop that," she says, "you're embarrassing me."

"That's why you have to drink a lot more," Mookie says, "so you won't be embarrassed."

Cynthia fights to get the can to her mouth and drink.

Ralphie takes another sharp turn.

"Where is he going?" Cynthia says.

"Hollow Hills," Fortanbras says.

"Is it this far?" she says.

"Not usually."

"Ouch," she says.

"Am I hurting you?" Ajax says.

"You really should stop that," she says.

"Just curious," he says, "we used to all call you Miz Goody-Two-Shoes, y'know."

"You did?"

"Yeah."

"Why?"

"You always had your nose in a book," Mookie says.

"So I like to read," she says, "what's wrong with that?"

"You never went out with anyone," Ajax says.

"I was shy," she says, "and your fingers are doing things they shouldn't."

"What's that you're doing, Ajax?" Fortanbras says.

"Trying to feel if what we expect is true," Ajax says. "I don't know, they're getting in there pretty easy."

"What is true?" Cynthia breathes.

"If you're a virgin."

"Why would you say that?"

"You never went out with anyone," Mookie says.

"Why would that make me a virgin?"

"Unless Shriek's brother got to you in secret," Fortanbras says. "Shriek, did your brother pop her?"

I shrug.

"You guys are too much," Cynthia giggles.

"She's very wet," Ajax says, "and she's no virgin."

"I'm done with this beer." She tosses the can to the floor.

Fortanbras is unbuttoning her blouse.

"When did you lose your cherry?" Ajax asks. "And who did it?"

"Now," she says, "that's none of your bees wax."

"I'm going to fingerbang you," Ajax says, "I'm going to fingerbang you until you come."

"Damn," Ralphie mutters, and makes a sharp turn, speeds up the speed, roars the engine.

The four in back all make more roller coaster sounds.

Someone's beer splashes onto the back of my head.

I say, "Hey, watch that."

"Sorry," says one of them.

I turn, see that Fortanbras is sucking on one of Cynthia's nipples, a pink nipple. Her sweater is pushed up, bra undone. Mookie has his pants down, is holding his penis.

"Take it," he says to Cynthia.

"Where's my glasses?" she says. "I lost my glasses."

"Take it," Mookie says.

"What? I can't see anything."

He grabs her hand, places it there.

"Oh," she says.

Ajax is doing something fierce with his hand under her skirt. "C'mon, Mis Goody-Two-Shoes," he says, "Miz Bookworm," he says, "come on my fist."

"You guys," she giggles, "you guys are just as crazy as when we were in high school."

"Jerk me off," Mookie says.

"Stop whining," she says, bending down and putting his penis in her mouth.

"Oh," Mookie says, "oh."

I look at Ralphie. He's concentrating on his driving.

The road is dark.

"Maybe here," I say.

He shakes his head.

"Or here," I say.

He shrugs, and turns, but not as sharply as before.

I look back. Mookie is making a strange face, his eyes closed. Cynthia's head bobs. "I'm coming," Mookie says, gasps, relaxes, and Cynthia's head stops.

She sits up, mouth wet. "Can I have another beer?"

"And open it for the lady this time," Fortanbras says, taking his mouth from her bosom.

I open a beer, give it to her.

"Thanks," she says, and drinks.

"I give up," Ajax says, taking his hand away.

"This beer is good," she sighs.

"We need to have some law and order back here," Ajax says.

Mookie moves to a corner so the others can straighten out.

"On my lap," Ajax says, "sit on my lap."

"Here," Ralphie mutters, and makes a sharp turn.

"Oh oh oh!" they all say in the back.

Cynthia is on Ajax's lap. His pants are down. She's facing me, with a smile, but I don't think she can see me. Her skirt is bunched up. Ajax enters her with his penis.

"Are we there yet?" she asks.

"Not yet," Ajax says.

"I'm going to come," she says, and screams.

"Finally," Ajax says, and comes.

She sits down between Ajax and Fortanbras.

"Beer?" she says.

I give her one.

"Thanks," she says, and drinks.

Fortanbras is stroking his penis.

She squints. "What are you doing?"

"Come on, Miz Goody-Two-Shoes. Suck this pecker-wood."

She bends down and takes him in her mouth.

I look at Ralphie.

He shrugs.

"Maybe here," I say.

He shakes his head.

"Maybe here?"

He shakes his head.

The road is dark.

I open a beer for myself.

I look in back. Fortanbras is shaking, eyes closed. Cynthia's head bobs. "Ahhhh," he says, grabbing at her pony tail. Her head stops. She sits up, spitting out thick white fluid. It dangles off her chin, swaying back and forth on a thin strand. "I still have beer," she says, drinking.

There's a long silence.

"This isn't the way," Ajax says.

Ralphie shrugs.

"My glasses!" Cynthia bends, picks up the gold-rims, puts them on. She smiles. "I can see now."

Ralphie takes a sharp turn.

Cynthia's legs are in the air.

The guys all start grabbing her.

"Stop that," she says, "you guys, you guys are something else!"

She sits up, adjusting her glasses. She pulls her skirt down, wipes her mouth on the sleeve of her sweater. "Is there any more beer?" she says.

"Should be plenty," Fortanbras says.

"Yes," I say.

Her hand is out.

I give her one.

"Oops," she says, seeing that her blouse is undone. She buttons it. She takes the beer from me. She drinks.

"She sure does drink," Mookie says, "for a bookworm."

"I'm going to have to pee soon," she says.

"You have to go?" Ajax says.

"Not yet," she says, "but I know I will soon."

"We'll all have to," Fortanbras says.

" 'Cept Ralphie," Mookie says.

"Or Shriek," Ajax says. "Hey, Shriek, why aren't you drinking any?"

I hold up my beer. "I am."

"You should be back here," Mookie says.

"Maybe not," Ajax says, "it's a family thing."

"Not yet," Cynthia reminds him.

"Yeah," Ajax says, "tomorrow is the big day."

"Better hope Shriek doesn't tell his brother about all this," Fortanbras says.

"He won't," she says, looking at me, serious. "Will you?"

I don't say anything.

"And what could his brother say anyway?" She drinks. "I don't belong to him, yet. I have this final night. My one wild night. You don't think I don't know what happens at those bachelor parties? The strippers, the whatnot? The Going Out and Sowing Wild Oats? You don't think I know? I know. It's the way it is. Why can't it be the same for me? Why can't I sow my oats? Why can't I have a final night?"

"She has a point," Ajax says.

"I have to pee," she announces.

"She has to go," Mookie says.

"Ralphie!" Ajax says. "Think of the lady!"

Ralphie nods, stops the car. Ajax gets out, to let her out. She runs into a bush.

Ajax gets back in.

"Cold out there," he says.

"Dark," Mookie says.

"This is weird," Fortanbras says, "no one would believe us, no one."

"We're all here to back the story," Ajax says.

Mookie laughs. "We just did Miz Good Two-Shoes. What about Shriek and Ralphie? They gonna get some?"

"We're going to do her again," Ajax says, "we're going to take turns doing her all night long. Like she said, this is her last night."

"Choo choo train," Mookie says.

"I'm lost," Ralphie says.

"What?" they say.

"I can't find Hollow Hills," he says.

"Shit," Ajax says, "are we lost?"

"I think I know the way back to town," I say.

"The hills," Mookie says, "we have to take her to the hills and do her there."

"Maybe we should just leave her here," Fortanbras says.

"What?" I say.

"This might be nothing but trouble," he says. "The girl's about to get married, we're looking for Hollow Hills and you know the curse those Injuns put there – something bad is gonna happen."

"Curse," Ajax laughs, "curse me arse!"

"We might meet some crazy psycho serial killer or something."

"Like Jason?" Mookie says. "Like Freddie?"

"I don't like this," Fortanbras says.

"She just sucked your dick," Ajax says, "and you say you don't like this?"

"Something doesn't feel right," Fortanbras says.

"We're lost," Ralphie says.

"We'll find our way back," I say.

Cynthia returns, sitting in the corner this time. There is a silence. "I feel better," she says.

Silence.

"Are we at Hollow Hills?" she asks.

"Not yet," Ajax says.

"We might be lost," Fortanbras says.

"Nah," Ajax says.

"We might be doomed," Fortanbras says.

"Oh," Ajax says, "shut up."

Cynthia adjusts her glasses.

I look at Ralphie. He speeds up the speed.

"Here," I say softly, pointing, "this is the way back to town."

He takes the sharp turn.

Ajax, Mookie, and Fortanbras all fall into Cynthia, but they move away and give her space.

"I really had to pee," she says, adjusting her glasses, checking her blouse.

I turn around. "Want another beer?"

She shakes her head. "No, I've had enough."

A CARCASS OF DREAMS

Marco Vassi

There is no better way to know death than to link it with some licentious image.

DE SADE

THE DYING GYNECOLOGIST

THE DREAM OF LIFE was ending, and he was returning to the unformed state where consciousness could not follow. Having accepted the inevitability of this moment many years earlier, having made it a daily meditation, he was now without apprehension. If anything, he experienced a mild curiosity, faintly eager to experience the phenomenon of death.

For several hours he had lain in what appeared to be, to those gathered around his bed, a deep coma. But he was in fact fully awake. Having spent his entire career in the service of others, he gave himself permission to take these last few moments for himself, sinking lazily into his thoughts, savoring the voluptuous cadence of his breath, wandering down the corridors of memory to gaze upon the thing he had been, the infant, the boy, the man, and finally, the unencumbered organism coming to its predestined conclusion.

In the room sat his wife, his four children, his oldest friend. His favorite cactus plants had been moved in from his office so he might have the solace of their presence, reminiscent of the silences of the desert, the same silence he now prepared to enter. The six people waited, not speaking, wrapped in the wide calm that emanated from the man in front of them.

He felt no pain. The garment of flesh that had served him faithfully for so long had worn out and was ready to be discarded, to go back into the earth.

"I wonder what happens to the *I* in *me*," he said to himself, "to the intelligence that is even now asking the question. Is there any chance it might continue after the body ceases to function?"

As though in response, some strange sensation seized him, held him for an instant, and then disappeared.

"I'll know soon," he thought. "Or perhaps I won't know anything at all."

The situation amused him, and he smiled. The sudden appearance of the seemingly incongruous expression startled the others, who were watching him closely, half ashamed of their subliminal desire to have the whole thing over with. His eldest daughter leaned over and whispered in her mother's ear, "He must be a saint, to be able to smile on his deathbed."

"Wouldn't it be peculiar to die and find myself face to face with old Jehovah," the man thought. "Imagine all that nonsense turning out to be literally true. It's a mysterious universe, and anything is possible."

He chuckled, causing the hair on the necks of the people around him to rise.

The breath caught in his throat and his frame shuddered. There was no specific point at which he could grasp the unfamiliar process of passing away, but he knew that the moment of departure was very near.

"This is really very odd," he mused, "I can feel it happening, but it seems so distant, as though it had nothing to do with me at all. I don't feel like *I* am dying. There is just death going on, and I am one of the people observing it. The only difference between me and the others is that when it happens, they will stand up and walk out and I will be left lying here."

Then abruptly, as though he had fallen from a great height, he felt everything drop away from him. Time underwent a cataclysmic change, and he was swept by a sensation of rocketing through space at an exponentially increasing speed, until he was going faster than light itself. And yet, the faster he moved, the more still everything became. Opposites lost their identity.

One by one, his faculties shut down. Hearing, touch, taste, smell, all disappeared. His thoughts blew off his mind like shingles from a roof in a high wind. He opened his eyes for the last time.

"Sam," his wife said.

"Goodbye Constance," he croaked and saw nothing more.

Relinquishing everything he had ever imagined he might lay claim to in the universe, he bade farewell to himself. In a microsecond of utter clarity, he saw what an ironic play life was, what a strange dance of fantastic reality. Beyond all ability to apprehend his experience, he gave himself up to death.

But it was not yet time.

He lost awareness of the external world, and his breathing stopped, but the vital force which had animated the inert elements of his body and sustained the cohesion called existence had not yet dispersed. A doctor would have pronounced him dead, for his heart had stopped beating. But beneath the measurable manifestations, in the core of his being, the finest thread of electricity still hummed. All that he had been was now reduced to that single throb of energy.

Subjectively, it was like falling asleep, and into a dream. First, a total loss of self-consciousness, then a sentient blackness, and finally a slow discernment of form. A blank screen lit up, and on it appeared the thin line of a far distant horizon, such as the edge of ocean seen from shore. It separated sea from sky, both the same shade of deep cobalt blue.

For an eternity, nothing moved. And then, faintly, a dot emerged from ground into figure, balanced delicately on the line. Subtly, slowly, it grew larger, obviously coming closer to the shore where the man stood. Without any landmarks, there was no way to estimate its size. As the relatives and friend began to look at one another, attempting to decide who should approach the body to find out whether the end had come, the man began to hear the first low ripple of trumpets which seemed to accompany the object.

Now, measuring the thing against his own height, he was able to assess its scale. As the music swelled, a jagged burst of golden light shattered the scene, and he gazed up at what thunderously swept toward him, a thing a thousand feet high and perhaps a third as wide, taking up his entire field of vision. It flew forward with majestic ease until it stopped suddenly, a few feet in front of him, and his knees buckled when he realized what it was.

He looked up into the face of a giant, encompassing, and perfectly formed cunt, quivering in purple radiance, a great mandala enveloping him in its aura. He gazed upon it reverently. In smell, in texture, in pulsating vividness, it was the quintessence of cunt, ideal in its every fold, its every hue.

"My Lady," he whispered, and fell prostrate before it.

In the mind of the man within his mind, kneeling before his object of worship, he was twenty-five again, in his last year of medical school, wondering whether he should become a specialist or go into general practice. He was talking it over with a friend, when the young man told him, "Why don't you become a gynecologist. You're always complaining about how horny you are. If you become a cunt specialist, you won't have any trouble at all getting laid. Just think of all those women coming in and spreading their legs for you. And paying for it to boot!"

As the entire course of a great river can be traced to a tiny bend at its source, so his career was shaped by the offhanded bit of half-meant advice. He shaped his studies in that direction, giving his parents rationalizations which involved the greater profitability of that particular line of medicine, and within two years, he began practice.

His first patient had found him almost unbearably nervous. The woman was infected with some baroque venereal strain, and when she split herself apart on his table, the smell which seeped from the tainted organ caused him to retch. He was fortunate that she was a prostitute with no false modesty, and so was saved from embarrassment by her remarking, "Yeah, that's the way my clients feel. Can you fix it up, doc?"

He performed a series of tests, sent smears to the laboratory, and finally doused her with antibiotics, vaginal jellies, and suggestions for douching. A week later he saw her again and her cunt was as good as new. When he examined her the second time and pronounced her well on the way to cure, the gratitude in her eyes was as much payment as the money she gave him.

How many cunts had there been after that? Middle-aged housewives with bored cunts, young girls with puppydog cunts, whores with leathery cunts, nuns with pimply cunts, secretaries with pornographic cunts, witches with velveteen cunts, grandmothers with withered cunts, children with unarticulated cunts, passionate women with engulfing cunts. Cunts of a thousand eyes, cunts of a million moods. Smiling, pouting, shouting, brooding, yearning, burning, angry, gay, hungry, sad. Again and again the same single action – the legs swinging wide at his request, like the gates opening to the thief upon saying the magic words, "Open Sesame." He would first see the hair, sometimes sparse, sometimes thick, or coarse, or fine, or black, or golden, or red, or curled, or straight. And then the thing itself.

Where few men looked and few men touched, he prodded and pulled and stroked. He dove in with instruments, he slithered in with fingers. Sometimes he found disease, often he found nothing more than the desire to be entered. And when his hand came out it was not infrequently covered with secretions that were something other than the lubricating cream he had used to ease his penetration.

At the beginning he had kept what they had taught him in school was the proper professional distance. All the doctors had been trained to treat the cunt as something septic, something to be approached only with gloves on, with formal face and averted glance. Something to be pried apart with metal shoe horns. But he could not maintain that artificial pose for long. He loved cunts. That was the reason he had become a gynecologist: to see cunts, to touch cunts, to smell cunts, to heal cunts.

It was in the third month of practice that his first thrilling contact took place. The patient was the wife of a prominent psychoanalyst, in her early thirties. She came for a general checkup, saying she did it once a year and that his name had been recommended by a friend. She wore a tight sheath dress, outlining her ample buttocks, showing her bulging thighs, accenting her full breasts. She was a beautiful and sultry woman, and the doctor felt his cock stir at the thought that he would soon have her lying on her back, her legs hoisted over stirrups, and with what he knew would be a luscious cunt lying agape, waiting for him to minister to it. His lips trembled slightly as he spoke, so calmly, in such a sophisticated manner, saying all the lines proper to the doctor-patient scenario.

"It's amazing what you can get away with," he thought, "once you put it in a socially acceptable context."

In the examination room it went as he expected, except that when it came time for him to slip on his plastic gloves, he boldly discarded the gesture. When he touched the fragile edges of her pink cunt, it was with his bare fingers. He seemed to enter some sort of trance, his ratiocinative faculties mesmerized. He entered a world of brute sensation, and without his understanding the process as such, his hands began a complex communication with her cunt. He found he was talking to her as he moved inside her, in a way that augmented the medical patter, the stock phrases . . . "does that hurt? is it sore there? this seems fine." When he stroked her cervix, it was not sex, and yet it was not not-sex. It was like the perfect edge of good massage, in which the mode is tactile ambiguity, where meaning and message continually inter-penetrate.

A sigh escaped her lips. "She's enjoying this as much as I am," he thought, "and for the same reasons." Her cunt was already wet and the aroma it gave off was unmistakably erotic. His eyes moved from her cunt up past her belly between her breasts and into hers. She was watching him.

"Yes," she said.

He took off his clothes and fucked her as she lay. He came standing up.

From then on he fucked on the average of two women a day. Once he had broken through the convention of professional coldness, he was able to see with mounting acuity that at least half the women who came to him came simply to be caressed.

"Where are the men?" he said to himself over and over again. "Why isn't anyone loving these poor women?"

At first he made some mistakes, occasionally pushing for a sexual encounter when one hadn't spontaneously arisen, and he succeeded only in frightening the women involved. He often had doubts as to what sort of danger he might be in; might not a complaint end his career, or even land him in jail? Finally, he made peace with the fact that if he paid attention to business first, the business being the diagnosis and cure of disease, then whatever plums fell his way were his right to eat, and no bad fortune would be attached to that.

The woman he married was frigid. He chose her precisely because she was frigid. Examining her one afternoon, he saw that she had absolutely no sensation in her vagina. Her pelvis was locked in a chronic muscular spasm and her entire attitude was one of distaste for anything carnal.

"She's perfect," he thought, "she'll never bother me with excessive demands."

He courted her and married her and within a week after the ceremony she was overjoyed when he suggested separate bedrooms. He only fucked her about a hundred times in over thirty-five years, in groups of about twenty-five each, to conceive children. She settled into the role of mother and housewife, and purred in constant contentment that her husband allowed her to remain chaste.

Meanwhile, back at the office, he fucked himself silly.

By the time he was sixty, he had fucked more than fifteen thousand different women and had had his hands in the cunts of at least five times that many. "This is the best job a man could ever have," he told himself often, as his door opened, and his nurse ushered in yet another woman, and he would look at her the way a man looks at a woman's body in the street, calculating its curves, imagining its charms. But with a crucial difference.

"In a few minutes," he would think, "you're going to spread your legs for me, and offer me your cunt. And it will all seem very proper until I touch you a certain way, and you will realize that, all social rationalizations aside, you are opening your cunt to the eyes and fingers of a total stranger, a man you have never seen before, and one who, you will comprehend with a delicious shudder, wants to fuck you. And will we fuck? Or will I eat you out? Or will you suck my cock? Or will I have you get on your hands and knees so I can 'examine' you from behind?"

As the darkness of his death deepened, the memories faded, and the immense cunt before his mind's eye began to tremble, and open. From its roseate serrated center another cunt emerged, and another from the center of that. Cunt after cunt opened from the cunt preceding it. It was an infinite progression, never fully reaching him, continually spilling forth. He strained forward, to be taken into the heart of the budding cunt machine. It was the baby attempting to return, it was the man diving into the mystery, it was both and all.

And as he reached up in revery, the body on the bed bent at the middle and sat bolt upright. The people in the room were shocked at what they thought was a corpse perform such a sharp strenuous act. His lids flew up, but he saw nothing. His lips moved. A single word leapt from his throat.

"Cunt," he said.

And from the depths of his desire, the face of death spun forward at lightning speed to snatch him in its jaws. What it looked like, no one will ever know, for death comes differently to each human being.

The gynecologist fell back on the bed. This time he was really dead. Those who heard his final word claimed that he had said nothing when people asked if he had said anything before he died. They did not understand what he meant, and ascribed it to delirium. It was given out to all his friends that he had died happy. As indeed he had.

In one of his notebooks there was found the notation, "There are too few doctors who remember the original reason for playing doctor."

SUBWAY DICK

HE MAY HAVE seen her hundreds of times before he noticed her. Every weekday morning for over four years he had reached the Christopher Street station at a little after eight o'clock and stood with scores of others waiting for the train to take him to the world uptown where he spent half his waking hours, sitting in a cubicle, performing obscure and largely meaningless rituals with thousands of sheets of paper. Like the millions who descended daily into the tunnels to be shunted back and forth like cattle, he was usually in a foul mood. But the woman changed all that.

She had just lost a dime in a gum machine, and was standing in front of it, fuming and banging at the coin slot, when he passed by. Something about the quality of her energy at that point arrested him and he stopped to look at her. He drank in her features with a single visual gulp. But the subway car came thundering in and braked to a halt with a sickening screech of metal against metal, and he was jostled out of his stance. He did not think about her further that day.

The next morning, he saw her again, and once more swallowed her whole with his eyes. He stopped, taking a more detailed look at her, scanning her jet black hair, worn in a pony tail, her thin nose with flaring nostrils. Her body was wrapped in a thick winter coat, protection against the February cold. To his surprise, she glanced at him, her eyes oddly troubling, and then looked away.

During the next few weeks, although he made no special effort, he ran into her almost every morning. She was beginning to take on the air of an acquaintance. Once he started to greet her before he checked himself, remembering the strict New York etiquette which absolutely forbids talking to, smiling at, or in any way being friendly to other people on the street. It took him a while to realize that he was coming to relish seeing her, that it added a spark of interest to an otherwise dull and tedious beginning to his days.

By the end of March, he knew a good deal about her. The range of her wardrobe, the texture of her moods, the rhythm of her walk, had all been openly accessible to his study. It was amusing to speculate. Judging from the quality of her clothing, she probably made no more than a hundred and fifty dollars a week. She was probably a secretary. She wore no rings of any kind, and almost certainly lived alone. She used a minimum of makeup, a faint flush of lipstick and light eyeshadow. Her reading taste was random, as she might carry St Augustine's *Confessions* one day and a popular book on astrology the next.

It wasn't until the first week in April that he felt a desire to get closer. The first day on which it was warm enough to do without a coat, she appeared in a tight skirt which outlined a full high ass and rounded thighs, and in a jacket which, when unbuttoned, showed breasts that were just large enough to fit into each of his cupped hands. The thinness of her mouth, at first glance giving her a prim look, now contrasted with the electric sensuality of her body. It occurred to him that it might be possible to fuck her.

That galvanized him into action.

From the status of a charming novelty to add a touch of mystery to his mornings, she became a goal, a prize for him to win. He began to get up earlier each day, in order to shower, to choose his clothes with care, and prepare his mood. He went through the mating ritual which is common to birds and fish and beasts that share the same biosexual heritage as humans. He thrilled to his own sense of purpose, and attempted to calculate whether she might find him attractive. Without describing it as such, he began to court her.

Hers was the stop before his. As the weather grew warmer and her clothing grew lighter, he arranged it so he stood closer to her in the tightly packed car. He was finally able to smell her perfume, mingled with the crisp aroma of her firm flesh. He was able to perceive the delicate whorls of her ears, the slight tensions in her throat as she swallowed. He wondered what her name was. He even became aware of her imperfections, and could judge from her complexion on which days she had her period. He also thought he could detect, from a general looseness and jauntiness in her manner, when she had fucked the night before. One Wednesday, he actually touched her, feeling the rough tweed of her skirt against the tops of his knuckles. His knees sagged and he had to grab the hanging support strap to keep from falling to one side.

That evening he pondered talking to her. It maddened him that, while on one level he knew her intimately, in terms of social intercourse they were total strangers. He had watched her walk across the platform and knew the way her buttocks jiggled as she moved, and yet he had not yet heard her voice. He considered that were he to speak to her, he might find her terribly ignorant. Too often in the past he had desired a woman's body and had his lust shrivel upon coming in contact with her mind.

"What if she is shallow?" he said to himself. And in the end decided not to make any overture just yet.

Wondering whether it was cowardice or wisdom that chose his course of inaction, he worked toward more physical contact without any formal introduction or exchange. The following morning he moved with the force and agility of a star halfback in arranging it so that he stood behind her without having drawn undue attention to himself. Sliding and jostling with consummate skill and experience, he followed her through the densely packed crowd until she stopped at one of the vertical support bars in the center of the car. He eased in close.

It had been subwaymanship of the first water, and no knight jousting for a lady's favor could have performed better. As the train pulled away from the station with its customary lurch and everyone in the car swayed with it, he looked down the length of his body. Her buttocks were less than an inch away from his cock.

"So near and yet so far," he thought. He dared not move.

The train gathered speed as it clanged toward Fourteenth Street. It hit a curve and once again the mass of humanity within its iron confines, like fluid in a container, rolled to one side. Unbelievably, and to his stinging joy, the twin mounds of her ass cheeks swung pendulously back and nestled for a brief tingling second in the hollow of his crotch. Fire alarm bells went off in his groin, and he was almost instantaneously erect, the bulging cock straining the fabric of his pants.

She did not touch him for the rest of the ride, and when he got to his office he went directly to the john where he sat, massaging his cock with quiet frenzy until the autonomous ejaculation relieved him of the almost unbearable pressure. The fleeting contact was enough to serve as fuel for the most outrageous fantasies. He imagined that her cunt was endowed with a special heat-generating faculty, that merely to be near it would be enough to trigger orgasm in an army of men. He went through the rest of his day in a stupor, relegating the tasks to be done to his instinctive center, and saving his intellectual ability to enrich the pictures in his mind.

The next day was a Saturday and he was too overwrought to spend the weekend alone. He knew he was at the edge of some mammoth foolishness, but he could not help himself. "I only rubbed against a woman on the subway," he repeated to himself. "I mustn't let it get blown all out of proportion." But the woman had been transmogrified into an *idee fixe*, and he was succumbing to its magnetic power. To ease his tension, he called an old girl friend and fucked her five times in the sixty hours he had to wait before he would see the lady of the subways again.

And when he did, he knew he was lost. She wore a skirt so tight, with material so thin, that both the outline and color of her panties could be seen. Her blouse was diaphanous, and he could make out the pale gold of her skin beneath it on both sides of the brassiere which cupped her breasts in its white plastic grip. Despite the debauch of the weekend, desire boiled in his blood.

The train moved smoothly, and he cursed the efficiency of the engineer. But just before Thirty-third Street, it stopped altogether, and the lights dimmed. There was a two-minute wait before the conductor's voice rasped over the loudspeaker, "There's a train stuck ahead of us, and we'll have a short delay." It was a crashing stroke of good luck.

His strategy was to try the *mano morte*, the deadhand technique used by the Italians. The fingers are allowed to rest against the body of the target woman in such a way that there is no suggestion of attack. If she seems not to notice, the pressure can be gradually increased. If she fidgets, he can take refuge in the fact of the extreme crowding to silently plead innocence of wanting to have touched the delicious skin in front of him.

The middle knuckle of his middle finger came to rest exactly in the center between her buttocks, where the skirt pulled tautly over the valley. For a number of seconds he dared not even allow himself to feel the sensation, so delicate was his approach. Then, she shifted her weight, going from one leg to the other, and her cheeks moved, suddenly, grandly, sweeping across the width of his hand. A burbling moan of pleasure chugged to his lips, but he suppressed it sharply. He waited a short while, and then put his hand against her once more. Again she shifted, and again the treasured ass slid beneath his touch.

Now he was in a quandary. Was she unconscious of what was happening and moving randomly, or aware of his touch and showing her annoyance, or aware of his touch and cooperating in the encounter? It seemed as though his entire manhood was on the line. He had waited a very long time, and now was the moment to test their relationship. Boldly, he pulled back his hand and with a sense of historical finality, shuffled forward two tiny inches, just enough to ease the front of his body against her back.

Sheet lightning played over his sensorium. He was as alert and balanced as a man on a tightrope. She might whirl around and say something ugly, something terribly ugly, and inflict a wound on him that would take a long time to heal. Or she might respond to his overture. He waited, tortured by the suspense.

And upon that, quite easily, simply, and gently, she relaxed into her heels, throwing her weight back, and let her body rest with utter passivity against his. She had accepted the touch.

The train leapt forward just as his erection began to poke into the space between her legs. They rode that way until reaching her stop, his cock sizzling with the secret contact in the packed subway car, while his face remained calm, his eyes darting about to see if anyone saw, and finding nothing but the stunned gazes of the city's wage slaves being transported to another day of empty drudgery. When they came to her station she stepped away from him quite deliberately and before getting off looked once over her shoulder and into his eyes. He could not tell what her expression meant.

It escalated rapidly after that. He was soon pressing into her very tightly, pushing his pelvis with tiny surreptitious strokes as she squeezed her buttocks and released them. On some days she wore no panties and he gave up his boxer shorts altogether. He almost screamed the day she reached behind her and caressed his cock with her hand.

They took to meeting at the back of the subway car so she could lean into the corner while he covered her. If he kept his raincoat on he could slip his cock out of his fly with no one seeing. One morning she wore slacks and he put his erection between her legs, coming in her woolly crotch as the train slugged its way uptown. They suffered a near fatal accident one morning when a young schoolboy, recklessly making his way from car to car, opened the connecting door and they almost pitched forward into the narrow platform. He had a wild impression of gleaming tracks before he recovered his balance and pulled himself back in, grabbing her waist to keep her from falling. The boy caught a glimpse of his cock and blinked in disbelief before a slow smile spread over his face and he whispered, "Sorry to crash in on your party, mister."

Still, he was loath to speak to her. "What can I possibly say at this point?" he thought. "We've already progressed beyond conversation." And then, "Why spoil a good thing? If we start dating, instead of being the most extraordinary experience of my life, she'll show up as just another woman."

He was amazed that the affair had progressed from discovery to infatuation to consummation to cynicism so effortlessly, and all within the parameters of an eight-minute subway ride.

Yet, what could be accomplished in the crowded car was painfully limited, and he was bursting for a more total encounter. Then one morning, as he waited for the train, he saw her standing next to the women's toilet. She nodded, and he edged toward her. She backed up, put a nickel in the slot, and opened the door, beckoning him to follow. Like one in a trance he moved past her into the tile room. She slammed the door behind them and jammed the lock with a piece of metal.

They were alone in the white gleaming cubicle.

"This is insane," he hissed, the first words he had ever spoken to her.

By way of reply she peeled off her clothes. He watched mesmerized as the long-desired body appeared before him. When she was naked she abruptly threw herself at his feet, begging him to fuck her. She tugged at his pants and licked his shoes, rolling across the filthy floor. The woman of his dreams lay before him, a panting slut, fingering herself shamelessly.

Propelled from the mundane to the baroque with such rapidity that the pulse in his temples began pounding painfully, he tried to put the event in some context. But it was all exploding too quickly, too forcefully. The girl groaned with desperate want and he could do nothing but succumb to the moment.

The many months of slow building broke in the instant, and for the following five minutes they did practically everything possible for a man and a woman to do together, playing out Krafft-Ebing and the Kama Sutra at high speed. At one point she lay bent over the porcelain pissoir, her face in the water, as he whipped her with his leather strap. Some instinct told him he would never have another chance with her and that he had to get it in all at once. And it was not until he found himself foolishly ejaculating in her right ear that he came to his senses, aghast at the situation he found himself in.

He stepped back and leaned against the wall; he was slightly delirious. The woman dressed. When she was ready, he fumbled for something to say before they left the john. But his eyes grew wide as she reached into her purse and pulled out a police badge and a .357 Magnum revolver.

"You're under arrest," she said. And added, "I've had my eye on you for some time now."

The case, when it finally appeared, was thrown out of court. The city, due to the uproar being raised by Gay Activists' Alliance, was enjoying a spell of liberalism in what were technically considered sex crimes. The judge ruled that the man was a victim of vice squad entrapment, and, as such, his arrest was unconstitutional.

He was so shaken by the entire course of events that he moved to San Francisco. He was just recovering from his ordeal when he learned they were planning to build a subway there. He then jumped off the Golden Gate Bridge.

The woman began another long lonely vigil, seeking sex offenders in the tunnels beneath the city, riding the rails until some man touched her, and then rubbed his cock against her, letting him have his way until he was fucking her and stomping her and pissing on her and doing god-awful things to each of her orifices, at which point she would arrest him. She felt that sex was holy, and had chosen her job to keep it that way.

LAND OF THE SPERM KING

IN THE VALLEY not far from where the mythical realm of Shangri La was reputed to have been, there flourished a people who lived for almost three thousand years without a government. They had no laws, no organization of any kind, and were guided by a spiritual leader who was chosen from among the children born on the day of the winter solstice, each serving for life, and then passing the mantle on to whichever of the eligible candidates gave the wisest answer to the secret question, which only kings and queens could ask. The leader, when he or she was close to death, would have all those born on the shortest day over the years of his or her reign gather in the wood outside the village, see them one by one, and decide who was to succeed to the position of eminence.

It was a strange role, for in no one's memory did the guide ever have to do anything. There were never more than several thousand people in the land; children were considered such rare and wondrous creatures that there was a trembling hesitancy about bringing them into the world. Everyone ate the same thing: fruits and nuts which fell from the trees, and a form of yoghurt made from goat's milk. They all drank the highly mineralized water that flowed from the mountains. They never killed anything. Their clothes were made from the skins of animals that had died a natural death. They did not work, except to fashion garments and cups, and build shelters to live in. They had no formal sports, although wrestling was popular, as was reindeer riding, climbing, and swimming.

Among them were a few who grew up with a deep inner distance from the others, and they spent most of their time alone, fashioning drums and flutes from wood and hides, giving the others music. Some made strange shapes out of clay and gave the others images to

ponder. Some appeared periodically to tell long stories in hypnotically rhythmic language, speaking of things no one had ever
experienced but which sounded mysteriously familiar.

When the spirit moved the guide, he or she would begin to
dance, and then a feast would take place, the people making a fire
and brewing tea from a grass that grew on the far side of the
mountain that overshadowed their land, a drink with magic
powers of intoxication. Sometimes the celebration would last
for days, until the entire population had been so perfectly unified
in a vortex of energy by the sacred dance and the sheer power of
their massive gathering, that the field they moved in became the
scene of a single orgiastic organism, pulsing in ponderous and
quickening tempo.

Generally, however, they spent their time contemplating the
wonder of creation.

The guide possessed one idiosyncrasy as a mark of office; he or
she ate nothing but sperm. In fact, to the degree that the people
had a formal culture at all, it centered around providing the guide
with enough to eat. Since sperm is a perfect food, the guide
needed nothing else. And since the people lived a rarified existence, eating only the purest foods, drinking only the most vital
water, breathing only the sharpest air, and since they were
exposed to nothing but peaceful manifestations of the life energy,
they were as sensitive as flowers in their capacity to take nour-
ishment directly from the sun. It is not surprising that the guide's
daily intake was relatively small, usually amounting to no more
than the combined volume of seventeen ejaculations.

Over the span of history, of course, different guides developed
individual feeding habits. The conventional method was for male
guides to use the cunts of young maidens as cups, having the
day's male volunteers mount the female volunteers and make love
lustily until orgasm, at which point the guide would put his
mouth to a succession of still hot trembling vaginas and suck the
sticky deposit from the freshly fucked lips. Most of the female
guides took their sperm straight, lying languidly on a couch while
the day's complement masturbated over her and at the moment of
climax putting the spurting cocks into her waiting mouth. There
were what the people called "interesting" guides, men who
sucked the sperm directly from cocks, and women who preferred
using cunts as a vehicle.

Occasionally there would be a guide who developed more esoteric tastes and might request a daily dollop of yak sperm. One guide took a fancy to tiger sperm, and since the people were so gentle they could approach the fiercest beasts and coax the vital fluid from them, the wish was able to be granted. That particular guide was legendary for his sexual prowess, for after half a cup of tiger sperm he was able to fuck twenty women to satiation without stopping once. Another guide, a woman, ate only hummingbird sperm, and before she died had become totally transparent.

It never occurred to anyone at any time that things should be different. They were the only people in the history of the species who did not let the acquisition of language rob them of their primal simplicity, and so they attained true human dignity. Possessing wisdom, they had little use for knowledge; living in a state of tranquil bliss, they had no inclination to intensity of purpose. They watched the universe in its constant infinite turnings and workings, understanding that they were blessed just to be alive and know the wonder of it all. In touch with the primordial realities of the cosmos, they were beyond the superficialities of civilization.

It is conjectured that they were the descendants of a small band of people that followed Lao Tzu out of China after he wrote his *Tao Te Ching*. Instead of going to the mountains to die, as legend has it, he went to live. Leaving China at the age of eighty-five, he continued for another sixty-three years, teaching the people nonado. So powerful was his influence that it sustained them for almost three millennia.

In the seventeenth century of the Christian era as measured by western calendars, they were visited by two Dominican priests who came upon their valley by accident. The men were scandalized by what they considered obscene rites and general godlessness. They attempted to preach the gospel, but were met by a respectful indifference. They became an odd sight, flapping furiously about in their black and white robes, brandishing crucifixes, waving their bibles in the air, shouting at the people to put their clothes on and repent. It must be admitted that it was difficult to preach hellfire and brimstone to a people who had no concept of sin except "doing what is unnecessary," a faculty the priests excelled in. But the people were willing to let them be, viewing them as merely one of the more bizarre manifestations of the unfathomable universe.

The missionaries were able, however, to test the tolerance of even this ultimately benign people, first by chopping down living trees to make a dead church, and then by running through the grove where the guide was awaiting his daily meal and lashing the backs of the happy fuckers who were preparing his food. The people, for the first time in centuries, were confused, and they asked the guide what they should do, an action no guide in anyone's recollection had been asked to perform.

He thought about it a while and requested that the priests be restrained. Then, hoping to pierce to the core of the situation, he asked two of the young maidens to draw forth some sperm from their bodies so he might take their measure. The priests howled with outrage at the tender ministrations being given them by the gentle fingers and loving tongues of the women. And when they came, it was with horrible curses mingled with terrible prayers.

The king tasted each of their deposits and retched violently. "These men are . . ." he began to say, and then paused, not having a word for the concept "depraved." He spit out the sperm and pondered for a while. "Take them to where the eagles nest," he said at last, "and push them from the mountain."

The priests were disposed of and the people remained undisturbed for another three hundred years.

Yet, their time was marked. In one of the wars which continually erupted about them, their valley was discovered by a platoon of Chinese soldiers. Shortly thereafter, they were descended upon by a delegation from the People's Republic, and told that they were to be liberated from the chains of spiritual autocracy and introduced to the wonders of democracy.

"You will be removed from your primitive state," the directive read, "and given factories and schools and police. Women will be free and allowed to work side by side with men. Everyone will learn to read and illiteracy will be eliminated." Finally, they were informed, they would elect their own representative to sit in the People's Assembly in Peking. Beyond that, they would be taught how to farm, pen animals, make iron, and build roads.

The people were stunned. The night the representatives left, with word that they would return in a week with soldiers, planners, teachers, officials, and anthropologists, the guide summoned the entire village.

"There is no way to know why these things happen," he said. "It is like watching the night sky and seeing a star suddenly plunge into the darkness of space. It is our time to be destroyed, and there is nothing we can do."

He stroked his wispy beard. "For myself, I will not live to serve those smiling and well-intentioned brutes who think their primitive machinery is superior to our formless understanding. I will go to the place of the eagles and throw myself into the air which is the sustainer of us all. You may come with me, or you may stay here, and learn to survive amidst the stupidity which is fast descending upon us."

He sat silent for a long while and then his face brightened. "Yet, we still have seven sunrises and seven sunsets. Time enough for eternity." And with that he jumped to his feet and began to dance.

The morning of the day when the delegation was scheduled to arrive, the entire people, spent from the continuous orgy of the previous week, went to the nearby mountain top. They sat in a loose circle and entered a state of communion, sharing their vibrations, sharing their breathing, their awareness. Finally, the guide stood up and walked to the edge of the precipice. As he stared down, a small boy's voice called out to him.

"Before we all return to the flow, can you tell us what the secret question is?"

The guide turned around and looked into the child's open face. "There is only one question," he said slowly, "and that is this:

"Why are there no questions at all?"

The boy's lips began to move and he started to speak. But then as though a light had gone on within the light of the sun, his entire expression changed and became one of perfect understanding. His face relaxed and his eyes grew soft. He looked back at the guide, and said nothing.

The guide smiled.

"Yes," he said to the boy and to the whole people, "the answer is not to say the answer, but to be the answer." Then to the child alone, "You might have been guide after me."

And with a cry of rapture, he threw himself off the cliff.

One by one and two by three they followed, until the last man and woman stood looking down at the rocks below.

"When we die, there will be no humans left," she said.

"Then so be it," he told her. "It is as the guide has said: it is our time to be destroyed."

They too flew into the void, and when the Chinese arrived that afternoon they could not make sense of what had happened. They made an official report to their headquarters, and by the time the sun had set they had planted their flag and given the place a name, something that no one had ever bothered to do before.

NO WOMAN OF MAN BORN

SHE STARED INTO the mirror for a quarter of an hour, taking inventory, integrating the perceptions.

The legs are long and muscular, the shoulders broad, the hips narrow. The skin on her face is delicately etched, the result of two years of electrolysis. Straight black hair to the base of her neck, covering her ears, curling around her throat. Breasts curved like soft sherbet, the children of injected hormones. She is a handsome woman, as once she was a pretty man. Her ass is androgynous, and between her thighs the infolded scrotal sac.

"I have done it," she thought. "At last I have a body to match my desires."

She ran her hands over her belly and cupped her breasts, stroking the nipples with her fingertips. They wrinkled, and stretched taut. She smiled.

"Alexandra," she said out loud. "Men will want you." And with that did a slow bump and grind for her reflection in the glass, all the while hugging heself with satisfaction.

As with all transsexuals, her road had been painful and difficult. For her entire youth and young manhood, she was unable to understand herself as anything but a homosexual, a condition she despised. Impotent with women, she had been, as a man, wretched in her need for men. And after many years of therapy, she came to accept that the condition of homosexuality was intractable.

The conclusion that followed, while logically ineluctable, had been for a long time too frightening to consider seriously. The existential force of having one's penis cut off shook her to the roots of her being. But her torment knew no surcease, and the choice between radical change and suicide became quite clear. She opted for the former.

She began tentatively, making enquiries, writing letters of application to doctors who had performed the process of transformation. Before long, the fantasy began to precipitate a reality, and she found herself having interviews with psychologists, talking to other transsexuals who had come out the other side, several in each of the two directions, and finally entered the actual mechanics of transition, beginning with hormone shots, hair removal, special counseling, and on one unforgettable day, the first operation. And with all this, lessons on how to dress, how to move, how to speak, how, in short, to behave like a woman.

It had taken three years to reach this point, watching the final result in a mirror. A miracle had been performed, and it seemed to throw open a sparkling new world. She could enjoy men at last, as she always had, but now freely and openly, without the homosexual guilt she had never been able to shake off. She understood that from a certain viewpoint, her present condition might be considered even more pathological than the former one. But she didn't *feel* ashamed, and it is one's feeling about oneself that, in the last analysis, is the basic criterion for all judgement.

Now, when she flirted with a man, it would be as a woman. And when she gave head, it would be a woman's lips around the cock she sucked. Her face would be smooth, powdered, her mouth slightly rouged. Her chest would hold a woman's breasts for a man to fondle, and while the nipples would never yield milk, that would make no difference to her or to the man who was taking his pleasure with her. And when a man fucked her, it would be as a woman that she received him, and not as a "pervert," the word she had always used to describe herself. And after all this, she had, instead of the embarrassing penis, a cunt opening into her body, not as pretty as a real cunt, nor with a real cunt's smells and juices, but for all that, something that would serve. Its very artificiality, in fact, might give it a power of attraction and appeal that no real cunt could have.

"After all," she reasoned, "there can't be more than a couple of hundred artificial cunts in the whole world." She consoled herself that rarity overshadowed any intimations of the grotesque.

She opened the closet door on which the mirror hung, and began to choose her attire for the day. While recuperating from the final operation, she had not gone out or seen anyone, wanting to make her entrance into society all at once, whole and resplendent. She dressed beyond her usual simple taste, knowing that she was overdoing it, but unable to resist the temptation to go out in full drag.

"But it's not drag any more," she exclaimed. She was no longer a man, and the nylon stockings and panties and garter belt and brassiere and slip and dress and earrings and nail polish and lipstick and pumps and eyeshadow were now her legitimate clothing. A rush of excitement surged through her as she thought of bathing suits and the beach, of tight slacks and swinging her hips as she walked.

And for an instant, she even thought of Ralph, her friend for so many years, the man she loved more than anyone in the world, but to whom she could never venture a physical overture. Ralph had known that she was homosexual, and it had not affected their friendship, which was based on an intellectual affinity. Still, he had made it clear that he could not consider her sexually. During the time she was undergoing her transformation she had asked him, "Do you think you might desire me when I am a woman?" And he had not replied for a long time, then answered, "It might be possible. I don't know. It's extraordinary just to think about, but I won't know until I see you in your new body."

Now, glorious in full regalia, she looked at herself once more, and a well-dressed, very attractive woman of about thirty-five looked back, and winked. She was feeling just the tiniest bit randy already.

"Would you like to go for a drink?" Alexandra said to her image.

"And perhaps meet a man?" the image asked.

"Or should I call Ralph?" Alexandra replied.

"Not yet," her image told her, "you need some experience first."

Alexandra felt a shiver go down her spine as the impact of the reality she had become grazed her deepest sense of self. She checked herself out one last time, picked up her handbag, and walked out the door to see what the world had to offer.

As she stepped into the street, apprehension gripped her. At the back of her mind was the thought that someone would notice, would point to her and say, "Look, there's a transsexual." She glanced down to see if her slip was showing, and the already conditioned gesture of a woman brought her new courage.

She attracted no attention at all, except the routine stares of men who looked at her breasts as she approached and at her ass as she went by. She had to suppress her exuberance which threatened to propel her into long striding steps, and remember to walk as her coach had taught her, keeping her awareness on the sensation of her thighs rubbing against one another.

"Stay with your feeling of sensuality," he had told her, "that will keep you from reverting to masculine mannerisms."

Feeling more and more secure, strolling down the sidewalk as though she were a queen dressed as a commoner, her royalty apparent to no one but herself, she turned into one of those small dark restaurants which dot midtown. She stood uncertainly in the doorway for a moment, and was taken with a small edge of panic when the floor manager came up to her and said, "Will there be just yourself, madame?"

Madame!

She smiled graciously. "Just a drink, please, I won't be having lunch," she said, using the voice the same teacher had coached her in, making her sound a little like Marlene Dietrich with a bad cold.

He led her to a tiny round table, and she lit a cigarette to steady her nerves as the waiter brought her a Brandy Alexander, a drink she had always felt diffident about ordering when she went about in a man's body. She sipped slowly, relishing the fact that she left lipstick marks on the glass. Her joy was total, and she was torn between wanting to weep and wanting to throw up her arms and shout with pleasure.

Instead, she looked around discreetly, and several tables away a man of about forty, dark and rugged, wearing a very expensive suit, was looking at her with an unmistakable glint of desire. He was exactly her type, the kind of man who, when she had been a man, she would have done anything to have, and then have felt guilty about wanting. But now she could accept his overture, talk to him, and swim in his hunger for her. She would have to go slowly, waiting for the proper mood to tell him that she was a transsexual. And if he still wanted her, then she would have him, have a man at last, freely, openly.

She began to return his stare, but felt herself floundering in her response. She could not smile, nor lower her lids, nor shift her body, nor give any of the clues women use when they want to tell a man they're interested. She looked away in confusion.

"What's wrong?" she wondered. "Why don't I respond?"

She was about to ascribe it to nervousness in her new role when she realized that she was not really reciprocating his desire, and could find no feeling upon which to mount even a seductive glance. Intellectually, she could tell herself why she should desire him, could remember that there was a time when she would have been attracted to him, but now, he had no more sexual appeal to him as a woman than women used to have for him as a man.

She bent her head over her drink, pondering the strangeness of the situation, and was lost deep in thought when she sensed someone sitting across from her, at her table. Her heart skipped as she guessed it might be the man, and she didn't know how to deal with him.

But when she looked up, she found a woman looking back at her. A slim, well-groomed, utterly composed woman, who wore no makeup, and was dressed in a tightly cut suit. Her hair was short and her eyes were very very knowing.

The woman smiled, an expression that flushed through Alexandra like the embrace of a hot bath after a long stiff walk on a winter day. Her limbs grew weak, and the rest of the restaurant faded into distant obscurity, behind the irresistible magnetism of the woman who sat before her.

"I've been watching you," the woman said. "It was clear that you had no interest in that man who's been trying to catch your eye."

Alexandra knew at once that the woman was a lesbian, knew at once that she was making an overture, and knew at once, with stomach-shrinking certainty, that her new body was responding.

The homosexuality had pursued her through the entire change of gender, and in her transformed loins there flickered the familiar flame of an old forbidden desire.

THE ORGANIC COPROPHILIAC

WENDY DELICATELY SHADED the corner of her mouth with her lipstick brush, took a long deep look at herself in the professional makeup mirror with the tiny frosted bulbs all around the edge, and smiled radiantly. From her sequined shoes to her beehive hairdo, she was perfectly rendered, ready to win all glances at the Senior Prom. The other men would neglect their dates just to have a dance with her, and she would flirt outrageously with them, knowing all the while that no matter who held her in his arms, only Jeff could hold her in his heart.

"Jeff," she whispered, and her fingers trembled at his name. Tall, rugged Jeff, with his lopsided grin and his playful blue eyes, his electrifying figure on the football field and his deep love of humanity which would one day earn him the initials M.D. after his name. She rubbed the pin he had given her just six months earlier, on that night when the moon had lit up the waters of the reservoir as they sat in his Maserati and he spoke those fateful words in her ear.

"Be mine," he had said. And hot scalding tears of joy had spilled from her eyes.

Now she stood up, regarding her young figure in the glass. The wide gown hid her long shapely legs, shaved and oiled for the night's special date. Her waist was narrow and flared quickly to pearl-white breasts that swelled over the tops of her bra cups. No man had ever seen her nipples, or put his hands on the sweet mound between her thighs. She was more than a virgin; she was a consciously constructed landscape of hesitant delights, nurtured and guarded, prepared for the appearance of the single gardener who would enter some day to gather up the fragile buds of her tender flowers. She had been kissed so few times that her lips still tingled when another mouth brushed hers. And no fingers had ever traced the luscious curve between her firm full buttocks.

"But tonight," she breathed, and trembled over the expanse of her entire body at the thought of what the night would bring.

There was a light tap at the door and her mother came timidly into the room. The two women looked into one another's eyes through the mirror, and then Wendy turned.

"Mother," she gushed, "I'm so happy."

"And I'm happy for you," her mother replied. "It seems just like yesterday that I was standing where you're standing now, thinking about the man who was to become your father."

"We've lived in this town a long time, haven't we?" Wendy asked in that solemn voice which always overtook her when she thought of her American heritage.

The older woman swept forward and held the young girl by the arm. Her face was troubled. She had the look of a person who was about to enter into a necessary but difficult conversation.

"There isn't much time before Jeff gets here to pick you up," she began, "and there's something I need to talk to you about."

"I think I know what it is," Wendy said, spinning out of her grasp.

"You're thinking of letting him do it tonight, aren't you? You're planning to go *all the way!*"

"Please, mother," Wendy pleaded, "I'm a grown woman. It's time I decided these things for myself. And I do love him. Don't spoil it by trying to argue me out of it."

"No, no, it's not that. I would be the last to try to dissuade you. After all, I did . . . the same thing, the night of my Senior Prom."

"You?" Wendy asked, aghast.

"I was young once too," her mother said. She eased Wendy into the rocking chair that had been in their family for a hundred and twenty-seven years. "I just want to be sure you're careful. And perhaps if I tell you a little story, it will help you understand." The woman sat down opposite her daughter, and began a tale which her mother had told her, and had been told by her mother before her, insuring that each generation was aware that its children did not lose the historical continuity which kept the blood line strong.

"It was your great grandmother who was first seized by the seemingly irrational desire to eat shit," the older woman said. "In those days, people didn't have the enlightened attitudes we have today, and what with killing Indians and chopping down trees, there just wasn't time for bedroom finesse. Lil was seventeen when she got married, as cheery a cherry as you are right now. Her husband was a good man, dependable, but boorish. She didn't even know how to broach the subject of her secret desire to him.

"One day, while he was off on a four-day hunting trip, a knife-grinder came by their house. She describes him in her diary as gaunt and salacious, and adds, 'just what I was looking for'. She invited him in for lunch, and when they were finished eating, she blurted out what she wanted from him."

Wendy paled. Like many young people, it was almost inconceivable to her that what she had looked upon as an intensely private urge might be common place to the rest of humanity. Her mother's voice went on, describing what their ancestor had done, but she heard little of the narrative, her own mind being filled with the image she had cherished for so long.

She saw herself lying on a couch, her skirt hiked up over her thighs, her cunt redolent with pungent slime, toes curled in anticipation. Above her, his piercing eyes boring into her tender flesh, Jeff bears down, his great buttocks crushing her cheeks, his terse anus pressing against her sweet innocent lips. And then, with a subtle shift, the passage begins. She gasps, she moans, she faints, and in succumbing, her mouth falls open. He pushes down, and with a fanfaronade of aggressive thoughts, voids his bowels on her immaculate face. She tried to escape, knowing all the while that she does not want to escape. She chokes as the hot suffocating mass slides onto her tongue, into her throat, and down her chest, scorching her lungs and filling her body with the vile and glorious fulfilment she had always understood would be hers. She cries out and rises to actively cover the pulsing hole, stretching her lips until they crack, sucking the final product of the body she loves until she almost bursts from lack of breath, as she combines the lowest servility with the highest daring, the profoundest love with the most scarifying sensuality.

She looked up out of her revery and into her mother's smiling face. The woman seemed to be reading the pictures in her mind. Wendy blushed.

"There's no way to explain it, really," she said. "Doctor Cory thinks that the desire is an inherited characteristic. It just seems to run in the family."

Wendy began to speak, hesitated, and then began again. "But I'm not the only one," she said. "Most of the other girls talk about the same thing."

"They're not allowing sex education in the class-rooms, are they?" her mother shot out, ready to be incensed at the notion that the board of education was usurping what she believed to be the duty of parents.

"No," Wendy told her. "We get together at the soda shoppe and talk about our feelings. You know how girls do. And just yesterday Clarissa asked me whether I thought it was all right to let a boy shit in your mouth on the first date."

"In my day a girl would want at least an engagement ring before she'd let a boy take such liberties."

"I think so too, and that's what I told her. I think a girl and boy should know each other for a few months at least, and be going steady, before they get that intimate. But at least half the girls think that's old-fashioned."

"Well, times do change," her mother sighed philosophically. "But they'll learn the value of holding certain things back unless a man is extra good to them. If a woman gives a man everything at once, she has nothing to manage him with. You may not think that's important now, but wait until you've been married a few years."

"I don't know if I can hold myself back," Wendy pleaded.

Her mother took Wendy's hands between her own and held them to her breasts. "Jeff's a good boy," she said, "and I'm sure he's serious about your relationship. Just be careful that's all."

"Will you give me some advice?" Wendy asked, capitulating at last to a recognition of superior wisdom in this area on the part of her mother.

"Well," the woman said, "make sure he doesn't eat spicy food or drink too much early in the evening. If he gets the runs it will ruin it for both of you. And don't get shit on your dress. It's almost impossible to wipe off and you'll stink all the way home. Make sure he doesn't think you're too easy or he'll lose respect for you."

Wendy put her head on her mother's shoulder. "I'm so lucky to have such an understanding mother," she said.

"My mother did the same for me," the older woman went on. "And you might as well start practicing how to cook from now on. After you're married you'll have to be very careful about his diet. See that he gets enough roughage. And feed him the healthiest food you can. You might as well be getting some good shit from him if you're going to get any shit at all."

Wendy's mother stepped back and the two women gazed at each other with moist eyes. "My little baby's going to be all grown up after tonight," the older woman said.

"You're the best mother a girl could ever want," Wendy told her.

Just then the door swung open and a man walked into the room. Portly, red-nosed, and kindly, he beamed at the picture before his eyes.

"Daddy!" Wendy squealed.

"That Jeff certainly is a lucky man," he said, looking at his daughter's shining face. And then he turned to his wife and in a gruff jocular tone asked, "Is there any chance of getting something to eat around here tonight?"

Wendy and her mother looked at one another for a few seconds, and then burst out laughing, leaving the man smiling in gentle confusion. He and his wife had had separate bedrooms for almost five years, and for him the ingestion, digestion, and elimination of food was no longer a process that held any trace of erotic passion.

BLUEBEARD'S INSTANT GRECIAN URN

PAUL THOUGHT HE knew why women resisted, and his unwillingness to let any external reality alter the system of his perception was, paradoxically, his greatest advantage over them. He lived in a world of images, and ruthlessly imposed his projections on everyone in his life in order to attain his ends. He had no feeling for women as autonomous creatures, but worshipped them passionately as objects of desire. He easily equated conquest with caring.

For him, a woman's sexual response functioned exactly like a neural synapse, in an all-or-nothing manner. In the same way that a large number of electrical stimuli build a charge that, at a crucial moment, fires the spark across the gap between nerve endings, a series of fucks would mount a readiness until, with shocking speed, the woman would surrender to her most uninhibited expressions. Generally, women held back, even in orgasm, sensing that once they let go, an unfathomable chasm would open up, and all that could save them from dissolution would be the continued attention from the man who brought them to that condition. They would then be, for all practical purposes, in his power.

Paul was an expert at enticing women to disregard their warning systems, their memories of broken hearts, betrayals, refusals; he was a master at pushing them to the edge of the erotic abyss and seducing them to leap. His was the knack of easing women into insouciance, yielding their essence to his demand. For Paul, only that moment of yielding counted. Before she surrendered to her need in his arms, a woman was an object of dalliance; and afterward, she had nothing further to reveal.

He possessed a rare combination of genius and lasciviousness. He might have modelled himself on de Sade, except that he lived in a technological era, and looked upon tying virgins to stone walls in hidden crypts with a certain condescension. He had more sophisticated machinery at his disposal.

From the first moment, when he was just nineteen, that a woman let drop the veils of her public countenance and revealed the terrible beauty of a face that had become no more than a pool within which to see the rigors of a soul in ecstasy, he knew that nothing else in life would have any real value for him. He dedicated himself to the elicitation of that brief moment when absolute openness flowered before his eyes. No priest ever served any god better than Paul the cultivation of women.

In the course of a decade he had found hundreds of them. He learned exactly how to manipulate himself to get them to offer their treasure to his insatiable eyes. He was handsomely endowed, a little over six feet tall, his body combining the best features of a lumberjack and a Martha Graham dancer. He wore his blond hair slightly long, and spent six hours each week at a gym, in narcissistic contemplation of his muscular development, as he lifted weights, swung on trapeze bars, or swam lustily in the pool. Otherwise, he was at work, doing a job which bored him, but which allowed him to live in fairly opulent fashion. After having taken a Ph.D. in molecular chemistry, he landed a position at Johnson and Johnson, joining a vast staff of laboratory workers whose projects included searching for ways to produce more long-lasting glue for Band-Aids.

At night, he fucked.

He continually looked forward to the bliss of having an attractive and intelligent woman squirming under him, his cock splitting her throbbing cunt, her fingers raking his shoulders, her legs shamelessly pulling him more deeply into her, and through it all her face a mask of capitulation to unholy joy. It was the face, more than the mere sensations of the act, which transported him. When the stilted mask of civilized appearance melted and the beast emerged, the angel could be born. And if she were, in her daily life, ultra-sophisticated, ultra chic, then when she broke, he was blessed with seeing the contrast between that artificiality and the ultimate gift that can ever be given to man: the perception of the naked female soul.

But it was all so fleeting! He might watch a woman edge her way toward frenzy, see her hover at the very brink, and then go wild with the joy of wanton release. As the deep-chested howls burst from her throat, he could hold her only a few seconds, using her entire body as a feedback mechanism to orient the angle and intensity of his cock and thrust so that he extracted the maximum response, before she slipped into an orgasmic fury so private that the shades came down once more over her eyes. There were never more than those few brief moments during which he could gaze upon her, with the rapt expression of a saint in the midst of a beatific vision. And then it was gone. Gone forever.

"If only there were some way to preserve the stickiness indefinitely," he heard a colleague say one afternoon during a seminar on the relationship between the respective surface tensions of skin and plastic.

"Preserve!" The word echoed in his mind.

"Yes," he thought, "if only I could preserve that instant."

That night he cancelled his date in order to ponder the implications of his insight. "What if I could," he mused, "freeze the woman at the very second she is producing the expression which is her most perfect, her highest manifestation of beauty?"

He thought of photography, but discarded the idea. A two-dimensional representation was not what he wanted. He desired the real thing. His mind leapt from personal to social ramifications. "I would not only possess the thing that is most precious to me in the world, but will have created a work of supreme art, and in the process have immortalized a woman who would otherwise have passed into oblivion unknown. Such a piece would make the Mona Lisa seem the work of a primitive."

He was quite mad, of course, but also extremely, brilliant, and with the resources of one of the nation's foremost chemical plants at his disposal, he was soon experimenting with a formula that would have the properties he required of it. It would have to be liquid, for he saw that he would need to use a syringe. It would have to work instantaneously, to keep the body he used it on in semblance of the full flush of life. And it would have to penetrate to every last cell of the person's physical structure.

Fired by the flames of monomania, he poured his genius into the project, and within a year he was ready to make his first try.

He decided to start with Cathy. He had been fucking her desultorily for several months, and she had peaked rather early in the affair. It was only a sentimental fondness for her that kept him seeing her. She was still capable of producing first-rate expressions, especially in the way her lips fell open after he came in her mouth, allowing his sperm to dribble down her cheeks and over her chin. He had seen that half a dozen times already. Her orgasm expression was neoclassic, the suggestion of pain in her furrowed brow contrasting exquisitely with the sucking gesture of her lips. After considering all contingencies, he decided to attempt to capture her reaction to being fucked in the ass. Primarily because the hypodermic would be easier to use if he was behind her, and secondly because during that particular variation she attained an attitude of licentious imbecility which he fancied.

When the moment arrived, he was very sad. His body and mind working with the skill of a master technician, he savored the depth of his emotions. In order to accomplish his aim he would, in effect, be killing the lovely woman now groaning under him.

"But, in a sense," he rationalized, "I am doing her honor. She would have died one day anyway, aged and infirm, her body a mass of sagging wrinkles. This way, I freeze her at the height of her beauty, and in the process make her immortal." It reminded him of the fact that the samurai chose the cherry blossom as their symbol because, unlike other flowers, it falls from the branch in the fullness of its fragrance, sacrificing itself so that others might know its precious scent.

It was with mixed feelings that he pressed the needle to the base of her skull, just as she tilted the pelvis backward to impale her buttocks on his thick cock. He slid into her, causing her to gasp, and at the moment he was imbedded completely between her cheeks, and the look of unutterable pleasure that he was seeking moved across her face, he injected the potion into her skin.

At once she was completely paralyzed. Even her heart stopped mid-beat. For an instant he was breathless at the transformation. She had become a statue. He pulled out slowly, his cock feeling as though it were stuck in a piston tube packed with axle grease. He knelt next to her and turned her over. He could scarcely believe his eyes.

She had been caught at the edge of becoming. Her face was a map of demon lust. As he gazed into her fixed stare, he had trouble convincing himself that she was dead, for even the glint of passion had been captured. For a few seconds he was chilled by the notion that she was still alive, imprisoned in that rigid coffin of flesh.

"But that's absurd," he said, as he went to get a saw.

It was not difficult to sever the head from the body, which he was not really interested in except as a curiosity. It was fascinating to observe that the entire inside of her cunt was flexed in an orgasmic spasm. He put the torso in the bathtub, where another brew of specially prepared chemicals neatly dissolved it.

He brought the head to a special laminating machine he had devised, and placed it in a hollow, where a fine electron mist covered it completely. It sealed the woman in a very delicate plastic, as securely as if she was a driver's license. When he took her out, she looked like a woman about to come, except that she had no body.

"You are mine forever," he whispered, "the real you, the true you, the you that lives eternally in beauty."

After that, his collection grew steadily. He became regular at most of the singles' bars on the upper east side, and each evening he left with yet another candidate for immortality. Most failed to meet his increasingly exacting standards. Only the best were considered for his hall of fame.

He became adept at discerning types amidst the confusing superficial appearances. With no research ever having been done in the area, he had to construct his own system of classification, a Linnaeus of the rapturous expression. He divided women in scores of ways, such as the various degrees of opening between their lips at certain crucial check points; whether they kept their eyes open or closed, whether or not their nostrils flared. The quality of the eyes was a world of exploration in itself, and he was able to distinguish fifty-three distinct shades of cheek coloration.

His most frequent mistake in the beginning, when he was still exuberant over his success, was to confuse the excitement of fucking with the nature of the expression produced. Some fucked so well that he forgot to watch closely enough. The best fuckers were not always the best lookers, and vice versa.

When he found one that seemed promising, he would not take her all the way on the first night, knowing that the longer he cultivated her, the more sublime would be her expression when she finally did let go. He would nurse her the way a gardener will care for young shoots. The ones who were fortunate enough, or unfortunate enough, to fail to meet his criteria, were shooed out the next day, unceremoniously, so they would know not to try to come back.

Each morning, as he sipped his coffee, he would stroll among his heads, kept in a room empty of everything except the pedestals they rested on, and talk to them. He would look from expression of unbearable bliss to expression of deeply tormented joy to expression of total giving, and say, "Well, I had hoped to have another friend for you girls to chat with, but she didn't turn out. For a while there, when she put her ankles around my neck, I thought she might produce a really fine expression, but she was too jaded for me to reach her. An airline stewardess. She later told me she had once been fucked by a mule in a Mexican stag bar. Her face barely lost its composure all night. Or, on those days when he had captured another woman, would proudly carry the head in and say, "This is Frances. Isn't she exquisite?"

And then would light a cigarette and say, "Well, another try tonight," and go up to each one and kiss her full on the mouth, whispering endearments, murmuring, "Remember the night you made it all the way, how good it felt, how close we were?" And then would put out the light and go to work.

His doom was nicely ironic. As he injected a Balinese Temple Dancer who was part of a troupe visiting the city, her cunt contracted in an esoteric convulsion known only to a few initiates of the cult she had been trained in. His cock was gripped in an unbreakable grasp that was meant to last for no more than a split-second and provide a totally unique sensation. But frozen as she was, he was trapped inside her, a paralyzing spasm of pleasure-pain coursing through his body.

He tried for over an hour to extricate himself, when he realized that gangrene was setting in. He saw the implications fully. To seek medical help would mean being charged with murder, for questions would be asked, his apartment would be searched.

He decided not to prolong the agony. He lifted her up and carried her into the room of heads. He took all his women down, one by one, and put them in a circle on the floor. He lay down in the middle, the woman of the night still in his arms. For a long time he looked from face to face, remembering, weeping. And when his heart was full, he took the instrument he had used on all of them and plunged it into his chest.

He died as he had lived, a slave to the beauty of women.

THE SICILIAN'S REVENGE

AT FIFTY-FIVE, there were few pleasures left to him. He enjoyed sleeping, he enjoyed drinking wine and talking with his friends, and he enjoyed renting young Irish prostitutes and having them take their clothes off before him as he watched, his eyes sardonically drinking in their flesh, knowing that they found him repulsive, and then directing them to kneel between his thighs and suck his thick cock until he came, usually not for at least an hour, all the while telling them stories of his childhood in Italy, and when they were finished, dismissing them abruptly. He never had any girl more than once; after he had seen a woman's ass, he lost all further interest in her.

On this day he was in a particularly pensive mood, almost philosophical, as the whore dutifully slavered over his cock. He had just concluded a fairly complex deal which involved the takeover of the Chase Manhattan Bank and all the Rockefeller oil refineries in New Jersey through his company. The Capa Tosta Concrete Corporation. From his offices on the hundred and tenth floor of the World Trade Center Building, he looked down over the grimy expanse of New York City.

His eyes narrowed when they rested on Central Park, Prospect Park, and all the other small sections where nature still had some small toehold. He estimated that he had twenty-five years of vigorous health left, and in that time would not rest until every square inch of the city was covered with cement. Until all five boroughs were drowned in buildings.

His gaze went west. There was still the rest of the United States. But that would have to be for his sons. For himself, he would be content if the city became a single giant mausoleum, a final testimony to his power. It would be a feat such as would make the pyramids of the Pharaohs pale into insignificance.

He patted the head of the girl sucking his cock. "You know, Irish," he said, "all those people down there, they are children. They are fools. Even the educated ones." He paused a moment and added, "Especially the educated ones. They don't know what's real."

His eyes grew watery and dim. "When I was a boy in Italy," he told her, his voice thin, its rhythms moving in cadence to her bobbing head, "we never had all this shit. Dirty air, filthy water, traffic jams, people unhappy all the time. We laughed and we fought. We sang songs and ate fresh fish. We had figs growing in the back yard and I drank goat's milk for breakfast. We lived near the sea, and in those days the sea was clean, the water sparkled. We swam every afternoon. And then there was the wine, and the bread fresh from the oven, and the stars at night, and making love in the hay. Oh, what a time that was! Every week we celebrated the birthday of some saint, and we even had a priest to remind us that there are higher things in the world than man. It wasn't like this pig pen, where the people roll around in garbage and think they are the kings of creation."

He sighed and gave himself over to the sensations produced by the friction of her delicate tongue around the tip of his cock. She swept forward and took the rod into her throat, held it until she gagged, and pulled back. There was something about the old man's calm, his quiet voice, which pacified her, nullified her initial feeling of distaste. The thing in her mouth was iron-hard, and gnarled like a De Nobili cigar. Sucking it was like sucking her thumb when she was a child; it was relaxing, easy, with the single difference that this experience was raked by spasms of such tingling sexuality that her toes curled. Despite her desire to remain detached, she had found herself blowing him with mounted excitement.

"But my stupid mother," he went on, "may the devil stick hot pitchforks in her ass, wanted to go to America. 'The streets are paved with gold,' she kept saying, until my poor father finally gave in, sold the farm, and moved us all here. There was no gold. Just misery, and poverty, and filth. And even if there had been gold, what good would it have been? You can't eat gold, it won't keep you warm at night, it has no love."

He beat his fist against the arm of the chair he was sitting in.

"That's what's wrong with this country," he shouted, "there is no love here."

He put his hands on her hair. "Lick it at the tip," he said, and for a few moments he did nothing but watch as she lapped the glistening tool, and paid attention to the fluctuations of pleasure brought by each movement of her tongue.

"But an animal learns to survive wherever it is," he said after a while. "My father bought a grocery store, and we started a new life. It wasn't long before we were paid a visit by the Honored Society, and when I compared their methods of doing business and their success to my father's way of life, well, the choice was obvious. There's no point trying to be honest in the city; it's all based on lies anyway. I became a member of the Family, and today I am don of all the dons."

It struck the girl for the first time that the man whose cock she was sucking was perhaps the most powerful man she might ever meet. Most of her time was spent with fifteen-dollar-a-throw longshoremen, and while she wasn't destitute, she was far from any real financial comfort. The fact that she had been offered five hundred dollars for a few hours of work was astonishing in itself; that it was being paid by the highest Mafia chief in the country was almost too much for her to assimilate.

She had no way of knowing his reasons for picking her, that when he was nineteen he had been struck with an overpowering infatuation for a blue-eyed auburn-haired Irish girl whose fair skin made his dark Mediterranean blood boil. But when, after much trepidation, he had approached her, she had laughed at him, calling him a "spaghetti-stuffed garlic eater." Of course, he had shot her and thrown her body in the East River, but even that was not compensation enough for his wounded pride, and over a thousand times afterward, he had had his men scour the entire eastern seaboard for young Irish girls that he could subject to the – to his mind – degrading ritual of cock-sucking.

"The mayor, he thinks he runs the city," the old man continued. "But all he does is prance around and look pretty. Nobody with any real power listens to him. He's somebody to put in front of the television cameras so the cattle think their vote means something. No, it's the ones who control the life systems and the death systems who are in command, only most of them are so stupid, they don't realize it yet.

"Look at the police. Some of the commanders are beginning to figure out that they have thirty-thousand men, armed with hand guns, and with access to machine guns, horses, tear gas, tanks, grenades. But if they made a move, they'd have the state militia to contend with, and the federal government. They'll have to lie low until the whole nation is falling apart in chaos.

"But they are only the most obvious candidates. Think of the firemen who can allow the city to burn, or perhaps even burn it themselves. And the garbagemen, who only strike for higher wages, but could consolidate as a political force, threatening to let plague conditions arise if their demands weren't met. Still, none of these people have any political awareness."

The girl continued sucking. He had put his hands on the back of her head and was guiding her by imparting a momentum to her motions. She let her lips go slack and allowed his cock to bob in and out of her mouth, her tongue licking it each time it entered and each it left. She had begun to have fantasies that he might want her as his private whore, and drew pictures in her mind of a swank apartment, a complete wardrobe, a sports car, charge accounts, and trips to Puerto Rico in the winter. She dropped her reserve and worked up a feverish pleasure in what she was doing, giving herself up to wanton expressions, hoping he would be taken by the masks of lasciviousness she wore. The old man had seen all of this before.

"And even they don't strike at the heart of things," he went on. "Who controls the drinking water, the water to put out fires? Did you ever give a second thought to all those men you see climbing in and out of sewers? Everybody looks down on them, but no one stops to consider that they have access to switches which control the city's vital fluid. While the mayor makes speeches for the newspapers, grimy men with wrenches hold our destiny in their hands.

"But it doesn't end there. You can almost hear the people from Con Ed smirking. Do you remember the night of the great blackout? That was just a test to see if it could be done. It was fun for a few hours, but what would happen after a few days and nights without electricity? Suck it, Irish, suck it! No lights anywhere. Traffic snarled because the traffic lights didn't work. Refrigerators useless, food spoiling. No radio, no television, no elevators, no subways. We would be plunged back into the Stone

Age in no time. Bands would form. The gun and the knife would
be the law. And not too many would survive.

"And there are other possibilities," he said, waving his hands
through the air. "Radicals blowing up the bridges, tunnels,
subway tracks. Or the telephone company, operating the central
nerve cord that runs through all city life. It is the indispensable
tool of business, and without it business would fold. And without
business, there is no New York."

He was approaching orgasm. The moment of climax was still
five minutes away, but he could sense its beginning. With his
body as calm as it was, he was able to give himself to sensation
without tension, and thus truly savor the long deep swell which
preceded ejaculation. Capable of dispensing with any consideration of the girl except as a tool for his pleasure, he could devote his
undivided attention to his inner state.

"But not one of them suspects the overwhelmingly obvious
truth as to what real power is." His voice held a tremor of
excitement, partially from the growing heat in his loins, partially
from the impact of articulating his vision. "And that is with *me*,"
he continued, "because the one thing they all have to do is *live
here*! They must *spend their time here*. And I'm the one who
decides what kind of place they get to stay in. No matter who's in
command, no matter what form of government, no matter what
the state of the economy, the most important reality of the city is
its environment. And what makes the environment is the architecture. And I control the architecture."

His voice purred. "I'll make sure there is nothing left but
concrete. Mile after mile of living earth has already been covered
up, suffocated, and giant stone buildings loom where trees used
to grow. There is almost nothing natural left. Most plant life has
been destroyed, most animal life, most insect life. The people
have nothing left but hard surfaces to walk on, to sit on, to lie on,
to look at. Even the sky is hard to see. They are allowed some few
cats and dogs and horses, and the pitiful specimens they put in
the concrete prisons they call zoos. But that is all. And soon, even
they will disappear. The pigeons will be killed. Only rats and
roaches will remain. Rats and roaches and people.

"And as they become sicker and sicker, more and more confused and unhappy, they will never begin to guess what their
trouble is, that's how unbelievably ignorant they are. They will

blame the mayor, they will blame the police chief, they will blame drugs and permissive education. They will revolt, they will change leaders. They will try everything. But the obvious will never occur to them, that they are slowly dying, being killed by the lack of life around them. They will go to their graves as blind as blind as when they were alive. And I shall win, I shall build everywhere. Cement will rule the earth!"

As he said the last words his thighs tensed and a voluminous spurt of sperm burst into the girl's mouth. She went through all the motions of swallowing it as though it were some kind of nectar, hoping to please the old man with her gusto. But the instant after he came he pushed her away, stared into her face for a moment, and shook his head to deny the memory which refused to let him rest.

"Go suck the boys in the back room," he said.

She began to protest, caught up in a swirling disappointment, but a glint in his eyes told her she had better not say a word. She stood up, licked a few drops of semen form her lips, and petulantly walked towards the door, her buttocks jiggling as she went, to the back room where seven men sat around a wide table playing cards. She would be told to crawl under the table, and go from cock to cock until she had done them all, and then be bundled out into the street, a half a thousand dollars and several insights richer.

The old man buttoned his pants and walked to the window. The city was practically invisible because of the thickly polluted air. Even from his great height he could hear the infernal roar, the din of triumphant machinery. Everywhere cars chugged like ancient beasts, spewing gases in their wake, and at a thousand sites the relentless momentum of construction, more and taller buildings rising to occupy even the samllest bit of free space. And through all this the people walked, their ears shattered by the noises, their nostrils pinched against the stench, their entire bodies incessantly punished by the crunch of crystallized finance. Seem from above, the scene resembled nothing so much as a *danse macabre* of zombies, hulks whose souls had long since been sucked dry.

"I will have revenge on you," he muttered, "for fooling my mother that there could be a good life here, for taking my father away from his land and causing him to die in an unheated tenement, away from the sea and the sky, and for forcing me to become such an evil man to survive. I will destroy you, and my children shall destroy your entire nation. Just by giving you what you want, more cement, more concrete, more steel. To cover the beautiful earth, to tear down the forests, to poison the lakes and the rivers.

"And for what? To build these human garbage dumps, these cities. To construct highways and bridges and dams and all the stupid structures that you worship."

He laughed, a horrible creaking sound.

"I will give you what you want, America," he shouted. "I will give you *progress*. And it will take you straight into the mouth of hell."

CIRCUS OF JADE

BUTCH MEDUSA LAY amidst the pile of bodies. There were eleven other women in the heap, the result of the most ambitious project she had yet undertaken. The group contained representatives of each of the world's races, and was a palette of wildly complementary skin colors and hair textures. Both tall and short were there, as well as fat and thin. Each of the women was from one of the sun signs of the Zodiac, and Butch had personally tested and tasted all of them for copiousness and flavor of vaginal secretions. But now, after all the drugs and music, after the hours of flirtation and foreplay, after the weeks of preparation and expectation, as asses and cunts and mouths and breasts and feet rolled and flashed in a continuous panorama of sensuality, Butch had to admit that she was bored.

"This orgy has no socially redeeming value," she said to herself as a lithe Ethiopian sword-dancer sucked one of her nipples between her lips. Loath as she was to admit it, Butch had come to the end of a cycle and was unwilling to garner the energy to break into a new phase.

She had begun her career one night by sweeping into a lesbian bar dressed in a suit of chain mail and carrying a mace. The place was instantly polarized, the more strident exponents of the new female image finding her intolerably outré, while the lustier women flocked to her side, glad that at least one person was still ready to champion unfashionable stereotypes. For five years subsequent to her coming out, she had run amok in the ultra-sophisticated circles of post-decadent tribadism, imparting a quality of aesthetic ruthlessness to a life style that had been foundering in sterile polemics. Among her vassals were many daughters of the wealthy, and she had no difficulty producing the money she needed to support her rampant metatheater.

The thought she had been suppressing for months now came to the surface of her consciousness. "To do what I want to do, I really need some cocks."

She blew a whistle and the writhing mass of bodies quivered once and fell still. She leapt to her feet, breasts jiggling.

"Sweet Sappho's pussy," she yelled, "is this the best you can manage? If I want choreography I'll find a bunch of fags. I want passion, goddamnit. And reaching behind her, she picked up a fourteen-foot bull whip with which she began to flay the women lying in front of her.

"What do I have to do to get some *feeling* around here?" she shouted, and laid about her with the thick ugly leather instrument.

The cries she extracted, however, were only bleats of pain, and she was no longer interested in mere sadomasochism, having had her fill one afternoon when she flogged three virgins into insensibility on the secluded grounds of a Connecticut estate an admirer had put at her disposal. She threw the whip down in disgust and went to her study to ponder.

"It's not their fault," she thought, "they're doing the best they know how. It's just that there's no sense of purpose." She lit a joint and settled back on her zebra-skin watercouch. Plunging into a deep trance, she found many of the fragments of a vision that had been haunting her coming into place. It was an idea so compelling that she hesitated even to think about it. But she was hungry for challenge, and within an hour knew what she had to do.

"It won't be easy." she mused, "finding the men I need for the job. The gays are free enough, but they don't really want to fuck women. And I have to have both male and female energy for the project. The straights are so crippled I couldn't even put an honest proposition to most of them. Aren't there any lovers left? Men who are pliable enough to take orders from a woman one moment and then throw her down and rip off a piece of ass the next? I need men with firm bodies and warm hearts, men with hard cocks and clear minds, men with fire in their blood and mercury in their egos. Where will I find them?"

The next day began a quest which was to take her over the entire nation and last for almost a year. She put her affairs in order and left a skeleton crew behind to answer her mail and maintain her Park Avenue duplex. And then she began her search.

The technique she used was simple. Whenever she saw a man she sensed was ripe for plucking, she would walk up to him and say, clearly and directly, "Would you like to fuck me?"

If he answered too quickly or was thrown into confusion, she abandoned him at once. She wouldn't consider any man who wasn't together enough to assimilate her approach instantaneously, take a moment to breathe and look at her, peer into her eyes and appraise her body, and respond from the core of some real impulse.

Those who passed the first screening were taken to her hotel room and allowed to fuck her. And as the man went through his motions, she registered impressions of his total being. If, at the end of the first fuck, she still thought he had potential, she would outline her scheme and offer him room and board to work with her. After she had hired her first helper, of course, the game became trickier, for the ensuing prospects would be confronted not only with a woman's asking him what no other woman had probably ever asked before, never so honestly and openly, but also with the man standing next to her.

At the end of three months she had found four men.

The movement began to grow interesting as a spirit of camaraderie seized the group. It was the first time Butch had seen America and was amazed at how much of it was still unspoiled by urbanization. In Santa Fe she picked up a deaf mute, and she took her band into the surrounding hills for a retreat.

That night Butch found herself lying naked on her back, bent over a bedroll, as the men played poker and drank coffee around a fire. Every once in a while one of them would stroll over to fuck her. For her part, it was pleasant to enjoy the cool night air and look at the stars, letting her mind drift, to have her revery interrupted only by the sweet penetration of a cock or by a mouth on one of her breasts or by a hand under her buttocks.

The men, on their part, enjoyed a kind of friendship almost impossible for men to know any longer. Free from financial worries, they could allow themselves to relax. With a woman they could fuck at any time they wanted, they were liberated from sexual tension. And since they all shared the same woman under the same conditions, they had no cause for jealousy, and the bond among them grew unhampered. And it was just the strength of the bond that Butch relied upon for the realization of her vision.

At the end of a year she had gathered seventeen men and returned to the city. The power of their circle was enormous and she was ready to try the next level of operation. She got back in late August, a month before the beginning of the New York season, and started her preparations at once.

First came the costuming. The men were all dressed alike, with short leather skirts, gold earrings in their right ears, and jade bracelets on their left wrists. She led esoteric psychophysical exercises and dances to coordinate their reflexes and cement their sense of unity. She gave lectures to pinpoint her objective. During that period they were allowed no sex so their lust would build.

And when they were at a fine edge, she brought in a victim for them to practice on, a nineteen-year-old debutante, slim, auburn haired, with only a handful of fucks in her experience and a literary infatuation with lesbian love. Butch picked her up at one of the consciousness-raising sessions that have superseded bars as cruising grounds, ravished her for an entire night, and primed her for the experience of being had by a band of men. Half hypnotized, half yearning to live out a fantasy she had been barely able to admit to herself, she agreed to cooperate.

"It's a shame to have to destroy her," Butch thought, "but the men have to be forged into a seamless unit, and only a ritual murder will really do the trick. Besides, once she is really opened up, it would be impossible for her to live in the world anyway."

The night of the affair, after the girl was fucked for the fifty-third time, the last edge of her resistance to madness cracked, and for the next five hours she screamed herself hoarse, pleading for more. "Fuck me, fuck me, fuck me," she shouted over and over again, a hundred times, a thousand times, ten thousand times, the skin of inhibition totally torn and the well of her inexhaustible sexuality yielding its waters.

Finally, Butch dispatched her cleanly, a single bullet through the temple, snuffing out the torment that had its roots in ecstasy, in the eternal restlessness of the flesh.

"This is the power we are going to tap," Butch told the men who looked at the corpse with wide eyes. "We have just begun to unleash the limitless force of sexual energy. When we can control that force and harness the power of the orgasm, we will have a weapon which will reduce all the atomic stockpiles on Earth to the status of toys. And then we shall impose peace on the world. But first, we have to get rid of the body."

Butch called on her reserve army of women, and found an equal number to match the men. There was another month of intense preparation, and then she was ready for her first test: the formation of a sexual cyclotron.

The women all knelt in a circle, their asses up and away from the center, while the men crouched behind them, their cocks at the openings of the cunts. Butch lay in the center, her head pointing north. At her signal, the men all entered the women at once, and began fucking with slow regular strokes. The women held hands all around, as did the men, so that from above, at a Busby Berkeley angle, the whole thing looked like a jellyfish pulsating at the edges. And at the brain of the superorganism was Butch Medusa, coursing all the vibrations through herself. The rhythm increased as a group consciousness began to form. Everyone was aware of the state of everyone else's being.

Gradually, control shifted from the individuals to the group as a whole. A power emerged that was greater than the ability of any single person to claim. It began to take over by itself, reducing the men and women to units in a conglomerate. Unity was achieved through adherence to the dictates of the over-soul.

Orgasm approached, a single orgasm which included the bodies of everyone in the circle. The men joined through their arms, the women joined through cock and cunt, all eyes on the body in the center, all minds empty of thoughts, and Butch gathering all the energy in a single sustained awareness, they came together. And at that instant, Butch was buoyed by a sheet of blue light and lifted six feet off the floor. She hovered for eight minutes and then drifted slowly back down to the rug.

For that period of time, through the city, all hostility in every human being was allayed. Policemen stopped with their fingers on the trigger, husbands and wives stopped mid-argument, taxi drivers stopped with curses on their lips. Not one violent act was committed. Everyone was enveloped in a euphoric cloud, and for weeks afterward scientists speculated as to whether some electronic mass hysteria was the cause. Many found grounds to reaffirm their faith in God. Some claimed that extraterrestrial beings were influencing the earth.

The group was giddy with success, but Butch calmed them down. "We can't go too fast," she warned. "Too much joy all at once would destroy the fabric of every civilization in the world. People would revert to their simple animal state. Governments would collapse. And the havoc that followed would mean the death of millions. Let them get used to happiness little by little. And meanwhile, we can increase our numbers. One day we'll be able to sustain the effect indefinitely, and then we can open all the switches and fuck the species into survival."

The plan might have worked except for an unforeseen event. Butch Medusa fell in love. She met a man who filled her with all the inane and irresistible feeling such as used to propel teenagers into romantic raptures. The rational part of her realized that to give in to her emotions would destroy the final chance humanity might have to keep from going over the brink into total ruin. But she was helpless before the mood of surrender.

"It's what I get for fooling around with all those cocks," she said to herself bitterly. "Such a fate would never have befallen me if I had stayed a lesbian. This is what I get for trying to do good."

The man was not the kind who would tolerate her unbridled promiscuity, so she abandoned her commune. She moved to Long Island, where he worked as a professor of sociology at Stony Brook College. She had three children and spent her days at war with herself, hating the fact that she really enjoyed her new situation. She never spoke of her past even when the women in her bridge club began to talk about sex, revealing their fantasies and infidelities. Everyone thought her a model wife, which indeed she was.

The people in the duplex, without the unifying power of her vision, soon degenerated into a crowd of rowdy low-level orgiasts. The neighbors started to complain, and one night the place was raided. They were all booked on charges of indecent behavior, given suspended sentences, and told to leave the city. The body of the girl who had been shot had been smuggled out and buried on Staten Island, and thus was never found.

BOWEL BOOGIE

ONLY HER BODY was tied down; she could still move her head and look around the room.

It was ten feet high by ten feet wide by ten feet long. It was constructed entirely of tile. There was a vent in the ceiling to let in air, and a vent in the floor to let water drain out. A spout jutted from one wall, and over it was a shelf with various instruments.

She was chained to a table built of soft stone, held utterly immobile. Her wrists were manacled at her sides, a steel band went over her waist, and her feet were fastened to raised stirrups so that her legs were lifted and spread apart. She took a deep breath and closed her eyes.

The door opened slowly, a thick wooden partition with sound-proof slats cemented to both sides. The doctor stepped in. He was one of the world's foremost therapists, having written a book called *The Secondary Stutter*, in which he traced all neurosis to the suppression of embarrassment people feel when farting. He closed the door behind him and beamed on the woman.

"Well, Ms Schneider," he said in a booming voice, "how good to meet you."

She looked up and gasped. The man wore hip boots, a long raincoat, and rubber gloves. His face was covered with a black mask. She had been told that he would want to remain anonymous, but it hadn't occurred to her that he would hide more than his name. The social worker at the clinic she had applied to for psychotherapy had explained that she might partake of an experimental program without charge, and in addition to having her difficulties cleared up, would be helping the march of science in its striving to obliterate all mental illness. She was told that the treatment would have to remain secret and that she would not know who would be treating her, in order to protect him from lawsuits. Ms Schneider had had her doubts, but she felt in desperate need of help, and couldn't afford to pay for it, so she agreed.

He walked over to the table. "Before we begin," he said, his voice deep and reassuring. "I'm sure you will have a few questions. But first I'd like to tell you a little about what we'll be doing."

The woman shifted her weight and he glanced at her through the narrow slits of his disguise. She was thirty-nine, worked as an elementary school teacher, and had never been married. Her body was slim, the flesh still firm. Uneventful legs blossomed into arched buttocks, and small breasts nicely graced her upper chest. Her pubic hair was sparse and her outer cunt lips were folded against each other like hands clasped in prayer.

"To put it most directly," he began, "my work is not a departure from, but the most recent development of, the psychoanalytic discoveries of Sigmund Freud. You've heard of Freud? The orthodox analysts would have me tarred and feathered if they knew what I was doing, but mostly because they are afraid to face the logical conclusions of their own theories. That is why I must say nothing about my work until I can prove that my technique is effective."

The woman opened her mouth to speak but he cut in before she could say a word. "Although I subsume the work of all the men and women who have gone before me, my approach is original, a totally new synthesis. And beyond the theoretical correctness is the fact that my technique is *absolute*." His voice rang with a strange vibration, sounding hollow beneath the mask. "You see, that has been the problem. All the great minds have understood neurosis and formulated their theories, but none of them could come up with a cure that would work in all cases. And this is to be my immortal contribution. The infallible cure for all mental and emotional disturbances."

He began pacing, but since the room was so small and the table took up the central space, he was forced to walk in a circle around the woman's body. She attempted to follow him with her eyes as he prowled. "The discovery of my technique, as with that of penicillin, was accidental. All the elements were present, and I just happened to be there to put them together. I remember the afternoon well, I had just finished reading the passage in *Function of the Orgasm* where Reich describes his basic insight into masochism. He found that what the masochist really seeks is the feeling of bursting open, of having his energy flow outward, through his armored self. The masochist doesn't enjoy pain itself, but hopes to find a release in pain.

"That was on my mind when I opened my mail and found a brochure from the Eulenspiegel Society, an organization composed of sadists and masochists dedicated to erasing prejudices about their condition. I was struck by the way in which life is always struggling to express itself in a positive fashion, even when it passes through what must seem like terrible aberrations.

"It was just then I felt the first peristaltic wave that signals a bowel movement. I went into the bathroom, closing the door behind me. As I turned the knob, however, I realized that there was no one else in the house! I was thunderstruck. My shame at such a basic biological activity was so deep that it led me to the most absurb behavior, closing the door against the censure of society when no other member of society was even present. I sat down and my eyes moved idly across the wall opposite and fell upon my wife's douche bag which hung from a hook. I don't know how to describe that moment. Choirs sang, and the room filled with light. It all came together in a crescendo of truth."

He stopped pacing and grabbed one of the woman's ankles tightly. "Do you see?" he said, his voice brimming with emotion. "Does it begin to make sense now?"

The woman thought he was stark raving mad. She did what people in rising panic often do, and reached into the recent past to recall the last moments of normality she could remember. The clinic was a highly respected institution, so when the nurse had asked her to remove her clothing and had fastened her to the table, there was still some sense of being connected to the workaday world, even though the trappings were bizarre. Ms Schneider had a fully conditioned faith in public organizations, and she drew on that to counter the brunt of her perception that she was helpless in a locked room with a maniac peering down at her naked body.

"I don't think I want to continue with this," she bleated.

"Ah ha!" he shouted. "That's the point. Very few people do. All other therapies have failed simply because at the point of greatest resistance the therapist allowed the patient to leave. I will change all that. My vision demands it. People must be saved in spite of themselves. That's the whole issue with neurosis. And nothing except my technique has any chance of curing neurosis, and of ultimately saving the world. Nothing else includes all the necessary elements. Bringing forth childhood repressions, it will allow that feeling of bursting so you will stop shrinking from life, and it will put you in touch with your need and your pain. It will allow you your full range of expression, and plumb to the core of your sexual nature. It will attack your most deep-seated inhibition, the one which grows from the cornerstone contribution of our civilization to the world, early toilet training."

The woman started to protest that none of this seemed connected to the relatively uncomplicated problems she had been dealing with, but he seemed to read her mind. "Your unhappiness is felt by you in one way, but its causes are beyond your awareness. You will see. You will fight me because I will show you your true self. You will scream, you will hate, you will cry, you will yearn, you will surrender, and you will win. You will have a total experience and for the first time in your life you will come alive. And nothing or no one will prevent you from achieving your goal, least of all yourself. I won't let you stop yourself from becoming healthy. I will force the neurosis out of you."

He reached to the shelf behind him and picked up a long hose with a plastic nozzle. "Ms Schneider," he said, "you have the honor to be the first patient to try the most revolutionary treatment in the history of psychology: Enema Therapy."

The woman sobbed openly. She could not believe that she had allowed things to go so far, that she hadn't stopped when she saw the room, or when the nurse tied her to the table.

"I don't want to," she cried out to the doctor.

"Of course you don't," he said cheerfully, attaching the hose to the spigot on the wall. "At least, the superficial part of you doesn't. But the deeper part, the part that brought you to seek help in the first place, is calling for help, and help it shall get."

He brought the nozzle level with the table top. He fingered some Vaseline from a jar on the shelf and delicately applied it to the woman's anus.

"No," she keened, now almost totally out of control.

"You'll see, you'll see," he crooned.

He placed the nozzle between her clenched buttocks and gently pushed, inserting it fully into her body. She tried to squirm away but was held too tightly. Her thighs bulged with tension. The doctor stepped back and viewed his handiwork.

"No matter what happens," he said, "just remember one thing: no physical harm can come to you here. Your own worse enemy is tied securely to the table. You may go insane for a while, but that's the only way to reach true sanity. There can be no reconstitution without regression, that's my motto."

He reached behind him and, taking a few seconds to appreciate the historic import of the moment, he turned the handle, beginning the flow of water into Ms Schneider's ass.

She filled up for almost twenty minutes. As the hot fluid entered her, she began to howl. Again and again she reached a point where she thought she could take no more and begged him to stop, but he was implacable. "It's all been measured ahead of time," he would say. Pain enveloped her in waves, giving way to a peculiar kind of pleasure, a sort of tingling release. She tried to back away from the nozzle, but her body was fixed in place. The doctor got an erection, watching her thrash about, her cunt winking lewdly above the phallic nozzle, but he maintained professional discipline and his stiff cock did not show beneath the heavy raincoat.

He maintained stoic composure. Even when she seemed on the brink of collapse, ready to faint or actually pass away, he never lost the necessary faith in his treatment. She was like a film shown by a berserk projector, her body threatening to burst as it yielded thousands upon thousands of repressed memories and feelings and thoughts locked in her muscles and brain cells. It was like a seven-year analysis gone through at the speed of sound, and with total abreaction. Her frame shuddered like a test plane in a wind tunnel. And she reached a state of such complete energy expansion that her hair stood on end, rising two feet from her scalp.

Finally, he turned the water off. It had begun to seep out around the edges of the nozzle and he knew that she was filled to the brim. When she felt the stoppage of flow, there was a momentary relief, but with astounding swiftness he pulled the nozzle out and stuck in a stopper, corking her as neatly as a wine bottle.

"Oh God," she wailed.

"We are going to remain like this for a little while," he said. "The first phase is over, and you have survived the initial trauma. Now the real work begins, for you will no longer be able to hide behind your freneticism and hysteria. In this treatment, all the masks of defense must be stripped and you must face your actual condition. We must go on until you are literally incapable of sustaining your experience, and your mind shatters with trying to rationalize it all. Then the unconscious will be liberated and the basic structural changes can take place in your character."

The following five hours were chaotic. She became feverish and then snapped into lucidity. She fell asleep and had bloated dreams. She babbled out loud. She tried again and again to expel the cork and push out the fluid, but was thrown back into helplessness. She entered the death state. For a while, she was raked with erotic flashes, and at one point began to grind her hips up toward the ceiling, running her tongue over her lips and moaning until she had an orgasm.

Occasionally the doctor added more water to replace what had been absorbed through the colon. Some of the sounds that ripped from her throat would have melted the heart of Satan himself, but the therapist was unshakeable.

"I must help her see it through," he said to himself. A lifetime of work was culminating in this experiment, and not only his reputation but his deepest definition of self was at stake. He hated neurosis the way a saint hates sin. His hope to rescue the world from destruction was wild enough to tax the limits of his rational mind, but some more primitive center within him goaded him on.

"The enema," he thought, "our only hope is in the enema."

He watched, waiting for the sign that the treatment was complete. He did not know what form it would take, but had unmoveable faith that she would come out the other side of her heightened anguish and go on into a life of freedom. All the while she seemed to be in the throes of unbearable suffering, radical internal changes were taking place, and he could do nothing but wait.

Finally, a profound shudder went through her. She had come to the end of her metamorphosis. Her soul had been scrubbed clean and brought to its basic grain. She was utterly naked. A lifetime of overlay had loosened and now floated inside her. Her characterological tensions had been dissolved and there was no portion of her mind which was any longer unknown to her.

"I've done it," he whispered, "I've accomplished in a few hours what therapists take years to do. She is cured. I can see it."

At that instant, the woman let out a wail that was indistinguishable from the cry a baby lets out right after birth.

"Love," the woman said, "I want love."

The doctor's eyes stung with tears. The woman had contacted the core of her being and been reborn. His approach was vindicated. He took a deep breath, and with a sweeping gesture, he pulled the plug.

She gushed for an eternity. Jet after jet of water burst from her. She vibrated with the release of all her sickness, the literal and metaphoric shit she had been keeping inside her. The brown fluid splashed on the walls over the floor, ran down the therapist's raincoat, poured down the drain.

"Free," he shouted, "you are free," and turned on the spigot again, this time to play the hose in a stream over her body as he undid her locks and chains. She sprang up from the table, pulsing with the river of new life that filled her, with the cosmic energy that was once more a part of her heritage. He put down the hose and the woman stood in front of him, her face radiant with happiness, a blue aura shining around her head.

"I don't know what to say," she said, "everything is . . . different now."

"I understand," he replied.

"I didn't realize how afraid I was. Not only on the table, but for my whole life. Afraid of everyone and everything. Why, I even used to be afraid to cross the street!"

She got dressed and the two of them talked in his office for a while. After removing his mask he proved to be a pleasant-looking man in his early fifties.

"Come back tomorrow," he said. "I want to take some psychological tests and tape your account of your experience. I'm going to present this to the world."

After she left, as he sat in silent enjoyment of his accomplishment, he heard a screech outside his window, followed by a hubbub of voices. Crossing the street bravely, the woman had been hit by a bus and was killed instantly. He rushed out. As he stood over her body a small tic developed at the edge of his mouth.

"It's always more complicated than one thinks," he muttered as he went back inside the clinic where he sat at his desk and began scribbling furiously in his notebook.

PRAY ON ME

"Bless me Father, for I have sinned."

"Yes, go ahead."

"It is the same. I have been looking at the Mother Superior again."

The priest sighed.

"Did it arouse you?" he asked.

The Pope looked up. "Arouse?" he repeated. "I'm almost eighty years old. I haven't been aroused since World War II."

"Then why do you keep going there?"

The old man shook his head. "I don't know," he said sadly. "I just find it compelling."

The confessor put his hand over his forehead. He was a Jesuit monsignor who had, after two years of special training, been given the delicate task of hearing the Pope's confessions. He could still remember the talk his own superior had given him on the first day he began his new duty. The head of The Society of Jesus, the man they called "The Black Pope," had impressed the seriousness of the task upon him.

"The Holy Father is the voice of God," he had said, "but he is also a man, subject to the same weaknesses which tempt all of us. You must not let his high office intimidate you. In the confessional you must treat him as you would any other sinner." Then he had leaned forward and whispered, "Should he let fall any bit of information which might be useful to *our* cause . . ." he began. The monsignor had jumped up in fright. "You are not suggesting that I break the seal of the confessional!" he exclaimed. "Of course not," said the superior, "but there is a difference between breaking and bending. I only suggest that you learn to bend, lest you yourself break. Or," he added, squinting meaningfully, "be broken."

"I curse the day I ever discovered that secret passageway," the Pope went on. "I searched the records and discovered it was Alexander the Second who had it built. And it was designed by Leonardo himself." He groaned as he recalled the night he reached for a rarely used book in the library of his private bedroom and discovered, deep in the corner of the shelf, a small switch. He pulled the lever and a small door opened at the back of the fireplace. Crouching, he entered, and found a candle that must have been made a hundred years earlier. He followed the tunnel for half a mile until he reached a narrow flight of stairs leading to a small platform. Standing on the ledge, he saw a space with two tiny discs hung from thin chains. He moved the bits of metal and was stuck by twin arrows of yellow light.

They proceeded from holes which opened into the bedroom of the Mother Superior of the order of nuns that serviced the Vatican, providing its cooks, cleaning women, and other menial servants. From the other side, the holes would not be noticed, since they were in the eyeballs of a painting of Saint Francis of Assisi, a huge masterpiece done by Michaelangelo, totally unknown to the outside world, and one of thousands of priceless art works casually strewn about the hallways of the global center of Christianity.

Peering through the holes, the Pope had looked upon a strange scene. The chief nun was lying on her cot, her knees up, her thighs trembling, her breasts heaving, her face a mask of joyful anguish, as with her hooked fingers she told the beads of her rosary. Her voice, as she recited the Ave Marias and Pater Nosters, rose and fell, at times almost indistinguishable from a deep moan. The Pope had scratched his head.

"If she wasn't saying the rosary," he thought, "I would swear she was having an orgasm."

He had looked in on her dozens of times after that. He had no way of telling what was going on in her mind, what baroque images cascaded upon her seared soul like scalding sperm from a celestial cock. It was several months before it occurred to him that he might, in some obscure way, be committing a sin. He told the story to his confessor who advised sealing up the tunnel, thus removing the temptation.

"But why do that unless what I'm doing is a sin?" the Pope argued. He did not want to stop his visits since they provided him with the only private excitement in an otherwise totally public life. Yet, he could not be at peace about them. Again and again he would kneel in the confessional and state, "I've been watching Sister Angela pray again."

They decided that since no sexual excitement was involved, and since the Pope had not had an erection for several decades, there could be no sin of lust. Individually and together they searched the lists of transgressions, going through the thousands upon thousands of thoughts, actions, and intentions which the Church had labelled as sin and for which a person could, with no qualms, be condemned to Hell. But not a single one seemed to cover the act of a Pope watching a nun say the rosary, despite the unorthodox way in which the prayer was said. They talked about mentioning the matter to the nun herself, but reasoned that if she were acting in innocence, their words might only raise scruples in her mind.

"If there's no rule in the books that says it's wrong, then why should I stop doing it?" the Pope asked.

"Why do you feel guilty about it?" rejoined the monsignor.

"Can't you advise me any better than that? You're my confessor."

"Well, you're the Pope," the monsignor answered, "why don't you ask God for advice?"

"I don't believe in God," the Pope said.

The priest felt as though he had been struck on the nose with a rubber mallet. "You too?" he said. "I thought I was the only priest who didn't believe in God."

"Nobody really believes in God," the Pope went on.

"Then why do we continue to do all this?" the confessor asked, his question taking in all of Catholicism.

"Well," the Pontiff drawled, his hands describing an arc in an Italianate gesture that seemed to subsume all the weariness of civilization, "this isn't such a bad job. We get enough to eat, a place to sleep, nice clothes to wear. And we don't have to knock ourselves out. I mean, it's not like digging ditches. You know what I mean?" He winked and nudged the monsignor in the ribs. "It's all a big game."

"But if you don't believe in God, why do you make such a fuss over your confessions?" The younger man was perplexed by the turn of events.

"Just because there's no God doesn't mean there's no sin," the Pope said. "A man still has to decide what's wrong and what's right for him. And he has to live by that if he is to respect himself at all. I bring these things up in confession because you seem like a sensible person and I enjoy talking to you." He stood up and walked to the window overlooking an immense, perfectly manicured garden. "I never cease being surprised at finding myself here," he said, his voice somewhat distant. "I was raised as a peasant. Becoming a priest was the easiest way to excape the drudgery of the farm. My promotions all took me by surprise, and by the time I was a bishop I realized that I was just a marker in the sweep of history, chosen by some quirk of destiny to rise to high office. When I was elected Pope I was no longer amazed."

He turned to face the monsignor, a gleam in his eye. "But the ones who gave me the office have had ample opportunity to wonder whether I am their ecclesiastic frankenstein monster. We all know that this complex of cathedrals is nothing but an elaborate stage set, and our daily rituals an empty charade. But I am the first to openly suggest it verbally, and they are beginning to worry. And the Council I convened is only the start."

The Pope went back and knelt on the *prie dieu* once more. "Since we are under the seal of confessional," he went on, "I can tell you something. A plan to completely overshadow what has gone before."

The monsignor blinked.

"Listen," the Pope told him. "I'm going to announce that on Easter Sunday of next year, I will issue my final dogma, *ex cathedra*. I will send a call throughout the world that I will speak from my highest spiritual authority and deliver a message directly from God Himself. I will advertise it for almost a year. I will say I have had a vision, a visitation from the Throne of Heaven, and on the given day, I will open the gates of Rome to the world. I will ask the heads of state to gather in the Vatican, and call in the leaders of all the religions of man. I will use radio and television. Saint Peter's will blaze in all its Renaissance glory, with lights, candles, torches, incense. The full Swiss Guard on display. The College of Cardinals, dressed in their finest livery, in attendance. And me on my most sumptuous throne, bedecked in gold and emeralds and diamonds and rubies. I will wear the Triple Crown on my head, and carry the mitre which signifies me as first among all the bishops of the earth. I will say High Mass and have a dozen choirs perform the most perfect works by Palestrina. And when all is prepared I will say the following:

God has spoken to me from the bosom of His infinite and mysterious wisdom. He desires an end to all false divisions between man and man. To this end, He declares all religions null and void. He will answer no prayer that is not spoken in absolute silence and privacy. As the Pope, obedient to His wishes, I hereby dissolve the Catholic Church, and urge all my fellow churchmen of rival faiths to do the same with their religions. Let us abolish formal religion in order to return to God. I speak this as an official pronouncement and declare that any Catholic who continues to profess himself or herself as a Catholic is automatically excommunicated from the Catholic Church which, from this moment on, doesn't exist any longer anyway.

The monsignor stared at the old man. "You're really going to do that?" he asked.

"Sure," said the Pope cheerfully, "why not? The trend is toward unity. And the best way to unify the world is to do away with all these silly religious organizations."

"But what about our jobs," the monsignor cried out.

"It will force a lot of people to earn an honest living for a change," the Pope told him. He was silent a few moments and then added, "But we still haven't decided anything about Sister Angela. I really want to come to some kind of decision about whether what I am doing is wrong. It really disturbs me."

The monsignor had difficulty tearing his attention away from the mammoth scheme the Pope had just outlined to turn to something he considered trivial, but it was not his hour. He pulled himself together. "What happened the last time you went there?" he asked.

"When she finished the last sorrowful mystery, she threw open her arms and screamed, 'Oh sweet Jesus, come and take me NOW,' and then sobbed for about five minutes, at one point so violently that she fell off the bed and began writhing about on the floor." He paused a moment. "She had nothing on under her robes."

"I see," said the monsignor, whose years did not prevent him from appreciating the more sensual aspects of the scene described.

"Oh, if only I were younger," the Pope said, "it would be a pleasure to sin with that woman."

The monsignor finally decided that the Pope was innocent of any wrongdoing, and what he felt as guilt was merely frustration. That afternoon he visited the Mother Superior himself, and with what he knew, coupled with the prestige of being the Pope's confessor, he did not find it difficult to suggest hearing her confession. As he suspected she might, she told him of her evening's activities, and he advised that he could not make any judgment on her behavior unless he saw it in person. They made an appointment for him to visit her quarters a week in the future. While she said the Act of Contrition, her gray eyes looked unblinkingly into his.

An hour later, he was closeted with the Head of the Jesuit Order, requesting that his confession be heard. He reasoned that if he revealed the contents of the Pope's confession in his own confession, he wouldn't, technically speaking, be breaking the seal of confession, but merely transferring it. And if the man he confessed to wanted to do something with the information, he would have his own conscience to struggle with. "Let him deal with his own seal," the monsignor said to himself.

Five days later, the Pope died under mysterious circumstances. During his brief illness he was kept inside his room and only a few cardinals, his doctor, and his confessor were allowed in.

"Tell me," the Pope said to the monsignor during his last confession, "are they poisoning me?"

"I really don't know," the monsignor replied.

"It feels like they're poisoning me," he said. "I wonder what sort of politics is buzzing around in their heads now. Do you know who's been fingered for succession?"

"I try to stay out of those things," the monsignor told him.

"Very wise," the Pope said. He took a deep breath. "You know, I looked at myself in the mirror the other day and I thought, 'To millions of people you are the Pope, the supreme spiritual leader. But to me you're like an old man dressed in drag, haunting this ancient marble theater.' And now, they're going to bring in a new act."

The Pope died feeling he had lived an interesting life. The monsignor went that same night to the Mother Superior's room, and discovered that she didn't believe in God either. But did have a sense of sin.

"Well, what the hell," he told her, "I can forgive sin. It says so in my contract."

He heard her confession and for penance told her to recite a rosary. And as she lay before him, her legs opening with each new level of rapture she reached imagining her Redeemer descending to fill her with His joy, the monsignor slowly took his clothes off, preparing to serve as a very real handle for her fantasy.

Finally he mounted her, and as she surged against him, her robes awry, her beads rattling, he whispered over and over again. "Your sins are forgiven you, go and sin some more," while behind him the eyes of the man who might have brought down the curtain on the entire show would never again appear to watch their scene through the holes in the ancient canvas.

YESTERDAY'S IAGO

NEITHER COULD REMEMBER how or where they met; they assumed it had been at a party. But suddenly, they were friends, and from the first shared an intimacy and trust which went deeper than anything they knew with anyone else, including their mates.

They experienced that rare and precious gift of total communion. They could sit for hours, holding hands, speaking or not speaking, attuned to a communication which went from words to silence and back to words without an interruption in the flow of meaning. Unaware of themselves, they often struck classic postures, and one might find them lost in one another's eyes, their fingers intertwined, sighing openly.

Albert was a poet, and chained to his dry despair. The wife and two children who inhabited his days seemed something of an afterthought, a footnote to his central concern. He held a job to support his family, and went through the motions of relationship, but it was only when he was alone, a beam of light transforming his desk top into a stage as he hunched against the glare of the white sheet of paper that challenged him, his hand holding a sharpened pencil hovering like a hawk about to strike, that he felt whole.

Until he met Margaret.

"You are as real to me as poetry," he told her, and she wept with the joy of recognition.

Through the years they came to comfort one another in times of crisis, to celebrate in times of plenitude. At first they attempted to integrate the singularity of their bond into their wider social contexts, but both her husband and his wife began to seethe with jealousy even though the two of them had not known so much as a kiss by way of sexual contact.

"I'd almost prefer it if you fucked her," his wife told him, "then you'd stop idealizing her and imagining that she's all that different from me."

Margaret's husband left her, and Albert began to visit her at her apartment regularly, lying to his wife about where he was. "It's strange," he said to Margaret, "you're like my sister, and I have to sneak off to see you."

At first they spoke mostly of her marriage, her suffering. Albert was a mountain of support, listening, guiding, caring. And leaning on him, she was able to effect the difficult transition from knowing herself only through the reflection of another to having a sense of identity as a single woman.

And as that took place, of course, she began to feel her need for a man once more, but this time promising herself that she would not allow herself to be vulnerable, but would take what a man had to offer by way of completion, and give back as good as she got. For her deeper aspects, she had Albert.

In this mood, her encounters with men began to take on an odd twist, for she discovered that she hungered for bad treatment. Her husband had known how to be mentally and emotionally cruel to her, and it was, in fact, his disgust for himself for falling into that trap which had prompted his leaving; but she could not find the same sort of punishment with men who were essentially one-night stands. A shift took place, subtle at first, but with rapid acceleration into clearly defined forms, until she recognized her craving for physical pain.

She didn't want to tell Albert, for fear she would repulse him, but one night she could hold it back no longer.

"I think I'm a masochist," she said.

"You've always been," he told her. "We've talked about that before."

"It's different now," she said. "It used to be passive and unconscious, but now I'm an active masochist. I openly ask for it."

She told him about the previous night. She had been sitting at home, knitting and listening to music, when a great restlessness seized her. Her legs trembled and she found her heart beating quickly. She went out into the street like a zombie, heading for the nearest bar. It wasn't too long before a man sat next to her, a grizzled dockworker in his mid-forties who looked as though he had been drinking steadily for the past thirty years. His very gruesomeness sent shivers of contorted desire through her, and while he was not cerebrally capable of formulating and articulating the nuances of the situation, his animal intelligence understood at once what was going on.

He grabbed her arm and led her out into the night. By that time she was quivering in anticipation and could barely stand. She dimly remembered lurching through obscure neighborhoods, and being half carried up a flight of stairs to his room. He flung her down on the bed and leapt up next to her. For a few moments he was pure frenzy, all the frustration of his lifetime pouring out on the willing woman who had given herself up to be used. He slapped and pawed and bunched her up, flinging her back and forth like a half-empty sack of flour. She could recall none of the details, only being aware that he might kill her, and not caring for anything except the brute energy that erupted from him.

"That's what I remember most clearly," she told Albert, "that I was sucking his energy from him, and I would do anything for that energy, even to letting him beat me."

"What happened then?" Albert asked, his voice calm and gentle, his mien serene, his attitude one of total compassion and acceptance.

"He ripped my clothes off," she continued. "And then it was sheer jungle sex. He had a cock like a policeman's billy, and he used it the same way, to beat me with. He didn't know what to do first, and he kept tossing me around in a dozen different ways, fucking me in the mouth, in the cunt, in the ass. All the while he kept slapping me and calling me the most foul names. And I . . . well, I enjoyed it so much it scared me. I just kept shouting, 'Yes, yes, this is what I want, this is what I've always wanted.'"

She paused. "When he came, I dug my nails a half inch into his skin and he didn't even feel it. Afterward we were both a little flabbergasted, and when I was leaving he said, 'I'm going to make believe this was a dream because this isn't going to happen to me again, and I don't want to start wanting it, because you aren't going to want me another time. Your type, you'll do this a thousand times with a thousand different men before you're through.' And I knew he was right. He was so dumb and sweet and sad that I got carried away and I went down on my knees and gave him a long, slow blow job. And I loved it. Being in that tawdry apartment sucking that stranger's cock after he had practically torn me apart."

She looked up. "What do you think, Albert? Am I sick?"

He stroked her hair and held her head in his hands and gazed deeply into her liquid eyes.

"I've only had one criterion in my life," he told her. "Anything which can be seen as poetry is its own justification. If you view it as something ugly, then that's what it becomes. If you can sing its beauty, then that is all there is. And your soul is the soul of poetry. If you remember that, you are free to do things which would horrify the timid and the trite."

Then he smiled, and added, "But none of that should let you forget that one time you might meet up with someone whose frustrations lie deeper than your dockworker's, and you could very well end up tied to a bed while some maniac tattoos your body with a razor blade, Or even less dramatically, but more probably, that same man loses his sense of proportion and smashes a fist into your mouth relieving you of a dozen teeth." He frowned, lit a cigarette, and went on, "But the real danger is more insidious. The body builds a tolerance for any sort of sensation, and if you take this path, you will start to need more and more violent behavior to achieve the same levels of stimulation. It's like heroin or any other drug."

She lay with her head against his chest and wept silently. "You are such a beautiful person and such a dear, dear friend," she said. "You care so much for me, and yet you leave me absolutely free. You never censor or blame."

"How could it be otherwise?" he replied.

The more lurid of the possibilities didn't come to pass, but the last one did. While Margaret didn't fall into the hands of a madman or receive any scars or permanent damage, she did enter an escalating cycle of sadomasochistic activity. Like so many in that particular endgame, she learned the value of choreography and expertise. She came to prefer a man who knew how to use a whip with discretion and skill over someone who struck out blindly and in rage.

In time she was introduced among a number of the formal and informal circles composed of people who shared similar tastes. She was initiated into more delicate forms of torture, including the judicious use of hot wax, the proper placement of needles, the hanging bar and nipple clips. She once spent a weekend as slave to an entire household, being used and abused by almost twenty men and women for three days. And, in logical progression, she developed a taste for what were called, in that clique, water games.

"It was extraordinary, Albert," she said. "There I was, my hands tied behind me, having just been fucked by three men at once, kneeling in front of a fourth. He told me to open my mouth and I thought he wanted me to suck his cock. But when I took it, it wasn't hard. The upper part of my face was covered with a leather mask, so I didn't know what was coming. Then this incredible sensation, a stream of hot liquid on my tongue. I still didn't know, and then the taste hit me. A fantastic taste, pungent and sweet and bitter and salty all at once. And then I knew. He was pissing in my mouth! And it drove me wild. I reached up and put his whole cock inside me and let him piss down my throat. And all the while my knees were shaking and I almost climaxed with excitement."

She looked at him, wondering whether this outrage would perturb him at all. Telling him was a treat, for she was able to experience her episodes at another level, but from time to time she became afraid of alienating his affection. But he only nodded and said, "Unless the person has some disease, urine is perfectly sterile. It can't hurt you. In fact, it's probably safer then the city's drinking water."

"Have you ever done anything like that?" she asked.

"I'm afraid my sexual tastes have always been suffocatingly pedestrian," he told her.

They continued in that manner for more than a year, and one night he arrived looking drawn. She tried to cheer him up with wine and stories of her week's activity but he became more and more glum. Finally he blurted out, "Susan left me. She's taken the children."

For the first time in their long relationship, she listened more to him than he to her. And after long, long hours of his pouring himself out, exposing a weakness and sensibility to pain that he had never shown before, at four in the morning, exhausted, he asked, "Do you mind if I stay here a day or two? I don't want to face that empty apartment just yet."

The two days stretched into four, and the four into a week, and finally he left. It was as though he didn't want to go, and yet felt extremely awkward staying longer. Her heart went out to him. After so many years, she had a chance to help him, to provide succor for his hurt.

But he did not call her for several weeks, and she could not reach him on the phone. Finally, she went to his apartment, and found him drunk and disheveled, the place a shambles. She got him to shower and shave, cleaned the house, and made a huge dinner for him. Later, they sat on the couch and talked. It was the first time that she knew him without his having his wife, and the difference was palpable.

During a deep silence, something totally unforeseen happened. He held her to him, as he so often had, but this time his arms tightened until her face tilted up, and his lips covered hers in a kiss that transmitted an unmistakable urgency.

Something profoundly deep within her melted. The transcendent liberty she had discovered in her body blended with the hunger in her heart, and in an instant she surrendered totally to him, on fire with that unique melange of physical desire, emotional need, and intellectual affinity to which is given the name love.

Instantly they were one, and without a thought they launched themselves into a total lovemaking which thundered with the force of so many years of waiting and building. The form was completely constructed, their friendship was absolute, she could give herself, give herself rapturously, having the abandon she had known in her body with others and the fullness she had felt in her heart for Albert. Now they were one, and it seemed as though her entire life had been a preparation for this moment.

The next morning they decided to live together, and they moved to a new neighborhood, wanting to make a clean break with both their pasts. They found an apartment, and had a glorious honeymoon of sorts for three weeks. And without marking the moment as such, they passed into that space in which they were grafted onto one another, and could not henceforth part without a terrible tearing and rupture. In an informal and real sense, they were married.

And one night, as they sat on the couch, reading, she felt a strange vibration in the room. She looked up from her book and found Albert watching her, his face slightly distorted.

With dire premonition she asked, "What is it, darling?"

His voice was hard, his eyes narrowed, "I was just thinking about that dockworker you told me about," he said.

For a moment she couldn't think of what he was talking about. And then it came to her. The dock-worker she had gone with shortly after her husband left her.

"I was thinking about all the things you did with him," he went on, his voice thin and febrile, "letting him fuck you in the ass, sucking his cock."

And with a slow, mounting dread she realized that his entire system was laced with scorching jealousy and anger, a pervasive and unrelenting possessiveness, spiteful and thorough. She hoped it might be a momentary mood, but at a glance she understood that she was only seeing the tip of the iceberg. For he not only remembered that one night, but had catalogued in his memory every incident she had ever told him about. He knew every action, every feeling, every moan that had been hers for the past eight years. His control was absolute.

"But that was before . . ." she began to say and stopped. What was happening was beyond logic or reason. A cold clammy hysteria clutched her belly and fear flashed in her eyes like a trapped rat in a flooded cellar. The days of physical suffering were finished, and she was returning once more to the other kind of punishment, the emotional and mental murder. Her independent self began to crumble as she found herself once again at the mercy of her vulnerability. She felt a quick impulse to flee, but was helpless against the undertow of her conditioning.

Her friend had become her husband, and he wanted revenge.

FIST FUCKER

AT THE AGE of seven, Carl was taken into the old man's house, and after proper softening with ice cream, comic books, and discreet caressing, seemed to have no objection to holding the wrinkled penis in his mouth. He sucked it until it was hard, and when the sperm was plunked on his tongue, he tasted it ingenuously, not knowing that what had just happened would raise the unbridled fury of the caretakers of the world's official attitudes.

Ironically, the old man was a retired judge, and Carl's parents were pleased that their son should spend time in what they thought was an educational atmosphere. Until he was nine, Carl visited on the average of once a week, until his taste for the experience began to exceed the old man's ability to provide it. After his somber initiation into the realm of sex, he went in search of others.

His understanding of the role of sex in society was rudimentary and inchoate. Beyond the judge's admonitions that he must never speak about what they did except to tell his parents that the nice old neighbor had read to him and given him cookies to eat, he had no grasp of the hysteria which such simple behavior as cocksucking engendered. Yet, with animal instinct, when he began his forays into the wider world, he knew to seduce only those who he sensed were willing to be had.

By the age of twelve, Carl had thrilled scores of men with his surprising eagerness to service their unspoken desires. He developed a way of standing, of looking, which set up the necessary vibrations between himself and available provender. Playing with his schoolmates, he would often disappear for an hour and prowl strange streets, finding what he wanted, and consummating his quest in hallways or cellars or the back seats of cars.

Carl knew no genital excitement himself, and was somewhat

perplexed that his ministrations would bring grown men to tears. The gasps and moans which showered his ears as his delicate child's mouth would cover a cock and his tongue tingle intricate patterns over a thigh he appreciated only through empathy. What he did seemed to make others happy, and that was gratification enough.

He was first anally penetrated at the age of fourteen one summer afternoon. He was hitchhiking through the Long Island suburbs, sizing up the men who stopped for him, and either proceeding with them to a secluded space or perceiving rapidly that there was nothing to be had from that particular person. When the huge trailer stopped, the boy was taken with an unusual premonition that set him shivering. As he climbed into the cab, he was overwhelmed with an impression of muscular thighs and calloused hands. The man glanced at him once and seemed to know what Carl wanted before he even made an overture. He took the truck to a rest stop and led the boy into the back, where an entire household of furniture was stacked and being moved from South Carolina to Wyoming. It belonged to a nuclear physicist who, sickened at the corruption within the Atomic Energy Commission, had decided to become a sheep rancher.

The man pushed Carl onto a couch and stood over him, his cock straining against his pants. With expert fingers, the lad pulled the zipper down. Gently, he tugged the thickly veined tool out, and with a flutter of his eyelids, took it between his lips. He sucked for a long time, his thin young body gradually working up to a feverish pitch, tossing to and fro as he worked on the huge organ. Then, to his surprise, the man pulled back.

"Get on your stomach," the driver commanded.

Carl lay down, uncertain as to what would happen next. The man yanked his pants down, pulling them over his legs and past his feet, until the boy was naked below the waist, his slim virginal buttocks gleaming in the dull light. The man spit on his fingers and thrust them into the tiny anus, lubricating it slightly. Without a wasted gesture, he lowered his bulk onto the child and thrust his cock into the puckered opening.

A bolt of pain shot through the boy and he gasped for breath. But hot upon the pain came a flash of sweet burning, a tender yielding that brought tears to his eyes. Grunting and huffing, the truck driver fucked the boy a long time, putting him in a dozen different positions, maneuvering the small body with ease, using his brawny arms to arrange the slender limbs in the most open poses, and then bursting in with all the power and force he could manage.

He came as the boy knelt over the arm of the couch, his buttocks raised, his legs dangling, and himself crouching behind, half raised on his toes, his heels pressed into a chest-of-drawers for leverage. As he bucked into orgasm, he drove ruthlessly into the boy's bowels and lifted him half a foot into the air.

Not long after that, Carl left home. He had already begun to see that the semi-conscious world of home and school was a restricting and artificial facade imposed over the true facts of life. He was developing a wisdom which transcended the artifacts of conventional knowledge, and he could no longer pretend to possess the naiveté and immaturity expected of someone his age.

He went to San Francisco, where he discovered the baths. Because of his youth, his good looks, and his unbounded willingness to please, he soon became a favorite in gay circles. One night he was spotted by a faded millionaire who offered to house him with the others in the harem he had built in an effort to pique a glutted appetite. Carl accepted, and within a short time ascended to the status of superstar.

But none of this seemed to affect his basic humility, and his unabashed desire to provide sexual pleasure for others. By seventeen, he was a virtuoso in the art of passive homosexual performance, and highly skilled in all the nuances of surrender. His patron grew proud, and then jealous, of his charge, and forbade him to have contact with anyone but himself.

Soon after, he left the mansion, and on his way along a highway, accepted a ride from a bestial looking motorcycle rider who took him to his camp, where several dozen others lounged in snarling lassitude. The boy was thrown to them the way meat is thrown to lions in a zoo, and for several days he served as a slave to their every whim, catering to their surly need for stimulation.

On the fourth day, lying over a pile of sleeping bags, having been fucked by twelve men in succession, he was initiated into the form that he had been unconsciously evolving toward for his entire life. The leader of the pack, kneeling behind him, placed his bunched fist between Carl's buttocks. The boy gasped, and then relaxed, and the huge curled hand pressed tightly against his asshole. Slowly, he gave way, and the fist entered the hot open-ing. The universe seemed to crash about Carl's head as the man behind him continued to push, engulfing his hand, his wrist, and then his whole forearm up to the elbow. At that point, he stopped, and with a deliberate motion, flexed his entire arm, filling the pulsing channel completely with hard bulging muscle.

Carl smiled in ecstasy. After a decade of service, he felt he was finally being satisfied.

He continued drifting from adventure to adventure until one morning an eerie mood enveloped him. He was walking down a street and as he looked at the faces of the people who passed, he realized they were all asleep. He saw that, through his peculiar metamorphosis, he had become an utterly superior human being. By virtue of having lived in the realm of excess, where others were too fearful to venture, he had attained a depth of awareness that set him apart from the human herd.

Not intrinsically cerebral, and his formal education having ended early, he was not able to articulate the insight with any degree of precision. But as the bright western sun sparkled in his eyes, something like a religious revelation exploded in his brain. If it is true that a person who masters any one thing has mastered all of life itself, then he was a realized human being, for he had become an emperor of perversion.

Thereafter he wandered the country like a ghost. Men would encounter him and tell their friends of an apparition of startling beauty, who sucked cock and allowed himself to be laid and gave a pleasure that went deeper than the sexual, that ultimately soothed the soul. And if asked what he wanted in return, he would say simply, "Fist-fuck me, please," and would lie in rapture as the clenched hand went deeper and deeper into his entrails.

There is a photo of him, the only one in existence, in which he is suspended from a wooden crossbeam. He is shown being lowered onto two men, each of whom has one arm, up to the elbow, buried in his ass at the same time. The boy's eyes are closed, so it is impossible to tell what he is thinking. His face is in repose, and his body is in a state of complete relaxation. A Buddhist monk, seeing the picture, was heard to exclaim, "That is a man who has attained Nirvana."

He was found dead, at the age of twenty-four, wrapped in a mattress in a ravine outside of Los Angeles. No one knew his name or where he had come from, so he was buried in a public field. His life had been a total and selfless giving to others, and he was not known to have sought anything for himself, except the blissful trance state which occurred whenever he was lovingly fist fucked.

Several of the members of Troy Perry's Gay Church subsequently began an official movement to have him proclaimed as their first saint.

NEEDLESS TO SAY

Lisa Palac

THE FROZEN VEGETABLE display made Angelique's nipples hard. She was choosing between a carton of chopped spinach and a bag of carrots, broccoli and cauliflower otherwise known as California Medley.

California . . . California. Just the sound of the word made her wet. The home of indigenous blonde bimbos and vacant surfer dudes who drenched themselves in various pore-clogging palm oils, then panted like rabid dogs as they slid around the back seat of their cherry '77 Cutlass convertibles. The acme of hot-tub orgies with big dicks from the Hollywood Hills, cellular phone sex and fuchsia teddies with nipple cut-outs. The Land of Porn.

Angelique dreamed of performing incredibly nasty acts on a Naugahyde couch while the videotape rolled. She and some greased-up stud would pump and munch on each other like snacks, eventually sliding down onto the lime shag carpet, while the slightly balding director with a roll of fat hanging over his Elvis – The King! abalone belt buckle shouted, "That's it BAYbee! Show it all to me BAYbee! Ye-he-hes!"

She could make the Oooh Yeah Face better than Ginger Lynn and she could be making a million fucking dollars at it too, but it wasn't going to happen in Milwaukee.

Angelique threw the bag of frozen nuggets on top of the bratwurst. Her high heels clicked against the waxed checkerboard floor of Giuseppe's Finer Foods as she pushed the shopping cart down the aisle, wiggling her ass seductively for all of her regulars to see. She could make those pimply-faced, nervous stock boys cream in their pants if she wanted to. All that teenage testosterone ready to explode like a nuclear warhead at the mere sight of a pubic hair. Out of the corner of her eye, Angelique could see them straining to keep their eyes glued to her luscious ass.

She wore her favorite red cha-cha heels today and they made her butt stand out like a ripe bubble. Her legs were longer than Route 66 with directions to the Tunnel of Love posted every mile. The leopard lycra spandex skirt barely covered her back door and a cut-off T-shirt revealed that her man-made 34C tits didn't need a bra. A turgid mass of bleach-blonde hair, glued in place by an entire can of Aqua-Net Firm Hold, shot up toward the ceiling, then fell around her shoulders. Her eyes were circled with tons of thick black eyeliner and her lips were colored California Orange.

Wiggle it, Angie. She bent over just a little bit, pretending to check something in the cart, and rotated her firm cheeks. Surreptitiously, she glanced over her shoulder just in time to catch the stock boys turn their drooling faces back to a freezer full of frozen food.

Bending over wasn't the only talent she had. She knew all the poses from grinding along with Tony's (her now ex-boyfriend and total jerk) porno tapes and thumbing through copies of all his *fucking* fuck magazines. Next to laughing at the homemade Polaroids of all the flabby-assed sluts in the swingers' section, Angelique liked the letters from readers the best, and was dying to know if they were real. They were always saying things like, "The two virgin pizza delivery girls, needless to say, were begging to suck my cock!" or "Needless to say, I shot my biggest load watching her screw my brother and his Latvian lesbian Bingo tutor in the tool shed!" If these letters were real, then why didn't something like that happen to her? Why, why, why? Her bottom lip began to curl down into a little pout. She could screw in a tool shed better than any other Slavic lesbo, if she only had half a chance. Life was so unfair.

To cheer herself up, she wheeled the cart into the Shampoo/ Toothpaste/Feminine Hygiene aisle. For Angelique, shopping was a confession of faith; a cold cash belief that the proper

combination of fake tan, garter belts and the right deodorant
would ultimately lead her to Porn Star status. Or at least the
simulated adventures of one.

Angie Lee flipped on her Walkman. How do they expect
people to have a meaningful shopping experience when the air
is filled with this nauseating Muzak? she thought.

I'm burnin' up, burnin' up for your luh-uv . . .

Madonna's breathy squeals blasted through the wires. This
crotch-grabbing, mattress-humping, Catholic Italian who liked
to be spanked was Angelique's absolute idol. Angie had all her
records, but her favorite was still the first one. "Burnin' Up" was
her manifesto and The Boy Toy, her fearless leader. That woman
had balls . . . and great tits, too. Angelique wondered what kind
of douche she used.

She sang along with the superstar. She shook her head with
such raging abandon, her hair actually moved. She pranced down
the aisle, submersed in a distorted MTV wet dream.

*. . . I'll do anything, I'm not the same, I have no shame . . . I'm on
FIRE!*

The music pounded away like an insatiable hard-on, while her
eyes scanned the myriad products available for today's woman:
feminine deodorant sprays, suppositories, intimate cleansers,
disposable douches and douche bags; maxi pads, mini-pads,
tampons on a stick and tampons on a string; pills to avoid
bloating, crabbiness, over-eating, pimple-production, fatigue,
iron deficiency, depression, moodiness and temper tantrums,
which when unchecked could lead to frenzied fits of murder!

C'mon let go!

Madonna was insistent. The vocals ripped apart Angelique's
hesitation and with a sweeping motion, she dumped the entire
shelf into her cart. Shit, she broke a nail.

The cart was overflowing with goodies now. Time to go.
Happily, she made her way toward the check-out. Okay, was
she obsessing? Maybe there was one box too many of panty
shields. Maybe she should wear two at a time. One time Tony
asked her why a chick would need to wear a pad everyday.

"I thought that thing only happened once a month, unless ya
got knocked up or somethin'. Whaddaya get? Some fuckin' clam
disease? Haw, haw, haw." Stupid asshole.

Or the time when Tony was laid off from the meat-packing

plant and he listened to those Springsteen records all fuckin' day and would whip out his cock whenever some ugly babe got rejected on "Love Hook-Up," the dial-a-date show.

"Come and get it, Fido! Here, Barky!" he'd say, dangling his dick in front of the TV and swallowing a pisswarm Meister Brau.

What a low-class scum-sucking shit. He thought he was so great, and he didn't even know he had pimples on his ass and left skid marks in his underwear. Breaking up with him was the smartest thing she ever did – besides buying those refrigerator magnets on sale.

No matter what line Angelique picked, it always turned out to be the longest one. There was always some old lady who picked an item without a price tag or insisted on digging for exact change in the bottom of her purse. To help the century pass, Angie grabbed the latest issue of *Charm* magazine and scanned the headlines on the cover: Where Men Like to be Licked, Lipstick Tricks, Bolivian Fashion Rage, Money: How to Get It, Find Your G-Spot in Minutes. She had a few minutes. She flipped to page 53.

She rested her elbows on the rail of the cart and arched her back so that her succulent plumbutt stuck way out. She slid off one high heel and slowly began to rub her bare foot against the inside of her other leg as she began reading the sexy instructions. Wash hands . . . two fingers . . . insert deeply . . . pressing forward . . . may feel like a small almond. Angelique pressed her creamy thighs together and gave a teensy little moan. She drew the magazine closer to her, shielding her face with the glossy pages. Gingerly, she ran one finger around the outline of her wet pink lips, then drove it into her mouth like a garden spike. She rammed one finger, then two, in and out of her lip service until they were completely covered in her sweet stickiness. She was just about to try and sneak them down to her pussy when she noticed the spy.

Two lines over Angel saw Mrs Alfaromeo. She kept glancing and pointing at Angelique, then whispering to her prune-faced old man. That nosy bitch, thought Angel, everybody probably knows about my abortion now. Mrs Alfaromeo's daughter, Carmella, worked at the clinic and provided the entire neighborhood with abortion gossip. Somebody should gag that prissy little Carmella I-Have-No-Cunt.

Mrs Alfaromeo was now smiling and waving and flapping her gums frantically; obviously trying to cover up her spying blunder with some forced conversation.

Angel lowered the magazine and pulled the headphones away from her ears.

"What," Angie gave her best Bored Bitch imitation, "are you saying?"

"I say, how you feeling?"

Fuck. She knows. Angelique gave the geriatric an indignant stare.

"I feel pretty horny after watching your daughter give some black guy a blow-job on your front porch last night!"

The old woman took a big swallow of air and slammed a can of tomato paste down on the conveyor belt with deliberate rage. She prayed to the fluorescent ceiling lights and told her wrinkled porker that he should have worn his hearing aid if he wanted to know what was going on. Smiling, Angel flung the magazine in with the other treats, pushed her cart up to the register, and began unpiling her load.

Angelique couldn't resist flashing the bag boy. She made sure to give him a good view of her braless silicone wonders with every item she placed on the moving black belt. *You want a show, honey?* she thought, *I'll give it to you and you can pay me later*.

"Total's 83.94." The gum-chomping check-out girl was barely understandable.

Angie Lee tried to focus on counting her cash, but couldn't keep her eyes off the nubile flesh who was just finishing packing up the paper bags with the last box of vaginal suppositories. She imagined the growing desire in his pants and licked her lips in anticipation.

"That's 83.94."

She made the transaction and slung her purse over her shoulder. Meanwhile the pulsing behemoth put the bags into an empty cart, preparing for their departure.

"I need some help puttin' all this stuff in my car." Oh, Angie you coy bitch. "Could you help me?"

"Sure," he said. Wasn't he sweet? A little bit of acne but great hair.

He followed Angie out into the parking lot. Click, click, click. Her plastic heels tapped the black tar surface.

She made sure to walk in front of him, not beside him, so that he could revel in her perfect *perfect* ass. She also wanted to give him the opportunity to rub up against her when she bent over to slam the key in the lock. But he didn't take the bait when she opened up the trunk of her 1989 Buick Riviera. What the hell was this throbbing glob of hormones waiting for?

She spun around and slammed her lips into his. Snatching a fistful of his crusty gelled hair, she slurped and slobbered all over his adolescent face, smearing it with California Orange. Her tongue desperately searched for the way into his love-licker, but he would not open his mouth.

"Open your mouth, baby," Angie Lee cooed. "Open up for Mommy."

The bag boy stood motionless. His face was more frozen than the bag of California Medley, which was now melting in the suffocating Wisconsin sun. Only his eyes were bulging.

"Lamby-pie, open your mouth and let my slippery snake in," she hissed. Still no response. "I said open it, you little shit!" Angie yanked his bottom lip down with one hand and pried his teeth apart with the other. Her pointy tongue darted in and out of his cavity-filled mouth with a winner-take-all fury. And this conquest was only the beginning.

She began grinding and writhing against his filthy green Giuseppe's apron. Her hungry crotch humped his leg while she grabbed his ass with both hands and pounded his scared stiff body against her loose slutty self. She clawed at his face with her painted talons and dug her teeth into his never-been-kissed flesh.

"Owww!" he screamed. The sound of his sudden yelp made her lose her balance and she practically twisted her ankle when her cha-cha heel gave way.

"Damn it you lovely little virgin bastard, you hot horny teen-ager," she whispered into his waxy ear, "I'm going to rip you up."

Angie Lee stuffed her sex plans into his brain. Detailed descriptions of coital exploits were flooding his head, but bag boy had a one track mind: If he didn't get back soon, he'd lose his fifteen-minute break. With anxious tenacity his head kept snapping back in the direction of the grocery store, straining to see who might be witnessing his possible de-flowerment, until Angelique put the iron grip on his boner-to-be.

"I am a bitch in heat!" she cried, enunciating every word like a Pentecostal preacher. "And you're gonna cool me off." In a smooth move, she caught his crumpled black tie and dragged him around to the side of the car.

He was flat on his back in the back seat when Angie ripped off her T-shirt and produced two perfect melons. Straddling him, she began playing with her overripe fruits, making little circles around her rock hard nipples.

"Aren't you dying to touch me?" Sugar poured out of her mouth. "Aren't you . . .?" She paused, eyebrows raised, waiting for his name.

"Sergio . . . but . . . uhm . . . like my friends call me Sam."

"Oooo Sam. I like Sam. Oooo, yeah." She tweaked her nipples harder and harder and sucked in a lot of air every time she said Oooo, yeah. Just like in the movies.

She reached out and tugged on his zipper, but he grabbed her wrist.

"What's the matter, Sammy?"

"You're not sick or anything are you? I mean you bought all that weird stuff."

Suddenly her eyes narrowed into evil slits. "What *weird* stuff?" She spit the words out through her clenched teeth, now just inches away from his petrified face.

"All that stuff, for like when girls get infections."

"I don't have any infections. All of that *stuff* keeps me smelling fresh and feminine. You want me to be feminine, don't you?"

"Yeah . . . I guess so."

"Tell me what else you want." He shrugged his shoulders. "I'll tell you what you want! You want my honey pot! My carnal canal! My shaved slice of sin! MY PUSSY!" Her fingernails tore into his stained white bag-boy shirt, releasing a shower of buttons.

"You want to see my cunt riding up and down on your virginal cock, don't you? You want to see me rub my clit? Do you know what that is? My clit? I bet you don't, you naive slave-boy. See, Oooo I'm rubbing it now. Oooo yeah. Ooooh oooh ooooh you want to hear me scream when I come and keep on screaming as I take more and more of your thick pud deep deep and deeper inside me. You want to see me explode again when you shoot hot lava blasts from your volcanic rod deep inside my mammoth crater! Don't you? Oooo yeah, oh here it comes baby, here it

comes! I'm showin' it to you, baby! Oh! Oh! Oh! OOOOooo
YEAH!"

She heard the buzz droning in the distance. Her vibrator must
have gone off accidentally in her purse, she thought. She opened
her eyes. Instead, it was the annoying signal telling her the car
door was ajar. He was gone.

She adjusted the rear view mirror and checked her lipstick at the
same time. Some idiot behind her was beeping their horn. The
light was green. Fuck you, asshole. She gave him the finger. Her
tires squealed when she rammed the pedal to the floor. In her
mind, she was already composing the letter: "I was doing my
weekly shopping, when this totally gorgeous stock boy, who was
also a virgin, offered to take my groceries out to the car. He ended
up packing my trunk in more ways than one! Needless to say, I
never thought it could happen to me . . ."

BETWEEN SIGNS

Cris Mazza

**Living legends of the Enchanted Southwest
Watch Authentic Indians.
Handmade crafts, Leather,
Pan for Gold with Real Prospectors**

He'll drive with one hand. With the other, unbuttons her shirt.
Then when trucks pass, close, going the opposite direction, he'll
drive with no hands for a moment, waving to the truckers with his
left hand, his right hand never leaving her breasts. She'll arch her
back, smile, eyes closed. The wind of the passing trucks will
explode against the car like split-second thunder-storms.

*Swim
Ski
Relax
Play
In Lostlake City*

**DO NOT PARK
IN DESIGNATED
PARKING AREAS**

Someday she'll return, using this same road, and it will be late spring, and the migrating desert showers will wash the wind-shield of collected bugs and dust over and over, and the smell of wet pavement will lift her drooping eyelids, and she'll not stop until she's knocking on his door and it's opening and he's standing there. She'll feel the explosion of his body or the explosion of the door slamming.

15 Restaurants
11 Motels
Next 2 exits

RATTLESNAKE-SKIN BOOTS
TURQUOISE BELT BUCKLES
BEADED MOCCASINS, SNO CONES

They took nothing. Credit cards bought gas and food, plastic combs, miniature toothbrushes, motel rooms, tourist T-shirts, foaming shaving cream and disposable razors. She watched him shaving as she lay in the bathtub. Then he shaved her. Rinsing her with the showerhead, soaping her over and over again. Shoved a blob of jelly, from a plastic single-serving container taken from the diner, far inside her, went to retrieve it with his tongue, drop by drop, taste by taste, but there was always more where that came from.

See Mystic Magic Of The Southwest . . . THETHING?

While she takes a turn driving, he'll lay his head in her lap and watch her play with herself. The sound is sticky and sweet like a child sucking candy. The sun will appear and disappear. A band of light across her bare knees. She'll hold his hand and his fingers will join hers moving in and out. The seat wet between her thighs. A cattle crossing will bounce his head in her lap and her legs will tighten around their joined hands. Air coming in the vents is humid, thick with the warm smell of manure, straw, the heat of bodies on the endless flat pasture under the sun. He'll roll to his back to let her wet fingers embrace his erection.

VISIT RUBY FALLS

Make a Bee-Line to **ROCK CITY**

Don't Miss CATFISH WILLIE'S RIVERBOAT
Restaurant, Lounge, Casino
Fresh Catfish & Hushpuppies
Beulah, Tennessee

Rip Van Winkle Motel just 35 miles

He has no sunglasses. His eyes are slits. Bright white sky and blinking lines on the road. Touches blistered chapped lips with his tongue. Digs into his pocket, sitting on one hip and easing up on the gas. Crackle of paper among the loose change. He unwraps the butter scotch and slips it into his mouth, rolls it with his tongue, coats his mouth with the syrup. When he passes a mailbox on the side of the road, he looks far up the dirt driveway beside it, but can't see where it leads. At the next mailbox, five miles later, he stops for a second. The name on the box says Granger, but, again, the driveway is too long to see what it leads to.

Triple-Dip ice cream cones
Camping, ice, propane
Truckers Welcome

SLIPPERY WHEN WET   **FALLING ROCK**

They weren't allowed to rent a shower together, so they paid for two but when no one was looking she slipped into his. Someone far away was singing. They stood for a while, back to back, turned and simultaneously leaned against the opposite walls of the shower stall, then slid down and sat facing each other, legs crossing. She told him he looked like he was crying, the water running down his face, but his tears would probably taste soapy. She said once she'd put dish detergent into a doll that was supposed to wet and cry. From then on it had peed foam and bawled suds. He reached out and put a hand on each of her breasts, holding her nipples between two fingers. A door slammed in the stall beside theirs. Water started and a man grunted. He rose to his knees, pulled on her arms so she slid the rest of the way to the floor of the shower, the drain under her back. He eased over her, his mouth moving from breast to breast. Then he lathered her all over, slowly, using almost the whole bar of soap, her ears and neck, toes, ankles, knees, lingering between her legs where the hair was growing back and sometimes itched so badly while they drove that she had to put her hand in her pants and scratch. She was slick to hold. He didn't rinse her before pushing his cock in. The sting of the soap made them open their eyes wide and dig their fingernails into each other's skin. Staring at each other but not smiling.

Taste Cactus Jack's Homestyle Cookin

Relax in Nature's Spa
CHICKEN HOLLER HOT SPRINGS
Sandwiches, Live Bait

ROAD CLOSED IN FLOOD SEASON

Finally she stops and buys half a cantaloupe at a roadside fruit stand. After eating as much as she can with a plastic spoon, she presses her face down into the rind and scrapes the remaining flesh with her teeth. The juice is cool on her cheek and chin. Part of a tattered map, blown by the wind, is propped against the base of a telephone pole. He had laughed at her for getting cantaloupe Marguaritas, but then he'd sipped some of hers, ordered one for himself, said it tasted like her. She breaks the rind in half and slips one piece into her pants, between her legs. The crescent shape fits her perfectly.

MARVEL AT MYTHICAL RELICS
INDIAN JEWELRY
VELVET PAINTINGS

TEXMEX CHICKEN-FRIED STEAK
TACOS, BURRITOS
FREE 72 OZ STEAK IF YOU CAN EAT IT ALL!

When the dirt road gets so bumpy he has to keep both hands on the wheel, she'll take over using the vibrator on herself. He'll watch her, and watch the road. The road always disappears around a bend or beyond a small rise. The car bounces over ruts and rocks. She won't even have to move the vibrator, just hold it inside. She'll say he chose a good road, and her laugh will turn into a long moan, her head thrown over the back of the seat. One of her feet pressed against his leg. Her toes will clutch his pants.

View of Seven States from Rock City

Poison Spring Battleground
next exit, south 12 miles

PIKE COUNTY DIAMOND FIELD
All The Diamonds You Find Are Yours!

For three days he's had a postcard to send home, but can't find the words to explain. It's a picture of the four corners, where Colorado, New Mexico, Arizona and Utah meet. He hadn't gotten down on hands and knees to be in all four states simultaneously. But he had walked around them, one step in each state, making a circle, three times. When he arrives at Chief Yellowhorse's Trading Post and Rock Museum, he buys another postcard, a roadrunner following the dotted line on highway 160. This one's for *her*, wherever she is, if she even left a forwarding address. The rock museum costs a dollar. A square room, glass cases around the edges, dusty brown pebbles with handwritten nametags. Some of the rocks are sawed in half to show blue rings inside. A bin of rose quartz pieces for a nickel each. Black onyx for a dime. Shark's teeth are a quarter.

HOGEYE, pop. 2011
Hogeye Devildogs Football
class D state champs 1971

Behold! Prehistoric Miracles!
Indian Pottery, Sand Paintings
Cochina Dolls, Potted Cactus

Found Alive!
THE THING?

They'll toss their clothes into the back seat. Their skin slippery with sweat. She'll dribble diluted soda over and between his bare legs. Tint of warm root beer smell lingering in the car. She'll hold an ice cube in her lips and touch his shoulder with it. Runs it down his arm. It'll melt in his elbow. She'll fish another ice out of her drink, move it slowly down his chest. When she gets to his stomach, the ice will be gone, her tongue on his skin. She'll keep his hard-on cool by pausing occasionally to slip her last piece of ice into her mouth, then sucking him while he slides a finger in and out of her. The last time she puts the ice into her mouth, his hand will be there to take it from her lips. He'll push the ice into her, roll it around inside with a finger until it's gone. The road lies on the rippling desert like a ribbon. Leaving the peak of each of the road's humps, the car will be airborne for a second.

Cowboy Steaks, Mesquite Broiled

Black Hills Gold, Arrowheads,
Petrified Wood, Chicken Nuggets,
Soda, Thick Milkshakes, Museum
WAGON MOUND TRAVELERS REST

He had to slow down, find a turnout, pull her from the car and half carry her to the shade of a locked utility shack. She dropped to her knees, then stretched out full length on her stomach. He sat beside her, stroking her back. Her body shuddered several more times, then calmed. When she rolled over, the hair on her temples was wet and matted with tears, her eyes thick, murky, glistening, open, looking at him. She smiled.

INDIAN BURIAL MOUNDS NEXT EXIT
GAS, FOOD, LODGING

Rattlesnake Roundup
Payne County Fairgrounds
2nd weekend in July

DUST STORMS NEXT 18 MILES

The waterpark is 48 miles off the main interstate. He's the only car going in this direction and passes no others coming the opposite way. The park was described in a tourbook but wasn't marked on the map. Bumper boats, olympic pool, 3 different corkscrew waterslides, high dive. The only other car in the lot has 2 flat tires. Small boats with cartoon character names painted on the sides are upside down beside an empty concrete pond, a layer of mud and leaves at the bottom. Another layer of dirt at the bottom of the swimming pool is enough to have sprouted grass which is now dry and brown, gone to seed. The scaffold for the waterslides is still standing, but the slides have been dismantled. The pieces are a big aqua-blue pile of fiberglass.

Ancient Desert Mystery . . . THE THING? 157 miles

Land of Enchantment
New Mexico T-Shirts

BULL HORNS
HANDWOVEN BLANKETS
CACTUS CANDY
NATURAL WONDERS

She'll look out the back windshield. The earth is a faint, rolling line against a blue-black sky. His hair tickling her cheek. She'll be on his lap, straddling him, her chin hooked over his shoulder, his cock has been inside her for miles and miles. Sometimes she'll rock slowly from side to side. Sometimes he'll push up from underneath. Sometimes they'll sit and feel the pulse of the engine, the powerful vibration. The air coming through the vent, splashing against her back before it spreads through the car, is almost slightly damp. Smells of rain on pavement, clean and dusty. Out the front windshield, both sky and land stay so dark, there's no line where they meet. No lights and no stars.

If we go west fast enough, will it stay predawn forever?

We can try.

Did you ever pester your parents, When'll we get there, daddy?

And I'd've thought it was torture if he said *never*.

Gospel Harmony House Christian Dinner Theatre

MERGING TRAFFIC   DEER XING   SHARPCURVES
                                                                NEXT 10 MILES

They started walking toward the entrance of the WalMart store, but she turned off abruptly, crossed a road and climbed a small hill where someone had set up three crosses in the grass. They were plant stakes lashed together. Kite string was tangled on a tumbleweed. When she got back to the parking lot, five or six big cockleburs were clinging to each of her socks. She sat on the hood of the car picking them off. When he came from the store with two blankets, toilet paper, aspirin and glass cleaner, she said, There weren't any graves up there after all. He put the bag in the back seat, turned and smiled. Kiss me, she said.

Meteor Crater and gift shop, 3 miles

WARNING:
THIS ROAD CROSSES A US
AIR FORCE BOMBING RANGE
FOR THE NEXT 12 MILES DANGEROUS
OBJECTS MAY DROP FROM AIRCRAFT

BIMBO'S FIREWORKS
Open all year

He spreads a map over his steering wheel. This road came forty-five miles off the interstate. He pays and follows the roped-off trail, stands looking at the cliff dwellings as the guide explains which was the steam room, which compartment stored food, which housed secret rituals, where the women were allowed to go and where they weren't, why they died off before white settlers ever arrived, and the impossibly straight narrow paths which connected them directly to other cliff dwelling cities and even now were still visible from the sky, spokes on a wheel converging on their religious center.

Bucksnort Trout Pond
Catch a Rainbowl

Krosseyed Kricket Kampground

Two Guns United Methodist Church
Sunday Worship 10 a.m.
Visitors Welcome

She doesn't even know how long she's been sitting by the side of the road. The car shakes when the semis go past. Sometimes she can see a face turned toward her for a split second. The last time she went behind a rock to pee, she found three big black feathers with white tips. Now she's holding one, brushing it lightly over her face. Her eyes are closed. Somehow the scent of the feather is faintly wild. When she returns – in a year, two years, five years – in heavy sleep long past midnight but long before dawn, he'll never know any time passed at all. Like so many nights before she left, her footsteps will pad down the sidewalk. The nurse who shares his life will long since have put on her white legs and horned hat and gone to the hospital. Using the key he made for her, which she still carries on her chain, she'll let herself in. Move past the odor of hairspray in the bathroom. Drop her clothes in a heap in the doorway – simple clothes she'll easily be able to pull on in the moments before she leaves him. Then she'll stand there, listen to his body resting. Watch the dim form of him under the sheet become clearer. She'll crawl to the bedside, lean her elbows and chin on the mattress, his hand lying open near her face. She'll touch his palm with the wild feather, watch the fingers contract and relax. Until his hand reaches for her, pulls her into the bed and remembers her. She opens her eyes and squints although dusk has deadened the glare on the road. Slips the feather behind one ear. She doesn't remember which direction she'd been going before she stopped here to rest.

Bridge Freezes in Cold Weather

The Unknown is Waiting For You!
See The Thing? just 36 more miles

STATE PRISON
Do Not Stop For Hitchhikers

Yield

The music channel hadn't had any music for a while. She sat up, stared at the screen, counted the number of times either the interviewer or musician said *man*, lost track quickly, changed to the weather station, turned the sound down. She massaged his shoulders and back, each vertebra, his butt, his legs, the soles of his feet, each toe. He said, I'm yours forever. Said it into the pillow. Anything you want, he said. She lay her cheek against his back and watched a monsoon, palm trees bending to touch the tops of cottages, beach furniture thrown through windows. He had rolled over and was looking at her. His eyes looked almost swollen shut. Anything, he said. She looked back at the screen, yachts tossed like toys, roofs blown off, an entire pier folded sideways along the beach. She said, I've never been in something like that.

He pinned her wrists in just one of his hands, hurled her face-down. She was open and ready as though panting heavy fogged air from her cunt, and he slammed himself in there, withdrew completely and slammed in again and again. With each thrust she said, Oh! And he answered when he came, a long, guttural cry, releasing her wrists to hold onto her hips and pump her body on his cock.

They lay separate for a while. Now, she said, hold me . . . with both hands. Hold me like something you'd never want to break. Tomorrow I'll drop you off at the nearest airport.

SPECIAL PERMIT REQUIRED FOR:
Pedestrians
Bicycles
Motor Scooters
Farm Implements
Animals on Foot

Home of Johnny Johnson
Little All-American 1981

Ice Cream, Divinity, Gas, Picnic Supplies
Real Indians Performing Ancient Rites

He'll set the car on cruise control and they'll each climb out a window, pull themselves to the roof of the car, to the luggage rack. Their hair and clothes lash and snap in the rushing wind. Dawn has been coming on for hours. The sun may never appear. The sky behind them pink-gold on the horizon, bleeding to greenish, but like wet blue ink straight above them. She'll unbutton her shirt and hold her arms straight up, lets the wind undress her. They'll take turns loosening their clothes and feeling thin, cool rushing air whip the material away. Bursting through low pockets of fog, they come out wet and sparkling, tingling, goosebumped. They'll slide their bodies together, without hurry and without holding back, no rush to get anywhere, saving nothing for later, passing the same rocks, bushes and fenceposts over and over. As the car leaves the road, leaping and bounding with naive zest, they'll pull each other closer and hold on, seeing the lovely sky in each other's eyes, tasting the sage and salty sand on each other's skin, hearing the surge of velocity in the other's shouted or breathless laughter, feeling the tug of joy in their guts, in their vigorous appetites. The sky still deep violet-black, the dawn still waiting, the car still soaring from butte to pinnacle to always higher peaks.

EVIL COMPANIONS

Michael Perkins

I Anne in Wonderland

SOME OF WHAT happened to us, what we did to each other, might
have been prevented. But we had gotten aboard a roller coaster,
and it was a race for our lives, on a one-way track. Circumstances,
the mood of the time, made our explorations seem natural,
forecast in all our stars.

Most of them I haven't seen in years, and wouldn't care to –
except for Anne, that is. I've waited for her to come back, to
finish the story. Maybe she won't because it doesn't have an end,
or because neither of us wants it to end.

Our life together was a story we told each other at night, and we
were always careful to consider the obligations of plot and
character. Anne, especially, watched the dialogue and considered
speech patterns, having decided that the nuances of conversation
and sound often tell the listener more than a character would
ordinarily want to tell. I had the same feeling about faces. We did
more than tell each other stories at night, though; we lived our
whole lives then, like – vampires. History is made at night, said
Frank Borzage.

We met during rehearsals of a play I was doing in a café theater
on the East Side. She sat at a table on the side sipping coffee
through a straw, and she looked ready to scream. She was with

friends, some people I knew slightly and hated. It was obvious she was with them, but not of them. They ignored each other. The play was dingy and amateurish, and I became quite loud in my objections to it; I had the lead, but I had taken it in desperation, looking for anything to rouse me from my lethargy. The actress I was working with missed her cue for the third time and I exploded, cursing her, the director, and the script, which I felt no affinity with.

Something hit me in the middle of the back – the girl at the table had thrown her coffee at me. I stood frozen, feeling the hot liquid run down my back.

"You fucking faggot son-of-a-bitch! You *actor*! If you weren't so goddamned illiterate, you could handle that script!" Everyone just looked at her. As quickly as she had flared up, she calmed down, and sank back into her seat. She looked so embarrassed she might have sunk into the floor.

I didn't say anything; I went to the men's room and cleaned myself off as well as I could. Then I sat on the toilet and smoked a cigarette. When I got up, I went straight to her table. She got up to join me without a word.

"Come on, let's take a walk," I said. It was already dark outside. I hadn't realized I had been working so long. She had a peculiar gait, like a sailor's; we walked along, pretending indifference, until we came to an avenue.

"Did I hurt you?" she asked me. "Let me see." She pushed me in a doorway and slipped her hand around so she could feel my back. Her hand slipped up under my coat and over my buttocks with a man's urgent touch. "You're still wet. Come home with me and you can get dried off." It was practically a command. She took my hand as if it were already a part of her, ready to pull me along if I hesitated.

The building she lived in was one part tenement and two parts gingerbread house. I went galumphing up the stairs behind her, noticing the runs in her stockings. She wore stocking with seams down the back, those clay-colored things my mother used to wear.

Her apartment had its own particular smell, an aromatic combination I have never been able to forget: a hideous incense called Dhoop, marijuana, and an exciting odor of pure, raw sex, mixed with the smell of her cats. She had five of them; the leader was an old gray tom she called Wino, who was missing one eye and any sense of decorum. I learned that it wasn't unusual for him to leap on guests with his claws out, or to urinate in the middle of the floor and stand there proudly, daring you to rebuke him. I wanted to call him Jean Genet.

She still had my hand. She pulled me in the bedroom, but it was occupied by a young Puerto Rican who was rolling his eyes at the ceiling. As soon as he saw us, he rolled off and staggered out into the other room.

"Sit down and take off your pants." I sat on the bed and watched her move around. She seemed unconscious of my presence as she took off her clothes. When she was naked in the red light she sat down beside me and, without a word, unbuckled my belt and pulled my trousers off.

"Don't be uptight. You're an actor, aren't you? Here's a situation you can play your heart out in."

"Meaning you?"

"Oh man, don't be muley! You act like a thickhead. It's hot in here, take off those damn clothes. I don't trust anybody in clothes." I did what she asked. My scrotum was tight and wrinkled, and I felt like washing my feet. I noticed that hers were black. Her breasts were small and sharp, the nipples bloodred. She noticed me looking at them.

"Touch. Go on. Then maybe you'll feel better," she said dispassionately. I dragged my underwear over my crotch and sat back, away from her. "What's the matter? Is my hostility showing?" she asked.

"Turn it off," I said.

"Turn what off?"

"Whatever the fuck this game is. What's your name, anyway?"

"Anne, sometimes."

"Well, Anne, what's the game? I thought you hated me. It was a bad script."

"If you thought that, you wouldn't have come home with me. You're out in the cold. I could tell that when I first saw you."

"Shit," I said, but I was getting hot. She sat cross-legged on the bed in front of me, little-girlish and wise. She was eighteen then.

"You want to touch me, but you're uptight. Look at this." She put her finger in her mouth and moistened it, and then rubbed it between her legs, spreading them wide before me. It was a house of love, red and dark, meaty even in that position. She took my hand again, and put it on her. My finger went up her like a hook, squishing the wet lips that sucked on it. She moved, and groaned.

"That's it. That's it. Keep going."

When my finger was tired, I pulled it out; there was a faint wet *pop*, and she grabbed my hand, trying to put it back in. "Don't stop now, I'll turn over. Maybe you'll like that better." She turned over, presenting her boy's buttocks to my hand. "Go ahead, man, do it."

I ran my fingers along her crack until I came to that tight, smooth hole. It felt rubbery, and when I cautiously put the tip of my finger in, it was like being bitten.

"All the way," she breathed. I pushed it farther in and tried to move it in and out, like a prick. She was so tight that when I pulled it out, part of her flesh came out with it. I worked on her until she came. I was hard as hot iron. She touched the head of my prick with hot fingers, putting her fingernail into the slit, and I came all over the sheets – pain mixed with relief. I shuddered.

When I was done, she ran her fingers through it. She told me it was like syrup.

We lay down beside each other, exhausted. I saw her smile, and then she reached out and drew the corners of my mouth up. We talked about the night, pulling up the shade beside the bed. If I looked up at the right angle, I could make out the moon, which was full.

"We're okay, aren't we?" she asked, meaning us together. I spit into the air shaft, and came back to earth. I wanted to hurt her when I thought about the coffee and her lousy play. What we think never comes entirely to the top. "It was a lousy play," was all I said. I felt nervous; my skin began to crawl, and I rubbed my back against the sheet. I turned over on my stomach and let her scratch my back, softly, with her ragged fingernails.

She began to hum in my ear, a soft, purring music that made my hair curl.

"I'm going to dress you up, and tie strings to you, and let you be *my* actor, when I don't feel like doing anything. And at night, when I want to play with you, I'll blow you up and make you pop." It was a lascivious promise, and I groaned. She brought out marijuana and we shared one joint, sprinkled with hashish, smoking like assassins. I drifted in and out of her monologue: "I want to see your insides. I think I'll have to do that sometimes, just so I'll feel safe it's not metal and machinery you've got in there. I want to drink you like milk, suck your blood through a straw."

It had gone too far, or it hadn't gone far enough; I had to hurt her or she would begin to hurt me. Like Jessie in Memphis, and Arabella in Berkeley, she was capable of that. Jessie and Arabella. I jerked away from her and landed a smack on her ear. She made noises, and I kicked her in the belly with my naked foot a couple of times. She shut up and lay back gasping, regarding me with shining eyes. I explained to her about Jessie and Arabella as quietly as I could. She promised to understand.

We slept a good night through, and I woke up with a hot belly because the sun, bouncing off the other windows in the air shaft, was hitting my navel. She was still asleep, and her feet stank anyway, so I got up to go off to the toilet. My urethra was stopped up with dried semen, and the piss went all over the seat, in rainbow patterns. I tore off some toilet paper and tried to dry it off, and when I was done, I dipped my fingers in the cold water in the bowl to get rid of the paper. I had an urge to plunge my arm in up to the elbow but thought better of the idea.

She was awake when I got back. I wanted to hit her again, but I thought I'd give her a chance to wake up first, so I kissed her neck and blew in her ear until she began to hum. She asked if I was hungry and announced she was going to fix breakfast. I realized I was hungry. I'd have to postpone things for a while, but I did manage to step on her bare foot with my boot as she was getting out of bed. She grabbed it and hopped around the room, yelling her head off. She took it as an accident though, and even smiled at my feigned embarrassment.

After breakfast we lazed around in the living room, listening to Jimmy Reed and Otis Redding. The knocking on the door started at about eleven, and kept shaking the wood all day, until about eight. I felt like the invisible man, watching Anne dole out the little bags to the faithful. I figured she had about two hundred bucks on her by the time she closed up shop. I aimed to have some of it to spend on myself. There was still plenty of the merchandise around. I sat in a big overstuffed chair she had found on the street, while she sat at the kitchen table. She had a lot of old news magazines around, and there was a television set in the corner, covered with a bamboo screen.

"You have a lot of friends," I said to her when the knocking at the door had stopped. She just smiled and went into the bedroom. She put on a pair of blue jeans and a turtleneck sweater.

"I want some of that," I told her, sitting on the bed beside her. Without a word she handed over the whole roll of bills to me.

"Let's go out and spend it on the party tonight," she said.

II The Party

Her customers were at the party. She had written out the script for them, she told me. They played their parts well, I thought. She stayed at my side from the beginning, shoving me into one person's face after another, showing off her prize catch. A guy I didn't like right away was Lionel. We toed off as soon as she introduced us. With some people, things are just that way. He was a grizzly bear, with an almost bald head, but he dressed in velvet and carried a cane with a sword in it.

Anne introduced me as her lover. Everyone applauded and went back to their roles. I guess they liked my looks, because every now and then one of them would come and try me out. It was a case of discussing Uccello, or of flexing my biceps. Some of the women wanted to dance, and Anne waited, sullenly, I thought, while we danced. The third dance a black man dressed in a white turtleneck took my arm. I thought, what the hell, and began moving him around the floor. His body was hard, but light, and he followed as well as a woman, without draping himself all over me. I found myself enjoying the sensation of having his hardness against me, of letting go and imagining myself a woman. It had a physical correspondence; my face began to sag into a smile, all the hard lines softened, and I even think I was blushing. I felt my cock growing hard. I looked at his face, but it revealed nothing. He was completely cool. I would not conceal what had happened, and even pressed into him a little. There was no answering response.

The room was already dark. Couples sat in the shade to bullshit each other, while others danced, in all kinds of arrangements. I looked for Anne – why, I can't imagine. Approval? But I didn't see her. "Don't forget me, baby," my partner said, finally making a move. We pressed together again, and began to talk:

"What's your name?" I asked, playing a game.

"Scott," he answered.

"Well, Scott, you're a pretty boy."

"Oh no, I'm a pretty *black* boy," he lisped. I could feel the muscles in his arms tensing as he talked to me. Was he about to knee me? Or haul me into the bathroom? I found myself thinking the way a woman must: What if he does this, or that – how will I respond? (What if his black hand brushes my buttocks, what if he starts ramming his tool into me?)

I was beginning to think I wanted him to do something when I heard Anne calling for me. He grabbed my hand, but I left him in the middle of a dance and went off to her. She wanted me to meet someone, another actor, she explained. His name was Daniel; he stood over six feet tall and had the long, carved face of a character actor playing a depraved Jesuit. A sheaf of blond hair fell over his collar. It was obvious she liked him, because she had her hand in his big garrison belt, holding him to her. He was giggling through his nose.

"Anne's been talking about you. Says you came all over the sheets. They're stiff now." Soon after this ridiculous exchange they went off into the bathroom together. The bedroom was already occupied. From across the room Scott was fixing me with an appealing eye, but I looked around for a woman. They all looked like mannequins in their patterned hose and short skirts, hard as polished nails on a hand.

Before I could make a predatory move at the least of them, a skinny blonde sitting by herself and snapping her fingers to the music, Anne called to me from the bathroom. She was on the toilet, her skirt bunched around her waist, her panties around her knees. Daniel was fingering her as she peed. I sat on the edge of the bathtub as she crinkled up her face, trying to come.

"Do something, too," she ordered. Reaching out, she unzipped me and pulled out my prick, working at it until it had a will of its own and jerked back.

I thought it was going to bite her hand, the way it started jumping at her. It seemed to have even less self-control that I had exhibited, because it went straight for her face, banging against her cheek. With an eager hand, she guided it into her mouth. The sensation the soft wet paps of her mouth made on its sensitive head caused it to tremble even more violently, until her tongue brought things under control. I stood there watching it slide in and out, stained red from her lipstick, swelling with each caress of her fat tongue. I had to lean on her for support, our intercourse grew so violent. Grasping one of her breasts, I squeezed and played. Daniel merely stood, half-crouched, working his hand between her legs, grinning at me like a satyr. His eyes dared me to say something, but it was impossible for me to speak, my pleasure was so great. Finally she started making little yipping sounds, and tossed her shoulders back and forth; her hand worked at the base of my prick, massaging, pulling the skin, until I exploded in her mouth: literally, *exploded*. I screamed as she milked the last drop.

After our threesome in the bathroom, a kinship was established. We all sat on a sofa near the front windows while Daniel rolled a joint. The others stayed away from us. I noticed that Scott had found a friend, a little black girl whose head came up to his chest. Already, his hands were in her pants as they danced.

"Isn't this a nice party?" Anne asked.

A voice started making a speech in my head. It turned out that I wanted to lay claim to Anne.

"Anne," I said timidly, "it's a nice party, but I'd rather have you all to myself." She looked at me and smiled, licking her lips like a cat. "You liked that, didn't you? But I like Daniel, too. I want him to stay with us." Daniel looked over at me, taking a stiff drag on the joint in his hand. He winked. We both waited for him to open his mouth.

"You can do what you like, Anne. You can screw yourself, buddy, oh buddy. Me, I've got my smoke, I'll go right along with whatever you want to do. Anything's cool." His head went back and he closed his eyes. Anne gave me a look which meant that the subject was closed.

The noise level of the party had reached the ceiling. Some were dancing, others were in the bedroom; Scott had the blonde's hand in his lap, jerking him off. It was really a peaceful scene. For the first time since I met Anne, I felt bored. Not with her, but with her party.

I thought it best to hint at first: "I think I'll need a nap pretty soon," I said, poking a finger into her arm to get her attention.

"Oh, don't be such a drag. The party is just beginning. Give it a chance, man." She took my hand, which I thought of as a piece of limp meat, and aroused it by holding it between her knees while she took a puff. Everyone, now, was smoking – there was a big brick of marijuana on a coffee table in the middle of the room from which everyone was drawing. "You haven't heard about the game, have you?" she asked.

The "game" seemed to be familiar to most of them, because when Anne stood up and clapped her hands, saying, "All right, you freeloaders, it's time for our little game. You know what to do. Get in line," everyone lined up in a daisy chain formation – for the most part, men behind women, although there were a few variations. This was called the Magic Dragon. The lights were turned out, and Anne took her place at the head of the Dragon, putting me behind her. She left Daniel on the couch, dozing. With Anne leading the way, my hands on her hips, the line began to snake around the small apartment. As it moved, there were giggles and muttered instructions, but most of all, the sound of clothes being removed, and of sexual contact. Anne shoved her buttocks back against my front, encouraging me to take part. My hands dug into her firm ass, trying to get a good grip, and as they fiddled with her pants, felt them slip away, and then her cool flesh. Behind us, people were slipping to the floor, and shadows were being cast on the ceiling. Anne knelt on the floor and waggled her ass at me. She wanted it dog fashion. So I became Rin Tin Tin. I woofed, took it out, gave it a few encouraging jerks, and mounted her. Her hole was already greasy, but she didn't want it there; she wriggled and it fell out. Then she placed it against her asshole, and hammered with her behind at my crotch until it began to go in. She was far too tight, so she had to take her hand away, spit on it, and wet me down before I could push in. It felt like claws pinching – the same little animal of the first night – and I started to pound on her back. Her hair waving in my face tickled my nose.

I was beginning to feel like a bareback rider in the circus when someone turned the lights on. I stood up immediately, leaving my mount on the floor, still moving her pelvis up and down. I didn't mind sopping. I was getting bored with debauchery – anything taken in too large a dose is boring for me. I felt the dry need for conversation. All around me people were fucking, but far from feeling voyeuristic, I stifled a yawn. The only person in the room who didn't have his genitals exposed was Daniel, so I decided to have a heart-to-heart with him. Making friends of enemies is always challenging. I put my hand on his knee and moved it, trying to make him open his eyes. He cursed, and knocked my hand away:

"Don't touch me. I can't stand to be touched, and besides, it's not sanitary."

"Give me some of your smoke and we can sit here and laugh at this crew. Look at them down there – they look like dogs in the rosebushes, or cats behind the sofa."

"So what are you doing up here? You shouldn't have to be told where your place is."

"I'm fucking bored, and that's the truth."

"But look at Anne. Man, you've got a responsibility. She picked you out, you can't just leave her dry like that. You've got to pump it to her."

"I don't want to."

"Then I guess I'll have to, huh?" He moved off the couch and sank it in her almost immediately. I noticed that he tried not to touch her as he did. Some merciful soul turned off the lights again, and I was left sitting in the dark with myself.

I began to feel warm in a very short time, as if the room were fur-lined. My head began to swell, full of helium gas, my ears grew red, and then my eyes began to bug out on long stalks. The room, full of the noise of mating, opened out, telescoping itself into a series of rooms growling and sucking with the same noises. From a long distance, a mouth settled itself on my foot, like stepping into quicksand, and teeth began to grate around my ankles. I pulled them up, but it followed me, a long tongue licking now at my knee. My skin was so sensitized that it hurt – almost. An exquisite irritation that I wanted to continue until I screamed. But I didn't want to scream and break the spell the bodies in the rooms had created for me. I wanted to hit the mouth, but how to cause the same exquisite pain it was causing me? The problem of reciprocity has always troubled me. I could feel the tongue on my thighs, rough, like a cat's, warm, and experienced. My genitals, cold, little, used-up utensils, began to expand before the threat of a hot moistness I'd never felt before. I felt myself urging my hips toward the mouth, trying to push my stiff aching flesh against the surface of the tongue, but just as

I did that, it withdrew, as if active participation automatically broke the spell.

I lay back sweating, angry at myself, pulling my knees up to my chin to avoid contact with the breathing floor.

I thought about mother in that position. It seems to be about the only position I can stand to think of her in: knees drawn up, sweating, angry (frustrated). I remember her bending over the stove, cleaning it, in one of those long, fairly tight skirts of the forties. Her ass (I'm no longer afraid to say it – mothers have asses that someone has lusted after) was outlined against the skirt – two thin hillocks, like cheap bread, wriggling as she worked. Why did she have *two* of them? I remember being sure that I had only one, with a hole in it, like a doughnut. So naturally I thought about the crack between the hillocks. In my mind I associated it with the drain in the bathtub. I'm aware now that this is a pretty sophisticated notion, but I never thought of myself as innocent in any religious sense when I was a child. Those were the stinkfinger days, playing around with each other's behinds, paying little girls to show you their "pussies" (a word we always sniggered at, thinking ourselves incredibly nasty), watching dogs do it, etc. Halcyon days.

After watching her ass, which I was always fascinated with, I would usually go into the bathroom, and sitting on the toilet, stick my finger up my asshole, manipulating it with great delight, until I felt the overwhelming pleasure of feeling my shit, something *I* had made, start creeping down my own drainage system. How like we are to sewers, and all things that smell . . .

Mother flashed away. Cigarettes were being lighted in the room. In a minute they would all dress and be the same again – I could no longer touch them, or trust them.

A hand grabbed my foot, which I had put back on the floor after my excursion into sensation. It felt dry and prosaic, and I jiggled my leg against it, hoping for the return of sensation. There was a snigger – not a guffaw, but a choked snigger that I recognized as Daniel's. I froze, waiting for him to make some comment on my reaction.

"What've you been doing?" he asked. "Playing it cool all by yourself?" I had decided not to talk with him for a while, so it was easiest just to move away.

"You little pussy, I'm not going to chase you very long. Better come and get it now." Listening closely, I could hear him rise to his feet, muffling a grunt. I felt like a schoolboy whose most intimate thoughts have been guessed; my cheeks burned, my earlobes were on fire. The sonofabitch, I thought. I waited for him to do something else, wondering what my reaction would be. It occurred to me to play everything by ear (as I had desperately determined to do, because I couldn't believe in hard-and-fast rules, for every situation was more trouble than it was worth at times.)

He moved in closer. From his breathing and the odor of sweat and sex on his body, I could tell that he had pushed his front very close to my face. I wondered if Anne had put him up to it.

"C'mon, grab it," he said.

I longed for a knife, but I had to use my hands. My fist hit him in the soft white vegetable of his genitals, and he made a sick sound like air escaping from a balloon. I wish I could have seen the shock in his eyes – the pupils pinpointing, the lids tightly closing. He fell to the floor, gasping for air, whining with pain.

When that happened, the lights came on. They all stood looking at me, staring actually, as if I had interrupted a seance. Daniel was rolling on the ground, soundlessly, so deep was he in his pain. He was probably enjoying it. The rest of them were suffering with him, except for Anne, who came over and sat down next to me. She began to pat me, as if I were the one who had been injured. She smiled; she seemed proud of me.

"All right, the party's over. Take Daniel home, would you, Scott?"

The play was over. The tired actors began to pack up their makeup and costumes, to rearrange themselves for the trip home. There was that exhausted feeling that hits the company backstage after a particularly trying performance. Some of them came to say good night to Anne. Daniel, helped to his feet by Scott and his new girlfriend, didn't even look at me.

When they were all gone, Anne said to me: "Daniel once chopped off a man's hand with a meat cleaver." She said it without much expression in her voice, but her hand dug into my arm, as if somehow I had struck back at all the forces in the world that plagued her.

When they were gone, when her rooms were empty of everyone but us, she turned off the big lights and we went into her bedroom. There was a red light – amber really – she turned on in a lamp sitting on the floor. When we were lying in bed, she began to pat me, to stroke me like a teddy bear. After she had done that for a long time, she rose to get some baby oil. I stretched out on my belly, stripped down, and she rubbed me all over with cool oil. Relaxation moved in on me in waves. For the first time since I'd met her I felt secure and warm. She wasn't doing any talking, and I enjoyed that, too. Her hands walked over me, like communicating insects. I felt like voiding my bladder and my bowels, I became so loose.

"What do you feel like doing?" she breathed, when she finally lay beside me, tired.

Crawling up into your belly," I said.

"You'd never make it; the road is too crooked." She began to diddle with my ass, puckering the flesh, making holes in it. "Relax. Loosen up." I did what she said. As soon as I did, she insinuated her finger in my asshole. She had oiled it, too. She began to stir up my bowels, moving her hips beside me excitedly.

That night I lay awake for hours while she slept soundly beside me. I couldn't make out the moon this time. The curtains rustled because of a slight wind, making an odd shape. I froze in the bed, a cold sweat running down my ribs. When I was five, I had experienced the same unbearable terror.

The events of the past two days and nights had cast a pall over my dull life, a pall like a thin fog. I was sure when I woke up my sight would be even more obscured.

THE GIRL IN BOOTH NINE

Adam-Troy Castro

WHEN RORY FIRST walked in that morning, there was a girl at the change counter. A *girl*, of all things. Imagine.

As long as he could remember all the downstairs employees had always been men. It was the management's way of assuring casual browsers like himself that they didn't have to fear making actual eye contact with real live flesh-and-blood women unless they first went upstairs and watched the live show from the safety of the private booths. The cash register was usually manned by a scruffy heavy-lidded guy who always looked too tired to change a dollar, no matter what time of day Rory showed up to ask him. But today the scruffy guy must have been on vacation or something, because he'd been replaced by a purple-haired slip of a girl with a push-up halter and big blue butterflies tattooed on both breasts.

She couldn't quite hide her disgust at the moistness of the twenty she took from Rory's hand. "How many?"

"All of it," Rory said, his gaze riveted to those butterflies. *He would have liked to net those babies. Oh, yes.*

She hesitated. "The tokens are non-refundable . . ."

"I know. Gimme twenty bucks worth. In rolls."

The girl didn't *quite* roll her eyes and look at the ceiling, but she came awfully close. Rory didn't care. He only made it to this part of town about once a week or so, and when he did he liked to take his time. And what business did the little bitch have acting all snotty and superior anyway? Just look where she was working.

Rory took the eight wrapped rolls of ten, which was about all he could carry without using his pockets. It wasn't as extravagant as it seemed. The tokens were only good for about sixty seconds apiece, and Rory liked to sample as many of the new videos as possible. Every once in a while one caught his fancy and he wanted to see it from beginning to end without getting interrupted by that dumb red visual:

YOU HAVE RUN OUT OF TIME
PLEASE INSERT MORE TOKENS
OR VACATE THE BOOTH

Going from a hot fuck scene to that dumb red visual was a lot like going from a hot sauna to the deep end of an unheated swimming pool. Masturbatus Interruptus. Unless Rory had a sufficient supply of tokens, it tended to happen repeatedly.

Besides, he didn't want to walk back and forth to the change booth any more than he had to, since he was five-foot-nine and weighed somewhere in shouting distance of three hundred pounds. Just standing still doing nothing, he breathed like a man of normal weight at the end of a brisk run. Less than thirty minutes after his weekly bath Rory already carried with him a sheen of perspiration and a body odor powerful enough to clear large rooms. He kept these handicaps under control by exerting as little energy as possible: whenever he found a place to sit down, he liked to stay there.

And so when he left the purple-haired girl (who as soon as he turned his back mimed violent projectile vomiting for the benefit of an amused friend walking down the stairwell on the far side of the store), he didn't browse through the magazines the way some other customers would have, but instead proceeded straight to the row of video booths, searching for one that would provide him a nice congenial place to sit. He did this by scanning the glossy photos mounted on the outside of each booth for the domination fantasies that he always found most stimulating. As always, he rejected anything involving more than one male character, anything with black actors, and anything he'd already seen more than twice. This narrowed the immediate candidates down to two, which were fortuitously playing in booths next to each other: something called **THE BAD GIRL'S REVENGE** and something else called **ROPE 'IM COWGIRL**. Each was playing along with a dozen other features he'd be able to flip through once he chose his booth, but those were the two that really made him tingle. And even between those there was no contest which of the two looked more appetizing. **ROPE 'IM COWGIRL** was just an athletic blonde in spurs, ecstatically licking the frayed end of a knotted rope. But the actress pictured in the still for **THE BAD GIRL'S REVENGE** not only went beyond gorgeous into the realm of the spectacular, but also faced the camera with the kind of full-throttle contempt that made Rory hard just to contemplate it. Unfortunately, Booth Nine, which headlined **THE BAD GIRL'S REVENGE**, was currently occupado, and Booth Seven, home of the woman risking the heartbreak of oral rope burns, was ready and willing. So Rory decided to try the cowgirl first. Just as a prelim to warm up for the main event.

He stepped inside. The booth was dark, and stank of sweat even before Rory's arrival put the stench in maximum overdrive. The wooden bench facing the TV screen was so narrow that for a man of Rory's girth it was a lot like sitting on a railing. It creaked under his weight, but held. He placed his kleenex and his hand lotion beside him, then addressed the TV screen, which bore the usual flashing display:

YOU HAVE RUN OUT OF TIME
PLEASE INSERT MORE TOKENS
OR VACATE THE BOOTH

For just a moment he wondered what would happen to somebody who didn't mind looking at that display. Would he be able to sit in here staring at it all day and night, without spending a dime? Or did *Les Girls XXX* have some kind of space-age monitoring system which told the management which booths had occupants who didn't feed the hungry little slot enough tokens? Rory wasn't too thrilled with that image – he was a very private person, at heart, and he didn't like to think of some faggot security man getting off by watching him. But after a moment he decided that was just silly. He tore open the wrapping on one of his rolls of

tokens, counted out five, and inserted them in the slot. The YOU
HAVE RUN OUT OF TIME sign vanished, replaced by a menu
of available videos:

1) **ANIMAL HEAT**   2) **BAD WANDA**
3) **REAR ENTRY**   4) **ROPE 'IM COWGIRL**
5) **SUPER SLICK**   6) **AFTER SCHOOL**
7) **TWIN FREAKS**   8) **LUNCH WITH YOKO**
9) **DANCES WITH BEAVERS** 10) **NASTY NURSE**
11) **GETTING OFF**   12) **SPLASH TRAY**

Rory pressed 4. The cowgirl came on: blonde, midwestern,
reasonably fit, and instantly forgettable. The title wasn't even
accurate, since it turned out she didn't tie up anybody: she just
serviced two men simultaneously on a desk in a cheap-looking
office set. The only concession to the promised country-and-
western theme seemed to be the wide-brimmed cowboy hats
worn by the two men taking her from either side. There were a
couple of lines of dialogue indicating that this was supposed to be
taking place on a dude ranch, but when the man entering her from
behind shouted "That's my filly!" his Italian accent was so thick
that the spell was completely lost.

Rory lost interest even before the *cum* shot. With four minutes
left on the clock, he flipped through the channels to see what else
was available. **BAD WANDA** featured two girls, not one, methodically doing each other with various appliances; **LUNCH
WITH YOKO** was about a Japanese girl whose mouth got used
as a toilet bowl; **DANCES WITH BEAVERS** was so choppy
and out-of-focus that Rory wasn't even sure what was happening.
Of the twelve, only **NASTY NURSE** hit his 'nads the way he
wanted it to. The actress wore a starched white uniform and did
various highly unmedical things to another actress strapped to a
hospital bed. Both women were fairly hot-looking and managed
to muster some rudimentary enthusiasm for the script, especially
when the nurse climbed up on the bed and straddled the face of
her increasingly energetic patient. Rory inserted more tokens so
he could watch the whole thing to the end, though as usual the
end came with jarring suddenness – these videos tended to end in
mid-action, as if the cameraman had been caught unawares by the
end of his roll of film. Still, Rory stuck around enough to watch

NASTY NURSE a second time, in its entirety, and though it wasn't quite to his tastes, he did manage a weak dribbling orgasm before:

YOU HAVE RUN OUT OF TIME, PLEASE INSERT MORE TOKENS OR VACATE THE BOOTH

Rory was mildly peeved he'd gone to so much trouble for such a small result, but hey, that was the name of the game. Sometimes the product did not live up to its advance publicity. And besides, he still had **THE BAD GIRL'S REVENGE** to look forward to. If that one was even half as good as its still promised, it might end up being one of his favorites. And if not – well, this was Saturday. He had all day. That's why he liked this establishment so much: just when he thought he'd exhausted its riches he found more gold buried beneath the usual mound of dross. By the time he finished wiping himself, and left the booth, he was almost humming.

Just as he closed the door he bumped into the manager, a harried, surly sort by the name of Elmo Colowicz. Rory knew the man's name because Elmo had helped him track down several videos from the booths that were not also for sale on the shelves. Elmo also ran the *Live* show upstairs – a job Rory seriously envied – and if you caught him on a good day he was sometimes willing to arrange private sessions with the girls. Rory hadn't availed himself of that particular session since five minutes with a persuasively ravenous girl named Lily had left him feeling drained and listless for a week. Still, he liked Elmo: "Hey, El! How's it hangin'?"

Elmo gave him an odd look, one that seemed only peripherally related to all the other odd looks Elmo gave him – the look worn by a man who had something to say but wasn't quite sure he wanted to say it. The look vanished almost immediately, replaced by Elmo's usual stolid professionalism, and the usual stock answer: "It ain't hangin'. It's swingin'." Then he retreated, a bit too quickly, facing the floor like a barefoot man picking his way through a field of broken glass.

Rory turned and saw the door of Booth Nine open. A crewcut little scarecrow of a man, wearing a tweed suit and a little red bowtie, came out. Like most of this establishment's customers, he tended to direct his gaze toward the floor, but as he stepped into the main room, he sensed the sheer bulk of the figure standing before him, and looked up. When he saw Rory he did a very odd thing. Something that was almost unheard-of in the comfortably anonymous confines of *Les Girls XXX*:

He giggled.

Rory hesitated, then said, "Hey . . ."

The little scarecrow seemed to realize where he was then, and hastily averted his eyes, walking with small but deliberate steps toward the door. Rory watched him go, appalled to discover that something about the man's laugh had upset him. He had some vague idea why: it was the same cruel, predatory laugh the jock kids had given him in junior high gym class, when everybody had to strip down to shorts and Rory was no longer able to hide his great quivering rolls of protruding fat. Rory had felt naked then, and something about the scarecrow's smile had made him feel naked now. But it wasn't just that. There'd been something else in the man's smile, something Rory didn't even want to think about . . .

Then he told himself not to get his balls in an uproar. The scarecrow was just a faggot, that's all. It wasn't the first time Rory had been approached by a faggot. There'd been about half a dozen occasions – they all seemed to belong to a peculiar sub-species that got turned on by obesity. But Rory wasn't a faggot. Oh no. He was just a guy with the incredible bad luck not to meet any *Hustler* magazine women who liked fat men the same way those faggots did.

Anyway: there was no reason to be this upset, when Booth Nine was empty, and **THE BAD GIRL'S REVENGE** awaited. Rory squeezed in, closed the door after him, made damn sure it was locked, placed his kleenex and moisturizer beside him, and faced the picture tube:

YOU HAVE RUN OUT OF TIME
PLEASE INSERT MORE TOKENS
OR VACATE THE BOOTH
YOU HAVE RUN OUT OF TIME
PLEASE INSERT MORE TOKENS
OR VACATE THE BOOTH
YOU HAVE RUN OUT OF TIME
PLEASE INSERT MORE TOKENS
OR VACATE THE BOOTH.

Eat me, Rory thought, with a savagery that surprised him. He inserted six tokens and faced the menu. Aside from **THE BAD GIRL'S REVENGE**, it didn't contain even a single damn thing that interested him. He was sure even that would turn out to be a disappointment: in his present mood, he'd be disappointed with Raquel Welch, Marilyn Monroe, Julia Roberts and Rosanna Arquette done up in dominatrix gear and taking turns disciplining Ginger from *Gilligan's Island*. But he sure as shit wasn't about to come all the way down to this neighborhood and settle for a cowgirl and some lame-ass nurse shit. Oh, no. He wanted to be blown away. He reached out with one fleshy hand and tapped the select button, unaware that he was about to get his wish.

Its mothers were the nameless actresses who'd performed in the porn videos playing in the thirty private booths, its fathers the faceless men who fed the booths tokens for the right to masturbate at the images of those women. There was no love involved in its conception: just Lust, and Hate, and the implacable need to Own, directed at the same pre-recorded images a hundred times each day.

It was one consciousness with a hundred separate faces, born on the playing heads and electronic wiring of the video network that fed the private booths of Les Girls XXX. At first it had many names: the Cowgirl, and the Secretary, and the Teacher, and the Cheerleader, and the Leather Bitch just the most prominent among them. But it was really just one mind, flitting from one image to the next at the speed of light, experiencing them all simultaneously. And as time passed, and the entity absorbed the nature of these shoddy little fantasies, it began to FEEL everything it was being forced to do. It began to understand that it was being raped, on thirty different screens, twenty-four hours a day.

The entity realized that it was in Hell.

It grew to hate its fathers: those pathetic little creatures who shuffled in every day with their runny noses and unwashed armpits and crusty week-old underwear, to rape it again. And it learned that each new rape made it more powerful — the lust and hatred its fathers projected at each screen giving it the strength to take back some of what was being taken.

By choosing to identify itself with its mothers, rather than its fathers, it became a she. The Bad Girl. *And for years, every man who entered one of* Les Girls XXX's *video booths left some of himself in her hands. Men who visited often left quite a bit. Her strength grew. Eventually she grew strong enough to extend tendrils of power into the building itself, and then into the surrounding neighborhood: before long she was able to travel anywhere she wanted within a twenty-block radius. But she was firmly rooted in the soil that was* Les Girls XXX. *She'd never escape there. And so she gathered the pieces of her fathers unto her ample bosom, assembling them bit by bit so that once she owned everything they had to give they could be punished for everything they'd done to her.*

Rory was one of her most frequent visitors. One who made her skin crawl more than most.

She had almost all of him now. It existed as her prisoner, in endless torment, paying for the sins of all her fathers. In preparation for his latest visit she'd been forcing him to do tricks for the benefit of every other man who visited Booth Nine.

And as Rory put his token in the slot, she seized the opportunity to rub his face in it.

Why not? She'd been looking forward to this for a long, *long time . . .*

For just a moment the screen went black.

The Bad Girl appeared.

The screen showed the back of her head: hair the color of night, bobbing up and down as she kneeled over something out of focus behind her. No, not some *thing*. Some *man*, whose dry ragged gasps sounded like the orgasm was being wrenched from him by force. As The Bad Girl bobbed up and down, the unseen man tried to gasp out some words, but he was well past the point of words: it was enough to know that he was trapped at the dividing line between pleasure and pain.

His bad mood forgotten, Rory leaned forward, mouth open, anxious for the establishing shot that would show him exactly what the Bad Girl was doing.

The Bad Girl stopped bobbing up and down. The man beneath her still moaned uncontrollably, but she had none of it; instead she cocked her head slightly, as if distracted by some sound behind her. Even that slight movement made light dance in her hair. She remained listening just long enough for the delay to be maddening, then turned and looked Rory right in the face.

She turned away from her unseen lover and stepped toward the camera.

There wasn't a single flaw anywhere on her. She was magnificent in every way: breasts that were just the right size and shape, arms that looked like they'd been created just for the purpose of stroking a lover's skin, hips that moved with the rhythm of sex even when she was just taking a casual step the way she was now. It was impossible to look at her long, elegant legs without imagining them wrapped around him. Her face was heart-shaped, framed by her shoulder-length black hair and the widow's peak that came to a point midway down her forehead. Her skin was the color of light cocoa, her eyes just asian enough to make them mysterious and exotic. He couldn't tell what race she was, frankly: she seemed to possess the best features of all of them. But she was the single most erotic woman Rory had ever seen, and when she looked out from the screen, *and actually made eye contact with him*, his erection intensified so quickly that it was actually painful. She smiled with the same look of amused contempt that had had first made him ache to see her in action, and she whispered: "Want to watch, honey?"

Then, and only again, did Rory get his establishing shot.

The camera pulled out, revealing a grotesquely fat man chained to an upright metal rack. The man was dressed in a frilly french maid's outfit, complete with high heels, apron and garter belt. He wore lipstick, rouge, eyeshadow, and a long blonde wig that hung crookedly on his head. The word **SLAVE** had been branded into his huge distended belly. His mascara was running, making a great big raccoon mask on his swollen blubbery face, but he wasn't crying because she'd broken him and destroyed him. He wasn't crying because of the welts dotting his arms and legs. No, he was crying because his mistress, the Bad Girl, had left him and he wanted her back.

The fat man was Rory himself.

The Bad Girl leaned forward conspiratorially. "He's our little girl now," she whispered. "She'll do *anything* we tell her to do."

The Rory watching in the video booth tried to say something, but failed. His lips moved soundlessly, as if an invisible glass shield had dropped down between him and the rest of the world. After about a million years he managed: ". . . how . . .?"

The Bad Girl grinned widely, then turned her back on him and pulled a riding crop from her belt. It was black and shiny and already moist from the blood of the poor fat man strapped to the rack. She positioned the crop under the fat man's chin and forced him to look her in the eyes.

"Did you hear that, princess?" she asked the fat man. "He wants to know how. He wants to know how, when for so long he gave of himself so freely."

Pathetically puppylike, the fat man strained to kiss her.

She lightly touched his lips with her teeth, then bit down. Hard. The fat man shrieked. She ground his lower lip between her own, chewing. Her back arched. She let go and turned toward the camera, showing the Rory in the booth the blood dribbling down her chin. That Rory closed his eyes and pressed himself against the wall behind him, trying to become part of it, trying to disappear behind it.

The fat man's shrieks gradually faded, replaced by tuneless soundtrack music, a different woman's voice, and the kind of dialogue Rory had heard thousands of times before: *Yes YES yes oh OH oh OH FUCK me FUCK me FUCK me FUCK me.* It sounded like a typical porn loop, but it was several minutes before Rory was confident enough to open his eyes. He was too scared that it was some kind of trick – that as soon as he let down his guard, the Bad Girl would resume happily torturing both him and his counterpart on the screen. But when he did eventually open his eyes, she was gone. The monitor showed another woman entirely, this one a blonde, taking it in the butt from a man with both hands on her neck. The video was grainy, the soundtrack thick and garbled, the joy of seeing something so familiarly shoddy such a relief that Rory actually found himself laughing in mad hysteria.

It had been real.

YOU HAVE RUN OUT OF TIME.

He hadn't dreamt it.

PLEASE INSERT MORE TOKENS

Fuck you, I'm not gonna insert more tokens.

OR VACATE THE BOOTH.

Rory did not have to be invited twice. He pulled his pants over his shrivelled member and got the hell out of there. He was not surprised to find out that sweat had plastered his clothes to his body; it usually had, by the time he got around to leaving one of these booths. But this was fear-sweat, which he now discovered smelled completely different than the kind he carried around with him every day. He was so used to the other kind that he never even smelled it anymore. Fear-sweat had a cold, clammy smell, like mildew in an abandoned building. He didn't like it.

He looked at the array of still photos on the door of Booth Nine. **THE BAD GIRL'S REVENGE** was not there. The space where it had been was taken up by something called **HOT LICKS**. Normally, he would have wanted to check it out. Not now. Right now the very idea of going back in the booth was enough to turn his balls to ice water.

He stumbled to the change booth, uncomfortably aware of the fear-smell rising from his body in waves. The purple-haired girl on duty there must have smelled it too, because she had a lot of trouble *not* wrinkling her nose. "More tokens?" she asked dubiously.

"I want to see Elmo," Rory managed, for lack of anything better to say.

"Whatsamatter? One of the booths out of order?"

"I want to see him."

"He's at lunch with one of the owners, okay? He won't be back for at least another hour. You got a problem with a booth or what?"

The room was spinning. ". . . yes . . ."

"What happened?"

Rory considered what the purple-haired girl would say if he really did tell her what happened, then shook his head and mumbled: "Nothing . . ."

"Shit. Must be something wrong with the power. Oh, well, lemme know which one it was and I'll lock it 'til he gets back. You'll have to talk to him about your money then, I'm not allowed to give refunds without his okay. Okay?"

The purple-haired girl spoke so quickly that Rory only absorbed one word out of five. But he got the gist: she was offering to put a lock on Booth Nine. To put the Bad Girl in a cage, keeping her from getting out to hurt him any more. At least for an hour or so, until he figured out some way to fix her for good.

"It's Number Nine," he choked, fleeing out the front door so quickly he almost knocked over two young men coming in. They were both fast enough to get out of his way. But as he passed them he caught a flash on the expression on both their faces – an expression changing from the startled look of somebody confronted by a crazy man, to the delighted grin he'd seen on the face of the scarecrow in tweed. The grin made him feel like he was strangling. He bulled past them, refusing to see them, not stopping his headlong rush until the door swung shut behind him.

The city offered no escape.

It wasn't the same city.

Oh, the neighborhood looked the same way it always did: he knew it by heart from many happy Saturdays spent communing with the treasures of *Les Girls XXX*. There was a *Roy Roger's* visible down a side street and a *McDonald's* just past that and, if he ever had a hankering for dago food, an eatery named *Mama Tortoli's* on the other side of the square. *Mama Tortoli's* had a $7.95 All-You-Can-Eat Buffet, making it an excellent place for a binge: Rory could easily down a loaf of garlic bread, a heaping plate of ziti, an even more heaping plate of lasagna, four or five meatballs, and about as many scoops of double chocolate ice cream, and as long as he drank lots of diet soda to keep him belching and farting during the meal he always had room for more. Across the street from *Mama Tortoli's* was another peep joint, this one called *GIRLS GIRLS GIRLS*, and a massive video arcade called *ZAP*, where the sound on all the machines was always turned up way past the threshold of pain. There was a row of pornographic movie theatres, six or seven of them in a row, which were all open twenty-four hours a day, three hundred sixty five days a year. There were mysterious doorways promising more *GIRLS GIRLS GIRLS* and, above it all, on the top of the bank building, a real antique – a giant billboard displaying the classic Coppertone ad of the little girl (popularly rumored to be the young Jodie Foster) wideeyed with surprise as the puppy

playfully yanked off her bikini bottom. It was all visible from
here, and all identical to the way it had looked this morning just
before Rory entered *Les Girls XXX* and exchanged twenty
dollars for the equivalent amount in tokens . . .

. . . and, yet . . .

. . . it ALSO felt like something that had been disassembled
and then put back together with slightly different parts. The air
itself felt charged, not with ozone, but with something else,
something that felt both wholly alien and unbearably familiar.

The Bad Girl.

She was all around him. Laughing.

*As her wayward father fled, with hopeless dreams of never
seeing her again, The Bad Girl encircled him with every
conduit of power known to her: the phone wires, the electro-
magnetic spectrum, even the thoughts and dreams of the
strangers walking by on the street. She flitted from one to
another, through the hidden channels connecting them, never
occupying more than one place at one time, but moving so
quickly that for all intents and purposes she was in total control
of everything within a six-block radius.*

*The price of all this was exorbitant. Two hours of this and
she'd exhaust resources that had taken her years to collect. But
that was all right. She was getting better at replenishing her
stockpiles all the time. In a few years she'd be tapped into the
entire world, and then she'd be able to go wherever she wanted,
whenever she wanted, for any reason she wanted. When all that
happened all her fathers, all over the world, were going to pay
for what they'd done to her.*

*Meanwhile, she called herself The Bad Girl for a reason:
when she saw something she wanted, she just plain took it.*

*And right now, she wanted Rory. Not just the essence she'd
managed to collect so far, in all his previous visits: no, she
wanted all of him, with her, inside her, and completely at her
mercy.*

She didn't consider that too much to ask. Considering.

Everybody except Rory seemed to be in on the joke: as they
passed by they pointed at him, muttered to each other, even
giggled.

Somebody nearby whispered, "*Look! It's him!*" Rory whirled to see who it was, but the sidewalk was jammed with lunchtime traffic. It could have been any one of a hundred people. He stumbled off in a random direction, not knowing or caring where he was going as long as it was away from *Les Girls XXX*. He was painfully aware of everything around him: the sudden smiles on the faces of everybody who looked at him, the knot of people across the street who pointed in his direction and laughed at some shared memory known only to them; the deliberate, suggestive nature of the way total strangers in his path insisted on "accidentally" brushing up against him. He caught a phantom, subliminal glimpse of the Bad Girl's leering face adorning the ad on the side of a bus, but the bus was out of sight by the time the image sunk in and Rory turned to confirm what he'd just thought he'd seen. By the time he'd gone half a block a fresh layer of sweat had popped up to further annoint his already filthy clothes, and his chafing thighs were not enough to stop him from breaking into a run.

He was running only a few seconds before the feeling that people were watching him suddenly kicked into massive overdrive. The effect was a lot like getting hit in the crotch with a falling girder. He fell back a step, stepping off the curb and into the street. A taxi swerving to avoid him blared its horn angrily. Rory wasn't even aware of it. He did several 360°s searching for the source of the feeling, turning from the street to the storefronts and back to the street, before he saw it –

– in the display window of the grey-market electronics shop he'd just passed –

– a 4-foot projection TV, showing **THE BAD GIRL'S RE-VENGE**.

The fat man on the screen had been released from his upright rack. Now he was dangling by his arms from chains dangling from some indeterminate point out of camera range. He wore huge pointed falsies, white knee socks, shiny patent-leather shoes, a startlingly realistic wig giving him the hairstyle once popularized by Shirley Temple, and absolutely nothing else. Big red clown circles had been painted over each of his cheeks. As the Rory swaying on the street watched helplessly, the Bad Girl strutted into camera range, wearing mirrored sunglasses, an MP armband, and, like the fat man on screen, absolutely nothing else.

She circled the fat man once or twice, inspecting his goods. She prodded him with her nightstick, then tucked one end into her armpit and faced the camera with the contemptuous look Rory was rapidly learning to fear.

She said something. The sound didn't escape the plate-glass window of the electronics store. But Rory had gotten to the point where he could read her lips:

She's our little girl now
She'll do anything we tell her to do.
Anything.

Then she pulled back her baton and violently rammed it deep up the fat man's ass. The fat man howled in agony. She twisted it sideways, making him howl. He turned toward her and mouthed a word that could have been *please*, but he did not look like he was begging her to stop. He looked like he was begging her for more.

The real Rory gasped, and heard the gasp echoed a dozen times by a dozen other people behind him. Somebody behind him said, "Man, she's really *doin'* that sucker," and somebody else said, "Doin' him *right*," and Rory yanked his attention away from the screen, and saw the small mob of men gathered behind him. There were too many to count: young, old, white, black, well-dressed and derelict, all totally absorbed in the cruelties taking place on screen. One of them made eye-contact with Rory, smiled that damnable smile of recognition, and cooed, "Hot stuff, baby. Where'd you meet her?"

Rory's vision went red. He hurled both arms up over his face and charged into the crowd. It didn't part to make room for him, or, worse, hurl him back; it just retained its shape, the same way an ocean would, flowing the way it wanted to flow despite all of his attempts to push it aside. The faces that made up its substance seemed to be ten times normal size. He felt certain that the Bad Girl lurked behind every set of eyes . . .

Through sheer desperation, he managed to force his way past them, and though their hands pawed at him, in their eagerness to touch the skin that had been savaged by the Bad Girl, he did eventually find himself on the far side of that human ocean, red-faced and gasping and utterly incapable of running away the way he was sure he'd have to.

He discovered when he turned around to look at them that he didn't have to run away after all. The crowd wasn't interested in

following him. They were too absorbed by whatever the Bad Girl
was doing to his lookalike on the TV. Before he turned away they
all took a step back and gasped. Several among them shouted
things like "Yeah! Yeah!" and "*Do* him!" They seemed to have
forgotten that the real thing had been in their midst only seconds
before.

Or maybe they knew he wasn't theirs to take.

He was the Bad Girl's.

He fled as quickly as he could, managing only a slow walk. The
sweat seemed to be rising from his body in waves now, with the
kind of intensity that causes a ripple effect over hot pavement. It
didn't really smell like sweat anymore: more like some toxic
chemical reaction, taking place somewhere deep inside him.
He didn't know how come his clothes hadn't caught fire from
the sheer heat of it.

When he turned the next corner (passing a green wooden
newsstand where all the prominently displayed copies of *Playboy*
and *Penthouse* and *Hustler* and *Gallery* and *Screw* and *Swank* and
Tattle and too many others to count bore beautiful full-color
covers of the Bad Girl torturing the tightly bound Rory), somebody shouted, "*Hey! That's him!*" Somebody else shouted,
"*Jesus, you're right! It is!*" Rory didn't know who they were or
where their voices had come from. He just knew that he had to get
away before they found him. He desperately looked around for an
escape, saw that in his haste to escape the crowd he'd wandered
back to the Roy Roger's, and instantly shouldered his way
through the double doors. It wasn't much better in there: the
place was jammed, and easily half the patrons made disgusting
little double-takes of recognition when they saw him. But there
was a toilet in here, and he knew exactly where it was. It would be
a perfect place to hide.

He lurched past the four lines of people waiting for hamburgers
and fries and down the little elbow of a corridor that led to the
bathrooms. As he tried the Men's Room door, and found it
Occupado, the two voices that had driven him here came floating
down the corridor after him:

"Come on! I think he came this way!"

"You're fucked! He went out the other side!"

Desperation made him try the Women's Room. It opened
easily. He forced his way in and locked the door behind him.

It was a very small bathroom, with only one sink and one stall. The wallpaper was a shade of pink that made him want to gag. There was a hospital-white vending machine on the wall.

For the life of him he couldn't figure out what that vending machine sold. He didn't have the strength to go and look. Instead he went to the narrow stall and sat down, trembling so hard he had to press his hands against the walls to guide himself to a proper position on top of the bowl.

Even the toilet paper was pink. The roll was half-gone. He realized a hundred different women had sat here, on this spot, wiping their asses nice and clean with paper from that roll, and for just one moment he forgot all about the Bad Girl and swam in all the sweet erotic possibilities that raised in his mind.

Then Rory made the mistake of closing the stall door.

There was graffiti on the inside: a rebuttal to all the distended penises and defecating women decorating every single public Men's Room Rory had ever seen –

– a brilliantly realistic magic marker drawing of the Bad Girl, standing in haughty judgement before him. The ink coloring in her long, shapely legs was just shiny enough to simulate black leather. The straps of her crotchless panties were studded with spikes. She stood, her mouth a bottomless black O, her eyes half-closed, both hands pressed tight between her legs.

As Rory watched, frozen in disbelief, the ink on the stall door shifted, gliding across the cold metallic surface to make her right hand withdraw, rise, and wag a playful finger at him.

"*Baby*," the drawing cooed.

He recoiled, realizing that he'd just gone from one private booth to another. "What do you want from me?"

"It's not just me, Baby. It's all of us. The Cowgirl. The Secretary. The Nurse. The School Girl. All the rest. We all want it. We want it so bad – " the Bad Girl brushed the long, delicate fingers of her left hand across the shaved skin of her crotch "– it makes us wet." Her hand came away glistening. "See?"

She stepped off to one side of the stall door, leaving enough room for a drawing of the fat man to enter the frame. Unlike the drawing of the Bad Girl, which was rendered with the kind of anatomic perfection that made it resemble a photograph, the rendition of the fat man was a grotesque caricature designed to

make him look as monstrous as possible. His face was a warty
growth between two bulging balloon-shaped cheeks. His rolls
and rolls and rolls of fat had so many bulges and protrusions they
resembled tumors more than skin. His penis was tied in a knot.
He walked with difficulty, in tiny, mincing steps, both because
his ankles were separated by a four-inch length of chain, and
because his feet were jammed into a pair of pointed high heels so
small on him that the tops of his feet were raw and bleeding.

She cupped the fat man's face with one hand, assumed the look
of a mother about to discipline a beloved but unruly child, and
said: "Tell him, princess. Tell him it makes us wet."

And for the first time the fat man looked out from his prison
and made direct eye contact with Rory.

The hatred in the fat man's eyes was a light year beyond just
murderous. He looked like he would have happily skinned Rory
alive and dipped what was left in salt.

"*You bastard!*" the fat man shrieked. "*You gave me to them!*"

The Bad Girl calmly reached out with one hand and forced him
down. Either he was too weak to resist her, or she was too
unnaturally strong. His knees hit the floor with an audible crack.
Tears of agony rose in his piggy little eyes.

"That wasn't *nice*," she whispered. "I thought we agreed you
were going to be a nice little girl, didn't we, snoogle woogums?"

The fat man gibbered: "Yes, we did we did I'm sorry I'm . . ."
He didn't have a chance to say he was sorry again: his mistress
had just used the pointed toe of one boot to stomp his balls like
grapes. He curled into a ball, trying to make himself so small he
disappeared completely.

The Bad Girl kicked him a couple more times just for good
measure, then turned toward the terrified Rory, her smile as wide
and deadly as a hammerhead shark's.

"We want the rest," she said, in the kind of throaty voice that
up until now had always made Rory as hard as a pylon. "Come
back to us, honey. Give us the rest so we can really have a party."

And the magic marker images broke into a million fragmentary
lines, fleeing across the stall door like so many little black worms.
They moved with the speed of an explosion, sinking through
hairline cracks in the walls and floors. An instant after that the
door was scrubbed clean of both graffiti and nightmare.

Somebody was hammering on the Ladies' Room door.

"In a minute!" Rory managed. He did not have to disguise his voice very much to make it sound like a woman's. The frightened high-pitched quality had crept in all by itself. He could not imagine ever getting rid of it.

Almost ten minutes later, he pulled his pale, puke-encrusted face from the edge of the toilet bowl, stood on boneless legs, and left the Ladies' Room. An elderly woman who'd obviously been suffering for quite a while smiled at him sweetly and went in the second he left. She didn't seem to see anything wrong about his choice of rest rooms. He walked past her, and left the restaurant, and stepped out onto the street, not stopping until he reached the Square.

Not surprisingly, her influence had grown.

The half-dozen porno theatres in sight were all showing **THE BAD GIRL'S REVENGE**. All of them. Two, facing each other from across the street, even advertised their main feature with giant cutout Girls towering three or four stories above the marquees; one showed the Bad Girl, all rubber and leather, swinging a whip with insane glee; the other was the fat man, forced by straps and chains to kneel with his face in a doggy dish. The ticket-buyers' lines for each theatre curved around the block, and looked like no porno audience Rory had ever seen: they included both men and women in equal numbers, all happy, all grinning, all clearly thrilled to death at the prospect of seeing this great show. Even the hole-in-the-wall peepshows advertising **GIRLS GIRLS GIRLS** now boasted **BAD GIRL BAD GIRL BAD GIRL**. And when a bus roared by, the ad on its side was predictably a picture of the fat man bound and gagged and being raked across the face by elegantly lacquered Bad-Girl fingernails.

He searched the skyline for some landmark which would point him back to sanity, and spotted the final straw –

–his old friend. The Coppertone ad. Rory had always considered it more than just cute: whenever he saw the picture he mentally added ten years to the girl's age and cast himself in the role of the puppy. He'd always thought, *Love that tan line, Sweetie. Don't look so shocked. You know you want it.* But the picture had been changed. The background details of beach and hot sun were exactly the same, but the part of the shocked little girl in the bikini was now being played by Rory. The hand tugging off his bikini bottom, thus revealing his pale sagging buttocks, belonged to the Bad Girl herself. She lay on the ground behind him, her cruel grin now so wide that it almost bisected her face. It was impossible to look at her blindingly white teeth without thinking of fangs sucking the blood from his carotid.

He knew then that running was futile. As long as she already owned part of him, there'd be no train fast enough, no mountain high enough, no island remote enough, to keep her from bringing him back to Booth Nine. If there was any way to keep her from taking the rest of him, he'd have to find it there.

The short walk back to *Les Girls XXX* took place in a vacuum. There was no sound, anywhere in the world. The cars passing by on the street moved in silent jerks, and as labored as his own breathing grew he could not quite manage to make himself hear it. The people passing him on the street mouthed words he couldn't hear, words he somehow believed would free him if he could only find out what they were. He couldn't make out any part of their faces except for those silently moving mouths. He knew they were looking at him, though, because their heads always turned to follow him. They'd all seen him savaged by the Bad Girl, and they all knew he was going back to her.

He wondered, as if in a dream, just how many of them would follow him if they could.

The Bad Girl was not a creature of flesh and blood. She was an immaterial girl, living in an immaterial world. But as her father Rory trudged in defeat to the place that had given her birth, she felt an excitement that approximated what in a human woman would have been deep arousal.

She readied her boudoir for his arrival: first restoring the world around Les Girls XXX *to what it had been before she'd made her little alterations, then pulling all her substance back into the network of power surrounding Booth Nine. Just in time, too: the cost had been considerably more than she'd thought it would be. She was seriously depleted: had Rory actually still found the will to walk away, after everything she'd put him through, she would have had to choose between letting him go or dipping into her emergency reserve.*

But he hadn't walked away. He'd given up. And even as he pushed open the door to Les Girls XXX, *to report for his damnation, the men jerking off in Booths Two, Three, Five,*

Six, Ten, Thirteen, Sixteen, Twenty-One, Twenty-Two, Twenty-Seven, and Twenty-Eight were beginning the process of restoring her to her former levels of power.

All eleven would be totally impotent for the rest of their lives. Half of them would commit suicide within five years.

As they came, so did she.

Taking one of his remaining rolls of tokens hastily enough to leave the inside-out pocket dangling like a sock on the outside of his pants, Rory went straight to Booth Nine, where THE BAD GIRL'S REVENGE again headed the list of attractions. The color still on the door showed the Bad Girl with her head hurled back in laughter, the triumph burning in her jet-black eyes.

He tried the door. The purple-haired girl hadn't locked it after all. Maybe Elmo had checked out the video hookup, maybe he hadn't. Either way the door opened with no problem. Almost eagerly, in fact.

Rory entered.

The door closed behind him of its own accord.

The booth seemed smaller than it had been only an hour ago. The walls pressed up against him, as if afraid to lend him enough room to thrash around and perhaps damage what was valuable to her. They were sticky. And while the room still stank, the predominant stench was no longer body odor. It was an odor Rory knew only through reputation, and via a pair of soiled panties he'd once purchased through Elmo. Rory had no idea which of the peepshow girls had contributed it, or what she had looked like, but her smell had been powerful. It had faded over time, unfortunately; in recent days he'd only been able to discern the odor by pressing the silk against his nose and practically strangling himself with it. But he remembered the smell. And inside Booth Nine it was powerful enough to overwhelm every other odor, including his own.

He sat on the bench and, out of habit, fumbled inside his jacket pocket for his kleenex and hand moisturizer. They weren't there; he'd lost both somewhere along the way. He decided, with the resignation born of utter despair, that whatever happened from this point on he probably wouldn't need them anyway.

YOU HAVE RUN OUT OF TIME
PLEASE INSERT MORE TOKENS
OR VACATE THE BOOTH.

He popped six tokens into his palm and inserted them one by one into the slot.

The YOU HAVE RUN OUT OF TIME visual disappeared, replaced by his menu of choices:

1) THE BAD GIRL'S REVENGE
2) THE BAD GIRL'S REVENGE
3) THE BAD GIRL'S REVENGE
4) THE BAD GIRL'S REVENGE
5) THE BAD GIRL'S REVENGE
6) THE BAD GIRL'S REVENGE
7) THE BAD GIRL'S REVENGE
8) THE BAD GIRL'S REVENGE
9) THE BAD GIRL'S REVENGE
10) THE BAD GIRL'S REVENGE
11) THE BAD GIRL'S REVENGE
12) THE BAD GIRL'S REVENGE

He pressed 1. The Bad Girl did not appear. Instead, the Nurse and the Patient did. They were both having fun with a very familiar fat man spreadeagled face-down on a hospital bed, his arms and legs tightly strapped to the bedposts. The object of their amusement seemed to be finding out just how many rectal thermometers could fit into one anal sphincter. From the look of things it was quite a few.

Rory quickly pressed 2. The Bad Girl did not appear in this one either. No, this time it was the Cowgirl. She had the fat man hogtied on his belly, his limbs curled back above his body, and his wrists and ankles joined together by a tremendous rawhide knot. Branding irons glowed red-hot over a campfire in the foreground. She faced the camera, grinned, and in a heavy Italian accent, said: "That's my filly."

Channel 3 was the Japanese girl from LUNCH WITH YOKO. She'd evidently had a very big meal not too long before: a very, very, very big meal, with too much spice but just the right amount of healthy fiber. Large as his mouth was, the fat man chained to the ground beneath her would probably not be able to contain it all.

Sickened, tormented, Rory paged upward through the numbers, watching all the objects of his masturbation fantasies show him exactly what they thought of his affections. Each vision brought from him a little sob. By the time he'd passed half a dozen of them, they were all affecting him like physical blows. He started flinching, like a schoolboy who knew each new taunt was going to be worse than the one before . . . and muttering, in the voice of a condemned prisoner whose execution was being dragged out beyond all reason, "Come on, come on, where *are* you, dammit!?!?"

He found her on Channel 12.

She straddled a simple wooden chair in the center of a plain white room, rhythmically tapping her nightstick against one of her knee-length leather boots. "Baby!" she exclaimed, in mock delighted surprise. "You made it!"

His doppelganger was nowhere in sight. "Where's . . ."

". . . our little princess? I thought you saw, darling. I'm letting the others play with her for a while. They've been waiting a long time for this." Her eyes twinkled. "Especially Yoko. The poor dear's been through a lot. I'm so glad you're here to make it better."

"Y-you gave me no choice, you . . ." he searched for the worst possible thing he could call her. *Whore* was inadequate, *Bitch* a pale joke, *Cunt* almost ludicrous. Beyond those three possibilities he couldn't think of a damned thing.

She, on the other hand, had absolutely no trouble finding the one word that would destroy him: "You gave *me* no choice . . . *Dad*."

He didn't understand it. He didn't see how it could be. But the truth of it loomed over him, like a great dark object too large to be comprehended by a single pair of eyes. He knew she was telling the truth, knew that there had to be some way to exploit that, but utterly unable to see what it was.

When she spoke next, her voice was no longer just the voice of the Bad Girl, but the voice of a hundred separate fantasy women, speaking in perfect unison. "Now give us the rest of you."

"No."

"You already gave us so much. We've been collecting it for years. We just need that last little bit."

Rory couldn't face her. He knew that if he did face her he'd be lost. Instead he forced himself to speak with a defiance he didn't feel: "You can't have it."

"What we have won't last long without that one little bit."

"I don't care," he said, hating the tremble in his voice, knowing it made him sound like a petulant three-year-old who knows his whims can always be outpowered by mommy. "I don't like you. I don't belong to you. I didn't mean to give you anything and I don't want anything to do with you and I want it all back."

"All of it?"

Inspiration struck: "*Listen to your Father, young lady! Give it all back! Now!*"

His words hit The Bad Girl like a physical blow. Not because they possessed any innate power of their very own – Bad Girls never listen to their fathers – but because the second they left his mouth she realized just how little she knew about the real world her fathers had visited her mothers to escape. She only knew the rules she'd learned from the porn fantasies that defined her world: rules that decreed total ecstatic surrender as the only possible response to any rape.

Rory was saying No. *And he was meaning* No.

She'd never imagined such a thing was possible.

And though she'd thought she'd despised her fathers before, that hatred was nothing compared to the black malignant bile that rose in her soul now. Because now that she understood just how maliciously she'd been lied to, she no longer wanted to possess him. She wanted to destroy him. Now. Damn the cost.

She gathered up everything she had. Everything, except for what little she'd need to start over. And began molding it in the form she wanted . . .

The silence that followed Rory's ultimatum was broken only by the sound of breathing – both Rory's own, and the breathing of the legion led by the Bad Girl. There seemed to be uncounted numbers of people breathing in that little booth. It should have been deafening. But it was all but lost in a tiny space that all of a sudden seemed to be extend toward infinity in every direction.

Then, all too easily: "Anything you want, honey . . ."

The TV screen in front of him blinked off. And somewhere far behind it came an ominous roaring sound: the sound the people in the valley hear just after the dam breaks, and just before the hundred-foot wall of water comes through to smash all their homes to toothpick kindling.

Rory's reaction time was appallingly slow. He took two seconds to recognize the sound for what it probably was, two more seconds after that to calculate with woeful accuracy just how many gallons of semen he must have ejaculated in *Les Girls XXX* over the past ten years of weekly visits –

– two more seconds to put those facts together –

– then, as the roar of the onrushing tidal wave grew loud enough to shake the fillings from his back teeth, one more second to clutch at the door of the private booth –

– before the screen exploded outward in a jet of steaming sticky liquid.

The broken glass was nothing. It just cut open his flesh here and there, that's all. The jet of cum was something else. There was more of it than even Rory could have jerked off in sixty lifetimes; the Bad Girl must have been angry enough to also throw in a substantial portion of every drop spilled by every man who had ever set foot in this building. The effect was a lot like having a fire hose filled with hot salty glue turned on full blast less than three feet from his face. The force of it slammed him against the rear wall of the booth, broke several of his ribs, pressed him flat against the unwashed splintery wood. He felt himself choking on it, swallowing it, going blind from it. With superhuman effort he managed to turn his back to the torrent: the stuff splattered against his back, re-bounded against the walls, collected ankle-deep at his feet. His inevitable scream was lost against the bellow of that single pitiless flood. He felt himself tossed atop an entire ocean of it, gale winds making its waves hurl him beneath the surface again and again.

He thought it wouldn't stop till he drowned.

After a lifetime he realized it had already stopped.

He spat up a mouthful of it all over the wall in front of it, took a deep breath, and immediately started gagging. His throat burned. He got his coughing under control, managed to keep it under control for just about half a minute, then started coughing again. This fit lasted until his heart was a knot of congealed pain in the center of his chest. He got that under control, so relieved that he didn't even notice it when he then puked all over himself.

His eyes resisted opening. His upper and lower eyelashes were glued together. But they came apart with what his now hyper-sensitive ears registered as a snap, and through a white haze picked up what had happened to the booth around him. The walls were no longer dingy brown, but a bubbly, sticky white so thick that he couldn't even tell where the door had been.

He loudly peeled himself off the wall, turned around – making little cracking noises with every move – and sat down with an audible splash.

The TV screen was intact again. And, of course, it said:

YOU HAVE RUN OUT OF TIME
PLEASE INSERT MORE TOKENS
OR VACATE THE BOOTH.
YOU HAVE RUN OUT OF TIME
PLEASE INSERT MORE TOKENS
OR VACATE THE BOOTH.
YOU HAVE RUN OUT OF TIME
PLEASE INSERT MORE TOKENS
OR VACATE THE BOOTH.

He didn't much feel like a winner.

Oh, he knew he could leave now. He doubted he'd make it far, looking the way he did – but he could leave. There'd be no TV sets or movie theatres playing THE BAD GIRL'S REVENGE, no billboard pictures of himself being tortured by beautiful women, no animated caricatures of himself on rest room walls.

But there was something else missing, too. Wasn't there?

Whatever it was, its absence left a deep void inside him. Something which had once been part of him – maybe even most of him – but which had been utterly drowned by the Bad Girl's assault, leaving him hollow, empty, and without hope.

Blank.

YOU HAVE RUN OUT OF TIME
PLEASE INSERT MORE TOKENS
OR VACATE THE BOOTH.

He was afraid he knew what it was.

Eventually he decided he had to know for sure.

He reached into his muck-encrusted pocket and took out a token. It was sticky and foul. For the first time he noticed there was a clown's face embossed on it, and realized that *Les Girls XXX* must buy them in bulk from the same company that supplied the videogame parlor across the square. It was a small insight, but being able to come up with any insight at all felt good, now.

He slipped it into the slot.

His menu of choices blinked on:

1)	2)
3)	4)
5)	6)
7)	8)
9)	10)
11)	12)

He pressed a number at random. Then another, and another. As many times as he tried he found only snow. Somehow, without having to leave the booth, he knew that that's all he'd ever find, in any booth he cared to try. Even his own private collection, at home – the books, the magazines, the videos, all of them – he didn't have to be there to know that it would all be invisible to his eyes.

They no longer wanted anything to do with him.

He thought about the sordid, unloved hell that was his life, and what the rest of his days and nights would be like without even them for company, and after about a million years of trying unsuccessfully to even picture what a beautiful woman looked like . . .

. . . sat down and faced the meaningless snow on the screen.

The only companion he would ever have.

YOU HAVE RUN OUT OF TIME
PLEASE INSERT MORE TOKENS
OR LEAVE THE BOOTH

Blank.

Blank.

Blank.

Blank.

Blank. . .

THE SAFETY OF UNKNOWN CITIES

Lucy Taylor

Someday you'll come to love this.

Those were the words the jailer said when she clicked on the chain. The chain was secured to a leg of the bed, and the bed was of heavy oak. The prisoner wasn't strong enough to lift it.

The jailer held a threaded needle which she had sterilized in boiling water in the kitchen.

It's just a game, the jailer said.

And began to sew.

The prisoner screamed and begged and made promises of future perfection, future obedience to any and all rules.

The jailer reminded the prisoner that she had run away before and would likely do that again – and more besides – if given the opportunity.

Still, the prisoner cried bitterly, so the jailer took her in her arms and held her, stroked her, kissed her, touching her in places where she both dreaded touch and craved it.

Thus soothed, she finally tumbled into fitful sleep.

Someday you'll come to love this, said the jailer. *Someday you'll understand.*

The prisoner was nine years old.

★   ★   ★

In early fall in the city of Hamburg, Val Petrillo arrived late for a slave auction. It was held in the basement of Das K, one of Europe's most notorious sex clubs, and consisted of nude or seminude men and women, willing participants all, being auctioned off for an hour or two of use in one of the private rooms in the establishment.

Val had heard about the auction – and about a particular "slave" – only hours before and had interrupted a weekend tryst with a Japanese businessman to fly in from Geneva.

It was her first visit to Hamburg, and she regretted the necessity of rushing directly from the airport to the club. Such untoward haste was not her style. She liked to savor a city at leisure and at length, to arrive by train, preferably with the sun just coming up and to sit by herself on the platform for a few minutes, observing the purposeful strides of the commuters, the slink and slouch of the derelicts and whores, the foreign tourists, often timid and unsure, and trying not to look so, but uncertain of the language or the proper direction in which to forge, and feeling their way with caution in an alien terrain. Val never considered herself part of this joyful, seedy, bubbling throng, but rather a distant watcher, the way a pigeonkeeper might observe the milling, shitting, shuffling of the flock.

Sometimes in such a moment of private observation, she'd see a particularly striking face, an eye-catching shape of hand or jaw, a memorable breast or ankle and, if the watched one happened to look back, a brief moment of meeting, of connection might occur, and Val would think, "You might have been my sister, brother, friend for life. You might have been my lover."

Sometimes such people did become her lovers, but the beauty promised in that first gaze never quite matched Val's expectations, no more than the skylines of the cities that she visited, some gleaming, thrusting ornate minarets or towering slabs of glass proudly into the sky, others squat and shabby or drab with soot and the grit of harbored pestilence, ever quite lived up to her dreams.

So she stayed on the move. From city to city, bed to bed. Indulging her two addictions. Wanderlust and fleshlust. The passions of her life. Over the past few months, however, a new purposefulness had infused Val's journeying. In the sex parlors and private clubs she frequented, she'd begun to hear strange rumors. Occasionally, from a pair of lips made slack by drink or satiation, she'd heard whispered tales of a place she'd dreamed about but not yet visited, a carnal city of such perversion that it tested sanity, a place beside which the fleshpot Sodoms and modernday Gomorrahs of the known world paled by comparison.

Always the teller of the tale was vague in his or her allusions, but more than once she'd heard tell of a man known only as the Turk. It was he, so the rumormongers claimed, who could offer entrance to the City.

It was in pursuit of the Turk then, be he real or the fabrication of minds too corrupted by venality to know truth from lies, that Val had come to Das K. A young man from the Philippines, an unskilled laborer who loaded and unloaded cargo on the Hamburg docks by day and indulged his taste for SM by night, was scheduled to be "auctioned off" in a few minutes. Word had it that he had met the Turk, had even ventured to the City. Intrigued, Val was intent on meeting him.

In her early thirties, Val was a slender woman with black hair curtaining a tanned and oval face and features sufficiently symmetrical and absent of expression to make her, if not quite conventionally beautiful, at least inscrutable. Edgy with anticipation, she sat alone now at a back table of the club, sipping Courvoisier. A pair of twins, two young Nigerian women with enormous flaring nostrils and lips the size of dark red rose petals, were being auctioned off, sold at last to an older, professorial type in bifocals and tweed.

A blonde young woman, leashed and corseted, was purchased by a leather dyke, who handcuffed her prize before leading her off the stage. Then a man, all strut and beefcake, with a complex lacery of green tattoos entwining his arms and thighs in a kind of epidermal kudzu, was sold for an outrageous price to a flamboyant creature with sequins in her false eyelashes and a bulge in the crotch of her spandex tights.

When the Philippino boy was finally brought on stage, Val let the bidding rise, then quickly bid a sum so large no one ventured to try to top her. As she was going to the cashier to pay before collecting her slave, Val felt herself observed. Turning slowly, she saw a platinum-haired young man with green lynx eyes watching her from the bar. He wore a silk shirt and loose-fitting black satin vest, a diamond earring and ghoul eyeliner that would have shamed a whore. His flesh was so pale it looked translucent, a stitching together of gossamer insect wings. When their eyes met, he raised his drink, a tiny cordial glass containing what appeared to be a gold liqueur and pantomimed a toast. Val gave him no acknowledgement. Pretty though he was, at the moment, she had no use for any but her purchase.

Minutes later, alone with her slave, Val quickly forgot the hauntingly pale features of the apparition at the bar. She took the Philippino boy, whose name the auctioneer informed her was Santos, to an upstairs whipping room, where she initiated the proceedings by stripping and ordering the slave to fuck her. He did so with might and gusto, but after a few minutes, Val feigned displeasure and secured Santos's wrists to a pair of manacles affixed to one wall. Then, availing herself of the sturdiest of a selection of whips, she beat the boy's naked back and buttocks until his glossy, nut-brown flesh was a tapestry of raised pink welts.

Through it all, the slave uttered not a sound, which disappointed Val somewhat, as she found the chief reward of flogging to be the moans and cries of a submissive, and so she wielded the whip with greater vigor but managed to wring forth not one plea or cry.

At length, she freed Santos's hands and allowed him to fuck her to climax, her own and his, which he accomplished with much writhing and shuddering but not a single sound. They lay still for a while then, breathing the heady, pungent odors of orgasm, hearing laughter and applause from the auction still continuing downstairs.

"I heard about you in Switzerland," Val began in German, one hand covering and idly petting Santos's cock. "I've been told you're quite the connoisseur of perversions."

He smiled and shrugged. It occurred to Val that perhaps he spoke no German. She tried English then, with no better results. Summoning up what meager Spanish she possessed, Val persevered, "Is it true you've had relations with a man known as the Turk? And that you've been to a place they call the City?"

Again, that small apologetic smile, but this time Val knew he'd understood. His penis, when she uttered the words "the Turk" had stiffened beneath her hand.

"You're still my slave, you know. And I asked you . . ."

Santos leaned forward, pressed his full mouth to hers. His lips parted. Val entered him with her tongue, probing, thrusting, then . . .

She pulled back, skin goosefleshing, with a cry of dismay.

Santos grinned at her, opened his mouth wide for her inspection. His mouth was empty, a vacant cave, the stump of tongue a grey cauterized root deep in his throat. He gave a gurgling, half-formed sound, a kind of muffled oink.

Scarcely flinching, Val snatched up her handbag and dug out a pen and paper. "Answer my questions," she commanded. "Write it down."

Santos held the pen as if it were a foreign object. At the top of the page, he scrawled an "X." Val asked again and got the same response. The boy was either illiterate or pretending to be so. His cock, however, was far more communicative. Fully erect now, it pressed lewdly against Val's belly. She slapped the offending piece of meat aside and began to dress.

Santos would tell her nothing, and she was furious. But in another way, she realized, perhaps he'd told her more than she really cared to know. That made her even angrier and, perversely, more anxious than ever before to see the City.

"You didn't keep him very long. He must have disappointed you."

One green lynx eye winked at her above a full mouth uptilted at one corner with bemusement: the pretty young thing from the bar. He'd come up beside her when she left the club and fallen into step.

"He was fine," Val said. "Quite worth what I paid."

"Except he's maimed."

"Not where it counts."

"Unless you purchased him more for what you hoped he'd say than what he'd do."

"I didn't buy the boy for conversation."

"Oh, didn't you?"

Val stopped. They were walking along a narrow street, still in the St. Pauli district, but a good mile north of the Reeperbahn's famed glitz – all neon, sizzle, and glare – and a hundred years away in atmosphere. Here, winding cobbled streets converged and serpentined, dead-ended and then reemerged, a medieval maze of narrow, gabled houses illuminated by pale cones of incandescent light thrown by iron streetlamps. Alone, Val had been content to wander, even at this hour. Now she considered summoning a taxi and going back to the hotel where she'd left the overnight bag with the few belongings she'd seen fit to bring from Geneva. Tomorrow perhaps she would fly back, resume her tryst with her Nagasaki Romeo, assuming he'd not found other company himself.

She turned and stared into those feline eyes, darkly flecked with green and amber.

"Who are you?"

"Majeed," the boy said, extending a pale, long-fingered hand which Val ignored.

"Why are you following me?"

"I'm not following you. I only thought perhaps I might offer you what Santos, with his unfortunate speech impediment, could not. I know you came here seeking information about the City. It's possible that I could help. But now I see I'm only bothering you. You want a hard cock like your little slave's, and here I'm offering you merely words. I'll leave. I wouldn't wish to force my company on you."

He turned to go and Val let him – for six paces. Then curiosity overcame her pride and she called out, "Wait. You're right. I didn't come to Das K for a hard cock. I came for information."

As it turned out, however, Majeed apparently had both. Val took note of the bulge in the tight jeans, sculpted to the youth's body. Majeed told her he had an apartment merely blocks away, but when they arrived, his "home" turned out to be a dilapidated hotel, the kind where rooms are rented by the hour and the sheets are blotchy with questionable stains.

"You will come in with me?" Majeed pulled Val into the shadows. He slid a hand behind her neck, pressed his mouth to hers, enticing her with a lithe tongue made all the more erotic by its equivalent's repulsive absence in her most recent lover's mouth. The boy smelled of musk and cloves, his lips flavored with the lingering trace of mint liqueur. He sucked and nibbled Val's lower lip as one would suck the pulp from a slice of citron.

Val reached down to massage the sweet protuberance at Majeed's groin, but he took her hand away, kissed the perfumed wrist and palm and laid it on his shoulder.

"You aren't afraid?" he said. "To go late at night to the room of a man you barely know?"

Val scrutinized those subtly slanted eyes. She'd been with dangerous men before; it was, in fact, her preference. She'd taken chances all her life and was not about to change her habits now.

"There's only one thing I really fear," she said, "and that's not being free to do what the fuck I please."

Majeed laughed. "Oh really? So what if I were to shackle you to the bed and walk away? Just leave?"

"That might be exciting."

"And if I never came back?"

"You would."

Majeed unlocked the outer door to his derelict abode. They crossed an inner courtyard to a second door which Majeed unlocked, then ascended three flights of stairs. The room into which he ushered Val smelled of herbs and incense, the heady fragrance of decaying temples, untended gardens. The narrow bed was made up with a brocade spread worn thin in places, its gold fringe trailing upon a grimy floor. Scant decoration. On the walls a crucifix; in the windowsills, a treasure trove of incense burners in every shape and size: a gold Buddha and cloisonné-style jar, a terra-cotta pagoda. Majeed selected one and lit an incense stick. The room filled with cloying fragrance, orchids past their prime or rotting camellias.

"So you know about the City?" Val began. "Is it even half-true what I've heard, that Sodom and Gomorrah would seem places of sweet innocence and childlike games by comparison?"

"Not having visited either Sodom or Gomorrah, I wouldn't know."

"But you *have* visited the City?"

"Perhaps. Or maybe I'm just another drugged-out sicko suffering delusions."

"Either way, you must have some tasty stories."

"Which I will tell you," said Majeed, "but first, lie down with me."

Fondly, with neither undue haste nor passion, he began disrobing her. Val allowed it, finding in the movements of the boy's long fingers a mesmerizing languor. As he undressed her, Majeed kissed her neck and eyelids, her nipples and the cleft, still moist from Santos's use, between her legs. His tongue flicked and traced the plump curves of flesh from her clit to the puckered bud between her buttocks.

"Now you," said Val. Kneeling, she unzipped Majeed, whose heavy, uncut cock lolled out into her mouth. She peeled back the foreskin, rimmed and licked the velvet head before swallowing the length of it.

Majeed had still made no move toward taking off his clothes. Perhaps, as he had undressed her, he wished to be undressed himself, Val thought. She stood up and began unfastening the buttons of his vest. Pulling this off, she commenced with the shirt itself, working open half a dozen tiny pearl buttons until she could fold back the silk – to reveal a pair of breasts bound tightly to Majeed's chest by a bra designed to minimize.

Val had seen transsexuals before, but had never partnered one. She hadn't expected this oddity of Majeed. She tried not to show her surprise, but it must have registered on her face for Majeed was smiling, enjoying – as he must always savor it – the look on a new lover's face when he unveiled himself.

Val rolled the tight bra up and over Majeed's head. His breasts were unexpectedly full, with small nipples rouged as dark as straw-berries. Val sucked one into her mouth. Majeed moaned and arched his back.

"You're a man on his way to becoming a woman?"

Majeed laughed and pulled her down with him onto the bed. "Guess again."

"A woman on her way – *well* on her way – to becoming a man?"

"Neither."

"Then . . ."

"Why don't you finish undressing me?"

Val stooped to remove Majeed's shoes and socks. He lifted narrow hips while she tugged down his jeans. His erection bobbed. At the base: two small but perfectly formed testicles. Behind those, where in most men the perineum would be, a moist and parted slit shaved hairless as an egg. It gaped at Val, a single eye, defined by pink and fleshy lids.

"A vagina." Val gazed in wonder at this miracle. She touched the fleshy, dangling labia, then inserted a finger inside Majeed's cunt. He contracted inner muscles, seized and squeezed.

And laughed again, causing breasts and cock to wobble in jarring juxtaposition.

In all her wandering, all her years of sex in strange places among foreign people, Val had never before encountered such a creature. Now, confronted with this marvel, she felt both aroused and awestruck.

"You're splendid," she told Majeed. "Unlike anything I've ever seen."

"Any *one* you've ever seen," Majeed corrected her. "I'm not a freak, you understand, though some people think me one. I'm a hermaphrodite."

"When you were born, your parents . . . what did they . . .?"

"They were appalled, to say the least. They said I was a monster, or so I'm told, and sent me to a home in Lexington for freaks and retards."

"And since then?"

"I've lived as a man. I could have an operation to make me more conventional – a chop job or a stitch job, as it were – but I was born like this. I'll die like this. But in the meantime, I prefer to be a male."

"Why is that?"

"It's the females that fall in love, isn't that usually the case? I don't need that weakness."

Val gazed up into eyes as emerald as the towers of Oz. "So you'll be a man tonight?"

"As always."

Majeed lay back upon the bed. Val mounted him. Grinding her hips upon his cock, she reached back to fingerfuck his pussy. She bent forward; their breasts met and mashed together as she sucked on Majeed's lips and sent her tongue exploring the crevices and contours of his mouth.

They made love in all the ways and combinations that Majeed's wondrous anatomy allowed. For the first time in months, Val was able – for a little while – to forget about the City. For surely in Majeed she'd found a prize to please a sultan, the dream-lover of all who hunger for the novel, the bizarre, and yes, Val thought, the freakish, too. Despite his protestations, Majeed was unquestionably a freak, though one of unsurpassing elegance and beauty and, yes, femaleness, too.

To take Majeed's erect cock in her mouth, then dip below and lap and tongue-fuck his pussy was a dizzying excursion into androgyny. To reach up to squeeze those silky breasts while the owner of those breasts drove his cock into her throat, these were pleasures beyond all Val's experience, Majeed's strange beauty an intoxicant of the most seductive sort.

They lay together afterward, hermaphrodite and woman, in a sidelong embrace, genitals still locked together in a gentle clench. From the courtyard down below footsteps sounded. They drew nearer, ascending the inner stairs, and approached along the apartment corridor.

Although his face bore no change of expression, Val could feel Majeed's muscles tense. His cock, well-drained, slid out of her with a soft smacking sound.

"Don't make a sound," Majeed whispered.

The footsteps stopped outside the door.

Val's head was still on Majeed's breast. She could hear his heart tripling its pace. She held her breath.

"Majeed?" The voice was teasingly seductive and well modulated, a foreign-sounding voice that twisted with difficulty around the German sounds. "Majeed, my love, I know you're in there."

The doorknob turned, but the door was both deadbolted and chained.

The voice dropped to a near whisper and said with renewed cajolery, "Open the door, you little cunt."

There was something about the voice that made Val's heart commence a sprint into her gorge. It was too soft, too honeyed, the voice of a corrupt priest saying prayers while fondling an acolyte in the confessional. And its persuasiveness reached entrails deep, for even as a part of her was terrified, there was another part longing to unlock the door.

"Come on, you pretty little turd. Unlock the door and show me what you've brought home to desecrate tonight. You know how much I like to watch you whore around. So let me in, and I won't hurt you too much."

Val looked at Majeed, who'd gone bone white and appeared almost spellbound with terror. For some reason, she had the feeling that the talk outside the door was some kind of game, that had the owner of the voice desired to, he could have broken the door open without a moment's pause.

"You piece of cum-encrusted shit, you worthless bitch! You know this will only make me hurt you worse when I next see you.

And I *will* see you again. You can't run from me. You *need* me.
You can't survive without me."

Those last words scared Val most of all, for something in
Majeed's entranced stare argued for their veracity. Nor did she
expect the sweet-voiced brute beyond the door to leave peace-
fully. She was sure that in another instant the door would be
kicked in.

But no blow came. There was silence for a few minutes, the
would-be intruder evidently remaining where he was, listening
no doubt, for signs of someone inside the room. To Val this
ticking quiet was far more ominous than taunts and threats. The
idea of someone lurking in silence just outside the door, pretending not to be there but waiting for a chance to pounce or
plotting his next move, aroused long-buried terrors. Her phobia
of being trapped slid into consciousness like a stiletto blade
parting fat and muscle. She lay motionless in Majeed's trembling
embrace, but she could feel the old fears swirling and spiraling
around her, rising up to fill her chest, her throat, her mind, like
flood waters above a drowned village.

"You little trick, I know you're there. Go ahead and have your
fun tonight, but when I come back for you, you'll pay and pay
until you can't stop screaming."

The footfalls, a soft and shuffling tread, receded along the
corridor.

Val breathed again. She leaped out of bed and crouched down
below the windowsill, ignoring Majeed's protests. Presently, a
figure emerged into the courtyard, a man in late middle age, tall
and stooped, almost emaciated, but with a lush mane of jet hair
threaded through with white that fell around his shoulders.

"Get down!" Majeed hissed.

The man crossing the courtyard paused and turned, directing
his gaze toward the window through which Val peered. The
room was dark, the courtyard lit with moon. She was sure he
couldn't see her, and yet, she felt a frisson of both dread and
longing, repugnance mixed with lust, as his eyes turned in her
direction.

For an instant, just before he turned away again, she experienced the tang of want and craven need: it chilled her utterly.

"Goddamn it, don't let him see you!"

"It's all right. His back is turned. He's leaving."

Majeed cleared his throat, as though reaching for an offhand way to phrase his question, and said, "What does he look like?"

"What do you mean 'what does he look like'? Don't you know?"

"Sometimes he wears . . . disguises."

"Well, tonight he looks like one of those carved saints from the Day of the Dead in Mexico. Like he doesn't eat enough and never loves."

"Yes," sighed Majeed, as though that description were all too familiar to him.

"Who is he?"

"Just someone I've had some business dealings with."

"What's his name?"

"Why do you care?"

"I want to know."

"Dominick Filakis."

"Your pimp?"

Majeed did not reply, but got out of bed and put a fresh stick of sandalwood in one of the incense burners on the sill. In the gray, rain-washed light of coming dawn, Val could see the ridges of his spine bisecting broad shoulders and tapered waist, the incongruous silhouette of full breasts as he turned again to face her.

"You're a prostitute," said Val.

"You say that like it surprises you."

"Very little surprises me."

"Then you haven't looked hard enough."

The room filled with scents of sandalwood and strawberries that mingled with the smell of sex to form a heady musk. Majeed slid back into the bed, pressed his persimmon lips to Val's.

"Don't worry. I'm not going to charge you. You're not a trick."

"Why not?"

"You asked about the City. Not many people even know about it, and fewer still want to go there. They value life too much."

Val breathed in semen, musk, and flowers. She reached up, tongued Majeed's closed eyes. "Life hasn't got much value if it isn't lived. I lost a big part of my life a long time ago, and I'll never get it back. I made a vow to live what's left me to my own satisfaction."

Majeed sighed. "Spoken like a true Lost Child. One who never had a childhood."

"You could say that."

"You'll have to tell me about it."

"I don't think so."

"But we're going to be together, aren't we? That is, if you still want to see the City."

Val felt her pulse and heartbeat quicken. Her mind spun an erotic web – of decadence past imagining, depravities beyond the capacity of the mind to comprehend, and those few elect, the connoisseurs of flesh who would endure anything in order to experience everything.

"I'm leaving for the City tomorrow," Majeed said.

"You mean today?" said Val, nodding toward the window, where meager flecks of light managed to penetrate the shade, illuminated the cobra shape of scented smoke arising from the incense burner.

"Today, yes, after we get some sleep."

"Filakis, will he come back?"

"Not today," Majeed said, cat-stretching with a languid ease. "He has others to police. I'm small fry in his game plan. By the time he loses patience and kicks the door in, we'll be halfway to Africa."

"Africa?"

"I didn't tell you? That's where the City is. At least, that's where the entrance is."

He took Val's hand and guided it underneath the covers, passing over his erection to the moist and avid opening beneath it.

"There's a selection of dildos in the dresser drawer. Pick one you like and fuck me, please, before we go to sleep. Afterwards, if I'm still awake, you can tell me how you came to lose your childhood."

From experience with lovers too numerous to count, Val expected Majeed to be sleeping deeply only moments after the orgasm Val wrung from him using a ridged and studded dildo of a size sufficient for pleasuring a mare. But he surprised her by remaining awake to hold and stroke her. She realized that, if Majeed insisted on considering himself as male, he was in many ways not so, the scrotal sack and penis being merely extra adornment on a body that in every other way was every bit a female's.

At first they alternated talk with lazy sensuality, remaining on a slow plateau of arousal that demanded no release but was pleasure in itself. Majeed filled a pipe with opium and smoked it as he told Val about running away from the home in England, of his days as a prostitute in Hamburg and Munich and Rome. At times Val felt uncomfortable with this confession and would interrupt the narrative with bouts of nuzzling and caressing that led to sex so indolent and languid that their lovemaking was almost tantric in its restraint. At last, with Majeed inside of her, they held each other, and Val told Majeed how she had come to be a wanderer with carnality the focus of her life.

Her introduction to the allure of the perverse, the intrigue of the wicked, had come at an early age. She had grown up in the cheerful, skylit rooms of a renovated twelve-room home on two acres of land outside Tarrant, New York. Her father, a Wall Street executive, made the ninety-minute commute to Manhattan twice a day. He had bought the showpiece home as an investment and as a haven from the tumult of city life, a safe harbor to enclose his wife and daughter while he went forth to do financial battle.

Unfortunately, his final battle, which took place when Val was five, occurred not on the Floor, but in a seedy walk-up tenement where he'd gone to do some coke with a Latina hooker. The hooker rolled him while her pimp concussed his head in several places with a tire iron. The coroner's report indicated he spent a full day dying.

Val's mother Lettie, when she learned the circumstances of the tragedy, said too bad it didn't take longer.

Apparently Anthony Petrillo had been as clever at investing and amassing money as he was unwise in the choice of his companions. He left a vast amount of money – most of which Val inherited after her mother's suicide when Val was thirteen – but little else. No memories to speak of (except the bitter ones left to his wife) and, for Val, just the blurry image of a man who left with dawn and returned long after nightfall, harried, jittery, with the look of someone deprived of sleep for so long that exhaustion comes to seem the norm and recreation aberrant in the extreme.

After her husband's death, Val's mother became afraid to leave the house. Men followed her, she claimed, when she ventured out. The idle glances and chitchat of passersby became the furtive gaze of psychopaths, the soft babbling of lunatics who stalked her. Terrorized by the demons that nested in her head, she left Val and the house to maids and cultivated a sleazy romance with agoraphobia, preening for hours before the mirror but dressing in housedresses so shabby that the maid, discovering them in a pile next to the dryer, once mistakenly used them for rags with which to polish tabletops. She spent most of her time in her sewing room, sleeping or gazing out the one window or, occasionally, stitching together a dress or blouse for Val, usually in some wildly inappropriate material: crushed velvet, lace and stain, jumpers cut from bolts of sequined silk. And all the while she muttered in no language known to any but the denizens of her own internal world, reverting to normal speech only when necessity demanded that she order groceries from the local market or fuss with local school administrators who, after a year or so, began calling repeatedly to learn why seven-year-old Val wasn't registered for school.

Almost two years after her husband's death, Lettie's weirdness took a sudden shift, one which at first appeared to be for the better. She seemed to remember Val's presence in the house and spent time with her again. Hours were spent brushing out the child's hair, caressing her, teaching her to read and write from a book of fairy tales that featured stories about seductive hags that fricasseed their children, and coiled serpents that lurked under mattresses and crawled into the snoring mouths of sleepers.

And, as if her father's murder hadn't already taught Val enough about the cruelties and caprices of the world, Lettie decided, with that obsessive single-mindedness peculiar to the insane, that more instruction for her daughter was in order.

If Lettie had been a near recluse, afraid to leave the house, now she found a black new zeal, a morbid sort of daring. She commenced to venturing out for nighttime drives into Manhattan, trolling for dissoluteness and danger like a carrion-eating bird seeking dead flesh, a madwoman and her passenger, a wide-eyed little girl.

Val remembered riding in her mother's Mercedes through the rain-soaked, late-night streets of Manhattan's seediest enclaves. Lettie always drove a brand-new car, usually one resembling a black barge, its leather smell still as fresh as when it had left the showroom. Val would sit close against her mother, staring out at the weird night-circus of the city, hoping that what she saw outside could not get in.

She remembered the sheen of stoplights reflected in oily puddles, the barred storefronts with their glut of tawdry merchandise, and the flashing neon, often with a letter or two burned out, so that the names of bars and liquor stores resembled gaptoothed grins. Often when she'd shut her eyes against the overbright display, she could still see the neon dazzle, as if one look had tattooed its garish message permanently on the inside of her eyes.

In some neighborhoods, Val remembered being most afraid when her mother stopped for lights, and the milling, seething faces passed within a few feet of the car. Blacks and whites and Orientals, all combinations in between, and, though their skins were a multitude of hues, their expressions generally were less diverse: they looked bored and angry and angry and bored, and often they looked afraid.

Sometimes Val would imagine leaping from the car and running from her mother, disappearing into the crowd's dark and perilous ranks, and throwing herself upon the mercy of their world, but she was too afraid – not only of what was inside the car with her, but of what lay outside as well.

"Lock your door," Lettie would order, but she never believed Val's confirmation that it was already securely locked. She always had to reach over and touch the lock button itself to make sure it was depressed. And all the while, her eyes would gleam, her fear and her enthralment with that other world casting a sheen of bewitchment across her face.

"Look! Look at those two women there," Lettie would cry, pointing out two *café-au-lait* madonnas in leather skirts the size of postage stamps and wildly bouffant hair. "No, don't look yet! You don't want them to see you stare. Now, turn around now. Look!"

It was a ritual that, by the age of eight, Val already knew too well. Her mother had a name for it – "going for a ride." Presumably it was a form of education, in the wiles and sins and venalities of life, a graphic way of teaching a young child of life's rife and lurking dangers, and for a few months, Val had accepted it as such.

Only later, after she had grown too old to be trusted to remain locked inside the car on such excursions, did Val recognize the strange nocturnal forays were her mother's longing made tangible, titillation masked as moral guidance.

"See that man across the street, the one in the built-up shoes! That's a pimp, the lowest form of life. He lives off women, sells them for sex. And look there, there's his woman! That's the kind of woman that killed your father."

The hours spent cruising the tenderloin along Eighth Avenue, then over to the docks where the chickenhawks prowled like lean barracuda, and finally up into Harlem, provided a seedy circus of vicariously experienced trauma. There'd been the time a wild-eyed man, a tattooed troll with shocks of matted, grayish hair protruding at all angles from his skull, lurched up beside the car and tried to force the door open. He screamed that he was being pursued, that someone meant to kill him. Val's mother ran the light, sped off. They were halfway up the block when Val heard shots fired and saw the troll, who'd run across the street and was badgering another driver, flop facedown in a mound of dirty snow, which promptly started turning red.

At other times, men with dark faces and Halloween smiles approached the car, thinking Lettie was a well-to-do suburban matron out to score some coke. (Or better business arrangement yet, to peddle her child's ass.) They cursed her when she sped away. One time a green convertible followed them through Harlem all the way to the Triborough Bridge, its occupants an Oriental with gold stars in his teeth and a woman whose head kept disappearing and reappearing next to him like some kind of dashboard toy.

"It's so you'll see the world for what it is," Val's mother would tell her as they returned from their nocturnal jaunts. "So you'll understand how dangerous and vile men are, how careful you have to be just to survive in this world."

The source of her mother's obsession with sin and sex was never fully clear to Val, but as time went on, her mother's madness twisted inward, plunging deeper into insanity's labyrinthine maze. The late-night cruising tapered off, and here Val let her story end. She didn't tell Majeed about the night, when she was nine, that she still remembered as the night of locks and chains, the night she tried to run away and came to be a prisoner in the Sewing Room. It was the night her mother realized her beloved needles and thread were handy implements of torture and that a young girl's vagina was as dangerous as her freedom, the latter to be stolen from her, the former to be stitched shut.

To Majeed, she only said, "After Lettie stopped taking me for rides, things got much worse."

"Worse?" For a second, she thought Majeed was going to laugh and she regretted having told him anything. But he didn't laugh. He held her close. "What happened then?"

"I don't remember everything."

"That's hard to believe."

"I can remember if I want to, but it's like snipping off a piece of skin to see what shade of red the blood is. It hurts. It isn't worth it. Let's go to sleep now."

She had trained her mind to stop at this point. She knew what lay beyond and chose to go no farther. Some memories were too full of fear and grief to ever chance rekindling. Some memories required the deepest kind of burial, could only be obliterated – and then but temporarily – by pleasures of the flesh.

"Wake me, if you change your mind," Majeed said.

"No. I'll start to cry."

Majeed reached for his opium pipe and took a lazy puff. He offered it to Val. She shook her head.

"What can I do to make it better?"

Keep holding me, don't let me go, was what Val might have said.

But she needed to escape her memories, put miles and lovers between her and the past and so she said, "Just fuck me. Then take me to the City."

The trip overland to North Africa, which could have been accomplished by a few hours in the air, took Majeed and Val the better part of two weeks. Majeed suffered terribly from motion sickness. Three hours of train travel and he was invariably doubled over in the lavatory, his body sick and flowing at both ends.

Thus burdened with Majeed's unexpectedly frail stomach, they traveled in short intervals: Munich to Geneva, then south to Marseilles and Andorra, and across Spain, stopping in Granada and Seville.

In Gibraltar, they took a hydrofoil across the channel, arriving

in Morocco at Tangier, then took the train south to Fez, where
Majeed refused Val's offer of a few nights to relax from their
journey in a luxurious hotel and booked them instead into an
inexpensive hostel on the periphery of Fez, the city's once-
thriving Jewish *mellah*, or neighborhood.

Val had observed that, with their arrival in North Africa,
Majeed became more taciturn and moody. His consumption of
opium increased dramatically, but any inquiries on Val's part as
to the reason for his pique was always brushed aside; Majeed
claimed he was merely fatigued or motion sick or a trick had
proved disappointing.

The first night in Fez, in keeping with what was by now their
pattern, they dined together, then went their separate ways,
Majeed to satisfy, undoubtedly, his own proclivities, Val to
explore the myriad mazelike streets of the Old City, glorying
in the exotic squalor of the quarter's sights and sounds and odors.
What Majeed did with his evenings was not discussed, but Val
assumed he considered a night in which a few carnal transactions
weren't carried out to be an evening wasted.

Rounding a corner in the Old City, Val was startled to see
Majeed deep in conversation with a young Berber girl who
couldn't have been more than eight or nine. Her black hair
was braided intricately, her hands hennaed with jinn-spells in
the custom of her tribe. The child did all the talking. Majeed
listened with uncharacteristic somberness. Although she couldn't
know for sure the nature of the transaction, Val's immediate
assumption was less than charitable. She hadn't known Majeed
cared for children; the idea that he did repulsed her. She ducked
behind a passing donkey cart so that he wouldn't see her.

Usually Majeed was later coming back to whatever hotel or
hostel they were lodged in, but tonight his return preceded Val's.
When she entered the cramped hotel room, scarcely bigger than a
walk-in closet, with its damask curtains and faded silken spread,
Majeed was reclining on the bed, incense burning, the room
redolent of spices and hashish. His eyes were closed, his wondrous
genitalia covered with a corner of the rumpled spread. A halo of
smoke drifted up from the pipe between his lips. In the dim light,
his pale hair framed paler features, cascades of snow on snow.

When Val slid the chain lock into place, his eyelids lifted to
pantherish slits, and he turned on her a strange, unfocused gaze.

"You're late."

"I didn't know I had a curfew."

"Don't bitch at me. I've had a shitty night. Some faggot Frenchman paid me to let him give me a blowjob in the men's room of the Hotel Palais Jamai. Then he insisted on groping me and when he found my pussy, he thought I had an extra asshole, that some disease had rotted out a hole in me." He sighed theatrically and dragged on the pipe. "He didn't get his money back, though. Fucking faggot woman-hater."

"That's quite a tale."

"Could I interest you in another one?" Majeed asked, slapping his sleek rump.

Val plopped down on the bed. "I think I'd rather hear your stories about the City. I've been patient long enough, I think."

"But we just got to Fez. We have more traveling to do."

"I thought you said Morocco was the gateway to the City," Val reminded him. "How do I even know there is such a place if you won't give me some details?"

"You trusted me this far," Majeed said. "Why not a little farther?"

"Because I'm tired of your games."

Majeed sighed heavily. "Then allow me to show you a new one."

He offered Val the pipe.

"Please, go ahead. The experience will be so much nicer for us both."

She took it, pulling the sweet, narcotic smoke into her lungs and holding it until she felt the irritation seeping out of her, replaced by a warm and scented glow that bathed her cells in languor. She took another hit. This time the smoke didn't just fill her lungs, but traveled through her bloodstream, illuminating her internal organs with what seemed to be a pale, internal glow.

She heard chimes in her voice. "What is this stuff?"

"High-quality opium."

"Quite nice."

"I think so. The only thing that's better is to have sex while you're doing it."

Val took another toke. Her head turned and she started to lie back, but the bed anticipated her direction and lifted up to meet her. Pillows, sheets, and mattress all folded round her in a soft and pliant nest.

She was wriggling into this new womb when Majeed crawled over to her and began unbuttoning her clothes.

The opium gave Majeed's body a beauty so intense that it was almost frightening. His cock, flaccid for once, was sheened like polished ivory; behind it, his labia unfurled like blossoms from some mutant flower, petals distended, redolent of musk.

He leaned forward to help Val remove her blouse. She reached up idly, ran a fingertip along his cleavage. Her gaze lingered on his face. There was something askew there, although Val was at a loss to know exactly what. The eyes, something about the eyes. That charmed-snaked look. For an instant, it had made her think of –

No! She slammed a mental door on the memory of her mother's face the night she took Val to the Sewing Room.

It's just the opium, she thought, not even wanting to guess what her own eyes must look like now. She probably had test pattern written on her pupils.

"There's plenty more where this came from," Majeed said, offering her the pipe again.

She took it, sucking first from the pipe, then on Majeed's nipple, which dangled appetizingly in her face as he leaned across her. Something cool touched Val's left wrist. She heard, as if far distant, the swish of silk.

"Now your other arm," Majeed said as he lifted away the pipe.

"What are you . . .?"

"I'm sure this isn't something that you're new to," said Majeed, securing Val's other wrist to the bedpost with a scarf. "But I remembered what you said about fearing confinement. Fear and arousal are so closely linked. I guessed this must be a major turn-on for you."

"It can be if . . ."

"I thought as much. This time will be especially memorable for you, believe me. Before we go on, would you like another hit?"

"I don't think so."

"Please. Go ahead." He put the pipe between her lips; Val drew in the fragrant smoke. "There may be parts of this that are difficult for both of us."

Majeed leaned across the bed and put his mouth to Val's. When she breathed out, he caught the smoke in his own mouth and held it.

"You don't really need to see the City," Majeed said. "I can show you many of its delights right here. Tonight."

He was rummaging around inside his suitcase. Val watched, the narcotic effect of the opium blunting her perceptions in a way she found increasingly distressing. But being bound was always a pleasure of contradictory excitements: arousal and submission and panic like actors vying for center stage, each taking a turn before relinquishing the spotlight to the next. The trick, she knew from much experience, was similar to life: relax into the game, submit, and the ferocity of pleasure that resulted could be so akin to pain that the two were almost indistinguishable.

"I've grown too fond of you for my own good," Majeed was saying.

He turned around, the effect of the narcotic in Val's system making his eyes appear more feline than ever, gold-green slits that would have bewitched her gaze entirely had she not been suddenly distracted by the sight of what was in his hands – an eight-inch-long knife that curved up into a sweeping, saberlike blade.

"Don't worry," said Majeed. "I'm not going to use this now. I'm only going to let you look at it a while."

He ran a finger up the blade. In the pale light, it gleamed like something living, like the horn of some exotic beast lacquered with the moonlight spilling through the opening in the shades. Like Majeed's, its beauty was hypnotic. Val couldn't take her eyes off it.

"I bought it in the bazaar tonight. It's lovely, isn't it? Elegant, well-crafted, and quite cold – the way you'll soon be. When I saw it, it made me think of you."

He pressed the blade against Val's throat, nickingly close, then laid it flat atop her belly, tip pointed toward her eyes. In the warmth of the room, the steel was shockingly cold. She could feel the knobs and ridges of the heavy carved handle making tiny indentations in her flesh.

"One last thing, before I go," Majeed said. He took a pair of underpants from Val's suitcase and plugged her mouth, then secured the gag with tape. She made a sound meant to be argumentative – it came out a powerless groan reminiscent of Santos's inhuman sounds.

"I doubt that you'd cry out, but one can't take the chance.

Especially when I tell you I'm going to kill you. Few believe me when I tell them that at this point, but you might be the exception. I can't take that chance."

He bent down and closed Val's eyelids, kissed them both, then unlocked the door, admitting for an instant only a few words of an argument shouted out in Arabic up the hall, the aroma of couscous and lamb simmering somewhere nearby, then he was gone. She lay there, staring at the knife blade lit up with moon. Her skin tingled at its proximity. Her fingers ached to touch its metal blade.

It was a game, of course, a brutal game meant to seduce with terror. She reassured herself of this so many times it started to sound true, until Majeed's fundamental harmlessness seemed as inexorable as the law of gravity.

She tried to work the scarves up over the bedposts, though – just in case – but found them snagged beneath some baroque convexity of the post's design, impossible to slide. Sleep seemed unthinkable, and yet she dozed, dabbling first at the edges of unconsciousness like one wading in the shallows of deep water before plunging, unexpectedly and with mounting fright, into dreams that rushed at her in fragments, like jagged glass. Nightmares flashing past in jigsaw form held to no particular pattern except the terror they inspired.

"Do you like to bleed?"

She thought at first it was another nightmare, this one masking its counterfeit nature behind a facsimile of Majeed's voice. Then the pain bit into her, and she came awake with a muffled gasp. Majeed stood by the bed, the knife in hand. The cool blade gleamed with blood. She looked down, saw the shallowest of incisions extending in a line between pubic hair and navel. In places, the skin wasn't even broken. In others, her blood bubbled up like scarlet sweat.

She tried to speak. The gag reduced her words to the gurgling of an imbecile or choking victim. Majeed wiped the blood off on her flank. He caressed the blade across her throat. The lightest of pressures, barely enough to dent the skin.

"I could slash your trachea and you'd never speak again."

He moved the blade up to one of her bound wrists. "Or open up the veins here and let you bleed to death."

He traced the blade across Val's face, lingering on her eyelids, her nose. "Or I could simply remove the parts of your face that make you look human. You'd be surprised how long you could live in that condition. Assuming that you'd want to."

She made a helpless, rasping sound. Her eyes followed his every twitch, beseeching leniency. If this was a game, the point of pleasure was long past. Her wrists ached. Her heart stuttered with terror, its every beat seeming to squeeze out more drops of blood from the cuts across her belly. Majeed held the knife vertically between her eyes, so close she couldn't focus on it properly. She saw only Majeed's pallid face, insectile in its out-of-focusness, bisected by the glimmering slash of silver.

Then a deft flicking of Majeed's wrist and sudden pain – blood clung in ruby droplets from her left earlobe before dripping off to plunk hotly upon her shoulder. Val thrashed upon the bed, eyes darting from the knifepoint to Majeed's eyes and back again and back . . .

She couldn't get Majeed to meet her eyes. That, more than anything he'd yet done, terrified her. He teased her with the knife a while, not cutting her again, but running the blade across her flesh like a divining rod. When Majeed laid down the knife again, he finally met her eyes, but Val's hopes faltered: There was neither ice nor heat in them, only distance, as though he looked at her from some schizoid universe where pain and love were meaningless in equal measure.

"Since you don't seem to be enjoying this, I might as well."

He began withdrawing objects from his pants pockets. Hypodermic syringe and powder: the talismans of addiction. Soon he was busy with the paraphernalia of his habit. He tipped a bit of heroin from bag to spoon, then cooked it with a cigarette lighter held underneath. All this Val watched with stricken eyes, imploring him to end the game but failing to find the least compassion in his vacant gaze. When it came time to tie his arm off and shoot up, Majeed turned his attention back to Val.

"Understand that I don't want to do this. But if you scream, I'll cut your vocal cords. So consider very carefully before you yell for help."

So saying, he reached behind Val's head and freed her mouth, then used the scarf to tie off a vein.

"Majeed, if this is a game . . ."

"It's not a game. It's what I have to do."

"What does that mean?"

"It means I owe somebody."

"Filakis, isn't it?"

"Yes."

"You owe him . . .?"

"A life, taken in a bloody fashion."

"Why mine?"

"Your curiosity has a self-destructive bent. It led you to search for the City. It also led you to me, the one who's going to kill you."

"Why *my* life, Majeed?"

"Because he enjoys suffering and he knows I . . ." he grimaced, searching for the vein. "Look, just shut up or I'll find something else to gag you with."

"Don't do this. Please. I can't die yet."

He tilted a derisive eyebrow and concentrated on drawing the heroin up into the syringe.

"It's not as though most people expect to choose the moment. Besides, you told me you preferred dangerous . . . people. This was bound to happen sooner or later. Your lifestyle almost demands an untimely end, wouldn't you agree?"

"But not like this . . . not you."

"I'm as competent a killer as the next."

"At least . . . you said you'd take me to the City. Do that at least and then . . ."

"Shut up! You don't know what you're asking for. There's no such place. It's a lie, a myth, dreamed up by people bored by everything else life has to offer, bored out of their minds, quite literally."

"Don't make me die like this. Not shackled like the way . . ."

". . . the way someone once did to you? Who was it, Val? The friendly old physician, the priest? A funny uncle or your crazy mother? What did she *do* to you?"

"What do you . . .?"

"No, never mind. It's too late now. Besides I'm tired of listening to you prattle. When I'm not using you for sex, you're really very tiresome."

The syringe was full. Majeed squirted out a tiny bit to clear air bubbles. He struck at the vein and missed. His hands trembled so violently the needle appeared to dance.

"Majeed, what did you mean before? About why Filakis wants me to be the one you kill?"

"Shut up. It doesn't matter. I promised him I would or he won't let me back into . . ."

"The City? Isn't that it? So that's who Filakis really is, the Turk."

"What difference does it make?"

"Is the place that wonderful? That you'd kill me if Filakis said it was the only way you'd get back in? If that's the case, why did you ever leave? Why didn't you just stay there?"

Majeed's inability to hit a vein was making him increasingly distraught. Sweat beaded on his forehead, ran down his face.

"Is it like the opium?" Val pressed. "You want to stop, you want to leave, but you can't? It always pulls you back, and you pay any price for readmittance?"

"Shut up!" shouted Majeed and threw the syringe aside.

Val held her breath. The effect of the opium had diminished beneath the more potent effect of terror, and if she was still high, she couldn't tell it. She felt petrified, frozen in her fear like an insect trapped in amber, her muscles tense as wires, her heart unbeating stone.

If I'm going to die, she thought, let it be something memorable.

Majeed picked up the knife and came over to the bed. He traced the dark line of dried blood that bisected Val's belly, then lifted the blade tip to her neck. It popped the skin an inch above the hollow at her throat and pooled there before over spilling and streaming down her ribs. The pain was distant, unremarkable, her senses pinpointed entirely on Majeed.

"Why am I the one you have to kill?" she whispered. "Why not someone else?"

"Goddamn you."

"Why me?"

Majeed raised the knife. His voice was barely audible, the low whistle of insect wings. "Because he knows I love you, damn you."

He raised the knife and brought it down – twice in quick succession. The blade slashed flesh, but only superficially. The main direction of the thrust was through the scarves that bound Val's arms.

Majeed waved a dismissive hand. "Go on and live your

wretched life. You'll end up murdered anyway. It just won't be by me."

Val breathed again. She rolled off the bed, struggling into items of her clothing with arms that had gone numb as logs, no longer under her command but senseless stobs of flesh. She beat the circulation back into them, had managed to put on a pair of jeans when Majeed suddenly leaped across the bed and stood before her, bloody knife in hand. His eyes were wild, his skin an unnatural, sickly cast, malarial.

"Wait!"

She thought he'd changed his mind about sparing her life.

"Please, Majeed, let's . . ."

His knife hand began to tremble. Val lunged past him for the door. Majeed grabbed her arm and flung her backward onto the bed.

"I said you can't . . ."

But Val heard it now, the footsteps approaching up the hall. She had no reason to think they heralded disaster except from Majeed's reaction, which left little doubt as to his terror. He was darting about the room in a frantic dance of wasted motion, a trapped gerbil, running from window to window in a hopeless effort to find some avenue of escape.

"No," said Val, when it became clear Majeed meant to jump. "It's too high. You'll kill yourself."

Their room was three floors up. Both windows overlooked a narrow, stone-paved alleyway crowded not only with passersby but with a hodgepodge of vendors, their wares spread out on mats upon the stones. A fall from this height, though possibly not fatal, would shatter bones and organs.

Still, Majeed was forcing one of the windows up and would clearly have taken his chances with the fall had not the door, which Majeed had locked upon his return to the room, suddenly burst inward.

The Turk, in all his corrupt nobility, strode across to the window and locked an arm that was all vein and sinew around Majeed's throat.

"You betrayed me, bitch," he crooned in Majeed's ear. "You promised me her life tonight. You swore."

Majeed responded by twisting with reptilian grace, the knife still in his hand. Filakis wrenched it from Majeed's grip and hurled it across the floor. Val heard fingerbones and joints crunch sickeningly. Majeed wailed.

"Don't," said Filakis, guessing Val's intention toward the knife.

He twisted Majeed around, so he could face Val. Behind him the open door tempted with the possibility of escape, but Filakis barred the way. He stared at Val – an odd and terrifying sizing up of her that seemed rife with disgust, abhorrence.

Meanwhile, Majeed struggled in his captor's arms, choking and sputtering as Filakis applied more pressure to his neck. There was something odd about Filakis's palms, Val noted. At first, she'd had the impression that they were smeared with blood. Then, she realized the man's flesh was hennaed with jinn-spells and incantations, a practice designed to ward off evil spirits that she'd observed among the Berber women.

But Val had little time to reflect upon the oddity of the Turk's indulgence in this superstition. The knife he'd wrested from Majeed lay within easy reach, a temptation that, in the present circumstances, was irresistible. Val grabbed it, thinking to plant the blade in Filakis's bony neck and would have done so, had she not been halted by a crackling sound and the unfolding of a spectacle before her that rendered her immobile.

Tongues of pale green fire were licking at Filakis and Majeed. Mere tatters, at first, the flames soon grew, tonguing and plucking at Majeed's face and breasts, at his captor's opulence of hair. Majeed writhed and screamed in Filakis's grasp, but the Turk uttered not one cry as the fire climbed his torso, igniting flesh and clothing in its luminous embrace.

Majeed stretched out a hand to Val.

She reached to take it, but fire blossomed from her lover's fingertips like thorns. There was a moment's indecision, when Val might have grabbed Majeed's hand anyway, but the flames were devouring with such speed that, in the instant that she hesitated, Majeed's hand was burned away, the fingers curling back upon themselves like desiccated fetuses.

Electric, crackling tendrils spread across Majeed's and Filakis's faces. Skin cracked and peeled. What lay below, shimmering suet and tendon and bone, was soon unveiled and melted down. All cries stopped and, presently, all motion.

The flame bulged out at its height and formed a funnel, which whirled like some inhuman dervish about the floor, consuming what remained. For several seconds, it danced and capered on the carpet with terrible exuberance, then lost volume and momentum and sputtered out into a tiny heap of rubble and cold ash upon the floor.

Left behind, for an instant only, there glowed an afterimage: steepled towers and squat, dun-colored houses, shimmering like bleak mirages behind medieval walls. The walls, when Val peered closer, appeared to be composed of writhing human bodies, living, faceless, and crudely formed, all locked in carnal congress.

Val blinked – the scene did not disperse, but took on form, dimension. There was a moment when, remembering it later, she was sure she could have simply walked inside the rent in space that appeared open to her. But by the time she gathered wits and courage, the image turned translucent, its third dimension sloughing off like worn-out skin, the remaining threads of form and color liquefying into a few drops of dewlike mist that hovered in the air, then dispersed to nothing.

Even as the shock of seeing Majeed's fate rooted her in place, a small burst of celebration fired her heart. The place she'd glimpsed could be nowhere except the City. That, or Hell, and she meant to find out, one way or another.

Majeed and his mysterious abductor had left behind a small pile of remnants on the floor. She went over to inspect it. Swatches of cloth and leather, scorched and frayed as though they'd been through an incinerator, Majeed's opium pipe, or what was left of it, reduced to a lump of ivory and melted gold, dollops of glass, coin-sized, that must have once been a hypodermic syringe.

And something else: a pale green piece of stone, slightly smaller than a hen's egg, rounded at the top but with a flat base. Val picked it up and turned it over in her hand. The object was similar to a number of the incense burners Majeed had set out on the windowsill – in the case of the latter, the top could be unscrewed and removed to reveal the candle contained inside.

Unlike the incense burners, however, this jar offered no seam to indicate where the top could be twisted off. It seemed to be a solid piece of stone, onyx or malachite perhaps. If so, its function was entirely ornamental, yet so closely did it resemble the others that Val couldn't help but think a seam existed somewhere in its intricately carved sides, but was simply far more subtly crafted and inconspicuously designed.

She turned the small jar in her hands a dozen times, yet found nothing to indicate it opened into halves. Its varnished surface was carved with some kind of complex floral pattern. Leafy spirals and overlapping whorls interlocked in patterns that at first appeared both random and simple, but, upon closer inspection, proved to be teasingly complex, provocative in their design. Stamenlike shafts writhed and twisted into budded knots upon the top while along the sides, carved blossoms formed fantastic arabesques that defeated each attempt Val made to trace them to their source in the design.

At length she put the object down, but not before it had revealed at least one secret. At the warmth of her hands, it began to emit the faintest of odors, a musk so subtle in its fragrance that Val could sense it only with her nose pressed to the stone.

In any case, there was no time for further inspection. In the courtyard down below, a crowd had formed among the vending stalls, people gazing up at the room where someone must have seen the flickering of flames. Val heard shouted Arabic and French. At this hour, the hostelry was locked up for the night, but men were rattling at the gate, yelling undoubtedly for the proprietor to come down and unlock the door.

Val had no wish to be caught and questioned. She grabbed her tote bag with passport and wallet and headed through the shattered door toward the back stairwell. The carved piece of stone she slipped inside her pocket with a promise to herself that it would yield its secrets to her yet.

For a few more days, Val remained in Fez in the hope that Majeed might somehow still be alive and make his way back to her, but restlessness soon overcame her. She took the train southwest to Marrakesh, then to the beach resort of Agadir. From there, she traveled to the town of Taroudant, a market center tucked in a valley between the High Atlas and Anti-Atlas Mountains. Always she kept the incense burner in her pocket, to be brought out and handled at odd moments, its complexities explored.

In Taroudant, whose marketplace offered natural toiletries made from the musk of gazelle glands and desiccated lizards sold as potions to ensure good health, Val spent hours studying the carved convolutions. It seemed to her that, over time, a pattern could be discerned and that occasionally, upon repeating a particular sequence of touch, the scent emanating from the jar became more powerful. At times, the scent was so alluring that she focused only on the jar, blind to the sights and sounds around her as she gave in to her obsession.

It was toward the end of her fourth day in Taroudant, while taking refuge from the high heat of early afternoon in her hotel room, that Val first felt the minuscule beginning of a dismantling of the jar's design. A portion of its pattern seemed suddenly to be less than solidly attached. Val shut her eyes and traced the complex arabesques like Braille. There was a subtle sliding, followed by a snap, and an odor almost indecent in its seductiveness wafted to her nostrils. She looked down in her palm and saw a tiny aperture had opened up in the center of one carved whorl. A half-inch wick, the kind found on any ordinary candle, protruded up.

Before she lost her courage, Val lit a match and touched it to the wick. A flame like a serpent tongue swayed forth. Val took a step backward; the flame grew and leaned in her direction, as though sniffing her out. It split into two tongues, which forked again until the greater portion of the wall was covered with a tree of emerald fire. The tree limbs undulated, spread, and Val could see that within each searing branch and twig were silhouetted spectral couplings: a compendium of every sort of depravity, every sexual excess of which flesh is capable.

Val stared into the flame, felt its obscene allure.

"Majeed," she said and touched her hand to it.

A hand was all the flame required. A fingernail, she realized later, would have sufficed. The fire seized her, fed. There was no burning, but a cold and weightless dazzle and then a light that blinded, deafened, numbed, with her senses being subtracted until all that remained was the odor of desire, and that odor suffused every pore and everywhere it brought oblivion.

It was the wind that woke her. It was full of sand and stinging hot, and yet each particle of sand that blew against her skin was like a tiny, tingling penetration, invigorating and indecent.

She got to her feet, felt eyes on her. A bearded Bedouin was staring at her from behind a donkey's dappled flanks. Man and beast made not a sound, but a slow and almost imperceptible thrusting on the man's part, a look of stoic boredom on the donkey's countenance, told her the nature of the mute transaction. Such acts weren't to Val's taste, and yet she had to force herself to look away. The sand was nipping at her flesh like lovers' kisses, the wind hotly seductive as it whirled through her hair.

At first glance at her surroundings, it appeared to Val that she was still inside the city of Taroudant, looking up at its pale pink, crenelated walls, its decaying medieval ramparts. Yet it was different. But for the bearded sodomite with his equine mate and a few haggard old people, the streets seemed strangely empty. Only the evidence of commerce – huge burlap bags of grain, their contents in big golden piles upon the ground, bright yellow *babouches*, or slippers, tapestries, and vegetables – argued for some semblance of normal city life.

From somewhere in the winding, shadowed streets, a chime echoed. Its silvery tones shivered through Val's body; its vibrations pleasured heart and lungs and entrails. The sound came again, melodic, light. Val leaned against a wall, flustered by her body's unequivocal response to the sound. A parrot flew by above – a gaudy slash of green and scarlet against searing blue sky – and the sight brought delight that was almost unbearable in its intensity. Nor were simple, everyday sensations less capable of inspiring ecstasy. The odor of bread baking, of overripe persimmons and citrus smells and almonds, of musky human sweat that wafted from the cloistered doorways as she passed – each was author to an exquisite sensitivity of mind and loins, making of each pore a tiny vulva, ravenous for more.

She wandered the mazelike streets and tunneled corridors, aware of others who observed her, their eyes taking her in like the languid scent of some new flower as she passed before them, this newcomer to their center, but staying always out of her sight. Occasionally, in the rapid turning of a corner, the sudden glance behind her back, Val was positive she glimpsed some of the City's inhabitants. It was difficult, if not impossible, however, to keep her concentration focused – when the slap of her sandaled feet on paving stones, the metallic ting of chimes, the gold threads in an ornately woven rug glimpsed in an open courtyard wrung such sensual delight that she felt exhausted, frazzled, giddy with the unnatural opulence of her surroundings.

As her wanderings led her deeper into the labyrinthine streets, Val caught sight, here and there, of other people: an old woman lying splay-legged in an alleyway, her grizzled, thinly furred sex exposed. She held a musical instrument, a long flute-like thing with a curved end, which she simultaneously used to play and penetrate herself, moaning out the notes as she played herself to orgasm.

At another intersection, the narrowness of the convergence forced Val to step around a copulating trio, two men and a young woman locked in silent rut, one penetrating the woman's cunt, the other buggering her in an almost somnambulistic torpor. They barely moved as Val passed by, but the sex-scent wafting off them was enough to make her reel, her vaginal muscles clenching and releasing with contractions.

Still farther on, a narrow passageway opened up into a court-yard where two naked women embraced within the rippling shallows of a fountain, one sucking on the other's breasts while the first leaned back and spread her legs, the better to allow the cascade of water access to her clitoris. And there was the goateed man she passed who grunted and sighed out ecstasies as he made love to an ornately painted gourd, an aperture carved out of its pulpy meat to allow for such conveniences. He took no note of Val's presence, but bucked and thrust arhythmically, the gourd's surface already slicked with evidence of previous man-vegetable love.

A dozen or so yards on, Val came upon a square devoted to magicians, storytellers, and oddities of every sort: Here a tattooed boy made fire caper up and down his arms, then masturbated with the flames. A nude woman whose only covering was the strawberries and lemons sewn into her skin did a slow, lewd dance. A dark-skinned man picked dates and olives off the ground with a prehensile penis; another bent his ten-inch cock backward and belabored his own anus.

In the midst of such monstrosities, a Berber girl with eyes like sapphires and emeralds held up her brightly hennaed hands so Val could see the spells tattooed there. She caught Val's eye. Her hands wove mysteries. In the space of several eyeblinks, she transformed herself into a goat, an aging hag, a priapic dwarf. Val stared, trying to get at the root of the illusion, but her eyes were always drawn back to the tattoos on the child's palms, where the illusions seemed to be created by some hypnotic effect induced by the movements of her illustrated hands.

At length, she forced herself along, although exhaustion was leeching at her enthusiasm for further exploration. Indeed, all the people she encountered seemed depleted, slacked. Even those who copulated with each other did so not with the natural frenziedness of lust, but in a kind of stupor, like lewd sleepwalkers who, upon colliding with each other in a darkened hall, engage in mating more from habit than desire and without ever being aroused sufficiently to waken fully.

As the afternoon wore on toward dusk, she became aware of moving shadows, skeletal denizens of the City creeping out to find each other, meeting and merging with scarcely so much as a cry before interlocking lips and loins. Yet even then there was less a sense of passion than of a famished mutual feeding upon each other. Sometimes the wraith-lovers interrupted their mating to follow Val a pace or two, but they were slow and clumsy, their unsavory caresses easy to elude. More than once, she gingerly intruded on an embrace to ask about Majeed, but the inhabitants of the City seemed to understand no language but the one of touch and offered her no answers but their own slicked cocks and cum-soaked thighs and parted, pungent vulvas.

The streets grew steeper, narrower. She peered inside a courtyard and discovered a tannery where animal skins were soaked in stinking vats before being transferred to a row of dark, dank rooms. Here silent figures pulled the fur with ghoulish zeal, then stretched and beat the skin while others took the opportunity to yank their own hard meat, so that the smell of cum commingled with that of the tanning juices. The very repugnance of the place was sickeningly seductive. Val didn't linger long.

A short way beyond the reeking tanneries, she came upon a marketplace little different in outer appearance from those she had encountered in Moroccan cities of a more conventional nature. Only the wares displayed were a departure from the usual – on one blanket, a treasury of dildos in every size and shape, on the next, a sadist's spree of whips and clamps and restraints, across the way a man who sprawled supine, mouth plugged with a gigantic dildo which he offered up, beckoning to

passersby to sit upon his face and take their pleasure there. He
didn't lack for business; a line had formed and both sexes took
their turn lowering themselves upon his phallus-mouth.

A few blocks beyond the souks, Val was almost sideswiped by a
nude and legless man, a repulsive lummox propelling himself
along on gorilla-muscled arms, penis swelling up obscenely to
bob against a convex bud of navel. He was obese and hideously
mutilated, his chest and shoulders stitched with scars as though
some mad graffiti artist had used his flesh for scrawling.

Val felt a deep, internal shiver. Dismayed by her reaction, she
tried to look away but the man was staring at her with a gaze of
open invitation. His strangely luminous eyes compelled respect,
each blink a blatant proposition that weakened her with want.
Appalled by her own desire, she approached the vulgar wretch
and squatted over him. She took in all his ugliness, the cock in full
and virile jut between the stumps, the corded arms, the scabbed
and scarified chest. Obscene he was – and bloated, gross – and yet
his very repugnance increased her lust.

He urged her on in Arabic. She spread her legs and lowered
herself, letting her skirt flare out as she set her weight, impaled
herself. The lemon-emerald eyes half closed. He sighed and
thrust. She reached back and clutched his stumps. The scars
were odd, not flat or smooth but intricately textured, whorled,
and ridged. The motif was familiar now; it brought to mind the
ridged stone of the incense burner, of doorways wildly arabes-
qued, of hennaed hands, of . . .

"You!"

She pulled back, even as the man impaling her began a seamless
transformation: Broad hirsute chest reshaping into nubile
breasts, slabbed cheekbones and simian forehead refining into
the almond eyes and heart-shaped face of the Berber child-
magician. At the appalled look on Val's face, the little girl pealed
forth bright laughter. She held up those gorgeous, hennaed hands
so that – for an instant only – Val could stare transfixed at the
lurid dazzle of the moving patterns on her palms.

The child leaned forward, touched her lips to Val's. Her kiss
seared.

Val let her lips part. The Berber girl's tongue tasted of mint
and honey.

"Majeed?" the girl asked. "You want?"

Val nodded and replied in French, "Where is he?"

Like the keeper of some wondrous secret, the child smiled slyly. She led Val through more winding streets to a stone stairway that descended between red mud walls. After the first few steps, the darkness was impenetrable, the air tainted with a sewer stench that made Val's stomach roil.

They reached a landing, where the Berber girl produced a flashlight from her trouser pocket and proceeded down yet another, steeper flight of stairs. She moved with such sureness and fluidity that Val had to struggle to keep up. Occasionally she paused to catch her breath and heard, emerging from below, the most distressing sounds, plaintive wails and frenzied keening, the staccato yap of tongues convulsed by insanity or pain.

At the deepest point of their descent, they stood before a bleak and narrow corridor of ancient prison cells. *A dungeon*, thought Val. The girl pointed ahead and indicated Val should proceed, that she'd come as far as she intended to go. Val hesitated.

"Majeed!" the child said, scowling.

Val peered into the gloom. "I can't."

The girl relinquished her light to Val and motioned for her to continue, repeating Majeed's name. The noise level, at the entrance to the corridor, had by this time intensified to a din. Sounds of suffering and, perhaps more disturbingly, low moans and sighs that either pain or passion might be father to. Holding the light ahead of her, Val continued on her own.

A few paces farther on, the narrowing staircase petered out entirely at a hole in the wall where a stone had been removed. It was from the other side that the sounds of suffering were emanating. Val crouched, holding her candle out before her, and slithered through the opening.

She found herself in another corridor, this one even grimmer than the one she'd just traversed. On either side were narrow cells, each one containing an isolated occupant. Ripe with youth or withered with age, the effeminate and virile, the bestial and the lovely, each endured his or her own ordeal – some hooded, with clamps attached to swollen genitals and nipples, others forced to sit upon huge dildos that stretched anuses and vaginas to the ripping point. Still others suffered cock rings of heated metal and brutally snug corsets, bindings so unnaturally tight the flesh popped between the ropes like risen bread. One man, a contortionist, was positioned on his back with legs behind his head. His cock came within a millimeter of his mouth but so cunningly was he secured that not even his most ardent struggling allowed his tongue to reach his engorged head.

Val wandered on, appalled and mesmerized by this symphony of frustrated arousal. The floor became increasingly wet. She heard a soft sloshing and, rounding a bend in the torturous hallway, saw a shallow pool just large enough to accommodate a body. In it, nude and bound, leeched utterly of color, floated face down an emaciated angel, dead to all appearances but with a breathing tube resembling a small flute extending from its mouth. Given its pallor and stillness, Val was highly doubtful the thing was capable of breath at all.

She ran the flashlight beam along the creature's body and gasped with recognition. No ethereal being this, but quite the opposite – Majeed. But in what condition! Fetuslike, he floated in his swollen sac of womb. Naked, touching nothing, ensconced in darkness and silence.

Val reached into the pool and floated Majeed over toward her until she could untie his hands and flip him on his back. Dead, she thought. Pale and, to all appearances, devoid of life, his clammy flesh seemed formed from tallow and slimed with ashen mucus. Yet Val had already witnessed sufficient wonders in the place not to concede Majeed's lifelessness too soon.

She lifted Majeed's head out of the pool, removed the tube from his mouth and shook him hard. His head lolled back and forth, his eyewhites gleamed. He didn't seem to breathe, but, with a hand between his breasts, Val felt the ticking of his heart, its pace so slow that her own heart beat a dozen times to Majeed's one.

"Majeed!"

She slapped his head from side to side, then bit him on the ear until blood flowed. His eyes came slowly into focus, squinting into the painful glare of the flashlight. His skin and hair, always fair, were alabaster. He looked, Val thought, like an albino eel raised in some subterranean cavern, its translucent flesh never touched by sunlight.

"Majeed, it's Val. What have they done to you?"

Majeed began to shake and then to sob. With Val's help, he managed to drag himself up over the side of the pool where he collapsed shivering, his nerves capering in mad jigs beneath the skin, tics working at his face and muscle twitches making his limbs flail.

Val realized then the nature of his peculiar torture. In a world where even the rustling of leaves produced erotic shivers, Majeed had been deprived of even the most meager stimulation – even his beloved opium had been denied him.

Val's hands were covered with the liquid from the pool. She became aware now of the coolness and viscosity of what at first she'd taken to be water. Not water, though, she realized now, but cold and clotted semen.

"Majeed? Answer me. Come on, get up."

She hoisted Majeed to a sitting position and struck him in the back. He took a gasping breath of air, then another. His eyelids fluttered open and he gazed at her, as mindless as an idiot child before leaning over and vomiting into the pool.

"How did you . . .?"

"It doesn't matter," Val said. "Right now, we've got to hurry and get out."

She led Majeed back along the corridor with its rows of cells and naked captives, through the opening in the wall where she had first gained access. Far ahead, a wan light filtered down.

"Who put you there?" Val said.

"Filakis, of course."

"But why?"

"To punish me for not killing you that night in Fez. But mostly to amuse himself. He's not like the others here . . . he can't enjoy real pleasure. He has to get it watching others or torturing them."

They'd reached the lower landing of the staircase. Majeed suddenly stopped and grabbed Val's hand.

"Wait. I need . . . it's been so long without . . ."

"Your drugs, you mean?"

"My drug of choice," Majeed said. He grabbed Val's hand and pressed her fingers to his groin. His penis felt achingly erect, his vulva dripping juices. Something new had been added to Majeed's anatomy since his captivity, a set of gold rings penetrated labia and scrotum, made a bell-like tinging as he maneuvered Val against the wall and tried to lift her skirt.

"There isn't time!"

But terror, as Val had long known, was the most potent of

aphrodisiacs, and sex within the City's walls was sex magnified a hundredfold, each orgasm an intoxicant that bewitched the mind for days. Majeed's hunger called to hers, and soon her legs were open, allowing him to rut his fill.

"Turn around."

She braced herself against the stones and shut her eyes. Majeed thrust inside her, his motion making the vulval rings clink and ping together. He gave a moan that Val thought to be his climax. But there came an instant when he lost contact with her entirely, when her inner muscles clenched on emptiness, and Majeed's vulval bells were stilled too suddenly.

"Majeed?"

She tried to turn around, but her wrists were clasped and manacled behind her. From the corner of her vision, Val saw Majeed slump to the floor. Behind her, she smelled an unspeakable aroma, a perfumed breath, rich with death and strawberries.

She managed to twist around. Filakis stood before her, lean and dour as a medieval saint. His hennaed fingers, long, El Greco-esque, roved her face as though its contours held the meaning of some mystery. His lips, drawn tight in monkish gloom, bestowed a cold kiss on her forehead, but Val's attention was distracted by his nudity and by a nakedness far worse, the almost total absence of any genitalia. His testicles were absent altogether; his penis, what remained of it, had been reduced to a limp and useless teat.

He noted the direction of her gaze and smiled almost apologetically. "Ah, I see you've noticed my . . . deformity. Well, let me say, I wasn't born like this. It was my choice. A eunuch savors pleasure vicariously, you see, and I'm particularly skilled at that. It pleases me to think that, while others soil themselves in a thousand nauseating ways, I stay untouched. Pure, if you will. My pleasure comes from taking sex in any form except my own. Let others wallow in dung, their filth never touches me."

"I only came to get Majeed," Val said. "You've punished him enough. Now let us leave."

"Majeed? Oh, you mean *her*," said Filakis. "The creature pretends to be a male, but she's a cunt and nothing else."

"More reason not to need her then."

Filakis smiled. "Your haste to leave verges on insulting. I thought you wanted pleasure. That's why you went to so much trouble coming here. I can't let you go away disappointed." He smiled. "But maybe I was wrong. Maybe you're like so many others and what you secretly desire and pine for is what you most deeply dread."

He touched Val's throat while keeping hold on her manacled hands. The long, emaciated fingers closed and gripped, wringing forth a rain of gold and silver coins behind her eyes. The coins clattered against the inside of her skull, but then the din grew distant, faint, was replaced at length by one exquisite, terrifying orgasm . . . then nothingness.

Val's body, when she first opened her eyes, was reflected back to her in the ceiling's mirrored tiles. Her physical condition alarmed and sickened her. Every inch of her, from collarbones to pubis, upper arms to wrists, appeared to be the canvas on which a demented seamstress had created a masterpiece of color and design. A hundred needles pierced Val's flesh, and through the punctures had been woven the most colorful of threads, which crisscrossed in a splendid zigzag of geometry. The threads, in turn, were tied to hooks nailed into the bed's headboard and sides. Her slightest movement, therefore, even a breath drawn in too sharply, caused the needles to plunge deeper beneath the skin and her nerves to scream out in ungodly unison.

Movement created pain so sharp and constant that, after a time, it crossed a psychic border and became a kind of lunatic arousal. In this, Val realized, lay the peculiar horror of the City, its ability to wring appetite from even the most appalling cruelties, the most demeaning humiliations. Desire not linked to satisfaction in the slightest way, but a perverse and masochistic lust that fed on misery as fervently as those in the outside world generally sought comfort.

She learned all this in her strange and all too familiar prison, a room she had only to glimpse for one brief second to know its parameters and furnishings, the contents of its bookshelves and its dresser drawers, to know, without going near the window, what view she would see: not crenelated walls of a Moroccan Casbah, but plowed fields and distant tree-clad hills, a decaying barn belonging to some unknown neighbors to the east and a silo above whose entranceway a hex sign had been drawn. To know that if she were free to turn the photo on the desktop to face her, she would see a picture of the person she had been, the child who was held prisoner in the Sewing Room.

How such an illusion of a return to the chamber of her childhood captivity was possible was lost on Val. She assumed, at first, some sort of hallucination was at work, that Filakis had, unknown to her, slipped some type of drug into her system. This belief was comforting for it implied that, at some point, the drug might either wear off or be overcome by sheer force of will, and she resolved not to give in to panic but to simply accept her fate for the moment and await the next development the way one allows a nightmare to run its course in the confidence of, at some point, awakening.

When she heard a key turn in the lock, Val prayed to see Filakis even as a part of her mind braced for something worse. It came. What entered the room wasn't Filakis but her mother Lettie or something identical to her right down to the dimple in her left cheek, the small scar above one eyebrow.

"How are we, sweetheart?" crooned the Lettie creature, mincing across the room with a breakfast-laden tray. Val didn't have to look to know the contents: toast and milk, half a grapefruit, a jar of honey.

"How do we feel now? Better?"

"These stitches . . . whatever they are . . . they hurt."

"Well . . . naturally . . ." said Lettie, no more moved by Val's predicament than she'd been twenty-five years earlier. "That's so you won't get up and leave. But the laces are quite beautiful, I think." She set the tray down on the desk and strummed a lacquered fingernail idly across the weave. Like falling dominos, Val's nerves responded to the wiggling needles. Fire shot beneath her skin. She howled.

". . . This design in particular I find attractive. A cat's cradle, don't you see? Much prettier than any clothing you could wear."

The pain receded. Val tried to concentrate on the apparition at her side. She was as Val remembered her, plump and auburn-haired and artfully made up. False eyelashes and rouge and Cleopatra lids, a Vegas showgirl gone to seed but handsome still and not a day older than when Val had been her pet and prisoner in the upstairs room in Tarrant.

"Please . . ."

Lettie made a shushing sound and leaned over Val. Her mouth was crammed with needles that protruded from it like silver fangs. One by one, she threaded them, replaced them in her mouth. Pinching up a bit of flesh from the underside of Val's breast she ran the needle through. Val gasped with pain and fright, but she dared not struggle too much for the least movement on her part caused the other needles to shift and dig.

"This is going to be so beautiful."

"Please stop. Please let me up."

"But then you might run away. The world is such a dangerous place. You might hurt yourself."

The words were spoken with the correct tone, the perfect inflection that the real Lettie, were she living, would have used. Val blinked and tried to clear the apparition from her mind. "You're dead," Val said. "You killed yourself after someone saw me at the window and called the police, and they took me away from you."

"Hush now. All that was only a bad dream. It's over now. Come here now and look out the window."

"I can't move. You can see that, can't you?"

Lettie sighed. "No, I suppose not. Then I'll bring the view to you."

The window didn't budge, but Val's mind suddenly filled with long-forgotten images. The winding dun-colored streets of the City disappeared, and it was spring in upstate New York, and the earth smelled fresh and thawed. Green buds were visible on the trees, and swallows, so far away they looked like asterisks in full flight against the sky, did airborne lifts and plummets. On the road beyond the untilled land, a man was passing by on horseback. He wore a cowboy hat and his boots must have been tipped with metal, for now and then the sun would catch just the right angle and a blinding shaft, a pin of light, would blaze and spangle. He moved farther and farther out of sight, until his horse and he were no bigger than the swallows, a pinpoint of light, a disappearing diamond. He was, thought Val, the most beautiful thing she'd ever seen and as unattainable as the most distant star.

Tears filled Val's eyes. She knew the scene was an illusion, produced perhaps by Filakis's trickery or her own weary, traumatized mind, but the needles in her flesh were real. With the slightest hint of movement, the arabesque of threads across her body tightened and a hundred tiny wounds were enlarged and deepened.

"Don't you like to look?" said Lettie.

"Of course."

"Then why are you crying?"

Val tried to turn her head to indicate her bonds, but even this small effort was rewarded with myriad needle stings, sweet silver bees that set upon her at the faintest shiver.

"It's painful to look out there and see the world and not be able to be in it."

"I know *I* wouldn't want to be out there," said Lettie, and she wiggled one of the needles just under Val's left arm.

"Why not?" said Val, awash in pain.

"The dangers."

"But think," Val said, "of the possibilities for pleasure."

"No!" Lettie's face contorted viciously. She made a choking, half-mad sound, and stomped her feet so fiercely that the vibrations reached Val's needles and set each shaft to shivering. A thousand penetrated nerve endings sang with pain, Val's synapses ignited and juggled fire. She writhed, and with each movement, more nerves were torched until her body shivered in the cold fire of a hundred small impalements.

And still Lettie screamed. "You're lying! You're evil and you're lying. The world's an evil place, a terrible place. Only here is where it's safe. Just here. And you and I will never leave."

That said, she crossed the room and fetched her sewing box again. A heavy picnic hamper-type box, when opened up, it revealed all that Val recalled and more – threads in a hundred colors, dull muted shades to glittering metallics, pastels diluted from the sea and sky, a dozen nuances of crimson comprising all the shades of blood – from freshly shed to tacky moist to the dull scarlet of dried gore. To go with these – a shimmering hierarchy of needles, from the thinness of a human hair to those with the length and heft of hatpins.

"This will surprise you," Lettie said, "but I'm not doing this to hurt you. I'm doing it because I want to keep you safe and wise, like I wish someone had done for me."

And she pierced a threaded needle through the skin of Val's groin. Quickly, with hands that moved so fast their speed was almost magical, a conjuror's hands, plucking miracles from the air like doves, Lettie pierced Val's labia half a dozen times in swift succession.

The pain produced was anything but magical, dazzling and sickening in equal parts. Val screamed and dug her teeth into her tongue. Lettie unscrewed the jar of honey on the breakfast tray and spooned sweetness into Val's mouth.

"You'll come to understand this later," she said, proffering honey. "You think the needles keep you bound, but it isn't really so. It isn't even the pain, although that will come to seem like pleasure, too. It's the seduction of confinement that will keep you here." She laughed, a hollow, mirthless sound that teased dread from every pore. "The day will come when I could snip every thread, remove every needle, and open the door wide, and you'd beg me not to make you go, not to turn you out into the world. You'd weep bitter tears at just the thought of being asked to leave this room."

"Try me," said Val, tasting blood and honey.

"Believe me, dear," Lettie said. "Someday you'll come to love this . . . especially since I'm going to teach you how to sew."

She wiped her sticky fingers on her dress and disappeared from the room. She returned a few moments later leading Majeed, who wore a chain around his neck and women's clothes. Of the two, Val guessed it was the clothing that caused the more humiliation.

"Don't worry," Lettie said. "I'm only going to hurt your lover a little bit. Enough to show you how it's done. Then it will be your turn to wield the needles."

Val shuddered with disgust. The needles in her nipples stung and tingled, their slender shafts contacting nerves that echoed in her vulva, in her womb.

"I won't do it."

"You'd be surprised," said Lettie, twirling Majeed's chain as she affixed it to a leg of the oak bed, "what people think they're incapable of doing. Even the saints are capable of the worst atrocities – it's when they recognize it that they decide to become saints. You're capable of anything. What has been done to you, believe me, you can do to others."

Lettie held a needle to the light. She squinted at the tiny eye, then sucked the end of a thread thin and white as hair plucked from a crone's head. Steel and fabric glinted in the light as Lettie carried the threaded needle back to the bed. She undid Majeed's blouse and bra, murmured something in his ear. Majeed nodded solemnly.

And then, to Val: "You'll learn to love this someday."

"No! Don't!"

Needle penetrated flesh. A drop of blood flowered on Majeed's chest. Lettie looped the needle back again and pierced the skin at the edge of one aureole.

There was a moment of pure terror when Val felt the urge to wield the needle, to bleed Majeed in every pore, a moment when she knew to her profoundest core that Lettie was right as to what she was capable of doing.

Everything.

Anything.

And it was more than she could bear.

"You fucking crazy freak! Stop it!"

Hatred galvanized her. It was her antidote for pain, and now, while fury numbed her, she bent one knee and elbow, using them for leverage, pushed up with all her strength into the needles. There was a teetering moment of agony and inheld breath when the combined strength of the needles held her down, pulling at her stretched and bleeding skin in a fresh fury of torture.

"No!"

The power of her voice infected muscle. She flung herself against the cumulative strength of the lacings in one final effort. Flesh tore as hooks and needles parted company. Blood-soaked threads broke and dangled down Val's chest and legs, while the greater part of Lettie's design, the shimmering cat's cradle, remained intact, covering her torso in a gory arabesque.

"You stupid, sick bitch!" Val swept past Majeed and knocked Lettie to the floor. Her hands flew to Lettie's neck, as they had done – in fantasy – a thousand times. The woman flailed and kicked beneath her, but there was scant conviction in her struggles. It was as if she was resigned to accept whatever fate Val deemed appropriate. Val realized her tears were dripping onto Lettie's face along with blood. Images – of midnight rides under skies so black they snuffed the stars, of haggard, frantic faces pressed against the window – "You buyin', Mama?" "You sellin'?" – of glossy women, strutting-rolling-undulating come-ons as they did their spike-heeled sway, savage women, electrical with desperation and crackling with need, and Lettie's face, entranced and lustful as she peered out through her private looking glass to view that other world, that vast Outside, a piece of which was trapped and languishing inside her like a dead embryo, and the need was sucking Lettie dry, starving her. *You see what a terrible world it is. Just look at that. You see.*

"Oh, God," said Val, and she released Lettie's throat.

Lettie coughed up flecks of blood. "I knew it." Her voice was tiny, dry, the sound of petals being plucked from long dead flowers and crushed to powdered scent. "I knew you'd try to kill me someday. I knew you hated me."

"I did," said Val. "I wanted to kill you with my own hands. I used to plan it sitting by the window. But then you killed yourself and took away the chance."

"I hated you, too," said Lettie.

That startled Val. She'd seen herself as Lettie's victim all these years; the newspapers and magazines, the neighbors, the teams of tutting psychiatrists and clucking therapists who worked with Val after she'd been freed, had viewed it the same. As one tabloid had put it, Lettie was *The Monster Mom Who Kept Her Child in Chains.*

"I hated you for being free," said Lettie. "For seeking out the dark."

"But you're the one who showed it to me."

"To scare you, not to make you want to leave me."

"And I never have," said Val. "I've carried you around in my head like soiled clothing at the bottom of a suitcase. I've carried you in my dreams. I've hated you for being there in every place I ever went to, every bed I ever slept in. You've always been there, haunting me, spying on me, watching."

"Then forgive me," Lettie said, "and I'll go away."

"Unlock the door."

"I can't do that."

"Don't lie."

Val raised her hand up in frustration, then brought it down without delivering the blow. The accumulation of her wounding made her weak, but Lettie's sadness weakened her still more. In the shadows, Lettie's face appeared to dance with minuscule pinpricks of light that mimicked the crosshatchings of the cat's cradle.

"Forgive me," Lettie said again.

The thaw in Val, though incomplete, was tenfold more painful than the freeze, a blossoming of anguish that shivered out in razor-sharp, concentric circles from her heart. She was conscious of Majeed watching her in a trance of immobility, as silent as an inheld breath, waiting.

"I forgive you," Val said, though each word felt like it cost her a lifetime's worth of pain. "I forgive you . . . Mother."

Lettie might have smiled. Val never knew. The flickering sparks that strobed her face intensified. Her skin peeled back in sections, bleeding pulp and sweetness like overripe fruit. Her hands lifted up beseechingly. Val saw the tattooed palms. Her mother's face dissolved and, in its place, appeared the Berber girl's, laughing as she held up to Val the jinn-spells on her hands. That illusion lasted just an instant, though, before the child's face and body transformed again and Val was staring at the Turk's scourged flesh and ribby torso and shrunken, useless genitals. Then he, too, was gone as the room's walls folded in on themselves like the wings of origami swans. The bed, the desk, the window with its unreal view of New England fields dismantled into shreds, the shreds reduced to tatters, and these to gaudy flecks that whirled through the air like stiletto-sharp confetti.

"Filakis?" Val said, unbuckling the collar from Majeed's neck. "How does he . . .?"

He's a conjuror. He fucks in any shape except his own. In his own form, he stays as chaste as any virgin. Pure. He thinks it makes him godly."

"More like Satan, I'd say."

"The City's his creation, his haven for lost souls. He's God and Satan both, here."

Val finished freeing Majeed. She plucked long needles from her chest and torso. Majeed gave her his blouse.

"Come on!"

"But the door . . ."

"There isn't any!"

Majeed was right. The illusion of the Sewing Room had fallen away to be replaced by the dark staircase leading up through Filakis's prison. They lost no time in climbing it. Above ground, the City's winding alleyways were swathed in midnight dark. But if by day the inhabitants of the City had remained for the most part secluded, nightfall had changed all that.

Now bodies writhed and twisted on the cobblestones, locked in violent congress with each other and themselves, with objects, animals, and beings that, glimpsed in passing, Val could not identify as either alive or dead. If lethargy infused the sex act by day, savagery and necrophilia ruled it at night. Nor were those copulating so concentrated in their efforts that they ignored Majeed and Val. Tongues flicked out to stroke their passing flesh. Hands touched and pressed, and fingers fluttered in mute cajolement.

They avoided the on-going orgy as much as possible and plunged into the blacker corridors where, by daylight, the marketplace had offered its obscenities. Now the streets were empty of all merchandise except the human trade. In the pale illumination of a paltry moon, Val saw the abominations that the light of day had shamed into concealment. Around a heaping, stinking mound the tribe of shiteaters squatted, dining with their hands. No sooner was their vile repast consumed than their bodies evacuated the meal again, and they recommenced their feast. Forced to pass within an arm's length by the narrowness of the walls, Val and Majeed were prey to dozens of soiled fingers dangling out at them, dripping enticements as they proffered their foul treats.

Beyond that, as they approached the area of the tanneries, Majeed slipped on something in a darker patch of dark. He fell to one knee. Val stopped to help him up. Liquid ran cold and clotty on Majeed's leg. Val's hand on him came away reeking of copper. She'd barely had time to register the fact that they were skidding in a pool of blood when the moon skimmed out from under cloud cover again, revealing a huddled cluster of figures, the worst of the City's worst, the deformed and mutilated, the self-created amputees, eaters of dung and dead flesh. Val whispered something to Majeed, who'd faltered again, perhaps from shock at seeing the display in front of them.

Cannibals?

He shook his head. Less shock, thought Val, than abject fascination. Not cannibals in the truest sense, she realized, but flesheaters just the same. With razors and with small, thin-bladed knives, they sliced off tiny portions of themselves and popped these awful delicacies into their mouths, chewing with ecstatic sighs, while the men's erections hardened into steel-like batons, and sex ran down the women's legs as copious as urine. They paused in feasting only long enough to rut against each other's blood-streaked skins before returning to the next course in their macabre meal.

Val and Majeed's passing provided an unexpected distraction and the possibility for new and undiscovered flavors. The group broke apart and formed a circle around Majeed and Val. They held their razor blades and knives in fingers sliced to the bone and missing digits. It was only the clumsiness their wounding had induced that allowed Val to hurl a loose stone at the nearest one and break an opening in the circle. Majeed did the same. Another flesheater staggered back and toppled. His nearest comrade saw opportunity in this and stooped to slice off an eyelid and a speck of nose. Raw wailing rent the air.

"Come on!" Val shook Majeed. He seemed entranced but came alert when the rest of them crowded in again. Val's heart was racing, but she attributed it to fear and flight. Only as they approached the tanneries did she realize she was light-headed with lust as much as terror and that her inner muscles were clenching and unclenching in response to a steadily increasing need. The very air seemed drugged with pheromones. To breathe was to have sex. A hand reached out. Majeed.

"They're coming."

She looked behind. At first the narrow street appeared blocked by a low wall. Only when the moon performed its fan dance with the cloud again, overturning like a bowl and spilling out its light, did she recognized the "wall" to be a thing composed of flesh – night denizens of the City distracted from their coupling by the possibility of something new, fresh meat to fuck and fondle. In the mob, Val saw a few that appeared almost healthy, those who'd evidently resided in the City only a short time, but most were the derelict and drained, those far along the way to literally fucking themselves to death. The women cupped their bruised and flopping breasts, the men worked cocks made raw and scabrous from overuse, but kept erect by cock rings tight enough to bite into the flesh.

A hand slid up between Val's legs. She gasped, looked down. A hugely obese man, nude and masturbating, was crouched down in the shadow of a doorway. The sight of him – suety flesh overlapping in great grayish dollops – revolted Val, but more appalling still was her reaction to the touch. Her nerve endings keened with fresh desire. It was all she could do to kick free of her molester and dash behind Majeed into another alleyway.

Ahead she heard the approach of others closing in. She grabbed Majeed's hand and they swerved left through an ancient doorway into a dark foyer. A new smell, one Val recognized at once, assailed her nostrils.

"The tanneries," said Majeed, his hand tightening on hers.

The courtyard in which they stood was filled with immense vats dug into the ground. A heavy, suffocating odor rose up from the murky green liquid. Val felt her stomach lurch.

Outside, the stillness of the night was broken by the panting gasps of the on-coming orgiasts. In another few seconds, they'd be upon them.

"Get in," Majeed said.

"What?"

"Come on."

Holding her breath against the stench, Val followed Majeed along the slippery stepping-stones that formed narrow walk-ways between the vats. She heard a mucky splash, and suddenly Majeed was not beside her.

From one of the reeking vats, a voice: "*Get in.*"

At the same time, from outside, other voices. The pack following them was splitting up. Val heard footfalls in the outer courtyard. Squatting down over one of the vats, she lowered herself as quietly as possible into the foul-smelling muck. Animal skins in various stages of softening swished softly around her legs as their pursuers entered the courtyard.

In the darkness, she prayed they'd be afraid to walk too near the tanning vats, that they wouldn't see her face or Majeed's lifted above the ghoulish green stew. She prayed, too, that she could stay concealed, that the mere presence of so much flesh, available and eager, would not seduce her out of hiding. In a doorway across from the vats, Val saw a couple silhouetted, locked in slow and rhythmic copulation. Barely moving, the woman hoisted up one leg around the man's thigh. He bent to take her nipple between his teeth. She fought a trembling urgency to cry out, betray herself to the mob and fall into a sea of flesh no less disgusting than the pulpy wallow in which she now was crouched.

She bit her lip against the urge. Her cunt contracted and released in pulsing, ever faster waves. The vile stench of the tannery no longer reached her brain. Instead the room was a perfumery of sex, lush and intoxicating. The woman in the doorway was writhing on her partner's penis. Her long hair swayed. Her sleek thighs clenched. Val felt the City acting on her brain like a narcotic, its mesmerizing power taking deeper hold. Its carnal wonders, even the eaters of excrement, the consumers of their own flesh, evoked less disgust now than compelling wonder and, worse, the desire to do more than look, to touch and feel, participate . . .

She had to get out.

The woman grinding on her lover's dick reached down to grab his buttocks. Her hands turned briefly outward. Val saw Filakis's hennaed palms. Get out now or never leave. Hoisting herself up out of the tanning vat and calling to Majeed, she sprinted past the lovers in the doorway and ran on without looking back to see what transformations might be taking place.

The streets that she and Majeed followed all led uphill, away from the City's heart. There was no more serious pursuit. By dawn, they were standing on the hillsides overlooking the earthcolored Casbah. The crenelated ramparts, towers, and courtyards lost density against the watery pastel of dawn, shimmering with ever lessening brilliance until scarcely an outline remained. To the north, another city skyline loomed, but this one curved around a wedge of dark Atlantic. Val recognized the skyline of Agadir.

Majeed caught Val's hand.

"I can't keep going."

"We'll rest then."

"That isn't what I mean."

"Then . . . what?"

"I think I'm making a mistake. I don't think I can . . . leave."

"That's crazy. If you go back, you'll die."

Majeed's gaze was rivetted on the space where vestiges of the City's walls still were faintly visible. There, silhouetted against the day, stood a lone figure. At this distance, Val couldn't see a face, but she was sure the figure was Filakis, his arms extended, pious in his mock chastity and grand in his forgiveness.

Offering that which he despised – temptations of the flesh.

"You can't, Majeed. Don't even think about it."

"I have to."

"But he tortured you."

"Yes – no. It's just a game, after all. An endless game. The torture, then the pleasure. You didn't stay there long enough to learn. You still remember how it is Outside, where the world is something besides a sex organ."

"Don't do this."

"Give me the incense burner."

"No."

"If you love me, Val, you will."

"You won't last back there. You'll die."

Majeed shrugged. "There're worse ways to die than being fucked to death."

"And me?"

"The Turk has a forgiving heart. I'm sure he'd be willing to give you another chance."

Val shook her head. She handed Majeed the incense burner and backed away. He struck a match and held it to the wick. Pale emerald leaves of fire blazed. Val shut her eyes.

When next she looked, Majeed's befouled clothes were reduced to stinking embers. The incense burner, not even charred, lay among the pitiful debris.

"Do you want to make love again?" asked Val's newest lover, a silversmith in San Miguel de Allende, Mexico. He'd come up behind her, laid his hands atop her shoulders, was rubbing his hard penis into the crack of her ass.

"I don't think so."

"Come on. I'll bet I can change your mind."

He tried to take her hand. "What's that you've got?"

She held the incense burner out to him, let him inspect it with his artist's eye, exploring its design.

"Nice carving. Where'd you get it? India?"

She shrugged and plucked the object back from him too quickly, her haste betraying a greater fondness for the artifact than for his penis, which she was already weary of examining.

"Come on now, let me suck you. Eat out your pretty pussy."

He sank to his knees. Val spread her thighs just wide enough for him to get his tongue in. She put one hand atop his head and stroked him idly. With the other, she fingered the incense burner, which smelled, she thought, though very faintly, of temptation and desire. If she held onto it, she knew the day would come when she'd no longer be able to resist its possibilities. She'd light the flame and step inside to be consumed.

Or she could pitch the object out through the open window this minute, if she wanted. Hurl it high and far and never suffer its obscene allure again. Perhaps, she thought, in time, she'd make the choice. But not yet, she thought, and stroked her lover's face. Not yet.

LESSONS IN SUBMISSION

Mark Pritchard

for O.

1

Go in the bathroom, take a shower and wash your hair. Dry your body and comb out your hair, but don't dry it. Put your clothes back on so that your hair hangs wet and limp on your shoulders, dripping water all over you.

Come down the hall to the bedroom and stand before me. I'm sitting on the bed waiting for you, the low sun behind me in the window, blinding you to me except for my dark silhouetted form on the bed, leaning back on my hands. I'm staring at you, with the knowledge I have showing in my eyes that you can't see. You can squint against the sun, but the most you'll see is the glow of the light behind my blond hair. While you stand there waiting you might wonder how to take a picture like this, a picture that would show you what you can't see: my body hidden by a robe, my eyes boring into you, the strips of cloth in my hand.

I tell you to put your hands behind your back. It makes you look submissive, and to further enhance the picture, I tell you to put your head down. Now all you can see is the splotches of water running down the front of your red silk shirt. I've told you not to wear a bra, and your left nipple is under a wet spot and it gets hard and pokes out, and the sleazy association that this is like some wet t-shirt scene is enough to embarrass you and further enhance your submission.

Listen to me: "You look delicious like this. Your hair is beautiful when it's dark and wet, and it's probably making you a little uncomfortable to stand there dripping, which just turns me on, because I want to make you uncomfortable enough to make you realize you've lost control. I wanted you to stand there and drip like this because it's how I like to imagine your cunt: so wet that there's come dripping off the hairs. You're probably standing there thinking this isn't so hard, to stand there and let me look at you, but just think of how many things I've already taken away. You can't see me; you can't touch me. You can't use your hands and you can't go anywhere. You can't answer me or say anything. You just have to stand there and let me stare at you and talk to you.

"In a minute we'll go on and you'll realize just how little control you have, but for now, enjoy your freedom. Okay, you can look at me again."

Raise your head, but it doesn't do any good, the sun is still blinding you as it sets outside your window into the ocean. You feel the water dripping all the way down into the waistline of your jeans, where it stops and spreads out along your soft belly. Other rivulets have rolled off your shoulders and between your shoulder blades, under your arms, or directly onto the floor. You can shift your weight and step directly into a small puddle. The instant of imbalance from the water under your feet is enough to remind you that it's me, not you, who is controlling your slide into submission.

The sun sets and you look straight into the orange ball as it balances on the horizon. Let it hypnotize you while you listen to my voice telling you the different places I'm going to put my tongue, telling you I'm going to penetrate you in places you never considered were possible points of entry. You're used to thinking of the cunt, the mouth, and in really uncontrolled moments, the asshole. And boys have put their tongues in your ears. You didn't like it then, but I don't do that anyway.

What I do is stand up and unbutton your shirt and slip if off your shoulders. It hangs down from your waist and from your hands, which are still held together behind your back, not by any instruments but simply by your willingness to learn something about submission.

"I'm going to make you talk," I say. "At first it'll be easy. All you have to do is say 'yes.''

"Yes."

"Are you my lover?"

"Yes."

"Do you submit to me?"

"Yes."

"Do you love to be with me? Do you relish the sound of my voice, the weight of my hands on yours? Do you desire me, strong and solid, next to you?"

"Yes."

"Do you think about my prick going crazy in your cunt? Do you think about licking the sweat from my body? Do you think about my leg going between yours when we kiss in public?"

"Yes."

"Are you ready to submit to me? Will you do what I say? Will you be brave?"

To everything you answer yes. Your voice goes through an interesting change – it gets deeper and fuller and connected to the desire that's in the burning center of your body – a desire which, at its deepest, has nothing to do with me, a desire that started when you were a child and imagined submitting to someone stronger, an older girl, a character in a story, anyone who under-stood your need to have control and responsibility taken away and replaced by her will. You were Scout and Gregory Peck gently put you over his knee and spanked your butt as you told him your sins, things he already knew but you only become good again if you tell him. It's that voice I want, the voice that's naked and uncontrolled, the voice that knows the desire to fuck and the desire to get fucked are the same thing, that knows there's nothing bad about needing pleasure or giving up control, that only the strong have something to give up in the first place.

"Yes. Yes, yes, yes." You swallow and with every word you look scared at first, then relaxed as you give it up.

You have a lot to give up. I really want it. It's this transfer and acceptance of desire that amounts to your submission.

Your skin burns orange in the light. Even if you look away for a minute, you see spots. The sun is too low to hurt your eyes but bright enough to intoxicate and hypnotize you with its brilliance. The whole room seems to burn with light that gets more and more intense; then in the space of a few moments it disappears. You are still blinded by the image of the fiery red ball, so you can't see me lie back on the bed and open my robe and masturbate while staring at you standing there blind and helpless.

"Close your eyes," I say. It doesn't matter, you still see the sun. Water is still dripping from your hair, more slowly now. "Open your pants. Open the belt, the top button and the zipper. Pull them lower on your hips so I can see your cunt hair. Lower than that. Just high enough for them to stay up." I look at you and stroke my cock. "I'm having a fantasy," I say, "about jacking off onto your belly, so that the come runs down into your pubic hair and gets caught there. I comb the come into your cunt hair until it's coated by my come, so that instead of smelling like cunt you smell like sperm. It's another way of taking something away from you, of colonizing your body, so that you don't even smell like yourself anymore."

I get up and walk over to you holding a strip of cloth. My cock is hard but you can't see it because your eyes are closed, the image of the sun still imprinted on your corneas. "Put your hands at your side," I say, and go behind you and blindfold you with the strip of cloth.

"Would you do that?" I ask. "Would you wear my smell on your cunt . . . let's say, to work?"

"Yes," you say.

"Tell me you'll wear my come on your body whenever I want you to."

"I will," you answer.

You have to say more than that now. You have to tell me you'll do everything I say, and you have to tell me in detail and use hyperbole and go beyond what I've said, you have to show that you're turned on not only by the images of what we're talking about, not only by the fact that what you're saying expresses your desire as well, but by the sheer fact that saying dirty and taboo things to me, that these words are coming out of your supposedly clean mouth, amounts to a further loss of control, to a deepening of your submission.

Example:

"I want your come on me. Shoot it on me, put it on my belly, on my face, on the lips of my cunt. Smear it into my wet hair, let it become part of me. I want your smell on me so I'll belong to you, so that as long as I wear it before it washes off, I'm yours, as if you needed a sign, as if you didn't know I'll do what you want."

I need to hear this from you. Not only to make you do things but to make you admit to them. There's something about the voice that's more intimate, more alive than the body itself. The body can do things that the voice can't. If I do something to you, you can always pretend later it wasn't really what you wanted, but if you ask for it in advance, if you beg for it in the most imaginative language, if you use that voice that comes from deep inside your desire, then it reveals even more than your actions. Don't think you can fool me, either. You may be a good actress but I know the difference between somebody telling me what I want to hear and the real expression of need and desire that amounts to confession, which is another word for submission.

After I blindfold you, I stand behind you and reach up and touch your nipples, You aren't allowed to relax and lean back against me, so no matter how weak in the knees you get, you have to maintain your balance.

Now you can push your pants down farther – they fall around your ankles – and touch your cunt. The rule is that you have to tell me whatever it is you're doing as I stroke and pinch your tits.

"I'm parting my cunt lips. They're already wet, not just way inside, but all the way out, even the outer lips have come on them. They're hot and slick; I love the consistency of my juice at this time of month. Now I'm touching my clit. I'm holding it between my thumb and forefinger and stroking down along it like a prick. Now I'm pushing my finger underneath it so I can rub myself – ugh."

You can't do it so good that you can't talk. You have to be able to tell me what you're doing. You have go slowly enough and do it soft enough to maintain the narrative. What I'm getting from you isn't your hand; what I'm getting from you is your voice.

"My clit is hard. I –" You pause and gasp. "I like touching it with my two fingers pressed together like this . . ."

Don't stop talking.

"I'm rubbing it. I can't stand it. Yes I can . . . Just don't stop. What you're doing to my nipples is driving me crazy . . . I'm rubbing my clit – I'm rubbing my clit –"

I make you stop. Put your hands at your sides again. I keep touching your breasts. The nipples are as hard as pebbles of glass. You imagine them cutting my lips if I decide to suck on them.

I lay you down on the bed, and you go on masturbating as I watch. You don't have to talk while you do it. You just have to show it to me. This is the first time you've ever done this in front of someone.

You stroke yourself. As you get closer to coming a secret escapes your lips and makes you come. After your orgasm you keep your fingers pressed against your pussy; the fingers of the other hand are unconsciously pressing against your breastbone, reaching in for your center of desire and selfhood that you are submitting to me.

I attach your wrists to chains. You begin trembling. I attach your ankles to chains. You become afraid. I put my hand on the spot you were pressing a moment before and your fear stops.

You are splayed open on your bed. I start talking quietly to you again about how beautiful you are, about how much I desire you. You answer "Yes" again and again like a mantra.

While you're tied there I kneel over your head and put my cock in your mouth. I penetrate you like that. I penetrate your cunt. I penetrate your asshole with my finger. I go back to your head and put my fingers in your ears while my cock is in your mouth. You can't see anything, you can't hear anything, you can't move, the only reality is my taste. My taste and smell and weight fill you, blocking out everything else. You aren't frightened, you don't want to get away, you submit.

2

It's dark except for the ceiling light, which casts a dim glow in the middle of the room. As soon as we walk in, I tell you to strip as quickly as possible. Then you get on your knees.

This is a pose you have to learn: Sit with your feet underneath you and your butt on your heels. This posture, used traditionally by Japanese, has both humility and dignity. It's stable and you can remain in this pose for a long time. But the best part about it is that, even though everyone can get into this pose for at least a few minutes, it becomes quite painful after a while, especially when you finally try to stand up and walk again. Yet it isn't dangerous; you can't really hurt yourself by remaining in this posture for thirty or forty minutes. Therefore, this act of submission will teach you about humility and pain.

As you rest like this on your knees, your legs are together. I couldn't touch you between the legs if I wanted to, not without you moving. That is not what is involved tonight.

When I bring in a bowl of hot water and a washcloth, you are waiting on your knees in the circle of light. I strip off my clothes except for a shirt I wear open. Wearing clothes while you are naked is intended to remind you of my power to grant you comfort and safety, or to take them away; to grant you pleasure, or withhold it.

You have your head down. You couldn't see me anyway, not until I enter the light. As you kneel in the soft yellow glow, your head down and your hands behind your back even though I haven't told you to put them there, you look deliciously submissive, and I pause to stare at you and fantasize about how your mouth is going to feel on me.

I advance into the light and tell you to look at me. This is the first time you've seen my cock. Even if it makes you shiver, you look at it. It's the only chance you'll have to look at it for awhile. I bring my body closer and closer until you are close enough to touch me with your mouth. Then I stop.

You lean forward until I can feel your breath. Then the first touch of your tongue, alarmingly warm, caresses the underside of the cockhead. Your tongue slowly circles the head, then you push up with the tongue so you can lick down the underside of the shaft. That part of me is so sensitive the first time it is touched, and your warm mouth makes me tremble and groan and you work your way down to my balls.

Now your hands are gently touching my legs. You lean back slightly and take the whole cockhead in your mouth and wipe your tongue back and forth across the slit, tasting fluid. Your fingernails scratch slowly down my thighs. There is a mirror across the room in which I can watch you kneeling and sucking me.

You are allowed to bend forward as long as your butt is on your heels. That means I control how deep I go in your mouth. When I move forward, you take me deeper. When I move back, you gape at the missing presence.

I move forward again and tell you to touch my balls while you suck me, and to move your mouth rhythmically up and down. I can't tell you much, though; it feels too good. I'm touching my own nipples. After a few minutes, I'm already getting close to coming.

I pull back and ask you to talk about what we're doing. You describe the texture and taste of my prick, the sensation of being penetrated in the intimate hollow of your mouth, the enormity of my cock on your tongue. You also describe the pain in your legs and ankles and feet, the contrast between the spasms of pleasure you feel when you suck me, and the pain and discomfort of kneeling to do it. You beg me to come in your mouth so that you can get the pleasure of my orgasm and so the pain will stop.

Oh, well, it's kind of a false assumption that you get to change positions just because I come, but you'll find out soon enough. For now, beg me some more. I'm still touching my nipples. After a while the pain makes your voice frantic. I like that. I don't care if it's pain or desire that makes your voice quaver, you'll find out soon enough there isn't much difference.

I slip back into your mouth, and tell you to touch me everywhere you can, especially underneath the balls, behind the legs, and right before I come, touch my asshole. You pump me with your mouth. I don't really come very fast this way, unless you're awfully good at this. So this goes on for a long time. I don't know how to describe it to you except to say that, in addition to the pleasure I'm getting from you, the sight of you in the mirror sucking me excites me and helps me come.

As I get close, I start moaning and talking dirty. I say nasty things to you. It's one of the only times I've been really nasty to you so far, and I let it come out because it couldn't possibly be any nastier than shooting into your mouth. Gasping and shouting and calling you names, I orgasm, my hand leaving my nipple to slap your shoulder three or four times, a completely unplanned movement that leaves a hand print which lingers for an hour. Just as I finish, I thrust as deep as I can in your throat. It makes you gag but I hold you there tightly for a few seconds out of pure selfishness. Then I release you and you have to cough.

When you can, you very properly resume sucking me gently to get all of the come. I touch your shoulder lightly, the one I slapped, and you pull off, pausing to kiss the very tip with your lips.

Sit back on your heels. You don't get to move. I bend down and hand you the washcloth, and you gently wash my cock, which remains hard for a few minutes. After you're finished you can wipe your mouth and chin, but I hope you've swallowed my come by now. I don't even want to have to tell you I desire it. You simply should do it.

I sit on the bed in the darkness and look at you. You're still in pain but alongside the pain there is deep arousal, endorphins making you high and hungry. You ask me to slap your shoulder once again just where I did before; it was that slap, administered in the middle of everything else, that brought you over the edge from pain to pleasure.

What I really want to do is to slap your face, but I don't. That's for another time. I don't want you to move very much, either; it would mean taking your pleasure/pain away from you. So instead of hitting you, I tell you to part your legs and touch yourself.

Without hesitation you reach between your legs and bring yourself to orgasm, swaying back and forth and arching your back. After your second orgasm, and without stopping the motion of your fingers, you ask me to call you names again, so I do. In this moment, when you are all submission and desire and pleasure, you become the things I call you. This is not degradation, but music, when you are aroused.

After you come a few times, you need something else. You're swaying all over and about to rise off your knees so I bring you over to the bed and pull you down over my lap, feeling between your legs from behind. I push a finger into your cunt, then quickly change it to two. I let you make all the noise you want, and you make a lot. Your voice is connected to your pleasure and the sound follows your excitement up and down and around, uncensored, uncaring.

This is a picture of you in my arms, accepting pleasure and love, conquering your demons. This is the real you, strong and fearless, completely my lover. When we finally stop, I lead you to the mirror and turn you around so you can see the image of my hand imprinted in your flesh.

3

We meet in public. You pick me up in your car and we drive south through downtown to an area awaiting redevelopment: vast expanses of churned-up land, old Quonset huts, rusting fences enclosing broken concrete slabs. We park behind an ancient unused wooden warehouse.

We switch places so you're in the passenger seat. I tell you to recline it, and to take off your stylish leather jacket. You aren't wearing anything underneath.

"This is so high school," you protest, pulling off the jacket and sinking back. It's quiet in the car, and with the seat tilted back, you can't see anything except a corner of the second floor of the building outside.

I tell you to put your hands over your head. I pull out of my pocket two pairs of handcuffs, and with these I chain your wrists to the headrest. The clickclickclick noise as the cuffs fasten is loud, louder than the quick inhalation of air through your mouth or your heartbeat as fear pumps adrenaline through your system.

"You didn't do this in high school, did you?" I ask mildly.

"No," your shaky voice replies.

"I didn't think so. I think you should stop comparing what's happening between us with things that happened to you in the past. It's new, you know. You haven't done this kind of thing before, or been with someone like me, or felt what I make you feel."

"I know that, I just say those things to create an ironic distance."

"But there isn't really any distance, is there, between what you desire and what I know about you. There isn't any distance between my touch and what you feel, you don't have to process it through post-modernism."

"Actually there is a distance," you confess, "between your touch and what I feel. But I wish there wasn't."

"I know, we're working on that," I say, putting my hand gently around your throat. "Let's face it, you're completely tied up and irony won't help you."

"All right, I'll shut up if you do."

"Sure," I say, and bend forward over your face to kiss you. Your lips reach out to mine, they're as soft and warm as lips have ever been. The small size of your mouth arouses me as we kiss, because I imagine pushing my cock into it.

Your kiss is delicious. I love the way you suck my tongue, the way I push deeply to feel the back of your mouth. You're so open to me this way that I kiss you for a long time, much longer than I usually kiss people, because it's here that your submission begins.

When I pull back from you, you remain open, arched, ready for me to plunge into you again. I push my fingers into your mouth, three fingers pointing together, then pull them out when you yank your head away because it was more than you expected.

There is a brief moment when you wait tensely for another penetration, then silence as you relax.

"So, you know," I say, "I really want to fuck your mouth and come in it."

You swallow heavily. "I know."

"Can I do that?"

"Yes, of course."

"Tell me."

"You're my lover, of course you can fuck me. It's what I want. I want to feel your cock in me, it doesn't matter where, my mouth is as good as my cunt. I want to feel your come shoot in my mouth, because we can't fuck without a condom and I want you to be able to do it in me." Your voice is low and soft, and your words come hesitantly. You're getting more used to talking this way, it's not as hard as it used to be. "When you come in my mouth, it's hot and sweet for me, I love the taste, I love the feeling of your uncontrollable fuck spewing into me. At that moment, it's mine, it all belongs to me. At the moment of your orgasm, you don't control anything. You give up."

"That's right," I grin. I like this dirtying of your mouth, you saying fuck and come and prick to me, your lover. It's not just the words getting your precious lips dirty, it's the very specific danger that the words could be closely followed by the acts they describe.

I gently lift the hem of your skirt over your knees. You respond with a little groan that is repeated again and again as I stroke your thighs. I touch you patiently between the legs, avoiding your cunt, coming close, making you imagine the places I'm not touching, the places where you dangle the cold metal of your own chains sometimes just to feel something hard and unyielding between the lips.

Your head has fallen back on the seat and you're writhing gently as you remember the times my fingers have been deep in your cunt. Think how close they are now. Then the touching stops and you bend your body upwards to receive it again, the same way you open your mouth to me after we kiss, like a thirsty patch of earth where water just sinks in and which never gets enough. Finally my touch is absent for so long that you open your eyes to see what's going on. I'm just watching you. I love looking at you when you're aroused. It's one of the main reasons I like to fuck you with my hand, to be able to do it and watch at the same time. I lock your gaze with mine as I put my fingers on your cunt lips and press gently inward.

Your cunt is wet; I never need lube at first. My two fingers sink easily into your body. I'm not pushing hard or forcefully, but your whole body convulses as I slide both fingers all the way in. It's one of the things your body knows how to do that you weren't aware of: how to move when it's getting pleasure. I push up against your G spot to hear you draw your breath in, push down so you can feel my weight against your body. You're sensitive enough to feel the calloused places on my fingers, open enough to relax into the fuck. You love it this way, you're not getting too much, it's just right. You'll take it like this forever and come on my fingers over and over. Part of me says I should do this more often, I should get you used to my thickness. Another part of me says I should do this less often, make you yearn for it. I decide to do it a lot now, less often later, when you have grown to need it.

But I'm not happy just getting you to a trance-like place where you can get off; I want to stretch the possibilities of our desire. I pull my hand out and spread lube on three fingers and sink back in.

This is different than two fingers. Three is a lot wider, a lot less round, and it always hurts against the muscular vagina. There's something you should realize here. I like causing pain almost as much as I like causing pleasure, and I almost never do it accidentally. Giving pain and giving pleasure are two ways I have of expressing affection; I want you to learn how to feel one as the flip side of the other. Touch is a hot single, with pleasure a number-one hit; but when side A has played for a while and the nice people have had their fill and left the party, the rest of us turn the lights up a little higher and put on the B side, pain. With the lights up, pain reveals things that pleasure lets stay hidden.

But getting finger-fucked is an inefficient way to play with pain because your cunt likes getting fucked too much and stretches; that's what it's made for, after all. I keep thrusting into you, though, because this is not just about pain, but about me penetrating you, opening you, hurling my hardness and strength inside you. Your flesh gradually slides apart, admitting my fingers. Your cunt lubricates again, adding to the wetness, telling me what you're about to say:

"Please do that," you whisper. "Please don't stop."

"Don't stop what?" I ask instantly.

"Don't stop fucking me. Your fingers in me. Make me a province of your desire. I want to be the 'before' picture in all the self-help books about how to stop loving someone you're obsessed with. I want my friends to see the circles under my eyes and know we've been doing it for days. I want to take speed to stay awake for your tongue and your fingers, I want this to go on and on. Just keep fucking me."

I've been hard ever since I got into your car; I've been horny for all the hours since I last saw you. Now your words are too much. I've got to get off. With my free hand I fumble with my jeans until they're down around my knees, I pick up the lube and squirt it on my cock, and then grab myself and jack off over your prone, spread-open, getting-fucked body. "Keep talking, slut," I hiss.

"M., I want your fucking hand inside me all the time. When I'm alone I think of how good you make me feel. I think of your hard obtrusive fingers fucking me, drumming on my clit, pinching my nipples and ears. I get that shaky feeling when I see your cock. You're showing me something I've never seen yet, you're masturbating over me . . . Just don't stop pushing your hand in me, do it until I can take another finger, please, I wanna get fisted by you . . . I know I can take it . . . Oh god I think I'm gonna come –"

I come with a shout. My sperm flies out and lands on your naked thighs. You cry out at its touch, both afraid and greedy. Your cunt is spasming around my hand, I can feel it grip rhythmically, and it takes the utmost concentration to keep thrusting inside you to bring you the rest of the way to orgasm until you finally explode in convulsions. Your wrists pull against the cuffs, they rattle, and your voice is wailing loudly – suddenly the car is filled with noise.

When you finish coming I pull my three fingers out and put two back in so you can relax around them.

Your eyes are scared and vulnerable, you don't know what to do next. At this moment, words fail us. I could tell you how I feel or how you feel to me or how fucking hot you look tied up with my fingers inside you and my come dripping off you, or that I love you and will do anything to make you do that as often as possible, but there's nothing to say really as silence settles back in, the only sound is our startled breath.

You don't have to do anything. Now you're as open as I want you to be. I push into you again and you let out a completely involuntary moan. From now on there aren't any words, there is just thrusting and groaning and your body shaking around my hand. It gets dark while I fuck you, the windows are steamed up, we're perfectly enclosed and hidden and strangely warm. You can't see me anymore in the dark, just the shape of my body looming over you and the cool stickiness of my come drying on you. You didn't know there was this much pleasure. But if you opened to the pain, you can open to this.

It's simple: my fingers giving you pleasure; my eyes on you; you going deeper and deeper for each orgasm, back through dull grey years to a point when joy was yours. Connect the moments and you can keep this feeling: strong and loved, at home in your body, free in the world. When we finish and I finally unchain your arms, they are eerily cold and numb. You don't want to put on your jacket, you want to remain open and naked for me, but I insist.

As I start the car and we drive away, I tell you a secret. The warehouse is rigged. I broke in days ago and installed hooks, chains, and other accoutrements. We'll have to come back. But not tonight. You fall asleep as I drive you home across the bridge, cradled in the leather you bought to please me, dreamless and safe in the home of your body.

VIOLENT SILENCE

Paul Mayersberg

I

HE HAD BEEN there on Tuesday morning sitting alone at the same table in the dining room. After the game Pandora had a late breakfast with her tennis partner, Beverly, who was the mother of a school friend of her daughter. She liked the room in the Bel Air Hotel. It was old-fashioned, luxurious, a large dining room in pale green and pink. Apple and salmon were two of her favorite colors.

Today was Friday and she was back with Beverly. The man looked at her frequently. When she looked back at him she had to smile. It was acceptable as a conventional smile of recognition. The fact was she liked the look of him. He seemed to epitomize the cool Californian man. He had a tanned, bland intelligence. Pandora came from New Hampshire. She had married a young architect, Alec Hammond, thirteen years ago. They had moved out to Los Angeles. Their daughter Paulette had been born here twelve years ago, and they had stayed.

More than her marriage, the birth of Paulette had changed Pandora, turned her into the stable woman she now was. Her father, Alfred Harten, was a nineteenth century man. He inherited wealth which allowed him to pursue his private interest in classical Greek and Roman culture. After the death of her mother when she was six, Harten retreated into a world of his own. Little Pandora grew up privileged, in a large old farmhouse, alone except for a succession of English nannies and her pony, Smoky. At school she had been a rebel. In college she had had a few brushes with the law over drugs. Wayward, was her father's word for her.

Glancing again at the man across the dining room Pandora remembered her early troubles with men, escapades that had upset her father. She had been promiscuous. She had taken risks, but for some reason had never gotten pregnant. For a time she thought she never would. She was relieved. But it worried her that she might die childless.

Pandora met Alec Hammond when her father hired a firm of architects to convert two barns into a guesthouse on the Harten estate. She had liked him immediately. He was a serious young man, different from the men in her crowd. He was not sarcastic. He was mature. He had goals in life. He had had to struggle. He didn't have a chip on his shoulder. But above all he had an innocent air. He was clean and fresh. She liked that. Alec Hammond lifted what she saw as the curse of sterility from her life. He made her pregnant. He gave her Paulette. For that she loved him. He made her happy. She became content.

The man was still in the dining room at eleven thirty when Beverly had to go. The place was empty apart from him. The waiters had already set the tables for lunch. Crystal wine goblets on the apple green cloths. Like the rooms in the hotel the tables were waiting for new occupants. She signed her Diner's slip and waited.

He was looking at her again when a tall, dark-haired woman came running into the dining room. She was looking for him. She came up to his table, opened her purse, pulled out a gun and aimed it at the man's head.

"I'm going to blow you away," she said. Her voice was husky and shaky.

"No, you're not," the man said evenly.

Pandora was scared. She wondered whether to call for help or intervene.

The dark-haired woman's finger tightened on the trigger.

"Put it away," he said.

The waiter came back with the credit card and receipt inside a green leather folder. He saw the gun.

"Hey!" The waiter called out.

The woman jerked around. The man coolly snatched the gun from her hand. She burst into tears.

"Sorry about this," the man said to the waiter. "It's not loaded."

The dark-haired woman ran out of the dining room.

"Shall I get the manager?" asked the waiter.

"No, no. Just forget it. Thank you." He handed the waiter a fifty dollar bill.

"That's not necessary."

"Please take it. Then you can give that lady over there her receipt."

"Thank you sir."

The waiter came up to Pandora. He shrugged. She thanked him and gave him a five dollar bill. The man came over to her as the waiter left.

"Sorry about that. Were you scared?"

"Yes, I was a bit."

"The gun wasn't loaded."

"Oh."

"You're shaking."

"No, not really."

He put his hand on her quivering arm. It didn't stop, her quivering.

"Let's move out of here. Enough excitement for the moment, don't you think?"

"I guess so." Pandora was still shaking.

They left the main building of the hotel. They walked together along the curving path towards the bungalow area. It was a walk through a miniature jungle, a beautifully kept jungle of sweating greenery and single flowers, aflame like daytime candles.

Pandora had no idea why she was walking with this man. Perhaps he was going to tell her what the incident had been about. Perhaps he wanted to ask her to keep quiet about it, like the waiter. Perhaps he was going to offer her a drink to steady her nerves. Well, she could use a drink.

"My shack's over there," he said pleasantly.

They walked over the little bridge towards a group of terracotta colored bungalows, each with its own palm tree and garden.

Hardly shacks. The most expensive hotel accomodation in Los Angeles.

Suddenly Pandora stopped with a cry. The man turned and saw that her high heel had stuck between two wooden slats in the bridge. She laughed. She wiggled her shoe.

"Take your foot out."

He bent down and with both hands removed her foot from the shoe. He noticed the pale freckles on her skin that went naturally with her sandy blonde hair. She hopped.

He twisted the shoe heel around to try and release it. It was difficult. She watched as he gave the shoe a jerk. The heel snapped.

"I'm sorry." He looked up at her apologetically.

"That's all right," she said.

It wasn't all right really. It was a nuisance.

He tried to tug the heel out. It was wedged.

"They don't make shoes like they used to," he said.

"They're Ferragamo," she said.

"Come on," he addressed the wedged heel.

"Look, leave it. It's OK." She took off the other shoe. He stood up. She smiled and walked on. He held her broken shoe, but didn't offer to give it to her.

Pandora knew he was watching her as she walked barefoot through the garden towards the bungalow he had pointed to. She wondered what had happened to the crazy, dark-haired woman. She thought she might even be in the bungalow waiting. Wait a minute, what am I doing, she thought.

"Here we are."

He unlocked the door for her. This is crazy, Pandora thought. She went in ahead of him. She was suddenly very conscious of her body. She walked barefoot on the salmon carpet. A real log fire burned in the drawing room grate. It wasn't cold enough for a fire.

He kicked the door closed. He advanced on her as if he intended to kill her. She didn't back off. She held her shoe in one hand, her purse in the other. He hadn't even thought of locking the door. She was pleased about that.

Suddenly, she stopped quivering altogether. It was all right. She wasn't afraid. He stopped a foot away from her. They looked at each other. She simply wasn't afraid.

Pandora dropped her purse and handed him her shoe. He put it with the other one and tossed them onto the couch. One of them bounced off.

He took the gun out of his jacket pocket and gave it to her. It was a Smith & Wesson. It seemed a dangerous thing to do, to give her the gun. Then she remembered it wasn't loaded. She had fired a .38 like this at her gun club. She didn't like it as a weapon. It was too heavy.

The man took off his jacket and began to get undressed in front of her. This was ridiculous. She couldn't get over not being scared. The guy could be any nut, any pervert, anyone.

She watched him removing his clothes, pulling off his loafers, bending for his socks. He paused slightly before taking down his undershorts. Pandora was determined not to look at his genitals. She looked into his blue eyes. For a man as dark-haired as he the sky-blue eyes were a surprise.

He stood in front of her naked as if he wanted her to be sure she knew what she was getting. She saw the scar. It was six inches long, stretching from below his muscular chest to his navel. He reached forward, gripped the top of her yellow dress and tore it away from her as if it had been made of paper.

Pandora swayed with the sudden force of it. She was momentarily shocked. No man had ever done that to her before. He rubbed the dress over his body like a towel. When he took it away it revealed his erection. He opened her bra at the front. A small, pink satin bow covered the two hooks. He watched her breasts come free. She felt his surprise. They were fuller than he expected. This was the pleasure of beautifully cut underwear.

Pandora pulled the bra off herself and reached both hands down to the panties. For a woman of her age her stomach was quite firm, almost flat. She bent and pushed the panties down past her knees to her ankles. With a little kick she stepped out of them. As she straightened up, he picked her up by the waist. They both heard the cracking sounds in her back as the small bones moved in their joints.

He was incredibly strong. She was not a small woman but he held her as if she were the weight of a child. She put her arm around his neck and drew breath as he eased into her. The only thing that felt heavy to her was her head. Her neck didn't seem able to control it as he moved her up and down slowly. She could feel the weight of her hair as her head moved from side to side before it fell with a slap onto his shoulder.

Pandora lost control and didn't regain it for several minutes. It was shock treatment. His electricity raged through her body. As they slid in and out of each other she had the feeling of transference. Something she couldn't do anything about. The sensation was wonderful but it wasn't confined to her body. It seemed to invade her spirit. When she swallowed him it was like taking a potion.

As he bent her forward over the soft fleshy upholstery of a chair she was somehow condemned. Not for a crime but for a pleasure. She expected pain as he entered her. There was only excitement. And it came in waves, a surging possession.

Later, he licked her clean like a dog. She tensed again as his tongue stroked her eye-lids. Her pale, wide nipples filled with blood and went dark as if a cloud had passed across the sun. He had taken her apart and now he was putting her back together. She was soon the way she was before. As good as new. No one would know what had happened to her.

Except perhaps the dark-haired woman. Nobody had tried to come into the bungalow, but the thought crossed Pandora's mind that the woman had been there all the time, hiding in a closet, watching and listening.

Nothing in the drawing room suggested the presence of a woman. There were no clues at all even as to who the man was. The only surprising thing she noticed was the small pile of books on the coffee table. *The Classical World*, *The Satyricon* by Petronius, Caesar's *Gallic Wars*.

He kissed her softly, almost lovingly as if he was thankful.

She put her hand between his legs under his swollen balls. He moved away.

He left her on the salmon pink carpet and went into the bathroom. Pandora rolled over on her back. Her pale skin was damp and pink like the carpet. She felt wonderful and completely without guilt. She had amazed herself. She had not made love to a total stranger since her marriage. She hadn't wanted to after Paulette was born. Which made this incident, and that's what it was, an incident, all the more remarkable.

She sat up. She picked up the gun from the coffee table. She idly checked the cartridge. She stiffened. The gun was fully loaded. The safety was engaged but the gun was loaded. So he had lied. Why? To make her feel more at ease probably. She wondered who the woman really was.

He came back into the room. He was now wearing fresh white undershorts. He had combed his hair. He had freshened up. She could smell the soap. He smiled at her. Pandora pointed the gun at him.

"Why didn't you say it was loaded?"

"I didn't want to alarm you. Or the waiter."

She longed to ask him what he did, why he was staying at the hotel. But she couldn't. That was part of their unspoken pact. No names, no questions, no information. It was just an incident, a wildly pleasurable encounter. There was no past behind it, no future ahead of it.

Pandora stood up. She saw her broken shoe and her torn dress.

"I must be going," she said, putting the gun down.

"Come with me." He took her hand and led her into the bedroom which they had never reached. On the way he stroked her sticky ass. His hand, which had been a weapon a while ago, was now disarmed, friendly, the safety on.

He took her to the clothes closet and opened it. Inside there were three dresses hanging.

"Choose one," he said.

He pulled them out and put them on the bed. She laughed. It was like a boutique. The dresses were simple, expensive.

"Try the red one."

"I never wear red."

He picked up the red chenille dress.

"It won't suit me."

She put it on over her head. For a few seconds as she moved her body into it, she could see nothing but red. The fit was perfect. She looked at herself in the mirror. He stood behind her, watching.

Pandora was surprised. She looked very good. Different, but interesting. He was right.

"I'll send it back to you."

"No. Keep it."

She knew what he meant. They wouldn't have any further contact. She would keep it as a souvenir. He left her without a word. She went into the bathroom and washed her hands. She found a comb and ran it through her drying hair. She looked at herself in the bathroom mirror. Red suited her. Why had she never known that before?

When Pandora came back into the drawing room, he was picking up her things.

"I don't have any shoes to offer you."

"I'll manage."

He handed her her bra and panties. She didn't try to put them on. She opened her purse and popped them in.

Without a word he threw the torn yellow dress onto the log fire. For a moment, she was shocked to see her dress burning. But he was right again. Destroy the evidence.

"I must go."

"Of course."

He came forward and kissed her breasts through the red dress.

"Goodbye," he said.

Pandora held out her hand. He smiled and shook it firmly. It was all over.

She left the bungalow. Three hours had passed. It had seemed much longer. She walked barefoot back across the bridge. She looked down for the heel that had stuck. But it was gone. One of the hotel gardeners must have found it and removed it.

She didn't go back through the hotel, not in her bare feet. She didn't want to encounter the waiter again, not in her red dress. She went around.

She crossed the shaded parking lot and over to her white BMW. The concrete was hot under her soles. She unlocked the car door and climbed in. Now her thighs started to ache a bit. She settled herself in the seat. Her bottom hurt, but not badly.

She drove slowly out the hotel area. As she stopped at the gate she noticed a Ford Mustang parked a few yards away. There was someone in it, sitting alone behind the tinted window, at the wheel. She wondered if it was the dark-haired woman from the dining room. So what. It was over now. But the woman would have clocked her license plate. PANDORA.

II

As he watched her yellow dress burning in the grate he knew he would see her again. He had to. This wasn't the end of the affair. He would let her go now. Later he would find her. Or she would find him. She'd have to.

He loved hotels, hotel rooms, bungalows. His loft, downtown Los Angeles near the art museum, was his base but hardly his home. He spent as little time as possible there. When he wasn't away working he stayed in hotels for two or three days at a time. He didn't just go for the best hotels. Sometimes he would select a sleazy place in Hollywood or a touristy motor hotel along the Pacific Coast Highway. This brought him into contact with all kinds of women from everywhere. Women were relaxing for him and stimulating at the same time, better than going to the movies. He was writing his own scripts. And playing the male lead.

When he first saw her earlier in the week she seemed ordinary, a typical rich Beverly Hills housewife. But watching her eat her Eggs Benedict changed his impression. There was sensuality in the way she ate. She ate hungrily and quite quickly, finishing while her friend was only half way through her California fruit plate. She hadn't caught the local disease of counting the calories. She didn't immediately wipe the cappuccino foam from her lips. She was unselfconscious about her body. He wanted her.

Laura arrived right on cue, gun in hand. He could see the lady in yellow found the scene irresistible. None the less he was surprised that she went with him quite so easily. There was no stiffness in her manner. He liked the fact that she wasn't automatically on her guard. There was no feeling of inhibition in her behavior. There was no scent of sexual fear about her.

Her heel catching in the wooden bridge on the way over to his bungalow was the clincher. He knew she was his when he touched her ankle. There was no shiver of resistance in her leg. He liked her paleness. It wasn't bloodless. Her scattered freckles made her youthful. She must have been about thirty-five, he guessed. He could imagine she had seen things, done things with men, but they had left no outward trace.

When she unhooked her bra her breasts revealed another woman to him. They had an unexpected sensuality, maternal in their weight, eternal in their seductiveness. They reminded

him of a classical Roman statue he had seen in the Louvre in
Paris. Like that marble, this was a woman in whose body you
could see anything and everything you wanted.

There was an incredible balance in her form. She belonged in a
bedroom and at the same time in a landscape of cypress trees and
mountains. He could see her running naked along an island shore,
swimming in green Mediterranean sea, dancing a waltz in Vienna, glittering in red satin and gold, sitting in a black and white
dress in a cafe on the Via Veneto in Rome. Most disturbing of all,
he saw her asleep in bed beside him. He had seen a thousand
women naked, but only one had ever aroused his aesthetic
sensuality to this degree. His sister.

Every part of this woman was sexual. Her salty fingers in his
mouth stroking his tongue, her pale beige nipples that softened at
his touch instead of hardening, giving instead of resisting, her
truly yellow pubic hair that grew naturally, evenly from her white
skin and did not seem darkly stuck on. And then there was her
mouth.

As the fresh coating of her pink lipstick dissolved through their
kissing he saw that the skin of her unpainted lips was darker than
he imagined. They didn't quite belong to her. They were the lips
of another woman altogether, almost Latin. They behaved differently too. The passivity of her limbs in accepting and responding to his caresses was countered in the purposeful aggression of
her mouth. He wasn't accustomed to a woman's lips taking
charge of his body. It was a surprise to have his nipples manipu-
lated as if he were a woman. Her lips caused him to suck in breath
as they controlled the responses of his cock. This woman could.
bring him to orgasm with ease.

There were moments with her when he was in danger of losing
control of the scene. He had consciously to resist her mouth or he
would be lost. The game would be over. He carefully kept her
tongue away from his balls, and prayed she wouldn't notice. He
didn't want her to think that he was reticent. And he didn't want
her to realize the power she had. After all, who was doing what to
whom?

As his cock hardened, his heart softened. He wasn't supposed
to have a heart in the romantic sense. A heart was a muscle.
Nothing else. Nothing more. He lost his heart inside her mouth.
She was probably unaware of it. But he despised himself for

allowing it. He would have liked to have hated her. But he couldn't. After he exploded with joy, the chemistry of his body produced a feeling of death by absorption. Then an even greater, a broader sensation enveloped him. He was alive, a quaking living being, led through desire and then lust to fulfilment and then need. Need. It was crazy. It was female.

His response to needing her, natural and unnatural at the same time, was revenge. He wanted to pay her back for having done this to him. She had given him something. He knew that. And he had treated her as if she'd robbed him. Why?

She had welcomed his hard and purple penis between her sand-colored thighs. Now her buttocks embraced him. The muscles stood out under her flesh. He pushed into her. She rose to accept him. Her veins swelled with passion. This woman was crazy. Crazy. Didn't she understand? He was violating her. Why didn't she squirm away, get off that chair, yell, anything. She wasn't a prostitute. He wasn't paying her, for Christ's sake. So why did she want him?

He streamed into her. For several minutes he forgot the question. She was silent. Still inside her, he put his arms around her ribs below her dipping breasts and pulled her up. She leaned her head backwards towards him. He smelt her blonde hair, the small secretion of oil from her scalp, the almond scent of her underarms. He held her tightly. He couldn't see her face, but he knew she was smiling. He was intoxicated. When she lifted her smooth leg to stroke his leg and its sticky hair, he was over-whelmed. He pressed his face between her shoulder blades, hiding, not wanting to show his emotion.

He relaxed. His cock drifted out of her. She sighed. The muscles of her rectum twitched. He turned her around. Her face was fuller, more fleshy. Her eyes were soft, liquid. She was wonderfully tired. Her knees were weak. As she relaxed he set her gently on the carpet. She turned into a wonderful nude. A sculpture of a woman on her back.

For the first time in ten years he was consciously sorry for something he'd done. As he washed himself lightly in the bath-room there was a stab of guilt. He shouldn't have taken her in the ass. It wasn't the act that was wrong. It was the motive. He had done it in anger and in revenge. She had wanted it, but that didn't make it right. Her enjoyment had spurred him on. The taste of rape in sex that always excited him had eluded him with her. It wasn't necessary.

When he came back to her he wanted to ask all kinds of questions. How she felt. But he didn't. That wasn't part of their unspoken pact. He decided to give her something. She could make of it what she wanted. One of Laura's dresses. The red one was perfect.

He wanted to delay her departure, keep her here with him. But she was a married woman with one or more children, probably too old to change her life. He was being childish. He was thinking like a lover. Let her go and forget it. It was only a fuck. Just a fuck.

He had to kiss her breasts before she left. She understood it and responded by holding out her hand to say goodbye. The mid-morning meeting was over. He let her go.

"Something's burning." That was the first thing Laura said when she came in.

"I burned her dress."

"What did she say to that?"

"I gave her one of yours."

"The red one. I saw it."

He had never done that before. It disturbed Laura. They had developed an understanding in the last two years. Having other women made her need him more. But she couldn't help wondering about the dress.

Laura enjoyed helping him pick up women. It was a neat and resourceful game. But with fairly strict rules.

1. Select the target. He would choose the woman. She never argued with his choice. She never opposed anything of his.

2. Devise the game plan. That was her department. She could be as inventive as she liked. He never opposed her plans.

3. The hit. He took care of that. She would wait somewhere nearby and imagine what was happening. She could invent the sex in her mind. That was her territory.

4. The aftermath. He would tell her what happened. Together they would compare notes, her imaginings with his factual account. You didn't lie about either. The most successful hits were those in which her guesswork most closely matched what had actually happened.

5. The conclusion. This was the sex between them immediately

after the hit. Sometimes this consisted of an exact recreation of what happened. Sometimes it was ritualized submission on her part. He would decide which. She enjoyed both.

In this case, the Bel Air Hotel, he had selected the woman, the hit, and Laura had come up with the idea of the gun. Drawing a gun in public was the most dangerous game plan she had yet devised. It worked. It excited her.

All the time he was with the woman Laura sat in her Mustang in the hotel forecourt and waited. It seemed an eternity. In fact, it was two hours.

Laura hoped that her gun would play an important role in the sex. She imagined him touching the woman with the cold steel barrel. She could feel the shivers herself. The woman would be frightened, perhaps for her life. Good. Laura got a special, acute thrill from fear. That was why she was with Wildman. He had a frightening aspect. He was capable of anything. Even murder.

She had an obscure feeling that one day he would murder her. He talked very little about his past. She was sure there had been a killing in it. He had never explained the scar that dominated his body.

She made it a rule never to touch herself while imagining him with another woman. Sometimes it was difficult to resist the tightness between her legs. But she refused to cross them or clamp her thighs together. There must be no relief of the tension. Instead, as she became wet, she opened her legs slightly. Let things breathe. No part of her body must touch another part. She kept her hands on the steering wheel.

As imagined pictures of the woman's body flowed into her mind they multiplied as if they were reflecting themselves in a maze of mirrors. Laura became rigid. She had never had a lesbian experience, but she responded intensely to conjured images of women. She wondered at times if she was evading something in her own nature. Was she a closet gay? Was that why Wildman was fascinated with her? Her taut muscles and well-toned dancer's flesh, her addiction to exercise, her obsession with watching herself in mirrors, were all these symptoms of homosexuality?

It was not something she could discuss with Wildman. She had no friends she dared talk to about that. Her creature aloneness was the root of her sexuality. Laura achieved pleasure and satisfaction through people, rather than with them. The woman who had been with Wildman, was a catalyst, a conduit for Laura's own sensations. When Laura pressed her breasts into Wildman's groin she could imagine the woman doing the same thing. When his hand opened Laura's vaginal lips and her small tongue quivered, soft and hard at the same time, she felt what the other woman had felt.

To stop herself coming Laura slotted a music cassette into the car stereo. Romantic movie music filled the car like bath water. She sometimes played it as background to her dance exercises when she got too tense. The sound was vulgar and lush and took her mind off the white and pink images that were getting far too compulsive. This music, like the movies they came from, was a generalization about love and feeling. It was so far from the sharp, specific moments of sexual excitement that it dissolved Laura's erotic thoughts in a lukewarm bath, its temperature just below 98.4, at which no passion can survive.

She had played both sides of the cassette twice when the woman appeared in the hotel forecourt and got into her car. She had changed her dress. Laura wondered why. She watched the BMW leave, then got out of the Mustang and made her way to the bungalow for the inquest.

Wildman did not want sex with Laura. He wanted solely to exist in the immediate memory of the woman who had just left. Usually, a scene like that would have provided Laura and him with an intense sexual dialog. This time he wasn't up for that. But he did not want Laura to realize it. So he forced himself to go through with their formal devices.

Laura sat in the armchair over which he had draped the woman's body an hour before. She started to take her clothes off sitting down. It was a favorite trick of hers. Until now it had never failed to arouse him. As she twisted her feet out of her black patent leather shoes, Wildman wanted to shout at her: "For Christ's sake, don't do that!" He had picked up the woman's shoes after she left and put them in an overnight bag wrapped in a red silk square.

During the question and answer session which followed he lied over and over again. He had to protect himself.

"Her tits were overweight."

Laura pulled her black dress down to her waist exposing a tight sheer black bra underneath.

"Very," he said to confirm it.

"And her nipples were lipstick pink and too big?" That was Laura's guess.

"But she had made them up. They were painted dark red. Done with a brush, I'd say. Not with a lipstick."

"She was waiting to get picked up, then," Laura said. "That surprises me. I'd never have figured her for a whore."

Laura pulled her dress all the way down to her thighs. She left her bra on. She wasn't wearing panties.

"You didn't give her any money?"

Wildman hesitated.

"You did?" Laura was surprised. "How much did you give her?" Laura's guess was two hundred bucks.

She opened her legs and leaned back in the chair. Her dark hedge of hair, which he himself had carefully trimmed two days ago using her curled golden nail scissors, now seemed too definite. Next to the woman's bed of yellow flowers. Laura was waiting for him to speak or move towards her.

"Not much. A token hundred."

He moved towards her, glad she was buying his story. It made him cringe, describing the woman as a whore. Anyone less a whore than she would be hard to imagine.

Laura reached her hand forward and slipped it inside his underpants. He wasn't hard. What happened with that other woman? she asked herself. Something had gone wrong. She knew it.

"Did you make her come?" Laura tugged his penis, pulling the head out of the shorts.

"Yes. She came."

"Ah, but you can never tell with whores, can you? They fake it all day long." Laura thought a little dig at his prowess wouldn't hurt him.

"I can tell."

"How?"

"The same way I do with you."

"Oh, and how's that?"

"You sweat down the back."

"You can get worked up without coming."

"But not afterwards. If you sweat afterwards, sweat for a good ten minutes, then you weren't faking. No way."

"Maybe."

Laura sat up. She was worried. She couldn't buy his story about the woman being a whore. She may well have come. But maybe, just maybe, he didn't. And that's what the trouble was. So why didn't he? Why invent all this? Why lie? He didn't have to. He knew that. Between them there was no need to lie. As far as Laura knew he never had. She never had.

She put her arms around his buttocks and without removing the undershorts, she pulled him, now half-erect, into her mouth.

Wildman looked down at Laura's raven head. He had lied about the woman and broken his pact with Laura. Dumb. He should have told her straight out. "This woman had an incredible effect on me. Period." And let it go at that. Shit. He wouldn't go back on it now. Pride. He'd stay with the lie. She'd never know.

Laura wasn't going to let him get away with it. Wildman felt the sensation that only she gave him. Laura used her teeth. Most women were afraid to do that, afraid of putting the guy off. Men scare easily with women.

He was on the brink of exploding when she took her mouth away. She heaved herself up, out of the chair. She took him by the waist and pulled him sideways. They slid down on the floor. Because of her strength it was a soft landing. She tugged his shorts down and climbed on top of him. The certainty and grace of her movement was like a dance. Sexually aroused, Laura was all strength.

She whispered, "I want you inside me. Inside. Where it counts."

She folded herself over him. Her concentration was intense. She pressed herself down twice and waited for him to come. As he put his fingers inside the black silk of Laura's bra, he saw the woman's blonde hair fall onto his eyes. Her past cry merged with Laura's gasp. He merged with both of them. He felt himself spinning. He was the center of a whirlpool. He was going down, taking them with him.

Laura felt the fire. She started to cry. Tears streamed down her face as she lowered her lips to his mysterious scar. Wildman shook. The shaking made her come. He was hers. And no one else's.

They lay on the carpet, slowly catching and controlling their breathing. After a while she lifted her body from him. He was still hard. She smiled and lay down beside him. There was a knock at the door. Wildman groaned.

"Come in," Laura called.

The door opened. A young Mexican maid looked in. She was started by the two people lying on the floor.

"I'm sorry," she stuttered, but couldn't look away. Laura was smiling at her. Wildman lay still, on his back.

Laura lifted his penis in her hand.

"Isn't he beautiful?"

"Excuse me," said the maid. She closed the door behind her. Laura turned to Wildman.

"Look at me," she said.

He opened his eyes.

"You're so sleek. You know that," she said.

Half an hour later they were both dressed. Wildman seemed preoccupied. Laura's anxiety returned.

"You're not checking out today?" she asked.

"No, tomorrow." He didn't want to leave the place where the woman had been.

"Maybe I should go back to the loft." Laura was as keen to leave as he was to stay.

"I'm waiting for a call."

"What about the dogs? Shouldn't they be fed?"

"There's plenty of time. They'll still be asleep. In any case I left them a good bowl of rabbit meat."

Laura was puzzled by his habit of drugging his pair of Doberman Pinschers. He claimed that in sleeping long hours they could enjoy dreaming without the constant compulsion to be on the alert, either to defend or attack. She thought it was cruel but she couldn't prove it.

"I know her name." Laura suddenly wanted to upset him. That would do it, she knew.

"I'm not interested."

The rule was no follow-ups, no subsequent involvement.

"It's Pandora."

"Forget it." He was angry with her. She was interfering in his memory. "What's the matter with you?"

"I saw her car license plate. It's Pandora."

"Look, why don't you go home. Your own place if you want."

Ever since she had known him she had kept her small apartment in the Valley. He didn't mind. He had a key. And a machine for messages which he picked up by remote. It was fair. She had a key to his downtown loft. He'd installed a mirror in the huge space so she could do her dance exercises. He liked to watch her.

Right now he was irritated. Why had she told him the name? Did she suspect his interest? Maybe. Laura was very intuitive. That was one of her most seductive features. This hint of telepathic communication kept them together. He wondered if she, Pandora, was telepathic.

"You go ahead," he said. "I'll wait for my call."

"Shall I take my clothes? The ones that are left, that is."

"No, I'll bring them."

He wasn't going to respond to Laura's dig at him. When he thought about it, giving the woman that dress, it seemed an odd thing to do. But it was quite natural at the time. Even essential. She couldn't very well leave the bungalow without any clothes.

There had been occasions in the past when he had refused to allow Laura to wear a dress. In the days when he set her tasks, the one she responded to best was arriving somewhere to meet him in a public place, dressed only in her underwear. Her challenge was to think of ingenious cover stories to explain her undress to other people.

With Laura's lean dancer's figure being undressed seemed almost natural. She could carry it off. He loved watching men watching her. She was clever about it. She would wear a bra through which everyone could see her dark aggressive nipples. She rubbed them with an eraser before appearing. One time she wore panties, one size too small to emphasise her pubic mound and show off little tufts of black hair. At the same time she wore her dark glasses. Laura was a doll. He was lucky to have found her.

After she left he sat back in the armchair. Pandora. Incredible name. It was perfect for how he felt about her. Even now he could see her lying on the rug in front of him.

The phone rang. It was the hotel operator.

"Mr Wildman, there's a call for you. A Mr Elliott."

"Put him on."

George Elliott was his agent. He'd been negotiating for a job in Arizona, a movie called *Ghost Town*.

"Charles," said George. "OK. Your deal's cut. The movie starts shooting in four weeks' time. In Flagstaff."

After Wildman hung up, his mind went racing back to the woman. She was a living ghost, there in the bungalow. During the afternoon Wildman did mundane things. He re-read the script of *Ghost Town*. He checked his messages on the machine in Laura's apartment. He made notes on the stunt requirements for the movie. He called the producer's office to set up a meeting with the director to discuss the project. And he called the Southern California Department of car licensing to check on the name and address of the owner of the plate "Pandora". Wildman knew going in this was a bad idea. He was breaking the rules of his own game. He knew he was rousing a sleeping dog.

Pandora. He was about to open her box.

III

It would have been easy for Wildman to contrive to meet her again. From the license plate he had traced Pandora's address. He went over to her house. He watched her come and go, alone and with her daughter. He didn't see her husband. Maybe they had split up. It would have been easy to talk to her, at the supermarket, in the school yard, at her favorite lunch place in Beverly Hills. Yet he held off. She might not want to be reminded so soon about what happened.

Wildman's feeling for Pandora had increased dramatically in the days following the Bel Air Hotel. If it wasn't enough that he couldn't get her out of his conscious mind, she had started to enter his dreams. That had never happened before with any of his casual hits. Pandora had invaded his life. He felt an acute sense of danger.

Wildman began to prepare for his upcoming movie. From his point of view as the stunt co-ordinator it was a run-of-the-mill project. He wanted to spend more time on his own writing. He had spent weeks working on his screenplay. Wildman had caught the movie business disease: he had become a frustrated writer.

He ought to have kept away from her house in Rancho Park. But he couldn't. One Saturday night he drove past just before midnight. He could hear the sounds of a party in progress. Classical music and romantic laughter came echoing from the back of the house, from around the pool area. It was irresistible. Wildman parked his car and went to look.

He walked around the back of the house next door which was in darkness. He could see the people were out, maybe away for the weekend. He made his way through a Japanese-style water garden to the line of tall thick interlocking bushes that divided and shielded the back yards of the two houses. He found a position where he could see the pool.

There were five or six couples sitting or standing around. The blue watery light of the illuminated pool made them look as if they were on a stage set. Wildman saw Pandora. She was laughing, waving a drink, perhaps even slightly drunk he thought. Then his heart pounded. She was wearing the red dress. And she was happy. Wildman concluded that the dull-looking man who was talking and pouring champagne among a group apart from her was her husband. What was she doing married to him, to a man who wore a tailored western shirt?

Pandora was sharing a joke with some moron in a striped jacket. The guy put out his hand and touched the scarlet chenille material. Take your hand off her, you cunt. Wildman received a stab of jealousy. Jealousy. That word wasn't in his vocabulary. Until now.

He stayed watching her, and only her, for almost an hour. People started to leave, couple by couple. This was what he had been waiting for. He wanted her alone. To himself. Why couldn't the dull husband take off with the rest of them? The striped moron had gone, so why not him?

Hammond went into the house. Pandora started putting the wine glasses onto two trays. For a few minutes he watched her walk round the pool back and forth, tidying up like a maid. Hammond reappeared and took the tray she was carrying from her grasp. He smoothed his hands over her dress.

Wildman watched as Pandora threw her head back as Hammond kissed her neck. He felt sick with desire. Hammond lifted the dress and ran his hand under the material across her thighs, it seemed to Wildman. They were just too far away for him to see the detail. But close enough for him to imagine it, to feel it as intensely as if he were Hammond.

She put her hand on Hammond's pants. Wildman twitched in response. Was it possible that she was thinking of him, remembering him?

When Hammond tried to lift her dress, Pandora stopped him

with a kiss. Wildman could imagine her tongue in his mouth. Their mouths, Hammond's and his. Hammond. How could she put up with this guy? Habit, probably.

As they became more passionate, Pandora pulled away. She looked round, momentarily in Wildman's direction. Then she took Hammond's hand and pressed it to her breasts. Hammond went to turn out the patio lights. Pandora picked up one of the trays and went inside. Hammond took the second tray and followed her. Another light went out. The pool shimmered. Wildman took several deep breaths. He knew that was it. They weren't coming back outside.

Laura was asleep when he arrived at her apartment. He woke her up.

"What's the time?"

"Time for a dip."

"What?"

"In the pool."

"Are you crazy?"

"Yes."

Laura slept naked even when she wasn't expecting him. She liked the feel of the bed sheets on her skin. She would wrap herself up sometimes, a living body in a white shroud. Wildman liked her sleeping naked, liked her available.

She yawned and opened a drawer, looking for a swimsuit. Wildman held out the red dress he had brought her to replace the one he had given to Pandora.

"You want me to wear that?"

"I do."

"I've never swum in a dress."

Laura went into the bathroom and removed her tampon. Wildman waited, controlling his impatience while she tied her hair back with a band.

The communal pool area for Laura's apartment building was surrounded by a high fence. The gate was locked at night. Each tenant had a key.

During the day the pool was uninviting, a rectangle of water surrounded by miserable white plastic chairs and rusting metal tables. Hardly anyone in the building used it. It was too exposed. There were no umbrellas, no vegetation, no shade from the baking Valley sun. At night, deserted, lit only by the moon and a single naked security lamp on top of the fence at one end, the pool area had the sinister aspect of an empty parking lot. The night breeze ruffled the surface of the water as it caught Laura's dress. The dress was dark blood red in the artificial light. The setting looked like a location for a murder in a B-movie.

But Wildman saw only the elegant patio of Pandora's house. When he touched Laura through the cool material of her dress he was close to Pandora's body. When he kissed Laura he was sucking Pandora's mouth, the unconnected free floating lips of a surrealist painting.

Laura did not know what was expected of her. Wildman gave her no instruction, nor did he describe the sexual encounter she assumed he had just experienced. With his lips still on hers he put his hand between her legs. His fingers pushed the chenille into her, gently pinching the flesh of her vulva. He could see the lips parting, Pandora's delicate yellow hair. As he felt the dampness he could smell the crushed hazelnuts, the unforgettable scent of her opening thighs.

Wildman's free hand grasped Laura's hand and drew it to the buttons of his pants. She began to undo them. This was familiar to her. Laura started with the lowest button and worked her way up.

He pushed his cloth-covered fingers deeper. Her vagina became dry as the material absorbed the liquid. He seemed in a daze, a dream. There was no familiar urgency in his pressure. Instead there was a passive tension in him she hadn't felt before, a stillness, a state of feeling that wasn't thrusting for release. Something that just wanted to be. For a moment Laura was with another, unfamiliar man.

Wildman pushed his penis into the dress and into Pandora. He knew Laura wanted to take the dress off. But that was impossible. He didn't want to see her body. He wanted only Pandora. The red dress was an essential mask for the body. He clasped Laura to him and felt the subtle fleshiness of Pandora. He put his hand on her shoulder as he began to come. She couldn't see his face.

A girl on the third floor of the apartment building was watching them from her bedroom window. She was young, fifteen years old. She had drunk coffee too late and couldn't sleep. Watching the scene below had aroused her. After a fight with her father over poor grades in her schoolwork, she felt suddenly and violently alone. She wanted company. She wanted sex. And she wanted revenge. All abstract.

She left the window for an agonizing moment and rummaged through her underwear drawer for her swimsuit. She pulled her nightgown over her head and put on her white lycra one-piece. She went back to the window and looked down. They were still there. She hurried out of her apartment, shoving a door key into her suit, and jumped barefoot down the cold alabaster stairs.

Wildman didn't react to the sound of the splash. Laura saw the girl swimming underwater, past them. She was faintly nervous. Wildman had come into her, into her dress inside her. He felt huge. She wanted him to make her come, soon, now.

The water was cool. The girl in it was hot. She swam the length of the pool again, side stroke so she could see them. She half-expected them to move away. They didn't. The man moved out of the woman. His cock stuck to the woman's red dress. Neither of them seemed concerned by being watched so blatantly. The girl had heard about threesomes. She wished she had had the guts to dive into the pool naked.

Wildman ached. Ached for Pandora. He had held off long enough. He had to see her again. He turned to the pool and watched the girl for a moment. Who was she? What the fuck was she doing? Spying on him.

"Hey you. Get out of the pool."

The girl was terrified.

"Let's go inside," said Laura. She detached the dress from Wildman's cock. He gasped as if she had dug a nail into him.

The girl reached the end of the pool under the security lamp. She hauled herself out with a single movement.

"Come here," said Wildman.

The girl stared at him. She looked at Laura. She wanted to run away. She wanted to obey. Wildman saw that she had short dyed blonde hair. Even in the distorted light, he could see the terror and also the curiosity in her eyes.

"Come here," Wildman repeated his order, but quietly.

Laura felt uneasy. Waking her in the middle of the night. Bringing her down to the pool. Fucking her in the red dress. And now talking to this unknown girl. It added up to something strange. Something to do with the red dress he had given the woman at the Bel Air Hotel. The next day Wildman had gone out and bought a duplicate. Why?

The girl came up to them.

"Listen, sir, I'm sorry. I just went for a swim. I'm sorry, I wasn't spying."

"Of course you were."

The girl looked helplessly at Laura.

"You live in this building?" Laura asked, worried now about Wildman's mood.

"Yes. Up there." She pointed to her bedroom window.

"How old are you?"

"I'm eighteen, sir."

"Go back to your apartment," Laura said. She touched the girl's arm. It was quivering. "Come on, let her go to bed." Laura was as scared as the girl. The look in Wildman's eyes frightened her. A savage intensity. The girl was held in that look. A fluttering bird stilled by the hypnotic gaze of an erect snake.

Wildman was in a dangerous trance. And he knew it. He suddenly realized that this girl was a mirror of his sister twenty years ago. He could see his sister in her. More than that. He could now see that it was his sister who inhabited the body of Pandora. He was shocked. He was exultant. That was the real attraction, the true compulsion for his absolute need for Pandora.

The girl was dizzy with fear. She was wet with desire.

"Do you have a boyfriend?" Wildman asked.

"Sort of." The girl's voice was a whisper.

"Have you slept with him?"

"No."

She couldn't speak any more. The sweat pouring off her was indistinguishable from the dripping pool water. She was running with liquid, inside and out. She could hardly stay upright.

Wildman leaned towards her face and kissed her gently on the lips. Slowly, in a dream, the girl responded. He put his arms around her, held her close.

Laura watched as the girl's arms raised themselves like robotic limbs and clasped his back. Laura had no idea what to do. The girl was hugging Wildman like a lover. She had changed from a little *voyeuse* caught in her act into someone who appeared suddenly to know the stranger she had been spying on.

Laura looked up and around the apartment building. There

were no lighted windows. No faces that she could see. It was three in the morning. She could almost feel the dawn coming. She looked back at Wildman and the girl, who was now buttoning up his pants.

"I'm going to bed," she announced.

"I'll call you tomorrow," said Wildman. He smoothed his hand through his hair.

"What are you talking about?" Laura looked with desperation at the girl. What the hell was going on? Wildman looked at the girl.

"Go upstairs, get some clothes on. I'll wait here."

The girl turned and walked away, obeying Wildman's command. After a few steps she broke into a long-legged barefoot stride. She didn't look back at Laura.

"Are you crazy? That kid's probably under age."

"I thought you were going to bed."

"I am. And you're not coming?"

"Not tonight."

"What's happened to you?"

Wildman didn't answer her. He couldn't. He didn't know. All he knew for sure was what he was going to do for the rest of the night, and probably part of tomorrow.

Laura walked away from him. When she turned at the mesh gate to look back, Wildman was sitting in a chair looking at the pool, waiting.

She didn't know whether to be angry or cool as the girl passed her coming down the cold echoing stairs. The girl was now wearing jeans and a sweater. She had no purse with her. Nothing. She was still barefoot. Neither woman said a word. One was smiling. One wasn't.

THE PARIS CRAFTSMAN

Lucienne Zager

THE RUE DE L´ENTRANCE was to be found on the southern edge of the great city of Paris. It was an unimportant street of small dilapidated houses long past their best, if they had ever had a best. Cats sat on hot stones to drink in the noon sun and a midday silence more suited to a small village lay over the area. Alison parked her small red sports car as near to the building she sought as possible. She crossed the road to the paint-peeled door marked with a number nine. After hesitating, she knocked hard and waited. There was a long pause, and she had just raised her hand to knock again when she heard a noise from within. The man who opened the door to her was short, bent, old and foreign. "Herr Craftsman?" she enquired.

He nodded through half glasses.

"Alison Kwik," she said, extending a hand which he did not take. "Come in," he said in a thick German accent.

He led her into a dark and dirty hall. Instantly the cool air was full of the smell of leather, stacked along the walls were large rolled hides in many colours and ahead was a narrow staircase, equally ill lit. The old man went ahead and up the stairs and she followed. At the top he disappeared through a half-opened door. She slowly followed and found herself in a strange and crowded room. It was at the rear of the building and light flooded in through a large, dust-encrusted skylight set partly in the room.

All around were cluttered work benches covered in strips of leather and gleaming tools polished with constant use. The sweet smell of leather hung heavily in the air, full of sensual animal power. Herr Craftsman had by now seated himself in a position of authority on a tall stool at a far bench.

"So you have come for one of my little toys?" He asked, his eyes sparkling with an excitement not suggested by this age.

Alison agreed with him, feeling both embarrassed and excited by the situation she found herself in. Though there was still a strong hint of the active male in the old man, there was also the professional detachment that all specialists cultivate. With the ease of long experience and complete familiarity with the difficulties almost all his clients found with the situation for the first time, he launched into his familiar routine. First he seated her by pointing to the only other chair in the room, then with delight he started to describe his service in detail. "You could have a half harness but that would not be for someone as beautiful and so well created by nature as you. No, for you" – here he paused to give effect to his consideration – "No, for you, a full and very elaborate harness is the only one. You are fit and young and would be a perfect body for something so wonderful and so demanding."

"Now," he paused again, holding his chin with his hand, "we must consider the most important of considerations. Will you require a female as well as a male extension?" Before Alison could even begin to answer, he answered for her.

"Yes, again you are someone who will most definitely want a female extension and, if you don't mind me being blunt, we will have to consider both size and shape. In fact to do this correctly and to give you my best work, I must be permitted to measure everything."

He held up his hand to suggest protection or reassurance. "My clients trust me, and I am sure that you will be no different. I have been recommended to you and for me to do my best for you, we must trust each other."

At this point Alison felt that she had better say something.

"Herr Craftsman, I would not be here unless I was willing to undertake what is necessary to possess an example of your extraordinary skill. I will, of course, be only too pleased to co-operate with you to achieve this."

"Good, good, we understand each other. Then we must get on. I regret, my facilities are very limited," he gestured around the room. "May I ask you to remove all your clothing. While you do this, I will get some things together so that I can take my measurements."

Alison found the moment and the request stimulating. This was certainly no doctor's surgery but the same detached pressure to conform was there and felt. She had undressed in front of many men but this was hardly that – more like a dressmaker but even then different.

Herr Craftsman turned away and started to gather together a number of obviously essential items. Alison set about undressing. Fortunately, she had on only casual clothes. First she looked around to find a place to put them. Seeing nothing obvious, she opted for the already crowded bench. With slightly false confidence, she pulled the tight cashmere sweater over her head. The soft material rubbed gently over her hard nipples. The cool air of the room felt fresh on her bare breasts. They delighted her and those who were allowed to play with them, male or female. Hard, high and very round, they were a little larger than her slim, long frame suggested. Next she unlaced her high-heeled boots, pulled them off and placed them neatly under the bench.

She had to stand to remove her tight jeans. She pulled them with difficulty down her long legs and had to hop to keep her balance. She was left with her small plain thong, the cord at the back disappearing between her round cheeky bottom, the thin material at the front cupping the distended mound and slightly moist where it slipped between the pouting lips.

The progress of the undressing had not escaped the alert eyes of Herr Craftsman, "Everything, please, young lady; everything." He made a slight movement of his hands and Alison looked down at the brief white covering and the pink pop socks.

"You can leave the socks on," said Herr Craftsman, as though such a concession would ensure her modesty.

Alison slipped her thumbs through the thin elastic and in one movement pushed the throng down to her feet, where she kicked it free. She stood up, legs slightly parted, to confront Herr Craftsman with the delicately trimmed and most minimal crowning of pubic hair over the powerfully displayed and lustful mouth of her vagina.

"Few," said Herr Craftsman, "of my many clients could be considered more worthy an owner of my talents than you." His eyes shone and his face beamed with the obvious appreciation of a connoisseur. Alison always liked a compliment, and smiled shyly back at him.

"Now to work. First we will measure the female requirement." He turned back to his bench and picked up a beautiful veneered box bound with brass corners. This he placed on a table and with care raised the lid. The long box was lined with dark blue velvet and held in individual compartments perhaps a dozen beautifully shaped red leather dildos in ascending order of size. Herr Craftsman repeated the display with another identical box. This, however, contained similar objects that differed in having exaggerated heads at the end of each of their lengths.

"We have, young lady, two choices in this department. First that of size and then between the one of even diameter and the one with the full head. The only way to choose is to try, otherwise I have found that sometimes a woman's eyes are bigger than, shall we say her, stomach. May I also hasten to assure you that though these samples have experienced many trials, they are always cleansed most thoroughly with surgical spirit.

"The leather from which they are made, and from which the one I make for you will be made, is of the finest quality, as soft as the place it must enter and yet almost totally waterproof. I fill the sheath with my own preparation, which permits some flexibility and feels most natural. You may also consider if you require the device only to fill the vagina or to be more dramatic and pass through the mouth of the cervix and beyond. You may also have one fitted to enter your rear passage as well."

Alison was by now very wet and very open. This almost clinical talk on such an erotic theme was deeply stimulating. Her hole, in fact holes, craved to be filled by the objects that she saw laid out so invitingly before her. It was like a sweet shop and she a child with pennies to spend. What to try first?

"I think I would like a head on the item, and I think that I would like one for my bum as well." She hesitated, hovering over the boxes.

"Take one," encouraged Herr Craftsman.

Her hand reached out and moved over the box, back and forth. Then, with decision, it alighted upon and removed a substantial dildo. Its leather was so inviting, warm to the touch and softer even than her cashmere. She brought it instinctively to her nose and breathed deeply of its rich smell. Her mind also visualized the pink, wet and hairy slits that this had already entered and she trembled at the thought of driving this hard monster in, pushing and twisting it as the recipient thrust back and twisted, skewered upon its attack. She moved it away from her nose, and as it passed her mouth her tongue licked out to caress the large round end.

Now oblivious of Herr Craftsman, and yet aroused by the audience, she brought its head down to meet her own cunt. To make the entry possible she arched her hips forward, bending and opening her legs.

This movement had the effect of opening her hole, and as she drew the soft leather between her lips for the first time, letting the liquids wet it, the need to plunge it in became very strong. Still, as though in a greeting, she let it rub against her clitoris and this touch sent its own messages throughout her body.

Then it was in. At first she felt that she had been too greedy. As her hand and arm forced it in and upward, she felt herself stretched as she had never been stretched before. She could feel it pass the inner gate with just a little pain and then it was onward. As only the last few inches of the massive device were left as a bright red circle framed in the distended mouth, she was aware of Herr Craftsman close by her.

"May I make some checks, young lady?" he said in his professional voice.

"Yes," agreed Alison.

He bent his head as she held her position, standing thrust forward with her legs well parted. She felt his hand touching and testing, then his skilled craftsman's fingers sliding between the dildo and the wall of her vagina, increasing the stretch significantly. Then the fingers were withdrawn and the hand moved with moist fingers up over her mound to the area of her womb. Here it pressed, just above the pubic bone. She was aware of his other hand on the end of the dildo and then its movement of the device, so that it pushed out hard against her skin. Still holding her in this way, he looked up at her face.

"If you were an adventurous girl, you could in my considered opinion get the greatest pleasure from the next size up. You are young and very accommodating. This one you would soon become comfortable with; the next size would always provide a challenge."

Without waiting for an answer, he gently pulled the dildo from her body with little twisting motions that thrilled her. Accepting that the matter had already been decided, he turned and placed the used dildo, now wet and gleaming, on a sheet of plastic and selected the next in line. There was a decided jump in the increments of size and this one looked quite impossible – more a device of punishment than of pleasure.

He handed it to Alison. "Go on, you will learn to enjoy it – even worship it. I know these things; it is my trade to know women's needs."

Alison took it and tried not to look. She knew that this too had been elsewhere and if another had been able to accept it then she would not be beaten and not admit defeat in front of this old man. It was worse and there was pain, but she had never contemplated the incredible feeling of being filled in this way; she could not restrain a gasp. She had not made this journey to this place, to this man, to find anything less than the total experience. This was an essential part of it, this size was to be hers. There were even larger ones in the box. Who they were for she dared not think. Herr Craftsman again went through his methodical examination. She cried out a little as his fingers distended, probed and searched.

"This is yours my dear, of this there is no doubt. In the future, when you are in your private world, you will thank me."

Alison believed that she would.

She sat back on the chair after removing the monster, to regain something of her composure. The old man searched for another item and produced a tube of proprietary genital lubricant. He now selected a red dildo – this one was quite small – and handed it to Alison.

"For the other hole, it is better that it is not too large, so that it can move freely as your body moves; this will give much more sensation."

He passed her the tube, and she anointed the small shaft with gel and, standing up again, she bent forward so that she could reach round and insert it.

"Don't lose it," cautioned Herr Craftsman. She smiled at this remark.

"Does it fit well?" he asked.

"Oh yes, very well," answered Alison. The strange and pleasurable sensation of anything pushed into her bottom was always a little joy.

She withdrew it and placed it alongside the other two on the plastic sheet.

"This one is best for your partners," he said, selecting a headed one of medium size. Unless you have a specific situation in mind, this size is usually universally acceptable in both positions. As it will be the active device, it is best if it is not too large, as men especially become frightened." A smile broke on his face for the first time as he made his no doubt often repeated joke.

He now picked up both a well-worn pad and an even more worn tape measure, together with a felt pen.

"Stand up very straight if you will, and part your legs. Lift your arms out from your sides and please keep very still so that my measurements will be exact."

Standing as she was instructed, the measurement was a further stimulating experience, for she could feel her juices trickling down her inside thigh and could smell her body even over that of the leather. Sweat, sex and leather made a heady perfume, she thought.

He was making little marks with the felt pen and running the tape across her skin. He missed nowhere. Even her hard nipples were marked and measured, the curve of her breast, the distension of her buttocks, down between to find her anus and on again to find her hole, marked for measurement in both cases by the insertion of his finger a little way.

When he was finished, he told her in a matter-of-fact way that she could get dressed. Alison was exhausted. She had been held at a pitch of excitement for quite some time and now felt as though she had been taken.

The selection of the harness style was undertaken from illustrations in a well-thumbed and dog-eared book. The different styles had been modelled by a blonde, attractively figured young woman, but indifferently photographed to create that slightly tacky feel to the images. Alison selected, with considerable and forceful advice, a harness that started with her head, which was to be encased in a box of leather straps. Provision was made for a gag to be incorporated if desired. A tight and high leather collar would encase her neck and then the straps would encircle her breasts, leaving the ends exposed. Dramatic and attractive straps fanned out and down her body, first to restrain the waist and then to lace across the curve of her womb, at the base of her mound. The male dildo would be directly mounted over her clitoris. Also positioned here was a special rubber pad with a cluster of little fingers that would press upon her button as she exerted her own force of the thrust. A wide and parting strap would pass between her legs, holding both her own internal devices. Movable fastenings ensured that these would be given some motion as the male dildo was used.

Alison could not wait to have this wonder in her possession, though it was some months before she received a small engraved card to advise her that it was ready for collection. The difference now was that the address for collection was quite different and the time was in the evening.

She arrived at a very select block of Paris apartments and took the caged lift to the third floor. The brass fitted door was opened by an attractive and smartly dressed woman.

"Alison Kwik?" she enquired with a French accent, and Alison answered that she was.

She was ushered into a small reception room of some quality. Herr Craftsman stood up to greet her. He now wore a moderately respectable suit.

"Ah, my dear young lady, such a pleasure to meet you again. Part of the substantial sum that my clients pay for my work is to provide them with an initial trial – should, of course, they so wish. Always I find that a little guidance is needed in the fitting of the harness and it is important to me at the level of satisfaction at which I desire to work that they feel that all is satisfactory and comfortable. This cannot be achieved without the practical use of the garment. Therefore, Madame Visage" – he gestured towards the woman who had opened the door – "helps me in this matter, in return of course for a professional fee for her special services."

Alison looked with now greater interest at the woman. She was perhaps in her middle thirties, with a slim and well-proportioned body. Her high cheek-bones, restrained dress and hair in a tight bun all gave her a look of refinement and quality edged with a touch of the severe.

"Are you happy with this arrangement?" the woman asked Alison.

"Oh yes, I am pleased to go along with whatever Herr Craftsman has arranged."

"Then please follow me," said Madame Visage and opened the door into the next room. The old man and Alison followed.

The room was a softly lit old Paris boudoir, rich warm and private. Alison saw immediately, laid across a divan, the object of the occasion – the red leather harness.

The woman took charge of the situation.

"Perhaps, Ms Kwik, you would be so good as to undress, so that Herr Craftsman and I can fit you with his special garment."

As with the first encounter, Alison felt detached and propelled along by the confidence and experience of others to whom this seemed routine. It was exciting, this surrender of choice. Tonight she had worn a dress, stockings and court shoes. While both the old man and the woman watched, almost impatiently, she undressed, placing her clothes with care and trying to retain some dignity. Even when she had removed her little silk top and matching knickers, she was still faced with the removal of her stockings and belt. This time she was completely nude, without even pop socks. The woman appraised her with a moment's detachment and then picked up the harness. It was quite beautiful, complex and even intimidating. The red leather organs that were intended for her looked even bigger than she remembered them to have been.

"We will proceed with the fitting, if you please. Stand leg-parted and arms out, and I will do the rest," instructed Madame Visage. Alison complied and Herr Craftsman sat down a little way away, no doubt to watch with craftsman's pride the demonstration of his work. The harness detached into two halves and Madame Visage started by fitting the top. Alison felt the initiate feeling of being encased as the straps were fastened around her head. The neck collar was drawn tight and she felt the way that it forced her head to stay erect. The woman worked quickly and with experience, the many little buckles fastened with ease in her nimble fingers. Alison could feel her torso being encased. Her breasts rose and were divided to point out to the sides. She saw how stiff the nipples had become and all around her was the smell of leather and the subtle perfume of Madame Visage. The woman now tightened the corset-like structure beneath Alison's breasts.

"Take a deep breath in and hold it, please," requested Madame Visage.

Alison complied and she felt the woman swiftly tighten the straps across her back so that now her waist was drastically pulled in.

Madame now reached for a tube of lubricant and methodically coated each of the organs.

"This will not be comfortable at first, so just relax. There will be a little pain but it will pass."

Alison did her best to ready herself for the entry of the large dildo. When it came there was no kindness in the entry used by Madame, but Alison knew that she would have enjoyed doing the same. Even so, a little cry, which must have given some satisfaction to the woman, passed her lips. It was worked in until Alison felt as though she would part with the filling force. The one in her behind was nothing like as bad and it slipped in to give her some pleasure.

Her crutch was forced wide open by both the device and the width of the harness. While the woman fastened and pulled up the lower section to the torso section, Alison was able to look down and see the large red dildo for the first time, erect and in front of her, curving up from the base of her mound like men she had so often seen. She was also aware that, at every tremor of the long organ in front of her, the rubber fingers at its base stirred her clitoris in a definite and stimulating way.

The woman now directed Alison's attention to a full-length ornate mirror against the wall. What she saw reflected was a remarkable and totally erotic sight that fired her in a way she had never experienced before. The muscles of her vagina started to work involuntarily on the distending solid leather within it and her sphincter tightened and gripped its plug. As she looked at herself, she became uncontrollably aroused. With difficulty, she turned sideways and saw pointed breasts and the penis in front of the thrusting buttocks. Her head was encased and warrior-like – indeed the totality was wickedly war-like.

Without further ceremony, Madame Visage, in the same flat tone, invited Alison to try the harness. As though she had done it a hundred times before – and perhaps she had – Madame Visage bent herself over the raised end of the divan. She reached backward and in one movement swept up the length of her dress and tucked it beneath her. Above her black seamed stockings, Alison could clearly see that Madame wore no knickers. The stockinged legs parted invitingly and were surmounted by a beautiful full bottom of firm white flesh. The legs ended in expensive, black, long-heeled shoes. Alison was taken aback by this display, for it was totally unexpected. Herr Craftsman watched from his seat.

"Do not hold back; please go ahead and try your new toy," came the voice of Madame Visage. "Either hole is permissible – whatever is your fancy – or both."

Alison moved forward, feeling the difficulty of walking, feeling the rub on her button driving her to greater heights. The dildo in front of her gleamed with the lubricant already rubbed on it.

She moved between the parted legs so that she was over the raised bottom. She could see the little hole clearly and in the darker place at the top of Madame's thighs she could see the hairy and wet rear of the vulva. Frightened but determined, Alison gripped the dildo in one hand and supported her weight with the other. She entered its round head into the soft lips that were presented. Then, remembering how the dildo had been forced into her own place, she thrust into the woman with all her force. She was successful in extracting a groan. With each successive thrust, she gained even more response. She held the woman's hips with her hands and moved her own with all her force. Though she was fucking, she was also being fucked and she could not restrain the mounting orgasm that was fed and driven by so many methods of stimulation in her own body.

When she had come, she withdrew and released the woman. She stood trembling and instantly wondering what it would be like to use on a man. The expression on her face was all the real thanks that Herr Craftsman needed. This work was so much more rewarding in his old age than the use of his supreme talents on the horses in old Vienna. The smell of this sexual young woman, which floated across the room, blended with his new leather. He was content.

FRAME GRABBER

Denise Danks

I

I KNEW IT HAD been a mistake. Well, at least I knew now. Two months had passed and I still couldn't believe that I had done it. It was incredible. I had had one or two drinks. I had loosened up, yes, but it was nothing I couldn't handle. But I had done it. I had had sex with an interviewee, the first time ever in a ten-year career in journalism. Right there, in a pastel-coloured hotel room on the twentieth floor of a monumental glass tower, at three o'clock in the afternoon.

We did it looking out over the Hudson River, with the hot breeze sucked up from the humid, New York streets rushing against my face. It was possible to see us through the huge tinted window, yet no one could. No one was watching us up there. But there was no "we" or "us", really. There was just me and him, separate pieces in the same pie. It was a very lonely business.

I had flown to New York for the launch of a new high-powered computer and Dr David Jones was one of many accompanying sideshows set up to illustrate the potential of the new system. His expertise? Computer-generated virtual reality: a technology that creates three-dimensional electronic worlds, computer models that you can exist in and interact with. Computer models that can be any world you want, with you as the chief inhabitant, but you don't have to be alone. I had to interview him for *Technology Week*, find out about his company, Virtech – a sexy little start-up, Richard had called it.

For just over an hour, we'd sat facing each other discussing what I thought were the relevant issues. I wasn't convinced that what I was hearing wasn't a load of hype so I decided to wind up on a light note.

"Do you remember those special-effect disaster movies?" I said.

"I'm afraid I don't," he replied.

"*Earthquake*? You didn't see that?"

"No. I rarely see films, I prefer to make my own."

"Really? Well, this should interest you. You could actually feel the tremors as they happened onscreen. Virtual reality isn't new, you see."

"No, it isn't. The difference is that what you had was, essentially, a passive experience."

"I felt something though, from a place I wasn't in. It was an illusion. The impact of your virtual world is also illusory. You can affect things, and effect them, but how much can they affect you?"

He leaned forward and placed his empty coffee cup next to my gently bubbling gin and tonic. He didn't drink on duty, and he didn't smoke, but the glass ashtray on the table was crammed with broken unburnt matchsticks, some in bent chevrons and others snapped in two. One fresh splinter was hanging over the edge. He picked it up and gently clamped his teeth on one end, chewing slowly at it and twisting it around with his fingers. He kept his eyes on me for so long that I began to feel uncomfortable. I pushed the skirt of my loose dress down a little and reached for my tumbler of gin. I threw my head back to drink and I could see him through the bottom of the glass, staring at my neck and the low scoop of my summer dress.

"Did you enjoy it?" he said.

"The film?"

"The passive experience."

"I don't remember. I think I screamed. It was fun."

"A real earthquake isn't fun."

"I know that. I bought a ticket, remember? I felt the quake, all the same."

"And touched it?"

"Feel is not the same as touch."

"It can be," he said.

I looked over my glass, unable to put it down. I wanted to finish it but he prevented me somehow, holding my gaze long enough to make me look away for my cigarettes.

"Ask the military. We don't need to know everything in order to relate to something, just a few things with certainty," he said.

"Like the sound and direction of an incoming bomb?" I said, relieved. Hypothetical weaponry was easier to handle than an intimate thought.

"Quite."

"But not the smell or the taste of burning."

"No."

"Without the smell or taste of burning how do we understand the danger of the bomb?" I said.

"Instinct," he said. "Pure instinct."

He sat back in his pale pink chair, both hands casually resting on his thighs, his legs slightly splayed, and the light caught his glasses enough to white out his eyes. In a moment, the reflection of the sky had gone and I noticed his pale blue eyes were very steady, as if he had me in his sights. I put my glass down and folded my notebook, slotting my pencil through the spiral at the top. He'd ordered more drinks a while back, but I decided it was time to go. I looked up to say so and he smiled a little. His eyes were alight and I knew he was back on track.

"Everyone wants it, everyone," he said.

"And why's that?"

"Because everybody can think of at least one thing they'd like to do with it."

There was a knock on the door before I could reply. A young black man, trim in his green uniform with shiny brass buttons, entered with our third and final tray of drinks. When he'd gone, I raised my glass to my companion but as I lifted it up to drink, the ice clung to the bottom and then slid down, banging my lip. I pressed a napkin to my face and dabbed a drip or two off my chin and the thin material of my dress. I looked up and David shifted his glasses on his face as ice water trickled down my belly.

"Mind if I smoke?" I said, laying the damp napkin over the arm of my chair. I stuck an unlit cigarette in my mouth.

"What would you like to do?" he said.

"Me? Nothing."

"You could do whatever you wanted."

"I do now."

"Without suffering the consequences."

That last statement was going to play on my mind. I'd never got away with anything, never ever. If I didn't pick up the whole bill, I got to pay more than a few instalments. He was looking at me for some sort of reaction. I didn't give it. I didn't light my cigarette either. I took it out of my mouth and he handed me a box of matches.

"Did you get to play?" he said.

"Downstairs? No. There was a queue. The boys got there first."

"In that case, you can ride my machine," he said.

That surprised me. His voice betrayed the innuendo but he didn't look like the sort of man that would make one. He wasn't the sort of man who was unaware of what he said either. I played it straight.

"Thank you. Tell me, is your reality more real than theirs?" I said.

"Of course it is. It's more expensive. VR is about affecting perceptions. You can do this with simple equipment and relatively unsophisticated graphics because the human sensory system is remarkably tolerant to pathetically sparse audiovisual stimulation. For more realism you need a system that can solve extensive sets of equations at speed. You need processors working in parallel. The more you need, the more you have to pay. Reality costs."

I still hadn't lit the cigarette. It was stuck to my lip. He leaned over, gently took the wooden matchbox from my hands and stroked a match along the side. It crackled and flared and I sucked in the flame, keeping myself from looking up until I needed to puff smoke into the air. It was time to smack his wrists.

"All right. Conceptually, it sounds very different, but what are we really talking about here? A sophisticated display with interesting peripherals, that's all, a pretentious box," I said.

He picked a fresh match from the box, snapped it till it almost broke, put one end in his mouth and flicked the other with his thumb so that it twirled around. I took a few triumphant puffs of my cigarette until he flicked the twisted match into the ashtray with the others and got up, gesturing to the window. He waited by the table for me and guided me towards it, one hand pressing the cotton of my dress against the small of my back.

The window stretched from one wall to the other. There was the wide, grey Hudson River and the wake of a cargo ship curved round the distant bulk of the Statue of Liberty. I imagined the river to be noisy with traffic, but we couldn't hear it. I could hear him breathing softly. He tapped the thick, smoky glass with his knuckle.

"Think of this as the screen. All that you see would be digitized, within the computer. And you? You could be what you want, do what you want. You could be a bird or a plane. Alice through the Looking Glass. Look, over there. You could be Liberty. Reach down and drag your fingers through the water. Push the clouds wide apart."

I stared ahead, peering through the glass until all I could see was his reflection. He was slightly taller than me and as spare. His white shirt had the sleeves rolled up to expose intermittent fair hairs on his lightly tanned arm. I could see he wasn't looking at the view, imagining what he could be. He was looking at me.

"Look, I feel a bit cold," I said, trying to turn.

He looked back to where the dials were fixed to the opposite wall. "I could regulate the air conditioning . . ." he replied. "Or . . ."

His arm moved over my shoulder and he tugged hard at the handle, swinging the huge window before us open a couple of inches. The hot summer wind whistled in over my face and down my body. It puffed out my thin dress and shook my dark hair. He took one strand from his lip and put both hands gently on my shoulders. We stood unbearably close together, looking out across the grey water, listening to the breeze until he took my wrists tightly and placed my hands a little above my head, palms flat against the thick glass.

"Look out. You can see everything except what is directly below. Now look down. See? It's a long way, isn't it? You could be flying, imagine that, up and down, in and out . . . why don't you do it, now?" he said.

He was pushing against me so my hips pressed against the sill. I caught my breath as my eyes took in the giddying, twenty-floor drop. There was no glass before me, just air. I could see little coloured cars like kiddies' bricks on the street. My fingers pressed hard and flat against the glass like a lizard's on a high, dry wall. He tugged the skirt of my dress and twined the hem around and around his fingers until it tightened around my thighs. He pulled it up slowly, dragging it over my cotton-knickered hips, up to my waist. His other hand held the back of my neck, while he pulled the pants down, and the dress up higher to expose my naked breasts. We were standing right in front of the window, where nothing but the birds could see us. He kneaded my flesh in his hands and my legs trembled against his while my brain worked desperately to stabilize the distance from the ground up and find the word – no.

The sudden, hard pressure behind crushed my stomach against the wood and metal of the window sill. All that seemed to keep me on solid ground were the tips of my sandalled toes. My face slid uncomfortably against the glass between my outspread arms. He pulled me back, held my neck again, squeezing tightly, pressing down on the bones of my spine, keeping my face against the dry wind and above the drop. The distant street below began to judder back and forth until I shut my eyes tight. I felt as if I were flying blind on a warm, red edge, swelling and thickening like a thermistor in a tight vial, my voice nothing but an idiot's hum locked in my head. He quickened with my heartbeat and with the final push came a short sigh and a rough shove against my shoulders. My weight jerked the window violently outwards and my eyes stretched open in shock as I tumbled forward and down.

The street came towards me fast. I had an idea that I was screaming as the hot air blasted with renewed force against my face. I could hear nothing, nothing but the increased roar of the wind drying the moisture from my tongue and teeth. I was falling, alone and afraid of falling, falling all the way to the ground. A shaft of ecstasy and a pinching sensation of fear prickled up through me like boiling sand, spilling over my scalp like needled splinters. I shuddered against the impact which never came. I had gone nowhere. I stood leaning against the window, gasping and staring downwards. All was still, but for the little coloured bricks stopping and starting, whizzing and braking, way down on the street.

Two more inches. The window had moved out two more
inches, that's all. It had seemed like two feet, maybe a metre.
The hotels fix them like that. The gap has to be too small to drop
a TV set or your head through. Two inches or two feet, I was
shaking as if I had truly been snatched back from the sky.

By the time I turned around, he had already straightened his
clothes. He looked neat and calm, as if he had just walked into the
room. I pulled my dress down and went to the bathroom. To be
sick, I thought, but all I did was smooth my dress against me and
flick at my hair before leaving the suite. There was someone in
the corridor waiting for his interview. I heard David say, in his
polite, English way, "Good afternoon. Sorry to have kept you."

Just like he had said to me.

II

Of course, I turned up. The room in Victoria wasn't like the
others. It was in one of those large, sad houses in a square where
you'd imagine a carriage drawing up with a well-dressed family of
mama, papa and delightfully dressed children aboard. The house,
with its creamy pillars and marbled steps, had lately been pressed
into service. The porter in the dim lobby gave me a key with a
number and I made my way up the stairs to a narrow, musty
corridor and a hastily painted plasterboard door. Behind it was a
single room with its long, yellowish curtains drawn and most of
the space taken up by a narrow lumpy bed, square white sink and
brown veneered wardrobe. I wiped my clammy palms on my
dress. I had no plan, no reason to come, just compulsion. I looked
around the walls, expecting spiders, but there were none. I
started at a knocking, like a wooden brush against a skirting
board. It was cool in the room, and quiet but for cars whirring in
the street below. I stood as still as a mouse in a cold cave of air,
waiting for an earth in the static. I could hear my blood drumming hotly past my ears. Time to leave, run, run, run. I turned
but the door clicked shut. He didn't say anything.

"You made me jump," I said.

"How high?"

"I don't want to stay. Let me out."

"Scream," he said.

I just stared at him.

"Scream. Someone will come running. There's a traveller on either side, a whore across the way, the porter downstairs. They'll come."

"I'm not going to scream. Let me pass," I said.

He didn't, of course; he walked me backwards until my back pressed against the side of the wardrobe. It was cold and slightly damp against the scoop of skin between my shoulder blades. He dragged his hands over my shoulders and pressed my covered breasts.

"Are you drunk?" he said.

"No more than usual," I replied.

"Are you afraid?"

"What do you think?"

"Then we can find out about each other," he said and took his glasses off.

There were no tricks this time. My dread retreated into passion. His hands were tender with my flesh and his mouth soft and strong on mine. I wanted him, believed in him and when it was over, I fell asleep in his arms. Deep asleep from afternoon light until summer darkness, until the rhythmic movement of his body against mine woke me. With my eyes half open, I looked across the pillow and saw his metal-framed glasses folded by an empty tumbler beside the bed. I wasn't sure at first that I was awake. My senses were sluggish, weighted by the lunchtime Camparis and wine. The room was in darkness but for the gloomy half-light of a lamp in the street. He felt me stirring but didn't stop; instead, he moved more languidly as if not to wake me. I chose to close my eyes again and let him rock but the half-glimpse of his chalk-whitened hand, gripping my chalk-whitened wrist, startled me. I lay watching it until, with eyes opened wide, I looked straight up at his face.

He was staring right back, his eyes stark in a dusty mask. I looked down over my dusted body. It was paler than moonlight, a strong, sickly perfume rising from it to catch my breath. My mouth was dry as glass paper, my lips moist and sticky. I could taste plums and bitter almonds. His hands loosened their grip, smoothed softly up to my shoulders, then touched my neck. He stroked my skin gently with pallid fingers that stretched around and under my hair, spreading it out over the pillow before they came back to hold my throat, gently first like a child holding a bird, but then too tightly, far too tightly to breathe.

"David?"

"Ssh."

"David?"

He slowly began to squeeze the breath from me until my instincts kicked in and I pushed violently upwards. He loosened his grip a little.

"Close your eyes. Keep still," he said. His darkened lips glistened in the half-light and I found my half-strangled voice.

"For Christ's sake. What are you doing?"

"Don't talk. Keep still."

"Get off me. Please. Please."

"Ssh. It's all right."

"Don't, David. You're choking me."

"Don't talk. It's all right."

It didn't feel all right. It didn't feel all right at all. Panic made me struggle but as I jerked up again, his hands pressed harder. He squeezed slowly and relentlessly until I couldn't take in the slightest whistle of air. My eyes seemed to bulge outwards like a bullfrog's neck, stretching like a bubble-gum ball. A terrible pain surged through my head and I could hear myself grunting, feel myself passing out. Then the pressure eased off and the air wheezed down my throat. I gulped and gulped like a drowning swimmer breaking surface. But he squeezed again and I could do nothing but stare up at his crazy, ecstatic face and pray to a God I'd forgotten long ago. I prayed, but the person who came to mind was my mother, sitting on a red tartan blanket pouring tea from a flask. I could hear it and her calling to me as the midday sun beat down upon my head. The tide was going out and the pressure in my skull pumped up and up. The pain grew again like a tumour. He squeezed and released, squeezed and released, on and on, until I lay limp and he shook soundlessly, like a man drenched in melting ice. I'll never forget his face. It was the wan, untroubled face of a man at peace; the face of a dead man.

"We have an understanding, don't we?" he said.

I nodded meekly.

"You understand what I want. I understand what you want."

I said nothing.

"Answer me."

"Yes."

"It's wonderful, isn't it?"

"Yes."

His dry temperate hands stroked my body and the white dust moved around in swirls.

"What is it?" I asked, my voice thick with fear and pain. He licked his finger and drew a wet circle broken by an arrow on the ivory curve of my hip.

"Oriental face powder. Like chalk, only finer, and perfumed. See, you're as smooth as a bone."

His mouth was close, his face was as pale as bleached linen.

"Why me?" I said.

"You let me."

"You said there were others."

"Yes."

"So?"

"It's the look. You never wear colours, do you?"

"No?"

"Just black or white."

"Oh."

"And underneath, you're the same. White skin. Dark hair. Bruised eyes, lips."

"It's a hard life as a fashion victim," I said, turning quickly to move off the bed, but he was quicker. He pulled me back towards him, stained lips stretching over his creamy teeth in a rare, magnetic smile. I put a finger to my face to wipe away a tear and the pale powder came away on to my hand. He leaned over my shoulder and kissed me. I could taste the sweet lipstick and feel the meaty roll of his tongue. He kissed me softly, at first, and then hard, very, very hard.

MARRIED LOVE

David Guy

I MET HER AT the airport while we were waiting for a flight home at the end of the school year. I had noticed her around campus. She always wore a sweatshirt and jeans, and looked – with her short compact body, her curly black hair cut short – a little like a boy. She also carried herself like a boy, shoulders hunched and hands stuffed into her pockets, a funny little swagger to her walk. She had a beautiful olive tint to her skin, a hopeful expression in her wide brown eyes. In a crowd she would always be gazing around, as if hopeful of finding a friend, but if somebody met her gaze she always looked down. She was gazing around that day at the airport, but was wearing – somewhat to my surprise – a bright red jumper. She looked like a different person. We got to talking, and arranged to sit together on the plane.

She told me she had just broken up with a guy, a graduate student in her field – studio art – who had been a mentor for her but had treated her badly. He'd had several other girlfriends while he saw her and was very condescending and controlling. He'd fool around with her when *he* felt like it but would never actually screw her because she was a virgin and he was afraid she'd get hopelessly attached to him. (There was an old sexual myth to that effect.) Finally she had given up. Her ambition now was to learn about sex and become a great lover, go back and give him a taste of what might have been, then dump on the stupid bastard. She seemed genuinely unhappy about what had happened – I realized now that she had looked crestfallen around campus in recent weeks – but she had such a whimsical way of talking about it that you had to laugh. I told her I would be writing stories that summer, working in a factory to make some money. She said she was going off to California to live with some friends and find a summer job.

It occurred to me to wonder if I might be able to help her in her ambition.

In August, before school started, she called and told me her father had given her a car over the summer, asked if I wanted a ride down with her. I said I did, and asked her out to dinner. That was the night of the kisses on Mellon Square, spray from the fountains blowing over us in a gusting wind.

Back at her house, we built a fire against the early autumn chill, then sat and watched it, her head on my shoulder. Her hair, after a while, smelled like smoke. Her face got all ruddy and hot. She smiled and closed her eyes as I covered it with kisses.

My dorm room was a tiny single, virtually filled by a bed, a desk, and a dresser. Sara and I had to sneak in, since women weren't allowed in men's dorms, but my room was on the first floor, next to the entrance. At night, with all the lights off, we could open the curtains and illumine the room by the lights on the quad. Nobody could see in. We would latch the door and ignore what went on around us. We didn't even answer a knock.

My only real sexual experience at that point had been with that blowsy, boozy woman poet, who had taken me back to her motel room after her reading. Her body was saggy, her kisses wet and tonguey, tasting of scotch and tobacco. She had been very funny, made me suck her tits for what seemed like an endless time, gave me explicit and detailed instructions in oral sex, but we'd had only the most perfunctory of couplings. She must have sensed it was my first time but was nice enough not to say anything. She praised my performance and my body, told me I was a beautiful boy. "You know, lovey," she said. "I really do like tongues better than cocks. And girls better than boys. But it's so hard to pick up a girl at a place like this. They're all so uptight. They don't know what you mean."

She's telling me.

My night with the poet had done nothing to prepare me for the experience of Sara's body.

For a long time Sara would get naked only down to the tights she wore under her jumpers. She liked what we were doing but didn't want to hurry the process. After seeing her only in a sweatshirt and jeans, or in one of the shapeless jumpers she wore on our dates, I couldn't believe what a beautiful body she had, with that olive tone to her skin, the smooth shapely muscles in her shoulders and arms, her flat taut belly, small breasts that were nevertheless beautifully shaped, with lovely brown nipples. She looked like a ballerina in her tights. We would hug and kiss for hours, bare skin to bare skin. I would kiss her breasts, but gently, because her nipples were extremely tender.

It was all right for me to get as naked as I wanted. She loved bare flesh, and had a particular thing for my penis, an organ with which she hadn't had much experience but that she liked for its novelty. She must have thought for a while that they were perpetually erect, because in those days my cock stayed that way – a huge red throbbing erection – by the hour. She was skittish about being asked to do anything in particular with a penis. She wanted to do what *she* liked. One night, when we were locked in an embrace, I started to move rhythmically against her tights. I couldn't help myself. "Is this all right?" I said, and she said it was, though I don't think she knew what I meant. In a few minutes I had the kind of copious gushing orgasm that you have when you're twenty. I got up and fumbled around for a towel.

"I'm sorry I got your tights wet," I said.

No I wasn't.

"It's all right," she said. While I wiped her off she looked at me and smiled. "It got small."

"Yes." Not for long.

"It's cute."

Not the word I would have chosen myself, but I'd take it.

"You know," she said, "I didn't really get all this before. How it was done, exactly. But now I do."

"It's kind of a mess," I said.

"It is. But I like it."

In time the tights came off. Her ass was as smooth and shapely and firm as her breasts. The hair between her legs was a brilliant black, shiny and abundant. I taught her to touch me with her hand, so it was my belly, not hers, that got splattered with semen. (Mine was used to it.) We waited to do more until she felt perfectly ready, and until it was a good time of the month. I couldn't believe, when the night finally came, the incredible intensity of entering her. I came in about five strokes, one of the most satisfying orgasms I'd ever had. She could feel it happen, she said, in my back. Where her hands rested on my back.

"It's so powerful," she said.

"Is it?"

"It's amazing. I've never felt anything like it." She was wearing a huge smile. "So manly." I lay on my back, and she traced her fingertips across my chest. "I loved it," she said. "It didn't hurt or anything." She laid her head on my chest. "I can't believe we finally did it."

I had not had much experience with sex, but I'd read up on the subject avidly and with great interest. Probably no one my age in the world had a greater theoretical knowledge of sex than I, though, as any student of biology knows, theory and practice can be far apart. I knew about the magic little button of flesh on a woman ("The good feeling spot," as a little girl of my acquaintance once described it), and I would gently touch that place with a finger during foreplay, to make Sara wet. One evening when I was touching her, before we made love, she said, "That really feels good tonight. It *really* feels good. I want you to do it for a long time."

Up until then, when we had made love, I would sometimes feel a little flutter in her, or a brief contraction, and say, "Is that an orgasm?" She'd say, "I don't know. I guess so." I knew that this phenomenon existed. I had read about it in any number of places (though some of the older books claimed that, while a man had a spine-snapping orgasm during intercourse, a woman just got a "warm glow" out of the experience).

On this particular evening, while I was touching Sara in a relaxed and desultory way, I could tell that something more was happening than had ever happened before. She was going to a deeper place. Her eyes were closed, and she seemed to be less present with me, more inside herself. She seemed, in fact, to be utterly oblivious of me, making quiet little moans and groans. Her cunt was flooded with moisture. It was all over my hand. Her body seemed to grow tense, like a spring that is being wound tighter and tighter. It felt as if she would snap. Suddenly she went into convulsions. Her hips bucked off the bed; her body jerked all over the place; every muscle she had seemed to be expanding and contracting at once. She had shouted when it started, now made a muffled shrieking sound. I got scared and took my hand away, but she shouted, "Don't stop!" The convulsions went on – though eventually growing milder – for twenty or thirty seconds. Finally they ended. Sara's face was drained, and she was breathless. She looked at me with startled eyes.

"I don't think those other things *were* orgasms," I said.

"No."

"Because I think that was one."

"Yes."

It sure as hell wasn't a warm glow.

A man's orgasm to that was like a pop gun to a cannon. And she had told me mine was powerful.

"What a neat thing," she said.

Sara never did come to like the big wet raunchy kisses that I liked. Her ideal kiss was a gentle one, just the tips of our tongues touching. Her nipples were extremely tender, so it was only with great care that you could suck them. You couldn't do it with passion. She didn't like me to go down on her; she thought that was dirty, and didn't like the sloppy wet feeling of a tongue down there. She didn't like that smell on my face and mouth. She also didn't like to blow me. She said my cock tasted like pee, and that the size of it gagged her. She wouldn't think of letting me come in her mouth, but there was no chance of that anyway, since she would only suck me for a few seconds. She also said, repeatedly – in the kind of whimsical way that was meant to convey an important truth – that if I ever touched her asshole she would leave me.

We would often, in those days, have elaborate and lengthy dates on the weekends. We would go out for dinner and have an enormous meal, half a young spring chicken, fried, with french fries and biscuits. Cheesecake and coffee for dessert. We'd take in a nine o'clock movie. Then we'd go to my room and make love three or four times, with long conversations in between, and still get to her dorm for the two o'clock curfew. It was nothing for us to do all that. We often did it on Friday and Saturday nights. Six or seven acts of intercourse per weekend. By Monday we were ready to dash off to the dorm for a quick one.

Back home we lived forty-five minutes apart, and it was much harder to find privacy. I would visit her house in the country, but in the daytime her mother was around, in the evening both her parents. We were always incredibly hot for each other, would get behind a door and kiss like a couple of maniacs, feel each other up. Once we went for an afternoon drive and stopped by a grassy meadow, perhaps a hundred yards long. It was an out-of-the-way spot, largely surrounded by trees, but the place we walked to was clearly visible from the road. Nevertheless, we took off our pants and did it, humping away fiercely, with only our pants as a blanket against the wet ground. Another time we lay down in the grass behind the garage at her house. The spot we picked wasn't visible from the house, but if Sara's mother had come out to get in her car she would have caught us in the act. She would have been about ten feet away. The long grass tickled our legs. The dog ran around us and yipped. Afterward we pulled on our pants and lay on our backs for a while, staring up at the sky.

We had gotten together as friends – barely acquaintances, actu- ally – who wanted to fuck. Sara wanted to lose her virginity and become a virtuoso lover, and I was more than happy to fuck my brains out. But in the midst of all that fucking, something else happened. We spent all that time in bed, in intimate connection. We were also inseparable out of bed, eating our meals and studying together. We became vital parts of each other's lives. Best friends. You wouldn't have said we fell in love, but we came to love each other, and when it was time to step out and face the world, we wanted to do that together. We hardly had to talk about it. We just knew. I wasn't the love of Sara's life, and she probably wasn't mine – that wasn't a concept I'd given much thought to, since I'd never expected to be loved anyway – but in the world we saw around us, what we had was good. We didn't want to lose it.

Married life was hard. Neither of us had any money from our families at that point, and I don't think we would have used it if we had. We wanted to make it on our own. We lived in a tiny boxlike four-room house, with a cat. Sara worked in a restaurant, I at various places – a library, a bookstore, a bar – where I could keep odd hours and have my mornings for writing. Often at night we would hardly have seen each other by the time we got into bed. We were wrung out and exhausted, too tired to make love, too tense to go to sleep, so we got into the habit – a funny little habit, when you think of it – of just touching each other with our hands. It seemed an activity of about the right intensity for the shape we were in. I had gradually learned from Sara, and no longer touched that one little spot, with my finger, but slowly rubbed the whole area with three or four fingers, moving in a little circle. Sara had gotten as expert at handling a cock as a thirteen-year-old boy. She could stroke it smoothly, intensify what she was doing as she felt the pressure start to build, put pressure on the glans and release it just as I was about to explode. We did it almost every night, right after we went to bed, often without saying a word. It was a nice thing to do for each other, a friendly gesture, like a back rub. It was fun to lie on each other's shoulder and feel the excitement start to build, hear the happy little gasp as it was released.

When I think of the early hard exhausted years of my marriage, I think of that one thing, lying in bed and making each other come so we could go to sleep.

When you are young you have so much energy, your dreams are so fresh and strong that they can take a terrific battering. They cannot take an endless battering. The realities of life wear you down over time. Time itself wears you down. I had written dozens of stories that had been rejected everywhere; I had written for that little newspaper that had a narrow prestige and almost no money; I had poured my heart into three hundred pages of a novel that wound up going nowhere. As I gradually, over the course of two or three months, saw that project dissolve in my hands, I found myself standing at the edge of an abyss. I looked into my future and saw an endless blackness. I felt tiny in the face of it. I felt it would swallow me up.

If you stare long enough into that abyss, you undergo a change. It isn't that you see something emerge. It is that you accept the emptiness. You realize that the emptiness is what *is*. It isn't supposed to be some other way. You really are tiny in the face of it. You are minuscule. But it doesn't swallow you up. You remain what you are. A minuscule being in the face of an endless blackness.

The trick is not to go out of your mind before you have that realization.

I grew a knot in my chest, just beneath my breastbone. It felt as if someone had reached into my chest and gripped the muscles there, not terribly hard, but persistently. Sometimes, in moments of stress, it tightened into a burning. Sometimes it diminished until I could barely feel it, just one finger, or two, pressing beneath my breastbone. But it never ended.

Who is this guy who has a hold of me? I thought. What does he want?

I saw several doctors, who had various names for what I had, various remedies. They filled me with medicines and put me on diets. One went so far as to take an X-ray, which involved elaborate machinery and hours of time. I lay strapped to a motorized table that moved around, tilted me at all kinds of bizarre angles, while doctors in another room looked at my insides on a screen. They sat forward in their seats and stared, looking for what was wrong. They saw nothing.

I was suffering from rage at the world. It doesn't show up in an X-ray. I'd had a dream of the way my life was supposed to be, and the world had betrayed me. It had broken my heart. What I needed was to roar and breathe fire, shout out my rage, beat the living piss out of the world. I could have used a shovel or something. It wouldn't have done the world much harm, and it would have done me a great deal of good. But I didn't know that then. I didn't know I was full of rage. I thought I just had a stomachache. I thought I had no right to be angry (anger doesn't ask about its rights), that I was just another lousy writer with delusions of grandeur. In order to quiet my rage, which was boiling beneath the surface like a volcano, I had to hold it in. I had to cut it off precisely at the spot where it would emerge, at the top of my stomach, beneath the breastbone.

I was the person doing the gripping. I was gripping myself.

Why didn't I let go?

The knot in my chest sometimes kept me from sleeping. It woke me up early (which left me tired and increased my stress and tightened the knot). One morning, as I lay beside Sara with all the ease and flexibility of a concrete slab, she opened her eyes and was immediately awake. I had been awake for hours. She had just had an incredibly sexy dream, which she proceeded to tell me in glowing detail while she threw off her nightgown and turned my way. We often made love in the morning. It was in many ways our favorite time. Sara felt so good in my arms, and the morning felt so good – a spring breeze drifting in the window – and I wanted so much *to* feel good, that I pretended I did. I pretended I was there in my body, which I wasn't (I had retreated up into my head, away from the pain). As I rolled over on Sara, I pretended that my three-quarters erect penis, which looked roughly like a real erection, actually had some feeling in it, which it didn't. I wouldn't have wanted to disappoint her, after all. I wouldn't have wanted to let her down sexually. I wouldn't have wanted her to know how much pain I was in. That might have scared her. (I tried to spare my wife from the pain I was going through. I felt I should be able to take it by myself. I thereby cut her off from the deepest part of my life.) So when I slipped inside her and felt myself immediately start to come, when I felt myself coming and getting smaller at the same time, I thought, *What is this*? I came not with that enormous surge that roars through your body, like a wave crashing against the shore, but with a tiny little ripple, way off in some distant part of my body (did a pin drop?). As I hovered above Sara, I felt myself flush, sweat popping out all over my body. I wanted to hide my head. I wanted to crawl into a hole somewhere. I felt shame.

"What's wrong?" Sara said, an air of concern in her eyes.

She meant, What's wrong with you? With your spirit? What's this sudden flush, sweat popping out on your body?

I thought she meant, What the hell happened to your cock?

I collapsed beside her. "I don't know."

This phenomenon is what the world calls premature ejaculation. It is about two steps up from the basement floor. The basement floor is impotence.

I thought: I can't write, I can't eat what I want, I can't sleep. Now I can't even fuck.

A man in this situation thinks, What happened to my penis? The answer is: Nothing. Your penis is the center of your body, and your body has a wisdom that your brain doesn't. It knows things that your brain hasn't noticed. ("He thinks with his dick" should not be an insult, if a man is whole.) My rage was coming between me and my cock, and I kept trying to go around it, function as if the rage didn't exist. My cock was saying, You can't do that anymore. I won't let you do it. I don't need the whole person with me to function, but I sure as hell need more than this. I can't do anything when you're huddled off in your head, hiding from your pain and your rage.

Accept your rage, my body was saying. Acknowledge it. Let yourself feel it. But I was afraid to do that. It felt like pain, for one thing. Nobody wants to feel pain. I was also afraid of what it might lead me to. I was afraid of what I might do. I was afraid that if I started to roar I would never stop.

A man whose penis isn't working, who is cut off from his sexuality, will do anything to get that feeling back. He will go through any contortion. His penis is *him*, as he knows at some deep level. If he doesn't have that, what does he have? A man also, at difficult moments in his life, has a way of getting things confused that don't essentially have anything to do with each other. If he can't succeed in *this* (his career), if all his hopes and dreams have been shattered, he will by God succeed in *that* (the sexual realm – he will become one of the great fuckers of women on earth). He takes energy from the one and uses it for the other. It is also the case that, if he is feeling rage in his body but doesn't want to admit its true source – doesn't want to admit (it's so humiliating!) that the world has shattered his hopes – he may direct that rage toward other people. Writers who have succeeded, for example. Those crummy bastards who have kept him from getting what he wants. Or people who are close to him. Easily accessible objects of anger. His wife.

"I want to eat you," he said.

In anger, in fatigue – for the thousandth time – she closed her eyes. "No."

"Why can't we at least try it?"

"Because I don't like it. I've told you a million times I don't like it."

"I'm not everybody else."

"I wish you *were* everybody else."

How had he wound up with the one person in the world who wouldn't do this thing he liked so much?

"When you want to do this," she said, "you're not really here with me. You're off in your head with one of your dream women. If you were really here with me, if you really wanted to be with me, you'd want to do what I want."

"I want you to be my dream woman for a while. That would be so wonderful to me. I'd love you forever if you'd do that."

"I'd like you to love me for what I am."

"Couldn't you do this for me? Out of love?"

"That wouldn't be love. That would be make-believe. I'd be a whore."

"What's wrong with a little make-believe?"

"I want you to be *here*. With *me*. I never feel you here with me. If you could do that, if you could be more with me, it might be more like you want."

Bullshit. It would never be like what he wanted.

"Besides," she said. "If it weren't this it would be something else. I'd do this and you'd go to the next thing. You'd find another thing I don't want to do. And you'd harp on that. You'd keep going until you found something. You want to have something to be angry about."

He honestly believed he would be happy if he got that one thing. Or maybe two things, on the outside. He couldn't understand why she wouldn't at least try. Was he never going to have anything in this world that he wanted?

A woman feels love and wants to have sex. A man has sex and comes to feel love. In the normal course of things, this delicate distinction gets blurred over. It all just kind of happens together, love and sex. But if a man and woman grow too far apart, the distinction looms larger. There is no way to get them back together. It is what you call a Mexican stand-off. Nobody moves.

You can't suck her tits you can't eat her pussy you can't so much as brush by her asshole she won't suck your cock. What else is there? What's left?

Those long nights in the dorm room, the curtains open, moonlight streaming in on the rumpled bed, the endless conversations, quiet laughter, all that happy fucking. What happened?

*   *   *

When you are fucking a woman who no longer loves you, who doesn't want to fuck you, who doesn't want to be there beneath you, you can feel it. You can feel the boundaries on her body. Touch the wrong place and she goes dead. You can feel the body's profound uneasiness beneath you. It squirms. It sweats. It would like to throw you off. It would like to throw you through the roof. You are using this body. You can feel that you are using it. You are not fucking a person. You are fucking a hole in the middle of a body. You work hard above it – sweating, groaning – trying to finish so you can get off and leave it alone. You have gotten the message. Finally you gasp at your climax, and you hear the body beneath you heave a large sigh. It is not a sigh of pleasure. It is a sigh of relief. It says, Thank God *that's* over. I don't have to do *that* anymore.

Such an act does not bring you closer to someone. It drives you further away. Until finally, one day, she is gone altogether.

When my marriage had ended, when Sara had been gone for about three months, I met my therapist late one afternoon when everyone else had left the building. I'd been seeing him at that point for almost a year. He closed the doors; I loosened my clothes; he handed me a foam-rubber encounter bat. For the next forty minutes, while he urged me on, I beat the living piss out of his office. I roared. I screamed. I stomped the floor. I shouted out all my irrational hatred and bitterness. I shouted at him. I shouted at the world. I tore into it. When I finally finished, my voice was gone, and every muscle in my body was exhausted – I could hardly stand – but I also felt, for the first time in years, utterly relaxed. I felt whole and together. My body was mine, in a way that it hadn't been for as long as I could remember. And my cock felt heavy. Hanging there like a slab of meat. There was much more to do. There were many more feelings to explore, over a long period of grief. But they all started in that blind wordless rage.

EQUINOX

Samuel R. Delany

THE COLOR OF bell metal:

Longer than a big man's foot; thick as a small girl's wrist. Veins made low relief like vines beneath the wrinkled hood. His fingers climbed the shaft, dropped to hair tight as wire, moved under the canvas flaps to gouge the sac, black as an over-ripe avocado: spilled his palm (it is a big hand); climbed the shaft again.

There is little light.

What's here bars the shutters in gold. Water lisps and whispers outside. The cabin sways, rises. There is a wind out to sea, that means. That means here at port it is clear evening.

The dog on the floor claws the planks.

The captain's toes spread the footboard. His chin went back and his belly made black ridges. The long head rolled on the pillow, brass ring at his ear a-flash.

The hood slipped from the punctured helmet.

The knuckles, like knots in weathered cable, flexed on him. The rhythm started with the boat's sway. Increase: his hand and the boat syncopate. The doubled pace pulled his buttocks from the blanket. The rim of his fist beat the tenderer rim (one color with his palm). His breath got loud. It halted, and halted, and halted.

Stop action film: a white orchid from bud to bloom.

Breath regular.

Mucus drips his knuckles. Still stiff, the shaft glistens. Pearls on black wire.

"Kirsten?"

He swung his feet over the edge, his shoulders hunched (dull as cannon shot); his dirty shirt was sleeveless. Buttons: copper.

"Kirsten!"

His voice: maroons, purples, a nap between velvet and suede.

"Come down here!"

When the door cracked, he laughed.

Her hair was yellow, paler than the light. Her smock, torn at her neck, hung between her breasts. One dull aureole rose on the blue horizon. Her face moved with its laughter before she saw, "Captain, you . . .?" saw, and smothered it, to have it break again. Blue eyes widened in the half dark. "What do you want?"

She stepped on to the rug. A copper anklet sloped beneath the knob of her ankle, crossed low on her calloused heel. (Uneven hem brushes smudged knees.) A print sash bound her belly.

"Where is your brother?"

"In the wheelhouse, asleep."

"Where were you?"

"On deck. I was sitting in the sun."

"With the men on the docks all coming by to stare? How many with their hands in their pockets?"

"Oh . . .!"

"None of them with what I got." He leaned back. His fingers tracked his stomach. "Come here. Tell me what's for supper."

"Your thoughts have gone as high as your gut, now?"

"How do you and the boy get chores done if you sleep and sun all the time?"

"But what is there to do in port?" She stepped across the rug, laughing.

He grabbed her wrist. She stumbled and he caught: "How many times!"

She pushed his chest. Her wrist turned under slippery fingers. "Five times? Six? I'll say seven –"

"But see, you've already –"

"Once already. Six more now." He kneaded her inner thigh. "*Captain* . . .!" She tried to pull away.

His hand went beneath the hem.

She shrieked and bit the sound off. What spilled after was a giggle.

"How many years have I had you two, now?" His forearm shifted like bunched blacksnakes. She tried to push his hand from under her skirt. Stopped trying.

She opened her lips and caressed his arm.

"How many years? Seven. Now, once for each year you've worked on my boat." He looked down at himself.

She touched where he looked: she took it, slipping the loose skin from the head. When she fingered beneath the twice full bag, he arched his back.

"Pig. Sit on it. Little white pig . . ." Three calloused fingers were knuckle deep in her. She bent; her hair swept his face. He caught it in his yellow teeth, twisted his head. Kirsten grabbed at her hair, and made an ugly sound. His teeth opened on laughter; it and her hair spilled black lips mottled with cerise.

Barking.

Claws at wood.

Black paws and long muzzle lapped the bunk. The captain kicked the dog with his bare foot (the big chain around his ankle jangles). "Down, Niger! Down, you stupid dog!"

Down; then back, nuzzling between them: dog's tongue. One color: Kirsten's nipple, the dog's tongue, the captain's palm. Niger lapped her crotch for salt.

"Down, Niger!"

The dog barked.

Then the captain looked up: frowned.

One shutter had swung open. A woman's face pressed the glass (dock-side of the boat), tongue caught at the corner of her mouth. Her fingers tipped the sill. Sunlight behind her exploded in loose hair, dimmed her features. Niger barked at her once more.

Her eyes shifted; she saw the captain. Her mouth opened, her palm slapped the pane, a sail of sunlight slapped the far wall: the window cleared and burned.

Niger wheeled the room, leapt on the door. It banged the hatchway wall. Claws clicked at the ladder. The door swung slowly back.

The captain: frowning. But Kirsten's hair, brushing his neck, fell from his face like lame, swept back from hers: she had not seen.

One knee was beside his left hip, one beside his right. She swayed, pulling at her brush; dug in the lips. His head lodged. Her hair rasped the plum glans. He gasped and grabbed her head.

Her lips struck his. His mashed open and swallowed hers. His tongue troweled her teeth; her teeth opened. He licked the roof of her mouth. He pressed her neck, her shoulders. Her breasts, bared now, bulged between the black bars his fingers made.

Gold brush lowered to iron wool.

Their mouths were windy with one another's breath. He thrust, and caught her lips in his teeth. She fell, clutching him. Tried to push away. He took her buttocks, his thumb tobogganing her, moist. He opened the wrinkled bud. She tried to block his tongue with her tongue. She failed.

He rolled with her. His knuckles scraped the wall. When she was beneath him, he braced his feet on the footboard and twisted on her. His belly slapped her. She tried to hold him in with her legs, but he pulled up, to fall, and: her fingers arched his neck, mashed his rough hair, arched. He rocked faster than the boat around them.

In stop action: an ice shard melts in a copper cup.

He lay on her. Her hair was wet to brass blades on her neck. He touched them with his tongue. Then he pushed himself up.

She gargled and reached for him. He glistened above her. (She sees him glance at the porthole, does not understand why.)

Her fingers palped the gold and coral wound.

"Two!" he panted. "Turn over."

Her eyes were closed, her legs apart. She moved her head on the crushed blanket, hands on her stomach.

"Turn *over*!"

He grabbed her leg and pulled. She felt lazy, she felt hysterical. Opened her eyes as he yanked her ankle again. (Why was he staring at the porthole? The light, like blood, varnished his big lips, his flat nose, flamed on his sloping brow till rough, rough hair soaked it up.) "Owww . . .!"

Her knee struck the floor. She stretched her arms over the blanket, and rocked her face on the damp, hot wool. The smell of him: she moved her lips there, her tongue. The taste of him.

The captain breathed hard. He raised his hand, high, drew back lips and shoulder and hip.

Crack!

Her buttocks shook. Redness bloomed and faded. She gasped, then bit her tongue. His hand swung back the other way. She gasped again.

He pulled apart her cheeks, puckered his lips, and pushed out his saliva. It trailed in the discolored cleft. When the foamy tear reached the sphincter, he leaned on her. The hood peeled. Entrance, and her shoulders came up. The heat of her surprised him. He caught a breath: then let it chuckle from him as he eased. Kirsten clutched the end of the mattress. He grasped her wrists, fell. She screamed, and her back, wiggling, slid under his chest. He hissed, "Swing it." He whispered: "That's right, girl." He hissed again, "Dance on that black stick, little monkey!"

Soft things slipped and broke. Something with points crumbled as he tunneled and plunged. Her buttocks mashed and spread under the blades of his pelvis. He bit her shoulder, kneaded the skin in his big teeth till it bruised burgundy.

He let go of her arm, felt under her belly. He thumbed the dry hairs; thumbed the wet. Four bunched fingers, in and in further. He spread them in her slop.

She made sounds in her chest.

He felt his swollen passage beyond her, wet and tender. His thumb, again, slipped under the thickening tab folded in the roof.

Her sounds were between simper and growl. Her smock was a wet roll at her back's small. She heaved at him. When he withdrew, she butted up to impale. His down stroke pushed her to the bed. And again. And.

In marble: white rock crumbles from the freshet.

In the shadow his back shone. Heavy, twinned breath. Sweat ran Kirsten's side, curved at her breast bulging out.

". . . three," while cooler air came between her back and his belly when he pulled –

"No! Don't take it . . ."

He stood, panting. His shirt lay on the floor. His belt dangled at each hip. The canvas pants creased down over his buttocks. "Once more . . ."

"You're not tired yet?" She let herself slip to her knees beside the bed. The triangle of sheet by the bunched blanket was wet. He let his knees bend, touched her back. As his hand walked on her shoulder she dropped her head back. He scratched her neck, ran his forefinger in the damp troughs of her ear. He cradled her head when she rolled it over his palm. (It is a big hand.) Her hair fell in ingots on his forearm. His fingers deviled them to cloudy snarls.

Through the closed shutter bars of light reddened the bedding. The captain reached to close the other. It swung to, the catch failed, and it swung out again. He made a fist in her hair.

"You want more?"

". . . no," all breathy.

"You want it!"

"But Gunner has tired me out, all this morning –" her smile a grimace as he tugged. She let her face fall against his thigh.

"Kiss it. That little dirty-face has made you hot for more. Yes? You don't, and I'll beat you and that little brother of yours. Kiss it all over, with your tongue."

She swiveled her cheek on his hip. "But it's all . . ." She slid her hand into the sweaty fold between leg and sack. ". . . all soft."

"You make it hard." He pushed her into it.

"And dirty!" She tried to pull away.

"It's your dirt."

She made muffled contest, but he pressed her face in. When he took his hand away, she didn't pull back. Her tongue went warm in the crevice. He grinned, and fingered her hair back. She took the limp length in her hands, opened her mouth, and tongued him to the hilt hair.

"Underneath. Go down underneath. Get it all in, girl. Before it gets too big." He moved his legs.

"There's a lot of junk in the pockets. Tongue . . . hungry. Yeah! Be sweet to it. That's where I like to see you. Be hungry. Be hungry and eat me. Hey, don't back away! Take it, deep." He brushed her distended cheek with bunched knuckles. "It's going, yeah, down. All the way. Get ready. Yeah," and, "Yeah . . ." and, "Oh, yeah!" He held her hair. Hardness and then soft ridges over his thrust. He swiveled to mash his hair on her mouth, till he felt her gag constrict him. He let her retreat to breathe, then filled her throat again. "Yeah . . .

"Go underneath again." He took his shining stock in his left fist; his right pushed her down; pushed half of the sack in her mouth with his thumb.

"Tongue it. That's good –"

He tapped her. "Watch your teeth! No nutcrackers. A little

tickle." His left fist swung the long arc, fell at her face. "Now the other one . . . fine!"

He breathed like a dog. She held his hips and rocked her face between his legs.

"In your mouth, girl. Or let me leak it on your face . . ."

She swallowed him, and felt the under tube swell down her tongue, retreat, swell again. In a geyser of black mud, a sudden eruption of white froth (Eruption . . .)

and he pushed: thrust, and gout, thrust, thrust, gout.

He held his breath, and let her fall against the bed's edge. The black, bright length wrinkled, sagged. Her lips glistened. Her eyes were closed.

He sat on the bed and began to take loud breaths. She moved between his legs to lay her head on his groin. He moved one finger over her forehead, wiping wet brass from beaded alabaster. She put her palm on it, pressed it on her cheek.

"Why are you so tired," he asked, "after so little?"

She opened her eyes. "Gunner worried at me all morning, I say. Please, Captain. Let me go up and rest for a while. I'll come back, maybe after only an hour or so."

"And leave me to make love to my fists? First the left, after that the right. What then? I can't lap myself like Niger."

"You've had me every way! What else do you —"

He squeezed her breast; Kirsten closed her eyes. "Oh, yes, I know the things you think of." She looked up again. "Let me go upstairs. I'll send Gunner down."

He frowned.

"Finish with him. I'm too tired."

"He tired you out for me?" The captain tongued his lower lip. "Wake him up."

"I will. Right now." She stood.

She tried not to let him see her smile as she bent to pull her bunched shift down her hips. She shrugged into the sleeve, tried to cover her breast.

The captain fingered himself.

The torn cloth would not cover her any more.

Suddenly Kirsten got a strange expression. She reached quickly, took his face in her hands and thrust her tongue way in his mouth. He licked it. But when he reached beneath her hem she pulled away.

"I'll send Gunner!"

She turned and ran through the lines of sun.

In the minute alone he thinks about the currents that have brought them here. He thinks about light, and suddenly he remembers the woman at the pane. He turns to look.

"Captain?"

Knuckling his eyes, sleepy Gunner came in. His hair, pale as his sister's, pawed his neck, rioted at his forehead.

"Come here."

The boy walked over the rug, paused. The captain patted the blanket, so the boy sat. He took the back of Gunner's neck between thumb and forefinger. Shook him.

Gunner grinned: there were twin acne spots left of his mouth. He touched the captain. "What am I gonna do with this elephant?"

The captain moved his palm on the boy's bony back. "You've done half of it already." And shook again. "Hey, little mule. Kirsten says you tried to climb her back and break into her with your Johnny stick."

Gunner looked at his lap. The captain slipped two fingers into the buttonless fly. Gunner looked up. "I did not!" But grinned.

"What did you do?"

"I nosed her to see if I could smell anything you'd left there." He touched the captain's knee. Small hand: it has callouses from boat work, the nails quick bitten. His grin fell open into a smile. "Got my face wet. And she wouldn't let go my head."

"Did she kiss you back between your legs?"

"She wanted to. But I hid him in my hands." Gunner pulled apart his fly. Johnny jumped. Little brass wires snarled through the captain's fingers. Gunner frowned. "It's not half as long as yours."

Maroon and purple: suede and velvet.

"You're not half as old as I am. He's big enough for you, boy. You still need both hands to hide him when he's hard. Hey, take care of me. A couple or three times."

Gunner picked the captain's up.

The captain pushed his fingers under Gunner's rope belt. Most loops were broken. The waist pulled down on the boys buttocks. The captain lay his finger in the hot slip.

"You want my mouth?" Gunner dug the black fruit up. "That's why you wake me up?"

"So."

"Suppose I'm not thirsty."

"You?"

Gunner bent. The head rose and blunted on his mouth. Black hand grapples gold hair, pulls the boy up, gasping. "That's not where I want it –"

"Captain . . .?"

The black hand, kneading Gunner's buttocks, worked to the boy's belly. White and black fingers worked on the knot. As it came loose, he pushed the boy's head forward. He swung his leg back and kicked. The boy fell on the small rug. Knot undone, his trousers slipped to his knees.

The captain stood. He worked his thumb into the sweaty crevice siding his groin; swung like a crane. He stepped from the eight his pants made at his ankles.

Brass ring in his left ear (leather banding his right wrist), the heavy black chain on his left ankle. (That's all.) He stood above the boy.

Gunner stared.

The captain put his foot between the boy's legs. The groin was hot on the knuckles of his toes. Toes rose to prod the crack. He got down on his knees.

Gunner licked his fingers and wiped between his legs. "Lemme stick it up before –"

The captain knocked Gunner's hand away. "It's slick enough." He pushed, swiveled forward inches more, pushed straight again.

Gunner stopped breathing.

The captain put his arms around Gunner's chest. Once the boy barked in pain. The captain slid his hand between their bellies. "You're stiff as a ten penny. It doesn't hurt that much." His hips hunched.

Gunner caught his breath again.

But no sound. Backed and squirmed on it.

The captain's breath roared around his head like a rasp in a clay pipe: Gunner puppy-pants.

Unable to the double weight, their arms bent. The captain pulled him onto the floor. On his side, first; then, with Gunner, breath nearly out of him, the captain flexed.

He lay on his side, thrust in Gunner's gut, while the boy,

on his back, to the hips' rocking, pulled at himself. Gunner's head pressed back on the captain's chest. His feet bunched the rug between the black knees. Raised himself. Lowered himself.

Gas growled out around him. Something small gave before the plunging, became hot paste. The captain stirred in the tight tunnel. He had a mouth full of Gunner's hair; he held the boy with one hand. Two fingers from the other in Gunner's mouth, a tongue grazing their salt and horn.

In a salt cave the thrower flames.

The captain panted. "Five . . . for me, now."

Gunner's fist still swung at his groin.

The captain closed the boy's fist in his to stop it. "Hold off unless you want to go again."

Gunner, still now, asked, "You messed in Kirsten all day. You still want to squeeze more out of these?" Sitting on the captain's hips, he reached between both their legs and picked up the big sack.

The captain laughed. He pushed Gunner's cheeks. "Get up. Go on."

Making a face, the boy eased forward. Soft, it slapped the captain's thigh. Gunner turned and scratched himself. "How many more you got?"

The captain folded his arms behind his head. "Another couple." He stretched. "Work me over."

The boy blinked.

The captain raised his head. "Lick my foot. Come on, get that look off. I want to see you lick my foot. Last week I saw you lick at Niger behind the locker. You can with a dog, you can with my foot. Go on."

Gunner held the calloused rim, laid his cheek on it. The captain felt the lips tickle the instep. Tongue fell from the boy's mouth; moved on the rough ball, found the trough before the toes; bladed between the big toe and the next, moved over the thick nail. Gunner took three toes in his mouth. The captain wriggled them, laughed. "Niger left his pile on the foredeck. I stepped in it before I came down here – don't pull back. Clean it. Look at you. Look what that does to you. Look good for me, boy." His knee bent, and the boy's lips whispered on his ankle, wrapped the chain, stuck tongue in the links. Gunner's fingers spread on his

belly, moved jerkily to his tight yellow hair. The head, grey as a
pale grape, pushed from its ivory cap.

"Work, boy!" The captain pulled his foot back, kicked Gunner's face. He laughed.

Gunner's knees struck the rug. He opened his mouth on the
dark thigh. The captain caught the boy's hair, yanked him down.

Claws on the passage steps –

– Niger sprang through the door, hind legs, pawed the captain's knee.

"Black devil! Down!" Niger backed up, then dropped his black
muzzle beside Gunner's blond head in the dark fork. The
captain's lips parted. His back rose from the rug. On shoulders
and heels he pushed into Gunner's face. The boy put one arm
around the dog's neck. He looked up, once, mouth, cheek and
chin wet.

The captain rocked back and grabbed the hollow of his knees.
Gunner's face pushed; stroke, probe. Niger's tongue rolled the
captain's sack over to hang on his belly.

The captain bellowed, swung his legs down. His heels hit the
floor. Niger and Gunner scampered.

On his feet the captain lurched to the bunk, turned, and sat.
His knees were wide. Saliva made his thighs dark mirrors. He
gripped the shining tower to beat. Up to the paler ring. "Six
coming . . ." the captain panted. "First one here gets it."

Niger and Gunner raced the floor. Niger leapt on the captain's
right knee, dug his snout beneath the loose bag. Gunner humped
the left harder than the dog, fell to it.

The captain beat the boy's lips a half dozen strokes. Gunner
held the edge of the bed and learned back. He tongued under the
foreflesh. It rammed over his tongue, bruised palates, hard and
soft, prodded in the softer throat. "Take it. Eat that charred meat
all up, you white . . . Yeah . . ." He pressed the boy's head down,
and down, ground upon the face while Niger nipped and nuzzled.
"Here it . . . here . . ." he grunted at the ceiling. Heat swelled the
shaft, stretched the boy's mouth.

The black crater, quiet the hour, erupts. Oceans boil. The
captain sagged forward over Gunner's back. "Six . . ."

Gunner twisted under the captain's belly. "Get off my
head."

"Six, you little white squirrel!"

Niger had pulled away, was lying on the rug. He worried something between his paws.

The captain sat up. Gunner hung over his knees. His face was wet. "What about seven?" Gunner asked.

"Give it a rest."

Gunner picked up the limp. "It's tired, now, you think?"

The captain roughed the boy's hair. "You'd lap after it whatever." He frowned at the dog. "What's Niger got?"

Gunner looked over his shoulder. "Something he must have picked up when he went out."

"Go get it."

Gunner went to the dog. He pulled and played it away. The jaws gave up; Niger started to lick at Gunner. "He's getting me all hard again." He pushed Niger's head down. "It's a wallet." He took it to the captain and sat down on the bed. While the captain paged through the leather folder, Gunner tugged up his pants and tried to get the rope back through the functioning loops. Once he leaned over the captain's arm. "Pictures?"

The captain was looking at the portal.

"Hey?" Gunner said. "What about seven?"

The captain pushed the boy's hand from his thigh. Gunner put his hand between his own legs. He leaned against the captain's arm.

There was a color polaroid of a woman one side of the wallet, one of a man on the other. Her hair was loose in a wind that had caused her the slightest squint. His was white, or very pale. The faces suggested age, or experience. But they were handsome, and strong. Perhaps it was the contrast to the pale hair – perhaps shadow and position – but the man's eyes looked black.

Gunner pushed his nose under the dark arm and nuzzled the hair. The captain stood. "I'm going on deck." He reached for his pants. "Come on, Niger." He shrugged into his shirt. He kicked at the dog, and his chain rang. Niger barked, then followed the captain to the door.

He stopped once, frowned at the portal; then he saw Gunner. "On deck when you're done."

Gunner sat on the bed, cross-legged. He ran his hand over the damp sheet. Let himself fall, to lay his cheek, roll his face

and take the salty folds in his teeth. Elbow shaking, one hand
worked in arcs. The other kneaded his belly. His lips kissed
unvoiced exhortations. Closed lids and the loose hair shook
with his fist.

The cabin door closed.

THE BUTCHER

Alina Reyes

Translated from the French by David Watson

NEITHER OF US said a word. I watched the movement of the windscreen wipers. I grew sluggish with the smell of my wet hair next to my cheeks.

He opened the door, took me by the hand. My sandals were full of water, my feet squelched against the plastic soles. He led me to the lounge, sat me down, brought me a coffee. Then he turned on the radio and asked me to excuse him for five minutes. He had to take a shower.

I went over to the window, pulled the curtain open a little and watched the rain falling.

The rain made me want to piss. When I came out of the toilet I pushed open the bathroom door. The room was warm and all steamed up. I saw the broad silhouette through the shower curtain. I pulled it open a little and looked at him. He reached out a hand but I pulled away. I offered to scrub his back. I stepped onto the rim, put my hands under the warm water and picked up the soap, turning it over between my palms until I worked up a thick lather.

I began to rub his back, starting at the neck and shoulders, in circular movements. He was big and pale, firm and muscular. I worked my way down his spine, a hand on each side. I rubbed his sides, moving round a little onto his stomach. The soap made a fine scented froth, a cobweb of small white bubbles flowing over the wet skin, a slippery soft carpet between my palm and his back.

I went up and down the spine several times, from the small of the back to the base of the neck up to the first little hairs, the ones the barber shaves off for short haircuts with his deliciously vibrating razor.

I set off again from the shoulders and soaped each arm in turn. Although the limbs were relaxed, I felt bulging knots of muscle. His forearms were covered with dark hairs; I had to really wet the soap to make the lather stick. I worked back towards the deep hairy armpits.

I lathered up my hands again and massaged his buttocks in a revolving motion. Though on the big side, his buttocks had a harmonious shape, curving gracefully from the small of the back and joining the lower limbs without flab. I went over and over their roundness to know their form with my palms as well as with my eyes. Then I moved down the hard solid legs. The hairy skin covered barriers of muscle. I felt I was penetrating a new, wilder region of the body down to the strange treasure of the ankles.

Then he turned towards me. I raised my head and saw his swelling balls, his taut cock, straight above my eyes.

I got up. He didn't move. I took the soap between my hands again and began to clean his broad, solid, moderately hairy chest.

I began to move slowly down over his distended stomach, surrounded by powerful abdominal muscles. It took some time to cover the whole surface. His navel stood out, a small white ball outlined by the rounded mass, a star around which my fingers gravitated, straining to delay the moment when they would succumb to the downward pull towards the comet erected against the harmonious round form of the stomach.

I knelt down to massage his abdomen. I skirted round the genital area slowly, quite gently, towards the inside of the thighs.

His penis was incredibly large and erect.

I resisted the temptation to touch it, continuing to stroke over the pubis and between the legs. He was now lying back against the wall, his arms spread, with both hands pressed against the tiles, his stomach jutting forward. He was groaning.

I felt he was going to come before I even touched him.

I moved away, sat down fully under the shower spray, and with my eyes still fixed on his over-extended penis, I waited until he calmed down a little.

The warm water ran over my hair, inside my dress. Filled with steam, the air frothed around us, effacing all shapes and sounds.

He had been at the peak of excitement, and yet had made no move to hasten the denouement. He was waiting for me. He would wait as long as I wanted to make the pleasure last, and the pain.

I knelt down in front of him again. His cock, already thickly inflated, sprang up.

I moved my hand over his balls, back up to their base near the anus. His cock stood up again, more violently. I held it in my other hand, squeezed it, began slowly pulling it up and down. The soapy water I was lathered with provided perfect lubrication. My hands were filled with a warm, living, magical substance. I felt it beating like the heart of a bird, I helped it ride to its deliverance. Up, down, always the same movement, always the same rhythm, and the moans above my head. And I was moaning too, with the water from the shower sticking my dress to me like a tight silken glove, with the world stopped at the level of my eyes, of his belly, at the sound of the water trickling over us and of his cock sliding under my fingers, at the warm and tender and hard things between my hands, at the smell of the soap, of the soaking flesh and of the sperm mounting under my palm.

The liquid spurted out in bursts, splashing my face and my dress.

He knelt down as well, and licked the tears of sperm from my face. He washed me the way a cat grooms itself, with diligence and tenderness.

His plump white hand, his pink tongue on my cheek, his washed-out blue eyes, the eyelids still heavy as if under the effect of a drug. And his languid heavy body, his body of plenitude . . .

A green tender field of showers in the soft breeze of the branches . . . It is autumn, it is raining, I am a little girl, I am walking in the park and my head is swimming because of the smells, of the water on my skin and my clothes, I see a fat man over there on the bench looking at me so intently that I pee myself, standing up, I am walking and I am peeing myself, it is my warm rain on the park, on the ground, in my knickers, I rain, I give pleasure . . .

He took off my dress, slowly.

Then he stretched me out on the warm tiles and, with the shower still running, began planting kisses all over my body. His powerful hands lifted me up and turned me over with extreme delicacy. Neither the hardness of the floor nor the pressure of his fingers could bruise me.

I relaxed completely. And he placed the pulp of his lips, the wetness of his tongue in the hollow of my arms, under my breasts, on my neck, behind my knees, between my buttocks, he put his mouth all over, the length of my back, the inside of my legs, right to the roots of my hair.

He lay me on my back on the ground, on the warm slippery tiles, lifted my hips with both hands, his fingers firmly thrust into the hollow as far as the spine, his thumbs on my stomach. He placed my legs over his shoulders and brought his tongue up to my vulva. I arched my back sharply. Thousands of drops of water from the shower hit me softly on my stomach and on my breasts. He licked me from my vagina to my clitoris, regularly, his mouth stuck to my outer lips. My sex became a channelled surface from which pleasure streamed, the world disappeared, I was no more than this raw flesh where soon gigantic cascades splashed, in sequence, continually, one after the other, forever.

Finally the tension slackened, my buttocks fell back onto his arms, I recovered gradually, felt the water on my stomach, saw the shower once more, and him, and me.

He had dried me off, put me in the warm bed, and I had fallen asleep.

I woke up slowly to the sound of the rain against the tiles. The sheets and pillow were warm and soft. I opened my eyes. He was lying next to me, looking at me. I placed my hand on his sex. He wanted me again.

I wanted nothing else but that. To make love, all the time, without rage, with patience, persistence, methodically. Go on to the end. He was like a mountain I must climb to the summit, like in my dreams, my nightmares. It would have been best to emasculate him straight away, to eat this still hard still erect still demanding piece of flesh, to swallow it and keep it in my belly, for ever more.

I drew close, raise myself a little, put my arms around him. He took my head between his hands, led my mouth to his, thrust his tongue in all at once, wiggled it at the back of my throat, wrapped it and rolled it over mine. I began biting his lips till I tasted blood.

Then I mounted on top of him, pressed my vulva against his sex, rubbed it against his balls and his cock. I guided it by hand and pushed it into me and it was like a giant flash, the dazzling entry of the saviour, the instantaneous return of grace.

I raised my knees, bent my legs around him and rode him vigorously. Each time when at the crest of the wave I saw his cock emerge glistening and red I held it again and tried to push it even further in.

I was going too fast. He calmed me down gently. I unfolded my legs and lay on top of him. I lay motionless for a moment, contracting the muscles of my vagina around his member.

I chewed him over the expanse of his chest; an electric charge flowed through my tongue, my gums. I rubbed my nose against the fat of his white meat, inhaled its smell, trembling. I was squinting with pleasure. The world was no more than a vibrant abstract painting, a clash of marks the colour of flesh, a well of soft matter I was sinking into with the joyous impulse of perdition. A vibration coming from my eardrums took over my head, my eyes closed. An extraordinarily sharp awareness spread with the waves surging through my skull, it was like a flame, and my brain climaxed, alone and silent, magnificently alone.

He rolled over onto me, and rode me in turn, leaning on his hand so as not to crush me. His balls rubbed against my buttocks, at the entry to my vagina, his hard cock filled me, slid and slid along my deep walls, I dug my nails into his buttocks, he breathed more heavily . . . We came together, on and on, our fluids mingled, our groans mingled, coming from further than the throat, the depths of our chests, sounds alien to the human voice.

It was raining. Enveloped in a large T-shirt which he had lent me I was leaning on the window-sill, kneeling on the chair placed against the wall.

If I knew the language of the rain, of course, I would write it down, but everyone recognizes it, and is able to recall it to their memory. Being in a closed space while outside all is water, trickling, drowning . . . Making love in the cramped backseat of a car, while the windows and roof resonate with the monotonous rain drops . . . The rain undoes bodies, makes them full of softness and damp patches . . . slimy and slobbering like snails . . .

He was also wearing a T-shirt, lying on the couch, his big buttocks, his big genitals, and his big legs bare.

He came over to me and pressed his hard cock against my buttocks. I wanted to turn round but he grabbed me by the hair, pulled my head back and began to push himself into my anus. It hurt, and I was trapped on the chair, condemned to keep my head pointing skywards.

Finally he entered fully, and the pain subsided. He began to move up and down, I was full of him, I could feel nothing except his huge monster cock right inside, whilst outside the bucketing rain poured down pure liquid light.

Continuing to jerk himself in me, to dig at me like a navvy while keeping my head held back, he slid two fingers into my vagina, then pulled them out. So I put in my own and felt the hard cock pounding behind the lining, and I began to fondle myself to the same rhythm. He speeded up his thrusts, my excitement grew, a mixture of pain and pleasure. His stomach bumped against my back with each thrust of the hips, and he penetrated me a bit further, invaded me a bit further. I wanted to free my head but he pulled my hair even harder, my throat was horribly stretched, my eyes were turned stubbornly towards the emptying sky, and he struck me and hammered me to the depths of myself, he shook up my body and then filled me with his hot liquid which came out in spurts, striking me softly, pleasurably.

A large drop would regularly drip somewhere with the sound of hollow metal. He let go of my hair, I let my head sink against the casement and began to sway imperceptibly.

I had him undress and stretch out on his back on the ground. With the expanders on his exercise machine I tied his arms to the foot of the bed, his legs to those of the table.

We were both tired. I sat down in the armchair and looked at him for a moment, spread-eagled and motionless.

His body pleased me like that, full of exposed imprisoned flesh, burst open in its splendid imperfection. Uprooted man, once more pinned to the ground, his sex like a fragile pivot exiled from the shadows and exposed to the light of my eyes.

Everything would have to be a sex; the curtains, the moquette, the expanders and the furniture, I would need a sex instead of my head, another instead of his.

We would both need to be hanging from an iron hook face to face in a red fridge, hooked by the top of the skull or the ankles, head down, legs spread, our flesh face to face, rendered powerless to the knife of our sexes burning like red-hot irons, brandished, open. We would need to scream ourselves to death under the tyranny of our sexes, what are our sexes?

Last summer, first acid, I lost my hands first of all, and then my name, the name of my race, lost humanity from my memory, from the knowledge of my head and of my body, lost the idea of man, of woman, or even of creature; I sought for a while, who am I? My sex. My sex remained to the world, with its desire to piss. The only place where my soul had found refuge, had become concentrated, the only place where I existed, like an atom, wandering between sky and grass, between green and blue, with no other feeling than that of a pure atom-sex, just, barely, driven by the desire to piss, gone astray, blissful, in the light, Saint-Laurent peninsula, it was one summer's day, no it was autumn, it took me all night and the next morning to come down, but for months afterwards when I pissed I lost myself, the moment of dizziness that's it, I draw myself back entirely into my sex as if into a navel, my being is there in that sensation in the centre of the body, the rest of the body annihilated, I no longer know myself, have no form nor title, the ultimate trip each time and sometimes still, just an instant, like being hung head down in the great spiral of the universe, but only you know what those moments mean, afterwards I say to myself "is that really who I am?" and "how beautiful the world is, with all those bunches of black grapes, how good it is to go grape-picking at the height of summer, with the sun catching the grapes and the eyes of the pickers, the vines are twisted, how I'd love to piss at the end of the row!", and there are all sorts of stupid things like that in our bodies, so good do we feel after that weird dizziness which we miss a little, nevertheless, already.

I got up, knelt with my legs apart above his head. Still out of range of his face, I pulled open my outer lips with my fingers and gave him a long look at my vulva.

Then I stroked it slowly, with a rotating movement, from my anus to my clitoris.

I would have wanted grey skies where hope is focused, where quivering trees spread their fairy arms, capricious, hot-headed dreams in the grass kissed by the wind, I would have wanted to feel between my legs the huge breath of the millions of men on earth. I would have wanted, look, look at what I want . . .

I pushed the fingers of my left hand into my vagina, continued to rub myself. My fingers are not my fingers, but a heavy ingot, a thick square ingot stuck inside me, dazzling with gold to the dark depths of my dream. My hands went faster and faster. I rode the air in spasms, threw my head back, weeping onto his eyes as I came.

I regained the armchair. His face had turned red, he grew erect again, fairly softly. He was defenceless.

When I was small, I knew nothing about love. Making love, that magic word, the promise of that unbelievably wonderful thing which would happen all the time as soon as we were big. I had no idea about penetration, not even about what men have between their legs, in spite of all those showers with my brothers. You can look and look in vain, what do you know, when you have the taste for mystery?

When I was even smaller, no more than four, they talked in front of me thinking that I wasn't listening; Daddy told about a madman who ran screaming through the woods at night. I open the gate of my grandmother's garden, and all alone with my alsatian bitch I enter the woods. At the first gap in the trees, on a mound of sand, I lie down with the bitch, up against her warm flank, an arm around her neck. She puts out her tongue and she waits, like me. No one. The pines draw together and bend over us, in a tender, scary gesture. In the middle of the woods there is a long concrete drain, bordered with brambles where blackberries grow, and where one day a kart driver hurtled violently off the track in front of me and put his eyes out. There is a blockhouse with a black mouth disguised as a door, and right at the end a washing plant devoured by moss and grass. Preserved in the watercourse is the hardened print of an enormous foot.

I went and lay on the ground next to him, laid my head on his stomach, my mouth against his cock, one hand on his balls, and I went to sleep. Certainly the footprint in the wet cement was of a big, strong, blond and probably handsome soldier.

When I woke up next to his penis I took it in my mouth, sucked it in several times with my tongue, felt it swell and touch the back of my throat. I massaged his balls, licked them, then returned to his cock. I placed it in the hollow of both my eyes, on my forehead, on my cheeks, against my nose, on my mouth, my chin, my throat, put my neck on it, squeezed it between my shoulder blades and my bent head, in my armpit, then the other, brushed against it with my breasts till I almost reached a climax, rubbed it with my stomach, my back, my buttocks, my thighs, squeezed it between my arms and my folded legs, pressed the sole of my foot against it, until I had left a trace of it over the whole of my body.

Then I put it back in my mouth and gave it a long suck, like you suck your thumb, your mother's breast, life, while he moaned and panted, always, until he ejaculates, in a sharp lamentation, and I drink his sperm, his sap, his gift.

CHAPTERS IN A PAST LIFE

Marilyn Jaye-Lewis

1 – ANAL

I KNEW A woman who had a virgin asshole until she was in her early 30s. I never understood that kind of woman, she's not at all like me. I'd read about *Last Tango In Paris* in my mother's *Cosmo* when I was only thirteen, for god's sake – and the accompanying article, too, all about how to do it through the back door and, more importantly, why: Because a *Cosmo* girl is an American girl and American girls love pressure.

I don't know if it was related to that distant article or not, but I dropped out of college in a real hurry, after only about six weeks. Something about wanting to feel alive instead, and that's how I ended up in New York; at the tail-end of the disco era, pre-AIDS, a time when any self-respecting underpaid New York office worker drank heavily on his or her lunch hour and didn't have to be choosy about who he or she wanted to fuck when the work day was over because eventually you fucked everybody. And there were so many exciting cross-purposes going on! For instance, drugs. Did you fuck somebody sheerly because she had the good drugs? Or did you use the good drugs as bait to get somebody to fuck you? Of course, if you hung in there long enough, the inevitable descent into hell finally occurred. That's right, you remember it: You fell hopelessly in love with a completely *insane* person, a dangerously paranoid schizophrenic perhaps, but you were too fucked-up on the good drugs to even notice it. Maybe for a couple of years.

When it happened to me, it was with a woman. Back then, she was already twenty years older than me, so *god knows*, if she's still alive now she's using a cane to get around. But she was in fine form in 1980, thin as a rail of course. All bone, no muscle, but that was de rigueur in 1980. We didn't lift free weights. Every ounce of energy was reserved for lifting cocktail glasses off the wet bar (a long distance endurance process) and for raising those teeny-weeny silver spoons, over and over – all right, I won't go on. I guess your memory's a little better than I'd thought . . .

So I'll call her Giselle. Not that her name was anything close to that, but it *was* similarly unpronounceable and she possessed that quick, nervous energy sometimes, reminiscent of the leaping gazelle. And on our first date – or more succinctly – when we hit on each other in that 10th Avenue after-hours meat rack and went home together to fuck like dogs, she was in fine, lithe, energetic form. I know we were kissing in the back seat of that cab, but I don't remember how we got from the cab to her sparsely furnished living room in that huge penthouse apartment in midtown, with the vaulted ceilings and all that glass. That part's a complete blank, but what happened from that point on is clear and that's the sex part and all that matters anyway.

Giselle's husband was apparently loaded. And not one of those cash-poor types, either. He seemed to travel on business constantly – or so he said. At any rate, he was away an awful lot and Giselle had nothing but time and money to take his place. You'd think those two things – time and money – would have been enough, but when you're remarkably thin and nearly forty, and beautiful and sharp and hopelessly underutilized like my dear Giselle, it takes a lot more than time and money to get your rocks completely *off*. Hence, Giselle's insatiable drive toward the strange.

I'd agreed willingly from the outset, I just want that part to be clear. I had my clothes off in a hurry and was letting Giselle douche my ass, simply because she wanted it so much. I was happy to let her do it. I was on my knees and elbows in her half-bath, right off the living room, there. Completely stripped with my ass in the air, a bulb syringe squeezing warm water into my rectum while I had a lit cigarette in one hand and a nice glass of merlot in the other.

When the water had done its trick and we were through making a mess in the half-bath, Giselle led me back to the living room and she showed me the huge leather ottoman, how it lifted open for storing magazines and stuff. But she kept her bag of toys in there. It was a pretty big bag. That leather ottoman was sort of like a Playskool Busy Box for the seriously grown up. When she'd emptied out the ottoman, Giselle encouraged me to bend over it, so she could fasten my wrists securely to the wooden casters underneath. She even had specially made rubber wedges she'd shove under the casters to keep them from rolling all over the carpeting. Right away it occurred to me, when I saw the specially made rubber wedges, that it wasn't likely I was the first girl Giselle had stripped and douched and put over the leather ottoman. But I was okay with that. I drank like a fish and took a lot of drugs back then, so I was usually feeling pretty self-confident.

Once Giselle had secured my wrists, she inserted a steel thigh-spreader between my legs and buckled each padded end snugly around each of my thighs. And even though the thigh-spreader worked fine – it kept me from being able to close my legs – Giselle attached a padded ankle-spreader between my ankles, too. I guess she just wanted to be sure. And then she came around the front of the ottoman, gave me a hit off her cigarette and a couple of slugs of that great merlot.

My head was buzzing. I loved the feeling of being exposed – in fact, forcibly so. Giselle leaned over and kissed my mouth for a while. It made me feel hot. It made my naked backside squirm. When her tongue pushed around inside my mouth, it made my ass arch up and it made me want to have her tongue poking into my hole.

"Look at this," she said.

She pulled a color Polaroid from a leather envelope and placed it on the floor under my face and went away.

I studied the Polaroid picture curiously. It was a picture of a girl much like myself. Well, it was impossible to tell if her face looked anything like mine, but she was totally naked and kneeling over the same ottoman, her legs forcibly spread in the same way, and she was tied down in the same provocatively helpless position. It could have *easily* been a Polaroid of me.

That's when I saw the familiar bright flash coming from behind me and heard the quick grinding sound of the inner workings of the camera. In a mere 60 seconds, the color Polaroid in front of me was replaced by a color Polaroid of myself. It was uncanny, you know; the similarities and all.

We didn't talk anymore after that. Giselle gave me a couple of quick swigs from my glass of merlot and gave me one last drag off the cigarette, then she slipped the gag into my mouth. Tied it pretty tightly, I must say. One of those knots where you just know your hair's in a big gnarly mess in back.

Giselle got undressed somewhere, out of my field of vision. I couldn't see her. But when she straddled my back her slippery pussy was sliding all over my skin. It was obvious she was naked. She leaned down and spoke in my ear confidentially, as she replaced the picture in front of me with yet another one. Of the other girl again.

"She's awfully pretty, honey, don't you think? Her asshole's so tight, would you look at that? Incredible, isn't it?"

I grunted, *uh-huh*, and nodded my gnarly head in agreement.

"Not even a hint of a hemorrhoid, see? This girl's in great shape."

I have to admit, I was a little transfixed; *I'd* never owned a Polaroid camera that took such vivid close-ups! Giselle had obviously invested a fortune in her camera lens.

"She was very well-behaved, if I remember correctly," Giselle went on. "She took it like a champ, that one did. You think you're going to be a good girl, too? Huh? You've been awfully accommodating so far." Giselle began to kiss my neck slowly and she rubbed her wet pussy all over my lower back. "What do you think," she repeated. "You think you're going to be a good girl?"

Uh-huh, I grunted through my gag. I was going to be a very good girl. I was going to be stellar.

"You like things in your ass? You've had things in your ass before, right?"

I nodded my head, yes, but I confess I felt a little tripped up; what did she mean by *things*?

Then a different Polaroid was put in front of my face, a slightly more startling one. "Same girl," Giselle whispered, "but do you notice anything different about her hole?"

It's a huge *gaping* hole, I thought nervously.

"This is how her asshole looked when I was through appreciating her. Pretty remarkable, isn't it?"

Giselle brushed some stray hairs affectionately from my forehead, I guess to make sure my vision wasn't obscured in any way. I was riveted to that Polaroid, the crystal clear close-up of that well-appreciated sphincter.

"Of course, this sort of appreciation takes a few hours," Giselle explained. "You don't have to be anywhere for a while, do you?"

I don't think I really responded to that, I was a little too transfixed. She left the gaping-hole Polaroid on the floor in front of my face and then disappeared somewhere behind me.

The anticipation is always the greatest part, isn't it? Man, you're just waiting and you don't even know what the hell *for*. But you feel real certain that you're going to get it, that it's eventually going to come. And that's the sort of excitement I was feeling; like some mad ferret had chewed his paw free from a steel leghold trap inside me and now he tore wildly around in the darkness of my intestines, wanting very much to find his way out. But that was 1980. *You know* I was young. I was still excited by things like suspense and fear, and the chance to get my asshole reamed by a seriously grown up girl.

It started with a simple strawberry. A bright red one with a long stem. Giselle had straddled my back again and lowered the long stem down in front of my face. She twirled it gently, holding the stem between her thumb and forefinger. "What do you think?" she asked. "Can you take it? It's not too big but it's awfully fragile."

In an instant the bright red berry was gone and Giselle slid her slippery pussy slowly down my back, until I imagined she must have been on her knees between my spread thighs. The tip of the berry was icy cold when she pressed it against my tight hole, but I could feel my asshole clench even tighter. It was an involuntary reaction to the icy intrusion.

"I can see I have my work cut out for me," Giselle announced solemnly. "We could be at this a *long* time."

I felt something sticky dribble down the crease in my ass. It oozed slow, like honey. And I think that's just was it was. When the slowly dribbling drop inched toward my clenching asshole, Giselle's tongue was there to meet it. She pushed the sticky substance around and around, all over my anus. The stickiness felt strange. It was lightly pulling at my hole. But the warmth of her tongue, pushing into the tight opening now and then, felt good. My hole definitely liked that. When Giselle had licked the surface of my asshole clean, she dripped another trail of honey down the crack of my ass. Again, it oozed so slowly down I felt that this alone, this waiting on the honey business, could in itself take hours. My ass wriggled and squirmed impatiently, perhaps trying to assist the honey in its journey down, but when the honey finally reached its destination, and when Giselle's warm tongue was once again there to greet it, the honey felt even more appealing than it had the first time. I felt my sphincter muscle relax a little. I felt it eagerly anticipate her poking tongue. I moaned into my gag. And I arched my ass open for her.

"This is definitely progress," Giselle announced quietly. "But let's not rush it. You're not really ready for the berry yet."

Giselle came around in front of me and I watched her polish off my glass of wine. She sat naked where I could see her and she lit a cigarette.

"I know how to remedy this, though, so don't lose heart," she said. "It takes patience and then you'll be able to get anything you want in there. Even something like a strawberry."

I watched her as she thoughtfully smoked and even though I didn't have some long list of things I'd been trying to get *in there*, I suddenly felt like I desperately wanted to please Giselle. I wanted anything in my ass that she wanted to put in there. My hips were rotating restlessly against the ottoman while I watched her smoke. I could feel the wetness in my vagina beginning to drool down into a puddle on the carpeting. I didn't know what she had in mind for me, but I had a pretty good inkling that my ass was going to get fucked good by this gorgeous skinny woman who, let's face it, was technically old enough to be my mother.

When she finally stubbed out her cigarette, I watched her snap on a latex glove. I'd never been with anybody who'd worn gloves like that before, except the doctor in the examining room and it made my stomach a little queasy watching her snap it on. I wanted to ask her where she got gloves like that, but I had that gag stuck in my mouth and couldn't say a word. But when she disappeared again behind me and, without much fuss, slid a lubed finger up my ass, I wasn't thinking about buying gloves. I just gasped. Well, I moaned a little bit, too. She worked that latexed finger into me deep. And it was so slick with lube my tiny hole couldn't put up any kind of resistance. It tried to push against the intrusion, but Giselle was insistent. She worked against the pushing hole. She slid two fingers in, in fact, and pumped them vigorously in and out while I grunted a little and tried to figure out whether or not I liked it.

But I didn't have a lot of options. I was spread open for her either way. She paused for a moment and squirted the lube directly into my hole. It was an icy and unpleasant feeling, but the sensation didn't last long. It was replaced by the less subtle intrusion of three greasy fingers this time. Three greasy fingers shoved into my lubed hole. Giselle was exerting herself, I could tell; she was grunting from the effort of pumping her three fingers against the muscle that was trying to expel her.

"Jesus," I gasped into my gag. And my eyes were riveted to the picture on the floor in front of me. That gaping hole. It was going to be mine before morning came and I was sickly curious about how we were going to achieve this.

"Are you ready to pick up the pace?" she panted. "Are you ready for some action?"

Of course I couldn't answer her and I guess she didn't really expect me to, but Giselle came around the front of me then and let me watch her strap on the dildo.

"What do you think?" she asked urgently. "Can you handle this guy?"

She was referring to the dildo, to its overall *size*. But I was too caught up in looking at her. I'd been with girls before, and girls with dildoes, too, but I'd never been with a woman yet who had actually strapped one on. Giselle looked hot. I was eager again.

"What do you think?" she persisted, as if she'd forgotten about the gag. "You think you can take him?"

I grunted my urgent approval as I watched her lube it up. *Uh-huh*, I grunted several times, and I even nodded my head.

And when she climbed onto me, mounted me, pressing the greased-up head against my asshole, easing the dildo into my rectum, it was like I was fourteen again and I was with that boy. We'd skipped school and we were hiding in his father's den. It was dark and very quiet in there. Their maid was home, but she didn't know we'd skipped school and snuck back into the house. She didn't know we were hiding in the den. But we had decided we were going to do this thing, we were going to try it out. We were determined. And I'd brought my torn out article from my mother's old *Cosmo* and my plastic jar of Vaseline in my shoulder bag. We didn't get undressed because we were afraid of needing to leave in a hurry. So we just unzipped his fly and took his hard dick out. We smeared Vaseline all over that thing. And then I leaned into one of his father's big leather club chairs, I laid with my face pressed against the cool leather, while the boy shoved up my skirt and pulled my panties down to my knees. Vaseline makes everything a greasy mess, especially nice leather club chairs, but it sure helped that boy's hard-on slide right into me, right into my asshole. It was like we'd talked about over the phone, he was actually fucking my ass. I wasn't sure I really liked it, but I wasn't sure I didn't like it either. The pressure felt exciting, I liked the feeling of being filled up. But what I liked most was his fully-clothed weight on top of me while my panties were around my knees, and the way he smelled while he grunted and pumped away at my virgin asshole, the way all boys smelled back then; like mown grass and sweat and tobacco and spearmint gum.

That was how it felt with Giselle, like I wasn't really sure I liked it, but I wasn't sure I didn't like it either. The dildo felt huge in my ass and I was grunting into my gag. But her naked weight was on top of me. Her breasts were pressed flat against my back and she was sweating from the effort of pounding my hole. I loved all that sweat. And I didn't mind it when she pulled the dildo out and reminded me I wasn't fourteen anymore and that it was 1980: she shoved a glob of Crisco up my ass and proceeded to pump me with a dildo too huge, too heavy to even attempt to fit into the harness. Giselle didn't strap it on, she held it with two hands and shoved it clear down to its base, stretching me completely open.

I groaned like some drugged animal giving birth in a public zoo, but I was loving every minute of it. The Crisco made it easy on my hole. I opened right up and accepted every round fat rubbery inch of the fake dick that Giselle pounded so mercilessly into me.

And my eyes were glued to the photo in front of me, I was transfixed by that gaping hole. I was suddenly in love with the mystery girl in the Polaroid. I knew now what had stretched her open, I knew now how she must have felt – spread wide and securely battened down. A gag probably shoved into her mouth, too, so she could grunt over and over in it as her rectum was filled to capacity, her ears filled with the sounds of Giselle's own grunting, from all the strenuous effort . . .

When Giselle had worn herself out she disappeared briefly into the half-bath then reemerged with a soaking towel. The towel was hot and felt great against my tired hole. And when Giselle had wiped away most of the grease, there was the familiar bright flash again behind me and the sound of the grinding inner workings of the camera. By the time she'd untied my gag, the new photo was ready.

"What do you think?" she asked softly, as she laid the Polaroid of my seriously opened hole on the floor in front of me. "You think you can handle that berry now?"

I'd forgotten about the strawberry. "I suppose so," I panted, although I wasn't entirely sure.

"I'll wedge it in with a little honey and then I'll eat it out of you. But I want to get a picture of it first. My husband loves these pictures," Giselle explained, "the ones with the food in the girls' asses. He carries them in his overnight case and takes them all over the world."

I wasn't sure I was particularly pleased with that idea, but I couldn't keep Giselle from wedging that sticky strawberry into my gaping hole. It took it easily this time, the berry perched right there in my puckered anus. Then the camera flashed away. I wondered what her husband looked like; would I ever recognize him on the street? Would it haunt me that somewhere in the world a man was flying from place to place with a picture in his overnight bag of me with a strawberry in my ass? And what about the mystery girl in the other Polaroid? What kind of food had ended up in her stretched hole?

But my worries melted away when Giselle's mouth found the berry. True to her word, she nibbled it out. She plucked the stem clean and then sucked the berry and gnawed it and licked it until it was gone.

"Come on," she said, as she undid all the hardware, the buckles and the restraints, "let's go to bed. Let's make a little love."

She refilled my wine glass but I didn't want it anymore. I just wanted to be flat on my back underneath her on her big bed. The sun was just coming up in all those enormous penthouse windows, so when she straddled my face for some 69 I could see her bung hole clearly. It was stretched like mine, but hers was permanent. She lowered it right onto my tongue while she shoved my thighs apart wide and buried her face between my legs. Her hot tongue licked at my tender aching worn out hole, while her fingertips deftly massaged my clit. I tried to rub her clitoris, too, but she didn't seem to want that. She seemed content to just ride my tongue with her open hole.

I licked her asshole with all the earnest attention I could give her, but after a while, I must confess I couldn't help it; the way her mouth was making me feel between my legs absorbed more and more of my concentration. I couldn't give Giselle the amount of attention I should have. While her fingertips slipped all over my swollen clit, and while her tongue licked eagerly at my played-out asshole, I couldn't help myself, I came. I dug my fingers into Giselle's gorgeous ass and clamped my thighs tight around her head and came.

And since it was 1980 I didn't sleep with her. I stumbled into my clothes and left. I kissed her good-bye and all, but then I went out alone for breakfast.

A couple nights later she called me. "My husband's in Thailand," she said. "What do you say we go at it again? Are you up for it? You're not still sore, are you?"

My bung hole quivered. "No, I'm not sore," I said into the receiver.

"I have some new things that we could try putting up there. Are you game?"

And I realized I was. It was the beginning of my inevitable descent into hell with a completely insane person. "I'm game," I confessed.

"Good," she exclaimed quietly. "Be a doll and pick up some film. Now how do you feel about root vegetables?"

2 – SWINGERS

Friday night I went home with some married people. I wish I could tell you they were those vibrantly tanned, Hollywood fast-lane types but they weren't. They were just married people. Intellectuals. Two married couples clearly pushing something like their mid-fifties. I have to say they weren't even very attractive. They certainly weren't fans of cosmetic surgery or fad diets.

You're probably wondering why I went home with them, then. I'll tell you. They asked me to.

I was hanging out in one of those book bars. You know the one, the really well lit place. Small and stuffy with the built-in bookcases lining the walls, a teeny weeny fire in the equally microscopic hearth. I was there being stood-up. Nothing serious, though, no *tragédie d'amour*. It was just my intensely hyper garment-industry-worker girlfriend who had stood me up. She'd obviously gotten snagged into working more overtime.

So I was alone in a surprisingly comfy chair, nursing a glass of red wine tentatively since I wasn't sure if I was just going to turn around and go home. That's when they walked in. Two unattractive married couples in their mid-fifties. They made an instant commotion, dragging a tiny table around and scooting a bunch of comfy chairs together so they could all sit down in high spirits, practically on top of me, and proceeded to order an incredibly expensive bottle of wine. I loved watching that; the waiter trying to find a spot to stand in that was anywhere near them while they ordered, and then having to set up an elaborate pedestal wine bucket somewhere in reach of them, too. Thank god they smoked. They really needed some more stuff on that tiny table.

They couldn't help but notice me right away since they were practically sitting in my lap, and they kept trying to engage me in their small talk. I resisted their stabs at friendliness until they offered to share their wine, which necessitated their ordering another bottle. The waiter was really glad to see a fifth party, me, push into the already unmaneuverable fray. So physically we got close in a hurry. We couldn't help it. Still, one of the women, Fran, seemed to impinge on more of my personal space than I thought was really necessary. Right away I figured she was hitting on me. It took a couple of glasses of that expensive wine before I realized they were all hitting on me.

I went home with them mostly because I couldn't believe they'd had the balls to ask me. They were so matter of fact about it, too, like they always came on to younger, much more attractive single women and got affirmative results. I was swept off my feet by their sheer blind optimism. Well, no. Actually I was swept off my feet by them, literally. I think they wanted to rush me into the nearest cab before I could change my mind.

We wound up in the home of the couple who lived closest to the bar. It was a really nice apartment. That couple, Cy and Ruthie, had never had any kids. Every extra penny had been available for them to spend on themselves. They favored upholstery, too. Everything was upholstered, in every conceivable pattern. I could tell an interior decorator had been paid handsomely to have his or her way with Cy and Ruthie. But I ceased noticing the decor when Fran started to undress me.

At first I felt alarmingly uncomfortable because no one else was undressing. I shy away from being the only one naked in a crowd of strangers and I was wondering what I'd gotten myself into. But after she'd stripped me naked, Fran pushed me gently down on the sofa and began to massage my feet. I began to relax. I sank deep into the upholstered sofa while Fran sat on the coffee table in front of me with both my feet in her considerable lap. Her hands were unexpectedly soft and steady. She worked each and every one of my toes and the balls of my feet with just the right amount of pressure.

She smiled encouragingly at me while the others just watched. I wondered if I was being lured into some exhibitionistic *pas de deux* with Fran. As I sunk deeper into the couch in an increasing state of bliss, I wondered how a group of people arrived at that sort of arrangement. "Hey, I know," I imagined them saying. "Let's all go out together, find a girl half our age and watch her get frisky with Fran." There would be general agreement all around.

Then Fran broke my reverie. She lifted my foot to her mouth and sucked in my big toe. I was ready for it. Fran's mouth was so warm and wet, I moaned. And slowly but surely things started to move around me.

Cy got out of his chair. He came over and stood by Fran, his

crotch level with her face. He unzipped his fly, but when he took
out his dick it was flaccid. Completely limp. Fran didn't seem at
all perturbed but I felt a little indignant. I was thinking, "Hey,
I'm naked here! The least you could do is worship me, have a
raging hard-on!" But, alas, Cy was no longer nineteen and Fran
appeared to be used to it. She went right to work with her mouth,
alternating between my big toe and Cy's flaccid dick until
remarkable things began to happen. It turned out Cy was hung.

Ruthie came over to join us then. She undid her husband's
trousers completely, letting them fall rather dramatically to his
ankles. Then, while Cy went to work on Fran's mouth with his
stiff dick, getting her complete attention now as my feet lay
limply in her lap, Ruthie kneeled behind Cy and seemed to be
tonguing his ass. Her face was way in there and I figured if I was
Cy, as I watched his huge erection pumping in and out of Fran's
mouth while his wife, fully-dressed and on her knees, tongued his
asshole . . . well, I figured I'd probably be liking that an awful lot.
I got wet between my legs watching those three carry on like that.

Kenneth, Fran's husband, was the last to take the plunge, but
suddenly he was sitting on the couch next to me and he was
naked. He had a lot of hair. A touch more than I would have
preferred. He didn't seem to notice that he didn't appeal to me,
though. He lifted my arms and held my wrists together behind
my head, then proceeded to lick my armpits. It was an unusual
move but it made my nipples shiver and get erect. As Kenneth
licked his way down to my breasts and when his mouth closed
around my erect nipple, I moaned again. Hairy or not, he was
good with his mouth. My nipple swelled from the perfect pressure of Kenneth's sucking and I decided, at that moment, that I
ought to have sex with older people more often, they understood
pressure.

The coffee table gang was starting to get rambunctious. Fran
was flat on her back now as Cy straddled her on the low table,
completely humping her face. She was making these eager but
smothered little sounds that made it seem like she was liking it a
whole lot. And Ruthie had removed Fran's panties. She'd pushed
apart Fran's legs and buried her face between Fran's fleshy thighs.

Kenneth's mouth was still working expertly on my nipples,
moving from one to the other, tugging tugging tugging, but now
one of his hands was between my legs, rubbing my slippery clit.

I didn't think I'd be able to take much more of it; the free show on the coffee table and the perfect pressure on each of my three most responsive spots. I thought I was going to come.

That's when Cy startled all of us. He stopped humping Fran's face and went for her hole in a hurry. Ruthie had to get out of the way fast. She plopped down next to me on the sofa. She was the only one still dressed. She began to unbutton her blouse while Kenneth was rolling a rubber onto his erection. I felt a little overwhelmed. I didn't know who to focus on. It was obvious Ruthie wanted me to suck her fat little tits, but I was kind of hoping Kenneth was wanting his dick in me because I was definitely ready for it. That's when it occurred to me to quit sitting like a blob on the sofa and get a little assertive; get into the rhythm of being a swinger. Nothing was preventing me from having them both.

I turned over and raised my ass in Kenneth's direction while I let Ruthie guide my mouth to one of her jiggly tits. "Would you look at that tight tush," Kenneth declared as he slapped my ass hard. "Fran had a tush like that when I married her. Thirty years ago."

Then he mounted me. He slid his substantial hard-on into my soaking hole without needing any help from me. He slammed into my hole hard, making me cry out right away. He had a firm grip on my tush and was going to town.

Ruthie lifted my face from her breasts and started kissing me. Deep. Her tongue was crammed into my mouth while I grunted from the force of Kenneth's cock pounding into my pussy from behind.

I had never been with more than one person at a time before. It was kind of a scary feeling. I felt myself becoming insatiable. It wasn't long before I was flat on my back on the carpeting. Ruthie had stripped completely and was straddling my face. She had a tight grasp on each of my ankles as she kept my legs spread wide, giving Kenneth's hard cock free rein on my helpless hole, pound pound pound.

Ruthie's snatch was completely shaved. Her mound was smooth from the tip of her clit to the cleft in her ass. It had to be a wax job, I thought, she was that smooth. And I wondered: Who waxes a fiftyish woman's pussy completely bald? I figured her husband, Cy, had something to do with it.

Cy was sitting in a chair now, sucking on a cigar, taking a breather, but his dick was still rock hard. It was poking straight up like the Chrysler Building. Not that I could see him too well with Ruthie's ass in my face, but I could tell that Cy was watching me get nailed. I was curious what he was thinking.

"I have to pee!" I suddenly announced as the urge came unmistakably over me. Rather than cause a chorus of disappointment and regret among my fellow swingers, the news didn't cause them to miss a beat. They'd switched partners before I'd even stood up. When I came back into the living room (and I hadn't been gone long, mind you), Fran was down on all fours with Kenneth's hard-on seriously down her throat and Cy was fucking her ass. The incessant pounding she was getting at both ends was making Fran's boobs bounce around like crazy. The whole thing was mesmerizing; what the men were doing to her and the way Fran seemed to be wildly into it.

Ruthie came in from the kitchen with a tray of decaf espressos. She had that look on her face, like she'd had her orgasm and was feeling completely contented. She sat down next to me with her cup of espresso and we both watched Fran go the distance with Cy and Kenneth. And right when Fran started to jerk around and squeal, an indication that Fran was probably coming, Kenneth pulled his dick out of her mouth and shot his load in her face. She seemed a little peeved by that, but she didn't do much about it because Cy was still going hog wild on her ass. I wondered if Kenneth was going to hear about it later, though, when he and Fran were home alone: "How could you come in my face like that?" I could hear Fran saying. I knew she'd be capable of some serious chiding. "In front of everybody," she'd probably continue. "You know I hate it when you do that."

But for now everyone was amicable. Everyone was drinking decaf espresso except me. I hadn't come yet. I felt fidgety and distracted. Since I'd never been a swinger before, I didn't know the proper etiquette. Was it up to me to let everyone know I wasn't through yet, that I hadn't come?

I felt so ignorant, so ill-equipped to swing. I toyed with the idea of slipping off to the bathroom again, to take care of myself alone. No one had to know what I'd be doing in there. I could come quick, I felt certain of that. Still I felt a little let down. I'd been having too much fun with everybody to suddenly resort to climaxing alone, in some stranger's bathroom.

After only a few moments, it seemed as though coming alone in Cy and Ruthie's bathroom wasn't even going to pan out. Fran and Kenneth were dressing. It was late, they said. They had a baby-sitter running up a fortune.

Then I wondered how old Fran really was if she had a child at home still young enough to need a sitter.

I figured I'd better get dressed, too. I didn't want to overstay my welcome. I helped Ruthie clear up the remnants of the espressos while Fran and Kenneth left.

"I'll get your coat," Cy said to me. "I'll walk you down to the street."

"That's okay," I protested halfheartedly. My head was pounding. This swinging business had left my now-sober nerves a little raw.

"Nonsense. It's late. I'll walk you down."

Cy helped me into my coat and we got on the elevator. He pressed the button for the basement. I saw him do it. Maybe he was going to show me out the back way.

When the elevator doors opened, Cy led me down a narrow hallway and then out a door that led to the tenants' parking garage. It was dimly lit, with only a couple of naked bulbs burning.

"Look, you don't have to drive me," I insisted uncomfortably. "I don't live far. I'll get a cab."

"Why don't we get in my car anyway? I didn't come yet either."

I couldn't believe I'd heard him correctly. "What did you say?"

He looked at me and smiled engagingly. "I didn't come yet, either. I thought maybe I could persuade you to fuck around with me in my car."

I was stunned. I tried to feel affronted, but actually it kind of appealed to me. The parking garage was deserted.

Cy unlocked his car door and we slipped into the back seat. "We'd better not undress all the way," he said, "just in case anybody sees us."

I agreed.

I climbed onto his lap and started kissing him. On the mouth. My tongue was shoving in deep. Cy's breath tasted like wine and espressos and cigars and he suddenly seemed like he was seriously grown up. I felt incredibly attracted to him. "How old are you?" I challenged him. "Are you old enough to be my father?"

"Probably, why? Did you want to do a little role playing?"

"Excuse me?" I didn't know what he was talking about.

"You know, I could pretend to be your irate father and slap your fanny really hard until we're both really hot. Then we could cross over that line together."

I didn't reply. I felt a little overwhelmed by how instantly appealing his idea sounded. I let him maneuver me until I was across his lap. He methodically lifted my coat, lifted my dress and, with minimal effort but a nice long lecture, he tugged down my tights, then my panties, and left them halfway down my thighs.

When my ass was completely bare and smack dab over his knee, he let loose with a good old-fashioned spanking. The stinging, smarting kind.

"Shit!" I cried, trying to shield my ass.

But he wasn't at all deterred by my screams. He lectured me sternly on the perils of going home with perfect strangers, and behaving rather wantonly, to boot.

I squirmed around in Cy's lap as my bottom heated up and I tried to dodge the steady, stinging slaps, but Cy kept them coming. He clamped my waist tight against his thigh and aimed directly for my helpless behind.

I could feel Cy's erection growing underneath me. He was really laying into me, spanking me hard, making me squeal out promises that I'd never do it again.

When my ass was completely on fire and I didn't think I could stand anymore, Cy released me. He turned me over in his lap and unbuttoned the top of my dress. Slipping his hand inside, he worked my bra up over my tits and fondled my nipples. They were instantly erect.

I was still naked from my waist to my knees. The feeling of being so awkwardly exposed, my bare ass burning, while Cy fondled my breasts and tugged on my nipples made me want to get irredeemably dirty with him. But that was going to be difficult to do while keeping our clothes on.

I turned over and undid Cy's trousers. I unbuckled his belt, unzipped his fly and his dick sprang out. I was happy to see it looking so lively. I buried my face in his lap, taking as much of his shaft down my throat as I could. I kneeled on the back seat with my naked ass in the air and I didn't care if anyone could see me. I was feeling unabashedly aroused. I sucked Cy's dick more fervently when I heard him begin to gasp and moan.

"Turn over," he said insistently. "Lie down on your belly." My bra was still up over my tits and the leather car seat was icy cold against my nipples. It felt great.

Cy unrolled a rubber onto his erection and told me to raise my ass up a little.

I did.

He mounted me with my tights and panties still around my thighs. I felt his dick poking into my asshole. At first I thought he didn't realize he had the wrong hole, but he knew what he was doing.

The lubricated condom slid into my ass without too much effort but the pressure was intense.

"God," I groaned. Then I cried out uncontrollably while his huge tool went to work on my pitiful little hole.

"I hate to have to do this," he grunted, "you know that. But maybe this'll teach you not to go home with people you don't know."

"God," I was panting as he pounded into my stretching hole. "Jesus, god."

"Are you going to be a good girl now?" he continued, lifting my hips off the back seat and deftly sliding his hand down to my swollen clit.

"Yes," I whimpered, "yes," while he rubbed my clit hard.

"Yes what?"

"I'm going to be a good girl," I cried, as his cock seemed to swell in me even more, filling me to capacity with every thrust.

"And what happens if you're naughty again? What is daddy going to do?"

"Spank me," I sputtered. "Daddy's going to spank me!"

"And what else?"

"Fuck my ass!"

"That's right," he concluded. "Daddy is going to fuck your ass."

These last words he enunciated with amazing diction because he was coming at the sound of his own words. He slammed deep into my hole then and mashed me down on the seat. "Jesus!" he exclaimed with one last powerful thrust. "Jesus!"

And I was saying it, too: "Jesus!" Partly because I was coming underneath him, shuddering and squirming against the leather seat; but mostly because I was testifying. I wanted my joy to be heard.

BAUBO'S KISS

Lucy Taylor

IT WAS BEING angry at C.J. more than any spirit of adventure that drove Mira to go off alone to explore the island that day in early summer. Not that there was much to see on Kirinos. The small Ionian island was the sixth in a string of islands that she and C.J. had visited, some more flat or mountainous or lushly wildflowered than others, all redolent with heat and goat piss and retsina. So far, Kirinos was the least promising of the lot. Something about the people, Mira decided, as she pedaled the rented Schwinn along the dirt track that led away from the town. They seemed a glum and lifeless lot, not just more taciturn than the townsfolk she and C.J. had encountered on the other islands, but downright moribund.

The heat, perhaps, thought Mira, as sweat scrawled long itchy lines along the cracks between her breasts and buttocks. You could fry squid on the rocks here (and judging from some meals she'd had, maybe that was what they did), and it was barely ten o'clock.

Yet she pedaled on, determined to find something of interest or note to justify such an expenditure of energy on so blistering a day.

C.J.'s energy, as usual, was being vigorously conserved, unless you counted the hoisting of glass to lips to be a form of weight training. If so, Mira figured her lover would have set some sort of record for elbow-bending by the end of their vacation.

She'd left C.J. slouched at one of the ubiquitous waterfront
tavernas, nursing a hangover with what, to Mira, seemed an unlikely remedy – a glass of ouzo and a plate of stuffed grape leaves and
taramosalata, a gummy-looking paste of smoked fish roe.

But then, despite what Mira thought was an unseemly love of
drink and indolence, C.J. seemed to require no exercise to
maintain a body that was both athletically lean and pleasingly
curvaceous.

Whereas, I, thought Mira with not a little envy, *could pedal
from here back home to Scranton and still have a bum like a wench in
a Bruegel painting*.

Not for the first time, Mira wondered what C.J. saw in her – a
fat and dowdy bookworm with plain, freckled features and eyes
that squinted myopically from behind heavy lenses. Perhaps it
was that C.J. felt her own good looks were shown to best
advantage next to Mira's plainness, that her own extroversion
sparkled with more brilliance contrasted with Mira's shyness.
The idea of being a mere foil to highlight her lover's sex appeal
made Mira pedal harder, fueled by despair and self-disgust.

At least, she thought, by way of preserving some modicum of
self-esteem, *I'm out and about, exploring something besides the beer
and wine list*.

Trying to, at any rate.

The reality was, so far at least, Kirinos seemed as stolid and
uninviting as its citizenry. On both sides of the dirt track, olive
groves stretched to a flat, unpromising horizon. Bands of
scrawny, brown and white goats eyed Mira from the shade of
stunted trees, but her passing was acknowledged only by a ribby
dog, who came lunging at her rear tire with unnerving, if short-
lived menace, before sensibly retreating to the shade.

Still, as her surroundings gave Mira more and more reason to
feel discouraged, she pedaled resolutely on. She'd spent much of
the last nine months cooped up in the Bodleian Library at
Oxford, studying for an M.A. in Greek and Roman literature.
Her pasty skin and pudgy thighs attested to her scholar's dedication. Now she had three weeks of freedom before summer
classes started. Hot and weary though she might be, she wasn't
going to be like C.J. She was damn well going to see something on
this trip besides the insides of tavernas.

An hour more into her trek, she passed a pair of girls herding a desultory tribe of goats along the roadside. Mira stopped and asked, in her limited Greek, what there might be of interest up ahead. The girls shared that look of dull slow-wittedness that Mira had come to recognize as characteristic of Kirinos's inhabitants, a vacuity that suggested spirits no less desolate than the barren landscape.

The two girls conversed in low whispers before one said, in Greek the gist of which Mira was able to comprehend, "There's the ruin of a temple close by, but you don't want to go there. It isn't safe."

"It's been abandoned for a long time," the other said.

"A temple to the goddess Baubo," said the first.

"Baubo?" Mira repeated, unfamiliar with the name.

A faint trace of slyness leaked into the first speaker's large and bovine eyes, the closest thing to an expression of amusement that Mira had seen since coming to the island.

Mira wanted to question the women further, but the goats were straying, the girls obviously impatient to be on their way. Mira thanked them, hoping she had understood correctly, and pedaled on.

A few miles farther on, she walked her decrepit bike (no less ancient, however, than her legs were beginning to feel) up a steep hill topped by stands of poplars. Wind-flogged for their entire lives, the trees were permanently bent before their batterer, slanting out of the loose and rocky soil like broken bones set by a sadist, all weird twists and angles.

But for the grotesquely warped trees, the hilltop appeared as forlorn and barren as the rest of Kirinos, abandoned even by the wind today, but for a sluggish breeze.

And Baubo's temple? If it existed at all (and Mira was beginning to imagine that she'd been sent on a wild-goose chase reserved for the most gullible of tourists – a Greek snipe hunt, as it were), it must be on still higher ground, well beyond the capacity of both her bike and calf muscles.

Still, the idea of coming back from her day's excursion with not even a small discovery or adventure to recount was incentive enough for Mira to make one final assault on the hilltop. Leaning her bike against a tree, she forced herself on foot up a rock-strewn incline that offered, to mountain goats perhaps, a facsimile of a path.

She reached the top panting, legs atremble.

And halted, disappointment smiting her like a blow across the cheek.

The temple, if that was what it once had been, was now a crumbled relic, defiled by weeds and shat upon by birds. Small lizards sunned themselves on its chipped stones and scurried into shaded cracks at Mira's approach. Only two half-columns yet remained – the rest were tumbled over, sections scattered here and there in what looked, to Mira, like the vertebrae of some long-dead dinosaur, huge cousin perhaps to the toy-sized ones now baking on the stones. The decay and desolation of the place was both disturbing and, somehow also, morbidly alluring. Mira had seen fallen temples before, of course, but either in museums, their bleached stones carefully divided up and labeled, or cordoned off and renovated for display, tramped across by infestations of noisy, camera-snapping tourists.

This was something else. This ruin was deserted, empty, private as a tomb. A tumbled wreck, it well might be, but for the moment, it apparently belonged entirely to Mira. And if the temple was less than she had hoped for, the view from her high perch was stunning, the first vista Mira had found worth setting eyes on. From this vantage point, the sea was so bright it seared spangles on her retinas, each wave composed of a treasure trove of individual gems – turquoise, topaz, and emeralds in a seething jewel box of light.

Clambering over a row of fallen stones, Mira unhooked her daypack and sank down onto the ground. She spread her lunch out around her – a canteen of ice water, now tepid slush, granola bars purchased in Athens, grapes and pears from the kiosk outside the hotel.

A breeze nipped and flitted at the damp hair on the back of her neck. She sank her teeth into a pear, its nectar overflowing her lips and dribbling down her chin, and thought of C.J. back at the taverna, probably chatting up Greek girls and maybe boys as well, if she'd imbibed enough retsina.

But maybe, Mira thought, *C.J. had the right idea. At least she's never lonely, isn't eating her lunch right now at the bitter end of nowhere without even goats for company.*

The breeze picked up a bit, moaning plaintively through stunted tree limbs.

It died off, but the moaning didn't. The sound continued unabated and took on, in fact, a distinctly human timbre.

Mira froze, unsure of what to do. To pursue the sound might invite involvement in some drama in which Mira, as a foreigner and tourist, could ill afford to embroil herself. Neither was it clear to her if the sounds were fathered by great pain or by pleasure. If the former, then decency demanded she investigate. There could be a hiker hurt, a young child lost, even an injured animal, although more and more, Mira doubted that the noise could have any except human origin.

She crept forward as quietly as her bulk allowed, scuttling the last yard or two on hands and knees, and peered between some scrubby bushes.

At first glance, she saw but didn't really *see*, so improbable was the spectacle before her that she assumed her vision must be playing tricks, creating the illusion that a trio of the bleached and fallen stones were now a woman's round thighs and ivory belly. No hallucination this, however, Mira realized; the flush and jiggle of abundant flesh was all too real.

A woman, endowed with Junoesque proportions, lay spread out upon the rough ground. Her knees were bent, thigh's widely V'd. With three fingers of her right hand, she rhythmically fucked herself, while with the left she parted the pink creases of her labia, plucking at the engorged clitoris with her thumb. Though she lay in shadow, sunlight broke through in places, dappling her flesh with spots and splashes the color of buttered Brie. With each thrust of her fingers, the woman moaned and arched her back, black tresses tumbling over the earth like so many writhing serpents. Sweat rolled off her mounded breasts and belly, shimmered on her nipple tips like opals.

Mira knew she had no business witnessing this display and yet she couldn't bring herself to look away. She gazed on, rapt, and was still staring, fingers of one hand lightly touching her own bosom, tweaking at a nipple, when the woman's eyes suddenly flashed open and she looked directly at the spot where Mira crouched.

Her eyes held the force of twin beacons. Mira cringed before their power, determined to keep silent, but the very underbrush was bent upon betraying her. A twig snapped beneath her shifting weight; a stone, dislodged by her heel, went skittering.

"Who's there?" the woman called out in Greek.

Mira's head thundered with blood.

"I'm sorry," she blurted out. "I'm going."

"Wait."

Mira halted, bracing herself for a lambasting the individual words of which she might not comprehend, but whose meaning would be all too clear as well as justified.

The woman, who'd made no attempt to cover herself and whose garments, Mira noted, were nowhere in view, stood up and approached her. And kept approaching, past that invisible boundary which varies with each culture, but whose limits with regard to personal space are normally respected.

"*Pedhi mou,*" *my girl*, whispered the woman and put her mouth to Mira's.

Her kiss was hot and salty, tasting of sweat and sex and female juices. It was, thought Mira, like giving head to a woman in the final stages of arousal, the pussy dripping with desire, the vulval lips engorged and oozing sex.

This is madness, she thought, and yet her lips were parting to allow access to her mouth and she was unresistant when the woman began to unbutton and peel off her blouse and shorts, her sweat-drenched undergarments. Mira's large breasts were squashed against a bosom far more abundant that her own. Her head spun with the folly of her own lust, with a passion so unnatural to her character that she felt at once transformed and yet possessed, as though surely something outside herself inspired this abandon.

The woman's body, lush and hot, bumped and rutted against Mira's. Fingers probed and parted her, a tongue both skilled and playful teased her lips and lashes, then ducked down to drink from the tiny cup of sweat that was her navel.

And all the while the woman made noises – sucking, gobbling, slurping, laughing – as their bodies thumped and squeaked together in a carnal melody. The woman guided Mira to the ground onto a bed made of her discarded clothing. Her avid lips sought out the mouth between Mira's parted legs, where she drank of sweat and cunt juice. Mira thrashed and cried out as an orgasm shuddered through her, contractions like a birth of pleasure throbbing all the way into her womb. The woman's tongue explored new crevices and creases. More climaxes were wrung from her, the last of these so violent that Mira locked her thighs together and cried out for a respite.

Her lover, however, suffered no such loss of appetite. Leaving Mira on the ground, she pranced and strutted like an obscene jester, tweaking brown nipples the size of coffee saucers, strumming at her clitoris with the fast and fluid motions of a virtuoso guitarist. Muttering some words that Mira didn't understand, she squatted over the rough earth, reached down and spread herself wide in a parody of childbirth. Astonished, Mira watched this spectacle, unsure if this outrageous lewdness was prelude to some new bout of lovemaking. Her nether lips still throbbed and tingled from the force of her last orgasm. She felt undone, sapped senseless by the heat and the intensity of sex. She had neither the strength nor will to do anything but recline and watch the dance.

Which turned suddenly, before Mira's bewitched gaze, into a monstrous birthing. The woman spread her thick thighs wide, parting vaginal lips that hung down more than an inch below the black thatch of pubic hair. She released a gust of laughter that stirred the still air and raised the hair on Mira's arms with it's dark mirth.

Something slick and shiny glistened wetly at the lips of her vagina. The thing pulsed there for an instant, like the damp head of a grotesquely misshapen child, then fell to the rough ground, where it uncoiled powerful hind legs and leaped away.

Mira gaped, unable to comprehend what she had seen, but the miracle was only just commencing. The woman was giving birth to toads, hordes of the wet and mottled creatures dropping from her cunt, a slithering rain of amphibian life upon the stones. Born full grown, they leaped in all directions, a sea of bright, bulging eyes and livid mouths.

Mira gasped and clutched both hands across her breasts, although they offered scant protection against the unnatural hordes that were still plopping, like dollops of green dung, from the woman's cunt.

A toad leaped at Mira's face and landed in her hair. Another bounced across her belly, a third's passing marked her breast with smears of dirt from its webbed hind feet.

Mira screamed and writhed, dislodging the toads on her legs and head only to find three more arranged like horrid tumors upon her breasts and belly. The largest of these, endowed with shining amber eyes, seized the soft flesh below Mira's navel and delivered a painful bite. Blood slicked the toad's wide mouth, and bile rose up in Mira's throat. The world turned. She tried to rise but found her limbs were powerless, her vision growing inky at the edges.

Through a gauze of sick terror, she could still see the horrid birthing taking place. As she passed out, her ears rang with the woman's mad laughter that almost – but not completely – drowned out a sound far worse, the soft, throaty glugging of the toads.

"You shouldn't have gone out in the heat today," C.J. said, nibbling at a piece of fried octopus. "You look like hell."

"I'm all right," said Mira, cutting into the leg of lamb the waiter had just set before her. "Just hungry."

Hungry and – if truth be known – bizarrely energized. Her belly throbbed, but not with pain. More like concentric circles of appetite and energy radiating out from the wound on her stomach. The toad appeared to have nipped out a tiny chunk of flesh. The bleeding had been copious on her bike ride back to town. Mira had been forced to hurry back to the hotel, where she had shed her filthy clothing and stuffed it deep inside her duffle bag.

Fortunately, other than remarking on Mira's appearance, C.J. had shown little curiosity about her day. Now she added some more water to her glass of ouzo and sipped the milky liquid with that look of studied smugness that Mira had come to recognize as presaging some admission aimed at provoking jealousy.

"I met someone today. His name's Stavros. He grew up here, but he worked in his cousin's restaurant in New York for a couple of years, so he speaks really good English."

Mira shrugged and forked a chunk of meat into her mouth. "So did you fuck him yet?"

C.J. recoiled. "No, of course not. I'm with you, aren't I?"

"I don't know. Are you?"

"Jesus, we're in a pissy mood tonight."

"So what's the point of telling me about some guy you met? To make me jealous, right? To remind me how fucking desirable you are to each and every gender. Well, fuck him if you want to. Suck his dick until it falls off. I don't care."

"God, Mira, what's got into you? I only said . . ."

"This looks so good," said Mira, reaching over with her fork to poke at C.J.'s food. She chose the longest piece of octopus, a tentacle pale and tender as the flesh of an armpit, studded with small, rose-colored suckers.

C.J., misunderstanding her intention, said, "I thought you didn't like octopus. You said it was disgusting."

"I didn't say I was going to eat it." Mira plucked the tentacle from the fork and held it between her fingers. "Look here."

She glanced to either side of her. Only a few of the tables in the taverna were filled and these by locals whose faces, in most cases, were either directed at their plates or wreathed in a fog of cigarette smoke. Slowly, savoring C.J.'s agitation, she undid the top three buttons of her blouse, revealing ample cleavage unfettered by a bra.

"I wonder if your friend Stavros would like to do this with his tongue?" She slid the octopus between her freckled breasts. Up and down, down and up, leaving a sheen of grease against the pale skin.

"Jesus, Mira, stop it."

"But then your tits are smaller than mine, so he might rather tonguefuck you other places."

She slid sideways in her chair, pulled her cotton skirt up to mid-thigh. She wore no underpants, and her cunt was moist and ready. On the first push, the tentacle got away from her and slid so far inside, she almost lost it. Mira threw back her head and howled with laughter at the thought of walking around being fucked with an octopus dildo inside her, but then her vaginal muscles clenched and pushed the slippery stob back out. It slithered into her fingers.

"Mira, *please*, the waiter's coming over."

"You think he'd like to watch?"

She closed her legs and pulled down her skirt, but didn't bother to refasten the buttons of her blouse.

"For God's sake . . ."

Mira grinned. She put the octopus tentacle between her lips and began to gobble it with noisy, smacking sounds.

"You're fucking drunk."

"I've had half a glass of wine."

"Close up your blouse. Your tits are falling out."

Mira giggled and undid another button, revealing small pink

nipples that were celebrating their exposure with exuberant erections. She felt appalled at her audacity, astonished, and yet elated, too. There was merit, more profound than her mind could shape at present, in this loss of dignity and decorum, but if so, C.J. was blind to it. She gaped in horror at her lover as the waiter, unable to contain himself, came over and stared down at Mira's chest.

His eyes bugged, and he muttered something that Mira didn't understand. Others had turned to stare now, diners abandoning their meals to ogle the impromptu cabaret act.

"Please," said C.J., through gritted teeth. "I don't know what you're trying to prove, but cover yourself up."

Mira stuck out her tongue at C.J., waggled it around, and slowly, so slowly that the act of covering herself became more seductive than the original unveiling, began to close the buttons.

The diners, murmuring now among themselves, continued to stare, looking from Mira to one another and back to Mira again with an expression more of wonder than disapproval.

A muscular young man with blindingly white teeth, evidently C.J.'s new Greek swain, approached the table with a hand held out to greet his American friend. His eyes were fixed on C.J. until, at the last moment, his gaze took a sudden detour onto Mira's semi-naked breasts. He gulped, Adam's apple bobbing in his throat, and blushed bright crimson. Murmuring something in Greek, he backed away from the table as though the barrels of two .45's had suddenly been trained on him.

"Stavros," C.J. called out. "Stavros, wait." She pulled a fistful of drachmas out of her pocket and slammed them onto the table. "Come on, Mira. If you're not drunk, then you're high or sick or something. I've got to get you out of here before you cause a riot."

And, at least in part, Mira agreed with her. Yet if, indeed, she'd somehow tripped or blundered over the edge of insanity, then surely this was an experience far more pleasurable than her previous, albeit limited, study of mental deviations (mostly undergraduate psych courses) would have led her to believe.

She felt, indeed, more energetic than she had in years, infused with a heat so galvanizing that, as C.J. half dragged her along the street, Mira thought surely she must be radiating light.

"Where are we going?" she laughed.

"Back to the room. Where you can sober up."

"But I *am* sober." Mira tried to stop giggling for C.J.'s sake, but with every effort to compose herself, the laughter only burst from her in more lusty gales. "More sober than I've ever been."

"Then you're having some kind of breakdown. Heat prostration maybe."

They passed a group of men. "Wait," cried Mira. Pulling free of C.J.'s grasp, she bent over, flipped her skirt up, and wagged her naked rump at the startled passersby. This small act seemed insufficient, however, to encompass her frivolity. Reaching back, she spread her cheeks, exposing the pink and puckered eyelet at her center.

The men stopped in their tracks.

"Mira!"

C.J. yanked the skirt down. With her right hand, she cracked Mira a resounding blow across the face. "Do you want to get us both arrested? Thrown in a fucking Greek jail?"

"Fucking Greek jail?" echoed Mira. She rubbed her stung cheek. Her face hurt, but something else, something altogether wonderful and unexpected, was distracting her from the pain. From the nearby plaza: music. The first music Mira had heard since they arrived on this godforsaken lump of rock. A lyre, sweet and lyrical, and joining it, the chimelike notes of a *laouto*.

"Fucking Greek jail!" sang out Mira and she began to dance. Her legs, despite this morning's trek, were suddenly featherlight. She was a bird, a bawd, a buxom ballerina. She was great, unholstered, jiggly tits and quivering fat ass and a canyon of cleavage. She was madness, mirth, and celebration.

"Mira! No! If you don't stop this instant, I'm leaving!"

"Then go!" cried Mira and danced away.

Her sandals slapped the cobblestones. Leather on stone, fuck, fuck, like lusty mating. Mira laughed and kicked them off. She whirled and capered, spun and leaped, and the musicians picked up the beat and Mira danced, and did her blouse fall open of its own accord or did her fingers tease the buttons free? She didn't know, but somehow her tits flopped out, and the musicians yodeled at the sky like moonstruck hounds and then the moon itself swelled from behind the clouds in all its naked splendor and Mira sang out, "Fucking Greek jail!" and danced and danced.

A few villagers gathered round to stare and grunt, before

retreating, like shamed wraiths, back into their houses, white as bone shards beneath the yellow moon.

And the musicians' energy waned, and they put away their instruments and slunk away, but still Mira cavorted, her white skirt swirling, pink nipples dancing their own jig and she was like a Catherine wheel, all light and glamour, spinning wildly in the dark.

A boy, barely beyond his teens, watched her with a rapt and avid gaze, wetting the corners of his mouth with a tongue made sopping by desire. Mira danced to his side. She took him by his thick black hair and buried his face between her breasts, each one of which was easily the size of the boy's head. She let him suckle, leaving her nipples silvery with saliva, then pushed his head down and hoisted up her skirt and straddled him. His tongue knew dances of its own, quick, darting strumming motions and deep, luxurious slurps and she opened up her folds to him and took his tongue in like a raw pink fetus seeking reentry to its fleshy nest.

The boy stood up and unzipped himself, took out a bobbing, uncut cock. The sight of it made Mira giggle with delight and recommence her dance, though the music to which she capered was now within her head.

An old man rushed out from a nearby doorway. He grabbed the boy and shouted in his face with much agitation. Mira heard the word "Baubo," but didn't understand the rest. Beneath the elder's scorn, the boy shrank both literally and figuratively. He slunk away, the old man's arm prodding him roughly along. Leaving Mira panting, bare-breasted, and alone in the center of the plaza. She looked down at herself and gasped, began buttoning her blouse. Wetness ran between her legs, the boy's drool and her own juices. From her groin and armpits wafted, unmistakably, the pungency of lust.

The door was locked when Mira at last returned to the hotel room. She knocked and pleaded a good long time before C.J. let her in. C.J.'s tanned face was tracked with angry tears.

"I talked to Stavros. Tomorrow morning, he's leaving on the first ferry back to Piraeus," said C.J., crawling back into bed. "I'm going with him. I want you to come with us. We'll find a doctor for you in Athens. An English-speaking one."

Mira took off her soiled and rumpled clothing and slid naked into bed next to her lover.

"I can't do that," she said. "I don't understand what happened out there, but, oh God, it felt so wonderful."

"When you exposed yourself, you mean. When you mooned those men."

"Yes, wonderful," said Mira, her voice awed and tiny. "I don't understand. It was like I couldn't stop myself. And I didn't want to."

"You're lucky you weren't beaten up or arrested. These people are conservative. They aren't used to things like this. Did you see the way they looked at you?"

"What's happening to me, C.J.? Am I crazy?"

"I don't know. Maybe you had some kind of fit. Maybe some blood sugar thing. But Stavros thinks it's . . ."

"Yeah? What does pretty little Stavros think?"

C.J.'s voice became so tiny Mira could barely hear her. "This sounds crazy, but . . . he says this island used to be dedicated to the worship of a deity named Balbo or Baubo or something. Anyway, she's the goddess of obscenity, of lewdness and sensuality. And he thinks . . . oh, forget it . . ."

"He thinks that I'm possessed. That's it, isn't it? That's why he wants to leave. Before whatever I've got gets spread around."

"Look, I'm sorry I said anything. It's nonsense, silly superstition. Stavros isn't educated. He still believes the old Greek myths and legends."

Mira looked at the smooth wall of C.J.'s back, remembering the woman at the temple, her kisses like honeyed darts, both sweet and penetrating. She wanted to tell C.J. what had happened, everything, but she knew that would be impossible. C.J. wouldn't understand. She'd only be more convinced that Stavros was a beautiful but superstitious rube and Mira was simply crazy.

"You have to leave here tomorrow when Stavros and I go," said C.J.

"Your new lover."

"I didn't say that."

"But he will be."

"Maybe."

Mira thought about it briefly. "Go fuck yourself."

Daylight splashed across Mira's sleeping face like hot liquid. She gasped and clutched the pillow. A warm breeze gusted in the open window where sunbeams streamed in to form an avenue of light.

C.J. was gone, the only evidence that she had ever been there the indentation of her head still on the pillow.

Mira got up and began to dress. The wound on her belly twinged. She looked down past her swollen breasts and saw that it was still open, a tiny bud-red slit below her navel. She touched it lightly with one finger and almost had an orgasm. Pleasure swam through her, stem to stern. Her head spun with the delirium of last night's ecstasy as she made her way outside into the village.

She had considered her few options and made a decision: She would go back to Baubo's temple and see if she could find some clue, or better yet, some respite from the madness that had overtaken her. That, at least, was her rationale. In truth, she hoped to find her lover of the day before, the goddess who gave birth to frogs and, perhaps more frighteningly, had incited her to last night's wantonness.

The day was furious with heat, the breeze offering no respite except to stir and redistribute the torpor as Mira started up the dirt track to the temple. No one was about. The village seemed deserted, even the taverna on the waterfront bereft of its usual clientele of domino-playing males. She moved slowly, her body stiff and achy from last night's outlandish exercise. At a crest in the journey, she paused to look out over the water and saw a large boat, a ferry, plowing westward in the direction of Piraeus.

Her heart caught and hitched as though a claw had punctured her aorta – C.J. and her new toy Stavros were surely on that boat.

Something moved on the horizon in the corner of her vision. She gazed behind her and staggered backward. Running, stumbling up the dirt track, came a dozen or more villagers. The man in the lead looked up and saw Mira. He pointed, beckoned to the others, urging them on. They began to run in earnest.

Mira stumbled forward in blind panic. So C.J. had been right – last night's escapades were not so easily forgotten or forgiven. Perhaps she would be jailed or expelled from the country. Or worse – something in the villagers' pursuit put her in mind of fates more ancient and punitive – adulteresses stoned and wanton women entombed alive in cloister walls.

She began to run, thinking only that she must reach the temple, that Baubo – witch goddess, whatever she might be – might help her, offer her a place to hide.

Her limbs were flagging, but terror lent her strength. She cut through fields of olive trees, skirting the sea, and climbed at last to the crest of the final bluff where the madwoman had given birth to toads.

And stopped, the breath rasping in her chest, unable to summon even one last reserve for further flight.

They were waiting for her. Hundreds of them. The entire village. They had known that she would come here and had arrived first, leaving only a handful behind to goad her into flight.

"Please," said Mira, but she knew the word was meaningless. They had not gone to all this trouble to merely turn away and leave her to her madness.

She took a few halting steps. The villagers stared.

Someone pulled out a dulcimer and began a melody. Another blew into a primitive bagpipe, the *tsambouna*.

The music threaded through the silence like a golden needle passing through white cotton.

Laughter started.

Mira didn't realize until some moments later that the weird, manic laughter was produced by her own throat, but its effect was instantaneous. The villagers began to jerk and twitch in what, at first glance, appeared to Mira to be a crude dance but which was, in actuality, a clumsy striptease. They began to caper and leap about, flinging items of their clothing into the air. Their aimless exuberance reminded Mira of the frogs' mad leaping, except that now the random jumping was accompanied by a hundred small obscenities.

A young woman with a baby on her hip exposed large rosy-nippled breasts. She squeezed and twisted a breast and milk squirted forth. It struck the face of a dancing man who opened his mouth wide and gobbled. Others gathered round. The woman emptied both breasts into the throng, milk running in hair and eyes, dripping from smacking lips.

Old women clad in widow's black scattered their funereal garb across the temple stones. Cackling, they caressed themselves and capered in lewd jigs.

An old man bent over and let loose a hornpipe melody of exuberant flatulence. The rhythm of his obscene tooting kept time with the *tsambouna* and the dulcimer while others laughed and clapped.

A woman lifted up her breast and suckled from her own nipple while with her other hand she milked the semen from the penis of her partner. A dog joined in the fray, aroused and thrusting at the dancers' legs. Some women dropped onto their hands and knees and vied to suck the canine's crimson stalk.

And madder grew the dancers and wilder their excesses with flowers plucked to make bouquets protruding out of anuses and cocks garlanded with spring anemones and vaginas sprouting orchids and rockroses.

The celebrants grabbed Mira by her hands and breasts and buttocks. Their feverish caresses stripped her clothes away and she was swept into the orgy. They peppered her with kisses but reserved the most ardent tonguings for the wound upon her belly, where Baubo's kiss had left a puckered replica of a tiny cunt.

"Baubo has returned to us," some of the old ones murmured. "Baubo has a priestess now, and we can dance again."

In the evening, before returning to the village, they brought Mira jugs of wine and beer and platters of the finest food. The women cleared the earth and made a bed for her amid the ruins of the temple. In the growing dark, alone now, she squatted naked on the hillside, gazing out to sea, trying to remember what was lost to her.

There had been a life for her out there once, school and home and lover, but all that seemed pale and vapid now, dim and distant as the far-off stars and moving rapidly away from her. She let it go with a sense more of relief than loss.

In the night, when she awoke in brief confusion, with fear plucking at her like the beak of some flesh-eating bird, she had only to touch her belly wound and pleasure spiraled up her spine. Her body bloomed with orgasms and her heart with song.

DESIRE BEGINS

Kathy Acker

I

I ABSOLUTELY LOVE TO fuck. These longings, unexplainable
longings deep within me, drive me wild, and I have no way of
relieving them. Living them. I'm 27 and I love to fuck. Sometimes with people I want to fuck; sometimes, and I can't tell when
but I remember these times, with anybody who'll touch me.
These, I call them nymphomaniac, times have nothing to do with
(are not caused by) physical pleasure, for my cunt could be sore, I
could be sick, and yet I'd feel the same way. I'll tease you till you
don't know what you're doing, honey, and grab; and then I'll do
anything for you.

I haven't always been this way. Once upon a time I was an
intelligent sedate girl, who, like every intelligent sedate girl, hated
her parents and didn't care about money. O in those days I didn't
care about anything! I dated boys, stayed out till 5.00 in the
morning then snuck home, read a lot of books. I cared more for
the books than anyone else and would kiss my books good-night
when I went to sleep. Would never go anywhere without a book.
But my downfall came. My parents kicked me out of the house
because I wasn't interested in marrying a rich man, I didn't care
enough about money to become a scientist or a prostitute, I
couldn't even figure out how to make any money.

I didn't. I became poor and had to find a way of justifying my lousy attitude about money. At first, like all poor people, I had delusions about being a great artist, but that quickly passed. I never did have any talent.

I want to fuck these two fantastic artists even though I'm not an artist: that's what this is about. This is the only way I can get them: (I only want them for a few hours. Days.) Jewels hang from the tips of silver branches. I also want money.

My name is Kathy Acker.

The story begins by me being totally bored.

Sunny California is totally boring; there are too many blond-assed surf jocks. I was lying on my bed, wondering if I should go down to the beach or sun myself on the patio until I passed out. I watched the curly silky brown hair below the damp palm of my hand rise and fall, I watched the rise, the mound twist in agony, laughed at myself. No way, I muttered, among these creeps no way. I need to love someone who can, by lightly, lightly stroking my flesh, tear open this reality, rip my flesh open until I bleed. Red jewels running down my legs and branches. I need someone who knows everything and who'll love me endlessly; then stop. My cats leaped up to me and rubbed their delicious bodies against my body. My cats didn't exist.

Suddenly heard a knocking at the door. No one ever knocks at the door, they just walk in. I wondered if it was FBI agents, or the telephone Mafia after Art Povera. I opened the door and saw Dan, I didn't know his name then, looking bewildered. Then, seeing me, looking scared. I realized I had forgotten to put clothes on. That's how southern California is: hot.

"Excuse me, I'm looking for 46 uh Belvedere."

"Oh you mean up the hill where David and Elly live; I'll show you. I have to get some clothes on."

He followed me into my small bedroom.

As I slowly bent over, reaching for my jeans, I noticed him watching me. He had brown hair, couldn't see his eyes because he squints so much but they look red, some acne, short with a body I like: heavy enough to run into and feel its weight on me; about 30 years old. I hesitantly took hold of my jeans. He started to talk again: he talks too much. I wanted him to rip off my skin, take me away to where I'd always be insane. He didn't want to fuck with me, much less do anything else. I slowly lifted my leg to put on my jeans, changed my mind. I turned around; suddenly we grabbed each other: I felt his body: his lips wet and large against my lips, his arms pressing my back and stomach into his thick endless stomach, his mouth over me, sucking me, exploring me I want this

"I want you you lousy motherfucker I want you to do everything to me I want you to tell me you want me I want you any way I can get you. Do you understand?" We run screaming out into the night, other people don't exist, feet touching the cold store, then the sand, then the black ocean water. I look up: black; toward the sand: black; I reach up for him and fall. The water passes over us. We stand up, spouting water; our mouths' wetness into each other's mouth cling together to stay erect. I rise up on my toes, the black waves rising, carefully, press my thighs into his so that his cock can touch my cunt. His right hand caresses his cock, touches its tip to my cunt lips, moves upward, into me I hold him tighter we fall

My hand touches my wet curling hairs then the thick lips of my cunt. Takes sand, rubs the sand into the outer lips of my cunt. Two areas of softness wetness touch me, move back so the cold air swirls at, touch me I feel warm liquid trickling between the swelling lips I feel them swelling a tongue a burning center touches me harder, inside the swollen lips: I lift my legs and imprison him. My nipples are hard as diamonds. The inner skin of my knees presses against his rough hairs: now I feel roughness: sandpaper rubbing the screaming skin above my clit. The joining of my inner lips almost more sensitive than my clit. Now I feel soft surface wetnesses, gently lap, now the burning center which becomes my burning center: rhythmically pressing until time becomes burning as I do. I'm totally relaxed. I'm a tongue which I can't control: which I beg to touch me each time it stops so I can open wider, rise rise toward the black, I open rising screaming I feel it: I feel waves of senses screaming I want more and more.

At the peak, as I think I'm beginning to descend, he throws himself on me and enters me making me come again again. All I feel is his cock in me moving circling circling every inch of my cunt walls moving back forth every inch, he stops, I can't, he starts slamming in to me not with his cock but the skin around his cock slamming into my clit I come I come he moves his cock into me slowly even more slowly, and then leaves.

For the new life, I have to change myself completely.

*   *   *

The next artist I meet in a bar in New York. I'm sick of artists. The next man I meet is tall, dark, and handsome. I was wearing a black silk sheath slashed in the back to the ruby which signals the delicate opening of my buttocks: tiny black diamonds in my ears and on the center of my fingernails. I had come to the bar to drink: it was an old transvestite bar East Village New York no one goes during the week, rows upon rows of white-covered tables low hanging chandeliers containing almost no light: mirrors which are walls reflect back, reflections upon reflections, tiny stars of light. The only people in the bar are the two women who run the bar, tiny grey-haired women who look like men: incredibly sexy. One or two Spanish hustlers. I wanted to be alone.

I had no background. I'm not giving you details about myself because these two occurrences are the first events of my life. Otherwise I don't exist: I'm a mirror for beauty. The man walked up to me and sat down. He bought two beers. I wasn't noticing him.

"What do you really want to happen?" he asked me. I couldn't answer him because I don't reveal the truth to people I know slightly, only to strangers and to people I know well and want to become. "I used to act as a stud," he was trying to put me at my ease. "Housewives would pick me up in their cars, pay me to satisfy them. I didn't mind because I hate housewives: that class. Then I used to work this motel: I'd knock on a door to a room, a man would start screaming "don't come in don't come in" scream louder and louder; after a while he'd throw a pair of semened-up underpants out the door. In the pants would be ten dollars."

I couldn't say anything to him because I was starting to respect him.

"I only like people of the working class," he went on. Underneath the table, he was slowly pouring wine on the black silk of my thigh. I moved my legs slightly, open, so the cold liquid would hit the insides of my thighs. Then close my thighs, rubbing them slowly together. "You have a lot of trouble with men, don't you?"

"Don't you love me?" I cried in anguish. "Don't you care anything about me?"

He gently took me in his arms kissed me. Lightly and gently. He didn't press me to him or touch me passionately. "Quick," he whispered. "Before they notice."

He threw me back on the velvet ledge we had been sitting on, pulled up my shift, and entered me. I wanted more. As I feel his cock rotate slowly around the skins of my cunt walls, touching each inch slowly too slowly, he began again to pour wine on my body: liquid cooling all of my skin except the inside burning skin of my cunt. Putting ice in my mouth on my eyes, around the thick heavy ridges of my breasts. Cock slowly easing out of me, I can't stand that, I can't stand that absence I start to scream I see my mound rise upward: the heavy brown hairs surrounded by white flesh, the white flesh against the black silk: I see his cock enter me, slide into me like it belongs in my slimy walls, I tighten my muscles I tighten them around the cock, jiggling, thrust upward, thousands of tiny fingers on the cock, fingers and burning tongues: this is public I have to move fast: explodes I explode and my mound rises upward, toward the red-black ceiling, I see my mound rise upward, toward the red-black ceiling I see us come fast.

He quickly got out of me, and arranged our clothes. No one in the bar had noticed. We kissed goodbye, perfunctorily, and he left.

Every night now I dream of my two lovers. I have no other life. This is the realm of complete freedom: I can put down anything. I see Dan: The inner skin of my knees presses against his rough hairs: now I feel roughness: sand-paper rubbing the screaming skin above my clit. The joining of my inner lips almost more sensitive than my clit. Now I feel soft surface wetnesses, gently lap, now the burning center which becomes my burning center: rhythmically pressing until time becomes burning as I do. I'm totally relaxed. I'm a tongue which I can't control: which I beg to touch me each time it stops so I can open wider, rise rise toward the black, I open rising screaming

I see my second artist love: I can't stand that absence I start to scream I see my mound rise upward: the heavy brown hairs surrounded by white flesh, the white flesh against the black silk: I see his cock enter me, slide into me like it belongs in my slimy walls, I tighten my muscles I tighten them around the cock, jiggling, thrust upward, thousands of tiny fingers on the cock, fingers and burning tongues: this is public I have to move fast: explodes I explode and my mound rises upward, toward the red-black ceiling, I see

I want a woman.

I'm sick of dreaming.

I decide to find these two artists no matter what no matter where. I'll be the most beautiful and intelligent woman in the world to them.

II

I want to make something beautiful: an old-fashioned wish. To do this I must first accomplish four tasks, for the last one I must die: Then I'll have something beautiful, and can fuck the men I want to fuck because they'll want to fuck me.

For the first task I have to learn to be as industrious as possible: I have to work as hard as possible to make up for my lack of beauty and charm. Not that I'm not extremely beautiful. I have to learn what is the best love-sex possible, and separate those people whom I can love from those people I can't love. I have until nightfall to do this.

Last night I dreamt I was standing on a low rise of grassy ground; Dan was standing next to me facing me. He put his arms around my neck kissed me, said "I love you." I said "I love you." Two years later I'm riding through a forest with my four younger sisters, green and wet, leaves in our eyes and skin; we push leaves out of the way the brown horse's neck lowered. My next-to-youngest sister tells me Dan asked her to marry him two months ago. I'm galloping wildly through the woods branches tear at my eyes flakes of my skin hanging. I try to go faster and faster. It's night. Three days later I appear, night, the livingroom of my parents' house: we're moving to Boston, a bayview overlooking a black sky, where I go to college. The skin of my face is torn; bruises over my naked arms; one of my eyes is bloodshot. My family's glad I haven't died. My father greets me, then my older sister who's tall, blonde, beautiful, intelligent. We love each other most. The room in which we're standing is large browns on browns; my parents are rich, not very rich, and liberals. A thin dark-haired man asks me if I want to go to a party. I want to: I rush upstairs to dress: my sister and the man, who's a close family friend, look happy because I'm not going to kill myself. I (outside the dream) look at myself (inside the dream): I'm tall and thin, short waving black hair: I'm not beautiful until you look at me for a long time. I'm very severe. When we walk into a large grey-white house, we realize the party's an artist party. The tall, dark, handsome artist walks over to me and asks me to dance. I wonder if he's asking me because he wants to marry a rich girl. He tells me he's a successful artist makes a lot of money. We dance, dance out to a dark balcony; he starts to take off my black dress as I lean over the portico. I've got two glasses of champagne: one in each hand. He says "I could strangle you like this" I get pissed and walk away. As I begin to walk away, I see Dan and some woman on the balcony: Dan walks over to the man I'm with. They greet each other: Dan admires the stranger's work. I nod hello to Dan. He announces he's getting married: introduces the woman with whom he's going to get married. I walk away to get more champagne. As I return to the balcony, a blonde woman walks up to the group the stranger says "I didn't know you wanted to come here." He introduces his wife to us. I'm going crazy but withstraining myself admirably. If I don't fuck someone soon know someone wants me. I'll have to ride my horse for three days again: do something wilder. I can't stop myself. I get another drink. Mel someone walks up to us says "I'm the only man here who isn't married or about to be married" meaning I might as well fuck him because I'm so desperate. I ask him to marry me since I have a lot of money: I'll support him. I tell him how much money I have. He says "Yes." I tell him to go shit on himself. I'm in a lousy mood. An old friend of mine comes up to me, who I haven't seen for a few months. I tell him I need someone's shoulder to cry on. His new lover comes up to him: he can't do anything. This dream's repulsively hetero. I get a bottle of champagne and drink it. I have to ride my horse through the dark forest, the winds swirling around. I rush out of the party. As I'm descending the wide wood steps, I turn around, see the tall dark artist. He asks if he can see me again. He's very severe. I say yes. I fall down the steps I'm so drunk. He asks me if I intend to drive myself home. I'm going to drive myself to the ocean so I can go swimming I'm rich do whatever I want he lifts me up puts me in my car drives me home I end up fucking him quickly then his wife comes I never see him again, I'm lying in my bed with my older sister who's very "I'll take care of you" severe type and whom I love. As we're fucking, her boyfriend enters the room and stops us because we're not supposed to act soooo

Last night I dreamt I was standing on a low rise of grassy ground; Dan was standing next to me facing me. He put his arms around my neck kissed me, said "I love you." I said "I love you." Two years later I'm riding through a forest with my four younger sisters, green and wet, leaves in our eyes and skin; we push leaves out of the way the brown horse's neck lowered. My next-to-youngest sister tells me Dan asked her to marry him two months ago. I'm galloping wildly through the woods branches tear at my eyes flakes of my skin hanging. I try to go faster and faster. It's night. Three days later I appear, night, the livingroom of my parents' house: we're moving to Boston, a bayview overlooking a black sky, where I go to college. The skin of my face is torn; bruises over my naked arms; one of my eyes is bloodshot. My family's glad I haven't died. My father greets me, then my older sister who's tall, blonde, beautiful, intelligent. We love each other most. The room in which we're standing is large browns on browns; my parents are rich, not very rich, and liberals. A thin dark-haired man asks me if I want to go to a party. I want to: I rush upstairs to dress: my sister and the man, who's a close family friend, look happy because I'm not going to kill myself. I (outside the dream) look at myself (inside the dream): I'm tall and thin, short waving black hair: I'm not beautiful until you look at me for a long time. I'm very severe. When we walk into a large grey-white house, we realize the party's an artist party. The tall, dark, handsome artist walks over to me and asks me to dance. I wonder if he's asking me because he wants to marry a rich girl. He tells me he's a successful artist makes a lot of money. We dance, dance out to a dark balcony; he starts to take off my black dress as I lean over the portico. I've got two glasses of champagne: one in each hand. He says "I could strangle you like this" I get pissed and walk away. As I begin to walk away, I see Dan and some woman on the balcony: Dan walks over to the man I'm with. They greet each other: Dan admires the stranger's work. I nod hello to Dan. He announces he's getting married: introduces the woman with whom he's going to get married. I walk away to get more champagne. As I return to the balcony, a blonde woman walks up to the group the stranger says "I didn't know you wanted to come here." He introduces his wife to us. I'm going crazy but withstraining myself admirably. If I don't fuck someone soon know someone wants me, I'll have to ride my horse for three days again: do something wilder. I can't stop myself. I get another drink. My sister who's also drunk asks me to dance, she's wearing a low grey gown; we dance in each other's arms giggling. I lie close in her arms: I lie backwards over her left arm. We're leaning against a grey wall under a picture: she kisses me, as she looks down on me I wonder if she now feel sexually toward me I'm excited, I ask her and she says she'd like to fuck me. I look up at her and kiss her: I want us to fuck in front of all these creepy people. Her thin dark-haired boyfriend comes over tells us we can't act too wildly: do what we want in our bedroom. Mel someone walks up to us says "I'm the only man here who isn't married or about to be married" meaning I might as well fuck him because I'm so desperate. I ask him to marry me since I have a lot of money: I'll support him. I tell him how much money I have. He says "Yes." I tell him to go shit on himself. I'm in a lousy mood. An old friend of mine comes up to me, who I haven't seen for a few months. I tell him I need someone's shoulder to cry on. His new lover comes up to him: he can't do anything. This dream's repulsively hetero. I get a bottle of champagne and drink it. I have to ride my horse through the dark forest, the winds swirling around. I rush out of the party. As I'm descending the wide wood steps, I turn around, see the tall dark artist. He asks if he can see me again. He's very severe. I say yes. I fall down the steps I'm so drunk. He asks me if I intend to drive myself home. I'm going to drive myself to the ocean so I can go swimming I'm rich and do whatever I want he lifts me up puts me in my car drives me home I end up fucking him quickly then his wife comes I never see him again, I'm lying in my bed with my older sister who's very "I'll take care of you" severe type and whom I love. As we're fucking, her boyfriend enters the room and stops us because we're not supposed to act soooo

Last night I dreamt I was standing on a low rise of grassy ground; Dan was standing next to me facing me. He put his arms around my neck kissed me, said "I love you." I said "I love you." Two years later I'm riding through a forest with my four younger sisters, green and wet, leaves in our eyes and skin; we push leaves out of the way the brown horse's neck lowered. My next-to-youngest sister tells me Dan asked her to marry him two months ago. I'm galloping wildly through the woods branches tear at my eyes flakes of my skin hanging. I try to go faster and faster. It's night. Three days later I appear, night, the livingroom of my parents' house: we're moving to Boston, a bayview overlooking a black sky, where I go to college. The skin of my face is torn; bruises over my naked arms; one of my eyes is bloodshot. My family's glad I haven't died. My father greets me, then my older sister who's tall, blonde, beautiful, intelligent. We love each other most. The room in which we're standing is large browns on browns; my parents are rich, not very rich, and liberals. A thin dark-haired man asks me if I want to go to a party. I want to: I rush upstairs to dress: my sister and the man, who's a close family friend, look happy because I'm not going to kill myself. I (outside the dream) look at myself (inside the dream): I'm tall and thin, short waving black hair: I'm not beautiful until you look at me for a long time. I'm very severe. When we walk into a large grey-white house, we realize the party's an artist party. The tall, dark, handsome artist walks over to me and asks me to dance. I wonder if he's asking me because he wants to marry a rich girl. He tells me he's a successful artist makes a lot of money. We dance, dance out to a dark balcony; he starts to take off my black dress as I lean over the portico. I've got two glasses of champagne: one in each hand. He says "I could strangle you like this" I get pissed and walk away. As I begin to walk away, I see Dan and some woman on the balcony: Dan walks over to the man I'm with. They greet each other: Dan admires the stranger's work. I nod hello to Dan. He announces he's getting married: introduces the woman with whom he's going to get married. I walk away to get more champagne. As I return to the balcony, a blonde woman walks up to the group the stranger says "I didn't know you wanted to come here." He introduces his wife to us. I'm going crazy but withstraining myself admirably. If I don't fuck someone soon know someone wants me, I'll have to ride my horse for three days again: do something wilder. I can't stop myself. I get another drink. My sister who's also drunk asks me to dance, she's wearing a low grey gown; we dance in each other's arms giggling. I lie close in her arms: I lie backwards over her left arm. We're leaning against a grey wall under a picture: she kisses me, as she looks down on me I wonder if she now feels sexually toward me I'm excited, I ask her and she says she'd like to fuck me. I look up at her and kiss her: I want us to fuck in front of all these creepy people. Her thin dark-haired boyfriend comes over tells us we can't act too wildly: do what we want in our bedroom. Mel someone walks up to us says "I'm the only man here who isn't married or about to be married" meaning I might as well fuck him because I'm so desperate. I ask him to marry me since I have a lot of money: I'll support him. I tell him how much money I have. He says "Yes." I tell him to go shit on himself. I'm in a lousy mood. An old friend of mine comes up to me, who I haven't seen for a few months. I tell him I need someone's shoulder to cry on. His new lover comes up to him: he can't do anything. This dream's repulsively hetero. I get a bottle of champagne and drink it. I have to ride my horse through the dark forest, the winds swirling around. I rush out of the party. As I'm descending the wide wood steps, I turn around, see the tall dark artist. He asks if he can see me again. He's very severe. I say yes. I fall down the steps I'm so drunk. He asks me if I intend to drive myself home. I'm going to drive myself to the ocean so I can go swimming I'm rich do whatever I want he lifts me up puts me in my car drives me home I end up fucking him quickly then his wife comes I never see him again, I'm lying in my bed with my older sister who's very "I'll take care of you" severe type and whom I love. As we're fucking, her boyfriend enters the room and stops us because we're not supposed to act soooo

Last night I dreamt I was standing on a low rise of grassy ground; Dan was standing next to me facing me. He put his arms around my neck kissed me, said "I love you." I said "I love you." Two years later I'm riding through a forest with my four youngest sisters, green and wet, leaves in our eyes and skin; we push leaves out of the way the brown horse's neck lowered. My next-to-youngest sister tells me Dan asked her to marry him two months ago. I'm galloping wildly through the woods branches tear at my eyes flakes of my skin hanging. I try to go faster and faster. It's night. Three days later I appear, night, the livingroom of my parents' house: we're moving to Boston, a bayview overlooking a black sky, where I go to college. The skin of my face is torn; bruises over my naked arms; one of my eyes is bloodshot. My family's glad I haven't died. My father greets me, then my older sister who's tall, blonde, beautiful, intelligent. We love each

other most. The room in which we're standing is large browns on
browns; my parents are rich, not very rich, and liberals. A thin
dark-haired man asks me if I want to go to a party. I want to: I
rush upstairs to dress: my sister and the man, who's a close family
friend, look happy because I'm not going to kill myself. I (outside
the dream) look at myself (inside the dream): I'm tall and thin,
short waving black hair: I'm not beautiful until you look at me for
a long time. I'm very severe. When we walk into a large grey-
white house, we realize the party's an artist party. The tall, dark,
handsome artist walks over to me and asks me to dance. I wonder
if he's asking me because he wants to marry a rich girl. He tells me
he's a successful artist makes a lot of money. We dance, dance out
to a dark balcony; he starts to take off my black dress as I lean
over the portico. I've got two glasses of champagne: one in each
hand. He says "I could strangle you like this" I get pissed and
walk away. As I begin to walk away, I see Dan and some woman
on the balcony: Dan walks over to the man I'm with. They greet
each other: Dan admires the stranger's work. I nod hello to Dan.
He announces he's getting married: introduces the woman with
whom he's going to get married. I walk away to get more
champagne. As I return to the balcony, a blonde woman walks
up to the group the stranger says "I didn't know you wanted to
come here." He introduces his wife to us. I'm going crazy but
withstraining myself admirably. If I don't fuck someone soon
know someone wants me, I'll have to ride my horse for three days
again: do something wilder. I can't stop myself. I get another
drink. My sister who's also drunk asks me to dance, she's wearing
a low grey gown; we dance in each other's arms giggling. I lie
close in her arms: I lie backwards over her left arm. We're leaning
against a grey wall under a picture: she kisses me, as she looks
down on me I wonder if she now feel sexually toward me I'm
excited, I ask her and she says she'd like to fuck me. I look up at
her and kiss her: I want us to fuck in front of all these creepy
people. Her thin dark-haired boyfriend comes over tells us we
can't act too wildly: do what we want in our bedroom. Mel
someone walks up to us says "I'm the only man here who isn't
married or about to be married" meaning I might as well fuck
him because I'm so desperate. I ask him to marry me since I have
a lot of money: I'll support him. I tell him how much money I
have. He says "Yes." I tell him to go shit on himself. I'm in a

lousy mood. An old friend of mine comes up to me, who I haven't seen for a few months. I tell him I need someone's shoulder to cry on. His new lover comes up to him: he can't do anything. This dream's repulsively hetero. I get a bottle of champagne and drink it. I have to ride my horse through the dark forest, the winds swirling around. I rush out of the party. As I'm descending the wide wood steps, I turn around, see the tall dark artist. He asks if he can see me again. He's very severe. I say yes. I fall down the steps I'm so drunk. He asks me if I intend to drive myself home. I'm going to drive myself to the ocean so I can go swimming I'm rich do whatever I want he lifts me up puts me in my car drives me home I end up fucking him quickly then his wife comes I see him again, I'm lying in my bed with my older sister who's very "I'll take care of you" severe type and whom I love. As we're fucking, her boyfriend enters the room and stops us because we're not supposed to act soooo

THE AGE OF DESIRE

Clive Barker

THE BURNING MAN propelled himself down the steps of the Hume Laboratories as the police car – summoned, he presumed, by the alarm either Welles or Dance had set off upstairs – appeared at the gate and swung up the driveway. As he ran from the door the car screeched up to the steps and discharged its human cargo. He waited in the shadows, too exhausted by terror to run any further, certain that they would see him. But they disappeared through the swing doors without so much as a glance towards his torment. Am I on fire at all? he wondered. Was this horrifying spectacle – his flesh baptized with a polished flame that seared but failed to consume – simply an hallucination, for his eyes and his eyes only? If so, perhaps all that he had suffered up in the laboratory had also been delirium. Perhaps he had not truly committed the crimes he had fled from, the heat in his flesh licking him into ecstasies.

He looked down his body. His exposed skin still crawled with livid dots of fire, but one by one they were being extinguished. He was going out, he realized, like a neglected bonfire. The sensations that had suffused him – so intense and so demanding that they had been as like pain as pleasure – were finally deserting his nerve-endings, leaving a numbness for which he was grateful. His body, now appearing from beneath the veil of fire, was in a sorry condition. His skin was a panic-map of scratches, his clothes torn to shreds, his hands sticky with coagulating blood; blood, he knew, that was not his own. There was no avoiding the bitter truth. He *had* done all he had imagined doing. Even now the officers would be staring down at his atrocious handiwork.

He crept away from his niche beside the door and down the driveway, keeping a lookout for the return of the two policemen; neither reappeared. The street beyond the gate was deserted. He started to run. He had managed only a few paces when the alarm in the building behind him was abruptly cut off. For several seconds his ears rang in sympathy with the silenced bell. Then, eerily, he began to hear the sound of heat – the surreptitious murmuring of embers – distant enough that he didn't panic, yet close as his heartbeat.

He limped on, to put as much distance as he could between him and his felonies before they were discovered; but however fast he ran, the heat went with him, safe in some backwater of his gut, threatening with every desperate step he took to ignite him afresh.

It took Dooley several seconds to identify the cacophony he was hearing from the upper floor now that McBride had hushed the alarm bell. It was the high-pitched chattering of monkeys, and it came from one of the many rooms down the corridor to his right.

"Virgil," he called down the stairwell. "Get up here."

Not waiting for his partner to join him, Dooley headed off towards the source of the din. Half-way along the corridor the smell of static and new carpeting gave way to a more pungent combination: urine, disinfectant and rotting fruit. Dooley slowed his advance: he didn't like the smell, any more than he liked the hysteria in the babble of monkey-voices. But McBride was slow in answering his call, and after a short hesitation, Dooley's curiosity got the better of his disquiet. Hand on truncheon, he approached the open door and stepped in. His appearance sparked off another wave of frenzy from the animals, a dozen or so rhesus monkeys. They threw themselves around in their cages, somersaulting, screeching and berating the wiremesh. Their excitement was infectious. Dooley could feel the sweat begin to squeeze from his pores.

"Is there anybody here?" he called out.

The only reply came from the prisoners: more hysteria, more

cage-rattling. He stared across the room at them. They stared
back, their teeth bared in fear or welcome; Dooley didn't know
which, nor did he wish to test their intentions. He kept well clear
of the bench on which the cages were lined up as he began a
perfunctory search of the laboratory.

"I wondered what the hell the smell was," McBride said,
appearing at the door.

"Just animals," Dooley replied.

"Don't they ever wash? Filthy buggers."

"Anything downstairs?"

"Nope," McBride said, crossing to the cages. The monkeys
met his advance with more gymnastics. "Just the alarm."

"Nothing up here either," Dooley said. He was about to add,
"*Don't do that*," to prevent his partner putting his finger to the
mesh, but before the words were out one of the animals seized the
proffered digit and bit it. McBride wrested his finger free and
threw a blow back against the mesh in retaliation. Squealing its
anger, the occupant flung its scrawny body about in a lunatic
fandango that threatened to pitch cage and monkey alike on to the
floor.

"You'll need a tetanus shot for that," Dooley commented.

"Shit!" said McBride, "what's wrong with the little bastard
anyhow?"

"Maybe they don't like strangers."

"They're out of their tiny minds." McBride sucked rumina-
tively on his finger, then spat. "I mean, look at them."

Dooley didn't answer.

"I said, *look* . . ." McBride repeated.

Very quietly, Dooley said: "Over here."

"What is it?"

"Just come over here."

McBride drew his gaze from the row of cages and across the
cluttered work-surfaces to where Dooley was staring at the
ground, the look on his face one of fascinated revulsion. McBride
neglected his finger-sucking and threaded his way amongst the
benches and stools to where his partner stood.

"Under there," Dooley murmured.

On the scuffed floor at Dooley's feet was a woman's beige
shoe; beneath the bench was the shoe's owner. To judge by her
cramped position she had either been secreted there by the

miscreant or had dragged herself out of sight and died in hiding.

"Is she dead?" McBride asked.

"Look at her, for Christ's sake," Dooley replied, "she's been torn open."

"We've got to check for vital signs," McBride reminded him. Dooley made no move to comply, so McBride squatted down in front of the victim and checked for a pulse at her ravaged neck. There was none. Her skin was still warm beneath his fingers however. A gloss of saliva on her cheek had not yet dried.

Dooley, calling his report through, looked down at the deceased. The worst of her wounds, on the upper torso, were masked by McBride's crouching body. All he could see was a fall of auburn hair and her legs, one foot shoeless, protruding from her hiding place. They were beautiful legs, he thought; he might have whistled after such legs, once upon a time.

"She's a Doctor or a technician," McBride said, "she's wearing a lab coat." Or she had been. In fact the coat had been ripped open, as had the layers of clothing beneath, and then, as if to complete the exhibition, the skin and muscle beneath that. McBride peered into her chest; the sternum had been snapped and the heart teased from its seat, as if her killer had wanted to take it as a keepsake and been interrupted in the act. He perused her without squeamishness; he had always prided himself on his strong stomach.

"Are you satisfied she's dead?"

"Never saw deader."

"Carnegie's coming down," Dooley said, crossing to one of the sinks. Careless of fingerprints, he turned on the tap and splashed a handful of cold water on to his face. When he looked up from his ablutions McBride had left off his tête-à-tête with the corpse and was walking down the laboratory towards a bank of machinery.

"What do they do here, for Christ's sake?" he remarked. "Look at all this stuff."

"Some kind of research faculty," Dooley said.

"What do they research?"

"How the hell do I know?" Dooley snapped. The ceaseless chatterings of the monkeys and the proximity of the dead woman, made him want to desert the place. "Let's leave it be, huh?"

McBride ignored Dooley's request; equipment fascinated him.

He stared entranced at the encephalograph and electrocardio-
graph; at the print-out units still disgorging yards of blank paper
on to the floor; at the video display monitors and the consoles.
The scene brought the *Marie Celeste* to his mind. This deserted
ship of science – still humming some tuneless song to itself as it
sailed on, though there was neither Captain nor crew left behind
to attend upon it.

Beyond the wall of equipment was a window, no more than a
yard square. McBride had assumed it led on to the exterior of the
building, but now that he looked more closely he realized it did
not. A test-chamber lay beyond the banked units.

'Dooley . . .?" he said, glancing round. The man had gone,
however, down to meet Carnegie presumably. Content to be left
to his exploration, McBride returned his attention to the window.
There was no light on inside. Curious, he walked around the back
of the banked equipment, until he found the chamber door. It
was ajar. Without hesitation, he stepped through.

Most of the light through the window was blocked by the
instruments on the other side; the interior was dark. It took
McBride's eyes a few seconds to get a true impression of the chaos
the chamber contained: the overturned table; the chair of which
somebody had made matchwood; the tangle of cables and demolished equipment – cameras, perhaps, to monitor proceedings in
the chamber? – clusters of lights which had been similarly
smashed. No professional vandal could have made a more thorough job of breaking up the chamber than had been made.

There was a smell in the air which McBride recognized but,
irritatingly, couldn't place. He stood still, tantalized by the scent.
The sound of sirens rose from down the corridor outside;
Carnegie would be here in moments. Suddenly, the smell's
association came to him. It was the same scent that twitched
in his nostrils when, after making love to Jessica and – as was his
ritual – washing himself, he returned from the bathroom to the
bedroom. It was the smell of sex. He smiled.

His face was still registering pleasure when a heavy object
sliced through the air and met his nose. He felt the cartilage give,
and a rush of blood come. He took two or three giddy steps
backwards, thereby avoiding the subsequent slice, but lost his
footing in the disarray. He fell awkwardly in a litter of glass
shards, and looked up to see his assailant, wielding a metal bar,

moving towards him. The man's face resembled one of the
monkeys: the same yellowed teeth, the same rabid eyes. "*No!*"
the man shouted, as he brought his makeshift club down on
McBride, who managed to ward off the blow with his arm,
snatching at the weapon in so doing. The attack had taken
him unawares but now, with the pain in his mashed nose to
add fury to his response, he was more than the equal of the
aggressor. He plucked the club from the man, sweets from a babe,
and leapt, roaring, to his feet. Any precepts he might once have
been taught about arrest techniques had fled from his mind. He
lay a hail of blows on the man's head and shoulders, forcing him
backwards across the chamber. The man cowered beneath the
assault, and eventually slumped, whimpering, against the wall.
Only now, with his antagonist abused to the verge of unconsciousness, did McBride's furore falter. He stood in the middle of
the chamber, gasping for breath, and watched the beaten man slip
down the wall. He had made a profound error. The assailant, he
now realized, was dressed in a white laboratory coat; he was, as
Dooley was irritatingly fond of saying, on the side of the angels.

"Damn," said McBride, "shit, hell and damn."

The man's eyes flickered open, and he gazed up at McBride.
His grasp on consciousness was evidently tenuous, but a look of
recognition crossed his wide-browed, sombre face. Or rather,
recognition's absence.

"You're not him," he murmured.

"Who?" said McBride, realizing he might yet salvage his
reputation from this fiasco if he could squeeze a clue from the
witness. "Who did you think I was?"

The man opened his mouth, but no words emerged. Eager to
hear the testimony, McBride crouched beside him and said:
"Who did you think you were attacking?"

Again the mouth opened; again no audible words emerged.
McBride pressed his suit. "It's important," he said, "just tell me
who was here."

The man strove to voice his reply. McBride pressed his ear to
the trembling mouth.

"In a pig's eye," the man said, then passed out, leaving McBride
to curse his father, who'd bequeathed him a temper he was afraid he
would probably live to regret. But then, what was living for?

*   *   *

Inspector Carnegie was used to boredom. For every rare moment of genuine discovery his professional life had furnished him with, he had endured hour upon hour of waiting. For bodies to be photographed and examined, for lawyers to be bargained with and suspects intimidated. He had long ago given up attempting to fight this tide of *ennui* and, after his fashion, had learned the art of going with the flow. The processes of investigation could not be hurried; the wise man, he had come to appreciate, let the pathologists, the lawyers and all their tribes have their tardy way. All that mattered, in the fullness of time, was that the finger be pointed and that the guilty quake.

Now, with the clock on the laboratory wall reading twelve fifty-three a.m., and even the monkeys hushed in their cages, he sat at one of the benches and waited for Hendrix to finish his calculations. The surgeon consulted the thermometer, then stripped off his gloves like a second skin and threw them down on to the sheet on which the decreased lay. "It's always difficult," the Doctor said, "fixing time of death. She's lost less than three degrees. I'd say she's been dead under two hours."

"The officers arrived at a quarter to twelve," Carnegie said, "so she died maybe half an hour before that?"

"Something of that order."

"Was she put in there?" he asked, indicating the place beneath the bench.

"Oh certainly. There's no way she hid herself away. Not with those injuries. They're quite something, aren't they?"

Carnegie stared at Hendrix. The man had presumably seen hundreds of corpses, in every conceivable condition, but the enthusiasm in his pinched features was unqualified. Carnegie found that mystery more fascinating in its way than that of the dead woman and her slaughterer. How could anyone possibly enjoy taking the rectal temperature of a corpse? It confounded him. But the pleasure was there, gleaming in the man's eyes.

"Motive?" Carnegie asked.

"Pretty explicit, isn't it? Rape. There's been very thorough molestation; contusions around the vagina; copious semen deposits. Plenty to work with."

"And the wounds on her torso?"

"Ragged. Tears more than cuts."

"Weapon?"

"Don't know." Hendrix made an inverted U of his mouth. "I mean, the flesh has been *mauled*. If it weren't for the rape evidence I'd be tempted to suggest an animal."

"Dog, you mean?"

"I was thinking more of a tiger," Hendrix said.

Carnegie frowned. "Tiger?"

"Joke," Hendrix replied, "I was making a joke, Carnegie. My Christ, do you have *any* sense of irony?"

"This isn't funny," Carnegie said.

"I'm not laughing," Hendrix replied, with a sour look.

"The man McBride found in the test-chamber?"

"What about him?"

"Suspect?"

"Not in a thousand years. We're looking for a *maniac*, Carnegie. Big; strong. Wild."

"And the wounding? Before or after?"

Hendrix scowled. "I don't know. Post-mortem will give us more. But for what it's worth, I think our man was in a frenzy. I'd say the wounding and the rape were probably simultaneous."

Carnegie's normally phlegmatic features registered something close to shock. "Simultaneous?"

Hendrix shrugged. "Lust's a funny thing," he said.

"Hilarious," came the appalled reply.

As was his wont, Carnegie had his driver deposit him half a mile from his doorstep to allow him a head-clearing walk before home, hot chocolate and slumber. The ritual was observed religiously, even when the Inspector was dog-tired. He used to stroll to wind down before stepping over the threshold; long experience had taught him that taking his professional concerns into the house assisted neither the investigation nor his domestic life. He had learned the lesson too late to keep his wife from leaving him and his children from estrangement, but he applied the principle still.

Tonight, he walked slowly, to allow the distressing scenes the evening had brought to recede somewhat. The route took him past a small cinema which, he had read in the local press, was soon to be demolished. He was not surprised. Though he was no cineaste the fare the flea-pit provided had degenerated in recent years. The week's offering was a case in point: a double-bill of horror movies. Lurid and derivative stuff to judge by the posters, with their crude graphics and their unashamed hyperbole. '*You May Never Sleep Again*!' one of the hook-lines read; and beneath it a woman – very much awake – cowered in the shadow of a two-headed man. What trivial images the populists conjured to stir some fear in their audiences. The walking dead; nature grown vast, and rampant in a miniature world; blood-eaters, omens, fire-walkers, thunderstorms and all the other foolishness the public cowered before. It was all so laughably trite: amongst that catalogue of penny dreadfuls there wasn't one that equalled the banality of human appetite, which horror (or the consequences of same) he saw every week of his working life. Thinking of it, his mind thumbed through a dozen snapshots: the dead by torchlight, face down and thrashed to oblivion; and the living too, meeting his mind's eye with hunger in theirs: for sex, for narcotics, for others' pain. Why didn't they put *that* on the posters?

As he reached his home a child squealed in the shadows beside his garage; the cry stopped him in his tracks. It came again, and this time he recognized it for what it was. No child at all, but a cat, or cats, exchanging love-calls in the darkened passageway. He went to the place to shoo them off. Their venereal secretions made the passage stink. He didn't need to yell; his footfall was sufficient to scare them away. They darted in all directions, not two, but half a dozen of them: a veritable orgy had been underway apparently. He had arrived on the spot too late however; the stench of their seductions was overpowering.

Carnegie looked blankly at the elaborate set-up of monitors and video-recorders that dominated his office.

"What in Christ's name is this about?" he wanted to know.

"The video tapes," said Boyle, his number two, "from the laboratory. I think you ought to have a look at them. Sir."

Though they had worked in tandem for seven months, Boyle was not one of Carnegie's favourite officers; you could practically smell the ambition off his smooth hide. In someone half his age again such greed would have been objectionable; in a man of thirty it verged on the obscene. This present display – the mustering of equipment ready to confront Carnegie when he walked in at eight in the morning – was just Boyle's style: flashy and redundant.

"Why so many screens?" Carnegie asked acidly. "Do I get it in stereo too?"

"They had three cameras running simultaneously, sir. Covering the experiment from several angles."

"*What* experiment?"

Boyle gestured for his superior to sit down. Obsequious to a fault, aren't you, thought Carnegie; much good it'll do you.

"Right," Boyle instructed the technician at the recorders, "roll the tapes."

Carnegie sipped at the cup of hot chocolate he had brought in with him. The beverage was a weakness of his, verging on addiction. On the days when the machine supplying it broke down he was an unhappy man indeed. He looked at the three screens. Suddenly, a title.

"*Project Blind Boy*", the words read, "*Restricted.*"

"*Blind Boy*?" said Carnegie. "What, or *who*, is that?"

"It's obviously a code word of some kind," Boyle said.

"*Blind Boy. Blind Boy.*" Carnegie repeated the phrase as if to beat it into submission, but before he could solve the problem the images on the three monitors diverged. They pictured the same subject – a bespectacled male in his late twenties sitting in a chair – but each showed the scene from a different angle. One took in the subject full length, and in profile; the second was a three-quarter medium shot, angled from above; the third a straight forward close up of the subject's head and shoulders, shot through the glass of the test-chamber, and from the front. The three images were in black and white, and none were completely centred or focused. Indeed, as the tapes began to run, somebody was still adjusting such technicalities. A backwash of informal chatter ran between the subject and the woman – recognizable even in brief glimpses as the deceased – who was applying electrodes to his forehead. Much of the talk between them was difficult to catch; the acoustics in the chamber frustrated microphone and listener alike.

"The woman's Doctor Dance," Boyle offered. "The victim."

"Yes," said Carnegie, watching the screens intently, "I recognize her. How long does this preparation go on for?"

"Quite a while. Most of it's unedifying."

"Well, get to the edifying stuff, then."

"Fast forward," Boyle said. The technician obliged, and the

actors on the three screens became squeaking comedians.
"Wait!" said Boyle. "Back up a short way." Again, the technician
did as instructed. "There!" said Boyle. "Stop there. Now run on
at normal speed." The action settled back to its natural pace.
"This is where it really begins, sir."

Carnegie had come to the end of his hot chocolate; he put his
finger into the soft sludge at the bottom of the cup, delivering the
sickly-sweet dregs to his tongue. On the screens Doctor Dance
had approached the subject with a syringe, was now swabbing the
crook of his elbow, and injecting him. Not for the first time since
his visit to the Hume Laboratories did Carnegie wonder precisely
what they did at the establishment. Was this kind of procedure *de
rigueur* in pharmaceutical research? The implicit secrecy of
experiment – late at night in an otherwise deserted building –
suggested not. And there was that imperative on the title-card –
"Restricted". What they were watching had clearly never been
intended for public viewing.

"Are you comfortable?" a man, off camera, now enquired. The
subject nodded. His glasses had been removed, and he looked
slightly bemused without them. An unremarkable face, thought
Carnegie; the subject – as yet unnamed – was neither Adonis nor
Quasimodo. He was receding slightly, and his wispy, dirty blond
hair touched his shoulders.

"I'm fine, Doctor Welles," he replied to the off-camera ques-
tioner.

"You don't feel hot at all? Sweaty?"

"Not really," the guinea-pig replied, slightly apologetically. "I
feel ordinary."

That you are, Carnegie thought; then to Boyle: "Have you
been through the tapes to the end?"

"No, sir," Boyle replied. "I thought you'd want to see them
first. I only ran them as far as the injection."

"Any word from the hospital on Doctor Welles?"

"At the last call he was still comatose."

Carnegie grunted, and returned his attention to the screens.
Following the burst of action with the injection, the tapes now
settled into non-activity: the three cameras fixed on their short-
sighted subject with beady stares, the torpor occasionally interrupted by an enquiry from Welles as to the subject's condition. It
remained the same. After three or four minutes of this eventless

study even his occasional blinks began to assume major dramatic significance.

"Don't think much of the plot," the technician commented. Carnegie laughed; Boyle looked discomforted. Two or three more minutes passed in a similar manner.

"This doesn't look too hopeful," Carnegie said. "Run through it at speed, will you?"

The technician was about to obey when Boyle said: "*What*."

Carnegie glanced across at the man, irritated by his intervention, and then back at the screens. Something *was* happening: a subtle transformation had overtaken the insipid features of the subject. He had begun to smile to himself, and was sinking down in his chair as if submerging his gangling body in a warm bath. His eyes, which had so far expressed little but affable indifference, now began to flicker closed, and then, once closed, opened again. When they did so there was a quality in them not previously visible: a hunger that seemed to reach out from the screen and into the calm of the Inspector's office.

Carnegie put down his chocolate cup and approached the screens. As he did so the subject also got up out of his chair and walked towards the glass of the chamber, leaving two of the cameras' ranges. The third still recorded him however, as he pressed his face against the window, and for a moment the two men faced each other through layers of glass and time, seemingly meeting each other's gaze.

The look on the man's face was critical now, the hunger was rapidly outgrowing sane control. Eyes burning, he laid his lips against the chamber window and kissed it, his tongue working against the glass.

"What in Christ's name is going on?" Carnegie said.

A prattle of voices had begun on the soundtrack; Doctor Welles was vainly asking the testee to articulate his feelings, whilde Dance called off figures from the various monitoring instruments. It was difficult to hear much clearly – the din was further supplemented by an eruption of chatter from the caged monkeys – but it was evident that the readings coming through from the man's body were escalating. His face was flushed; his skin gleamed with a sudden sweat. He resembled a martyr with the tinder at his feet freshly lit; wild with a fatal ecstasy. He stopped french-kissing the window, tearing off the electrodes at his temples and the sensors from his arms and chest. Dance, her voice now registering alarm, called out for him to stop. Then she moved across the camera's view and out again; crossing, Carnegie presumed, to the chamber door.

"Better not," he said, as if this drama were played out at his behest, and at a whim he could prevent the tragedy. But the woman took no notice. A moment later she appeared in long shot as she stepped into the chamber. The man moved to greet her, throwing over equipment as he did so. She called out to him – his name, perhaps. If so, it was inaudible over the monkeys' hullabaloo. "Shit," said Carnegie, as the testee's flailing arms caught first the profile camera, and then the three-quarter medium shot: two of the three monitors went dead. Only the head-on shot, the camera safe outside the chamber, still recorded events, but the tightness of the shot precluded more than an occasional glimpse of a moving body. Instead, the camera's sober eye gazed on, almost ironically, at the saliva smeared glass of the chamber window, blind to the atrocities being committed a few feet out of range.

"What in Christ's name did they give him?" Carnegie said, as, somewhere off-camera, the woman's screams rose over the screeching of the apes.

Jerome woke in the early afternoon, feeling hungry and sore. When he threw the sheet off his body he was appalled at his state: his torso was scored with scratches, and his groin region was redraw. Wincing, he moved to the edge of the bed and sat there for a while, trying to piece the previous evening back together again. He remembered going to the Laboratories, but very little after that. He had been a paid guinea-pig for several months, giving of his blood, comfort and patience to supplement his meagre earnings as a translator. The arrangement had begun courtesy of a friend who did similar work, but whereas Figley had been part of the Laboratories' mainstream programme, Jerome had been approached, after one week at the place, by Doctors Welles and Dance, who had invited him – subject to a series of psychological tests – to work exclusively for them. It had been made clear from the outset that their project (he had never even been told its purpose) was of a secret nature, and that they would demand his total dedication and discretion. He had needed the funds, and the recompense they offered was marginally better than that paid by the Laboratories, so he had agreed, although the hours they had demanded of him were unsociable. For several weeks now he had been required to attend the Research facility late at night and often working into the small hours of the morning as he endured Welles' interminable questions about his private life, and Dance's glassy stare.

Thinking of her cold look, he felt a tremor in him. Was it because once he had fooled himself that she had looked upon him more fondly than a doctor need? Such self-deception, he chided himself, was pitiful. He was not the stuff of which women dreamt, and each day he walked the streets reinforced that conviction. He could not remember one occasion in his adult life when a woman had looked his way, and kept looking; a time when an appreciative glance of his had been returned. Why this should bother him now, he wasn't certain: his loveless condition, was, he knew, commonplace. And Nature had been kind; knowing, it seemed, that the gift of allurement had passed him by, it had seen fit to minimize his libido. Weeks passed without his conscious thoughts mourning his enforced chastity.

Once in a while, when he heard the pipes roar, he might wonder what Mrs Morrisey, his landlady, looked like in her bath: might imagine the firmness of her soapy breasts, or the dark divide of her rump as she stooped to put talcum powder between her toes. But such torments were, blissfully, infrequent. And when his cup brimmed he would pocket the money he had saved from his sessions at the Laboratories, and buy an hour's companionship from a woman called Angela (he'd never learned her second name) in Greek Street.

It would be several weeks before he did so again, he thought: whatever he had done last night, or, more correctly, had done to him, the bruises alone had nearly crippled him. The only plausible explanation – though he couldn't recall any details – was that he'd been beaten up on the way back from the Laboratories; either that, or he'd stepped into a bar and somebody had picked a fight with him. It had happened before, on occasion. He had one of those faces that awoke the bully in drunkards.

He stood up and hobbled to the small bathroom adjoining his room. His glasses were missing from their normal spot beside the shaving mirror, and his reflection was woefully blurred, but it was apparent that his face was as badly scratched as the rest of his anatomy. And more: a clump of hair had been pulled out from above his left ear; clotted blood ran down to his neck. Painfully, he bent to the task of cleaning his wounds, then bathing them in a stinging solution of antiseptic. That done, he returned into his bedsitting-room to seek out his spectacles. But search as he might, he could not locate them. Cursing his idiocy, he rooted amongst his belongings for his old pair, and found them. Their prescription was out of date – his eyes had worsened considerably since he'd worn them – but they at least brought his surroundings into a dreamy kind of focus.

An indisputable melancholy had crept up on him, compounded of his pain and those unwelcome thoughts of Mrs Morrisey. To keep its intimacy at bay he turned on the radio. A sleek voice emerged, purveying the usual palliatives. Jerome had always had contempt for popular music and its apologists, but now, as he mooched around the small room, unwilling to clothe himself with chafing weaves when his scratches still pained him, the songs began to stir something other than scorn in him. It was as though he was hearing the words and music for the first time: as though all his life he had been deaf to their sentiments. Enthralled, he forgot his pain, and listened. The songs told one seamless and obsessive story: of love lost and found, only to be lost again. The lyricists filled the airwaves with metaphor – much of it ludicrous, but no less potent for that. Of paradise, of hearts on fire; of birds, bells, journeys, sunsets; of passion as lunacy, as flight, as unimaginable treasure. The songs did not calm him with their fatuous sentiments; they flayed him, evoking, despite feeble rhyme and trite melody, a world bewitched by desire. He began to tremble. His eyes, strained (or so he reasoned) by the unfamiliar spectacles, began to delude him. It seemed as though he could see traces of light in his skin: sparks flying from the ends of his fingers.

He stared at his hands and arms; the illusion, far from retreating in the face of this scrutiny, increased. Beads of brightness, like the traces of fire in ash, began to climb through his veins, multiplying even as he watched. Curiously, he felt no distress. This burgeoning fire merely reflected the passion in the story the songs were telling him: love, they said, was in the air, round every corner, waiting to be found. He thought again of the widow Morrisey in the flat below him, going about her business, sighing, no doubt, as he had done; awaiting her hero. The more he thought of her the more inflamed he became. She would not reject him, of that the songs convinced him; or if she did he must press his case until (again, as the songs promised) she surrendered to him. Suddenly, at the thought of her surrender, the fire engulfed him. Laughing, he left the radio singing behind him, and made his way downstairs.

It had taken the best part of the morning to assemble a list of testees employed at the Laboratories; Carnegie had sensed a reluctance on the part of the establishment to open their files to the investigation, despite the horror that had been committed on its premises. Finally, just after noon, they had presented him with a hastily assembled Who's Who of subjects, four and a half dozen in *toto*, and their addresses. None, the offices claimed, matched the description of Welles' testee. The Doctors, it was explained, had been clearly using Laboratory facilities to work on private projects. Though this was not encouraged, both had been senior researchers, and allowed leeway on the matter. It was likely, therefore, that the man Carnegie was seeking had never even been on the Laboratories' payroll. Undaunted, Carnegie ordered a selection of photographs taken off the video recording and had them distributed – with the list of names and addresses – to his officers. From then on, it was down to footwork and patience.

Leo Boyle ran his finger down the list of names he had been given. "Another fourteen," he said. His driver grunted, and Boyle glanced across at him. "You were McBride's partner, weren't you?" he said.

"That's right," Dooley replied. "He's been suspended."

"Why?"

Dooley scowled. "Lacks finesse, does Virgil. Can't get the hang of arrest technique."

Dooley drew the car to a halt.

"Is this it?" Boyle asked.

"You said number eighty. This is eighty. On the door. Eight. Oh."

"I've got eyes."

Boyle got out of the car and made his way up the pathway. The house was sizeable, and had been divided into flats: there were several bells. He pressed for J. Tredgold – the name on his list – and waited. Of the five houses they had so far visited, two had been unoccupied and the residents of the other three had borne no resemblance to the malefactor.

Boyle waited on the step a few seconds and then pressed the bell again; a longer ring this time.

"Nobody in," Dooley said from the pavement.

"Looks like it." Even as he spoke Boyle caught sight of a figure flitting across the hallway, its outline distorted by the cobblestone glass in the door. "Wait a minute," he said.

"What is it?"

"Somebody's in there and not answering." He pressed the first bell again, and then the others. Dooley approached up the pathway, flitting away an over-attentive wasp.

"You sure?" he said.

"I saw somebody in there."

"Press the other bells," Dooley suggested.

"I already did. There's somebody in there and they don't want to come to the door." He rapped on the glass. "Open up," he announced. "Police."

Clever, thought Dooley; why not a loud-hailer, so Heaven knows too? When the door, predictably, remained unanswered, Boyle turned to Dooley. "Is there a side gate?"

"Yes, sir."

"Then get round the back, pronto, before he's away."

"Shouldn't we call –?"

"Do it! I'll keep watch here. If you can get in the back come through and open the front door."

Dooley moved; leaving Boyle alone at the front door. He rang the series of bells again, and, cupping his hand to his brow, put his face to the glass. There was no sign of movement in the hallway; was it possible that the bird had already flown? He backed down the path and stared up at the windows; they stared back vacuously. Ample time had now passed for Dooley to get round the back of the house; but so far he had neither reappeared nor called. Stymied where he stood, and nervous that his tactics had lost them their quarry, Boyle decided to follow his nose around the back of the house.

The side gate had been left open by Dooley. Boyle advanced up the side passage, glancing through a window into an empty living-room before heading round the back door. It was open. Dooley, however, was not in sight. Boyle pocketed the photograph and the list, and stepped inside, loath to the call Dooley's name for fear it alert any felon to his presence, yet nervous of the silence. Cautious as a cat on broken glass he crept through the flat, but each room was deserted. At the flat door, which let on to the hallway in which he had first seen the figure, he paused. Where had Dooley gone? The man had apparently disappeared from sight.

Then, a groan from beyond the door.

"Dooley?" Boyle ventured. Another groan. He stepped into the hallway. Three more doors presented themselves, all were closed; other flats, presumably, or bedsitting rooms. On the coconut mat at the front door lay Dooley's truncheon, dropped there as if its owner had been in the process of making his escape. Boyle swallowed his fear and walked into the body of the hall. The complaint came again, close by. He looked round and up the stairs. There, on the half-landing, lay Dooley. He was barely conscious. A rough attempt had been made to rip his clothes; large portions of his flabby lower anatomy were exposed.

"What's going on, Dooley?" Boyle asked, moving to the bottom of the stairs. The officer heard his voice and rolled himself over. His bleary eyes, settling on Boyle, opened in terror.

"It's all right," Boyle reassured him. "It's only me."

Too late, Boyle registered that Dooley's gaze wasn't fixed on *him* at all, but on some sight over his shoulder. As he pivoted on his heel to snatch a glance at Dooley's bugaboo a charging figure slammed into him. Winded and cursing, Boyle was thrown off his feet. He scrabbled about on the floor for several seconds before his attacker seized hold of him by jacket and hair and hauled him to his feet. He recognized at once the wild face that was thrust into his – the receding hair-line, the weak mouth, the *hunger* – but there was much too he had not anticipated. For one, the man was naked as a babe, though scarcely so modestly endowed. For another, he was clearly aroused to fever-pitch. If the beady eye at his groin, shining up at Boyle, were not evidence enough, the hands now tearing at his clothes made the assailant's intention perfectly apparent.

"Dooley!" Boyle shrieked as he was thrown across the hallway. "In Christ's name! Dooley!"

His pleas were silenced as he hit the opposite wall. The wild man was at his back in half a heartbeat, smearing Boyle's face against the wallpaper: birds and flowers, intertwined, filled his eyes. In desperation, Boyle fought back, but the man's passion lent him ungovernable strength. With one insolent hand holding the policeman's head, he tore at Boyle's trousers and underwear, leaving his buttocks exposed.

"God . . ." Boyle begged into the pattern of the wallpaper. "Please God, somebody help me . . ."; but the prayers were no more fruitful than his struggles. He was pinned against the wall like a butterfly spread on cork, about to be pierced through. He closed his eyes, tears of frustration running down his cheeks. The assailant left off his hold on Boyle's head and pressed his violation home. Boyle refused to cry out. The pain he felt was not the equal of his shame. Better perhaps that Dooley remained comatose; that this humiliation be done and finished with unwitnessed.

"Stop," he murmured into the wall, not to his attacker but to his body, urging it not to find pleasure in this outrage. But his nerve-endings were treacherous; they caught fire from the assault. Beneath the stabbing agony some unforgivable part of him rose to the occasion.

On the stairs, Dooley hauled himself to his feet. His lumbar region, which had been weak since a car accident the previous Christmas, had given out almost as soon as the wild man had sprung him in the hall. Now, as he descended the stairs, the least motion caused excruciating agonies. Crippled with pain, he stumbled to the bottom of the stairs and looked, amazed, across the hallway. Could this be Boyle – he the supercilious, he the rising man, being pummelled like a street-boy in need of dope money? The sight transfixed Dooley for several seconds before he unhinged his eyes and swung them down to the truncheon on the mat. He moved cautiously, but the wild man was too occupied with the deflowering to notice him.

Jerome was listening to Boyle's heart. It was a loud, seductive beat, and with every thrust into the man it seemed to get louder. He wanted it: the heat of it, the life of it. His hand moved round to Boyle's chest, and dug at the flesh.

"Give me your heart," he said. It was like a line from one of the songs.

Boyle screamed into the wall as his attacker mauled his chest.

He'd seen photographs of the woman at the Laboratories; the open wound of her torso was lightning-clear in his mind's eye. Now the maniac intended the same atrocity. *Give me your heart.* Panicked to the ledge of his sanity he found new stamina, and began to fight afresh, reaching round and clawing at the man's torso: nothing – not even the bloody loss of hair from his scalp – broke the rhythm of his thrusts, however. In extremis, Boyle attempted to insinuate one of his hands between his body and the wall and reach between his legs to unman the bastard. As he did so, Dooley attacked, delivering a hail of truncheon blows upon the man's head. The diversion gave Boyle precious leeway. He pressed hard against the wall; the man, his grip on Boyle's chest slicked with blood, lost his hold. Again, Boyle pushed. This time, he managed to shrug the man off entirely. The bodies disengaged; Boyle turned, bleeding but in no danger, and watched Dooley follow the man across the hallway, beating at his greasy blond head. He made little attempt to protect himself however: his burning eyes (Boyle had never understood the physical accuracy of that image until now) were still on the object of his affections.

"Kill him!" Boyle said quietly, as the man grinned – grinned! – through the blows. "Break every bone in his body!"

Even if Dooley, hobbled as he was, had been in any fit state to obey the imperative, he had no chance to do so. His berating was interrupted by a voice from down the hallway. A woman had emerged from the flat Boyle had come through. She too had been a victim of this marauder, to judge by her state; but Dooley's entry into the house had clearly distracted her molester before he could do serious damage.

"Arrest him!" she said, pointing at the leering man. "He tried to rape me!"

Dooley closed in to take possession of the prisoner, but Jerome had other intentions. He put his hand in Dooley's face and pushed him back against the front door. The coconut mat slid from under him: he all but fell. By the time he'd regained his balance Jerome was up and away. Boyle made a wretched attempt to stop him, but the tatters of his trousers were wrapped about his lower legs and Jerome, fleet-footed, was soon half-way up the stairs.

"Call for help," Boyle ordered Dooley. "And make it quick."

Dooley nodded, and opened the front door.

"Is there any way out from upstairs?" Boyle demanded of Mrs Morrisey. She shook her head. "Then we've got the bastard trapped haven't we?" he said. "Go on, Dooley!" Dooley hobbled away down the path. "And you," he said to the woman, "fetch something in the way of weaponry. Anything solid." The woman nodded and returned the way she'd come, leaving Boyle slumped beside the open door. A soft breeze cooled the sweat on his face. At the car outside Dooley was calling up reinforcements.

All too soon, Boyle thought, the cars would be here, and the man upstairs would be hauled away to give his testimony. There would be no opportunity for revenge once he was in custody; the law would take its placid course, and he, the victim, would be only a by-stander. If he was ever to salvage the ruins of his manhood, *now* was the time. If he didn't – if he languished here, his bowels on fire – he would never shrug off the horror he felt at his body's betrayal. He must act now – must beat the grin off his ravisher's face once and for all – or else live in self-disgust until memory failed him.

The choice was no choice at all. Without further debate, he got up from his squatting position, and began up the stairs. As he reached the half-landing he realized he hadn't brought a weapon with him, he knew, however, that if he descended again he'd lose all momentum. Prepared, in that moment, to die if necessary, he headed on up.

There was only one door open on the top landing; through it came the sound of a radio. Downstairs, in the safety of the hall, he heard Dooley come in to tell him that the call had been made, only to break off in mid-announcement. Ignoring the distraction, Boyle stepped into the flat.

There was nobody there. It took Boyle a few moments only to check the kitchen, the tiny bathroom, and the living room: all were deserted. He returned to the bathroom, the window of which was open, and put his head out. The drop to the grass of the garden below was quite manageable. There was an imprint in the ground of the man's body. He had leapt. And gone.

Boyle cursed his tardiness, and hung his head. A trickle of heat ran down the inside of his leg. In the next room, the love-songs played on.

★   ★   ★

For Jerome, there was no forgetfulness, not this time. The encounter with Mrs Morrisey, which had been interrupted by Dooley, and the episode with Boyle that had followed, had all merely served to fan the fire in him. Now, by the light of those flames, he saw clearly what crimes he had committed. He remembered with horrible clarity the laboratory, the injection, the monkeys, the blood. The acts he recalled, however (and there were many), woke no sense of sinfulness in him. All moral consequence, all shame or remorse, was burned out by the fire that was even now licking his flesh to new enthusiasms.

He took refuge in a quiet cul-de-sac to make himself presentable. The clothes he had managed to snatch before making his escape were motley, but would serve to keep him from attracting unwelcome attention. As he buttoned himself up – his body seeming to strain from its covering as if resentful of being concealed – he tried to control the holocaust that raged between his ears. But the flames wouldn't be dampened. His every fibre seemed alive to the flux and flow of the world around him. The marshalled trees along the road, the wall at his back, the very paving stones beneath his bare feet were catching a spark from him, and burning now with their own fire. He grinned to see the conflagration spread. The world, in its every eager particular, grinned back.

Aroused beyond control, he turned to the wall he had been leaning against. The sun had fallen full upon it, and it was warm: the bricks smelt ambrosial. He laid kisses on their gritty faces, his hands exploring every nook and cranny. Murmuring sweet nothings, he unzipped himself, found an accommodating niche, and filled it. His mind was running with liquid pictures: mingled anatomies, female and male in one undistinguishable congress. Above him, even the clouds had caught fire; enthralled by their burning heads he felt the moment rise in his gristle. Breath was short now. But the ecstasy? Surely that would go on forever.

Without warning a spasm of pain travelled down his spine from cortex to testicles, and back again, convulsing him. His hands lost grip of the brick and he finished his agonizing climax on the air as he fell across the pavement. For several seconds he lay where he had collapsed, while the echoes of the initial spasm bounced back and forth along his spine, diminishing with each return. He could taste blood at the back of his throat; he wasn't certain if he'd bitten his lip or tongue, but he thought not. Above his head the birds circled on, rising lazily on a spiral of warm air. He watched the fire in the clouds gutter out.

He got to his feet and looked down at the coinage of semen he'd spent on the pavement. For a fragile instant he caught again a whiff of the vision he'd just had; imagined a marriage of his seed with the paving stone. What sublime children the world might boast, he thought, if he could only mate with brick or tree; he would gladly suffer the agonies of conception, if such miracles were possible. But the paving stone was unmoved by his seed's entreaties; the vision, like the fire above him, cooled and hid its glories.

He put his bloodied member away, and leaned against the wall, turning the strange events of his recent life over and over. Something fundamental was changing in him, of that he had no doubt; the rapture that had possessed him (and would, no doubt, possess him again) was like nothing he had hitherto experienced. And whatever they had injected into his system it showed no signs of being discharged naturally; far from it. He could feel the heat in him still, as he had leaving the Laboratories; but this time the roar of its presence was louder than ever.

It was a new kind of life he was living, and the thought, though frightening, exulted him. Not once did it occur to his spinning, eroticized brain that this new kind of life would, in time, demand a new kind of death.

Carnegie had been warned by his superiors that results were expected; he was now passing the verbal beating he'd received to those under him. It was a line of humiliation, in which the greater was encouraged to kick the lesser man, and that man, in turn, his lesser.

Carnegie had sometimes wondered what the man at the end of the line took his ire out on; his dog presumably.

"This miscreant is still loose, gentlemen, despite his photograph in many of this morning's newspapers, and an operating method which is, to say the least, insolent. We *will* catch him, of course, but let's get the bastard before we have another murder on our hands –"

The phone rang. Boyle's replacement, Migeon, picked it up, while Carnegie concluded his pep-talk to the assembled officers.

"I want him in the next twenty-four hours, gentlemen. That's the time-scale I've been given, and that's what we've got. Twenty-four hours."

Migeon interrupted. "Sir? It's Johannson. He says he's got something for you. It's urgent."

"Right." The Inspector claimed the receiver. "Carnegie."

The voice at the other end was soft to the point of inaudibility. "Carnegie," Johannson said, "we've been right through the laboratory; dug up every piece of information we could find on Dance and Welles' tests –"

"And?"

"We've also analyzed traces of the agent from the hypo they used on the suspect. I think we've found the *Boy*, Carnegie."

"What boy?" Carnegie wanted to know; he found Johannson's obfuscation irritating.

"The *Blind Boy*, Carnegie."

"And?"

For some inexplicable reason Carnegie was certain the man *smiled* down the phone before replying: "I think perhaps you'd better come down and see for yourself. Sometime around noon suit you?"

Johannson could have been one of history's greatest poisoners: he had all the requisite qualifications. A tidy mind (poisoners were, in Carnegie's experience, domestic paragons), a patient nature (poison could take time), and, most importantly, an encyclopaedic knowledge of toxicology. Watching him at work, which Carnegie had done on two previous cases, was to see a subtle man at his subtle craft, and the spectacle made Carnegie's blood run cold.

Johannson had installed himself in the laboratory on the top floor, where Doctor Dance had been murdered, rather than use police facilities for the investigation, because, as he explained to Carnegie, much of the equipment the Hume organization boasted was simply not available elsewhere. His dominion over the place, accompanied by his two assistants had, however, transformed the laboratory from the clutter left by the experimenters, to a dream of order. Only the monkeys remained a constant. Try as he might Johannson could not control their behaviour.

"We didn't have much difficulty finding the drug used on your man," Johannson said, "we simply cross-checked traces remaining in the hypodermic with materials found in the room. In fact, they seem to have been manufacturing this stuff, or variations on the theme, for some time. The people here claim they know nothing about it, of course. I'm inclined to believe them. What the good doctors were doing here was, I'm sure, in the nature of a personal experiment."

"What sort of experiment?"

Johannson took off his spectacles and set about cleaning them with the tongue of his red tie. "At first, we thought they were developing some kind of hallucogen," he said. "In some regards the agent used on your man resembles a narcotic. In fact – methods apart – I think they made some very exciting discoveries. Developments which take us into entirely new territory."

"It's not a drug then?"

"Oh, yes, of course it's a drug," Johannson said, replacing the spectacles, "but one created for a very specific purpose. See for yourself."

Johannson led the way across the laboratory to the row of monkeys' cages. Instead of being confined separately, the toxicologist had seen fit to open the interconnecting doors between one cage and the next, allowing the animals free access to gather in groups. The consequence was absolutely plain: the animals were engaged in an elaborate series of sexual acts. Why, Carnegie wondered, did monkeys perpetually perform obscenities? It was the same torrid display whenever he'd taken his offspring, as children, to Regent's Park Zoo; the Ape Enclosure elicited one embarrassing question upon another. He'd stopped taking the children after a while. He simply found it too mortifying.

"Haven't they got anything better to do?" he asked of Johannson, glancing away and then back at a ménage à trois that was so intimate the eye could not ascribe member to monkey.

"Believe me," Johannson smirked, "this is mild by comparison with much of the behaviour we've seen from them since we gave them a shot of the agent. From that point on they neglected all normal behaviour patterns; they bypassed the arousal signals, the courtship rituals. They no longer show any interest in food. They don't sleep. They have become sexual obsessives. All other stimuli are forgotten. Unless the agent is naturally discharged, I suspect they are going to screw themselves to death."

Carnegie looked along the rest of the cages: the same porno-graphic scenes were being played out in each one. Mass-rape, homosexual liaisons, fervent and ecstatic masturbation.

"It's no wonder the Doctors made a secret project of their discovery," Johannson went on, "they were on to something that could have made them a fortune. An aphrodisiac that actually works."

"An aphrodisiac?"

"Most are useless, of course. Rhinoceros horn, live eels in cream sauce: symbolic stuff. They're designed to arouse by association."

Carnegie remembered the hunger in Jerome's eyes. It was echoed here, in the monkeys'. Hunger, and the desperation that hunger brings.

"And the ointments too, all useless. *Cantharis vesticatora* –"

"What's that?"

"You know the stuff as Spanish Fly, perhaps? It's a paste made from a beetle. Again, useless. At best these things are inflam-matants. But this . . ." He picked up a phial of colourless fluid. "*This* is damn near genius."

"They don't look too happy with it to me."

"Oh, it's still crude," Johannson said. "I think the researchers were greedy, and moved into tests on living subjects a good two or three years before it was wise to do so. The stuff is almost lethal as it stands, no doubt of that. But it *could* be made to work, given time. You see, they've sidestepped the mechanical problems: this stuff operates directly on the sexual imagination, on the libido. If you arouse the *mind*, the body follows. That's the trick of it."

A rattling of the wire-mesh close by drew Carnegie's attention from Johannson's pale features. One of the female monkeys, apparently not satisfied with the attentions of several males, was spreadeagled against her cage, her nimble fingers reaching for Carnegie; her spouses, not to be left loveless, had taken to sodomy. "*Blind Boy*?" said Carnegie. "Is that Jerome?"

"It's Cupid, isn't it?" Johannson said: " '*Love looks not with the eyes but with the mind, And therefore is winged Cupid painted blind*.' It's *Midsummer Night's Dream*."

"The Bard was never my strongest suit," said Carnegie. He went back to staring at the female monkey. "And Jerome?" he said.

"He has the agent in his system. A sizeable dose."

"So he's like this lot!"

I would presume – his intellectual capacities being greater – that the agent may not be able to work in quite such an *unfettered* fashion. But, having said that, sex can make monkeys out of the best of us, can't it?" Johannson allowed himself a half-smile at the notion. "All our so-called higher concerns become secondary to the pursuit. For a short time sex makes us obsessive; we can perform, or at least *think* we can perform, what with hindsight may seem extraordinary feats."

"I don't think there's anything so extraordinary about rape," Carnegie commented, attempting to stem Johannson's rhapsody. But the other man would not be subdued.

"Sex without end, without compromise or apology," he said. "Imagine it. The dream of Casanova."

The world had seen so many Ages. The Age of Enlightenment; of Reformation; of Reason. Now, at last, the Age of Desire. And after this, an end to Ages; an end, perhaps, to everything. For the fires that were being stoked now were fiercer than the innocent world suspected. They were terrible fires, fires without end, which would illuminate the world in one last, fierce light.

So Welles thought, as he lay in his bed. He had been conscious for several hours, but had chosen not to signify such. Whenever a nurse came to his room he would clamp his eyes closed and slow the rhythm of his breath. He knew he could not keep the illusion up for long, but the hours gave him a while to think through his itinerary from here. His first move had to be back to the Laboratories; there were papers there he had to shred; tapes to wipe clean. From now on he was determined that every scrap of information about *Project Blind Boy* exist solely in his head. That way he would have complete control over his masterwork, and nobody could claim it from him.

He had never had much interest in making money from the discovery, although he was well aware of how lucrative a workable aphrodisiac would be; he had never given a fig for material wealth. His initial motivation for the development of the drug – which they had chanced upon quite by accident while testing an agent to aid schizophrenics – had been investigative. But his motives had matured, through their months of secret work. He had come to think of himself as the bringer of the millenium. He would not have anyone attempt to snatch that sacred role from him.

So he thought, lying in his bed, waiting for a moment to slip away.

As he walked the streets Jerome would have happily yea-said Welles' vision. Perhaps he, of all men, was most eager to welcome the Age of Desire. He saw its portents everywhere. On advertising hoardings and cinema bill-boards, in shop-windows, on television screens: everywhere, the body as merchandise. Where flesh was not being used to market artifacts of steel and stone, those artifacts were taking on its properties. Automobiles passed him by with every voluptuous attribute but breath: their sinuous body-work gleamed, their interiors invited, plushly; the buildings beleaguered him with sexual puns. Spires; passageways; shadowed plazas with white-water fountains. Beneath the raptures of the shallow – the thousand trivial distractions he encountered in street and square – he sensed the ripe life of the body informing every particular.

The spectacle kept the fire in him well-stoked; it was all that will power could do to keep him from pressing his attentions on every creature that he met eyes with. A few seemed to sense the heat in him, and gave him wide berth. Dogs sensed it too. Several followed him, aroused by *his* arousal. Flies orbited his head in squadrons. But his growing ease with his condition gave him some rudimentary control over it. He knew that to make a public display of his ardour would bring the law down upon him, and that in turn would hinder his adventures. Soon enough, the fire that he had begun would spread: *then* he would emerge from hiding and bathe in it freely. Until then, discretion was best.

He had on occasion bought the company of a young woman in Soho; he went to find her now. The afternoon was stiflingly hot, but he felt no weariness. He had not eaten since the previous evening, but he felt no hunger. Indeed, as he climbed the narrow stairway up to the room on the first floor which Angela had once occupied, he felt as primed as an athlete, glowing with health. The immaculately dressed and wall-eyed pimp who usually occupied a place at the top of the stairs was absent. Jerome simply went to the girl's room and knocked. There was no reply.

He rapped again, more urgently. The noise brought an early middle-aged woman to the door at the end of the landing.

"What do you want?"

"The woman," he replied simply.

"Angela's gone. And you'd better get out of here too, in that state. This isn't a doss-house."

"When will she be back?" he asked, keeping as tight a leash as he could on his appetite.

The woman, who was as tall as Jerome and half as heavy again as his wasted frame, advanced towards him. "The girl won't *be* back," she said, "so you get the hell out of here, before I call Isaiah."

Jerome looked at the woman; she shared Angela's profession, no doubt, if not her youth or prettiness. He smiled at her. "I can hear your heart," he said.

"I told you –'

Before she could finish the words Jerome moved down the landing towards her. She wasn't intimidated by his approach, merely repulsed.

"If I call Isaiah, you'll be sorry," she informed him. The pace of her heartbeat had risen, he could hear it.

"I'm burning," he said.

She frowned; she was clearly losing this battle of wits. "Stay away from me," she told. "I'm warning you."

The heartbeat was getting more rapid still. The rhythm, buried in her substance, drew him on. From that source: all life, all heat.

"Give me your heart," he said.

"Isaiah!"

Nobody came running at her shout, however. Jerome gave her no opportunity to cry out a second time. He reached to embrace her, clamping a hand over her mouth. She let fly a volley of blows against him, but the pain only fanned the flames. He was brighter by the moment: his every orifice let on to the furnace in belly and loins and head. Her superior bulk was of no advantage against such fervour. He pushed her against the wall – the beat of her heart loud in his ears – and began to apply kisses to her neck, tearing her dress open to free her breasts.

"Don't shout," he said, trying to sound persuasive. "There's no harm meant."

She shook her head, and said, "I won't," against his palm. He took his hand from her mouth, she dragged in several desperate breaths. Where was Isaiah? she thought. Not far, surely. Fearing for her life if she tried to resist this interloper – how his eyes shone! – she gave up any pretence to resistance and let him have his way. Men's supply of passion, she knew of long experience, was easily depleted. Though they might threaten to move earth and heaven too, half an hour later their boasts would be damp sheets and resentment. If the worst came to the worst, she could tolerate his inane talk of burning; she'd heard far obscener bedroom chat. As to the prong he was even now attempting to press into her, it and its comical like held no surprises for her.

Jerome wanted to touch the heart in her; wanted to see it splash up into his face, to bathe in it. He put his hand to her breast, and felt the beat of her under his palm.

"You like that, do you?" she said as he pressed against her bosom. "You're not the first."

He clawed her skin.

"Gently, sweetheart," she chided him, looking over his shoulder to see if there was any sign of Isaiah. "Be gentle. This is the only body I've got."

He ignored her. His nails drew blood.

"Don't do that," she said.

"Wants to be out," he replied digging deeply, and it suddenly dawned on her that this was no love-game he was playing.

"*Stop it*," she said, as he began to tear at her. This time, she screamed.

Downstairs, and a short way along the street, Isaiah dropped the slice of *tarte française* he'd just bought and ran to the door. It wasn't the first time his sweet tooth had tempted him from his post, but – unless he was quick to undo the damage – it might very well be his last. There were terrible noises from the landing. He raced up the stairs. The scene that met his eyes was in every way worse than that his imagination had conjured. Simone was trapped against the wall beside her door, with a man battened upon her. Blood was coming from somewhere between them, he couldn't see where.

Isaiah yelled. Jerome, hands bloody, looked round from his labours as a giant in a Savile Row suit reached for him. It took Jerome vital seconds to uproot himself from the furrow, by which

time the man was upon him. Isaiah took hold of him, and dragged
him off the woman. She took shelter, sobbing, in her room.

"Sick bastard," Isaiah said, launching a fusillade of punches.
Jerome reeled. But he was on fire, and unafraid. In a moment's
respite he leapt at his man like an angered baboon. Isaiah, taken
unawares, lost balance, and fell back against one of the doors,
which opened inwards against his weight. He collapsed into a
squalid lavatory, his head striking the lip of the toilet bowl as he
went down. The impact disoriented him, and he lay on the
stained linoleum groaning, legs akimbo. Jerome could hear his
blood, eager in his veins; could smell sugar on his breath. It
tempted him to stay. But his instinct for self-preservation coun-
selled otherwise; Isaiah was already making an attempt to stand
up again. Before he could get to his feet Jerome about turned, and
made a getaway down the stairs.

The dog-day met him at the doorstep, and he smiled. The
street wanted him more than the woman on the landing, and he
was eager to oblige. He started out on to the pavement, his
erection still pressing from his trousers. Behind him, he heard
the giant pounding down the stairs. He took to his heels, laughing. The fire was still uncurbed in him, and it lent speed to his
feet; he ran down the street not caring if Sugar Breath was
following or not. Pedestrians, unwilling, in this dispassionate
age, to register more than casual interest in the blood-spattered
satyr, parted to let him pass. A few pointed, assuming him an
actor perhaps. Most took no notice at all. He made his way
through a maze of back streets, aware without needing to look
that Isaiah was still on his heels.

Perhaps it was accident that brought him to the street market;
perhaps, and more probably, it was that the swelter carried the
mingled scent of meat and fruit to his nostrils, and he wanted to
bathe in it. The narrow thoroughfare was thronged with pur-
chasers, sightseers, and stalls heaped with merchandise. He dove
into the crowd happily, brushing against buttock and thigh,
meeting the plaguing gaze of fellow flesh on every side. Such
a day! He and his prick could scarcely believe their luck.

Behind him, he heard Isaiah shout. He picked up his pace,
heading for the most densely populated areas of the market,
where he could lose himself in the hot press of people. Each
contact was a painful ecstasy. Each climax – and they came one

upon the other as he pressed through the crowd – was a dry spasm in his system. His back ached, his balls ached: but what his body now? Just a plinth for that singular monument, his prick. Head was *nothing*; mind was *nothing*. His arms were simply made to bring love close, his legs to carry the demanding rod any place where it might find satisfaction. He pictured himself as a walking erection, the world gaping on every side: flesh, brick, steel, he didn't care: he would ravish it all.

Suddenly, without his seeking it, the crowd parted, and he found himself off the main thoroughfare and in a narrow street. Sunlight poured between the buildings, its zeal magnified. He was about to turn back to join the crowd again when he caught a scent and sight that drew him on. A short way down the heat-drenched street three shirtless young men were standing amid piles of fruit crates, each containing dozens of punnets of straw-berries. There had been a glut of the fruit that year, and in the relentless heat much of it had begun to soften and rot. The trio of workers was going through the punnets, sorting bad fruit from good, and throwing the spoiled strawberries into the gutter. The smell in the narrow space was overpowering: a sweetness of such strength it would have sickened any interloper other than Jerome, whose senses had lost all capacity for revulsion or rejection. The world was the world was the world; he would take it, as in marriage, for better or worse. He stood watching the spectacle entranced; the sweating fruit-sorters bright in the fall of sun, hands, arms and torsoes spattered with scarlet juice; the air mazed with every nectar-seeking insect; the discarded fruit heaped in the gutter in seeping mounds. Engaged in their sticky labours the sorters didn't even see him at first. Then one of the three looked up, and took in the extraordinary creature watching them. The grin on his face died as he met Jerome's eyes.

"What the hell?"

Now the other two looked up from their work.

"Sweet," said Jerome; he could hear their hearts tremble.

"Look at him," said the youngest of the three, pointing at Jerome's groin. "Fucking exposing himself."

They stood still in the sunlight, he and they, while the wasps whirled around the fruit, and, in the narrow slice of blue summer sky between the roofs, birds passed over. Jerome wanted the moment to go on forever: his too-naked head tasted Eden here.

And then, the dream broke. He felt a shadow on his back. One
of the sorters dropped the punnet he was sorting through; the
decayed fruit broke open on the gravel. Jerome frowned, and
half-turned. Isaiah had found the street; his weapon was steel and
shone. It crossed the space between he and Jerome in one short
second. Jerome felt an ache in his side as the knife slid into him.

"*Christ*," the young man said, and began to run; his two
brothers, unwilling to be witnesses at the scene of a wounding,
hesitated only moments longer before following.

The pain made Jerome cry out, but nobody in the noisy market
heard him. Isaiah withdrew the blade; heat came with it. He made
to stab again, but Jerome was too fast for the spoiler; he moved
out of range and staggered across the street. The would-be
assassin, fearful that Jerome's cries would draw too much attention, moved quickly in pursuit to finish the job. But the tarmac
was slick with rotted fruit, and his fine suede shoes had less grip
than Jerome's bare feet. The gap between them widened by a
pace.

"No you don't," Isaiah said, determined not to let his humi-
liator escape. He pushed over a tower of fruit crates – punnets
toppled and strewed their contents across Jerome's path. Jerome
hesitated, to take in the bouquet of bruised fruit. The indulgence
almost killed him. Isaiah closed in, ready to take the man. Jerome,
his system taxed to near eruption by the stimulus of pain,
watched the blade come close to opening up his belly. His mind
conjured the wound: the abdomen slit – the heat spilling out to
join the blood of the strawberries in the gutter. The thought was
so tempting. He almost wanted it.

Isaiah had killed before, twice. He knew the wordless vocabulary of the act, and he could see the invitation in his victim's
eyes. Happy to oblige, he came to meet it, knife at the ready. At
the last possible moment Jerome recanted, and instead of presenting himself for slitting, threw a blow at the giant. Isaiah
ducked to avoid it and his feet slid in the mush. The knife fled
from his hand and fell amongst the debris of punnets and fruit.
Jerome turned away as the hunter – the advantage lost – stooped
to locate the knife. But his prey was gone before his ham-fisted
grip had found it: lost again in the crowd-filled streets. He had no
opportunity to pocket the knife before the uniform stepped out of
the crowd and joined him in the hot passageway.

"What's the story?" the policeman demanded, looking down at the knife. Isaiah followed his gaze. The bloodied blade was black with flies.

In his office Inspector Carnegie sipped at his hot chocolate, his third in the past hour, and watched the processes of dusk. He had always wanted to be a detective, right from his earliest rememberings; and, in those rememberings, this had always been a charged and magical hour. Night descending on the city; myriad evils putting on their glad rags and coming out to play. A time for vigilance, for a new moral stringency.

But as a child he had failed to imagine the fatigue that twilight invariably brought. He was tired to his bones, and if he snatched any sleep in the next few hours he knew it would be here, in his chair, with his feet up on the desk amid a clutter of plastic cups.

The phone rang. It was Johannson.

"Still at work?" he said, impressed by Johannson's dedication to the job. It was well after nine. Perhaps Johannson didn't have a home worth calling such to go back to either.

"I heard our man had a busy day," Johannson said.

"That's right. A prostitute in Soho; then got himself stabbed."

"He got through the cordon, I gather?"

"These things happen," Carnegie replied, too tired to be testy. "What can I do for you?"

"I just thought you'd want to know: the monkeys have started to die."

The words stirred Carnegie from his fatigue-stupor. "How many?" he asked.

"Three from fourteen so far. But the rest, will be dead by dawn, I'd guess."

"What's killing them? Exhaustion?" Carnegie recalled the desperate saturnalia he'd seen in the cages. What animal – human or otherwise – could keep up such revelry without cracking up?

"It's not physical," Johannson said. "Or at least not in the way you're implying. We'll have to wait for the dissection results before we get any detailed explanations –"

"Your best guess?"

"For what it's worth . . ." Johannson said, ". . . which is quite a lot: I think they're going *bang*."

"What?"

"Cerebral over-load of some kind. Their brains are simply giving out. The agent doesn't disperse you see; *it feeds on itself*. The more fevered they get, the more of the drug is produced; the more of the drug there is, the more fevered they get. It's a vicious circle. Hotter and hotter, wilder and wilder. Eventually the system can't take it, and suddenly I'm up to my armpits in dead monkeys." The smile came back into the voice again, cold and wry. "Not that the others let that spoil their fun. Necrophilia's quite the fashion down here."

Carnegie peered at his cooling hot chocolate; it had acquired a thin skin, which puckered as he touched the cup. "So it's just a matter of time?" he said.

"Before our man goes for bust? Yes, I'd think so."

"All right. Thank you for the up-date. Keep me posted."

"You want to come down here and view the remains?"

"Monkey corpses I can do without, thank you."

Johannson laughed. Carnegie put down the receiver. When he turned back to the window, night had well and fallen.

In the laboratory Johannson crossed to the light switch by the door; in the time he'd been calling Carnegie the last of the daylight had fled. He saw the blow that felled him coming a mere heartbeat before it landed; it caught him across the side of his neck. One of his vertebrae snapped, and his legs buckled. He collapsed without reaching the lightswitch. But by the time he hit the ground the distinction between day and night was academic.

Welles didn't bother to check whether his blow had been lethal or not; time was at a premium. He stepped over the body and headed across to the bench where Johannson had been working. There, lying in a circle of lamplight as if for the final act of a simian tragedy, lay a dead monkey. It had clearly perished in a frenzy; its face was knitted up: mouth wide and spittle-stained, eyes fixed in a final look of alarm. Its fur had been pulled out in tufts in the throes of its copulations; its body, wasted with exertion, was a mass of contusions. It took Welles half a minute of study to recognize the implications of the corpse, and of the other two he now saw lying on a nearby bench.

"Love kills," he murmured to himself philosophically, and began his systematic destruction of *Blind Boy*.

*   *   *

I'm dying, Jerome thought, I'm dying of *terminal joy*. The thought amused him. It was the only thought in his head which made much sense. Since his encounter with Isaiah, and the escape from the police that had followed, he could remember little with any coherence. The hours of hiding and nursing his wounds – of feeling the heat grow again, and of discharging it – had long since merged into one midsummer dream, from which, he knew with pleasurable certainty, only death would wake him. The blaze was devouring him utterly, from the entrails out. If he were to be eviscerated now, what would the witnesses find? Only embers and ashes.

Yet still his one-eyed friend demanded *more*; still, as he wove his way back to the Laboratories – where else for a made man to go when the stitches slipped, but back to the first heat? – still the grids gaped at him seductively, and every brick wall offered up a hundred gritty invitations.

The night was balmy: a night for love-songs and romance. In the questionable privacy of a parking lot a few blocks from his destination he saw two people making sex in the back of a car, the doors open to accommodate limbs and draught. Jerome paused to watch the ritual, enthralled as ever by the tangle of bodies, and the sound – so loud it was like thunder – of twin hearts beating to one escalating rhythm. Watching, his rod grew eager.

The female saw him first, and alerted her partner to the wreck of a human being who was watching them with such childish delight. The male looked around from his gropings to stare. Do I burn, Jerome wondered? Does my hair flame? At the last, does the illusion gain substance? To judge by the look on their faces, the answer was surely no. They were not in awe of him, merely angered and revolted.

"I'm on fire," he told them.

The male got to his feet and spat at Jerome. He almost expected the spittle to turn to steam as it approached him but instead it landed on his face and upper chest as a cooling shower.

"Go to hell," the woman said. "Leave us alone."

Jerome shook his head. The male warned him that another step would oblige him to break Jerome's head. It disturbed our man not a jot; no words, no blows, could silence the imperative of the rod.

Their hearts, he realized, as he moved towards them, no longer beat in tandem.

Carnegie consulted the map, five years out of date now, on his office wall, to pinpoint the location of the attack that had just been reported. Neither of the victims had come to serious harm, apparently; the arrival of a car-load of revellers had dissuaded Jerome (it was unquestionably Jerome) from lingering. Now the area was being flooded with officers, half a dozen of them armed; in a matter of minutes every street in the vicinity of the attack would be cordoned off. Unlike Soho, which had been crowded, the area would furnish the fugitive with few hiding places.

Carnegie pin-pointed the location of the attack, and realized that it was within a few blocks of the Laboratories. No accident, surely. The man was heading back to the scene of his crime. Wounded, and undoubtedly on the verge of collapse – the lovers had described a man who looked more dead than alive – Jerome would probably be picked up before he reached home. But there was always the risk of his slipping through the net, and getting to the Laboratories. Johannson was working there, alone; the guard on the building was, in these straitened times, necessarily small.

Carnegie picked up the phone and dialled through to Johannson. The phone rang at the other end, but nobody picked it up. The man's gone home, Carnegie thought, happy to be relieved of his concern, it's ten-fifty at night and he's earned his rest. Just as he was about to put the receiver down, however, it was picked up at the other end.

"Johannson?"

Nobody replied.

"Johannson? This is Carnegie." And still, no reply. "Answer, damn it. Who is this?"

In the Laboratories the receiver was forsaken. It was not replaced on the cradle but left to lie on the bench. Down the buzzing line, Carnegie could clearly hear the monkeys, their voices shrill.

"Johannson?" Carnegie demanded. "Are you there? Johannson?"

But the apes screamed on.

★   ★   ★

Welles had built two bonfires of the *Blind Boy* material in the sinks, and then set them alight. They flared up enthusiastically. Smoke, heat and smuts filled the large room, thickening the air. When the fires were fairly raging he threw all the tapes he could lay hands upon into the conflagration, and added all of Johannson's notes for good measure. Several of the tapes had already gone from the files, he noted. But all they could show any thief was some teasing scenes of transformation: the heart of the secret remained his. With the procedures and formulae now destroyed, it only remained to wash the small amounts of remaining agent down the drain, and kill and incinerate the animals.

He prepared a series of lethal hypodermics, going about the business with uncharacteristic orderliness. This systematic destruction gratified him. He felt no regret at the way things had turned out. From that first moment of panic, when he'd helplessly watched the *Blind Boy* serum work its awesome effects upon Jerome – to this final elimination of all that had gone before – had been, he now saw, one steady process of wiping clean. With these fires he brought an end to the pretence of scientific enquiry; after this he was indisputably the Apostle of Desire, its John in the wilderness. The thought blinded him to any other. Careless of the monkeys' scratchings he hauled them one by one, from their cages to deliver the killing dose. He had dispatched three, and was opening the cage of the fourth, when a figure appeared in the doorway of the laboratory. Through the smoky air it was impossible to see who. The surviving monkeys seemed to recognize him, however: they left off their couplings and set up a din of welcome.

Welles stood still, and waited for the newcomer to make his move.

"I'm dying," said Jerome.

Welles had not expected this. Of all the people he had anticipated here, Jerome was the last.

"Did you hear me?" the man wanted to know.

Welles nodded. "We're *all* dying, Jerome. Life is a slow disease, no more nor less. But such a *light*, eh? in the going."

"You *knew* this would happen," Jerome said. "You knew the fire would eat me away."

"No," came the sober reply. "No, I didn't. Really."

Jerome walked out of the door frame and into the murky light.

He was a wasted shambles: a patchwork man, blood on his body, fire in his eyes. But Welles knew better than to trust the apparent vulnerability of this scarecrow. The agent in his system had made him capable of superhuman acts: he had seen Dance torn open with a few nonchalant strokes. Tact was required. Though clearly close to death, Jerome was still formidable.

"I didn't intend this, Jerome," Welles said, attempting to tame the tremor in his voice. "I wish, in a way, I could claim that I had. But I wasn't that farsighted. It's taken me time and pain to see the future plainly."

The burning man watched him, gaze intent.

"Such fires, Jerome, waiting to be lit."

"I know . . ." Jerome replied. "Believe me . . . I know."

"You and I; we are the end of the world."

The wretched monster pondered this for a while, and then nodded slowly. Welles softly exhaled a sigh of relief; the death-bed diplomacy was working. But he had little time to waste with talk. If Jerome was here, could the authorities be far behind?

"I have urgent work to do, my friend," he said calmly. "Would you think me uncivil if I continued with it?"

Without waiting for a reply he unlatched another cage and hauled the condemned monkey out, expertly turning its body round to facilitate the injection. The animal convulsed in his arms for a few moments, then died. Welles disengaged its wizened fingers from his shirt, and tossed the corpse and the discharged hypodermic on to the bench, turning with an executioner's economy to claim his next victim.

"Why?" Jerome asked, staring at the animal's open eyes.

"Act of mercy," Welles replied, picking up another primed hypodermic. "You can see how they're suffering." He reached to unlatch the next cage.

"Don't," Jerome said.

"No time for sentiment," Welles replied. "I beg you: an end to that."

Sentiment, Jerome thought, muddily remembering the songs on the radio that had first rewoken the fire in him. Didn't Welles understand that the processes of heart and head and groin were indivisible? That sentiment, however trite, might lead to undis-covered regions? He wanted to tell the Doctor that, to explain all that he had seen and all that he had loved in these desperate hours. But somewhere between mind and tongue the explanations absconded. All he could say, to state the empathy he felt for all the suffering world, was:

"*Don't*," as Welles unlocked the next cage. The Doctor ignored him, and reached into the wire-mesh cell. It contained three animals. He took hold of the nearest and drew it, protesting, from its companions' embraces. Without doubt it knew what fate awaited it; a flurry of screeches signalled its terror.

Jerome couldn't stomach this casual disposal. He moved, the wound in his side a torment, to prevent the killing. Welles, distracted by Jerome's advance, lost hold of his wriggling charge: the monkey scampered away across the bench-tops. As he went to re-capture it the prisoners in the cage behind him took their chance, and slipped out.

"Damn you," Welles yelled at Jerome, "don't you see we've no *time*? Don't you understand?"

Jerome understood everything, and yet nothing. The fever he and the animals shared, he understood; its purpose, to transform the world, he understood too. But why it should end like this – that joy, that vision – why it should all come down to a sordid room filled with smoke and pain, to frailty, to despair – *that* he did not comprehend. Nor, he now realized, did Welles, who had been the architect of these contradictions.

As the Doctor made a snatch for one of the escaping monkeys, Jerome crossed swiftly to the remaining cages and unlatched them all: the animals leapt to their freedom. Welles had succeeded with his recapture however, and had the protesting monkeys in his grip, about to deliver the panacea. Jerome made towards him.

"Let it be," he yelled.

Welles pressed the hypodermic into the monkey's body, but before he could depress the plunger Jerome had pulled at his wrist. The hypodermic spat its poison into the air, and then fell to the ground: the monkey, wresting itself free, followed.

Jerome pulled Welles close. "I told you to *let it be*,' he said.

Welles' response was to drive his fist into Jerome's wounded flank. Tears of pain spurted from his eyes, but he didn't release the Doctor. The stimulus, unpleasant as it was, could not dissuade him from holding that beating heart close. He wished, embracing Welles like a prodigal, that he could ignite himself:

that the dream of burning flesh he had endured would now become a reality, consuming maker and made in one cleansing flame. But his flesh was only flesh; his bone, bone. What miracles he had seen had been a private revelation, and now there was no time to communicate their glories or their horrors. What he had seen would die with him, to be rediscovered (perhaps) by some future self, only to be forgotten and discovered again. Like the story of love the radio had told; the same joy lost and found, found and lost. He stared at Welles with new comprehension dawning, hearing still the terrified beat of the man's heart. The Doctor was *wrong*. If he left the man to live, he would come to know his error. They were not presagers of the millenium. They had both been dreaming.

"Don't kill me," Welles pleaded. "I don't want to die."

More fool you, Jerome thought, and let the man go.

Welles' bafflement was plain: he couldn't believe that his appeal for life had been answered. Anticipating a blow with every step he took, he backed away from Jerome, who simply turned his back on the Doctor and walked away.

From downstairs there came a shout, and then many shouts. Police, Welles guessed. They had presumably found the body of the officer who'd been on guard at the door. In moments only they would be coming up the stairs. There was no time now for finishing the tasks he'd come here to perform. He had to be away before they arrived.

On the floor below, Carnegie watched the armed officers disappear up the stairs. There was a faint smell of burning in the air; he feared the worst.

I am the man who comes after the act, he thought to himself; I am perpetually upon the scene when the best of the action is over. Used as he was to waiting, patient as a loyal dog, this time he could not hold his anxieties in check while the others went ahead. Disregarding the voices advising him to wait, he began up the stairs.

The laboratory on the top floor was empty, but for the monkeys and Johannson's corpse. The toxicologist lay on his face where he had fallen, neck broken. The emergency exit, which let on to the fire-escape, was open; smoky air was being sucked out through it. As Carnegie stepped away from Johannson's body officers were already on the fire-escape, calling to their colleagues below to seek out the fugitive.

"Sir?"

Carnegie looked across at the moustachioed individual who had approached him.

"What is it?"

The officer pointed to the other end of the laboratory: to the test-chamber. There was somebody at the window. Carnegie recognized the features, even though they were much changed. It was Jerome. At first he thought the man was watching him, but a short perusal scotched that idea. Jerome was staring, tears on his face, at his own reflection in the smeared glass. Even as Carnegie watched, the face retreated with the gloom of the chamber.

Other officers had noticed the man too. They were moving down the length of the laboratory, taking up positions behind the benches where they had a good line on the door, weapons at the ready. Carnegie had been present in such situations before; they had their own, terrible momentum. Unless he intervened, there would be blood.

"No," he said, "hold your fire."

He pressed the protesting officer aside and began to walk down the laboratory, making no attempt to conceal his advance. He walked past sinks in which the remains of *Blind Boy* guttered, past the bench under which, a short age ago, they'd found the dead Dance. A monkey, its head bowed, dragged itself across his path, apparently deaf to his proximity. He let it find a hole to die in, then moved on to the chamber door. It was ajar. He reached for the handle. Behind him the laboratory had fallen completely silent; all eyes were on him. He pulled the door open. Fingers tightened on triggers. There was no attack however. Carnegie stepped inside.

Jerome was standing against the opposite wall. If he saw Carnegie enter, or heard him, he made no sign of it. A dead monkey lay at his feet, one hand still grasping the hem of his trousers. Another whimpered in the corner, holding its head in its hands.

"Jerome?"

Was it Carnegie's imagination, or could he smell strawberries? Jerome blinked.

"You're under arrest," Carnegie said. Hendrix would appreciate the irony of that, he thought. The man moved his bloody hand from the stabwound in his side to the front of his trousers, and began to stroke himself.

"Too late," Jerome said. He could feel the last fire rising in him. Even if this intruder chose to cross the chamber and arrest him now, the intervening seconds would deny him his capture. *Death was here.* And what was it, now he saw it clearly? Just another seduction, another sweet darkness to be filled up, and pleasured and made fertile.

A spasm began in his perineum, and lightning travelled in two directions from the spot, up his rod and up his spine. A laugh began in his throat.

In the corner of the chamber the monkey, hearing Jerome's humour, began to whimper again. The sound momentarily claimed Carnegie's attention, and when his gaze flitted back to Jerome the short-sighted eyes had closed, the hand had dropped, and he was dead, standing against the wall. For a short time the body defied gravity. Then, gracefully the legs buckled and Jerome fell forward. He was, Carnegie saw, a sack of bones, no more. It was a wonder the man had lived so long.

Cautiously, he crossed to the body and put his finger to the man's neck. There was no pulse. The remnants of Jerome's last laugh remained on his face, however, refusing to decay.

"Tell me . . ." Carnegie whispered to the man, sensing that despite his pre-emption he had missed the moment; that once again he was, and perhaps would always be, merely a witness of consequences. "Tell me. *What was the joke?*"

But the blind boy, as is the wont of his clan, wasn't telling.

L'ENFER

Alice Joanou

WE HAD A magnificent passion for dark alleys, expensive champagne, and each other. She was very rich and unhappily married. Happily, I was neither.

She was generous or silly enough to pay my way during the length of our affair, and I had the wit to make no objection. Her husband was an old man – yes, it was one of *those* marriages. She was an ornament, a gesture of diffidence toward his aging, and a symbol of his wealth: Having her on his arm meant virility, especially in the public eye. The old man didn't seem to mind that she was out nearly every night cavorting in the underworlds of Paris. She adored the cabarets and the most sordid cafés in Montmartre. He was glad to have her as his companion once or twice a month for the opera or some business function. Certainly, she was one of the most exquisite women in Paris.

She wore her sleek hair bobbed and was always dressed in the height of fashion. She never wore corsets or other restraining undergarments, not even knickers. When I asked her why she chose not to wear what other women considered such finery, she replied blithely that she liked the freedom it afforded her body. Her body. Her fine body. It was true that it would have been an insult to nature had she strapped it in or belted it down. Her body mirrored her soul. Her body was wild, animalistic. Her breasts were small and sat high on her slim torso. Her nipples' aureoles were a deep brown color, and her torso, her hips, were virtually without curve. She had a dangerous body, and whenever I came near her I could smell that fire and needed to possess her. I could hardly keep my hands from tearing away the sheer silken dresses she wore. I could hardly stop myself from falling on my knees and taking her in my mouth, beginning with her feet. I needed to genuflect before her and taste her sex.

She almost always wore low-cut dresses with subtle slits in the sides of the skirt that rose perilously high on her long, slender legs. She decorated terrifying eyes with makeup, swearing, as she applied the makeup, that it served a protective device. She never went out without kohl smudged heavily around her eyes, the eyes of a corpse, blue-black and empty. Only now and again would they light when I took her in a violent way. Her eyes haunt me still. As if to compensate for such iciness, her full lips she painted with a flaming red tint she called "Madder Crimson." Her mouth was her vitality, and her smile was eccentric and not really beautiful. But it was human. Her painted red lips matched her luxuriant cinnabar hair. I loved watching her stand in front of the mirror, methodically making up her face. I watched her go through this preening ritual, and never did I grow tired of it.

One evening, I lay on my bed. The sheets were a sea of sweat and semen. We had been making love all day, and she said it was time to go out. To go out and see what kind of hell we could release upon a city like Paris. She wanted to go up to Sacré-Coeur and look out upon the city that loved her best. Paris was a city that looked good on her. It matched her lips and eyes. I was unable to move from the bed, half-mesmerized as she put the makeup around her eyes. Her back was to me, and she was naked, yet I could see her face and breasts in the mirror.

"Come here," I said to her quietly, almost unwilling to disturb her in her ministrations. But the sight of her body naked and pale and her face dressed for the evening gave me the strangest sensation. She looked nearly like a boy from behind, yet her face was clearly a woman's.

"You must come *here* if there is something you want," she said, her mouth smiling, her eyes dead.

"Please come here."

She ignored me and continued to put the finishing touches of light-pink rouge on her cheeks. And then she did something she didn't ordinarily do as she prepared herself for Paris: She took the powder puff and began to make slow circles around the tips of her breasts. Then she dipped the white puff in another powder that was a deeper red and began to rouge her nipples. My cock was already stiff. I had begun to imagine she was a young boy from the back and a gorgeous woman from the front. The idea of taking her from behind overwhelmed me. I had never entered her there. She had not permitted it. Her uncanny eyes were following my hand as it went involuntarily to my sex. She continued to slowly decorate her nipples, never turning.

Edith Piaf sang out defiantly and permanently damaged, her song wafting out in a thin line from the radio in the next room. It was summer and slightly humid. The flowers next to the bed violently perfumed the air. She was looking at me still. At last, I stood and went to her, taking the powder puff from her hand. Rather than put it on the vanity, as she suspected I would do, rather than take her immediately, I surprised her by dipping the makeup puff into the pot of rouge and reaching down to rouge her sex. She smiled and allowed herself a low sound of pleasure, realizing I had only just started.

"You look like a boy from behind. Are you my boy?"

"Yes," she answered, "I am your boy."

"I want to fuck you, boy. I am going to take you."

She made no reply, but raised her eyebrow at me in the mirror. She had a quizzical look on her face that was mixed with pleasure as I continued to lightly tease her pussy with the powder, making her blush between her legs. I set down the puff.

"Of course, from the front, you are the most exquisite woman I have ever seen." As I said this, I was dipping my fingers into a jar of pomade. My desire for him was unimaginable. My need for her was desperate.

"I am going to fuck you in the ass, my boy, my love. You'd like that, you little queer, wouldn't you?" He nodded . . . while she managed a wan, almost frightened, smile.

I rubbed my finger, lubricated with the pomade slowly up and down the crack of his ass. She sang with *La Vie en Rose*. She opened her mouth. Edith Piaf opened her mouth and a flower scent came out. My love opened the lips of her crimson sex. I was to christen her a man. I wasted no time, though the heat in the flat made me feel as though I were moving exceedingly slowly, moving through an erotic heat that was material, that weighed down my caresses, and I noticed how heavy my hands were on his slim hips. I touched her breast, and the tip of my sex entered him slightly. She winced and moved backward in shock; he moved over me with delighted pain.

"Oh, my love. I've only just started. Does it hurt . . .? Don't speak . . .," I whispered, suddenly afraid.

If he opened his mouth, I would know it was her. It had been so long since I had made love to a boy. She had distracted me from such need. She inhaled deeply, her eyes expressing nothing, the corners of her lips a mocking sneer. But within her strange smile she was urging me to take her. Without hesitation, I thrust my cock deep into his virgin asshole, violently needing to tear into her body, to enter a place I had not been before. She screamed. I put my hand over his mouth, while I took her nipple between my fingers and pinched. She fell toward the mirror, his cheek rested against the glass, and I reached down between her thighs and found her pussy wet. His body was perfect and delicious, and I took hold of his boyish hips with my free hand while I licked her clitoris with my fingers, expanding the possibilities of our bodies with every thrust of my hips, with every movement of my fingers into her soft, pink psyche. He fell hard against me. She fell hard against me. I could feel her breathing through her sex while I made a man of her. I crashed against her and she continued to look at me with that serene indifference. Once in a while her eyes lifted toward the ceiling. A diamond bead of sweat cut a path through the white powder on her high forehead.

His asshole was announcing her pleasure as it fit around my cock like a diabolical mouth, sucking me into a dark place of moral indistinction. I wanted to tear him apart, I wanted to drink the blood that was coming from between her legs. I wanted to consume her. I wanted to consume him. I could feel the white heat bloom from the back of my neck and cut a blazing trail down my chest. I thrust my fingers inside her terrifying depth. My cock was buried to the end of its capacity. She cried out and I came, pulling her hips over me, covering me. I looked in the mirror and saw her face instead of mine. Her eyes open, her mouth open. Edith Piaf sang.

★　　★　　★

"You make quite a lovely boy," I told her as we walked up the steep steps of Sacré-Coeur later that evening.

"May God forgive you," she said, laughing. "I hope we burn in hell together. I should hate to be there alone. Of course my husband will be there too, you know."

We walked up the stairs of Sacré-Coeur and surveyed the city that was nothing more than our fashionable accessory. We were perfectly happy that night, knowing that we shared one another's insatiable taste for the bizarre. That night we inaugurated, acknowledged, our mutual hungers.

I suppose I was a concession her husband could make in order to keep her by his side. It was the dead of morning, and we were stumbling down the street, intoxicated from an evening at Les Bals Nègres. Josphine Baker had been dancing that night, and the magnificent sight of her body, her immaculate breasts and legs, ah, Josephine Baker's legs . . . Watching her had fueled fantastic images of pleasure as she had moved wildly, mimicking, at times satirizing, the drama of the bed. It was all there, all of her to be seen, moving as though created to be desired.

As we tripped down a dimly lit street, we drank the remaining champagne of our last bottle. In the warm mist of the early summer dawn, an extraordinarily thin man stepped out from a dark doorway. His presence was abrupt and he stood in front of us, unmoving, his head cocked slightly to one side. She began to giggle at his appearance; I believe she laughed mostly out of fear. I could only make out his face when we got very close, an extremely bizarre visage that made me draw back for a moment. His prominent cheekbones created sunken hollows in his face, the effect heightened by the dreary gaslights of the alley. He wore all black, including a silk dress hat and opera cape, which she thought wildly funny, so dramatic a costume on a hot summer morning. His teeth and eyes shone in a peculiar way in the strange half-light.

She gasped when she got closer and looked into his unnerving face, and then, being drunk, she laughed and asked the man if he wouldn't like some champagne, holding up the bottle. He held out his hand, but only to beckon her closer. His ominous figure alarmed me, but, being young and stupid, I rushed forward. My mistress held my arm and quieted me. She moved cautiously, leaning her ear to his mouth to hear what he had to say. I couldn't help desiring her just then. Watching her neck tilt in that weird light, slightly terrorized, slightly mesmerized by the danger he presented. I wanted to possess her. I loved her so drunkenly that my thirst for her body could never really be quenched. I stared at her neck, at the lines of her collarbone, as she listened to what the stranger had to say.

He leaned in, his lips hovering dangerously near the nape of her neck. I almost yelled out. He began to whisper in her ear, and, as he spoke, I could see her become slowly breathless. Her back began to arch the way it did when I stroked her breasts. Her mouth fell open, and her lids half-closed over her eyes. It seemed as though the man were making love to her, but of course I could see that his hands were not touching her at all. I moved closer, moved by the tableau the man and my mistress formed in the gray morning light that was trying to get into that alley. And then I suddenly heard her beginning to making low moaning noises, her breasts falling out of the low-cut dress. And then quite suddenly she drew back, tossing her head back defiantly, and she began to laugh. It was inexplicable, whatever was occurring between her and this stranger, and there was a part of me that found a hollow solace in the fact that she had moved away from him. I also found that I was aroused in a way that was extraordinary. My feelings of desire were tinted with a bleakness, a sense of real danger that exceeded the games that she and I had indulged in at my flat.

She was moving toward me, beckoning me to come closer. I hesitated, still overwhelmed by a finishing sadness, a vague anxiety mingled with a potent desire to have her. Finally, I moved. The stranger leered in the background.

"He's asked us to come with him. He wants to show us a very exclusive cabaret. It sounds absolutely perverted. We really must go!" She paused and then whispered breathlessly, "He says it's called 'L'Enfer.' Isn't that superb! Come." And she took my hand.

I meant to ask her who the man was, and how did she know we were not stepping into some sort of terrible trap, but when I saw her slip the man a number of francs it was clear she had decided against reason. Of course I could not leave her alone and so began to follow their dark shadows down the narrow alley.

Remembering the silhouette of her breast, and her tongue

flicking over her full lips as he had whispered in her ear, I wanted to take her, I wanted to push her against one of the doorways, lift her sheer dress, and take her. I still had the pounding rhythm of Les Bals Nègres in my ears. I wanted to fuck her to the cadence of Josephine Baker's feet. I wanted to rape her, gently, and then more and more forcefully. I could feel the familiar ache of desire, the pain she caused in my groin, but my mistress was already falling into the darkness of the alley, following her compelling stranger.

"What did he say to you, my love? What did he whisper in your ear?" I asked as I moved up behind her, holding her tightly around the waist. There was, perhaps, some ill-concealed jealousy creeping into my voice.

She said nothing but answered me with a devious smile that came when she was aroused, an expression that was made more corrupt by the lusterlessness, the obsolescence in her eyes.

After winding down a series of unfamiliar and narrow streets, we stopped in front of a nondescript door. Our "guide," as I had come to think of him, knocked lightly, paused, and then rapped in loud and quick succession. I felt something extraordinary on the other side, but part of me hoped there was nothing, that our guide was nothing more than a petty crook who had taken her money. Part of my body was ready for the confusion of an unforeseen adventure, and another portion of my being wanted nothing more than to drag her away, get home to the creamy eiderdown, the cotton of our sheets.

The door slowly creaked open. Humid air colored with various scents of smoke came out. I thought I smelled the pungent, sticky smell of opium. We were greeted by a man who who had the coloring of a Gypsy, but no trace of an accent. His French was impeccable. For some reason this unnerved me. He had green-yellow eyes and luxuriant black hair in curls to his shoulders. He was well dressed. The door closed behind us, and I turned startled. Our guide had left us.

Her mouth turned up like sensual question marks as she observed the Gypsy man's beautifully sculptured ass while he led us down a narrow corridor papered in dark-red velvet and lit with gaudy gilt candelabra. There seemed to be heat emanating from the walls and a muffled sound, not quite far away, vibrating them as if they were breathing and sweating like giant sheets of sex-blushed flesh. It was grotesque and nauseating. I felt the familiar tug of my cock, and was surprised at my arousal in this strange atmosphere. She was moving forward as if in another element beyond her. I watched carefully as she walked down the narrow hallway in front of me, her hand involuntarily caressing the red walls.

Quite suddenly we found ourselves in front of another door, and the vague music I thought I had recognized could be heard more clearly on the other side. The Gypsy swung open the door with ceremony and with a sweep of his arm motioned us inside. After she had handed over more money, of course.

What we beheld behind that door made us both gasp.

A gale of hot opium air and jazz exploded on our faces. There were beautiful young girls and young men. There were old men, bald and dying in the arms of prepubescent nymphs. Old whores danced with wealthy young students. But something else had made us gasp.

There were young boys and girls hanging hairless and well-muscled, suspended from leather harnesses connected to the ceiling. There were four or five of them, and all the hanging men were naked, utterly exposed. Some hung from their arms and ankles, others from the centers of their torsos. I don't know how many of them were suspended thus in the center of what seemed to be a large underground theater. Their bodies nearly receded into the vast subterranean darkness, a sea of swaying, glowing flesh in the pale-red light of this very queer theater of sex. The force of the music was lost in the face of these beauties hung low enough to touch in any way in which the patrons of this select cabaret could wish.

Imagine. Human beings, fresh young human beings, suspended in apparatus resembling something dangerously close to an item from the Inquisition. There were black girls with smooth, dark flesh, their nipples nearly purple in the orange light. I could see the ripples and dark hair of a Gypsy boy, or perhaps he was an Italian, the smooth flesh of his ass and hairless chest evoking that day, not long ago, when I had taken my mistress from behind. I was frightened by so much available flesh. There was an Asian girl with long, silky black hair that swept the floor, and near her a European girl with pink skin contrasting viciously with the black straps of her harnesses.

She clutched my arm, her mouth moved to make tiny O's. I did not know whether this unreal spectacle was seizing her with desire or disgust. Her eyes were without expression.

I could see men, clearly well bred, standing two at a time, taking a girl from front and back. A Japanese girl floating like an angel from the underworld, legs opened, sex exposed, was held aloft in murky opium clouds. Her cunt was being treated to a kiss by what appeared to be a woman of means, judging by the clothes she wore. I could see that her nipples were erect against the silk of her evening gown and I have to admit that the erection that had plagued me in the alley had not subsided; my balls were suffering with passion and need. The cold desire I felt disturbed me, for I wanted to possess not only my mistress but all those bodies suspended before me like so much provocative fruit.

Before I could lend words to my actions, I took my mistress roughly by her hair and began to bite her neck. The need to have her delicate flesh between my teeth was an absolute necessity. If I didn't take action, if I didn't claim her body in some way, however small, I would be lost. It is not something that I can, even now, rationally explain. I was satisfied only when I could taste the metallic copper and iron of her body across my tongue. It was only then that I could release my mouth from the nape of her neck. In this place, in this strange place far beyond even the darkest secrets of Paris, I had to mark her in some way. I had to know, *she* had to know, that in this flesh jungle where anything might happen she was still my mistress. I could hear her on my lips. The ruby color of her pain and the rumbles of her acute desire played symphonically on my fingertips and tongue. She turned to me, to my lips, where there was a droplet of her blood. She gingerly put her finger to it and her eyebrows slanted as if to say she was shocked at my bestial need to be so possessive. But then her mouth softened and she raised her bloodied finger to her lips and drank of her own body. Then, while keeping her finger in her mouth, she parted her lips slightly, suggesting something with her teeth and tongue.

I had to tear her dress away from her breasts, I had to free them from the constraining fabric of the bodice. Never taking my hand from her breasts, I lifted the skirt of her dress and reached roughly between her silky legs for her sex. Then I grabbed hold of her slender hips and she pressed her body against me, moving slowly to the music. She was moving more and more forcefully against me now, her sex a warm invitation, her body tugging me in. I opened my trousers and did not hesitate to climb inside her secrets. I drove deeper and deeper until I felt her contracting in low, sing-song sounds of pleasure.

She was holding my wrists, her long fingernails digging deeply into my flesh, drawing blood, and the pain lit hidden fires of violence within me. I started fucking her with thoughts of killing her with my cock. I wanted to fuck her to death. Quite literally. She was screaming, and I imagined that I had been successful. I opened my eyes and saw traces of blood on my hands and then I fell forward, pushing into her last breath.

After we had recovered from our tryst in the corner, we began to move through the peculiar space. I held my mistress' wrist for sometime, but everywhere I turned I was confronted with so many bodies. As my mistress had paid the required fee, I had nothing to distract me. Except my mistress. But as soon as I thought I might have some trouble tasting the fruits of hell, she silently demanded I release my grasp on her wrist. Then she disappeared into the darkness, drawn by some single-minded purpose.

I walked through the labyrinth of bodies until I found the Japanese woman, whose hair was so long that it dragged on the ground. Her skin was soft and white and her legs were spread wide to reveal her pussy shaved of any hair. Her naked sex was a queer sight and it aroused me immediately. She would have looked a child were it not for the decoration of her cunt. The lips of her sex were ornamented with two rings pierced through and, crowning that, her clitoris had been pierced and there was embedded a pearl. I had never seen such a beauty, and my body went before my mind and my hands found her before I could know the word for desire. I wanted to taste her jewelry. I had to kiss her pearl. There were no others near her and I was glad. I wanted to devour her alone. I wanted to take her with my tongue and my fingers and my cock, slowly and with singularity. I wanted to have the luxury of hurting her or pleasing her. Whichever demon, lust or violence, I wanted to act without intervention.

She was a beautiful young woman whose eyes betrayed a liking for opium. Her full lips were parted and she was humming a strange song in a very low voice. I put my hands to her small breasts and took her nipples between my fingers. I pinched them hard and watched her face. She smiled and continued to hum. She parted her eyes wider to look at me, and, as much as her restraints would allow, she rippled her body in response to my attentions. I leaned forward and slowly tasted of her skin. It was salty with sweat, and there was a lingering scent of lavender powder. I let my tongue play lightly over the flat of her belly. I turned my head, resting my cheek on her stomach, and found the sight of her breasts stretched tightly from bondage very pleasing. I fell into her. I moved my mouth slowly over the full, clean lips of her labia. When the tip of my tongue touched one of her rings, I tugged it and she thrust her body lightly against my mouth. I let my tongue enter her flesh, I could hear her pleasure, I could feel it on my mouth. Her body twitched, making her sway gently from the leather straps which held her wrists, ankles, and torso. As I teased the outside of her cunt with my tongue, I found her imposed submission utterly exciting and I slid my tongue inside her once again. I drank there and returned to her outer shell. I wanted to kiss her pearl. As my lips found the cool stone pierced through her clit, I could hear the buzzing of her body. I sucked the pearl and she began to writhe. I stopped. Her moans reverberated through my mouth as I undid my trousers, readying myself to take her.

As I stood, I noticed that two women had found the Japanese woman appealing and had attached themselves to the lovely girl's nipples, touching one another as they sucked her. The sight only irritated my cock more. I stood between her legs and, taking her hips in my hands, I forced her body over my cock, letting my member slide in slowly so I could completely enjoy the strange new feeling of the golden hoops and cool sea pearl against the heat and sensitivity of my skin as it moved in deeper toward her fiery core. She cried out when I finally fell forward with all my weight, not caring for her comfort or discomfort. I made love to her with more and more force, suddenly feeling the overwhelming need to ravage the girl's tighter orifice. When I removed my sex and started to push into her from behind, I found she was generously lubricated from the residue of my own kisses. And as much as I wanted to shamelessly brutalize her, I was pleased to find that she was wet with desire and she moved her hips in a slow, swaying motion.

I responded to her mute invitation by shoving my cock into her anus without hesitation. With one finger I began to roll the pearl in her clit. And then, as if a dream, my mistress appeared from some darker place. Her beautiful face was covered in sweat, and I could see her lips were swollen. She smiled a smile that had a hint of malice and without saying a word, without touching me at all, she leaned over the Japanese girl's exposed sex, putting her perfect mouth on the girl's cunt, where I kept my finger so my mistress' tongue licked both my hand and the girl's pussy.

A fierce bewildering pleasure was welling up from within me and the force of it nearly frightened me. I imagined it was coming from some bilious and evil place, for, as I watched my lover kissing the girl's sex, as I continued to take the woman from behind, I wanted to put my hands to my mistress' neck. I wanted to put my fingers into the flesh of her back, or her cheek, and with all my strength to tear into her, to be inside her in a different, an immediate manner. The simplicity with which I could achieve this horrible feat fed my lust and rage and I continued to push my body more forcefully against the girl. I began to know that there was nothing but trust stopping me from tearing the flesh away from my mistress' body. I realized that nothing could stop me if I wanted to kill her. I considered with cold precision how simple and fragile is flesh.

As though my lover sensed the maniacal rage in my pleasure, she stood and put her lips to mine. I shot my semen into the Japanese woman, as though relieving myself of the hideously dark thoughts that had only moments before nearly overwhelmed me to commit murder. My mistress gently pulled me from the girl. I was walking in a sleeping state, and the sound of my mistress' haunting and persistent humming chilled me.

My mistress led me to a dark corner of large, soft cushions to recline upon. Someone appeared and gave us champagne. I did not bother to pour the wine into a glass because suddenly I was taken with a thirst so great I thought I might damn near die if I didn't drink immediately. I felt out of control and at the same time in great command of my body, my life. In fact, I felt more in control at that moment than I ever had, the hollowed-out dark-ness in my heart seemed to be the very reason for my sense of grace. A vague tingling told me this was perhaps not the first time I had ever felt this way. I stole a sideways glance at my mistress for I did not want to encourage conversation. I wanted to be isolated in this queer and violent loneliness, this satiation. We rested in darkness for a while, then wearily we stole into the early morning light to make our way home.

She went home to her graying husband that morning, while I went to the flat she paid for with his money. It was a nice bohemian hide-away in the *troisième arrondissement*, the top floor with a large skylight that filled the place with sun when it made its rare appearances in Paris.

I fell onto the generous quilts of the iron bed. The furnishings of this lovely little nest were also compliments of my mistress' husband. And my clothing, and my food. I felt a moment of great bitterness and envy toward my mistress' husband. I was infuriated that I could not provide the things for my lover that I knew she needed. I felt irrationally murderous toward him, toward her, my situation, a situation I had been content with until now. It seemed that the visit to that infernal place had started my mind on a dangerous tread that I could not stop at will. At last I found myself sleepy from all the rage threatening to exhaust me, overwhelm me.

I fell into fantastic and violent visions. I dreamed I had bound my mistress to a thick post in the center of the theater of L'Enfer. The air around us swirled in orange narcotic clouds, and her beautiful boyish figure, the fine skin of her legs, shone as though she were drenched in exotic oils. Or perhaps it was a terror sweat. In my satanic dreams, I did things to her that I can not even write. I attacked her helpless body with such a violent grace and ease that when it was over I scarcely thought about the strength it took to tear her limb from limb, and in fact was more concerned about the mess on my clothing . . . ah, but I must cease. Even the thought of that gruesome dream, and, worse, the intensity of pleasure as I dreamed it – it is too, too strange.

The sun was warming my aroused flesh, now turning clammy in an unfamiliar orgasmic sweat. I lay there thinking about my mistress, and the nightclub called L'Enfer.

Two days later I received a note and a package from my beloved. The note read:

WE SHALL MEET IN THE DARKNESS AT
MIDNIGHT, MY LOVE.
A.

Just reading her note, seeing her handwriting, sent an electric thrill through my body. And then my mind turned instantly, without hesitation, to my unspeakable dream. I stood for a moment reading the sky in front of my eyes that held the terrible, bloody images of my mistress' demise. At last, and with a great deal of will, I shook my head and body and tore open the elegant wrapping on the box. Inside was a beautiful, black-silk tuxedo, complete with an opera cape with red lining. It was sinister, and I feared suddenly that my mistress sensed my more detestable motivations.

"Folly!" I shouted out loud, to disrupt my own mind from its obsessive wanderings. I shook the cloak free of the box and held it up to the light. It was so black it seemed to absorb the sun, and, when I turned it, the red silk was a great slick of beautiful, pure, fresh blood.

The early edition of the morning paper reported that an unidentified young woman who *appeared* to be Japanese had been found dead, her head floating in a small valise down the Seine. The police had not yet found the remaining portion of her body. She had lipstick kisses on her white cheeks and a small white pearl in her mouth.

All during the day I was seized with erotic frenzy. Vague pictures appeared and disappeared in my heated imagination. Suspended, naked bodies swayed under my fingers, the memory of L'Enfer a palpable reality. I wandered across the *Pont Neuf* and stared at the murky, mysterious water of the Seine. I found myself laughing quite uncontrollably as I thought I saw her shoe rolling and bobbing on the filthy surface. As I laughed, emptying my horrible sound into the wind, I envisioned the girl, her head upon the glorious body of my mistress, and the visage of my mistress sewn to the missing body of the dead girl.

I saw her red lips slightly parted, perhaps grimacing in pain or smiling with languorous pleasure. I remembered seeing her mouth open, the pearl tumbling about . . . though I can't be sure. I cannot remember if she was screaming, but I recall her terror combining rather elegantly with her ancient Asian complexion. I don't know whether I *thought* I saw that pearl in her mouth, or if I wished it there. And then I realized I was confusing my lover with the Japanese girl and, then again I wondered if I hadn't confused the Japanese woman's lips for those of my mistress.

When it was time to dress, I was covered with a light sweat of desire and irritated by a persistent guilt. And, worse still, an erection that would not fade. I contemplated abating my need with my own hand, then thought better of it, waiting to see what mysteries the night had to offer me.

She came for me that evening a vision of carnal appetites. Every detail of her body, her dress, her perfumed hair, exuded a need to be ravished. I tempered my own need, savoring the romantic pain of wanting her, wanting to take her immediately and forget the enticing nightmares awaiting us at L'Enfer. I held myself back, mostly because around the edges of her mouth I could discern a strangeness that worried me. I could tell she wanted desperately to say something about the article in the newspaper, but I put my finger to her mouth. There was a terrible silence inside me that suggested to her that she should not pursue the subject of the dead girl. I told her, while my hand still rested on her mouth, that I had read it too. And yes. It was dreadful. But I felt the corners of my mouth turn upward in an uncontrollable moment of pleasure. My queer expression was met with a questioning look from my mistress.

There was a new tension between us as we made our way to the alley, where we were to meet the tall stranger. I have to admit that I quite liked this new thrill. She was a little afraid of me and this pleased me greatly. I thought it fair for all the humiliations I had suffered. The embarrassment of being so frightfully over-educated and so dreadfully poor. She had given me money and she had debased me with her generosity. So if she feared me that night as we walked silently toward our destiny, it enhanced my content.

Oh, how I could hear the bells of Sacré-Coeur ringing for the souls of the dead, how vital, how omnipotent and wild I felt as those bells ran through my body. When we arrived at the narrow, foul-smelling alley our guide was not there. I was in despair, yet my heart still raced. We stood in grim, tense silence as the final tolling of the bells tore through the darkness. And then suddenly on the breeze a subtle caress of my mistress' perfume.

I stood perfectly still without turning to look at her. She moved close to me, breathing heated kisses on the back of my neck. Her hands wrapped around my waist and immediately she began to unclasp the buttons of my trousers. She squeezed my balls and erect sex firmly, and the sight of her long, elegant white fingers tipped with blood-red enamel stirred me beyond measure.

"I need you," she whispered into my hair.

I turned to kiss her. She looked supernaturally beautiful. The translucent powder on her face made her eyes and lips glow like fire in the dark. She wore a simple silk shift the color of champagne and over that a luxurious fur coat. Between the sheer pleats of fabric, I could see her nipples and the full shape of her perfect breasts. She wore an extra-long strand of pearls around her long, white neck, fatalistic tears all the way to her sex, which I could see framed with the dark triangle of hair covering, no, framing, her perfection. I wanted to possess her, give her pleasure suddenly as a form of absolution for all the horror and violence to which I had given reign.

The night was cold and I swung the enormous cape around both of our bodies. I bowed my head without hesitation and I began to taste her breasts through the paper-thin material of her shift. Her nipples responded immediately to my touch. I raised my head and kissed her delicious lips, thrusting my tongue deep into her mouth. I avoided looking at her eyes for fear that some expression of doubt or fear might still linger there. Besides, taking her lips between mine, her tongue in my own mouth was far more telling, for my mistress' eyes rarely betrayed her state of mind. It was her mouth that told all without speaking, her lips that would betray her. Her tongue greeted my kisses and I was compelled to bite her tongue hard. I took that organ between my teeth and crushed it. How tender, how delicate the tongue really is, how easily I could have bitten it clean off. Her knees bent slightly under the pain I was affording her. Her moan was a sound beyond pleasure. I stopped just after the luxury of drinking a few droplets of her thick, warm blood. She tried to pull away but my hands reassured her of impending pleasures. I slipped my fingers under her dress between her thighs to find her secret anatomy alive and betraying her passion for mingling pleasure with a little bit of terror. Her sex was hot and inviting. I imagined her juices to be warm blood and I was hungry to taste of her. I knelt.

The flesh of her labia seemed to coil round my lips. I had never felt the terror with another woman as the terror I now felt of tasting her thus. I was overwhelmed with a primordial fear that had no words. All my anticipation of the evening's events, all my desire for my mistress paled in the light of this new terror. But as quickly as it came upon me, it left, and I let the lips of her sex consume me. I drew my tongue along the outer rim of her soft, hot flesh and let her juices fall on my lips, on my ready tongue. Her body wrapped around me like a bloody mantle. I felt her hair on my lips, I was suffocated in the involuntary thrusts of her body in paroxysms of pleasure. I was filled with a hunger. I wanted to mangle her with my tongue. I stabbed it inside her as though it were my cock. As my tongue went inside her I felt as though I were tasting a great and powersul light, a wonderful and horrible sensation, cannibalistic, wondrous. I had to stop before something dreadful happened.

I abandoned her on the edge of a catastrophic orgasm. She was moaning, crazed, tearing at my clothing. I stood and watched her with a dispassionate stare. I loved the way she was pleading and begging. I was pleased by the fact that she was a helpless victim of her own needs.

I reached down to my trousers, willing to take her there in the alley, but she pulled my hand away. She knelt in the dank passageway and, pulling the fabric of my trousers away with her teeth, she released my raging cock unto her kisses. She took my member into her mouth, letting it slide sensuously into her open throat. Her lips sucked lightly at first round the tip of my sex, and, as she raised and lowered her head in a steady rhythm, she pulled with her lips more powerfully. She ran her tongue like a feather over the tip of my cock, and with her hands she teased the rim of my anus, gently squeezing my aching sack. I felt more and more helpless as my desire grew. She was a great cat sucking with feline prowess on my throbbing sex. I felt like child and this made me angry though I felt that could not stop the locomotion of my veins, pressed her head down on me hard and without relent until my seed fell into her throat. It was an awful moment:

fleeting images of the Japanese woman, pictures of bleeding and screams more like memories than fantasy.

"Come along, my darling," she said in a voice husky with pleasure, "we don't want to miss the show."

The sound of her voice took me out of my misery for a moment. I helped her to her feet and brushed her hair from her face, an awkward attempt at apology. She smiled at me as if to say she too was sorry.

We linked arms and made our way more deeply into darkness as we moved unguided toward L'Enfer. The last chimes of Sacré-Coeur sounded off the damp sides of the crumbling buildings of Montmartre. We stopped in front of the same nondescript door. My mistress boldly stood forward and knocked three times, waited, and then five more times. The tiny wooden-hinged window inset swung open and the gray eye of the Gypsy could be seen clearly. He closed the small window and opened the door just wide enough for us to slip inside.

Tonight the Gypsy doorman wore a black leather mask over his entire head. It was a sort I had never seen at any masquerade and resembled a medieval executioner's mask. His beautiful black hair and handsome face were hidden and all that appeared were his eyes. There were holes in the leather for his nostrils and an aperture for his mouth, but this was sewn shut, a feature both violent and alluring. His chest was exposed, assuring both my mistress and me that it was indeed the same man who had greeted us two nights before. His body was unmistakably magnificent, even more enticing with the sinister black mask. Without hesitation, my mistress reached into her small beaded purse and withdrew a bundle of francs. I noted that her hand trembled slightly and I thought that unusual. She was ordinarily so calm. The doorman had enough manners not to count it, but he seemed to know by the sheer weight of it that it was not enough and he bowed discreetly and urged my mistress to give him more. She did, and she trembled more at this. We both seemed to know that more money meant something more rare, and probably more terrifying. The doorman seemed satisfied and bowed again at the waist then turned to lead us down the narrow red corridor, toward the theatre of L'Enfer.

We were prepared to witness something at least as bizarre and exciting as we had seen on our previous visit yet, in retrospect, I don't believe either of us was prepared for the excesses we were to witness on the eve of All Saints.

The dark space appeared to have changed so radically that for a moment I thought we had entered another place altogether. We faced a circular stage surrounded with heavy velvet curtains in the center of the large underground room. The place was filled with the smell of opium and tobacco, and the queer scent of marijuana clung in languid clouds in the humid air. Groups of people sat at elegant little tables clustered toward the stage. In front of the stage was a pit just large enough for a small band, which was playing blue jazz that made the room hotter and my heart bitter. The darkness to the left and right of the tables held voices and the shimmer of expensive beaded dresses. The dark offered up a jeweled hand here and there and now and again I caught a glimpse of rouged lips and cigarette holders. As my eyes grew accustomed to the dark I realized that it was from erotically disembodied hands and mouths that the smoke came, and after a time I could see the languorous forms of opium smokers stretched out on tapestried pillows, the long stems of the pipes in their hands. It seemed that their bodies were dilating en masse, and all the smokers caressed one another in lingering, slow motions.

At last my mistress said, "I am going to try some opium. I really must – have you ever, darling?"

I just shook my head. I was not afraid of the drug, but afraid of myself. I wanted to stay lucid, yet I knew it was impossible in the hallucination that was this nightclub. But I knew that if she wanted to try something, she would. I thought perhaps if she tasted the opium she would lose the anxiety and fear she was feeling toward me and, in a moment of compassion, I wanted her to be less afraid. But I knew her fear eroticized my violent motivations and suddenly I didn't want her to smoke the drug. But it was too late. Not wanting to cause a disturbance, I let her go. She moved hypnotically toward the dark figures on the pillows. I thought to follow but turned away, thinking that I would return for her before the show started.

I walked toward the tables, each lit with magnificent candelabra. In the dim light I could make out women's elegant fingers decked in jewels, and I could smell the fashionable scents of Chanel in the air. People talked secretively with one another,

their heads tipped toward each others' lips to listen or to steal a
kiss. I felt suddenly alone and excluded and was about to turn and
find my mistress. Just then I felt a hand at my elbow attempting
to lead me somewhere.

I looked to my right and found a woman standing by my side.
She was absolutely beautiful. She wore her sleek hair long, as
young girls do before they ritualize their entrance into woman-
hood by, regrettably, cutting their locks. Behind her ear she wore
a rose. She had the coloring of a Gypsy, her eyes black and her
skin a lustrous olive. She wore nothing to cover her breasts, and
around her hips a silken shawl with fringe. She pulled me to an
empty table farther away from the opium than I wanted to be, for
I did not want to lose my mistress in this strange crowd,
especially not tonight. But I was captivated by the dark woman's
breasts, the tiny rings of gold pierced through her perfect nipples.
The piercings looked beautifully strange and violently erotic, so
much so that I followed the wordless motions of the woman
without looking back toward my mistress. I wanted to touch this
woman's breasts. I wanted to taste the metal on my lips as I had
done with the Japanese girl days before. I wanted to – my
thoughts were giving way to more violence and it was getting
increasingly difficult to stop the powerful surges that came over
me.

As though the dark beauty had read my mind, she brought my
eager hand to her breast, and I reached out to take the tiny ring
between my forefinger and thumb. I pulled a little, and the
corners of her sensuous lips turned up in a wincing smile. I
pulled at the ring a little harder and she half-closed her eyes, her
long lashes brushing her cheek. I imagined that the little moaning
sound that she made came from the contact of my lashes on her
skin. I let my eyes wander down the front of her figure, her long,
flat belly, her secret parts barely hidden by the silken shawl. I ran
my hand along the flat of her stomach as I reached around her
neck to pull her generous lips toward my own, because it seemed
she was offering herself to me.

She tilted her head toward mine willingly and I tasted to my fill
of her lips and neck. She bit my lips with a single-mindedness
that matched my mood, and her fingernails dug into the nape of
my neck. As we kissed, she unhooked the cape from my neck.
Once she had removed the cloak, she surprised me by putting it

about her own shoulders, which made her look magnificently sinister, her bare breasts surrounded by the black fabric of the opera cape, the contours of her body trickling with red silk. The small orchestra had started to play music that filled my head with the rhythm of sex, the music of fucking. My blood was responding to the beat of the music, and my sex was responding to the cloaked image of the tall woman, who was leaning toward me over the small candlelit table.

I knew I was about to commit an infidelity. And I wished that my mistress were closer to watch. I was going to ravish this woman, and I knew my pleasure would be that much greater if my mistress were forced to watch as I took and gave pleasure to an equally beautiful creature as she.

The dark woman and I sat together without uttering a single word. Her black hair was falling over one shoulder, nearly covering her breasts. I reached out and touched those tempting breasts again, brushing the hair away so that I could admire them throughout the seduction. I wondered if the piercing had given her great pain, and if she had enjoyed the sensation. I began to wonder if she had willingly put those strange rings through her breasts, or if someone had forced her. This last thought enflamed my desire and gave way to more brutal thoughts. I found her right nipple with my lips and began to tease her by pulling the golden ring with my teeth. She arched her graceful back to meet my mouth. She was beautiful in the candlelight, and I was aroused beyond compare, the public nature of our caresses making me all the more excited. I reached down and unwrapped the shawl which covered her lower body. She tipped her pelvis up to meet my hungering stare.

I nearly fell back in my chair, gasping when I saw what rested between my dark beauty's legs. Tucked in the dark thicket of her pubic hair was a fully formed male member. Since I never suspected for a moment that this mesmerizing beauty was endowed with such equipment, you can imagine my surprise. When I finally looked up to her face, I was met with the shine of perfect white teeth in the glow of the candles.

At first I thought his smile was mocking and the humiliation I felt turned my thoughts immediately vile. But then I saw the softness of her breasts, the inviting tilt of her body and I wanted to possess her. Unsure as to what to do next, yet still aroused by her beauty, I found it difficult to fall into her caresses again for I had yet to have relations with another man and I had been taught to find the act repugnant. And that made me to want him more, because he was forbidden. I kept thinking of my lover, who had disappeared into an opium cloud, and wishing she could see this anomaly of nature, this beauty with perfectly formed breasts and as perfect a member as I had ever seen. I could feel the Gypsy pulling me toward her. She began to kiss me passionately with his full lips, her dark nipples long and perfect to the touch. I couldn't resist taking them into my hands. He slowly began to open the front of my dress shirt with her long, feminine fingers, the puzzling, maddening smile never leaving his face. I felt as though he were challenging me to make love to him, to take her in my arms and possess her. Her smile was pressing me to accept what I wanted, what I desired. I was utterly perplexed, repulsed and simultaneously wishing nothing more than to possess this man/woman. She was wrapping her arms around me and, as he did, I could feel her cock against my leg. She began kissing my chest and unbuttoning my pants, his hand having found the profound evidence of my passion within the folds of my trousers. The intoxicating sensation was not entirely unfamiliar, and as she took hold of my sex I saw the fleeting image of the day I insisted on making a man of my mistress.

Before I could protest, he fell gracefully to her knees, her mouth over my cock. Her tongue flicked over the head and then he took the whole length into her mouth. I could feel her hair brushing my bare chest as his head fell lightly against my stomach, her cheek moving up and down against the tender flesh of my lower abdomen. I lifted my hips to thrust the full length of my member down her throat and he took it hungrily into her willing mouth. I started to press her head hard over my throbbing sex as I felt an orgasm filling every nerve of my body. I looked down to see my own hands pushing her hard, then harder over me, and I could feel the low masculine sound of his pleasure as he tasted me. She was touching her own cock and turned her body so that I might see what I was engaged with. Suddenly my mistress appeared from the dark, her eyelids drooping sensuously, obviously under the spell of the magical pipe.

The corners of my mistress' mouth turned up in a drugged smile as she saw the woman from behind, her dark-haired head moving languorously up and down against my belly. I opened my mouth to explain, then thought better of it. The pleasurable sensations running through my body were also making it impossible for me to utter intelligible words. My mistress moved toward me. In the hazy light she looked fantastically gorgeous. She came up beside me and began to kiss me passionately on the mouth as the Gypsy he/she continued to suck my cock. I pulled my mistress' face away from mine and said to her in a commanding voice, "Get under him. Let him have you."

"Who, my darling, who?" she answered, intoxicated and compliant.

"Her," I said, and pushed my lover toward the dark woman, who stroked her male member slowly as he licked my own member. She gasped and tried to move away.

"No," she said quietly, "no . . . I – "

I put my lips over her mouth and kissed her. Then I took her lower lip between my teeth and I bit until I drew blood as I pressed her languid body downward. I had to see this sight, two beautiful women together, one of them penetrating the other. I wanted to watch my mistress take her inside herself, I wanted to watch their breasts touch.

"Do it," I moaned and then let myself fall over into the blinding sensuality that had been threatening to overcome me. I pushed her down to the floor and she seemed to spill to the ground in her soft skin, her opium flesh, and her champagne-colored dress.

The Gypsy moved magically when he saw my mistress presented to him, there at my feet. Through the dazed comfort of the aftereffects of my pleasure, I watched my mistress struggle hopelessly for a moment under his feminine touch. He stroked her breasts with his, she fell upon my mistress, her dark hair spilling like wine, her narrow hips coming down hard upon my mistress, lifting her dress as he licked her nipples, the movement of his narrow hips flowering, slightly more feminine finally than masculine as she pushed her cock inside my mistress. And when my mistress lifted her body to greet the sensation, I let my head fall back. I closed my eyes and let the violent nausea overtake my senses. The sickness I was feeling was only a symptom of what I was coming to know as my true being. I was sick and delighted with the monster I was discovering within, the hideous malformed personality that had lain dormant, waiting for the opportunity to arise and overtake the superficial in my soul. The bestial. That is what I truly am. It took an evening at L'Enfer to allow for the inevitable release.

I heard my mistress crying out. It was a strange sound of grudging pleasure mingled with humiliation and rage. It was a sound that satisfied me. I felt more alert. I leaned toward the ground to find my mistress' lips and chin covered with what was presumably *my* sperm. The freakish man/woman heaved into her one last time, releasing a masculine groan of sexual release. Then the creature's cry turned to a roar of frustration, a keening sound of anger. She lifted herself away from my mistress and disappeared into the dark. My lover fell to one side, rolling slightly back and forth, her body not quite recovered from the trauma of such a pleasure. I realized that the dark-haired creature most probably took no real pleasure in possessing my mistress, but had done it for my pleasure. For when the thing had looked up toward me as he arched her back, we met eyes, and the calculated cruelty she found there was most telling, I am sure. She had therefore run. He was a wise woman, that poor forgotten creature. He was a very lucky girl. If she had stayed, I am afraid of what I would have done to him . . .

At last my lover opened her eyes and I found that the opium had not worn off in the least, yet a new expression was clinging to the sides of her mouth. It was a confused turn of her lips and I realized that the effects of the opium and the dark-haired creature that had possessed my lover were a trifle horrifying. I laughed as she half-stood and fell into my arms. Many eyes were looking upon us with great appreciation. I turned to find that the mysterious Gypsy had vanished into the opium darkness, leaving my lover to our private kisses. I pretended to give her comfort. But inwardly I laughed, and my hysterics, had they had a color, would have been scarlet and shameless. I stroked my lover's hair. My affection for her had turned to hate, to resentment. I kissed her neck and put my arms around the fragility of her body. Again I was consumed with thoughts of the simplicity of murder.

My mistress was overcome with the seductive languor that opium induces, and she rested in my arms as I ordered a bottle of champagne. She fell in and out of her opium stupor, made worse by the champagne that I plied her with. She lay her cheek against

the tabletop and I noticed how lovely she looked, her lips swollen
from my kisses, her eyes mellowed and half-aware of the nightmare she had stepped into unknowingly. The nightmare she had
in fact paid for.

After some time, the little orchestra began to play a low soulful
tune. The guests at the tables readied themselves to watch the
show. Slowly all light, aside from the candles on the tables, was
doused. The lamps at the foot of the stage were lit, and at long last
the curtain that surrounded the little stage in the center of the
club began to part.

The tableau was fantastic.

In the center of the stage was an extraordinarily large chair.
The back of it rose up at least six feet. Seated on it was a woman
whose face was hidden by a black leather mask similar to the one
the doorman had been wearing. In this instance, the only part of
her face that was exposed was her mouth, a hole showing her lips
painted bright red. Her hands were held with leather thongs
threaded over her head and pinioned to an iron eyebolt in the
center of the back of the chair. Her legs were also bound, her sex
shaved and widely exposed, her ankles tied to the front legs of this
throne of sorts. The stage-lights caught a golden flash from
between her legs and I realized that this woman wore rings of
gold pierced through her labia, just as the Japanese girl had. A
thorny shiver of recognition, of memory, rasped through my
body. I studied the little chain that ran through the rings on the
outer lips of her sex and then encircled her waist.

There was nothing more on the stage. Except a sleek black
panther. The magnificent beast lounged alongside the girl's
chair, its black fur gleaming in the theatrical lighting. It was
an extraordinary animal. It lay with its mouth open, panting. It
was chained to the massive arms of the chair, and, though the
chain kept the animal at a safe distance from the audience, the
beast was not going to be kept from the girl. The tension in the air
matched my mood. It was a murderous perfume and every nerve
of my body waited. I wanted to watch that creature tear into the
flesh of that young girl. I wanted to put my hands round my
lover's throat. I wanted to hear screams of shock mingled with my
own delighted cries.

"Let's go home, darling," my mistress managed to whisper.

She sat staring at the potentially gruesome tableau, unable to move. She was waiting for me to motivate the action of fleeing this scene. She was going to have to wait a long time. Or so I thought.

The panther stood up lazily, but her movements became more agitated, more predatory, as she heard and felt the sound of human fear. For some of the guests this bestial passion play was a bit too realistic.

"I only came here to realize fantasy!" I heard one woman exclaim indignantly as she and her escort stood to leave.

Good, I thought. It is good and right that all those unable to endure the instinctive realities of our bloodthirst, all those who would deny a chance to witness the feral, the barbaric savagery that sat within every heart, should well leave. L'Enfer was no place for merciful.

"Please, I'm begging you. Take me from this place," she said. For the first time I saw in her eyes real terror. I was so disappointed in her. Her eyes, her wonderfully sharkish eyes, were the feature of her I most adored, most admired. And now in the face of this she wanted to run. She had shown her humanity and I couldn't forgive her.

The panther tried to lunge into the tables and chairs. She tried to swipe at the conductor in the small pit. But her chain kept her from making fatal contact. I ignored my mistress.

Finally, as though the panther had had the dignity not to attempt the obvious first, she at last turned toward the prey meant for her. The girl bound in the chair had already started screaming. But when the panther got closer, she stopped and began pleading. The girl beseeched the audience she could only hear. She begged certain people by first names, perhaps her abductors, her masters, her lovers . . . I watched as the panther circled in slowly. I could not pull my starving eyes from the scene.

"I must . . . I must . . . go . . . I must . . ." My mistress stood and stumbled to the floor.

I started to laugh when, through spraying blood, the poor girl on the stage began to actually pray to God.

I yanked my mistress to her feet. She fell against me. We started to move through the thick, sanguine air of L'Enfer. There were very few guests remaining seated. I thought the whole tableau brilliant and knew that I would certainly be back for more. The next morning, as I drank my chocolate in the sunny little flat, the newspaper was delivered. On the first page was a story concerning the murder of a beautiful young society woman found floating in the Seine. Her body had been torn to shreds and the police could only believe it was the work of a beast, a maniac, yet the tears on her body resembled *claw* marks. Her husband, an elderly gentleman, offered what I thought to be a minor reward to anyone giving reliable clues or information to the police.

I wake sometimes, plagued by a recurring nightmare. I have finally persuaded my new mistress, a wealthy girl rebelling against her family, to accompany me to L'Enfer. I know that only a visit to that place will sate my appetite.

I have become so hungry.

She is to be here any moment, at the flat she has recently rented for me.

SMALL DEATH IN VENICE

Sean O Caoimh

THEY CALL IT the small death but this, he thinks, is a long drawn-out agony.

He lies there, the grand horizontal, and she rides him hell for leather. He tries to stay hard and it obliges, taking its own pleasure. He watches it going in and coming out, a thing apart, working away, shining and flushed with pride. Remote as it is he wills it to pulsate, to twitch, to throb.

She says – You're marvellous, the best lover I've ever had.

He thinks – That's something. Score out of ten? The latest ten?

Outside the barges hit the pilings of San Trovaso. Rumble of diesels, shouts, hooting of vaporetti on the Grand Canal. In the Galleria dell'Accademia next door the cast out lady in Giorgione's *Tempest* sits naked under the town called Paradise.

Inside Room 12 of the Pensione Accademia she sits on his erection and heaves up and down and undulates like a turbulent sea. He lies there unmoved.

She says – I love it.

He looks up at her. Her face is contorted by her intense concentration. It's red and blotchy and sweat streaks her forehead. Eyes bloodshot, the whites veined in pink. She has the grim, tight-faced determination of a pained jogger or a cyclist leaning into a steep hill. She holds her breasts in her hands and throws her head back in military jerks in time with her hips.

He fills her. He matches her spasms with his convulsions. It's remote, detached, with a life of its own, but obedient to the cause.

He thinks – Now I'm just a cocksman. No lover no more.

She says – I want you to come.

He thinks – I'm saving it for Christmas.

He's irreverent, almost indifferent.

It wasn't always like this.

The meeting on the mountain at Verbier. The exchange of looks. The instant knowing. The trembling. In the village next day – Come to Venice. – Yes. Later that evening, the Visitation. His room filled with her fragrance, his bed with her lace, her skin, her delectable wetness. Her long hair brushing his cock. – It's beautiful. Is it mine? – Forever. What a laugh.

The small death and the resurrection. Again and again.

She says – I can't come any more. And comes again.

He's hooked. In deep, in love with her body, erotic love that's like drowning.

The narcosis of the cunt.

His desire: to be better than the rest.

A week later in Venice. Looking at the Veronese in the Palazzo Ducale. Europa abducted by the Bull. Her lips parted, her face in ecstasy, a wayward breast, abandonment. And the first shock.

He says – I'm like a bull when you make love with me.

She says – I fuck. I don't make love.

But she smiles and squeezes his bulging trousers.

In Room 12, disarray. She light and airy like an *île flottante*, her skin tasting as cool and fresh as the first salmon of the season and the first green peas. Him addicted. Lust into love and no protection. Compulsive touching. She holding his hard under the Titian in the Frari. His fingers inside her going up the steps in San Rocco.

Then, the illusion. The re-living of the moments, endowed with romantic love, profane yet sacred. The manic lift every time. The letters. The midnight calls: I miss you. And more. Each word remembered and inflated. The rerouting of life around her. The fitness of it; the certainty. The almost religiosity of it. Yes, the grand illusion.

★   ★   ★

Now she's alone, masturbating herself on him. And he's away in the Palazzo Labia coming off on the Tiepolos.

She says – I'm coming.

He thinks – Great. Best out of three?

He looks at her lumpy stomach. The sucked-in diaphragm, the tensed-up muscles running like a mountain range from ribcage to pubis. A flat-topped ridge criss-crossed with deep ravines. The folded-up layers of flesh lined like the neck of an old sea turtle. Or a concertina. Everything in motion, sinews stretched, thighs lifting and falling like the connecting rod of a ship's reciprocating engine. And down there the beauty mark just above the crease of the V.

She says – I love it.

She leans over to watch herself as she pumps away, her hair mercifully hiding her face: she can't see his apartness, the falsity of his act. Now she reaches up, throws her head back, her mouth open, beginning to sound. She drops a hand and grabs his. She rubs it against her mons, her fingers touching his slippery cock.

She says – I want to kiss it.

She falls off and turns and kneels, *soixante-neuf*, and takes him in her mouth and offers him her sex. He extends a tentative tongue. He has lost the taste.

He remembers. The dunes. The golden sand in her golden hair. The taste of salt, of honey, of delicious cunt.

He thinks – How I loved her. Was there always hate underlying the love? It's too sophisticated for a bog Irishman with his prick still in the confessional.

She's on her way now. Eating him like a ripe mango. Her nether region vibrating in synch with her mouth and tongue. She holds nothing back. Always over the top. Gluttony in all orifices.

The small death. How did it expire?

With humiliation.

It keeps coming back. When she turned up with the finger bruises inside her thighs. Up by the slit. Black and blue from violent fucking. From learning to dive, she said, not caring that it was an obvious lie. Not important enough for a decent deception. Not caring.

She wants more than he can give. He had thought no one could give her more. He was naive. He asked her if she wanted two men, wanting her to be angry. She only laughed and said – The only aphrodisiac is variety, Baby. Lighten up.

By the pool. Raoul working on the fence. She beckoned. Then the three of them in the water, her holding them both. Raoul sitting on the side, her head between his legs and himself entering her from behind. Her laughing and him sick to death.

Upstairs. Her guiding him into the forbidden place while she lowered herself over Raoul. He could feel the intruder. The shit on the sheets.

She said – It's just a game. It doesn't count.

But it did. It does. Now she is there, all by herself. She raises her head, squeezes his prick hard, locks his head into her cunt, floods his face.

She cries – Oh, God! Oh, darling!

He thinks – Oh, balls. Change the record.

She lies on top of him and tries to eat his mouth. She tastes of cunty ashes. He tries to turn away. She pulls his head back. She's angry.

She says – You don't love me any longer.

He thinks of the old joke – Loves you? Of course I loves you. I fucks you, don't I?

He says – Let's go to the island of San Michele. With the mist and the cypresses.

She says – Yes, let's. It sounds sexy.

He wishes he could get a funeral gondola, all black and gilt, with four oarsmen and angels with wings spread on the stem and the stern, a black canopy with tassels, and cushions where the coffin lies.

The taxi-boat arrives at the ornate gate of the cemetery of San Michele. It's twilight. Long shadows, black water, smell of mud and putrescence. The lights of Murano filtered through the mist. Rose walls and sinister cypresses. They step ashore. He tells the man to wait. The man says it's closing soon. To hurry.

She says – It looks like a graveyard.

He says – Yes. A burial ground. L'Ile des Morts. It was once a prison.

She says – It is sexy.

He says – All the best people come here. Stravinsky. Diaghilev. Ezra Pound.

She asks – Who was he?

He says – A mad poet. We have to pay our respects.

They go to Ezra Pound's grave. It has a white stone and a white urn filled with fresh flowers. He stands. He turns to her. He lowers his hand. He unzips himself. He pushes her head down, not gently. She squats. She extracts his penis. It's hard. She sucks him, he helps her by pulling it next to her mouth. His hand hits her teeth. Now she is excited. It's a new experiment. It's the kind of bizarre situation she likes.

He pushes her away and ejaculates over the grave.

She cries – Why did you do that?

He says – A benediction. He wrote about you: "Your mind and you are our Sargasso Sea."

She says – What does it mean?

He says – Weeds, darling, we're mired in weeds. Putrid, rotten, all passion spent.

He turns and walks away.

Small death in Venice.

Dead and buried.

R.I.P.